FICTION

THE UNIVERSAL ELEMENTS

FICTION

THE UNIVERSAL ELEMENTS

Pearl Gasarch

NEW YORK CITY
COMMUNITY COLLEGE

Ralph Gasarch

NEW YORK CITY
BOARD OF EDUCATION

BROOKLYN COLLEGE

D. VAN NOSTRAND COMPANY

New York Cincinnati Toronto London Melbourne

D. Van Nostrand Company Regional Offices:
Cincinnati New York Millbrae

D. Van Nostrand Company International Offices:
London Toronto Melbourne

Library of Congress Catalog Card Number: 75-183938

ISBN: 0-442-22632-2

Manufactured in the United States of America.

Published by D. Van Nostrand Company
450 West 33rd Street, New York, N. Y. 10001

Published simultaneously in Canada by Van Nostrand Reinhold Ltd.

Painting on cover *The Lovers of Venice* by Marc Chagall.
Used by permission of A.D.A.G.P., 1972, by French Reproduction Rights, Inc.

Text design by Morris Karol
Cover by Saul Schnurman

8 7 6 5 4 3

PREFACE

IDEALLY, the literary experience should illuminate and expand the reader's life experience. Yet for many of today's students the standard fiction anthologies fail, with their explication of technique and literary history, to forge that connection between literature and life which is so vital to the discovery that reading good fiction is a means of learning more about one's life and the lives of all men.

In *Fiction: The Universal Elements,* we have grouped 31 stories around five universal life stages, and we have carefully searched out authors with diverse backgrounds. Our rationale has been that universality in fiction is most accessible to the broad spectrum of the present-day student body when it is presented in the language, styles, and themes of a greater diversity of writers than one finds in most anthologies.

The book therefore reflects our conviction that, for fiction to evoke an awareness of universal meanings in the student, he must be able to identify with a significant portion of the immediate reality of the literary work. Accordingly, the stories assembled here treat stages of the life cycle which we have found to be of greatest interest to contemporary youth: the decline of innocence in childhood, the search for identity in adolescence, the experience of love, the sharing of one's life with another person, and the complexities of later life.

Beyond this, the authorship includes representative literary expression from, for example, the black and Spanish-American experiences, which we have found highly effective when read in conjunction with more commonly anthologized fiction. The interesting paradox seems to be that, just as the successful writer derives his universal power from the selective reworking of a particular reality, so the reader's recognition of that power is best promoted through a variety of regional, ethnic, and other literary perspectives which are still slighted in many anthologies.

In a number of cases we were able to obtain from living writers whose work appears here statements about their lives and their work which they thought would interest readers of a collection such as we have assembled. Their commentaries appear within the editorial remarks about the author that precede each story.

We elected to restrict the book to short fiction, but we have included three longer stories ("The Bear," "The Loneliness of the Long-Distance Runner," and "The Death of Ivan Ilych") which are usually classified as novellas, to provide experiences with a somewhat more extended fictional form.

Once a reader has experienced the satisfaction that comes from rethinking his own experience in the larger perspective provided by literature, some consideration of the formal elements of fiction may add another dimension to his appreciation. The conclusion of the book (page 442 and following) therefore provides an alternate table of contents arranged by formal elements, as well as an introductory discussion of the chief formal devices in fiction, each of which is illustrated with reference to stories in this book.

ACKNOWLEDGMENTS

JAMES BALDWIN: "Sonny's Blues" from *Going to Meet the Man.* Reprinted by permission of The Dial Press and Robert Lantz—Candida Donadio Literary Agency, Inc. Copyright 1965 by James Baldwin.

ROBERT BOLES: "The Engagement Party" from *Best Short Stories by Negro Writers,* Langston Hughes, ed., Little, Brown and Company, 1967. Reprinted by permission of the author and by his agent, Cyrilly Abels.

CYRUS COLTER: "The Beach Umbrella" reprinted by permission of the author and the University of Iowa Press. Copyright © 1963 by Alfred A. Knopf, Inc.

PEARL CRAYTON: "The Day the World Almost Came to an End" from *Best Short Stories by Negro Writers,* Langston Hughes, ed., Little, Brown and Company, 1967. © 1965 by *Negro Digest* (now *Black World*). Reprinted by permission of the author.

WILLIAM FAULKNER: "The Bear" from *The Collected Short Stories of William Faulkner,* copyright © 1945 by Curtis Publishing Company and renewed 1970 by Estelle Faulkner and Jill Faulkner Summers. Reprinted by permission of Random House, Inc., Alfred A. Knopf, Inc., and Chatto and Windus Ltd.

F. SCOTT FITZGERALD: "Babylon Revisited" from *Taps at Reveille.* Reprinted by permission of Charles Scribner's Sons and the Bodley Head. Copyright © 1931 by Curtis Publishing Company; renewal copyright © 1959 by Frances S. F. Lanahan.

ERNEST GAINES: "The Sky Is Gray" from *Bloodline.* Reprinted by permission of The Dial Press. Copyright © 1964, 1968 by the author.

ERNEST HEMINGWAY: "The Short Happy Life of Francis Macomber" from *The Short Stories of Ernest Hemingway.* Reprinted by permission of Charles Scribner's Sons. Copyright © 1964 by Mary Hemingway.

JAMES JOYCE: "Arby" from *Dubliners.* Reprinted by permission of The Viking Press, Inc., Jonathan Cape, Ltd., on behalf of the Executors of the James Joyce Estate, and The Society of Authors. Copyright © 1967 by the Estate of James Joyce.

JONATHAN KARIARA: "Her Warrior" reprinted by permission of the author. Copyright © 1964 by the author.

D. H. LAWRENCE: "The Horse Dealer's Daughter" from *The Complete Short Stories of D. H. Lawrence.* Reprinted by permission of The Viking Press, Inc., and Lawrence Polbuger, Ltd. Copyright © 1922 by Thomas Seetzer. Renewed 1950 by Freda Lawrence.

BERNARD MALAMUD: "The Magic Barrel" from *The Magic Barrel* by Bernard Malamud. Reprinted by permission of Farrar, Strauss and Giroux, Inc., and Eyre and Spatteswoode. Copyright © 1954 by Bernard Malamud.

KATHERINE MANSFIELD: "A Dill Pickle" from *The Short Stories of Katherine Mansfield.* Reprinted by permission of Alfred A. Knopf, Inc., Random House Inc., 1961, 1920, and The Society of Authors. Copyright © 1948 by J. Middleton Murry.

PAULE MARSHALL: "Brazil" from *Soul Clap Hands and Sing.* Published by Atheneum Publishers, Copyright © 1961 by Paule Marshall. Reprinted by permission of Cyrilly Ables, Literary Agent.

CLAUDE MCKAY: "Truant" from *Gingertown.* Reprinted by permission of Harper and Row, Inc. Copyright © 1960 by Hope McKay Virtue.

FRANK O'CONNOR: "My Oedipus Complex" from *The Stories of Frank O'Connor.* Reprinted by permission of Alfred A. Knopf, Inc., and A. D. Peters and Company. Copyright © 1950, 1952 by the author.

I. L. PERETZ: "Bontsha the Silent" from *A Treasury of Yiddish Stories* edited by Irving Howe and Eliezer Greenberg. Reprinted by permission of The Viking Press, Inc., and Andre Deutch Ltd. Copyright © 1954 by The Viking Press, Inc.

KATHERINE ANNE PORTER: "Rope" from *The Collected Stories of Katherine Anne Porter.* Reprinted by permission of Harcourt Brace Jovanovich, Inc., and Jonathan Cape, Ltd. Copyright © 1930, 1958 by the author.

TED POSTON: "The Revolt of the Evil Fairies" from *Best Short Stories by Negro Writers,* Langston Hughes, ed., Little, Brown and Company, 1967. Reprinted by permission of the author.

JAMES PURDY: "Cutting Edge" from *Color of Darkness.* Reprinted by permission of New Directions Publishing Corp. and David Higham, Associates. Copyright © 1957 by James Purdy.

RICHARD RIVE: "Resurrection" from *Modern African Prose.* Published by and reprinted with permission of Heinemann Educational Books. Copyright © 1964 by the author.

PHILIP ROTH: "Defender of the Faith" from *Goodby, Columbus.* Reprinted by permission of Houghton Mifflin Company and Robert Lantz—Candida Donadio Literary Agency, Inc. Copyright © 1959 by Philip Roth.

IRWIN SHAW: "The Girls in Their Summer Dresses" from *The Selected Stories of Irwin Shaw.* Reprinted by permission of Random House, Inc. Copyright © 1939, 1967 by the author.

ALAN SILLITOE: *The Loneliness of the Long-Distance Runner.* Reprinted by permission of Alfred A. Knopf, Inc. Copyright © 1959 by Alan Sillitoe.

JAMES THURBER: "The Secret Life of Walter Mitty" from *My World and Welcome To It.* Published by Harcourt Brace Jovanovich, Inc., New York. Originally printed in *The New Yorker.* Reprinted by permission of Hamish Hamilton. Copyright © 1942 by James Thurber. Copyright © 1970 by Helen W. Thurber and Rosemary Thurber Sauers.

LEO TOLSTOI: "The Death of Ivan Ilych" from *The Death of Ivan Ilych and Other Stories,* translated by Louise and Aylmer Maude. Published by Oxford University Press and reprinted with their permission.

NICK C. VACA: "The Visit" from *The Mirror,* Octavio Romano V, ed. and reprinted by permission of Quinto Sol Publications, Inc. Copyright © 1969 by the author.

SILVIO VILLAVICENCIO: "The Mirror" from *The Mirror,* Octavio Romano V, ed. Reprinted by permission of Quinto Sol Publications, Inc. Copyright © 1969 by the author.

EUDORA WELTY: "Livvie" from *The Wide Net.* Reprinted by permission of Harcourt Brace Jovanovich, Inc., and Russel and Volkening, Inc. Copyright © 1962, 1970 by Eudora Welty.

THOMAS WILLIAMS: "Goose Pond" from *A High New House* reprinted by permission of The Dial Press and Harold Matson Company. First published in *Esquire Magazine.* Copyright © 1959, 1961, 1963 by the author.

RICHARD WRIGHT: "Big Boy Leaves Home" from *Uncle Tom's Children.* Reprinted by permission of Harper and Row, Publishers. Copyright © 1963 by Richard Wright.

CONTENTS

4 MARRIAGE
The Shared Life

5 LATER LIFE
New Joys, New Sorrows

TO THE READER:

A Note on Universality

THE BEST REASON for putting a collection of fiction together is to give pleasure to the reader. Our students—and we—have been delighted, astonished, distressed, and humbled by the stories gathered here. They are all different—in length, language, place, and "feel." Yet each rewarded us in some special way as we read and reread it. So we wanted each to have a larger audience because we had found it a source of pleasure.

The pleasures of reading are not altogether like the pleasures of hearing a favorite record or lounging on a beach. There is, to be sure, the sheer delight in enjoying the sounds and rhythms of well-constructed language or the skillful verbal depiction of sensory experience. But the most enduring pleasures of reading go deeper. They go as deep as the reader's experience is deep. And that, we believe, is what makes the stories that follow especially rewarding. Each has the power to jolt you out of your own experience and into the action of the story—then right back into your own feelings. Each writer knows at least a few things that you already know. Each can surprise you by using an idea or emotion that you have experienced and shaping it into a new notion that will fascinate you. You can find *yourself,* if you look, in these stories.

Discovering your own experience mirrored in a story is different from the uses to which fiction is often put. Because the simplest way to cope with painful or dull reality is to escape, stories are sometimes read simply to transport us to other places, other times, other ways of life, where we can temporarily forget the troubles of our here and now. But escapist pleasures fade all too quickly, and we return to the real world with nothing to show for our trip except the passage of an hour's time. This is not surprising, for our goal was to be taken *away from* rather than *into* our immediate reality.

The best stories, as far back as we can trace the tales, myths, and dramas of man, have always worked both ways. They sweep us out of our world into a new, intriguing setting, yet in the final analysis they return us to our present lives by reminding us of truths, character types, and patterns of experience we already recognize in our own existence. In this way, good stories help us to order our lives.

And we are eager for order, which often seems lacking in real life. Most of us are too much in the middle of things to find much meaning in them. Viewing our reality from one narrow point of view—our own—we often fail to see a single incident in perspective, or to relate it to other experiences—much less to the general condition of mankind.

Sometimes, looking back, we pause, reexamine, gain fresh insights. This is the point at which we begin to engage in something like the literary process that writers use. The author's raw material, like ours, is the disorder of life. But with his literary license an author is not restricted to the randomness, the uncertainties, the emotional blinders, and the gaps in knowledge that becloud any attempt to understand life while it is going on. Like an all-knowing god, he isolates a specific experience (from his own life or from his observation), gives it a past and a future, views it as it might appear through a particular pair of eyes he chooses, and, already knowing its final outcome, weaves a pattern through which we can recognize something that once happened to us.

Our first reaction is a response to the story's immediately familiar elements: setting, incidents, characters, the way of life depicted. At the same time, we react with interest about the unfamiliar: an earlier era, a foreign place, strange customs and traditions, a different point of view. Beneath the surface reality in a good story (strange as it may seem at first) we sense an identification. We may identify with a recognizable dilemma (facing an English reform-school boy), a familiar character trait (in a dying nineteenth-century Russian bureaucrat), or a similar memory (a Dublin adolescent worshiping his beloved from afar).

These underlying universal elements in fiction, feeding back as they do to our own experience, can expand our knowledge of ourselves in the larger context of mankind. How much of this analysis is stimulated by a work of fiction is a measure of its achievement. How much it changes the reader's view of himself and of life is a measure of its significance. That is what we mean when we say that reading a good story can be intensely pleasurable.

The forms of fiction are many. This book presents a sampling, including a wide representation of *short fiction,* which most readers find easiest to start with.

Limitation of length in a short story forces the author to view life from the other end of the telescope. A short story contracts reality to squeeze out the truth to be found in a mere thread of experience. Restricted in length, it can probe only a fragment of life: *one* sequence of events, usually illuminating *one* character trait, illuminating *one* aspect of reality. A few of the pieces of fiction in this book are longer than the average short story. You will probably not be particularly aware of length as you read, but you may find yourself thinking afterward that the author treated his subject differently from the way he might have treated it in half the space.

The themes of fiction are as various as life itself. We have arranged the stories that follow around five universal elements in the life of every person: childhood, youth, the search for love, marriage, and later life. Each story in a group is unique, yet each shares something with the others because of the life stage they all portray.

Within these five groupings you will find rich variety in style, setting, point of view, character, and way of life in stories dealing with a similar theme. At the same time, you will probably recognize universalities of the human condition that go beyond time and place. Although the stories reflect more than a century of writing and range in setting from the throne of the Almighty in heaven to the streets of Bayonne, Louisiana, they share common concerns which are boundless in time and space.

To help suggest how much of a writer's material is shaped not simply out of his imagination but out of his own direct experience, we attempted to contact each of the living writers represented here. We asked them to share with readers of this book whatever they thought would be of interest, either in their own life experience or in their writing. The majority have responded with messages that reveal the man or woman behind the writing. Others declined to comment, in the belief that no author can speak for a story or for himself better than the story itself can.

Our first criterion in choosing stories for this collection was their ability to communicate the universality that can be found in life's diversity. We also attempted to draw stories from a broad range of experiential sources, from a wide selection of authors with dissimilar backgrounds. If we have chosen well, you should not go very far in this book without encountering something that rings a bell, no matter what your own unique background may be.

FICTION

THE UNIVERSAL ELEMENTS

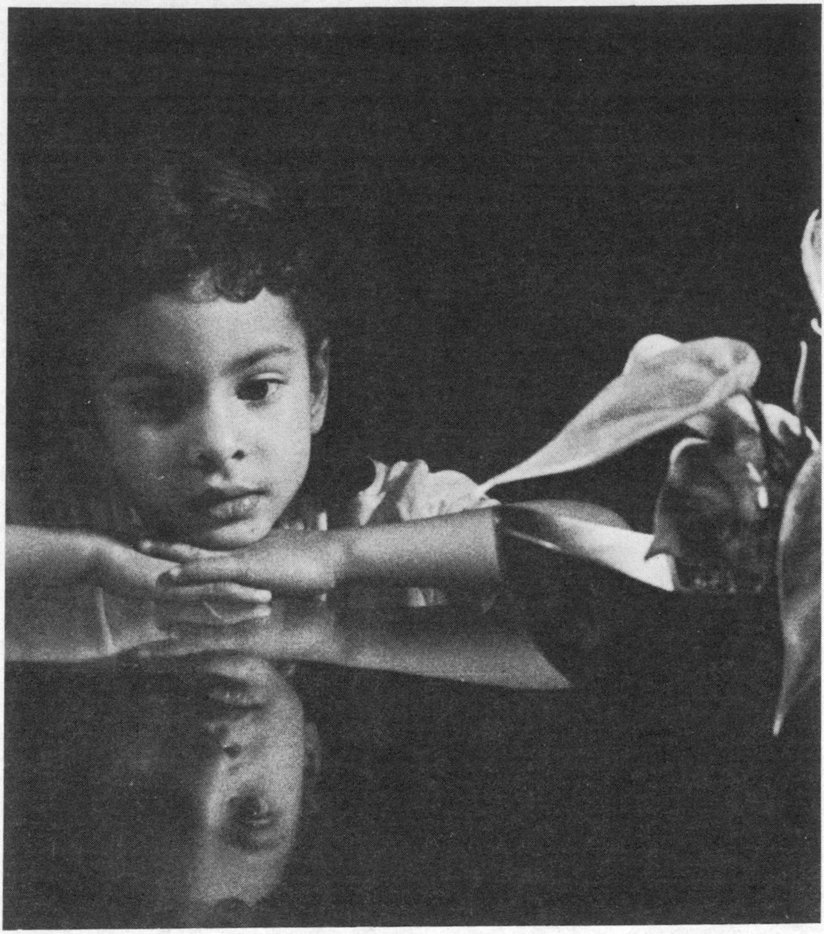

1

Childhood

The Loss of Innocence

A child is born in a state of innocence. That moment when he senses a difference between what the adult world has previously told him is true and what his own experience now tells him is true marks his first intimation of maturity. It is the beginning of his loss of innocence.

FRANK O'CONNOR (1903–1966)

Frank O'Connor was born in Ireland and lived and wrote there most of his life. Until he established his reputation as an author with his first collection of stories, Guests of the Nation *(1931), he was active in the Irish revolutionary movement and literary revival, during which time he supported himself by working as a librarian. Though best known for his short stories, he was also a novelist, playwright, and translator of ancient and contemporary century Gaelic poetry and prose.*

O'Connor's settings and the lilt of his language are unmistakably Irish, yet his insight into the ironies of human behavior is universal. His observation of the complexities and fallibilities of human nature is communicated with compassion and humor.

"My Oedipus Complex" is a warm and amusing presentation of a five-year-old boy's attempt to cope with the threat posed by a strange man (his father) returning from the wars to displace him in his mother's bed.

My Oedipus Complex

FATHER was in the army all through the war—the first war, I mean—so, up to the age of five, I never saw much of him, and what I saw did not worry me. Sometimes I woke and there was a big figure in khaki peering down at me in the candlelight. Sometimes in the early morning I heard the slamming of the front door and the clatter of nailed boots down the cobbles of the lane. These were Father's entrances and exits. Like Santa Claus he came and went mysteriously.

In fact, I rather liked his visits, though it was an uncomfortable squeeze between Mother and him when I got into the big bed in the early morning. He smoked, which gave him a pleasant musty smell, and shaved, an operation of astounding interest. Each time he left a trail of souvenirs—model tanks and Gurkha knives with handles made of bullet cases, and German helmets and cap badges and button-sticks, and all sorts of military equipment—carefully stowed away in a long box on top of the wardrobe, in case they ever came in handy. There was a bit of the magpie about Father; he expected everything to come in handy. When his back was turned, Mother let me get a chair and rummage through his treasures. She didn't seem to think so highly of them as he did.

The war was the most peaceful period of my life. The window of my attic faced southeast. My mother had curtained it, but that had small effect. I always woke with the first light and, with all the responsibilities of the previous day melted, feeling myself rather like the sun, ready to illumine and rejoice. Life never seemed so simple and clear and full of possibilities as then. I put my feet out from under the clothes—I called them Mrs. Left and Mrs. Right—and invented dramatic situations for them in which they discussed the problems of the day. At least Mrs. Right did; she was very demonstrative, but I hadn't the same control of Mrs. Left, so she mostly contented herself with nodding agreement.

They discussed what Mother and I should do during the day, what Santa Claus should give a fellow for Christmas, and what steps should be taken to brighten the home. There was that little matter of the baby, for instance. Mother and I could never agree about that. Ours was the only house in the terrace without a new baby, and Mother said we couldn't afford one till Father came back from the war because they cost seventeen and six. That showed how simple she was. The Geneys up the road had a baby, and everyone knew they couldn't afford seventeen and six. It was probably a cheap baby, and Mother wanted something really good, but I felt she was too exclusive. The Geneys' baby would have done us fine.

Having settled my plans for the day, I got up, put a chair under the attic window, and lifted the frame high enough to stick out my head. The window overlooked the front gardens of the terrace behind ours, and beyond these it looked over a deep valley to the tall, red-brick houses terraced up the opposite hillside, which were all still in shadow, while those at our side of the valley were all lit up, though with long strange shadows that made them seem unfamiliar; rigid and painted.

After that I went into Mother's room and climbed into the big bed. She woke and I began to tell her of my schemes. By this time, though I never seem to have noticed it, I was petrified in my nightshirt, and I thawed as I talked until, the last frost melted, I fell asleep beside her and woke again only when I heard her below in the kitchen, making the breakfast.

After breakfast we went into town; heard Mass at St. Augustine's and said a prayer for Father, and did the shopping. If the afternoon was fine we either went for a walk in the country or a visit to Mother's great friend in the convent, Mother St. Dominic. Mother had them all praying for Father, and every night, going to bed, I asked God to send him back safe from the war to us. Little, indeed, did I know what I was praying for!

One morning, I got into the big bed, and there, sure enough, was Father in his usual Santa Claus manner, but later, instead of uniform, he put on his best blue suit, and Mother was as pleased as anything. I saw nothing to be pleased about, because, out of uniform, Father was altogether less interesting, but she only beamed, and explained that our prayers had been answered, and off we went to Mass to thank God for having brought Father safely home.

The irony of it! That very day when he came in to dinner he took off his boots and put on his slippers, donned the dirty old cap he wore about the house to save him from colds, crossed his legs, and began to talk gravely to Mother, who looked anxious. Naturally, I disliked her looking anxious, because it destroyed her good looks, so I interrupted him.

"Just a moment, Larry!" she said gently.

This was only what she said when we had boring visitors, so I attached no importance to it and went on talking.

"Do be quiet, Larry!" she said impatiently. "Don't you hear me talking to Daddy?"

This was the first time I had heard those ominous words, "talking to Daddy," and I couldn't help feeling that if this was how God answered prayers, he couldn't listen to them very attentively.

"Why are you talking to Daddy?" I asked with as great a show of indifference as I could muster.

"Because Daddy and I have business to discuss. Now, don't interrupt again!"

In the afternoon, at Mother's request, Father took me for a walk. This time we went into town instead of out to the country, and I thought at first, in my usual optimistic way, that it might be an improvement. It was nothing of the sort. Father and I had quite different notions of a walk in town. He had no proper interest in trams, ships, and horses, and the only thing that seemed to divert him was talking to fellows as old as himself. When I wanted to stop he simply went on, dragging me behind him by the hand; when he wanted to stop I had no alternative but to do the same. I noticed that it seemed to be a sign that he wanted to stop for a long time whenever he leaned against a wall. The second time I saw him do it I got wild. He seemed to be settling himself forever. I pulled him by the coat and trousers, but, unlike Mother who, if you were too persistent, got into a wax and said: "Larry, if you don't behave yourself, I'll give you a good slap," Father had an extraordinary capacity for amiable inattention. I sized him up and wondered would I cry, but he seemed to be too remote to be annoyed even by that. Really, it was like going for a walk with a mountain! He either ignored the wrenching and pummeling entirely, or else glanced down with a grin of amusement from his peak. I had never met anyone so absorbed in himself as he seemed.

At teatime, "talking to Daddy" began again, complicated this time by the fact that he had an evening paper, and every few minutes he put it down and told Mother something new out of it. I felt this was foul play. Man for man, I was prepared to compete with him any time for Mother's attention, but when he had it all made up for him by other people it left me no chance. Several times I tried to change the subject without success.

"You must be quiet while Daddy is reading, Larry," Mother said impatiently.

It was clear that she either genuinely liked talking to Father better than talking to me, or else that he had some terrible hold on her which made her afraid to admit the truth.

"Mummy," I said that night when she was tucking me up, "do you think if I prayed hard God would send Daddy back to the war?"

She seemed to think about that for a moment.

"No, dear," she said with a smile. "I don't think he would."

"Why wouldn't he, Mummy?"

"Because there isn't a war any longer, dear."

"But, Mummy, couldn't God make another war, if he liked?"

"He wouldn't like to, dear. It's not God who makes wars, but bad people."

"Oh!" I said.

I was disappointed about that. I began to think that God wasn't quite what he was cracked up to be.

Next morning I woke at my usual hour, feeling like a bottle of champagne. I put out my feet and invented a long conversation in which Mrs. Right talked of the trouble she had with her own father till she put him in the Home. I didn't quite know what the Home was but it sounded the right place for Father. Then I got my chair and stuck my head out of the attic window. Dawn was just breaking, with a guilty air that made me feel I had caught it in the act. My head bursting with stories and schemes, I stumbled in next door, and in the half-darkness scrambled into the big bed. There was no room at Mother's side so I had to get between her and Father. For the time being I had forgotten about him, and for several minutes I sat bolt upright, racking my brains to know what I could do with him. He was taking up more than his fair share of the bed, and I couldn't get comfortable, so I gave him several kicks that made him grunt and stretch. He made room all right, though. Mother waked and felt for me. I settled back comfortably in the warmth of the bed with my thumb in my mouth.

"Mummy!" I hummed, loudly and contentedly.

"Sssh! dear," she whispered. "Don't wake Daddy!"

This was a new development, which threatened to be even more serious than "talking to Daddy." Life without my early-morning conferences was unthinkable.

"Why?" I asked severely.

"Because poor Daddy is tired."

This seemed to me a quite inadequate reason, and I was sickened by the sentimentality of her "poor Daddy." I never liked that sort of gush; it always struck me as insincere.

"Oh!" I said lightly. Then in my most winning tone: "Do you know where I want to go with you today, Mummy?"

"No, dear," she sighed.

"I want to go down the Glen and fish for thornybacks with my new net, and then I want to go out to the Fox and Hounds, and—"

"Don't-wake-Daddy!" she hissed angrily, clapping her hand across my mouth.

But it was too late. He was awake, or nearly so. He grunted and reached for the matches. Then he stared incredulously at his watch.

"Like a cup of tea, dear?" asked Mother in a meek, hushed voice I had never heard her use before. It sounded almost as though she were afraid.

"Tea?" he exclaimed indignantly. "Do you know what the time is?"

"And after that I want to go up the Rathcooney Road," I said loudly, afraid I'd forget something in all those interruptions.

"Go to sleep at once, Larry!" she said sharply.

I began to snivel. I couldn't concentrate, the way that pair went on, and smothering my early-morning schemes was like burying a family from the cradle.

Father said nothing, but lit his pipe and sucked it, looking out into the shadows without minding Mother or me. I knew he was mad. Every time I made a remark Mother hushed me irritably. I was mortified. I felt it wasn't fair; there was even something sinister in it. Every time I had pointed out to her the waste of making two beds when we could both sleep in one, she had told me it was healthier like that, and now here was this man, this stranger, sleeping with her without the least regard for her health!

He got up early and made tea, but though he brought Mother a cup he brought none for me.

"Mummy," I shouted, "I want a cup of tea, too."

"Yes, dear," she said patiently. "You can drink from Mummy's saucer."

That settled it. Either Father or I would have to leave the house. I didn't want to drink from Mother's saucer; I wanted to be treated as an equal in my own home, so, just to spite her, I drank it all and left none for her. She took that quietly, too.

But that night when she was putting me to bed she said gently:

"Larry, I want you to promise me something."

"What is it?" I asked.

"Not to come in and disturb poor Daddy in the morning. Promise?"

"Poor Daddy" again! I was becoming suspicious of everything involving that quite impossible man.

"Why?" I asked.

"Because poor Daddy is worried and tired and he doesn't sleep well."

"Why doesn't he, Mummy?"

"Well, you know, don't you, that while he was at the war Mummy got the pennies from the Post Office?"

"From Miss MacCarthy?"

"That's right. But now, you see, Miss MacCarthy hasn't any more pennies, so Daddy must go out and find us some. You know what would happen if he couldn't?"

"No," I said, "tell us."

"Well, I think we might have to go out and beg for them like the poor old woman on Fridays. We wouldn't like that, would we?"

"No," I agreed. "We wouldn't."

"So you'll promise not to come in and wake him?"

"Promise."

Mind you, I meant that. I knew pennies were a serious matter, and I was all against having to go out and beg like the old woman on Fridays. Mother laid out all my toys in a complete ring round the bed so that, whatever way I got out, I was bound to fall over one of them.

When I woke I remembered my promise all right. I got up and sat on the floor and played—for hours, it seemed to me. Then I got my chair and looked out the attic window for more hours. I wished it was time for Father to wake; I wished someone would make me a cup of tea. I didn't feel in the least like the sun; instead, I was bored and so very, very cold! I simply longed for the warmth and depth of the big featherbed.

At last I could stand it no longer. I went into the next room. As there was still no room at Mother's side I climbed over her and she woke with a start.

"Larry," she whispered, gripping my arm very tightly, "what did you promise?"

"But I did, Mummy," I wailed, caught in the very act. "I was quiet for ever so long."

"Oh, dear, and you're perished!" she said sadly, feeling me all over. "Now, if I let you stay will you promise not to talk?"

"But I want to talk, Mummy," I wailed.

"That has nothing to do with it," she said with a firmness that was new to me. "Daddy wants to sleep. Now, do you understand that?"

I understood it only too well. I wanted to talk, he wanted to sleep—whose house was it, anyway?

"Mummy," I said with equal firmness, "I think it would be healthier for Daddy to sleep in his own bed."

That seemed to stagger her, because she said nothing for a while.

"Now, once for all," she went on, "you're to be perfectly quiet or go back to your own bed. Which is it to be?"

The injustice of it got me down. I had convicted her out of her own mouth of inconsistency and unreasonableness, and she hadn't even attempted to reply. Full of spite, I gave Father a kick, which she didn't notice but which made him grunt and open his eyes in alarm.

"What time is it?" he asked in a panic-stricken voice, not looking at Mother but the door, as if he saw someone there.

"It's early yet," she replied soothingly. "It's only the child. Go to sleep again. . . . Now, Larry," she added, getting out of bed, "you've wakened Daddy and you must go back."

This time, for all her quiet air, I knew she meant it, and knew that my principal rights and privileges were as good as lost unless I asserted them at once.

As she lifted me, I gave a screech, enough to wake the dead, not to mind Father. He groaned.

"That damn child! Doesn't he ever sleep?"

"It's only a habit, dear," she said quietly, though I could see she was vexed.

"Well, it's time he got out of it," shouted Father, beginning to heave in the bed. He suddenly gathered all the bedclothes about him, turned to the wall, and then looked back over his shoulder with nothing showing only two small, spiteful, dark eyes. The man looked very wicked.

To open the bedroom door, Mother had to let me down, and I broke free and dashed for the farthest corner, screeching. Father sat bolt upright in bed.

"Shut up, you little puppy!" he said in a choking voice.

I was so astonished that I stopped screeching. Never, never had anyone spoken to me in that tone before. I looked at him incredulously and saw his face convulsed with rage. It was only then that I fully realized how God had codded me, listening to my prayers for the safe return of this monster.

"Shut up, you!" I bawled, beside myself.

"What's that you said?" shouted Father, making a wild leap out of bed.

"Mick, Mick!" cried Mother. "Don't you see the child isn't used to you?"

"I see he's better fed than taught," snarled Father, waving his arms wildly. "He wants his bottom smacked."

All his previous shouting was as nothing to these obscene words referring to my person. They really made my blood boil.

"Smack your own!" I screamed hysterically. "Smack your own! Shut up! Shut up!"

At this he lost his patience and let fly at me. He did it with the lack of conviction you'd expect of a man under Mother's horrified eyes, and it ended up as a mere tap, but the sheer indignity of being struck at all by a stranger, a total stranger who had cajoled his way back from the war into our big bed as a result of my innocent intercession, made me completely dotty. I shrieked and shrieked, and danced in my bare feet, and Father, looking awkward and hairy in nothing but a short grey army shirt, glared down at me like a mountain out for murder. I think it must have been then that I realized he was jealous too. And there stood Mother in her nightdress, looking as if her heart was broken between us. I hoped she felt as she looked. It seemed to me that she deserved it all.

From that morning out my life was a hell. Father and I were enemies, open and avowed. We conducted a series of skirmishes against one another, he trying to steal my time with Mother and I his. When she was sitting on my bed, telling me a story, he took to looking for some pair of old boots which he alleged he had left behind him at the beginning of the war. While he talked to Mother I played loudly with my toys to show my total lack of concern. He created a terrible scene one evening when he came in from work and found me at his box, playing with his regimental badges, Gurkha knives and button-sticks. Mother got up and took the box from me.

"You mustn't play with Daddy's toys unless he lets you, Larry," she said severely. "Daddy doesn't play with yours."

For some reason Father looked at her as if she had struck him and then turned away with a scowl.

"Those are not toys," he growled, taking down the box again to see had I lifted anything. "Some of those curios are very rare and valuable."

But as time went on I saw more and more how he managed to alienate Mother and me. What made it worse was that I couldn't grasp his method or see what attraction he had for Mother. In every possible way he was less winning than I. He had a common accent and made noises at his tea. I thought for a while that it might be the newspapers she was interested in, so I made up bits of news of my own to read to her. Then I thought it might be the smoking, which I personally thought attractive, and took his pipes and went round the house dribbling into them till he caught me. I even made noises at my tea, but Mother only told me I was disgusting. It all seemed to hinge round that unhealthy habit of sleeping together, so I made a point of dropping into their bedroom and nosing round, talking to myself, so that they wouldn't know I was watching them, but they were never up to anything that I could see. In the end it beat me. It seemed to depend on being grown-up and giving people rings, and I realized I'd have to wait.

But at the same time I wanted him to see that I was only waiting, not giving up the fight. One evening when he was being particularly obnoxious, chattering away well above my head, I let him have it.

"Mummy," I said, "do you know what I'm going to do when I grow up?"

"No, dear," she replied. "What?"

"I'm going to marry you," I said quietly.

Father gave a great guffaw out of him, but he didn't take me in. I knew it must only be pretense. And Mother, in spite of everything, was pleased. I felt she was probably relieved to know that one day Father's hold on her would be broken.

"Won't that be nice?" she said with a smile.

"It'll be very nice," I said confidently. "Because we're going to have lots and lots of babies."

"That's right, dear," she said placidly. "I think we'll have one soon, and then you'll have plenty of company."

I was no end pleased about that because it showed that in spite of the way she gave in to Father she still considered my wishes. Besides, it would put the Geneys in their place.

It didn't turn out like that, though. To begin with, she was very preoccupied—I supposed about where she would get the seventeen and six—and though Father took to staying out late in the evenings it did me no particular good. She stopped taking me for walks, became as touchy as blazes, and smacked me for nothing at all. Sometimes I wished I'd never mentioned the confounded baby—I seemed to have a genius for bringing calamity on myself.

And calamity it was! Sonny arrived in the most appalling hullabaloo—even that much he couldn't do without a fuss—and from the first moment I disliked him. He was a difficult child—so far as I was concerned he was always difficult—and demanded far too much attention. Mother was simply silly about him, and couldn't see when he was only showing off. As company he was worse than useless. He slept all day, and I had to go round the house on tiptoe to avoid waking him. It wasn't any longer a question of not waking Father. The slogan now was "Don't-wake-Sonny!" I couldn't understand why the child wouldn't sleep at the proper time, so whenever Mother's back was turned I woke him. Sometimes to keep him awake I pinched him as well. Mother caught me at it one day and gave me a most unmerciful flaking.

One evening, when Father was coming in from work, I was playing trains in the front garden. I let on not to notice him; instead, I pretended to be talking to myself, and said in a loud voice: "If another bloody baby comes into this house, I'm going out."

Father stopped dead and looked at me over his shoulder.

"What's that you said?" he asked sternly.

"I was only talking to myself," I replied, trying to conceal my panic. "It's private."

He turned and went in without a word. Mind you, I intended it as a solemn warning, but its effect was quite different. Father started being quite nice to me. I could understand that, of course. Mother was quite sickening about Sonny. Even at mealtimes she'd get up and gawk at him in the cradle with an idiotic smile, and tell Father to do the same. He was always polite about it, but he looked so puzzled you could see he didn't know what she was talking about. He complained of the way Sonny cried at night, but she only got cross and said that Sonny never cried except when there was something up with him—which was a flaming lie, because Sonny never had anything up with him, and only cried for attention. It was really painful to see how simple-minded she was. Father wasn't attractive, but he had a fine intelligence. He saw through Sonny, and now he knew that I saw through him as well.

One night I woke with a start. There was someone beside me in the bed. For one wild moment I felt sure it must be Mother, having come to her senses and left Father for good, but then I heard Sonny in convulsions in the next room, and Mother saying: "There! There! There!" and I knew it wasn't she. It was Father. He was lying beside me, wide awake, breathing hard and apparently as mad as hell.

After a while it came to me what he was mad about. It was his turn now. After turning me out of the big bed, he had been turned out himself. Mother had no consideration now for anyone but that poisonous pup, Sonny. I couldn't help feeling sorry for Father. I had been through it all myself, and even at that age I was magnanimous. I began to stroke him down and say: "There! There!" He wasn't exactly responsive.

"Aren't you asleep either?" he snarled.

"Ah, come on and put your arm around us, can't you?" I said, and he did, in a sort of way. Gingerly, I suppose, is how you'd describe it. He was very bony but better than nothing.

At Christmas he went out of his way to buy me a really nice model railway.

PEARL CRAYTON (b. 1930)

Pearl Crayton still lives in Louisiana, the state of her birth. She has been the editor of the Alexandria News Leader, *a weekly newspaper, and the author of articles on leading Louisiana Negroes, past and present. Her stories have been published in* The Texas Quarterly *and several anthologies of black literature.*

In response to our invitation to discuss her fiction with her readers, Pearl Crayton wrote the following: "Let he who wants to create with his pen worlds to entertain others always be sure that in each of his creations there is some light that will forever shine in the memory of his readers. And to do this, the creator must put into his works something that was a light in his own life, some light of joy, or love, or wisdom, or hope. He may create midnights, and storms, and the most horrid hell, but somewhere there must also be light or his works will not live, for without light there can be no life."

In the story "The Day the World Almost Came to an End," Crayton depicts the mixture of innocent gullibility and pure terror that the imminent end of the world would produce in a twelve-year-old Louisiana girl.

The Day the World Almost Came to an End

IF YOU haven't had the world coming to an end on you when you're twelve years old and a sinner, you don't know how lucky you are! When it happened to me it scared the living daylights and some of the joy of sinning out of me and, in a lot of other ways, messed up my life altogether. But if I am to believe Ralph Waldo Emerson's "Compensation," I guess I got some good out of it too.

The calamity befell me back in 1936. We were living on a plantation in

Louisiana at the time, close to the earth and God, and all wrapped up in religion. The church was the axis around which plantation life revolved, the Mother to whom the folks took their problems, the Teacher who taught them how the Lord wanted them to live, the Chastiser who threatened the sinful with Hell.

In spite of the fact that my parents were churchgoing Christians, I was still holding on to being a sinner. Not that I had anything against religion, it was just a matter of integrity. There was an old plantation custom that in order to be baptized into the church a sinner had to "get religion," a mystical experience in which the soul of the sinner was converted into Christian. A Christian had to live upright, and I knew I just couldn't come up to that on account of there were too many delicious sins around to get into. But a world coming to an end can be pretty hard on a sinner.

The trouble began when my cousin Rena came upon me playing in the watermelon patch, running like the devil was behind her. I was making a whole quarter of mud cabins by packing dirt over my foot in the shape of a cabin, putting a chimney on top, then pulling my foot out. The space left by my foot formed the room of the cabin. I'd broken some twigs off chinaberry and sycamore trees which I planted in the ground around the cabins to make "trees." Some blooming wild flowers that I had picked made up a flower yard in front of each cabin. It was as pretty a sight as you ever want to see before she came stepping all over everything. I let her know I didn't like it real loud, but she didn't pay what I said any attention, she just blurted out, "The end of the world is coming Saturday; you'd better go get you some religion in a hurry!"

That was on a Friday afternoon, getting late.

A picture of Hell flashed across my mind but I pushed it back into the subconscious. "The world's NOT coming to an end!" The confidence I tried to put in my voice failed; it quaked a little. "Who told you the world is coming to an end?"

"I heard Mama and Miss Daya talking about it just now. There's going to be an eclipse Sunday. You know what an eclipse is, don't you?"

I didn't know but I nodded anyhow.

"That's when the sun has a fight with the moon. If the sun whips, the world goes on; if the moon whips, then the world comes to an end. Well, they say that Sunday the moon is going to whip the sun!"

I wasn't going to be scared into giving up my sinning that easily. "How do they know the moon is going to whip?" I asked.

"They read it in the almanac. And it's in the Bible too, in Revelation. It says in Revelation that the world is supposed to end this year. Miss Daya is a missionary sister and she knows all about things like that."

"Nobody knows anything about Revelation, my daddy says so," I rebutted. "Ain't never been nobody born smart enough to figure out Revelation since that Mister John wrote it. He's just going to have to come back and explain it himself."

She acted like she didn't hear that. "And Reverend Davis said in church last Sunday that time is winding up," she said.

"He's been saying that for years now, and time hasn't wound up yet."

"That's what I know, he's been saying it for years, and all the while he's been saying it time's been winding right along, and now it's just about all wound up!"

That made sense to me and I began to consider that maybe she could be right. Then that Miss Daya happened by.

"Lord bless you down there on your knees, baby! Pray to the Lord 'cause it's praying time!"

I hadn't gotten up from where I'd been making mud cabins, but I jumped up quick to let her know I wasn't praying.

"Both of you girls got religion?" she asked, and without waiting for an answer, "That's good. You're both big girls, big enough to go to Hell. You all be glad you all got religion 'cause the Lord is coming soon! He said he was coming and he's coming SOON!" And she went on towards our cabin before I could ask her about the world ending Sunday.

Rena just stood there and looked at me awhile, shaking her head in an "I told you so," and advised me again to get some religion in a hurry. Then she ran off to warn someone else.

Although I was a sinner, I was a regular churchgoing sinner and at our church we had a hellfire-preaching pastor. He could paint a picture of Hell and the Devil in his sermons horrible enough to give a sinner a whole week of nightmares. Nobody with a dime's worth of sense wanted to go to a hot, burning Hell where a red, horned Devil tormented folks with a pitchfork, but I'd been taking a chance on enjoying life another thirty years or so before getting some religion—getting just enough to keep me out of Hell. I hadn't figured on time running out on me so soon, and I still wasn't taking anybody's word before asking my daddy about it first. But it was plowing time and Daddy was way back in the cornfield where I'd already run across a rattlesnake, so I figured even the world coming to an end could wait until suppertime.

I went around the rest of that day with my mind loaded down. Now I didn't exactly believe that the world was coming to an end, but I didn't exactly believe it wasn't either. About two years before, I'd went and read the worst part of Revelation and it had taken my daddy two weeks to convince me that I didn't understand what I had read, which still didn't keep me from having bad dreams about the moon dripping away in blood and a lot of other distressing visions aroused from misunderstood words.

Those dreams were only a vague and frightening memory the Friday I'm talking about, and Revelation an accepted mystery. Yet things like that have a way of sneaking back on you when you need it the least. I got to "supposing" the world did come to an end with earthquakes and hail and fire raining down from the sky and stars falling, exactly like it read in Revelation, and "supposing" the Devil got after me and took me to Hell like folks on the plantation said he would, and "supposing" Hell really and truly was as horrible as the preacher said it was. The way the preacher told it, in Hell a person got burned and burned up and never died, he just kept on burning, burning, burning. With "supposing" like that going through it, my mind was really loaded down! I figured there was no use talking to Mama about what was bothering me because that Miss Daya had stayed at our cabin for over an hour, and I was sure she had convinced Mama that the moon was going to whip the sun.

It seemed to me like it took Daddy longer than ever to come home. It was the Friday of Council Meeting at the church, and Daddy, a deacon, had to be there. I knew he wouldn't have much time to talk to me before he'd have to leave out for the church, so I started walking up the turnrow through the fields to meet him. When I finally saw him riding towards home on his slide I ran to meet him.

Daddy always hitched a plank under his plow to keep the plow blades from cutting up the turnrow when he came home from plowing the fields. The plank, which we called a slide, was long enough behind the plow for him to stand on and ride home, pulled by his plow horse. Whenever I ran to meet him he'd let me ride home with him on the slide.

"Daddy," I said as soon as he'd put me on the slide in front of him and "gee'd" the horse to go on, "is the world going to come to an end Sunday?"

"I don't know, honey," he replied. "Why do you want to know?"

I told him about Rena's prophecy. That really tickled him! He laughed and laughed like that was the funniest thing he'd ever heard! I laughed a little too, though I didn't get the joke in it.

"There's always somebody coming around prophesying that the world's coming to an end," he said after he'd laughed himself out. "Folks been doing that ever since I was a boy, they were doing it when my daddy was a boy, aw, they've been doing that for hundreds of years and the world is still here. Don't you ever pay any attention to anybody that comes around telling you the world is going to end, baby."

"But ain't the world *ever* going to end?" I wanted to know.

"Yeah, but don't anybody know when. Only the Lord knows that. Why, the world might not end for another thousand years, then again it might end tonight, we just don't know. . . ."

"TONIGHT! You mean the world might end TONIGHT!"

"Sure. I'm not saying it will but it could. A person never can tell about a thing like that. But if you let that bother you, why you'll be scared to death every day of your life looking for the world to end. You're not going to be that silly, are you?"

"Aw, shucks no," I lied. I was that silly. Right then and there I got to looking for the world to end, right there on the *spot!*

Like anybody expecting a calamity, I decided to sit up all night that night but Mama made me go to bed. My room was full of the plantation, the darkest of darkness. Before Daddy returned from church Mama put out the coal oil lamp and went to bed.

The lazy old moon was on its vacation again; there was no light anywhere, not a speck. Although my eyes couldn't see anything in that awful dark, my mind had always been very good at seeing things in the dark that weren't there. I got to "seeing" how it was going to be when the world ended, the whole drama of it paraded right before my mind. Then my imagination marched me up before the judgment seat to give account for my past sins and I tried to figure out how much burning I'd get for each offense. Counting up all the ripe plums and peaches I'd saved from going to waste on the neighbors' trees, neglecting to get the owners' permission, the fights I'd had with that sassy little Catherine who lived across the river, the domino games I'd played for penny stakes with my sinner-cousin, Sam, the times I'd handled the truth careless enough to save myself from a whipping, and other not so holy acts, I figured I'd be in for some real hot burning.

While I lay there in that pitch-black darkness worrying myself sick about burning in Hell, a distant rumbling disturbed the stillness of the night, so faint that at first I wasn't sure I'd heard it. I sat up in the bed, straining my ears listening. Sure enough there was a rumbling, far away. The rumbling wasn't thunder, I was sure of that because thunder rumbled, then died away, but this rumbling grew louder and louder and LOUDER. A slow-moving, terrible, loud rumbling that was to my scared mind the earth quaking, the sky caving in, the world ending!

I got out of there, I got out of there *fast!* I didn't even think about being dressed only in my nightgown or the awful dark outside being full of ghosts and bogeymen and other horrors, I just ran!

"The world is ending! The world is ending! Run! Run for your life!" I shouted a warning to Mama, and I just kept on hollering as I ran down the road past the other plantation cabins. "The world is ending! The world is ending! Run! Run for your life!"

Doors opened and folks came out on the cabin porches, some holding coal oil lamps in their hands. They'd look at me in my white nightgown running down the road as fast as a scared rabbit, then look up at the sky, rumbling like it was caving in, and a few of them hollered something at me as I passed by, but I couldn't make out what any of them said.

I might have run myself plumb to the ocean or death if Daddy and some other deacons hadn't been coming up the road on their way from church. Daddy caught me. He had a hard time holding me though. The fear of the Devil and Hell was stronger in me than reason. I was dead set on escaping them.

Daddy had heard my hollering about the world ending as I ran down the road towards them, so he kept telling me, "That's just an old airplane, honey, the world's not ending. That's just an old airplane making all that racket!"

When his words got through the fear that fogged my mind I calmed down a bit. "Airplane?" I'd only heard about airplanes, never had I seen one or heard one passing by.

Daddy laughed. "You were just about outrunning that old airplane and keeping up almost as much racket!" He pointed toward the sky. "Look up there, you see, it's gone now. See that light moving towards town? That's it. Those old airplanes sure have scared a lot of folks with all that racket they make."

I looked up. Sure enough there was a light that looked like a star moving across the sky. The rumbling was way off in the distance, going away slowly like it had come. And the sky was whole, not a piece of it had caved in! I broke down and cried because I was so relieved that the world wasn't coming to an end, because I'd been so scared for so long, because I'd made such a fool of myself, and just because.

Daddy pulled off his suit coat and wrapped it around me to hide the shame of my nightgown from the deacons. After I'd had a real good cry we walked home.

As we walked up the ribbon of road bordering the plantation on our way home I felt a new kind of happiness inside of me. The yellow squares of light shining from the black shapes of the plantation cabins outlined against the night made a picture that looked beautiful to me for the first time. Even the chirping of the crickets sounded beautiful, like a new song I'd never heard before. Even the darkness was beautiful, everything was beautiful. And I was alive, I felt the life within me warming me from the inside, a happy feeling I'd never had before. And the world was there all around me, I was aware of it, aware of all of it, full of beauty, full of happy things to do. Right then and there I was overwhelmed with a desire to *live,* really *live* in the world and enjoy as much of it as I could before it came to an end. And I've been doing so ever since.

ERNEST J. GAINES (b. 1933)

Although he left rural Louisiana for California at the age of fifteen, Ernest J. Gaines' writing largely reflects the Creole-Negro atmosphere of the Louisiana backwater of his childhood, particularly the conflicts arising from the resistance of its deeply embedded pride-ridden way of life to the infusion of new ideas and change.

After graduating from San Francisco State College in 1957, Gaines studied for a year at Stanford University on a creative writing fellowship.

His published novels to date are Catherine Carmier *(1964),* Of Love and Dust *(1967), and* Autobiography of Miss Jane Pitman *(1971). His short stories appeared in* Negro Digest *and several anthologies of black literature before publication in* Bloodline *(1968).*

"The Sky Is Gray" (1963) looks, through the eyes of an eight-year-old black boy, at the conflicting aspects of the rural Southern world in which his mother attempts to guide him toward manhood through the inner strength of her pride and independence.

The Sky Is Gray

GO'N BE COMING in a few minutes. Coming 'round that bend down there full speed. And I'm go'n get out my hankercher and I'm go'n wave it down, and us go'n get on it and go.

I keep on looking for it, but Mama don't look that way no more. She looking down the road where us jest come from. It's a long old road, and far's you can see you don't see nothing but gravel. You got dry weeds on both sides, and you got trees on both sides, and fences on both sides, too. And you got cows in the pastures and they standing close together. And when us was coming out yer to catch the bus I seen the smoke coming out o' the cow's nose.

I look at my mama and I know what she thinking. I been with Mama so much, jest me and her, I know what she thinking all the time. Right now it's home—Auntie and them. She thinking if they got 'nough wood—if she left 'nough there to keep 'em warm till us get back. She thinking if it go'n rain and if any of 'em go'n have to go out in the rain. She thinking 'bout the hog—if he go'n get out, and if Ty and Val be able to get him back in. She always worry like that when she leave the house. She don't worry too much if she leave me there with the smaller ones 'cause she know I'm go'n look after 'em and look after Auntie and everything else. I'm the oldest and she say I'm the man.

I look at my mama and I love my mama. She wearing that black coat and that black hat and she looking sad. I love my mama and I want put my arm 'round her and tell her. But I'm not s'pose to do that. She say that's weakness and that's cry-baby stuff, and she don't want no cry-baby 'round her. She don't want you to be scared neither. 'Cause Ty scared of ghosts and she always whipping him. I'm scared of the dark, too. But I make 'tend I ain't. I make 'tend I ain't 'cause I'm the oldest, and I got to set a good sample for the rest. I can't ever be scared and I can't ever cry. And that's the reason I didn't never say nothing 'bout my teef. It been hurting me and hurting me close to a month now. But I didn't say it. I didn't say it 'cause I didn't want act like no cry-baby, and 'cause I know us didn't have 'nough money to have it pulled. But, Lord, it been hurting me. And look like it won't start till at night when you trying to get little sleep. Then soon's you shet your eyes—umm-umm, Lord, look like it go right down to your heart string.

"Hurting, hanh?" Ty'd say.

I'd shake my head, but I wouldn't open my mouth for nothing. You open your mouth and let that wind in, and it almost kill you.

I'd just lay there and listen to 'em snore. Ty, there, right 'side me, and Auntie and Val over by the fireplace. Val younger 'an me and Ty, and he sleep with Auntie. Mama sleep 'round the other side with Louis and Walker.

I'd just lay there and listen to 'em, and listen to that wind out there, and listen to that fire in the fireplace. Sometime it'd stop long enough to let me get little rest. Sometime it just hurt, hurt, hurt. Lord, have mercy.

II

Auntie knowed it was hurting me. I didn't tell nobody but Ty, 'cause us buddies and he ain't go'n tell nobody. But some kind o' way Auntie found out. When she asked me, I told her no, nothing was wrong. But she knowed it all the time. She told me to mash up a piece o' aspirin and wrap it in some cotton and jugg it down in that hole. I did it, but it didn't do no good. It stopped for a little while, and started right back again. She wanted to tell Mama, but I told her Uh-uh. 'Cause I knowed it didn't have no money, and it jest was go'n make her mad again. So she told Monsieur Bayonne, and Monsieur Bayonne came to the house and told me to kneel down 'side him on the fireplace. He put his finger in his mouth and made the Sign of the Cross on my jaw. The tip of Monsieur Bayonne finger is some hard, 'cause he always playing on that guitar. If us sit outside at night us can always hear Monsieur Bayonne playing on his guitar. Sometime us leave him out there playing on the guitar.

He made the Sign of the Cross over and over on my jaw, but that didn't do no good. Even when he prayed and told me to pray some, too, that teef still hurt.

"How you feeling?" he say.

"Same," I say.

He kept on praying and making the Sign of the Cross and I kept on praying, too.

"Still hurting?" he say.

"Yes, sir."

Monsieur Bayonne mashed harder and harder on my jaw. He mashed so hard he almost pushed me on Ty. But then he stopped.

"What kind o' prayers you praying, boy?" he say.

"Baptist," I say.

"Well, I'll be—no wonder that teef still killing him. I'm going one way and he going the other. Boy, don't you know any Catholic prayers?"

"Hail Mary," I say.

"Then you better start saying it."

"Yes, sir."

He started mashing again, and I could hear him praying at the same time. And, sure 'nough, afterwhile it stopped.

Me and Ty went outside where Monsieur Bayonne two hounds was, and us started playing with 'em. "Let's go hunting," Ty say. "All right," I say; and us went on back in the pasture. Soon the hounds got on a trail, and me and Ty followed 'em all cross the pasture and then back in the woods, too. And then they cornered this little old rabbit and killed him, and me and Ty made 'em get back, and us picked up the rabbit and started on back home. But it had started hurting me again. It was hurting me plenty now, but I wouldn't tell Monsieur Bayonne. That night I didn't sleep a bit, and first thing in the morning Auntie told me go back and let Monsieur Bayonne pray over me some more. Monsieur Bayonne was in his kitchen making coffee when I got there. Soon's he seen me, he knowed what was wrong.

"All right, kneel down there 'side that stove," he say. "And this time pray Catholic. I don't know nothing 'bout Baptist, and don't want know nothing 'bout him."

III

Last night Mama say: "Tomorrow us going to town."

"It ain't hurting me no more," I say. "I can eat anything on it."

"Tomorrow us going to town," she say.

And after she finished eating, she got up and went to bed. She always go to bed early now. 'Fore Daddy went in the Army, she used to stay up late. All o' us sitting out on the gallery or 'round the fire. But now, look like soon's she finish eating she go to bed.

This morning when I woke up, her and Auntie was standing 'fore the fireplace. She say: " 'Nough to get there and back. Dollar and a half to have it pulled. Twenty-five for me to go, twenty-five for him. Twenty-five for me to come back, twenty-five for him. Fifty cents left. Guess I get a little piece o' salt meat with that."

"Sure can use a piece," Auntie say. "White beans and no salt meat ain't white beans."

"I do the best I can," Mama say.

They was quiet after that, and I made 'tend I was still sleep.

"James, hit the floor," Auntie say.

I still made 'tend I was sleep. I didn't want 'em to know I was listening.

"All right," Auntie say, shaking me by the shoulder. "Come on. Today's the day."

I pushed the cover down to get out, and Ty grabbed it and pulled it back.

"You, too, Ty," Auntie say.

"I ain't getting no teef pulled," Ty say.

"Don't mean it ain't time to get up," Auntie say. "Hit it, Ty."

Ty got up grumbling.

"James, you hurry up and get in your clothes and eat your food," Auntie say. "What time y'all coming back?" she say to Mama.

"That 'leven o'clock bus," Mama say. "Got to get back in that field this evening."

"Get a move on you, James," Auntie say.

I went in the kitchen and washed my face, then I ate my breakfast. I was having bread and syrup. The bread was warm and hard and tasted good. And I tried to make it last a long time.

Ty came back there, grumbling and mad at me.

"Got to get up," he say. "I ain't having no teef pulled. What I got to be getting up for."

Ty poured some syrup in his pan and got a piece of bread. He didn't wash his hands, neither his face, and I could see that white stuff in his eyes.

"You the one getting a teef pulled," he say. "What I got to get up for. I bet you if I was getting a teef pulled, you wouldn't be getting up. Shucks; syrup again. I'm getting tired of this old syrup. Syrup, syrup, syrup. I want me some bacon sometime."

"Go out in the field and work and you can have bacon," Auntie say. She stood in the middle door looking at Ty. "You better be glad you got syrup. Some people ain't got that—hard's time is."

"Shucks," Ty say. "How can I be strong."

"I don't know too much 'bout your strength," Auntie say; "but I know where you go'n be hot, you keep that grumbling up. James, get a move on you; your mama waiting."

I ate my last piece of bread and went in the front room. Mama was standing 'fore the fireplace warming her hands. I put on my coat and my cap, and us left the house.

IV

I look down there again, but it still ain't coming. I almost say, "It ain't coming, yet," but I keep my mouth shet. 'Cause that's something else she don't like. She don't like for you to say something just for nothing. She can see it ain't coming, I can see it ain't coming, so why say it ain't coming. I don't say it, and I turn and look at the river that's back o' us. It so cold the smoke just raising up from the water. I see a bunch of pull-doos not too far out—jest on the other side the lilies. I'm wondering if you can eat pull-doos. I ain't too sure, 'cause I ain't never ate none. But I done ate owls and black birds, and I done ate red birds, too. I didn't want kill the red birds, but she made me kill 'em. They had two of 'em back there. One in my trap, one in Ty trap. Me and Ty was go'n play with 'em and let 'em go. But she made me kill 'em 'cause us needed the food.

"I can't," I say. "I can't."

"Here," she say. "Take it."

"I can't," I say. "I can't. I can't kill him, Mama. Please."

"Here," she say. "Take this fork, James."

"Please, Mama, I can't kill him," I say.

I could tell she was go'n hit me. And I jecked back, but I didn't jeck back soon enough.

"Take it," she say.

I took it and reached in for him, but he kept hopping to the back.

"I can't, Mama," I say. The water just kept running down my face. "I can't."

"Get him out o' there," she say.

I reached in for him and he kept hopping to the back. Then I reached in farther, and he pecked me on the hand.

"I can't Mama," I say.

She slapped me again.

I reached in again, but he kept hopping out my way. Then he hopped to one side, and I reached there. The fork got him on the leg and I heard his leg pop. I pulled my hand out 'cause I had hurt him.

"Give it here," she say, and jecked the fork out my hand.

She reached and got the little bird right in the neck. I heard the fork go in his neck, and I heard it go in the ground. She brought him out and helt him right in front o' me.

"That's one," she say. She shook him off and gived me the fork. "Get the other one."

"I can't, Mama. I do anything. But I can't do that."

She went to the corner o' the fence and broke the biggest switch over there. I knelt 'side the trap crying.

"Get him out o' there," she say.

"I can't, Mama."

She started hitting me cross the back. I went down on the ground crying.

"Get him," she say.

"Octavia," Auntie say.

'Cause she had come out o' the house and she was standing by the tree looking at us.

"Get him out o' there," Mama say.

"Octavia," Auntie say; "explain to him. Explain to him. Jest don't beat him. Explain to him."

But she hit me and hit me and hit me.

I'm still young. I ain't no more'an eight. But I know now. I know why I had to. (They was so little, though. They was so little. I 'member how I picked the feathers off 'em and cleaned 'em and helt 'em over the fire. Then us all ate 'em. Ain't had but little bitty piece, but us all had little bitty piece, and ever-'body jest looked at me, 'cause they was so proud.) S'pose she had to go away? That's why I had to do it. S'pose she had to go away like Daddy went away? Then who was go'n look after us? They had to be somebody left to carry on. I didn't know it then, but I know it now. Auntie and Monsieur Bayonne talked to me and made me see.

V

Time I see it, I get out my hankercher and start waving. It still 'way down there, but I keep waving anyhow. Then it come closer and stop and me and Mama get on. Mama tell me go sit in the back while she pay. I do like she say, and the people look at me. When I pass the little sign that say White and Colored, I start looking for a seat. I jest see one of 'em back there, but I don't take it, 'cause I want my mama to sit down herself. She come in the back and sit down, and I lean on the seat. They got seats in the front, but I know I can't sit there, 'cause I have to sit back o' the sign. Anyhow, I don't want sit there if my mama go'n sit back here.

They got a lady sitting 'side my mama and she look at me and grin little bit. I grin back, but I don't open my mouth, 'cause the wind'll get in and make that teef hurt. The lady take out a pack o' gum and reach me a slice, but I shake my head. She reach Mama a slice, and Mama shake her head. The lady jest can't understand why a little boy'll turn down gum, and she reached me a slice again. This time I point to my jaw. The lady understand and grin little bit, and I grin little bit, but I don't open my mouth, though.

They got a girl sitting 'cross from me. She got on a red overcoat, and her hair plaited in one big plait. First, I make 'tend I don't even see her. But then I start looking at her little bit. She make 'tend she don't see me neither, but I catch her looking that way. She got a cold, and ever' now and then she hist that little hankercher to her nose. She ought to blow it, but she don't. Must think she too much a lady or something.

Ever' time she hist that little hankercher, the lady 'side her say something in her yer. She shake her head and lay her hands in her lap again. Then I catch her kind o' looking where I'm at. I grin at her. But think she'll grin back? No. She turn up her little old nose like I got some snot on my face or something. Well, I show her both o' us can turn us head. I turn mine, too, and look out at the river.

The river is gray. The sky is gray. They have pull-doos on the water. The water is wavy, and the pull-doos go up and down. The bus go 'round a turn, and you got plenty trees hiding the river. Then the bus go 'round another turn, and I can see the river again.

I look to the front where all the white people sitting. Then I look at that little old gal again. I don't look right at her, 'cause I don't want all them people to know I love her. I jest look at her little bit, like I'm looking out that window over there. But she know I'm looking that way, and she kind o' look at me, too. The lady sitting 'side her catch her this time, and she lean over and say something in her yer.

"I don't love him nothing," that little old gal say out loud.

Ever'body back there yer her mouth, and all of 'em look at us and laugh.

"I don't love you, neither," I say. "So you don't have to turn up your nose, Miss."

"You the one looking," she say.

"I wasn't looking at you," I say. "I was looking out that window, there."

"Out that window, my foot," she say. "I seen you. Ever' time I turn 'round you look at me."

"You must o' been looking yourself if you seen me all them times," I say.

"Shucks," she say. "I got me all kind o' boyfriends."

"I got girlfriends, too," I say.

"Well, I just don't want you to get your hopes up," she say.

I don't say no more to that little old gal, 'cause I don't want have to bust her in the mouth. I lean on the seat where Mama sitting, and I don't even look that way no more. When us get to Bayonne, she jugg her little old tongue out at me. I make 'tend I'm go'n hit her, and she duck down side her mama. And all the people laugh at us again.

VI

Me and Mama get off and start walking in town. Bayonne is a little bitty town. Baton Rouge is a hundred times bigger 'an Bayonne. I went to Baton Rouge once—me, Ty, Mama, and Daddy. But that was 'way back yonder—'fore he went in the Army. I wonder when us go'n see him again. I wonder when. Look like he ain't ever coming home. . . . Even the pavement all cracked in Bayonne. Got grass shooting right out the sidewalk. Got weeds in the ditch, too; jest like they got home.

It some cold in Bayonne. Look like it colder 'an it is home. The wind blow in my face, and I feel that stuff running down my nose. I sniff. Mama say use that hankercher. I blow my nose and put it back.

Us pass a school and I see them white children playing in the yard. Big old red school, and them children jest running and playing. Then us pass a café, and I see a bunch of 'em in there eating. I wish I was in there 'cause I'm cold. Mama tell me keep my eyes in front where they blonks.

Us pass stores that got dummies, and us pass another café, and then us pass a shoe shop, and that baldhead man in there fixing on a shoe. I look at him and I butt into that white lady, and Mama jeck me in front and tell me stay there.

Us come to the courthouse, and I see the flag waving there. This one yer ain't like the one us got at school. This one yer ain't got but a handful of stars. One at school got a big pile of stars—one for ever' state. Us pass it and us turn and there it is—the dentist office. Me and Mama go in, and they got people sitting ever' where you look. They even got a little boy in there younger 'an me.

Me and Mama sit on that bench, and a white lady come in there and ask me what my name. Mama tell her, and the white lady go back. Then I yer somebody hollering in there. And soon's that little boy hear him hollering, he start hollering, too. His mama pat him and pat him, trying to make him hush up, but he ain't thinking 'bout her.

The man that was hollering in there come out holding his jaw.

"Got it, hanh?" another man say.

The man shake his head.

"Man, I thought they was killing you in there," the other man say. "Hollering like a pig under a gate."

The man don't say nothing. He jest head for the door, and the other man follow him.

"John Lee," the white lady say. "John Lee Williams."

The little boy jugg his head down in his mama lap and holler more now. His mama tell him go with the nurse, but he ain't thinking 'bout her. His mama tell him again, but he don't even yer. His mama pick him up and take him in there, and even when the white lady shet the door I can still hear him hollering.

"I often wonder why the Lord let a child like that suffer," a lady say to my mama. The lady's sitting right in front o' us on another bench. She got on a white dress and a black sweater. She must be a nurse or something herself, I reckoned.

"Not us to question," a man say.

"Sometimes I don't know if we shouldn't," the lady say.

"I know definitely we shouldn't," the man say. The man look like a preacher. He big and fat and he got on a black suit. He got a gold chain, too.

"Why?" the lady say.

"Why anything?" the preacher say.

"Yes," the lady say. "Why anything?"

"Not us to question," the preacher say.

The lady look at the preacher a little while and look at Mama again.

"And look like it's the poor who do most the suffering," she say. "I don't understand it."

"Best not to even try," the preacher say. "He works in mysterious ways. Wonders to perform."

Right then Little John Lee bust out hollering, and ever'body turn they head.

"He's not a good dentist," the lady say. "Dr. Robillard is much better. But more expensive. That's why most of the colored people come here. The white people go to Dr. Robillard. Y'all from Bayonne?"

"Down the river," my mama say. And that's all she go'n say, 'cause she don't talk much. But the lady keep on looking at her, and so she say: "Near Morgan."

"I see," the lady say.

VII

"That's the trouble with the black people in this country today," somebody else say. This one yer sitting on the same side me and Mama sitting, and he kind o'sitting in front of that preacher. He look like a teacher or somebody that go to college. He got on a suit, and he got a book that he been reading. "We don't question is exactly the trouble," he say. "We should question and question and question. Question everything."

The preacher jest look at him a long time. He done put a toothpick or something in his mouth, and he jest keep turning it and turning it. You can see he don't like that boy with that book.

"Maybe you can explain what you mean," he say.

"I said what I meant," the boy say. "Question everything. Every stripe, every star, every word spoken. Everything."

"It 'pears to me this young lady and I was talking 'bout God, young man," the preacher say.

"Question Him, too," the boy say.

"Wait," the preacher say. "Wait now."

"You heard me right," the boy say. "His existence as well as everything else. Everything."

The preacher jest look cross the room at the boy. You can see he getting madder and madder. But mad or no mad, the boy ain't thinking 'bout him. He look at the preacher jest's hard's the preacher look at him.

"Is this what they coming to?" the preacher say. "Is this what we educating them for?"

"You're not educating me," the boy say. "I wash dishes at night to go to school in the day. So even the words you spoke need questioning."

The preacher jest look at him and shake his head.

"When I come in this room and seen you there with your book, I said to myself, There's an intelligent man. How wrong a person can be."

"Show me one reason to believe in the existence of a God," the boy say.

"My heart tell me," the preacher say.

"My heart tells me," the boy say. "My heart tells me. Sure, my heart tells me. And as long as you listen to what your heart tells you, you will have only what the white man gives you and nothing more. Me, I don't listen to my heart. The purpose of the heart is to pump blood throughout the body, and nothing else."

"Who's your paw, boy?" the preacher say.

"Why?"

"Who is he?"

"He's dead."

"And your mom?"

"She's in Charity Hospital with pneumonia. Half killed herself working for nothing."

"And 'cause he's dead and she sick, you mad at the world?"

"I'm not mad at the world. I'm questioning the world. I'm questioning it with cold logic, sir. What do words like Freedom, Liberty, God, White, Colored mean? I want to know. That's why *you* are sending us to school, to read and to ask questions. And because we ask these questions, you call us mad. No, sir, it is not us who are mad."

"You keep saying 'us'?"

" 'Us' . . . why not? I'm not alone."

The preacher jest shake his head. Then he look at ever'body in the room—ever'body. Some of the people look down at the floor, keep from looking at him. I kind o' look 'way myself, but soon's I know he done turn his head, I look that way again.

"I'm sorry for you," he say.

"Why?" the boy say. "Why not be sorry for yourself? Why are you so much better off than I am? Why aren't you sorry for these other people in here? Why not be sorry for the lady who had to drag her child into the dentist office? Why not be sorry for the lady sitting on that bench over there? Be sorry for them. Not for me. Some way or other I'm going to make it."

"No, I'm sorry for you," the preacher say.

"Of course. Of course," the boy say, shaking his head. "You're sorry for me because I rock that pillar you're leaning on."

"You can't ever rock the pillar I'm leaning on, young man. It's stronger than anything man can ever do."

"You believe in God because a man told you to believe in God. A white man told you to believe in God. And why? To keep you ignorant, so he can keep you under his feet."

"So now, we the ignorant?"

"Yes," the boy say. "Yes." And he open his book again.

The preacher jest look at him there. The boy done forgot all about him. Ever'body else make 'tend they done forgot 'bout the squabble, too.

Then I see that preacher getting up real slow. Preacher a great big old man, and he got to brace hisself to get up. He come 'cross the room where the boy is. He jest stand there looking at him, but the boy don't raise his head.

"Stand up, boy," preacher say.

The boy look up at him, then he shet his book real slow and stand up. Preacher jest draw back and hit him in the face. The boy fall 'gainst the wall, but he straighten hisself up and look right back at that preacher.

"You forgot the other cheek," he say.

The preacher hit him again on the other side. But this time the boy don't fall.

"That hasn't changed a thing," he say.

The preacher jest look at the boy. The preacher breathing real hard like he jest run up a hill. The boy sit down and open his book again.

"I feel sorry for you," the preacher say. "I never felt so sorry for a man before."

The boy make 'tend he don't even hear that preacher. He keep on reading his book. The preacher go back and get his hat off the chair.

"Excuse me," he say to us. "I'll come back some other time. Y'all, please excuse me."

And he look at the boy and go out the room. The boy hist his hand up to his mouth one time, to wipe 'way some blood. All the rest o' the time he keep on reading.

VIII

The lady and her little boy come out the dentist, and the nurse call somebody else in. Then little bit later they come out, and the nurse call another name. But fast's she call somebody in there, somebody else come in the place where we at, and the room stay full.

The people coming in now, all of 'em wearing big coats. One of 'em say something 'bout sleeting, and another one say he hope not. Another one say he think it ain't nothing but rain. 'Cause, he say, rain can get awful cold this time o' year.

All 'cross the room they talking. Some of 'em talking to people right by 'em, some of 'em talking to people clare 'cross the room, some of 'em talking to anybody'll listen. It's a little bitty room, no bigger 'an us kitchen, and I can see ever'body in there. The little old room 's full of smoke, 'cause you got two old men smoking pipes. I think I feel my teef thumping me some, and I hold my breath and wait. I wait and wait, but it don't thump me no more. Thank God for that.

I feel like going to sleep, and I lean back 'gainst the wall. But I'm scared to go to sleep: Scared 'cause the nurse might call my name and I won't hear her. And Mama might go to sleep, too, and she be mad if neither us heard the nurse.

I look up at Mama. I love my mama. I love my mama. And when cotton come I'm go'n get her a newer coat. And I ain't go'n get a black one neither. I think I'm go'n get her a red one.

"They got some books over there," I say. "Want read one of 'em?"

Mama look at the books, but she don't answer me.

"You got yourself a little man there," the lady say.

Mama don't say nothing to the lady, but she must 'a' grin a little bit, 'cause I seen the lady grinning back. The lady look at me a little while, like she feeling sorry for me.

"You sure got that preacher out here in a hurry," she say to that other boy.

The boy look up at her and look in his book again. When I grow up I want be jest like him. I want clothes like that and I want keep a book with me, too.

"You really don't believe in God?" the lady say.

"No," he say.

"But why?" the lady say.

"Because the wind is pink," he say.

"What?" the lady say.

The boy don't answer her no more. He jest read in his book.

"Talking 'bout the wind is pink," that old lady say. She sitting on the same bench with the boy, and she trying to look in his face. The boy make 'tend the old lady ain't even there. He jest keep reading. "Wind is pink," she say again. "Eh, Lord, what children go'n be saying next?"

The lady 'cross from us bust out laughing.

"That's a good one," she say. "The wind is pink. Yes, sir, that's a good one."

"Don't you believe the wind is pink?" the boy say. He keep his head down in the book.

"Course I believe it, Honey," the lady say. "Course I do." She look at us and wink her eye. "And what color is grass, Honey?"

"Grass? Grass is black."

She bust out laughing again. The boy look at her.

"Don't you believe grass is black?" he say.

The lady quit laughing and look at him. Ever'body else look at him now. The place quiet, quiet.

"Grass is green, Honey," the lady say. "It was green yesterday, it's green today, and it's go'n be green tomorrow."

"How do you know it's green?"

"I know because I know."

"You don't know it's green. You believe it's green because someone told you it was green. If someone had told you it was black you'd believe it was black."

"It's green," the lady say. "I know green when I see green."

"Prove it's green."

"Surely, now," the lady say. "Don't tell me it's coming to that?"

"It's coming to just that," the boy say. "Words mean nothing. One means no more than the other."

"That's what it all coming to?" the old lady say. That old lady got on a turban and she got on two sweaters. She got a green sweater under a black sweater. I can see the green sweater 'cause some of the buttons on the other sweater missing.

"Yes, ma'am," the boy say. "Words mean nothing. Action is the only thing. Doing. That's the only thing."

"Other words, you want the Lord to come down here and show Hisself to you?" she say.

"Exactly, ma'am."

"You don't mean that, I'm sure?"

"I do, ma'am."

"Done, Jesus," the old lady say, shaking her head.

"I didn't go 'long with that preacher at first," the other lady say; "but now —I don't know. When a person say the grass is black, he's either a lunatic or something wrong."

"Prove to me that it's green."

"It's green because the people say it's green."

"Those same people say we're citizens of the United States."

"I think I'm a citizen."

"Citizens have certain rights. Name me one right that you have. One right, granted by the Constitution, that you can exercise in Bayonne."

The lady don't answer him. She jest look at him like she don't know what he talking 'bout. I know I don't.

"Things changing," she say.

"Things are changing because some black men have begun to follow their brains instead of their hearts."

"You trying to say these people don't believe in God?"

"I'm sure some of them do. Maybe most of them do. But they don't believe that God is going to touch these white people's hearts and change them tomorrow. Things change through action. By no other way."

Ever'body sit, quiet and look at the boy. Nobody say a thing. Then the lady 'cross from me and Mama jest shake her head.

"Let's hope that not all your generation feel the same way you do," she say.

"Think what you please, it doesn't matter," the boy say. "But it will be men who listen to their heads and not their hearts who will see that your children have a better chance than you had."

"Let's hope they ain't all like you, though," the old lady say. "Done forgot the heart absolutely."

"Yes, ma'am, I hope they aren't all like me," the boy say. "Unfortunately I was born too late to believe in your God. Let's hope that the ones who come after will have your faith—if not in your God, then in something else, something definitely that they can lean on. I haven't anything. For me, the wind is pink; the grass is black."

IX

The nurse come in the room where us all sitting and waiting and say the doctor won't take no more patients till one o'clock this evening. My mama jump up off the bench and go up to the white lady.

"Nurse, I have to go back in the field this evening," she say.

"The doctor is treating his last patient now," the nurse say. "One o'clock this evening."

"Can I at least speak to the doctor?" my mama say.

"I'm his nurse," the lady say.

"My little boy sick," my mama say. "Right now his teef almost killing him."

The nurse look at me. She trying to make up her mind if to let me come in. I look at her real pitiful. The teef ain't hurting me a tall, but Mama say it is, so I make 'tend for her sake.

"This evening," the nurse say, and go back in the office.

"Don't feel 'jected, Honey," the lady say to Mama. "I been 'round 'em a long time—they take you when they want to. If you was white, that's something else; but you the wrong shade."

Mama don't say nothing to the lady, and me and her go outside and stand 'gainst the wall. It's cold out there. I can feel that wind going through my coat. Some of the other people come out of the room and go up the street. Me and Mama stand there a little while and start to walking. I don't know where us going. When us come to the other street us jest stand there.

"You don't have to make water, do you?" Mama say.

"No, ma'am," I say.

Us go up the street. Walking real slow. I can tell Mama don't know where she going. When us come to a store us stand there and look at the dummies. I look at a little boy with a brown overcoat. He got on brown shoes, too. I look at my old shoes and look at his'n again. You wait till summer, I say.

Me and Mama walk away. Us come up to another store and us stop and look at them dummies, too. Then us go again. Us pass a café where the white people in there eating. Mama tell me keep my eyes in front where they blonks, but I can't help from seeing them people eat. My stomach start to growling 'cause I'm hungry. When I see people eating, I get hungry; when I see a coat, I get cold.

A man whistle at my mama when us go by a filling station. She make 'tend she don't even see him. I look back and I feel like hitting him in the mouth. If I was bigger, I say. If I was bigger, you see.

Us keep on going. I'm getting colder and colder, but I don't say nothing. I feel that stuff running down my nose and I sniff.

"That rag," she say.

I git it out and wipe my nose. I'm getting cold all over now—my face, my hands, my feet, ever'thing. Us pass another little café, but this'n for white people, too, and us can't go in there neither. So us jest walk. I'm so cold now, I'm 'bout ready to say it. If I knowed where us was going, I wouldn't be so cold, but I don't know where us going. Us go, us go, us go. Us walk clean out o' Bayonne. Then us cross the street and us come back. Same thing I seen when I got off the bus. Same old trees, same old walk, same old weeds, same old cracked pave—same old ever'thing.

I sniff again.

"That rag," she say.

I wipe my nose real fast and jugg that hankercher back in my pocket 'fore my hand get too cold. I raise my head and I can see David hardware store. When us come up to it, us go in. I don't know why, but I'm glad.

It warm in there. It so warm in there you don't want ever leave. I look for the heater, and I see it over by them ba'ls. Three white men standing 'round the heater talking in Creole. One of 'em come to see what Mama want.

"Got any ax handle?" she say.

Me, Mama, and the white man start to the back, but Mama stop me when us come to the heater. Her and the white man go on. I hold my hand over the heater and look at 'em. They go all the way in the back, and I see the white man point to the ax handle 'gainst the wall. Mama take one of 'em and shake it like she trying to figure how much it weigh. Then she rub her hand over it from one end to the other. She turn it over and look at the other side, then she shake it again, and shake her head and put it back. She get another one and she do it jest like she did the first one, then she shake her head. Then she get a brown one and do it that, too. But she don't like this one neither. Then she get another one, but 'fore she shake it or anything, she look at me. Look like she trying to say something to me, but I don't know what it is. All I know is I done got warm now and I'm feeling right smart better. Mama shake this ax handle jest like she done the others, and shake her head and say something to the white man. The white man jest look at his pile of ax handle, and when Mama pass by him to come to the front, the white man jest scratch his head and follow her. She tell me come on, and us go on out and start walking again.

Us walk and walk, and no time at all I'm cold again. Look like I'm colder now 'cause I can still remember how good it was back there. My stomach growl and I suck it in to keep Mama from yering it. She walking right 'side me, and it growl so loud you can yer it a mile. But Mama don't say a word.

X

When us come up to the courthouse, I look at the clock. It got quarter to twelve. Mean us got another hour and a quarter to be out yet in the cold. Us go and stand side a building. Something hit my cap and I look up at the sky. Sleet falling.

I look at Mama standing there. I want stand close 'side her, but she don't like that. She say that's cry-baby stuff. She say you got to stand for yourself, by yourself.

"Let's go back to that office," she say.

Us cross the street. When us get to the dentist I try to open the door, but I can't. Mama push me on the side and she twist the knob. But she can't open it neither. She twist it some more, harder, but she can't open it. She turn 'way from the door. I look at her, but I don't move and I don't say nothing. I done seen her like this before and I'm scared.

"You hungry?" she say. She say it like she mad at me, like I'm the one cause of ever'thing.

"No, ma'am," I say.

"You want eat and walk back, or you rather don't eat and ride?"

"I ain't hungry," I say.

I ain't jest hungry, but I'm cold, too. I'm so hungry and I'm so cold I want cry. And look like I'm getting colder and colder. My feet done got numb. I try to work my toes, but I can't. Look like I'm go'n die. Look like I'm go'n stand right here and freeze to death. I think about home. I think about Val and Auntie and Ty and Louis and Walker. It 'bout twelve o'clock and I know they eating dinner. I can hear Ty making jokes. That's Ty. Always trying to make some kind o' joke. I wish I was right there listening to him. Give anything in the world if I was home 'round the fire.

"Come on," Mama say.

Us start walking again. My feet so numb I can't hardly feel 'em. Us turn the corner and go back up the street. The clock start hitting for twelve.

The sleet's coming down plenty now. They hit the pave and bounce like rice. Oh, Lord; oh, Lord, I pray. Don't let me die. Don't let me die. Don't let me die, Lord.

XI

Now I know where us going. Us going back o' town where the colored people eat. I don't care if I don't eat. I been hungry before. I can stand it. But I can't stand the cold.

I can see us go'n have a long walk. It 'bout a mile down there. But I don't mind. I know when I get there I'm go'n warm myself. I think I can hold out.

My hands numb in my pockets and my feet numb, too, but if I keep moving I can hold out. Jest don't stop no more, that's all.

The sky's gray. The sleet keep falling. Falling like rain now—plenty, plenty. You can hear it hitting the pave. You can see it bouncing. Sometimes it bounce two times 'fore it settle.

Us keep going. Us don't say nothing. Us jest keep going, keep going.

I wonder what Mama thinking. I hope she ain't mad with me. When summer come I'm go'n pick plenty cotton and get her a coat. I'm go'n get her a red one.

I hope they make it summer all the time. I be glad if it was summer all the time—but it ain't. Us got to have winter, too. Lord, I hate the winter. I guess ever'body hate the winter.

I don't sniff this time. I get out my hankercher and wipe my nose. My hand so cold I can hardly hold the hankercher.

I think us getting close, but us ain't there yet. I wonder where ever'body is. Can't see nobody but us. Look like us the only two people moving 'round today. Must be too cold for the rest of the people to move 'round.

I can hear my teefes. I hope they don't knock together too hard and make that bad one hurt. Lord, that's all I need, for that bad one to start off.

I hear a church bell somewhere. But today ain't Sunday. They must be ringing for a funeral or something.

I wonder what they doing at home. They must be eating. Monsieur Bayonne might be there with his guitar. One day Ty played with Monsieur Bayonne guitar and broke one o' the string. Monsieur Bayonne got some mad with Ty. He say Ty ain't go'n never 'mount to nothing. Ty can go jest like him when he ain't there. Ty can make ever'body laugh mocking Monsieur Bayonne.

I used to like to be with Mama and Daddy. Us used to be happy. But they took him in the Army. Now, nobody happy no more. . . . I be glad when he come back.

Monsieur Bayonne say it wasn't fair for 'em to take Daddy and give Mama nothing and give us nothing. Auntie say, Shhh, Etienne. Don't let 'em yer you talk like that. Monsieur Bayonne say, It's God truth. What they giving his children? They have to walk three and a half mile to school hot or cold. That's anything to give for a paw? She's got to work in the field rain or shine jest to make ends meet. That's anything to give for a husband? Auntie say, Shhh, Etienne, shhh. Yes, you right, Monsieur Bayonne say. Best don't say it in front of 'em now. But one day they go'n find out. One day. Yes, s'pose so, Auntie say. Then what, Rose Mary? Monsieur Bayonne say. I don't know, Etienne, Auntie say. All us can do is us job, and leave ever'thing else in His hand. . . .

Us getting closer, now. Us getting closer. I can see the railroad tracks.

Us cross the tracks, and now I see the café. Jest to get in there, I say. Jest to get in there. Already I'm starting to feel little better.

XII

Us go in. Ahh, it good. I look for the heater; there 'gainst the wall. One of them little brown ones. I jest stand there and hold my hand over it. I can't open my hands too wide 'cause they almost froze.

Mama standing right 'side me. She done unbuttoned her coat. Smoke rise out the coat, and the coat smell like a wet dog.

I move to the side so Mama can have more room. She open out her hands and rub 'em together. I rub mine together, too, 'cause this keeps 'em from hurting. If you let 'em warm too fast, they hurt you sure. But if you let 'em warm jest little bit at a time, and you keep rubbing 'em, they be all right ever' time.

They got jest two more people in the café. A lady back o' the counter, and a man on this side the counter. They been watching us ever since us come in.

Mama get out the hankercher and count the money. Both o' us know how much money she got there. Three dollars. No, she ain't got three dollars. 'Cause she had to pay us way up here. She ain't got but two dollars and a half left. Dollar and a half to get my teef pulled, and fifty cents for us to go back on, and fifty cents worse o' salt meat.

She stir the money 'round with her finger. Most o' the money is change 'cause I can hear it rubbing together. She stir it and stir it. Then she look at the door. It still sleeting. I can yer it hitting 'gainst the wall like rice.

"I ain't hungry, Mama," I say.

"Got to pay 'em something for they heat," she say.

She take a quarter out the hankercher and tie the hankercher up again. She look over her shoulder at the people, but she still don't move. I hope she don't spend the money. I don't want her spend it on me. I'm hungry, I'm almost starving I'm so hungry, but I don't want her spending the money on me.

She flip the quarter over like she thinking. She must be thinking 'bout us walking back home. Lord, I sure don't want walk home. If I thought it done any good to say something, I say it. But my mama make up her own mind.

She turn way from the heater right fast, like she better hurry up and do it 'fore she change her mind. I turn to look at her go to the counter. The man and the lady look at her, too. She tell the lady something and the lady walk away. The man keep on looking at her. Her back turn to the man, and Mama don't even know he standing there.

The lady put some cakes and a glass o' milk on the counter. Then she pour up a cup o' coffee and set it side the other stuff. Mama pay her for the things and come back where I'm at. She tell me sit down at that table 'gainst the wall.

The milk and the cakes for me. The coffee for my mama. I eat slow, and I look at her. She looking outside at the sleet. She looking real sad. I say to myself, I'm go'n make all this up one day. You see, one day, I'm go'n make all this up. I want to say it now. I want to tell how I feel right now. But Mama don't like for us to talk like that.

"I can't eat all this," I say.

They got just three little cakes there. And I'm so hungry right now, the Lord know I can eat a hundred times three. But I want her to have one.

She don't even look my way. She know I'm hungry. She know I want it. I let it stay there a while, then I get it and eat it. I eat jest on my front teefes, 'cause if it tech that back teef I know what'll happen. Thank God it ain't hurt me a tall today.

After I finish eating I see the man go to the juke box. He drop a nickel in it, then he jest stand there looking at the record. Mama tell me keep my eyes in front where they blonks. I turn my head like she say, but then I yer the man coming towards us.

"Dance, Pretty?" he say.

Mama get up to dance with him. But 'fore you know it, she done grabbed the little man and done throwed him 'side the wall. He hit the wall so hard he stop the juke box from playing.

"Some pimp," the lady back o' the counter say. "Some pimp."

The little man jump off the floor and start towards my mama. 'Fore you know it, Mama done sprung open her knife and she waiting for him.

"Come on," she say. "Come on. I'll cut you from your neighbo to your throat. Come on."

I go up to the little man to hit him, but Mama make me come and stand 'side her. The little man look at me and Mama and go back to the counter.

"Some pimp," the lady back o' the counter say. "Some pimp." She start laughing and pointing at the little man. "Yes, sir, you a pimp, all right. Yes, sir."

XIII

"Fasten that coat. Let's go," Mama say.

"You don't have to leave," the lady say.

Mama don't answer the lady, and us right out in the cold again. I'm warm right now—my hands, my yers, my feet—but I know this ain't go'n last too long. It done sleet so much now you got ice ever'where.

Us cross the railroad tracks, and soon's us do, I get cold. That wind go through this little old coat like it ain't nothing. I got a shirt and a sweater under it, but that wind don't pay 'em no mind. I look up and I can see us got a long way to go. I wonder if us go'n make it 'fore I get too cold.

Us cross over to walk on the sidewalk. They got jest one sidewalk back here. It's over there.

After us go jest a little piece, I smell bread cooking. I look, then I see a baker shop. When us get closer, I can smell it more better. I shet my eyes and make 'tend I'm eating. But I keep 'em shet too long and I butt up 'gainst a telephone post. Mama grab me and see if I'm hurt. I ain't bleeding or nothing and she turn me loose.

I can feel I'm getting colder and colder, and I look up to see how far us still got to go. Uptown is 'way up yonder. A half mile, I reckoned. I try to think of something. They say think and you won't get cold. I think of that poem, *Annabel Lee.* I ain't been to school in so long—this bad weather—I reckoned they done passed *Annabel Lee.* But passed it or not, I'm sure Miss Walker go'n make me recite it when I get there. That woman don't never forget nothing. I ain't never seen nobody like that.

I'm still getting cold. *Annabel Lee* or no *Annabel Lee,* I'm still getting cold. But I can see us getting closer. Us getting there gradually.

Soon's us turn the corner, I see a little old white lady up in front o' us. She the only lady on the street. She all in black and she got a long black rag over her head.

"Stop," she say.

Me and Mama stop and look at her. She must be crazy to be out in all this sleet. Ain't got but a few other people out there, and all of 'em men.

"Yall done ate?" she say.

"Jest finished," Mama say.

"Yall must be cold then?" she say.

"Us headed for the dentist," Mama say. "Us'll warm up when us get there."

"What dentist?" the old lady say. "Mr. Bassett?"

"Yes, ma'am," Mama say.

"Come on in," the old lady say. "I'll telephone him and tell him yall coming."

Me and Mama follow the old lady in the store. It's a little bitty store, and it don't have much in there. The old lady take off her head piece and fold it up.

"Helena?" somebody call from the back.

"Yes, Alnest?" the old lady say.

"Did you see them?"

"They're here. Standing beside me."

"Good. Now you can stay inside."

The old lady look at Mama. Mama waiting to hear what she brought us in here for. I'm waiting for that, too.

"I saw yall each time you went by," she say. "I came out to catch you, but you were gone."

"Us went back o' town," Mama say.

"Did you eat?"

"Yes, ma'am."

The old lady look at Mama a long time, like she thinking Mama might be jest saying that. Mama look right back at her. The old lady look at me to see what I got to say. I don't say nothing. I sure ain't going 'gainst my mama.

"There's food in the kitchen," she say to Mama. "I've been keeping it warm."

Mama turn right around and start for the door.

"Just a minute," the old lady say. Mama stop. "The boy'll have to work for it. It isn't free."

"Us don't take no handout," Mama say.

"I'm not handing out anything," the old lady say. "I need my garbage moved to the front. Ernest has a bad cold and can't go out there."

"James'll move it for you," Mama say.

"Not unless you eat," the old lady say. "I'm old, but I have my pride, too, you know."

Mama can see she ain't go'n beat this old lady down, so she jest shake her head.

"All right," the old lady say. "Come into the kitchen."

She lead the way with that rag in her hand. The kitchen is a little bitty thing, too. The table and the stove jest about fill it up. They got a little room to the side. Somebody in there laying cross the bed. Must be the person she was talking with: Alnest or Ernest—I forget what she call him.

"Sit down," the old lady say to Mama. "Not you," she say to me. "You have to move the cans."

"Helena?" somebody say in the other room.

"Yes, Alnest?" the old lady say.

"Are you going out there again?"

"I must show the boy where the garbage is," the old lady say.

"Keep that shawl over your head," the old man say.

"You don't have to remind me. Come boy," the old lady say.

Us go out in the yard. Little old back yard ain't no bigger 'an the store or the kitchen. But it can sleet here jest like it can sleet in any big back yard. And 'fore you know it I'm trembling.

"There," the old lady say, pointing to the cans. I pick up one of the cans. The can so light I put it back down to look inside o' it.

"Here," the old lady say. "Leave that cap alone."

I look at her in the door. She got that black rag wrapped 'round her shoulders, and she pointing one of her fingers at me.

"Pick it up and carry it to the front," she say. I go by her with the can. I'm sure the thing 's empty. She could 'a' carried the thing by herself, I'm sure. "Set it on the sidewalk by the door and come back for the other one," she say.

I go and come back, Mama look at me when I pass her. I get the other can and take it to the front. It don't feel no heavier 'an the other one. I tell myself to look inside and see just what I been hauling. First, I look up and down the street. Nobody coming. Then I look over my shoulder. Little old lady done slipped there jest 's quiet 's mouse, watching me. Look like she knowed I was go'n try that.

"Ehh, Lord," she say. "Children, children. Come in here, boy, and go wash your hands."

I follow her into the kitchen, and she point, and I go to the bathroom. When I come out, the old lady done dished up the food. Rice, gravy, meat, and she even got some lettuce and tomato in a saucer. She even got a glass o' milk and a piece o' cake there, too. It look so good. I almost start eating 'fore I say my blessing.

"Helena?" the old man say.

"Yes, Alnest?" she say.

"Are they eating?"

"Yes," she say.

"Good," he say. "Now you'll stay inside."

The old lady go in there where he is and I can hear 'em talking. I look at Mama. She eating slow like she thinking. I wonder what 's the matter now. I reckoned she think 'bout home.

The old lady come back in the kitchen.

"I talked to Dr. Bassett's nurse," she say. "Dr. Bassett will take you as soon as you get there."

"Thank you, ma'am," Mama say.

"Perfectly all right," the old lady say. "Which one is it?"

Mama nod towards me. The old lady look at me real sad. I look sad, too.

"You're not afraid, are you?" she say.

"No'm," I say.

"That's a good boy," the old lady say. "Nothing to be afraid of."

When me and Mama get through eating, us thank the old lady again.

"Helena, are they leaving?" the old man say.

"Yes, Alnest."

"Tell them I say good-by."

"They can hear you, Alnest."

"Good-by both mother and son," the old man say. "And may God be with you."

Me and Mama tell the old man good-by, and us follow the old lady in the front. Mama open the door to go out, but she stop and come back in the store.

"You sell salt meat?" she say.

"Yes."

"Give me two bits worse."

"That isn't very much salt meat," the old lady say.

"That'll all I have," Mama say.

The old lady go back o' the counter and cut a big piece off the chunk. Then she wrap it and put it in a paper bag.

"Two bits," she say.

"That look like awful lot of meat for a quarter," Mama say.

"Two bits," the old lady say. "I've been selling salt meat behind this counter twenty-five years. I think I know what I'm doing."

"You got a scale there," Mama say.

"What?" the old lady say.

"Weigh it," Mama say.

"What?" the old lady say. "Are you telling me how to run my business?"

"Thanks very much for the food," Mama say.

"Just a minute," the old lady say.

"James," Mama say to me. I move towards the door.

"Just one minute, I said," the old lady say.

Me and Mama stop again and look at her. The old lady take the meat out the bag and unwrap it and cut 'bout half o' it off. Then she wrap it up again and jugg it back in the bag and give it to Mama. Mama lay the quarter on the counter.

"Your kindness will never be forgotten," she say. "James," she say to me.

Us go out, and the old lady come to the door to look at us. After us go a little piece I look back, and she still there watching us.

The sleet's coming down heavy, heavy now, and I turn up my collar to keep my neck warm. My mama tell me turn it right back down.

"You not a bum," she say. "You a man."

TED POSTON (b. 1906)

In response to our invitation to discuss his life and work directly with his readers, Ted Poston has sent us the following:

"I was born in Hopkinsville, Kentucky on July 4, 1906 and attended the Booker T. Washington Colored Grammar School, which is the locale of "The Revolt of the Evil Fairies" and a half dozen other short stories now included in other anthologies.

"The story was written, between editions, in the City Room of the New York Post *and for my own amusement. I am glad I wrote it, and several others, because it captured, I hope, a period that no longer exists. There is less intra-racial tension and aggravation than that time when conflicts between light and dark Negroes were more intense than the present interracial tensions between whites and blacks. And, alas, the most redundantly-named educational institution in America is no longer called the Booker T. Washington Colored Grammar School, but something like Public School No. 2, and they've even got a few white kids there—thanks to the U. S. Supreme Court ruling of 1954.*

"I have been employed by the New York Post *since 1937, except for a*

five-year period during World War II when I went to Washington where I served, among other government assignments, as administrative assistant to Jonathan Daniels at the White House and later at the same post under David Niles during the Roosevelt and Truman administrations. Technically, I was deputy director of the Office of War Information during this period, under the late Elmer Davis.

I will probably retire from the Post *next year and after I get over my present horror of the sight of a typewriter I will again try to recapture my childhood in the Booker T. Washington Colored Grammar School."*

The Revolt of the Evil Fairies

THE GRAND dramatic offering of the Booker T. Washington Colored Grammar School was the biggest event of the year in our social life in Hopkinsville, Kentucky. It was the one occasion on which they let us use the old Cooper Opera House, and even some of the white folks came out yearly to applaud our presentation. The first two rows of the orchestra were always reserved for our white friends, and our leading colored citizens sat right behind them—with an empty row intervening, of course.

Mr. Ed Smith, our local undertaker, invariably occupied a box to the left of the house and wore his cutaway coat and striped breeches. This distinctive garb was usually reserved for those rare occasions when he officiated at the funerals of our most prominent colored citizens. Mr. Thaddeus Long, our colored mailman, once rented a tuxedo and bought a box too. But nobody paid him much mind. We knew he was just showing off.

The title of our play never varied. It was always Prince Charming and the Sleeping Beauty, but no two presentations were ever the same. Miss H. Belle LaPrade, our sixth-grade teacher, rewrote the script every season, and it was never like anything you read in the storybooks.

Miss LaPrade called it "a modern morality play of conflict between the forces of good and evil." And the forces of evil, of course, always came off second best.

The Booker T. Washington Colored Grammar School was in a state of ferment from Christmas until February, for this was the period when parts were assigned. First there was the selection of the Good Fairies and the Evil Fairies. This was very important, because the Good Fairies wore white costumes and the Evil Fairies black. And strangely enough most of the Good Fairies usually turned out to be extremely light in complexion, with straight hair and white folks' features. On rare occasions a darkskinned girl might be lucky enough to be a Good Fairy, but not one with a speaking part.

There never was any doubt about Prince Charming and the Sleeping Beauty. They were always lightskinned. And though nobody ever discussed those things openly, it was an accepted fact that a lack of pigmentation was a decided advantage in the Prince Charming and Sleeping Beauty sweepstakes.

And therein lay my personal tragedy. I made the best grades in my class, I was the leading debater, and the scion of a respected family in the community. But I could never be Prince Charming, because I was black.

In fact, every year when they started casting our grand dramatic offering my family started pricing black cheesecloth at Franklin's Department Store. For they knew that I would be leading the forces of darkness and skulking back in the shadows—waiting to be vanquished in the third act. Mamma had experience with this sort of thing. All my brothers had finished Booker T. before me.

Not that I was alone in my disappointment. Many of my classmates felt it too. I probably just took it more to heart. Rat Joiner, for instance, could rationalize the situation. Rat was not only black; he lived on Billy Goat Hill. But Rat summed it up like this:

"If you black, you black."

I should have been able to regard the matter calmly too. For our grand dramatic offering was only a reflection of our daily community life in Hopkinsville. The yallers had the best of everything. They held most of the teaching jobs in Booker T. Washington Colored Grammar School. They were the Negro doctors, the lawyers, the insurance men. They even had a "Blue Vein Society," and if your dark skin obscured your throbbing pulse you were hardly a member of the elite.

Yet I was inconsolable the first time they turned me down for Prince Charming. That was the year they picked Roger Jackson. Roger was not only dumb; he stuttered. But he was light enough to pass for white, and that was apparently sufficient.

In all fairness, however, it must be admitted that Roger had other qualifications. His father owned the only colored saloon in town and was quite a power in local politics. In fact, Mr. Clinton Jackson had a lot to say about just who taught in the Booker T. Washington Colored Grammar School. So it was understandable that Roger should have been picked for Prince Charming.

My real heartbreak, however, came the year they picked Sarah Williams for Sleeping Beauty. I had been in love with Sarah since kindergarten. She had soft light hair, bluish-gray eyes, and a dimple which stayed in her left cheek whether she was smiling or not.

Of course Sarah never encouraged me much. She never answered any of my fervent love letters, and Rat was very scornful of my one-sided love affairs. "As long as she don't call you a black baboon," he sneered, "you'll keep on hanging around."

After Sarah was chosen for Sleeping Beauty, I went out for the Prince

Charming role with all my heart. If I had declaimed boldly in previous contests, I was matchless now. If I had bothered Mamma with rehearsals at home before, I pestered her to death this time. Yes, and I purloined my sister's can of Palmer's Skin Success.

I knew the Prince's role from start to finish, having played the Head Evil Fairy opposite it for two seasons. And Prince Charming was one character whose lines Miss LaPrade never varied much in her many versions. But although I never admitted it, even to myself, I knew I was doomed from the start. They gave the part to Leonardius Wright. Leonardius, of course, was yaller.

The teachers sensed my resentment. They were almost apologetic. They pointed out that I had been such a splendid Head Evil Fairy for two seasons that it would be a crime to let anybody else try the role. They reminded me that Mamma wouldn't have to buy any more cheesecloth because I could use my same old costume. They insisted that the Head Evil Fairy was even more important than Prince Charming because he was the one who cast the spell on Sleeping Beauty. So what could I do but accept?

I had never liked Leonardius Wright. He was a goody-goody, and even Mamma was always throwing him up to me. But, above all, he too was in love with Sarah Williams. And now he got a chance to kiss Sarah every day in rehearsing the awakening scene.

Well, the show must go on, even for little black boys. So I threw my soul into my part and made the Head Evil Fairy a character to be remembered. When I drew back from the couch of Sleeping Beauty and slunk away into the shadows at the approach of Prince Charming, my facial expression was indeed something to behold. When I was vanquished by the shining sword of Prince Charming in the last act, I was a little hammy perhaps—but terrific!

The attendance at our grand dramatic offering that year was the best in its history. Even the white folks overflowed the two rows reserved for them, and a few were forced to sit in the intervening one. This created a delicate situation, but everybody tactfully ignored it.

When the curtain went up on the last act, the audience was in fine fettle. Everything had gone well for me too—except for one spot in the second act. That was where Leonardius unexpectedly rapped me over the head with his sword as I slunk off into the shadows. That was not in the script, but Miss LaPrade quieted me down by saying it made a nice touch anyway. Rat said Leonardius did it on purpose.

The third act went on smoothly, though, until we came to the vanquishing scene. That was where I slunk from the shadows for the last time and challenged Prince Charming to mortal combat. The hero reached for his shining sword—a bit unsportsmanlike, I always thought, since Miss LaPrade consistently left the Head Evil Fairy unarmed—and then it happened!

Later I protested loudly—but in vain—that it was a case of self-defense. I pointed out that Leonardius had a mean look in his eye. I cited the impromptu rapping he had given my head in the second act. But nobody would listen. They just wouldn't believe that Leonardius really intended to brain me when he reached for his sword.

Anyway, he didn't succeed. For the minute I saw that evil gleam in his eye —or was it my own?—I cut loose with a right to the chin, and Prince Charming dropped his shining sword and staggered back. His astonishment lasted only a minute, though, for he lowered his head and came charging in, fists flailing. There was nothing yellow about Leonardius but his skin.

The audience thought the scrap was something new Miss LaPrade had written in. They might have kept on thinking so if Miss LaPrade hadn't been screaming so hysterically from the sidelines. And if Rat Joiner hadn't decided that this was as good a time as any to settle old scores. So he turned around and took a sock at the male Good Fairy nearest him.

When the curtain rang down, the forces of Good and Evil were locked in combat. And Sleeping Beauty was wide awake and streaking for the wings.

They rang the curtain back up fifteen minutes later, and we finished the play. I lay down and expired according to specifications but Prince Charming will probably remember my sneering corpse to his dying day. They wouldn't let me appear in the grand dramatic offering at all the next year. But I didn't care. I couldn't have been Prince Charming anyway.

RICHARD WRIGHT (1908–1960)

Richard Wright was born on a farm near Natchez, Mississippi, and spent an impoverished and dismal childhood in the South. Moving to Chicago at the age of nineteen, he found the quality of life there hardly at all like that he had come to expect from his reading of H. L. Mencken, Sinclair Lewis, and Theodore Dreiser. He discovered instead that black people in Chicago were little better off or better treated than those in the South. As a consequence, he became active in the Communist movement and published in radical journals such as New Masses *and* The Daily Worker. *After about ten years, he became disillusioned with Communism too and he quit the Party. Eventually, he would leave America as well.*

Wright's first important book was Uncle Tom's Children *(1938), a collection of short fiction portraying black rural Southern sharecroppers who, unable to accept the position of an Uncle Tom, become alienated and find themselves involved in violent conflict with the white Southern society around them.*

Native Son *(1940), Wright's next book, was a landmark in American literature, the first black protest novel to place the burden of guilt for the degradation of the Negro in America clearly upon its white readers. Its brutalized, violent protagonist, Bigger Thomas, is emphatically a "native son," very much an offspring of American racism. Soon after publishing* Black Boy *(1945), the autobiography in which personal loneliness and frustration are strong notes, Wright left America for France, never to return. He died there in 1960.*

"Big Boy Leaves Home," from Uncle Tom's Children, *is a numbing, terrifying story of the violent coming of age of a young black boy who accidentally sets off a series of events that culminates in his pursuit by a lynch mob.*

Big Boy Leaves Home

I

Yo mama don wear no drawers . . .

Clearly, the voice rose out of the woods, and died away. Like an echo another voice caught it up:

Ah seena when she pulled em off . . .

Another, shrill, cracking, adolescent:

N she washed 'em in alcohol . . .

Then a quartet of voices, blending in harmony, floated high above the tree tops:

N she hung 'em out in the hall . . .

Laughing easily, four black boys came out of the woods into cleared pasture. They walked lollingly in bare feet, beating tangled vines and bushes with long sticks.

"Ah wished Ah knowed some mo lines t tha song."

"Me too."

"Yeah, when yuh gits t where she hangs em out in the hall yuh has t stop."

"Shucks, whut goes wid *hall?*"

"Call."

"Fall."

"Wall."

"Quall."

They threw themselves on the grass, laughing.
"Big Boy?"
"Huh?"
"Yuh know one thing?"
"Whut?"
"Yuh sho is crazy!"
"Crazy?"
"Yeah, yuh crazys a bed-bug!"
"Crazy bout whut?"
"Man, whoever hearda *quall?*"
"Yuh said yuh wanted something t go wid *hall,* didnt yuh?"
"Yeah, but whuts a *quall?*"
"Nigger, a *qualls* a *quall.*"
They laughed easily, catching and pulling long green blades of grass with their toes.
"Waal, ef a *qualls* a *quall,* whut IS a *quall?*"
"Oh, Ah know."
"Whut?"
"Tha ol song goes something like this:

Yo mama don wear no drawers,
Ah seena when she pulled em off,
N she washed em in alcohol,
N she hung em out in the hall,
N then she put em back on her QUALL!"

They laughed again. Their shoulders were flat to the earth, their knees propped up, and their faces square to the sun.
"Big Boy, yuhs CRAZY!"
"Don ax me nothin else."
"Nigger, yuhs CRAZY!"
They fell silent, smiling, drooping the lids of their eyes softly against the sunlight.
"Man, don the groun feel warm?"
"Jus lika bed."
"Jeeesus, Ah could stay here ferever."
"Me too."
"Ah kin feel tha ol sun going all thu me."
"Feels like mah bones is warm."
In the distance a train whistled mournfully.
"There goes number fo!"
"Hittin on all six!"
"Highballin it down the line!"
"Boun fer up Noth, Lawd, boun fer up Noth!"
They began to chant, pounding bare heels in the grass.

Dis train boun fo Glory
Dis train, Oh Hallelujah
Dis train boun fo Glory
Dis train, Oh Hallelujah
Dis train boun fo Glory
Ef yuh ride no need fer fret er worry
Dis train, Oh Hallelujah
Dis train . . .

Dis train don carry no gambler
Dis train, Oh Hallelujah
Dis train don carry no gambler
Dis train, Oh Hallelujah
Dis train don carry no gambler
No fo day creeper er midnight rambler
Dis train, Oh Hallelujah
Dis train . . .

When the song ended they burst out laughing, thinking of a train bound for Glory.

"Gee, thas a good ol song!"

"Huuuuummmmmmmmman . . ."

"Whut?"

"Geeee whiiiiiiz . . ."

"Whut?"

"Somebody don let win! Das whut!"

Buck, Bobo, and Lester jumped up. Big Boy stayed on the ground, feigning sleep.

"Jeeesus, tha sho stinks!"

"Big Boy!"

Big Boy feigned to snore.

"Big Boy!"

Big Boy stirred as though in sleep.

"Big Boy!"

"Hunh?"

"Yuh rotten inside!"

"Rotten?"

"Lawd, cant yuh smell it?"

"Smell whut?"

"Nigger, yuh mus gotta bad col!"

"Smell whut?"

"NIGGER, YUH BROKE WIN!"

Big Boy laughed and fell back on the grass, closing his eyes.

"The hen whut cackles is the hen whut laid the egg."

"We ain no hens."

"Yuh cackled, didnt yuh?"

The three moved off with noses turned up.

"C mon!"

"Where yuh-all goin?"

"T the creek fer a swim."

"Yeah, les swim."

"Naw buddy naw!" said Big Boy, slapping the air with a scornful palm.

"Aw, c mon! Don be a heel!"

"N git *lynched?* Hell naw!"

"He ain gonna see us."

"How yuh know?"

"Cause he ain."

"Yuh-all go on. Ahma stay right here," said Big Boy.

"Hell, let im stay! C mon, les go," said Buck.

The three walked off, swishing at grass and bushes with sticks. Big Boy looked lazily at their backs.

"Hey!"

Walking on, they glanced over their shoulders.

"Hey, niggers!"

"C mon!"

Big Boy grunted, picked up his stick, pulled to his feet, and stumbled off.

"Wait!"

"C mon!"

He ran, caught up with them, leaped upon their backs, bearing them to the ground.

"Quit, Big Boy!"

"Gawddam, nigger!"

"Git t hell offa me!"

Big Boy sprawled in the grass beside them, laughing and pounding his heels in the ground.

"Nigger, what yuh think we is, hosses?"

"How come yuh awways hoppin on us?"

"Lissen, wes gonna double-team on yuh one of these days n beat yo ol ass good."

Big Boy smiled.

"Sho nough?"

"Yeah, don yuh like it?"

"We gonna beat yuh sos yuh cant walk!"

"N dare yuh to do nothin erbout it!"

Big Boy bared his teeth.

"C mon! Try it now!"

The three circled around him.

"Say, Buck, yuh grab his feets!"

"N yuh git his head, Lester!"
"N Bobo, yuh git berhin n grab his arms!"
Keeping more than arm's length, they circled round and round Big Boy.
"C mon!" said Big Boy, feinting at one and then the other.
Round and round they circled, but could not seem to get any closer. Big Boy stopped and braced his hands on his hips.
"Is all three of yuh-all scareda me?"
"Les git im some other time," said Bobo, grinning.
"Yeah, we kin ketch yuh when yuh ain thinkin," said Lester.
"We kin trick yuh," said Buck.
They laughed and walked together.
Big Boy belched.
"Ahm hongry," he said.
"Me too."
"Ah wished Ah hada big hot pota belly-busters!"
"Cooked wid some good ol salty ribs . . ."
"N some good ol egg cornbread . . ."
"N some buttermilk . . ."
"N some hot peach cobbler swimmin in juice . . ."
"Nigger, hush!"
They began to chant, emphasizing the rhythm by cutting at grass with sticks.

Bye n bye
Ah wanna piece of pie
Pies too sweet
Ah wanna piece of meat
Meats too red
Ah wanna piece of bread
Breads too brown
Ah wanna go t town
Towns too far
Ah wanna ketch a car
Cars too fas
Ah fall n break mah ass
Ahll understan it better bye n bye . . .

They climbed over a barbed-wire fence and entered a stretch of thick woods. Big Boy was whistling softly, his eyes half-closed.
"LES GIT IM!"
Buck, Lester, and Bobo whirled, grabbed Big Boy about the neck, arms, and legs, bearing him to the ground. He grunted and kicked wildly as he went back into weeds.
"Hol im tight!"
"Git his arms! Git his arms!"

"Set on his legs so he cant kick!"

Big Boy puffed heavily, trying to get loose.

"WE GOT YUH NOW, GAWDDAMMIT, WE GOT YUH NOW!"

"Thas a Gawddam lie!" said Big Boy. He kicked, twisted, and clutched for a hold on one and then the other.

"Say, yuh-all hep me hol his arms!" said Bobo.

"Aw, we got this bastard now!" said Lester.

"Thas a Gawddam lie!" said Big Boy again.

"Say, yuh-all hep me hol his arms!" called Bobo.

Big Boy managed to encircle the neck of Bobo with his left arm. He tightened his elbow scissors-like and hissed through his teeth:

"Yuh got me, ain yuh?"

"Hol im!"

"Les beat this bastard's ass!"

"Say, hep me hol his *arms!* Hes got aholda mah *neck!*" cried Bobo.

Big Boy squeezed Bobo's neck and twisted his head to the ground.

"Yuh got me, ain yuh?"

"Quit, Big Boy, yuh chokin me; yuh hurtin mah neck!" cried Bobo.

"Turn me loose!" said Big Boy.

"Ah ain got yuh! Its the others whut got yuh!" pleaded Bobo.

"Tell them others t git t hell offa me or Ahma break yo neck," said Big Boy.

"Ssssay, yyyuh-all gggit ooooffa Bbig Boy. Hhhes got me," gurgled Bobo.

"Cant yuh hol im?"

"Nnaw, hhes ggot mmah nneck . . ."

Big Boy squeezed tighter.

"N Ahma break it too less yuh tell em t git t hell offa me!"

"Ttturn mmmeee llloose," panted Bobo, tears gushing.

"Cant yuh hol im, Bobo?" asked Buck.

"Nnaw, yuh-all tturn im llose; hhhes got mah nnneck . . ."

"Grab his neck, Bobo . . ."

"Ah cant; yugurgur . . ."

To save Bobo, Lester and Buck got up and ran to a safe distance. Big Boy released Bobo, who staggered to his feet, slobbering and trying to stretch a crick out of his neck.

"Shucks, nigger, yuh almos broke mah neck," whimpered Bobo.

"Ahm gonna break yo ass nex time," said Big Boy.

"Ef Bobo coulda hel yuh we woulda had yuh," yelled Lester.

"Ah wuznt gonna let im do that," said Big Boy.

They walked together again, swishing sticks.

"Yuh see," began Big Boy, "when a ganga guys jump on yuh, all yuh gotta do is jus put the heat on one of them n make im tell the others t let up, see?"

"Gee, thas a good idee!"

"Yeah, thas a good idee!"

"But yuh almos broke mah neck, man," said Bobo.
"Ahma smart nigger," said Big Boy, thrusting out his chest.

II

They came to the swimming hole.
"Ah ain goin in," said Bobo.
"Done got scared?" asked Big Boy.
"Naw, Ah ain scared . . ."
"How come yuh ain goin in?"
"Yuh know ol man Harvey don erllow no niggers t swim in this hole."
"N jus las year he took a shot at Bob fer swimmin in here," said Lester.
"Shucks, ol man Harvey ain studyin bout us niggers," said Big Boy.
"Hes at home thinkin about his jelly-roll," said Buck.
They laughed.
"Buck, yo mins lowern a snakes belly," said Lester.
"Ol man Harveys too doggone ol t think erbout jelly-roll," said Big Boy.
"Hes dried up; all the saps done lef im," said Bobo.
"C mon, les go!" said Big Boy.
Bobo pointed.
"See tha sign over yonder?"
"Yeah."
"Whut it say?"
"NO TRESPASSIN," read Lester.
"Know whut tha mean?"
"Mean ain no dogs n niggers erllowed," said Buck.
"Waal, wes here now," said Big Boy. "Ef he ketched us even like this thered be trouble, so we just as waal go on in . . ."
"Ahm wid the nex one!"
"Ahll go ef anybody else goes!"
Big Boy looked carefully in all directions. Seeing nobody, he began jerking off his overalls.
"LAS ONE INS A OL DEAD DOG!"
"THAS YO MA!"
"THAS YO PA!"
"THAS BOTH YO MA N YO PA!"
They jerked off their clothes and threw them in a pile under a tree. Thirty seconds later they stood, black and naked, on the edge of the hole under a sloping embankment. Gingerly Big Boy touched the water with his foot.
"Man, this waters col," he said.
"Ahm gonna put mah cloes back on," said Bobo, withdrawing his foot.
Big Boy grabbed him about the waist.

"Like hell yuh is!"

"Git outta the way, nigger!" Bobo yelled.

"Throw im in!" said Lester.

"Duck im!"

Bobo crouched, spread his legs, and braced himself against Big Boy's body. Locked in each other's arms, they tussled on the edge of the hole, neither able to throw the other.

"C mon, les me n yuh push em in."

"O.K."

Laughing, Lester and Buck gave the two locked bodies a running push. Big Boy and Bobo splashed, sending up silver spray in the sunlight. When Big Boy's head came up he yelled:

"Yuh bastard!"

"Tha wuz yo ma yuh pushed!" said Bobo, shaking his head to clear the water from his eyes.

They did a surface dive, came up and struck out across the creek. The muddy water foamed. They swam back, waded into shallow water, breathing heavily and blinking eyes.

"C mon in!"

"Man, the waters fine!"

Lester and Buck hesitated.

"Les wet em," Big Boy whispered to Bobo.

Before Lester and Buck could back away, they were dripping wet from handsful of scooped water.

"Hey, quit!"

"Gawddam, nigger! Tha waters col!"

"C mon in!" called Big Boy.

"We jus as waal go on in now," said Buck.

"Look n see ef anybodys comin."

Kneeling, they squinted among the trees.

"Ain nobody."

"C mon, les go."

They waded in slowly, pausing each few steps to catch their breath. A desperate water battle began. Closing eyes and backing away, they shunted water into one another's faces with the flat palms of hands.

"Hey, cut it out!"

"Yeah, Ahm bout drownin!"

They came together in water up to their navels, blowing and blinking. Big Boy ducked, upsetting Bobo.

"Look out, nigger!"

"Don holler so loud!"

"Yeah, they kin hear yo ol big mouth a mile erway."

"This waters too col fer me."

"Thas cause it rained yistiddy."

They swam across and back again.

"Ah wish we hada bigger place t swim in."

"The white folks got plenty swimmin pools n we ain got none."

"Ah useta swim in the ol Missippi when we lived in Vicksburg."

Big Boy put his head under the water and blew his breath. A sound came like that of a hippopotamus.

"C mon, les be hippos."

Each went to a corner of the creek and put his mouth just below the surface and blew like a hippopotamus. Tiring, they came and sat under the embankment.

"Look like Ah gotta chill."

"Me too."

"Les stay here n dry off."

"Jeeesus, Ahm col!"

They kept still in the sun, suppressing shivers. After some of the water had dried off their bodies they began to talk through clattering teeth.

"Whut would yuh do ef ol man Harveyd come erlong right now?"

"Run like hell!"

"Man, Ahd run so fas hed thinka black streaka lightnin shot pass im."

"But spose he hada gun?"

"Aw, nigger, shut up!"

They were silent. They ran their hands over wet, trembling legs, brushing water away. Then their eyes watched the sun sparkling on the restless creek.

Far away a train whistled.

"There goes number seven!"

"Headin fer up Noth!"

"Blazin it down the line!"

"Lawd, Ahm goin Noth some day."

"Me too, man."

"They say colored folks up Noth is got ekual rights."

They grew pensive. A black winged butterfly hovered at the water's edge. A bee droned. From somewhere came the sweet scent of honeysuckles. Dimly they could hear sparrows twittering in the woods. They rolled from side to side, letting sunshine dry their skins and warm their blood. They plucked blades of grass and chewed them.

"Oh!"

They looked up, their lips parting.

"Oh!"

A white woman, poised on the edge of the opposite embankment, stood directly in front of them, her hat in her hand and her hair lit by the sun.

"It's a woman!" whispered Big Boy in an underbreath. "A *white* woman!"

They stared, their hands instinctively covering their groins. Then they scrambled to their feet. The white woman backed slowly out of sight. They stood for a moment, looking at one another.

"Les git outta here!" Big Boy whispered.

"Wait till she goes erway."

"Les run, theyll ketch us here naked like this!"

"Mabbe theres a man wid her."

"C mon, les git our cloes," said Big Boy.

They waited a moment longer, listening.

"Whut t hell! Ahma git mah cloes," said Big Boy.

Grabbing at short tufts of grass, he climbed the embankment.

"Don run out there now!"

"C mon back, fool!"

Bobo hesitated. He looked at Big Boy, and then at Buck and Lester.

"Ahm goin wid Big Boy n git mah cloes," he said.

"Don run out there naked like tha, fool!" said Buck. "Yuh don know whos out there!"

Big Boy was climbing over the edge of the embankment.

"C mon," he whispered.

Bobo climbed after. Twenty-five feet away the woman stood. She had one hand over her mouth. Hanging by fingers, Buck and Lester peeped over the edge.

"C mon back; that womans scared," said Lester.

Big Boy stopped, puzzled. He looked at the woman. He looked at the bundle of clothes. Then he looked at Buck and Lester.

"C mon, les git our cloes!"

He made a step.

"Jim!" the woman screamed.

Big Boy stopped and looked around. His hands hung loosely at his sides. The woman, her eyes wide, her hand over her mouth, backed away to the tree where their clothes lay in a heap.

"Big Boy, come back n wait till shes gone!"

Bobo ran to Big Boy's side.

"Les go home! Theyll ketch us here," he urged.

Big Boy's throat felt tight.

"Lady, we wanna git our cloes," he said.

Buck and Lester climbed the embankment and stood indecisively. Big Boy ran toward the tree.

"Jim!" the woman screamed. "Jim! Jim!"

Black and naked, Big Boy stopped three feet from her.

"We wanna git our cloes," he said again, his words coming mechanically.

He made a motion.

"You go away! You go away! I tell you, you go away!"

Big Boy stopped again, afraid. Bobo ran and snatched the clothes. Buck and Lester tried to grab theirs out of his hands.

"You go away! You go away! You go away!" the woman screamed.

"Les go!" said Bobo, running toward the woods.

CRACK!

Lester grunted, stiffened, and pitched forward. His forehead struck a toe of the woman's shoes.

Bobo stopped, clutching the clothes. Buck whirled. Big Boy stared at Lester, his lips moving.

"Hes gotta gun; hes gotta gun!" yelled Buck, running wildly.

CRACK!

Buck stopped at the edge of the embankment, his head jerked backward, his body arched stiffly to one side; he toppled headlong, sending up a shower of bright spray to the sunlight. The creek bubbled.

Big Boy and Bobo backed away, their eyes fastened fearfully on a white man who was running toward them. He had a rifle and wore an army officer's uniform. He ran to the woman's side and grabbed her hand.

"You hurt, Bertha, you hurt?"

She stared at him and did not answer.

The man turned quickly. His face was red. He raised the rifle and pointed it at Bobo. Bobo ran back, holding the clothes in front of his chest.

"Don shot me, Mistah, don shoot me . . ."

Big Boy lunged for the rifle, grabbing the barrel.

"You black sonofabitch!"

Big Boy clung desperately.

"Let go, you black bastard!"

The barrel pointed skyward.

CRACK!

The white man, taller and heavier, flung Big Boy to the ground. Bobo dropped the clothes, ran up, and jumped onto the white man's back.

"You black sonsofbitches!"

The white man released the rifle, jerked Bobo to the ground, and began to batter the naked boy with his fists. Then Big Boy swung, striking the man in the mouth with the barrel. His teeth caved in, and he fell, dazed. Bobo was on his feet.

"C mon, Big Boy, les go!"

Breathing hard, the white man got up and faced Big Boy. His lips were trembling, his neck and chin wet with blood. He spoke quietly.

"Give me that gun, boy!"

Big Boy leveled the rifle and backed away.

The white man advanced.

"Boy, I say give me that gun!"

Bobo had the clothes in his arms.

"Run, Big Boy, run!"

The man came at Big Boy.

"Ahll kill yuh; Ahll kill yuh!" said Big Boy.

His fingers fumbled for the trigger.

The man stopped, blinked, spat blood. His eyes were bewildered. His face whitened. Suddenly, he lunged for the rifle, his hands outstretched.

CRACK!

He fell forward on his face.

"Jim!"

Big Boy and Bobo turned in surprise to look at the woman.

"Jim!" she screamed again, and fell weakly at the foot of the tree.

Big Boy dropped the rifle, his eyes wide. He looked around. Bobo was crying and clutching the clothes.

"Big Boy, Big Boy . . ."

Big Boy looked at the rifle, started to pick it up, but didn't. He seemed at a loss. He looked at Lester, then at the white man; his eyes followed a thin stream of blood that seeped to the ground.

"Yuh done killed im," mumbled Bobo.

"Les go home!"

Naked, they turned and ran toward the woods. When they reached the barbed-wire fence they stopped.

"Les git our cloes on," said Big Boy.

They slipped quickly into overalls. Bobo held Lester's and Buck's clothes.

"Whut we gonna do wid these?"

Big Boy stared. His hands twitched.

"Leave em."

They climbed the fence and ran through the woods. Vines and leaves switched their faces. Once Bobo tripped and fell.

"C mon!" said Big Boy.

Bobo started crying, blood streaming from his scratches.

"Ahm scared!"

"C mon! Don cry! We wanna git home fo they ketches us!"

"Ahm scared!" said Bobo again, his eyes full of tears.

Big Boy grabbed his hand and dragged him along.

"C mon!"

III

They stopped when they got to the end of the woods. They could see the open road leading home, home to ma and pa. But they hung back, afraid. The thick shadows cast from the trees were friendly and sheltering. But the wide glare of sun stretching out over the fields was pitiless. They crouched behind an old log.

"We gotta git home," said Big Boy.

"Theys gonna lynch us," said Bobo, half-questioningly.

Big Boy did not answer.

"Theys gonna lynch us," said Bobo again.

Big Boy shuddered.

"Hush!" he said. He did not want to think of it. He could not think of it; there was but one thought, and he clung to that one blindly. He had to get home, home to ma and pa.

Their heads jerked up. Their ears had caught the rhythmic jingle of a wagon. They fell to the ground and clung flat to the side of a log. Over the crest of the hill came the top of a hat. A white face. Then shoulders in a blue shirt. A wagon drawn by two horses pulled into full view.

Big Boy and Bobo held their breath, waiting. Their eyes followed the wagon till it was lost in dust around a bend of the road.

"We gotta git home," said Big Boy.

"Ahm scared," said Bobo.

"C mon! Les keep t the fields."

They ran till they came to the cornfields. Then they went slower, for last year's corn stubbles bruised their feet.

They came in sight of a brickyard.

"Wait a minute," gasped Big Boy.

They stopped.

"Ahm goin on t mah home n yuh better go on t yos."

Bobo's eyes grew round.

"Ahm scared!"

"Yuh better go on!"

"Lemme go wid yuh; theyll ketch me . . ."

"Ef yuh kin git home mabbe yo folks kin hep yuh t git erway."

Big Boy started off. Bobo grabbed him.

"Lemme go wid yuh!"

Big Boy shook free.

"Ef yuh stay here theys gonna lynch yuh!" he yelled, running.

After he had gone about twenty-five yards he turned and looked; Bobo was flying through the woods like the wind.

Big Boy slowed when he came to the railroad. He wondered if he ought to go through the streets or down the track. He decided on the tracks. He could dodge a train better than a mob.

He trotted along the ties, looking ahead and back. His cheek itched, and he felt it. His hand came away smeared with blood. He wiped it nervously on his overalls.

When he came to his back fence he heaved himself over. He landed among a flock of startled chickens. A bantam rooster tried to spur him. He slipped and fell in front of the kitchen steps, grunting heavily. The ground was slick with greasy dishwater.

Panting, he stumbled through the doorway.

"Lawd, Big Boy, whuts wrong wid yuh?"

His mother stood gaping in the middle of the floor. Big Boy flopped wordlessly onto a stool, almost toppling over. Pots simmered on the stove. The kitchen smelled of food cooking.

"Whuts the matter, Big Boy?"

Mutely, he looked at her. Then he burst into tears. She came and felt the scratches on his face.

"Whut happened t yuh, Big Boy? Somebody been botherin yuh?"

"They after me, Ma! They after me . . ."

"Who!"

"Ah . . . Ah . . . We . . ."

"Big Boy, whuts wrong wid yuh?"

"He killed Lester n Buck," he muttered simply.

"Killed!"

"Yessum."

"Lester n Buck!"

"Yessum, Ma!"

"How killed?"

"He shot em, Ma!"

"Lawd Gawd in Heaven, have mercy on us all! This is mo trouble, mo trouble," she moaned, wringing her hands.

"N Ah killed im, Ma . . ."

She stared, trying to understand.

"Whut happened, Big Boy?"

"We tried t git our cloes from the tree . . ."

"Whut tree?"

"We wuz swimmin, Ma. N the white woman . . ."

"*White* woman? . . ."

"Yessum. She wuz at the swimmin hole . . ."

"Lawd have mercy! Ah knowed yuh boys wuz gonna keep on till yuh got into somethin like this!"

She ran into the hall.

"Lucy!"

"Mam?"

"C mere!"

"Mam?"

"C mere, Ah say!"

"Whutcha wan, Ma? Ahm sewin."

"Chile, will yuh c mere like Ah ast yuh?"

Lucy came to the door holding an unfinished apron in her hands. When she saw Big Boy's face she looked wildly at her mother.

"Whuts the matter?"

"Wheres Pa?"

"Hes out front, Ah reckon."

"Git im, quick!"

"Whuts the matter, Ma?"

"Go git you Pa, Ah say!"

Lucy ran out. The mother sank into a chair, holding a dish rag. Suddenly, she sat up.

"Big Boy, Ah thought yuh wuz at school?"

Big Boy looked at the floor.

"How come yuh didnt go t school?"

"We went t the woods."

She sighed.

"Ah done done all Ah kin fer yuh, Big Boy. Only Gawd kin hep yuh now."

"Ma, don let em git me; don let em git me . . ."

His father came into the doorway. He stared at Big Boy, then at his wife.

"Whuts Big Boy inter now?" he asked sternly.

"Saul, Big Boys done gone n got inter trouble wid the white folks."

The old man's mouth dropped, and he looked from one to the other.

"Saul, we gotta git im erway from here."

"Open yo mouth n talk! Whut yuh been doin?" The old man gripped Big Boy's shoulders and peered at the scratches on his face.

"Me n Lester n Buck n Bobo wuz out on ol man Harveys place swimmin . . ."

"Saul, its a *white* woman !"

Big Boy winced. The old man compressed his lips and stared at his wife. Lucy gaped at her brother as though she had never seen him before.

"What happened? Cant yuh-all talk?" the old man thundered, with a certain helplessness in his voice.

"We wuz swimmin," Big Boy began, "n then a white woman comes up t the hole. We got up right erway t git our cloes sos we could git erway, n she started screamin. Our cloes wuz right by the tree where she wuz standin, n when we started t git em she jus screamed. We tol her we wanted our cloes . . . Yuh see, Pa, she wuz standing right *by* our cloes; n when we went t git em she jus screamed . . . Bobo got the cloes, n then he shot Lester . . ."

"*Who* shot Lester?"

"The white man."

"Whut white man?"

"Ah dunno, Pa. He wuz a soljer, n he had a rifle."

"A soljer?"

"Yessuh."

"A *soljer?*"

"Yessuh, Pa. A soljer."

The old man frowned.

"N then what yuh-all do?"

"Waal, Buck said, 'Hes gotta gun!' N we started runnin. N then he shot Buck, n he fell in the swimmin hole. We didnt see im no mo . . . He wuz close on us then. He looked at the white woman n then he started t shoot Bobo. Ah grabbed the gun, n we started fightin. Bobo jumped on his back. He started beatin Bobo. Then Ah hit im wid the gun. Then he started at me n Ah shot im. Then we run . . ."

"Who seen?"

"Nobody."

"Wheres Bobo?"

"He went home."

"Anybody run after yuh-all?"

"Nawsuh."

"Yuh see anybody?"

"Nawsuh. Nobody but a white man. But he didnt see us."

"How long fo yuh-all lef the swimmin hole?"

"Little while ergo."

The old man nervously brushed his hand across his eyes and walked to the door. His lips moved, but no words came.

"Saul, whut we gonna do?"

"Lucy," began the old man, "go t Brother Sanders n tell im Ah said c mere; n go t Brother Jenkins n tell im Ah said c mere; n go to Elder Peters n tell im Ah said c mere. N don say nothin t nobody but whut Ah tol yuh. N when yuh git thu come straight back. Now go!"

Lucy dropped her apron across the back of a chair and ran down the steps. The mother bent over, crying and praying. The old man walked slowly over to Big Boy.

"Big Boy?"

Big Boy swallowed.

"Ahm talkin t yuh!"

"Yessuh."

"How come yuh didnt go t school this mawnin?"

"We went t the woods."

"Didnt yo ma send yuh t school?"

"Yessuh."

"How come yuh didnt go?"

"We went t the woods."

"Don yuh know thas wrong?"

"Yessuh."

"How come yuh go?"

Big Boy looked at his fingers, knotted them, and squirmed in his seat.

"AHM TALKIN T YUH!"

His wife straightened up and said reprovingly:

"Saul!"

The old man desisted, yanking nervously at the shoulder straps of his overalls.

"How long wuz the woman there?"

"Not long."
"Wuz she young?"
"Yessuh. Lika gal."
"Did yuh-all say anythin t her?"
"Nawsuh. We jus said we wanted our cloes."
"N whut she say?"
"Nothin, Pa. She jus backed erway t the tree n screamed."
The old man stared, his lips trying to form a question.
"Big Boy, did yuh-all bother her?"
"Nawsuh, Pa. We didnt *touch* her."
"How long fo the white man come up?"
"Right erway."
"Whut he say?"
"Nothin. He jus cussed us."
Abruptly the old man left the kitchen.
"Ma, cant Ah go fo they ketches me?"
"Sauls doin whut he kin."
"Ma, Ma, Ah don wan em t ketch me . . ."
"Sauls doin whut he kin. Nobody but the good Lawd kin hep us now."
The old man came back with a shotgun and leaned it in a corner. Fascinatedly, Big Boy looked at it.
There was a knock at the front door.
"Liza, see whos there."
She went. They were silent, listening. They could hear her talking.
"Whos there?"
"Me."
"Who?"
"Me, Brother Sanders."
"C mon in. Sauls waitin fer yuh."
Sanders paused in the doorway, smiling.
"Yuh sent fer me, Brother Morrison?"
"Brother Sanders, wes in deep trouble here."
Sanders came all the way into the kitchen.
"Yeah?"
"Big Boy done gone n killed a white man."
Sanders stopped short, then came forward, his face thrust out, his mouth open. His lips moved several times before he could speak.
"A *white* man?"
"They gonna kill me; they gonna kill me!" Big Boy cried, running to the old man.
"Saul, cant we git im erway somewhere?"
"Here now, take it easy; take it easy," said Sanders, holding Big Boy's wrists.
"They gonna kill me; they gonna lynch me!"

Big Boy slipped to the floor. They lifted him to a stool. His mother held him closely, pressing his head to her bosom.

"Whut we gonna do?" asked Sanders.

"Ah done sent fer Brother Jenkins n Elder Peters."

Sanders leaned his shoulders against the wall. Then, as the full meaning of it all came to him, he exclaimed:

"Theys gonna git a mob! . . ." His voice broke off and his eyes fell on the shotgun.

Feet came pounding on the steps. They turned toward the door. Lucy ran in crying. Jenkins followed. The old man met him in the middle of the room, taking his hand.

"Wes in bad trouble here, Brother Jenkins. Big Boy's done gone n killed a white man. Yuh-alls gotta hep me . . ."

Jenkins looked hard at Big Boy.

"Elder Peters says hes comin," said Lucy.

"When all this happen?" asked Jenkins.

"Near bout a hour ergo, now," said the old man.

"Whut we gonna do?" asked Jenkins.

"Ah wanna wait till Elder Peters come," said the old man helplessly.

"But we gotta work fas ef we gonna do anythin," said Sanders. "Well git in trouble jus standin here like this."

Big Boy pulled away from his mother.

"Pa, lemme go now! Lemme go now!"

"Be still, Big Boy!"

"Where kin yuh go?"

"Ah could ketch a freight!"

"Thas *sho* death!" said Jenkins. "They'll be watchin em all!"

"Kin yuh-all hep me wid some money?" the old man asked.

They shook their heads.

"Saul, whut kin we do? Big Boy cant stay here."

There was another knock at the door.

The old man backed stealthily to the shotgun.

"Lucy go!"

Lucy looked at him, hesitating.

"Ah better go," said Jenkins.

It was Elder Peters. He came in hurriedly.

"Good evenin, everbody!"

"How yuh, Elder?"

"Good evenin."

"How yuh today?"

Peters looked around the crowded kitchen.

"Whuts the matter?"

"Elder, wes in deep trouble," began the old man. "Big Boy n some mo boys . . ."

". . . Lester n Buck n Bobo . . ."

". . . wuz over on ol man Harveys place swimmin."

"N he don like us niggers *none,*" said Peters emphatically. He widened his legs and put his thumbs in the armholes of his vest.

". . . n some white woman . . ."

"Yeah?" said Peters, coming closer.

". . . comes erlong n the boys tries t git their cloes where they done lef em under a tree. Waal, she started screamin n all, see? Reckon she thought the boys wuz after her. Then a white man in a soljers suit shoots two of em . . ."

". . . Lester n Buck . . ."

"Huummm," said Peters. "Tha wuz ol man Harveys son."

"Harveys son?"

"Yuh mean the one tha wuz in the Army?"

"Yuh mean Jim?"

"Yeah," said Peters. "The papers said he wuz here fer a vacation from his regiment. N tha woman the boys saw wuz jus erbout his wife . . ."

They stared at Peters. Now that they knew what white person had been killed, their fears became definite.

"N whut else happened?"

"Big Boy shot the man . . ."

"Harveys *son?*"

"He had t, Elder. He wuz gonna shoot im ef he didnt . . ."

"Lawd!" said Peters. He looked around and put his hat back on.

"How long ergo wuz this?"

"Mighty near an hour, now, Ah reckon."

"Do the white folks know yit?"

"Don know, Elder."

"Yuh-all better git this boy outta here right now," said Peters. "Cause ef yuh don theres gonna be a lynchin . . ."

"Where kin Ah go, Elder?" Big Boy ran up to him.

They crowded around Peters. He stood with his legs wide apart, looking up at the ceiling.

"Mabbe we kin hide im in the church till he kin git erway," said Jenkins.

Peters' lips flexed.

"Naw, Brother, thall never do! Theyll git im there sho. N anyhow, ef they ketch im there itll ruin us all. We gotta git the boy outta town . . ."

Sanders went up to the old man.

"Lissen," he said in a whisper. "Mah son, Will, the one whut drives fer the Magnolia Express Comny, is taking a truck o goods t Chicawgo in the mawnin. If we kin hide Big Boy somewhere till then, we kin put im on the truck . . ."

"Pa, please, lemme go wid Will when he goes in the mawnin," Big Boy begged.

The old man stared at Sanders.

"Yuh reckon thas safe?"

"Its the only thing yuh *kin* do," said Peters.

"But where we gonna hide im till then?"

"Whut time yo boy leavin out in the mawnin?"

"At six."

They were quiet, thinking. The water kettle on the stove sang.

"Pa, Ah knows where Will passes erlong wid the truck out on Bullards Road. Ah kin hide in one of them ol kilns . . ."

"Where?"

"In one of them kilns we built . . ."

"But theyll git yuh there," wailed the mother.

"But there ain no place else fer im t go."

"Theres some holes big ernough fer me t git in n stay till Will comes erlong," said Big Boy. "Please, Pa, lemme go fo they ketches me . . ."

"Let im go!"

"Please, Pa . . ."

The old man breathed heavily.

"Lucy, git his things!"

"Saul, theyll git im out there!" wailed the mother, grabbing Big Boy.

Peters pulled her away.

"Sister Morrison, ef yuh don let im go n git erway from here hes gonna be caught shos theres a Gawd in Heaven!"

Lucy came running with Big Boy's shoes and pulled them on his feet. The old man thrust a battered hat on his head. The mother went to the stove and dumped the skillet of corn pone into her apron. She wrapped it, and unbuttoning Big Boy's overalls, pushed it into his bosom.

"Heres somethin fer yuh t eat; n pray, Big Boy, cause thas all anybody kin do now . . ."

Big Boy pulled to the door, his mother clinging to him.

"Let im go, Sister Morrison!"

"Run fas, Big Boy!"

Big Boy raced across the yard, scattering the chickens. He paused at the fence and hollered back:

"Tell Bobo where Ahm hidin n tell im t c mon!"

IV

He made for the railroad, running straight toward the sunset. He held his left hand tightly over his heart, holding the hot pone of corn bread there. At times he stumbled over the ties, for his shoes were tight and hurt his feet. His throat burned from thirst; he had had no water since noon.

He veered off the track and trotted over the crest of a hill, following Bullard's Road. His feet slipped and slid in the dust. He kept his eyes straight ahead, fearing every clump of shrubbery, every tree. He wished it were night. If he could only get to the kilns without meeting anyone. Suddenly a thought came to him like a blow. He recalled hearing the old folks tell tales of bloodhounds, and fear made him run slower. None of them had thought of that. Spose blood-houns wuz put on his trail? Lawd! Spose a whole pack of em, foamin n howlin, tore im t pieces? He went limp and his feet dragged. Yeah, thas whut they wuz gonna send after im, blood-houns! N then thered be no way fer im t dodge! Why hadnt Pa let im take tha shotgun? He stopped. He oughta go back n git tha shotgun. And then when the mob came he would take some with him.

In the distance he heard the approach of a train. It jarred him back to a sharp sense of danger. He ran again, his big shoes sopping up and down in the dust. He was tired and his lungs were bursting from running. He wet his lips, wanting water. As he turned from the road across a plowed field he heard the train roaring at his heels. He ran faster, gripped in terror.

He was nearly there now. He could see the black clay on the sloping hillside. Once inside a kiln he would be safe. For a little while, at least. He thought of the shotgun again. If he only had something! Someone to talk to . . . Thas right! Bobo! Bobod be wid im. Hed almost fergot Bobo. Bobod bringa gun; he knowed he would. N tergether they could kill the whole mob. Then in the mawning theyd git inter Will's truck n go far erway, t Chicawgo . . .

He slowed to a walk, looking back and ahead. A light wind skipped over the grass. A beetle lit on his cheek and he brushed it off. Behind the dark pines hung a red sun. Two bats flapped against that sun. He shivered, for he was growing cold; the sweat on his body was drying.

He stopped at the foot of the hill, trying to choose between two patches of black kilns high above him. He went to the left, for there lay the ones he, Bobo, Lester, and Buck had dug only last week. He looked around again; the landscape was bare. He climbed the embankment and stood before a row of black pits sinking four and five feet deep into the earth. He went to the largest and peered in. He stiffened when his ears caught the sound of a whir. He ran back a few steps and poised on his toes. Six foot of snake slid out of the pit and went into coil. Big Boy looked around wildly for a stick. He ran down the slope, peering into the grass. He stumbled over a tree limb. He picked it up and tested it by striking it against the ground.

Warily, he crept back up the slope, his stick poised. When about seven feet from the snake he stopped and waved the stick. The coil grew tighter, the whir sounded louder, and a flat head reared to strike. He went to the right, and the flat head followed him, the blue-black tongue darting forth; he went to the left, and the flat head followed him there too.

He stopped, teeth clenched. He had to kill this snake. Jus had t kill im! This wuz the safest pit on the hillside. He waved the stick again, looking at the snake before, thinking of a mob behind. The flat head reared higher. With stick over shoulder, he jumped in, swinging. The stick sang through the air, catching the snake on the side of the head, sweeping him out of coil. There was a brown writhing mass. Then Big Boy was upon him, pounding blows home, one on top of the other. He fought viciously, his eyes red, his teeth bared in a snarl. He beat till the snake lay still; then he stomped it with his heel, grinding its head into the dirt.

He stopped, limp, wet. The corners of his lips were white with spittle. He spat and shuddered.

Cautiously, he went to the hole and peered. He longed for a match. He imagined whole nests of them in there waiting. He put the stick into the hole and waved it around. Stooping, he peered again. It mus be awright. He looked over the hillside, his eyes coming back to the dead snake. Then he got to his knees and backed slowly into the hole.

When inside he felt there must be snakes all about him, ready to strike. It seemed he could see and feel them there, waiting tensely in coil. In the dark he imagined long white fangs ready to sink into his neck, his side, his legs. He wanted to come out, but kept still. Shucks, he told himself, ef there wuz any snakes in here they sho woulda done bit me by now. Some of his fear left, and he relaxed.

With elbows on ground and chin on palms, he settled. The clay was cold to his knees and thighs, but his bosom was kept warm by the hot pone of corn bread. His thirst returned and he longed for a drink. He was hungry, too. But he did not want to eat the corn pone. Naw, not now. Mabbe after erwhile, after Bobod came. Then theyd both eat the corn pone.

The view from his hole was fringed by the long tufts of grass. He could see all the way to Bullard's Road, and even beyond. The wind was blowing, and in the east the first touch of dusk was rising. Every now and then a bird floated past, a spot of wheeling black printed against the sky. Big Boy sighed, shifted his weight, and chewed at a blade of grass. A wasp droned. He heard number nine, far away and mournful.

The train made him remember how they had dug these kilns on long hot summer days, how they had made boilers out of big tin cans, filled them with water, fixed stoppers for steam, cemented them in holes with wet clay, and built fires under them. He recalled how they had danced and yelled when a stopper blew out of a boiler, letting out a big spout of steam and a shrill whistle. There were times when they had the whole hillside blazing and smoking. Yeah, yuh see, Big Boy wuz Casey Jones n wuz speedin it down the gleamin rails of the Southern Pacific. Bobo had number two on the Santa Fe. Buck wuz on the Illinoy Central. Lester the Nickel Plate. Lawd, how they shelved the wood in! The boiling water would almost jar the cans loose from the clay. More and more pine-knots and dry leaves would be piled under the cans. Flames would grow so tall they would have to shield their eyes. Sweat would pour off their faces. Then, suddenly, a peg would shoot high into the air, and

Pssseeeezzzzzzzzzzzzzzzzzzz . . .

Big Boy sighed and stretched out his arm, quenching the flames and scattering the smoke. Why didnt Bobo c mon? He looked over the fields; there was nothing but dying sunlight. His mind drifted back to the kilns. He remembered the day when Buck, jealous of his winning, had tried to smash his kiln. Yeah, that ol sonofabitch! Naw, Lawd! He didnt go t say tha! What wuz he thinkin erbout? Cussin the dead! Yeah, po ol Buck wuz dead now. N Lester too. Yeah, it wuz awright fer Buck t smash his kiln. Sho. N he wished he hadnt socked ol Buck so hard tha day. He wuz sorry fer Buck now. N he sho wished he hadnt cussed po ol Bucks ma, neither. Tha wuz sinful! Mabbe Gawd would git im fer tha? But he didnt go to do it! Po Buck! Po Lester! Hed never treat anybody like tha ergin, never . . .

Dusk was slowly deepening. Somewhere, he could not tell exactly where, a cricket took up a fitful song. The air was growing soft and heavy. He looked over the fields, longing for Bobo . . .

He shifted his body to ease the cold damp of the ground, and thought back over the day. Yeah, hed been dam right erbout not wantin t go swimmin. N ef hed followed his right min hed neverve gone n got inter all this trouble. At first hed said naw. But shucks, somehow hed just went on wid the res. Yeah, he shoulda went on t school tha mawnin, like Ma told im t do. But, hell, who wouldnt git tireda awways drivin a guy t school! Tha wuz the big trouble awways drivin a guy t school. He wouldnt be in all this trouble now ef it wuznt fer that Gawddam school! Impatiently, he took the grass out of his mouth and threw it away, demolishing the little red school house . . .

Yeah, ef they had all kept still n quiet when tha ol white woman showed-up, mabbe shedve went on off. But yuh never kin tell erbout these white folks. Mabbe she wouldntve went. Mabbe tha white man woulda killed all of em! All *fo* of em! Yeah, yuh never kin tell erbout white folks. Then, ergin, mabbe tha white woman woulda went on off n laffed. Yeah, mabbe tha white man woulda said: *Yuh nigger bastards git t hell outta here! Yuh know Gawddam well yuh don berlong here!* N then they woulda grabbed their cloes n run like all hell . . . He blinked the white man away. Where wuz Bobo? Why didnt he hurry up n c mon?

He jerked another blade and chewed. Yeah, ef pa had only let im have tha shotgun! He could stan off a whole mob wid a shotgun. He looked at the ground as he turned a shotgun over in his hands. Then he leveled it at an advancing white man. *Boooom!* The man curled up. Another came. He reloaded quickly, and let him have what the other had got. He too curled up. Then another came. He got the same medicine. Then the whole mob swirled around him, and he blazed away, getting as many as he could. They closed in; but, by Gawd, he had done his part, hadnt he? N the newspapersd say: NIGGER KILLS DOZEN OF MOB BEFO LYNCHED! Er mabbe theyd say:

TRAPPED NIGGER SLAYS TWENTY BEFO KILLED! He smiled a little. Tha wouldnt be so bad, would it? Blinking the newspaper away, he looked over the fields. Where wuz Bobo? Why didnt he hurry up n c mon?

He shifted, trying to get a crick out of his legs. Shucks, he wuz gittin tireda this. N it wuz almos dark now. Yeah, there wuz a little bittie star way over yonder in the eas. Mabbe tha white man wuznt dead? Mabbe they wuznt even lookin fer im? Mabbe he could go back home now? Naw, better wait erwhile. Thad be bes. But, Lawd, ef he only had some water! He could hardly swallow, his throat was so dry. Gawddam them white folks! Thas all they wuz good fer, t run a nigger down lika rabbit! Yeah, they git yuh in a corner n then they let yuh have it. A thousan of em! He shivered, for the cold of the clay was chilling his bones. Lawd, spose they foun im here in this hole? N wid nobody t hep im? . . . But ain no use in thinkin erbout tha; wait till trouble come fo yuh start fightin it. But ef tha mob came one by one hed wipe em all out. Clean up the whole bunch. He caught one by the neck and choked him long and hard, choked him till his tongue and eyes popped out. Then he jumped upon his chest and stomped him like he had stomped that snake. When he had finished with one, another came. He choked him too. Choked till he sank slowly to the ground, gasping . . .

"Hoalo!"

Big Boy snatched his fingers from the white man's neck and looked over the fields. He saw nobody. Had someone spied him? He was sure that somebody had hollered. His heart pounded. But, shucks, nobody couldnt see im here in this hole . . . But mabbe theyd seen im when he wuz comin n had laid low n wuz now closin in on im! Praps they wuz signalin fer the others? Yeah, they wuz creepin up on im! Mabbe he oughta git up n run . . . Oh! Mabbe tha wuz Bobo! Yeah, Bobo! He oughta clim out n see ef Bobo wuz lookin fer im . . . He stiffened.

"Hoalo!"

"Hoalo!"

"Wheres yuh?"

"Over here on Bullards Road!"

"C mon over!"

"Awright!"

He heard footsteps. Then voices came again, low and far away this time.

"Seen anybody?"

"Naw. Yuh?"

"Naw."

"Yuh reckon they got erway?"

"Ah dunno. Its hard t tell."

"Gawddam them sonofabitchin niggers!"

"We oughta kill ever black bastard in this country!"

"Waal, Jim got two of em, anyhow."

"But Bertha said there wuz *fo!*"

"Where in hell they hidin?"

"She said one of em wuz named Big Boy, or somethin like tha."

"We went t his shack lookin fer im."

"Yeah?"

"But we didnt fin im."

"These niggers stick tergether; they don never tell on each other."

"We looked all thu the shack n couldnt fin hide ner hair of im. Then we drove the ol woman n man out n set the shack on fire . . ."

"Jeesus! Ah wished Ah coulda been there!"

"Yuh shoulda heard the ol nigger woman howl . . ."

"Hoalo!"

"C mon over!"

Big Boy eased to the edge and peeped. He saw a white man with a gun slung over his shoulder running down the slope. Wuz they gonna search the hill? Lawd, there wuz no way fer im t git erway now; he wuz caught! He shoulda knowed theyd git im here. N he didnt hava thing, notta thing t fight wid. Yeah, soon as the blood-houns came theyd fin im. Lawd, have mercy! Theyd lynch im right here on the hill . . . Theyd git im n tie im t a stake n burn im erlive! Lawd! Nobody but the good Lawd could hep im now, nobody . . .

He heard more feet running. He nestled deeper. His chest ached. Nobody but the good Lawd could hep now. They wuz crowdin all round im n when they hada big crowd theyd close in on im. Then itd be over . . . The good Lawd would have t hep im, cause nobody could hep im now, nobody . . .

And then he went numb when he remembered Bobo. Spose Bobod come now? Hed be caught sho! Both of em would be caught! Theyd make Bobo tell where he wuz! Bobo oughta not try to come now. Somebody oughta tell im . . . But there wuz nobody; there wuz no way . . .

He eased slowly back to the opening. There was a large group of men. More were coming. Many had guns. Some had coils of rope slung over shoulders.

"Ah tell yuh they still here, somewhere . . ."

"But we looked all over!"

"What t hell! Wouldnt do t let em git erway!"

"Naw. Ef they git erway notta woman in this town would be safe."

"Say, whuts tha yuh got?"

"Er pillar."

"Fer whut?"

"Feathers, fool!"

"Chris! Thisll be hot ef we kin ketch them niggers!"

"Ol Anderson said he wuz gonna bringa barrela tar!"

"Ah got some gasoline in mah car ef yuh need it."

Big Boy had no feelings now. He was waiting. He did not wonder if they were coming after him. He just waited. He did not wonder about Bobo. He rested his cheek against the cold clay, waiting.

A dog barked. He stiffened. It barked again. He balled himself into a knot at the bottom of the hole, waiting. Then he heard the patter of dog feet.

"Look!"

"Whuts he got?"

"Its a snake!"

"Yeah, the dogs foun a snake!"

"Gee, its a big one!"

"Shucks, Ah wish he could fin one of them sonofabitchin niggers!"

The voices sank to low murmurs. Then he heard number twelve, its bell tolling and whistle crying as it slid along the rails. He flattened himself against the clay. Someone was singing:

We'll hang ever nigger t a sour apple tree . . .

When the song ended there was hard laughter. From the other side of the hill he heard the dog barking furiously. He listened. There was more than one dog now. There were many and they were barking their throats out.

"Hush, Ah hear them dogs!"

"When theys barkin like tha theys foun somethin!"

"Here they come over the hill!"

"WE GOT IM! WE GOT IM!"

There came a roar. Tha mus be Bobo; tha mus be Bobo . . . In spite of his fear, Big Boy looked. The road, and half of the hillside across the road, were covered with men. A few were at the top of the hill, stenciled against the sky. He could see dark forms moving up the slopes. They were yelling.

"By Gawd, we got im!"

"C mon!"

"Where is he?"

"Theyre bringin im over the hill!"

"Ah got a rope fer im!"

"Say, somebody go n git the others!"

"Where is he? Cant we see im, Mister?"

"They say Berthas comin, too."

"Jack! Jack! Don leave me! Ah wanna see im!"

"Theyre bringin im over the hill, sweetheart!"

"AH WANNA BE THE FIRS T PUT A ROPE ON THA BLACK BASTARDS NECK!"

"Les start the fire!"

"Heat the tar!"

"Ah got some chains t chain im."

"Bring im over this way!"

"Chris, Ah wished Ah hada drink . . ."

Big Boy saw men moving over the hill. Among them was a long dark spot. Tha mus be Bobo; tha mus be Bobo theys carryin . . . Theyll git im here. He oughta git up n run. He clamped his teeth and ran his hand across his forehead, bringing it away wet. He tried to swallow, but could not; his throat was dry.

They had started the song again:

We'll hang ever nigger t a sour apple tree . . .

There were women singing now. Their voices made the song round and full. Song waves rolled over the top of pine trees. The sky sagged low, heavy with clouds. Wind was rising. Sometimes cricket cries cut surprisingly across the mob song. A dog had gone to the utmost top of the hill. At each lull of the song his howl floated full into the night.

BIG Boy shrank when he saw the first tall flame light the hillside. Would they see im here? Then he remembered you could not see into the dark if you were standing in the light. As flames leaped higher he saw two men rolling a barrel up the slope.

"Say, gimme a han here, will yuh?"

"Awright, heave!"

"C mon! Straight up! Git t the other end!"

"Ah got the feathers here in this pillar!"

"BRING SOME MO WOOD!"

Big Boy could see the barrel surrounded by flames. The mob fell back, forming a dark circle. Theyd fin im here! He had a wild impulse to climb out and fly across the hills. But his legs would not move. He stared hard, trying to find Bobo. His eyes played over a long dark spot near the fire. Fanned by wind, flames leaped higher. He jumped. That dark spot had moved. Lawd, thas Bobo; thas Bobo . . .

He smelt the scent of tar, faint at first, then stronger. The wind brought it full into his face, then blew it away. His eyes burned and he rubbed them with his knuckles. He sneezed.

"LES GIT SOURVINEERS!"

He saw the mob close in around the fire. Their faces were hard and sharp in the light of the flames. More men and women were coming over the hill. The long dark spot was smudged out.

"Everbody git back!"

"Look! Hes gotta finger!"

"C MON! GIT THE GALS BACK FROM THE FIRE!"

"Hes got one of his ears, see?"

"Whuts the matter!"

"A woman fell out! Fainted, Ah reckon . . ."

The stench of tar permeated the hillside. The sky was black and the wind was blowing hard.

"HURRY UP N BURN THE NIGGER FO IT RAINS!"

Big Boy saw the mob fall back, leaving a small knot of men about the fire.

Then, for the first time, he had a full glimpse of Bobo. A black body flashed in the light. Bobo was struggling, twisting; they were binding his arms and legs.

When he saw them tilt the barrel he stiffened. A scream quivered. He knew the tar was on Bobo. The mob fell back. He saw a tar-drenched body glistening and turning.

"THE BASTARDS GOT IT!"

There was a sudden quiet. Then he shrank violently as the wind carried, like a flurry of snow, a widening spiral of white feathers into the night. The flames leaped tall as the trees. The scream came again. Big Boy trembled and looked. The mob was running down the slopes, leaving the fire clear. Then he saw a writhing white mass cradled in yellow flame, and heard screams, one on top of the other, each shriller and shorter than the last. The mob was quiet now, standing still, looking up the slopes at the writhing white mass gradually growing black, growing black in a cradle of yellow flame.

"PO ON MO GAS!"

"Gimme a lif, will yuh!"

Two men were struggling, carrying between them a heavy can. They set it down, tilted it, leaving it so that the gas would trickle down to the hollowed earth around the fire.

Big Boy slid back into the hole, his face buried in clay. He had no feelings now, no fears. He was numb, empty, as though all blood had been drawn from him. Then his muscles flexed taut when he heard a faint patter. A tiny stream of cold water seeped to his knees, making him push back to a drier spot. He looked up; rain was beating in the grass.

"It's rainin!"

"C mon, les git t town!"

". . . don worry, when the fire git thu wid im hell be gone . . ."

"Wait, Charles! Don leave me; its slippery here . . ."

"Ahll take some of yuh ladies back in mah car . . ."

Big Boy heard the dogs barking again, this time closer. Running feet pounded past. Cold water chilled his ankles. He could hear raindrops steadily hissing.

Now a dog was barking at the mouth of the hole, barking furiously, sensing a presence there. He balled himself into a knot and clung to the bottom, his knees and shins buried in water. The bark came louder. He heard paws scraping and felt the hot scent of dog breath on his face. Green eyes glowed and drew nearer as the barking, muffled by the closeness of the hole, beat upon his eardrums. Backing till his shoulders pressed against the clay, he held his breath. He pushed out his hands, his fingers stiff. The dog yawped louder, advancing, his bark rising sharp and thin. Big Boy rose to his knees, his hands before him. Then he flattened out still more against the bottom, breathing lungsful of hot dog scent, breathing it slowly, hard, but evenly. The dog came closer, bringing hotter dog scent. Big Boy could go back no more. His knees were slipping and slopping in the water. He braced himself, ready. Then, he never exactly knew how—he never knew whether he had lunged or the dog had lunged—they were together, rolling in the water. The green eyes were beneath him, between his legs. Dognails bit into his arms. His knees slipped backward and he landed full on the dog; the dog's breath left in a heavy gasp. Instinctively, he fumbled for the throat as he felt the dog twisting between his knees. The dog snarled, long and low, as though gathering strength. Big Boy's hands traveled swiftly over the dog's back, groping for the throat. He felt dognails again and saw green eyes, but his fingers had found the throat. He choked, feeling his fingers sink; he choked, throwing back his head and stiffening his arms. He felt the dog's body heave, felt dognails digging into his loins. With strength flowing from fear, he closed his fingers, pushing his full weight on the dog's throat. The dog heaved again, and lay still . . . Big Boy heard the sound of his own breathing filling the hole, and heard shouts and footsteps above him going past.

For a long, long time he held the dog, held it long after the last footstep had died out, long after the rain had stopped.

V

Morning found him still on his knees in a puddle of rainwater, staring at the stiff body of a dog. As the air brightened he came to himself slowly. He held still for a long time, as though waking from a dream, as though trying to remember.

The chug of a truck came over the hill. He tried to crawl to the opening. His knees were stiff and a thousand needle-like pains shot from the bottom of his feet to the calves of his legs. Giddiness made his eyes blur. He pulled up and looked. Through brackish light he saw Will's truck standing some twenty-five yards away, the engine running. Will stood on the runningboard, looking over the slopes of the hill.

Big Boy scuffled out, falling weakly in the wet grass. He tried to call to Will, but his dry throat would make no sound. He tried again.

"Will!"

Will heard, answering:

"Big Boy, c mon!"

He tried to run, and fell. Will came, meeting him in the tall grass.

"C mon," Will said, catching his arm.

They struggled to the truck.

"Hurry up!" said Will, pushing him onto the runningboard.

Will pushed back a square trapdoor which swung above the back of the driver's seat. Big Boy pulled through, landing with a thud on the bottom. On hands and knees he looked around in the semi-darkness.

"Wheres Bobo?"

Big Boy stared.

"Wheres Bobo?"

"They got im."

"When?"

"Las night."

"The mob?"

Big Boy pointed in the direction of a charred sapling on the slope of the opposite hill. Will looked. The trapdoor fell. The engine purred, the gears whined, and the truck lurched forward over the muddy road, sending Big Boy on his side.

For a while he lay as he had fallen, on his side, too weak to move. As he felt the truck swing around a curve he straightened up and rested his back against a stack of wooden boxes. Slowly, he began to make out objects in the darkness. Through two long cracks fell thin blades of daylight. The floor was of smooth steel, and cold to his thighs. Splinters and bits of sawdust danced with the rumble of the truck. Each time they swung around a curve he was pulled over the floor; he grabbed at corners of boxes to steady himself. Once he heard the crow of a rooster. It made him think of home, of ma and pa. He thought he remembered hearing somewhere that the house had burned, but could not remember where . . . It all seemed unreal now.

He was tired. He dozed, swaying with the lurch. Then he jumped awake. The truck was running smoothly, on gravel. Far away he heard two short blasts from the Buckeye Lumber Mill. Unconsciously, the thought sang through his mind: Its six erclock . . .

The trapdoor swung in. Will spoke through a corner of his mouth.

"How yuh comin?"

"Awright."

"How they git Bobo?"

"He wuz comin over the hill."

"Whut they do?"

"They burnt im . . . Will, Ah wan some water; mah throats like fire . . ."

"Well git some when we pass a fillin station."

Big Boy leaned back and dozed. He jerked awake when the truck stopped. He heard Will get out. He wanted to peep through the trapdoor, but was afraid. For a moment, the wild fear he had known in the hole came back. Spose theyd search n fin im? He quieted when he heard Will's footstep on the runningboard. The trapdoor pushed in. Will's hat came through, dripping.

"Take it, quick!"

Big Boy grabbed, spilling water into his face. The truck lurched. He drank. Hard cold lumps of brick rolled into his hot stomach. A dull pain made him bend over. His intestines seemed to be drawing into a tight knot. After a bit it eased, and he sat up, breathing softly.

The truck swerved. He blinked his eyes. The blades of daylight had turned brightly golden. The sun had risen.

The truck sped over the asphalt miles, sped northward, jolting him, shaking out of his bosom the crumbs of corn bread, making them dance with the splinters and sawdust in the golden blades of sunshine.

He turned on his side and slept.

2

Youth

Self Awareness Takes Root

In primitive societies, every youth undergoes elaborate rites of initiation, ritualistic ordeals closely paralleling the realities of survival in his tribe. No such initiation ceremonies survive in our complex civilization, forcing each young person to grope for his own individual means of attaining maturity.

JAMES JOYCE (1882–1941)

All of James Joyce's fiction, including his collection of short stories, Dubliners *(1914), as well as his novels,* Portrait of the Artist as a Young Man *(1916),* Ulysses *(1922), and* Finnegans Wake *(1939), is set in the Ireland of his youth. Although he left Ireland forever at the age of twenty-two, Joyce never really left in spirit or in imagination.*

He fled because he felt himself becoming paralyzed emotionally and intellectually in the provincially repressive atmosphere of the Ireland of that day. But his writings in exile worked and reworked the experiences, characters, and images that his young life in Ireland had provided. Through his writing, Joyce attempted to liberate his countrymen from their moral and cultural stagnation by graphically depicting its effect on all areas of Irish life. He also attempted to liberate literature itself from its conventional form and content.

Joyce's writing grew progressively more internal and experimental. He employed a "stream of consciousness" technique which goes beyond recording what a character sees or thinks into an attempt to transcribe the disordered ramblings of the inner mind. In his final work, Finnegans Wake, *Joyce moves to the very brink of literate communication in an effort to record the main character's dream language, where almost every word is so full of allusions as to require translation.*

The frankness with which Joyce treated taboo subjects like sex, religion, and politics caused him many problems with publishers and censors. Ulysses *could not be published in the United States for over a decade until a landmark court decision in 1933 declared it was not obscene.*

In "Araby," a story from Dubliners, *the narrator looks back at the illusory romance of his boyhood and its inevitable clash with the drab reality of Dublin at the turn of the century.*

Araby

NORTH RICHMOND STREET, being blind, was a quiet street except at the hour when the Christian Brothers' School set the boys free. An uninhabited house of two stories stood at the blind end, detached from its neighbors in a square ground. The other houses of the street, conscious of decent lives within them, gazed at one another with brown imperturbable faces.

The former tenant of our house, a priest, had died in the back drawing room. Air, musty from having been long enclosed, hung in all the rooms, and the waste room behind the kitchen was littered with old useless papers. Among these I found a few paper-covered books, the pages of which were curled and damp: *The Abbot,* by Walter Scott, *The Devout Communicant,* and *The Memoirs of Vidocq.* I liked the last best because its leaves were yellow. The wild garden behind the house contained a central apple tree and a few straggling bushes under one of which I found the late tenant's rusty bicycle pump. He had been a very charitable priest; in his will he had left all his money to institutions and the furniture of his house to his sister.

When the short days of winter came dusk fell before we had well eaten our dinners. When we met in the street the houses had grown somber. The space of sky above us was the color of ever-changing violet and towards it the lamps of the street lifted their feeble lanterns. The cold air stung us and we played till our bodies glowed. Our shouts echoed in the silent street. The career of our play brought us through the dark muddy lanes behind the houses where we ran the gauntlet of the rough tribes from the cottages, to the back doors of the dark dripping gardens where odors arose from the ashpits, to the dark odorous stables where a coachman smoothed and combed the horse or shook music from the buckled harness. When we returned to the street, light from the kitchen windows had filled the areas. If my uncle was seen turning the corner we hid in the shadow until we had seen him safely housed. Or if Mangan's sister came out on the doorstep to call her brother in to his tea we watched her from our shadow peer up and down the street. We waited to see whether she would remain or go in and, if she remained, we left our shadow and walked up to Mangan's steps resignedly. She was waiting for us, her figure defined by the light from the half-opened door. Her brother always teased her before he obeyed and I stood by the railings looking at her. Her dress swung as she moved her body and the soft rope of her hair tossed from side to side.

Every morning I lay on the floor in the front parlor watching her door. The blind was pulled down to within an inch of the sash so that I could not be seen. When she came out on the doorstep my heart leaped. I ran to the hall, seized my books and followed her. I kept her brown figure always in my eye and, when we came near the point at which our ways diverged, I quickened my pace and passed her. This happened morning after morning. I had never spoken to her, except for a few casual words, and yet her name was like a summons to all my foolish blood.

Her image accompanied me even in places the most hostile to romance. On Saturday evenings when my aunt went marketing I had to go to carry some of the parcels. We walked through the flaring streets, jostled by drunken men and bargaining women, amid the curses of laborers, the shrill litanies of shop boys who stood on guard by the barrels of pigs' cheeks, the nasal chanting of street singers, who sang a *come-all-you* about O'Donovan Rossa, or a ballad about the troubles in our native land. These noises converged in a single sensation of life for me: I imagined that I bore my chalice safely through a throng of foes. Her name sprang to my lips at moments in strange prayers and praises which I myself did not understand. My eyes were often full of tears (I could not tell why) and at times a flood from my heart seemed to pour itself out into my bosom. I thought little of the future. I did not know whether I would ever speak to her or not or, if I spoke to her, how I could tell her of my confused adoration. But my body was like a harp and her words and gestures were like fingers running upon the wires.

One evening I went into the back drawing room in which the priest had died. It was a dark rainy evening and there was no sound in the house. Through one of the broken panes I heard the rain impinge upon the earth, the fine incessant needles of water playing in the sodden beds. Some distant lamp or lighted window gleamed below me. I was thankful that I could see so little. All my senses seemed to desire to veil themselves and, feeling that I was about to slip from them, I pressed the palms of my hands together until they trembled, murmuring: *"O love! O love!"* many times.

At last she spoke to me. When she addressed the first words to me I was so confused that I did not know what to answer. She asked me was I going to *Araby*. I forgot whether I answered yes or no. It would be a splendid bazaar, she said; she would love to go.

"And why can't you?" I asked.

While she spoke she turned a silver bracelet round and round her wrist. She could not go, she said, because there would be a retreat that week in her convent. Her brother and two other boys were fighting for their caps and I was alone at the railings. She held one of the spikes, bowing her head towards me. The light from the lamp opposite our door caught the white curve of her neck, lit up her hair that rested there and, falling, lit up the hand upon the railing. It fell over one side of her dress and caught the white border of a petticoat, just visible as she stood at ease.

"It's well for you," she said.

"If I go," I said, "I will bring you something."

What innumerable follies laid waste my waking and sleeping thoughts after that evening! I wished to annihilate the tedious intervening days. I chafed against the work of school. At night in my bedroom and by day in the classroom her image came between me and the page I strove to read. The syllables of the word *Araby* were called to me through the silence in which my soul luxuriated and cast an Eastern enchantment over me. I asked for leave to go to the bazaar on Saturday night. My aunt was surprised and hoped it was not some Freemason affair. I answered few questions in class. I watched my master's face pass from amiability to sternness; he hoped I was not beginning to idle. I could not call my wandering thoughts together. I had hardly any patience with the serious work of life which, now that it stood between me and my desire, seemed to me child's play, ugly monotonous child's play.

On Saturday morning I reminded my uncle that I wished to go to the bazaar in the evening. He was fussing at the hall stand, looking for the hat brush, and answered me curtly:

"Yes, boy, I know."

As he was in the hall I could not go into the front parlor and lie at the window. I left the house in bad humor and walked slowly towards the school. The air was pitilessly raw and already my heart misgave me.

When I came home to dinner my uncle had not yet been home. Still it was early. I sat staring at the clock for some time and, when its ticking began to irritate me, I left the room. I mounted the staircase and gained the upper part of the house. The high cold empty gloomy rooms liberated me and I went from room to room singing. From the front window I saw my companions playing below in the street. Their cries reached me weakened and indistinct and, leaning my forehead against the cool glass, I looked over at the dark house where she lived. I may have stood there for an hour, seeing nothing but the brown-clad figure cast by my imagination, touched discreetly by the lamplight at the curved neck, at the hand upon the railings and at the border below the dress.

When I came downstairs again I found Mrs. Mercer sitting at the fire. She was an old garrulous woman, a pawnbroker's widow, who collected used stamps for some pious purpose. I had to endure the gossip of the tea table. The meal was prolonged beyond an hour and still my uncle did not come. Mrs. Mercer stood up to go: she was sorry she couldn't wait any longer, but it was after eight o'clock and she did not like to be out late, as the night air was bad for her. When she had gone I began to walk up and down the room, clenching my fists. My aunt said:

"I'm afraid you may put off your bazaar for this night of Our Lord."

At nine o'clock I heard my uncle's latchkey in the hall door. I heard him talking to himself and heard the hall stand rocking when it had received the weight of his overcoat. I could interpret these signs. When he was midway through his dinner I asked him to give me the money to go to the bazaar. He had forgotten.

"The people are in bed and after their first sleep now," he said.

I did not smile. My aunt said to him energetically:

"Can't you give him the money and let him go? You've kept him late enough as it is."

My uncle said he was very sorry he had forgotten. He said he believed in the old saying: "All work and no play makes Jack a dull boy." He asked me where I was going and, when I had told him a second time he asked me did I know *The Arab's Farewell to His Steed.* When I left the kitchen he was about to recite the opening lines of the piece to my aunt.

I held a florin tightly in my hand as I strode down Buckingham Street towards the station. The sight of the streets thronged with buyers and glaring with gas recalled to me the purpose of my journey. I took my seat in a third-class carriage of a deserted train. After an intolerable delay the train moved out of the station slowly. It crept onward among ruinous houses and over the twinkling river. At Westland Row Station a crowd of people pressed to the carriage doors; but the porters moved them back, saying that it was a special train for the bazaar. I remained alone in the bare carriage. In a few minutes the train drew up beside an improvised wooden platform. I passed out on to the road and saw by the lighted dial of a clock that it was ten minutes to ten. In front of me was a large building which displayed the magical name.

I could not find any sixpenny entrance and, fearing that the bazaar would be closed, I passed in quickly through a turnstile, handing a shilling to a weary-looking man. I found myself in a big hall girdled at half its height by a gallery. Nearly all the stalls were closed and the greater part of the hall was in darkness. I recognized a silence like that which pervades a church after a service. I walked into the center of the bazaar timidly. A few people were gathered about the stalls which were still open. Before a curtain, over which the words *Café Chantant* were written in colored lamps, two men were counting money on a salver. I listened to the fall of the coins.

Remembering with difficulty why I had come I went over to one of the stalls and examined porcelain vases and flowered tea sets. At the door of the stall a young lady was talking and laughing with two young gentlemen. I remarked their English accents and listened vaguely to their conversation.

"O, I never said such a thing!"

"O, but you did!"

"O, but I didn't!"

"Didn't she say that?"

"Yes. I heard her."

"O, there's a . . . fib!"

Observing me, the young lady came over and asked me did I wish to buy anything. The tone of her voice was not encouraging; she seemed to have spoken to me out of a sense of duty. I looked humbly at the great jars that stood like eastern guards at either side of the dark entrance to the stall and murmured:

"No, thank you."

The young lady changed the position of one of the vases and went back to the two young men. They began to talk of the same subject. Once or twice the young lady glanced at me over her shoulder.

I lingered before her stall, though I knew my stay was useless, to make my interest in her wares seem the more real. Then I turned away slowly and walked down the middle of the bazaar. I allowed the two pennies to fall against the sixpence in my pocket. I heard a voice call from one end of the gallery that the light was out. The upper part of the hall was now completely dark.

Gazing up into the darkness I saw myself as a creature driven and derided by vanity; and my eyes burned with anguish and anger.

WILLIAM FAULKNER (1897–1962)

Winner of the Nobel Prize for Literature (1950), William Faulkner is generally considered one of the giants of twentieth century American letters. Most of his stories and novels depict the world around Oxford, Mississippi (fictionalized as Yoknapatawpha County), where he was born and to which he returned after the success of Sanctuary *in 1932 made it possible for him to subsist as a writer.*

In his short stories, and in novels like Sartoris *(1929),* The Sound and the Fury *(1929),* Light in August *(1932), and* Absolom, Absolom *(1936), Faulkner drew upon what he had observed in the South and what he could learn of his family history to evolve an epic portrait of the deterioration of the South. Writing of its inability to replace the vigor and individuality of the dying past with anything more than greed and bigotry, Faulkner probed deeply into the emotions and fears of characters caught and often destroyed in this conflict between decadence and crass materialism. Faulkner's characters are drawn so subtly, in fact, that, like Joyce, he skillfully leaves unsaid certain nuances of his meaning.*

In his acceptance speech upon receiving the Nobel Prize, Faulkner expressed a belief that man will prevail because he has a soul and spirit capable of compassion, sacrifice, and endurance. "The Bear" celebrates the coming of age of a boy who develops these qualities through his closeness to nature, in which he is initiated into manhood by an uncorrupted man of an untouched forest, the half-breed hunter Sam Fathers.

The Bear

HE WAS TEN. But it had already begun, long before that day when at last he wrote his age in two figures and he saw for the first time the camp where his father and Major de Spain and old General Compson and the others spent two weeks each November and two weeks again each June. He had already inherited then, without ever having seen it, the tremendous bear with one trap-ruined foot which, in an area almost a hundred miles deep, had earned itself a name, a definite designation like a living man.

He had listened to it for years: the long legend of corncribs rifled, of shotes and grown pigs and even calves carried bodily into the woods and devoured, of traps and deadfalls overthrown and dogs mangled and slain, and shotgun and even rifle charges delivered at point-blank range and with no more effect than so many peas blown through a tube by a boy—a corridor of wreckage and destruction beginning back before he was born, through which sped, not fast but rather with the ruthless and irresistible deliberation of a locomotive, the shaggy tremendous shape.

It ran in his knowledge before he ever saw it. It looked and towered in his dreams before he even saw the unaxed woods where it left its crooked print, shaggy, huge, red-eyed, not malevolent but just big—too big for the dogs which tried to bay it, for the horses which tried to ride it down, for the men and the bullets they fired into it, too big for the very country which was its constricting scope. He seemed to see it entire with a child's complete divination before he ever laid eyes on either—the doomed wilderness whose edges were being constantly and punily gnawed at by men with axes and plows who feared it because it was wilderness, men myriad and nameless even to one another in the land where the old bear had earned a name, through which ran not even a mortal animal but an anachronism, indomitable and invincible, out of an old dead time, a phantom, epitome and apotheosis of the old wild life at which the puny humans swarmed and hacked in a fury of abhorrence and fear, like pygmies about the ankles of a drowsing elephant: the old bear solitary, indomitable and alone, widowered, childless, and absolved of mortality—old Priam reft of his old wife and having outlived all his sons.

Until he was ten, each November he would watch the wagon containing the dogs and the bedding and food and guns and his father and Tennie's Jim, the Negro, and Sam Fathers, the Indian, son of a slave woman and a Chickasaw chief, depart on the road to town, to Jefferson, where Major de Spain and the others would join them. To the boy, at seven, eight, and nine, they were not going into the Big Bottom to hunt bear and deer, but to keep yearly rendezvous with the bear which they did not even intend to kill. Two weeks later they would return, with no trophy, no head and skin. He had not expected it. He had not even been afraid it would be in the wagon. He believed that even after he was ten and his father would let him go too, for those two weeks in November, he would merely make another one, along with his father and Major de Spain and General Compson and the others, the dogs which feared to bay at it and the rifles and shotguns which failed even to bleed it, in the yearly pageant of the old bear's furious immortality.

Then he heard the dogs. It was in the second week of his first time in the camp. He stood with Sam Fathers against a big oak beside the faint crossing where they had stood each dawn for nine days now, hearing the dogs. He had heard them once before, one morning last week—a murmur, sourceless, echoing through the wet woods, swelling presently into separate voices which he could recognize and call by name. He had raised and cocked the gun as Sam told him and stood motionless again while the uproar, the invisible course, swept up and past and faded; it seemed to him that he could actually see the deer, the buck, blond, smoke-colored, elongated with speed, fleeing, vanishing, the woods, the gray solitude, still ringing even when the cries of the dogs had died away.

"Now let the hammers down," Sam said.

"You knew they were not coming here too," he said.

"Yes," Sam said. "I want you to learn how to do when you didn't shoot. It's after the chance for the bear or the deer has done already come and gone that men and dogs get killed."

"Anyway," he said, "it was just a deer."

Then on the tenth morning he heard the dogs again. And he readied the too-long, too-heavy gun as Sam had taught him, before Sam even spoke. But this time it was no deer, no ringing chorus of dogs running strong on a free scent, but a moiling yapping an octave too high, with something more than indecision and even abjectness in it, not even moving very fast, taking a long time to pass completely out of hearing, leaving then somewhere in the air that echo, thin, slightly hysterical, abject, almost grieving, with no sense of a fleeting, unseen, smoke-colored, grass-eating shape ahead of it, and Sam, who had taught him first of all to cock the gun and take position where he could see everywhere and then never move again, had himself moved up beside him; he could hear Sam breathing at his shoulder, and he could see the arched curve of the old man's inhaling nostrils.

"Hah," Sam said. "Not even running. Walking."

"Old Ben!" the boy said. "But up here!" he cried. "Way up here!"

"He do it every year," Sam said. "Once. Maybe to see who in camp this time, if he can shoot or not. Whether we got the dog yet that can bay and hold him. He'll take them to the river, then he'll send them back home. We may as well go back too; see how they look when they come back to camp."

When they reached the camp the hounds were already there, ten of them crouching back under the kitchen, the boy and Sam squatting to peer back into the obscurity where they had huddled, quiet, the eyes luminous, glowing at them and vanishing, and no sound, only that effluvium of something more than dog, stronger than dog and not just animal, just beast, because still there had been nothing in front of that abject and almost painful yapping save the solitude, the wilderness, so that when the eleventh hound came in at noon and with all the others watching—even old Uncle Ash, who called himself first a cook—Sam daubed the tattered ear and the raked shoulder with turpentine and axle grease, to the boy it was still no living creature, but the wilderness which, leaning for the moment down, had patted lightly once the hound's temerity.

"Just like a man," Sam said. "Just like folks. Put off as long as she could having to be brave, knowing all the time that sooner or later she would have to be brave to keep on living with herself, and knowing all the time beforehand what was going to happen to her when she done it."

That afternoon, himself on the one-eyed wagon mule which did not mind the smell of blood nor, as they told him, of bear, and with Sam on the other one, they rode for more than three hours through the rapid, shortening winter day. They followed no path, no trail even that he could see; almost at once they were in a country which he had never seen before. Then he knew why Sam had made him ride the mule which would not spook. The sound one stopped short and tried to whirl and bolt even as Sam got down, blowing its breath, jerking and wrenching at the rein, while Sam held it, coaxing it forward with his voice, since he could not risk tying it, drawing it forward while the boy got down from the marred one.

Then, standing beside Sam in the gloom of the dying afternoon, he looked down at the rotted over-turned log, gutted and scored with claw marks and, in the wet earth beside it, the print of the enormous warped two-toed foot. He knew now what he had smelled when he peered under the kitchen where the dogs huddled. He realized for the first time that the bear which had run in his listening and loomed in his dreams since before he could remember to the contrary, and which, therefore, must have existed in the listening and dreams of his father and Major de Spain and even old General Compson, too, before they began to remember in their turn, was a mortal animal, and that if they had departed for the camp each November without any actual hope of bringing its trophy back, it was not because it could not be slain, but because so far they had had no actual hope to.

"Tomorrow," he said.

"We'll try tomorrow," Sam said. "We ain't got the dog yet."

"We've got eleven. They ran him this morning."

"It won't need but one," Sam said. "He ain't here. Maybe he ain't nowhere. The only other way will be for him to run by accident over somebody that has a gun."

"That wouldn't be me," the boy said. "It will be Walter or Major or—"

"It might," Sam said. "You watch close in the morning. Because he's smart. That's how come he has lived this long. If he gets hemmed up and has to pick out somebody to run over, he will pick out you."

"How?" the boy said. "How will he know—" He ceased. "You mean he already knows me, that I ain't never been here before, ain't had time to find out yet whether I—" He ceased again, looking at Sam, the old man whose face revealed nothing until it smiled. He said humbly, not even amazed, "It was me he was watching. I don't reckon he did need to come but once."

The next morning they left the camp three hours before daylight. They rode this time because it was too far to walk, even the dogs in the wagon; again the first gray light found him in a place which he had never seen before, where Sam had placed him and told him to stay and then departed. With the gun which was too big for him, which did not even belong to him, but to Major de Spain, and which he had fired only once—at a stump on the first day, to learn the recoil and how to reload it—he stood against a gum tree beside a little bayou whose black still water crept without movement out of a canebrake and crossed a small clearing and into cane again, where, invisible, a bird—the big woodpecker called Lord-to-God by Negroes—clattered at a dead limb.

It was a stand like any other, dissimilar only in incidentals to the one where he had stood each morning for ten days; a territory new to him, yet no less familiar than that other one which, after almost two weeks, he had come to believe he knew a little—the same solitude, the same loneliness through which human beings had merely passed without altering it, leaving no mark, no scar, which looked exactly as it must have looked when the first ancestor of Sam Fathers' Chickasaw predecessors crept into it and looked about, club or stone ax or bone arrow drawn and poised; different only because, squatting at the edge of the kitchen, he smelled the hounds huddled and cringing beneath it and saw the raked ear and shoulder of the one who, Sam said, had had to be brave once in order to live with herself, and saw yesterday in the earth beside the gutted log the print of the living foot.

He heard no dogs at all. He never did hear them. He only heard the drumming of the woodpecker stop short off and knew that the bear was looking at him. He never saw it. He did not know whether it was in front of him or behind him. He did not move, holding the useless gun, which he had not even had warning to cock and which even now he did not cock, tasting in his saliva that taint as of brass which he knew now because he had smelled it when he peered under the kitchen at the huddled dogs.

Then it was gone. As abruptly as it had ceased, the woodpecker's dry, monotonous clatter set up again, and after a while he even believed he could hear the dogs—a murmur, scarce a sound even, which he had probably been hearing for some time before he even remarked it, drifting into hearing and then out again, dying away. They came nowhere near him. If it was a bear they ran, it was another bear. It was Sam himself who came out of the cane and crossed the bayou, followed by the injured bitch of yesterday. She was almost at heel, like a bird dog, making no sound. She came and crouched against his leg, trembling, staring off into the cane.

"I didn't see him," he said. "I didn't, Sam!"

"I know it," Sam said. "He done the looking. You didn't hear him neither, did you?"

"No," the boy said. "I—"

"He's smart," Sam said. "Too smart." He looked down at the hound, trembling faintly and steadily against the boy's knee. From the raked shoulder a few drops of fresh blood oozed and clung. "Too big. We ain't got the dog yet. But maybe someday. Maybe not next time. But someday."

So I must see him, he thought. *I must look at him.* Otherwise, it seemed to him that it would go on like this forever, as it had gone on with his father and Major de Spain, who was older than his father, and even with old General Compson, who had been old enough to be a brigade commander in 1865. Otherwise, it would go on so forever, next time and next time, after and after and after. It seemed to him that he could never see the two of them, himself and the bear, shadowy in the limbo from which time emerged, becoming time; the old bear absolved of mortality and himself partaking, sharing a little of it, enough of it. And he knew now what he had smelled in the huddled dogs and tasted in his saliva. He recognized fear. *So I will have to see him,* he thought, without dread or even hope. *I will have to look at him.*

It was in June of the next year. He was eleven. They were in camp again, celebrating Major de Spain's and General Compson's birthdays. Although the one had been born in September and the other in the depth of winter and in another decade, they had met for two weeks to fish and shoot squirrels and turkey and run coons and wildcats with the dogs at night. That is, he and Boon Hoggenbeck and the Negroes fished and shot squirrels and ran the coons and cats, because the proved hunters, not only Major de Spain and old General Compson, who spent those two weeks sitting in a rocking chair before a tremendous iron pot of Brunswick stew, stirring and tasting, with old Ash to quarrel with about how he was making it and Tennie's Jim to pour whiskey from the demijohn into the tin dipper from which he drank it, but even the boy's father and Walter Ewell, who were still young enough, scorned such, other than shooting the wild gobblers with pistols for wagers on their marksmanship.

Or, that is, his father and the others believed he was hunting squirrels. Until the third day, he thought that Sam Fathers believed that too. Each morning he would leave the camp right after breakfast. He had his own gun now, a Christmas present. He went back to the tree beside the bayou where he had stood that morning. Using the compass which old General Compson had given him, he ranged from that point; he was teaching himself to be a better-than-fair woodsman without knowing he was doing it. On the second day he even found the gutted log where he had first seen the crooked print. It was almost completely crumbled now, healing with unbelievable speed, a passionate and almost visible relinquishment, back into the earth from which the tree had grown.

He ranged the summer woods now, green with gloom; if anything, actually dimmer than in November's gray dissolution, where, even at noon, the sun fell only in intermittent dappling upon the earth, which never completely dried out and which crawled with snakes—moccasins and water snakes and rattlers, themselves the color of the dappling gloom, so that he would not always see them until they moved, returning later and later, first day, second day, passing in the twilight of the third evening the little log pen enclosing the log stable where Sam was putting up the horses for the night.

"You ain't looked right yet," Sam said.

He stopped. For a moment he didn't answer. Then he said peacefully, in a peaceful rushing burst as when a boy's miniature dam in a little brook gives way, "All right. But how? I went to the bayou. I even found that log again. I—"

"I reckon that was all right. Likely he's been watching you. You never saw his foot?"

"I," the boy said—"I didn't—I never thought—"

"It's the gun," Sam said. He stood beside the fence motionless—the old man, the Indian, in the battered faded overalls and the five-cent straw hat which in the Negro's race had been the badge of his enslavement and was now the regalia of his freedom. The camp—the clearing, the house, the barn and its tiny lot with which Major de Spain in his turn had scratched punily and evanescently at the wilderness—faded in the dusk, back into the immemorial darkness of the woods. *The gun,* the boy thought. *The gun.*

"Be scared," Sam said. "You can't help that. But don't be afraid. Ain't nothing in the woods going to hurt you unless you corner it, or it smells that you are afraid. A bear or a deer, too, has got to be scared of a coward the same as a brave man has got to be."

The gun, the boy thought.

"You will have to choose," Sam said.

He left the camp before daylight, long before Uncle Ash would wake in his quilts on the kitchen floor and start the fire for breakfast. He had only the compass and a stick for snakes. He could go almost a mile before he would begin to need the compass. He sat on a log, the invisible compass in his invisible hand, while the secret night sounds, fallen still at his movements, scurried again and then ceased for good, and the owls ceased and gave over to the waking of day birds, and he could see the compass. Then he went fast yet still quietly; he was becoming better and better as a woodsman, still without having yet realized it.

He jumped a doe and a fawn at sunrise, walked them out of the bed, close enough to see them—the crash of undergrowth, the white scut, the fawn scudding behind her faster than he had believed it could run. He was hunting right, upwind, as Sam had taught him; not that it mattered now. He had left the gun; of his own will and relinquishment he had accepted not a gambit, not a choice, but a condition in which not only the bear's heretofore inviolable anonymity but all the old rules and balances of hunter and hunted had been abrogated. He would not even be afraid, not even in the moment when the fear would take him completely—blood, skin, bowels, bones, memory from the long time before it became his memory—all save that thin, clear, immortal lucidity which alone differed him from this bear and from all the other bear and deer he would ever kill in the humility and pride of his skill and endurance, to which Sam had spoken when he leaned in the twilight on the lot fence yesterday.

By noon he was far beyond the little bayou, farther into the new and alien country than he had ever been. He was traveling now not only by the compass but by the old, heavy, biscuit-thick silver watch which had belonged to his grandfather. When he stopped at last, it was for the first time since he had risen from the log at dawn when he could see the compass. It was far enough.

He had left the camp nine hours ago; nine hours from now, dark would have already been an hour old. But he didn't think that. He thought, *All right. Yes. But what?* and stood for a moment, alien and small in the green and topless solitude, answering his own question before it had formed and ceased. It was the watch, the compass, the stick—the three lifeless mechanicals with which for nine hours he had fended the wilderness off; he hung the watch and compass carefully on a bush and leaned the stick beside them and relinquished completely to it.

He had not been going very fast for the last two or three hours. He went no faster now, since distance would not matter even if he could have gone fast. And he was trying to keep a bearing on the tree where he had left the compass, trying to complete a circle which would bring him back to it or at least intersect itself, since direction would not matter now either. But the tree was not here, and he did as Sam had schooled him—made the next circle in the opposite direction, so that the two patterns would bisect somewhere, but crossing no print of his own feet, finding the tree at last, but in the wrong place—no bush, no compass, no watch—and the tree not even the tree, because there was a down log beside it and he did what Sam Fathers had told him was the next thing and the last.

As he sat down on the log he saw the crooked print—the warped, tremendous, two-toed indentation which, even as he watched it, filled with water. As he looked up, the wilderness coalesced, solidified—the glade, the tree he sought, the bush, the watch and the compass glinting where the ray of sunshine touched them. Then he saw the bear. It did not emerge, appear; it was just there, immobile, solid, fixed in the hot dappling of the green and windless noon, not as big as he had dreamed it, but as big as he had expected it, bigger, dimensionless, against the dappled obscurity, looking at him where he sat quietly on the log and looked back at it.

Then it moved. It made no sound. It did not hurry. It crossed the glade, walking for an instant into the full glare of the sun; when it reached the other side it stopped again and looked back at him across one shoulder while his quiet breathing inhaled and exhaled three times.

Then it was gone. It didn't walk into the woods, the undergrowth. It faded, sank back into the wilderness as he had watched a fish, a huge old bass, sink and vanish into the dark depths of its pool without even any movement of its fins.

He thought, *It will be next fall.* But it was not next fall, nor the next nor the next. He was fourteen then. He had killed his buck, and Sam Fathers had marked his face with the hot blood, and in the next year he killed a bear. But even before that accolade he had become as competent in the woods as many grown men with the same experience; by his fourteenth year he was a better woodsman than most grown men with more. There was no territory within thirty miles of the camp that he did not know—bayou, ridge, brake, landmark, tree and path. He could have led anyone to any point in it without deviation, and brought them out again. He knew the game trails that even Sam Fathers did not know; in his thirteenth year he found a buck's bedding place, and unbeknown to his father he borrowed Walter Ewell's rifle and lay in wait at dawn and killed the buck when it walked back to the bed, as Sam had told him how the old Chickasaw fathers did.

But not the old bear, although by now he knew its footprints better than he did his own, and not only the crooked one. He could see any one of three sound ones and distinguish it from any other, and not only by its size. There were other bears within these thirty miles which left tracks almost as large, but this was more than that. If Sam Fathers had been his mentor and the backyard rabbits and squirrels at home his kindergarten, then the wilderness the old bear ran was his college, the old male bear itself, so long unwifed and childless as to have become its own ungendered progenitor, was his alma mater. But he never saw it.

He could find the crooked print now almost whenever he liked, fifteen or ten or five miles, or sometimes nearer the camp than that. Twice while on stand during the three years he heard the dogs strike its trail by accident; on the second time they jumped it seemingly, the voices high, abject, almost human in hysteria, as on that first morning two years ago. But not the bear itself. He would remember that noon three years ago, the glade, himself and the bear fixed during that moment in the windless and dappled blaze, and it would seem to him that it had never happened, that he had dreamed that too. But it had happened. They had looked at each other, they had emerged from the wilderness old as earth, synchronized to the instant by something more than the blood that moved the flesh and bones which bore them, and touched, pledged something, affirmed, something more lasting than the frail web of bones and flesh which any accident could obliterate.

Then he saw it again. Because of the very fact that he thought of nothing else, he had forgotten to look for it. He was still hunting with Walter Ewell's rifle. He saw it cross the end of a long blow-down, a corridor where a tornado had swept, rushing through rather than over the tangle of trunks and branches as a locomotive would have, faster than he had ever believed it could move, almost as fast as a deer even, because a deer would have spent most of that time in the air, faster than he could bring the rifle sights up with it. And now he knew what had been wrong during all the three years. He sat on a log, shaking and trembling as if he had never seen the woods before nor anything that ran them, wondering with incredulous amazement how he could have forgotten the very thing which Sam Fathers had told him and which the bear itself had proved the next day and had now returned after three years to reaffirm.

And now he knew what Sam Fathers had meant about the right dog, a dog in which size would mean less than nothing. So when he returned alone in

April—school was out then, so that the sons of farmers could help with the land's planting, and at last his father had granted him permission, on his promise to be back in four days—he had the dog. It was his own, a mongrel of the sort called by Negroes a fyce, a ratter, itself not much bigger than a rat and possessing that bravery which had long since stopped being courage and had become foolhardiness.

It did not take four days. Alone again, he found the trail on the first morning. It was not a stalk; it was an ambush. He timed the meeting almost as if it were an appointment with a human being. Himself holding the fyce muffled in a feed sack and Sam Fathers with two of the hounds on a piece of plowline rope, they lay down wind of the trail at dawn of the second morning. They were so close that the bear turned without even running, as if in surprised amazement at the shrill and frantic uproar of the released fyce, turning at bay against the trunk of a tree, on its hind feet; it seemed to the boy that it would never stop rising, taller and taller, and even the two hounds seemed to take a desperate and despairing courage from the fyce, following it as it went in.

Then he realized that the fyce was actually not going to stop. He flung, threw the gun away, and ran; when he overtook and grasped the frantically pin-wheeling little dog, it seemed to him that he was directly under the bear.

He could smell it, strong and hot and rank. Sprawling, he looked up to where it loomed and towered over him like a cloudburst and colored like a thunderclap, quite familiar, peacefully and even lucidly familiar, until he remembered: This was the way he had used to dream about it. Then it was gone. He didn't see it go. He knelt, holding the frantic fyce with both hands, hearing the abashed wailing of the hounds drawing farther and farther away, until Sam came up. He carried the gun. He laid it down quietly beside the boy and stood looking down at him.

"You've done seed him twice now with a gun in your hands," he said. "This time you couldn't have missed him."

The boy rose. He still held the fyce. Even in his arms and clear of the ground, it yapped frantically, straining and surging after the fading uproar of the two hounds like a tangle of wire springs. He was panting a little but he was neither shaking nor trembling now.

"Neither could you!" he said. "You had the gun! Neither did you!"

"And you didn't shoot," his father said. "How close were you?"

"I don't know, sir," he said. "There was a big wood tick inside his right hind leg. I saw that. But I didn't have the gun then."

"But you didn't shoot when you had the gun," his father said. "Why?"

But he didn't answer, and his father didn't wait for him to, rising and crossing the room, across the pelt of the bear which the boy had killed two years ago and the larger one which his father had killed before he was born, to the bookcase beneath the mounted head of the boy's first buck. It was the room which his father called the office, from which all the plantation business was transacted; in it for the fourteen years of his life he had heard the best of all talking. Major de Spain would be there and sometimes old General Compson, and Walter Ewell and Boon Hoggenbeck and Sam Fathers and Tennie's Jim, too, were hunters, knew the woods and what ran them.

He would hear it, not talking himself but listening—the wilderness, the big woods, bigger and older than any recorded document of white man fatuous enough to believe he had bought any fragment of it or Indian ruthless enough to pretend that any fragment of it had been his to convey. It was of the men, not white nor black nor red, but men, hunters with the will and hardihood to endure and the humility and skill to survive, and the dogs and the bear and deer juxtaposed and reliefed against it, ordered and compelled by and within the wilderness in the ancient and unremitting contest by the ancient and immitigable rules which voided all regrets and brooked no quarter, the voices quiet and weighty and deliberate for retrospection and recollection and exact remembering, while he squatted in the blazing firelight as Tennie's Jim squatted, who stirred only to put more wood on the fire and to pass the bottle from one glass to another. Because the bottle was always present, so that after a while it seemed to him that those fierce instants of heart and brain and courage and wiliness and speed were concentrated and distilled into that brown liquor which not women, not boys and children, but only hunters drank, drinking not of the blood they had spilled but some condensation of the wild immortal spirit, drinking it moderately, humbly even, not with the pagan's base hope of acquiring the virtues of cunning and strength and speed, but in salute to them.

His father returned with the book and sat down again and opened it. "Listen," he said. He read the five stanzas aloud, his voice quiet and deliberate in the room where there was no fire now because it was already spring. Then he looked up. The boy watched him. "All right," his father said. "Listen." He read again, but only the second stanza this time, to the end of it, the last two lines, and closed the book and put it on the table beside him. "She cannot fade, though thou hast not thy bliss, forever wilt thou love, and she be fair," he said.

"He's talking about a girl," the boy said.

"He had to talk about something," his father said. Then he said, "He was talking about truth. Truth doesn't change. Truth is one thing. It covers all things which touch the heart—honor and pride and pity and justice and courage and love. Do you see now?"

He didn't know. Somehow it was simpler than that. There was an old bear, fierce and ruthless, not merely just to stay alive, but with the fierce pride of liberty and freedom, proud enough of the liberty and freedom to see it threatened without fear or even alarm; nay, who at times even seemed deliberately to put that freedom and liberty in jeopardy in order to savor them, to remind his old strong bones and flesh to keep supple and quick to defend and preserve them. There was an old man, son of a Negro slave and an Indian king, inheritor on the one side of the long chronicle of a people who had learned humility through suffering, and pride through the endurance which survived the suffering and injustice, and on the other side, the chronicle of a people even longer in the land than the first, yet who no longer existed in the land at all save in the solitary brotherhood of an old Negro's alien blood and the wild and invincible spirit of an old bear. There was a boy who wished to learn humility and pride in order to become skillful and worthy in the woods, who suddenly found himself becoming so skillful so rapidly that he feared he would never become worthy because he had not learned humility and pride, although he had tried to, until one day and as suddenly he discovered that an old man who could not have defined either had led him, as though by the hand, to that point where an old bear and a little mongrel of a dog showed him that, by possessing one thing other, he would possess them both.

And a little dog, nameless and mongrel and many-fathered, grown, yet weighing less than six pounds, saying as if to itself, "I can't be dangerous, because there's nothing much smaller than I am; I can't be fierce, because they would call it just a noise; I can't be humble, because I'm already too close to the ground to genuflect; I can't be proud, because I wouldn't be near enough to it for anyone to know who was casting the shadow, and I don't even know that I'm not going to heaven, because they have already decided that I don't possess an immortal soul. So all I can be is brave. But it's all right. I can be that, even if they still call it just noise."

That was all. It was simple, much simpler than somebody talking in a book about youth and a girl he would never need to grieve over, because he could never approach any nearer her and would never have to get any farther away. He had heard about a bear, and finally got big enough to trail it, and he trailed it four years and at last met it with a gun in his hands and he didn't shoot. Because a little dog— But he could have shot long before the little dog covered the twenty yards to where the bear waited, and Sam Fathers could have shot at any time during that interminable minute while Old Ben stood on his hind feet over them. He stopped. His father was watching him gravely across the spring-rife twilight of the room; when he spoke, his words were as quiet as the twilight, too, not loud, because they did not need to be because they would last. "Courage, and honor, and pride," his father said, "and pity, and love of justice and of liberty. They all touch the heart, and what the heart holds to becomes truth, as far as we know the truth. Do you see now?"

Sam, and Old Ben, and Nip, he thought. And himself too. He had been all right too. His father had said so. "Yes, sir," he said.

JAMES PURDY **(b. 1923)**

Born in Ohio, educated in Chicago, Mexico, and Madrid, employed for a time as a teacher at Lawrence College in Wisconsin, James Purdy now lives and writes in New York City. A group of his shorter works, written between the end of World War II and 1952, was first printed privately in New York and then, through the aid and influence of Dame Edith Sitwell, in England (1957), prior to their commercial publication in America as Color of Darkness. *That book has been followed by several other collections of short fiction and by five novels:* Malcolm *(1959),* The Nephew *(1960),* Cabot Wright Begins *(1964),* Eustace Chisholm and the Works *(1967), and* Jeremy's Version *(1970).*

In response to our invitation to discuss his work with his readers, James Purdy has written: "My work has always been by its nature and form 'against the grain.' At the beginning of my career Dame Edith Sitwell quoted John Cowper Powys's description of my fiction as an exploration 'under the skin' of my characters. To explore what is 'inside' will always be unpopular or taboo so far as any 'establishment' is concerned. Similarly, my style, based on the rhythm and idiom of common American speech, from my own small-town Ohio background, jarred and still jars on the ears of the spokesmen-salesmen for blue-skim homogenized prose à la New York City. The public, devourers of best-seller fiction, demand now as always candy-wrapped lies. They will applaud anything, provided they are not required to feel. Anaesthesia is the boon they have always asked of the writers applauded by the New York book trade.

"The advantages, in my case, however, of having no public are considerable. There is no one I need please except myself, and since I have never been 'in', I cannot fear being 'out'. Thus I am free to pursue my own way, while at the same time I am creating an audience or 'followers' who also are willing to go imaginatively 'under the skin,' through the medium of my stories, written in 'native American diction,' and in the 'cadence and idiom' of the psyche."

In "Cutting Edge," a college student's return home, sporting a beard, gets "under the skin" of his parents, trapped in a bleak, sterile marriage.

Cutting Edge

MRS. ZELLER opposed her son's beard. She was in her house in Florida when she saw him wearing it for the first time. It was as though her mind had come to a full stop. This large full-bearded man entered the room and she remembered always later how ugly he had looked and how frightened she felt seeing him in the house; then the realization it was someone she knew, and finally the terror of recognition.

He had kissed her, which he didn't often do, and she recognized in this his attempt to make her discomfort the more painful. He held the beard to her face for a long time, then he released her as though she had suddenly disgusted him.

"Why did you do it?" she asked. She was, he saw, almost broken by the recognition.

"I didn't dare tell you and come."

"That's of course true," Mrs. Zeller said. "It would have been worse. You'll have to shave it off, of course. Nobody must see you. Your father of course didn't have the courage to warn me, but I knew something was wrong the minute he entered the house ahead of you. I suppose he's upstairs laughing now. But it's not a laughing matter."

Mrs. Zeller's anger turned against her absent husband as though all error began and ended with him. "I suppose he likes it." Her dislike of Mr. Zeller struck her son as staggeringly great at that moment.

He looked at his mother and was surprised to see how young she was. She did not look much older than he did. Perhaps she looked younger now that he had his beard.

"I had no idea a son of mine would do such a thing," she said. "But why a beard, for heaven's sake," she cried, as though he had chosen something permanent and irreparable which would destroy all that they were.

"Is it because you are an artist? No, don't answer me," she commanded. "I can't stand to hear any explanation from you. . . ."

"I have always wanted to wear a beard," her son said. "I remember wanting one as a child."

"I don't remember that at all," Mrs. Zeller said.

"I remember it quite well. I was in the summer house near that old broken-down wall and I told Ellen Whitelaw I wanted to have a beard when I grew up."

"Ellen Whitelaw, that big fat stupid thing. I haven't thought of her in years."

Mrs. Zeller was almost as much agitated by the memory of Ellen Whitelaw as by her son's beard.

"You didn't like Ellen Whitelaw," her son told her, trying to remember how they had acted when they were together.

"She was a common and inefficient servant," Mrs. Zeller said, more quietly now, masking her feelings from her son.

"I suppose *he* liked her," the son pretended surprise, the cool cynical tone coming into his voice.

"Oh, your father," Mrs. Zeller said.

"Did he then?" the son asked.

"Didn't he like all of them?" she asked. The beard had changed this much already between them, she talked to him now about his father's character, while the old man stayed up in the bedroom fearing a scene.

"Didn't he always," she repeated, as though appealing to this new hirsute man.

"So," the son said, accepting what he already knew.

"Ellen Whitelaw, for God's sake," Mrs. Zeller said. The name of the servant girl brought back many other faces and rooms which she did not know were in her memory. These faces and rooms served to make the bearded man who stared at her less and less the boy she remembered in the days of Ellen Whitelaw.

"You must shave it off," Mrs. Zeller said.

"What makes you think I would do that?" the boy wondered.

"You heard me. Do you want to drive me out of my mind?"

"But I'm not going to. Or rather it's not going to."

"I will appeal to him, though a lot of good it will do," Mrs. Zeller said. "He ought to do something once in twenty years at least."

"You mean," the son said laughing, "he hasn't done anything in that long."

"Nothing I can really remember," Mrs. Zeller told him.

"It will be interesting to hear you appeal to him," the boy said. "I haven't heard you do that in such a long time."

"I don't think you ever heard me."

"I did, though," he told her. "It was in the days of Ellen Whitelaw again, in fact."

"In *those* days," Mrs. Zeller wondered. "I don't see how that could be."

"Well, it was. I can remember that much."

"You couldn't have been more than four years old. How could you remember then?"

"I heard you say to him, *You have to ask her to go.*"

Mrs. Zeller did not say anything. She really could not remember the words, but she supposed that the scene was true and that he actually remembered.

"Please shave off that terrible beard. If you only knew how awful it looks on you. You can't see anything else but it."

"Everyone in New York thought it was particularly fine."

"Particularly fine," she paused over his phrase as though its meaning eluded her.

"It's nauseating," she was firm again in her judgment.

"I'm not going to do away with it," he said, just as firm.

She did not recognize his firmness, but she saw everything changing a little, including perhaps the old man upstairs.

"Are you going to 'appeal' to him?" The son laughed again when he saw she could say no more.

"Don't mock me," the mother said. "I will speak to your father." She pretended decorum. "You can't go anywhere with us, you know."

He looked unmoved.

"I don't want any of my friends to see you. You'll have to stay in the house or go to your own places. You can't go out with us to our places and see our friends. I hope none of the neighbors see you. If they ask who you are, I won't tell them."

"I'll tell them then."

They were not angry, they talked it out like that, while the old man was upstairs.

"Do you suppose he is drinking or asleep?" she said finally.

"I thought he looked good in it, Fern," Mr. Zeller said.

"What about it makes him look good?" she said.

"It fills out his face," Mr. Zeller said, looking at the wallpaper and surprised he had never noticed what a pattern it had before; it showed the sacrifice of some sort of animal by a youth.

He almost asked his wife how she had come to pick out this pattern, but her growing fury checked him.

He saw her mouth and throat moving with unspoken words.

"Where is he now?" Mr. Zeller wondered.

"What does that matter where he is?" she said. "He has to be somewhere while he's home, but he can't go out with us."

"How idiotic," Mr. Zeller said, and he looked at his wife straight in the face for a second.

"Why did you say that?" She tried to quiet herself down.

"The way you go on about nothing, Fern." For a moment a kind of revolt announced itself in his manner, but then his eyes went back to the wallpaper, and she resumed her tone of victor.

"I've told him he must either cut it off or go back to New York."

"Why is it a beard upsets you so?" he wondered, almost to himself.

"It's not the beard so much. It's the way he is now too. And it disfigures him so. I don't recognize him at all now when he wears it."

"So, he's never done anything of his own before," Mr. Zeller protested suddenly.

"Never done anything!" He could feel her anger covering him and glancing off like hot sun onto the wallpaper.

"That's right," he repeated. "He's never done anything. I say let him keep the beard and I'm not going to talk to him about it." His gaze lifted toward her but rested finally only on her hands and skirt.

"This is still my house," she said, "and I have to live in this town."

"When they had the centennial in Collins, everybody wore beards."

"I have to live in this town," she repeated.

"I won't talk to him about it," Mr. Zeller said.

It was as though the voice of Ellen Whitelaw reached her saying, *So that was how you appealed to him.*

She sat on the deck chair on the porch and smoked five cigarettes. The two men were somewhere in the house and she had the feeling now that she only roomed here. She wished more than that the beard was gone that her son had never mentioned Ellen Whitelaw. She found herself thinking only about her. Then she thought that now twenty years later she could not have afforded a servant, not even her.

She supposed the girl was dead. She did not know why, but she was sure she was.

She thought also that she should have mentioned her name to Mr. Zeller. It might have broken him down about the beard, but she supposed not. He had been just as adamant and unfeeling with her about the girl as he was now about her son.

Her son came through the house in front of her without speaking, dressed only in his shorts and, when he had got safely beyond her in the garden, he took off those so that he was completely naked with his back to her, and lay down in the sun.

She held the cigarette in her hand until it began to burn her finger. She felt she should not move from the place where she was and yet she did not know where to go inside the house and she did not know what pretext to use for going inside.

In the brilliant sun his body, already tanned, matched his shining black beard.

She wanted to appeal to her husband again and she knew then she could never again. She wanted to call a friend and tell her but she had no friend to whom she could tell this.

The events of the day, like a curtain of extreme bulk, cut her off from her son and husband. She had always ruled the house and them even during the awful Ellen Whitelaw days and now as though they did not even recognize her, they had taken over. She was not even here. Her son could walk naked with a beard in front of her as though she did not exist. She had nothing to fight them with, nothing to make them see with. They ignored her as Mr. Zeller had when he looked at the wallpaper and refused to discuss their son.

"You can grow it back when you're in New York," Mr. Zeller told his son.

He did not say anything about his son lying naked before him in the garden but he felt insulted almost as much as his mother had, yet he needed his son's permission and consent now and perhaps that was why he did not mention the insult of his nakedness.

"I don't know why I have to act like a little boy all the time with you both."

"If you were here alone with me you could do anything you wanted. You know I never asked anything of you. . . ."

When his son did not answer, Mr. Zeller said, "Did I?"

"That was the trouble," the son said.

"What?" the father wondered.

"You never wanted anything from me and you never wanted to give me anything. I didn't matter to you."

"Well, I'm sorry," the father said doggedly.

"Those were the days of Ellen Whitelaw," the son said in tones like the mother.

"For God's sake," the father said and he put a piece of grass between his teeth.

He was a man who kept everything down inside of him, everything had been tied and fastened so long there was no part of him any more that could struggle against the stricture of his life.

There were no words between them for some time; then Mr. Zeller could hear himself bringing the question out: "Did she mention that girl?"

"Who?" The son pretended blankness.

"Our servant."

The son wanted to pretend again blankness but it was too much work. He answered: "No, I mentioned it. To her surprise."

"Don't you see how it is?" the father went on to the present. "She doesn't speak to either of us now and if you're still wearing the beard when you leave it's me she will be punishing six months from now."

"And you want me to save you from your wife."

"Bobby," the father said, using the childhood tone and inflection. "I wish you would put some clothes on too when you're in the garden. With me it doesn't matter, you could do anything. I never asked you anything. But with her . . ."

"God damn *her,*" the boy said.

The father could not protest. He pleaded with his eyes at his son.

The son looked at his father and he could see suddenly also the youth hidden in his father's face. He was young like his mother. They were both young people who had learned nothing from life, were stopped and drifting where they were twenty years before with Ellen Whitelaw. Only *she,* the son thought, must have learned from life, must have gone on to some development in her character, while they had been tied to the shore where she had left them.

"Imagine living with someone for six months and not speaking," the father said as if to himself. "That happened once before, you know, when you were a little boy."

"I don't remember that," the son said, some concession in his voice.

"You were only four," the father told him.

"I believe this is the only thing I ever asked of you," the father said. "Isn't that odd, I can't remember ever asking you anything else. Can you?"

The son looked coldly away at the sky and then answered, contempt and pity struggling together, "No, I can't."

"Thank you, Bobby," the father said.

"Only don't *plead* any more, for Christ's sake." The son turned from him.

"You've only two more days with us, and if you shaved it off and put on just a few clothes, it would help me through the year with her."

He spoke as though it would be his last year.

"Why don't you beat some sense into her?" The son turned to him again.

The father's gaze fell for the first time complete on his son's nakedness.

Bobby had said he would be painting in the storeroom and she could send up a sandwich from time to time, and Mr. and Mrs. Zeller were left downstairs together. She refused to allow her husband to answer the phone.

In the evening Bobby came down dressed carefully and his beard combed immaculately and looking, they both thought, curled.

They talked about things like horse racing, in which they were all somehow passionately interested, but which they now discussed irritably as though it too were a menace to their lives. They talked about the uselessness of art and why people went into it with a detachment that would have made an outsider think that Bobby was as unconnected with it as a jockey or oil magnate. They condemned nearly everything and then the son went upstairs and they saw one another again briefly at bedtime.

The night before he was to leave they heard him up all hours, the water running, and the dropping of things made of metal.

Both parents were afraid to get up and ask him if he was all right. He was like a wealthy relative who had commanded them never to question him or interfere with his movements even if he was dying.

He was waiting for them at breakfast, dressed only in his shorts but he looked more naked than he ever had in the garden because his beard was gone. Over his chin lay savage and profound scratches as though he had removed the hair with a hunting knife and pincers.

Mrs. Zeller held her breast and turned to the coffee and Mr. Zeller said only his son's name and sat down with last night's newspaper.

"What time does your plane go?" Mrs. Zeller said in a dead, muffled voice.

The son began putting a white paste on the scratches of his face and did not answer.

"I believe your mother asked you a question," Mr. Zeller said, pale and shaking.

"Ten-forty," the son replied.

The son and the mother exchanged glances and he could see at once that his sacrifice had been in vain: she would also see the beard there again under the scratches and the gashes he had inflicted on himself, and he would never really be her son again. Even for his father it must be much the same. He had come home as a stranger who despised them and he had shown his nakedness to both of them. All three longed for separation and release.

But Bobby could not control the anger coming up in him, and his rage took an old form. He poured the coffee into his saucer because Mr. Zeller's mother had always done this and it had infuriated Mrs. Zeller because of its low-class implications.

He drank viciously from the saucer, blowing loudly.

Both parents watched him helplessly like insects suddenly swept against the screen.

"It's not too long till Christmas," Mr. Zeller brought out. "We hope you'll come back for the whole vacation."

"We do," Mrs. Zeller said in a voice completely unlike her own.

"So," Bobby began, but the torrent of anger would not let him say the thousand fierce things he had ready.

Instead, he blew savagely from the saucer and spilled some onto the chaste white summer rug below him. Mrs. Zeller did not move.

"I would invite you to New York," Bobby said quietly now, "but of course I will have the beard there and it wouldn't work for you."

"Yes," Mr. Zeller said, incoherent.

"I do hope you don't think I've been. . . ." Mrs. Zeller cried suddenly and they both waited to hear whether she was going to weep or not, but she stopped herself perhaps by the realization that she had no tears and that the feelings which had come over her about Bobby were likewise spent.

"I can't think of any more I can do for you," Bobby said suddenly.

They both stared at each other as though he had actually left and they were alone at last.

"Is there anything more you want me to do?" he said, coldly vicious.

They did not answer.

"I hate and despise what both of you have done to yourselves, but the thought that you would be sitting here in your middle-class crap not speaking to one another is too much even for me. That's why I did it, I guess, and not out of any love. I didn't want you to think that."

He sloshed in the saucer.

"Bobby," Mr. Zeller said.

The son brought out his *What?* with such finished beauty of coolness that he paused to admire his own control and mastery.

"Please, Bobby," Mr. Zeller said.

They could all three of them hear a thousand speeches. The agony of awkwardness was made unendurable by the iciness of the son, and all three paused over this glacial control which had come to him out of art and New

York, as though it was the fruit of their lives and the culmination of their twenty years.

ALAN SILLITOE (b. 1928)

The son of a laborer in the slums of Nottingham, England, Alan Sillitoe left school at the age of fourteen to work in a factory. He subsequently spent two years in the Royal Air Force stationed in Majorca, where he met the poet, novelist, and scholar Robert Graves, who strongly encouraged his writing. Saturday Night and Sunday Morning *(1958), later made into a well-received film, was the first of several well-received novels by Sillitoe, all of which realistically depict the spiritual sterility and pent-up frustrations of English working-class life.*

In response to our invitation to discuss his work, particularly "The Loneliness of the Long-Distance Runner" with his readers Alan Sillitoe wrote the following: "What you ask for calls for a book in reply, not a letter, I am afraid. A writer has to write about people with whom he is in sympathy, and by this he may present something new about the people he is trying to show to the reader. Firstly, though, I do not write for an audience, but for myself, and through that, perhaps there is something that other people want to hear. If there is, then I am lucky, for it enables me to live by my writing, though I would still be writing even if it didn't.

"The story you are intending to use in your anthology was written by me in 1958—a long time ago—but I still believe in the principles which are enshrined in it. Authority which is imposed without sympathy or reason is always to be distrusted and fought against with all the power and integrity at the disposal of the person who feels threatened. This is vital to remember for anyone who values his or her self-respect. A person has to live by his or her own values, and not by alien values imposed from any other place. At the same time there is an obligation to help other people and not harm anyone—unless it can't be helped, or they are threatened with these alien values. We should never have anything to do with the truth with a capital T, only with human love and sympathy. Those who claim to know the truth, and who say they are right, and embody in themselves all the dangerous and false authority that this tends to give, are either to be fought when they are weak enough, or eroded if they are too strong. The world is changing, and they have to be made to realise it."

The Loneliness of the Long-Distance Runner

AS SOON AS I got to Borstal* they made me a long-distance cross-country runner. I suppose they thought I was just the build for it because I was long and skinny for my age (and still am) and in any case I didn't mind it much, to tell you the truth, because running had always been made much of in our family, especially running away from the police. I've always been a good runner, quick and with a big stride as well, the only trouble being that no matter how fast I run, and I did a very fair lick even though I do say so myself, it didn't stop me getting caught by the cops after that bakery job.

You might think it a bit rare, having long-distance cross-country runners in Borstal, thinking that the first thing a long-distance cross-country runner would do when they set him loose at them fields and woods would be to run as far away from the place as he could get on a bellyful of Borstal slumgullion—but you're wrong, and I'll tell you why. The first thing is that them bastards over us aren't as daft as they most of the time look, and for another thing I'm not so daft as I would look if I tried to make a break for it on my long-distance running, because to abscond and then get caught is nothing but a mug's game, and I'm not falling for it. Cunning is what counts in this life, and even that you've got to use in the slyest way you can; I'm telling you straight: they're cunning, and I'm cunning. If only 'them' and 'us' had the same ideas we'd get on like a house on fire, but they don't see eye to eye with us and we don't see eye to eye with them, so that's how it stands and how it will always stand. The one fact is that all of us are cunning, and because of this there's no love lost between us. So the thing is that they know I won't try to get away from them: they sit there like spiders in that crumbly manor house, perched like jumped-up jackdaws on the roof, watching out over the drives and fields like German generals from the tops of tanks. And even when I jog-trot on behind a wood and they can't see me anymore they know my sweeping-brush head will bob along that hedge-top in an hour's time and that I'll report to the bloke on the gate. Because when on a raw and frosty morning I get up at five o'clock and stand shivering my belly off on the stone floor and all the rest still have another hour to snooze before the bells go, I slink downstairs through all the corridors to the big outside door with a permit running-card in my fist, I feel like the first and last man in the world, both at once, if you can believe what I'm trying to say. I feel like the first man because I've hardly got a stitch on and am sent against the frozen fields in a shimmy ** and shorts—even the first poor bastard dropped on to the earth in midwinter knew how to make a suit of leaves, or how to skin a pterodactyl for a topcoat. But there I am, fro-

* *Borstal.* School (in England) for delinquent boys
** *shimmy.* Undershirt (from "chemise")

zen stiff, with nothing to get me warm except a couple of hours' long-distance running before breakfast, not even a slice of bread-and-sheepdip. They're training me up fine for the big sports day when all the pig-faced snotty-nosed dukes and ladies—who can't add two and two together and would mess themselves like loonies if they didn't have slavies to beck-and-call—come and make speeches to us about sports being just the thing to get us leading an honest life and keep our itching finger-ends off them shop locks and safe handles and hairgrips to open gas meters. They give us a bit of blue ribbon and a cup for a prize after we've shagged ourselves out running or jumping, like race horses, only we don't get so well looked-after as race horses, that's the only thing.

So there I am, standing in the doorway in shimmy and shorts, not even a dry crust in my guts, looking out at frosty flowers on the ground. I suppose you think this is enough to make me cry? Not likely. Just because I feel like the first bloke in the world wouldn't make me bawl. It makes me feel fifty times better than when I'm cooped up in that dormitory with three hundred others. No, it's sometimes when I stand there feeling like the *last* man in the world that I don't feel so good. I feel like the last man in the world because I think that all those three hundred sleepers behind me are dead. They sleep so well I think that every scruffy head's kicked the bucket in the night and I'm the only one left, and when I look out into the bushes and frozen ponds I have the feeling that it's going to get colder and colder until everything I can see, meaning my red arms as well, is going to be covered with a thousand miles of ice, all the earth, right up to the sky and over every bit of land and sea. So I try to kick this feeling out and act like I'm the first man on earth. And that makes me feel good, so as soon as I'm steamed up enough to get this feeling in me, I take a flying leap out of the doorway, and off I trot.

I'm in Essex. It's supposed to be a good Borstal, at least that's what the governor said to me when I got here from Nottingham. "We want to trust you while you are in this establishment," he said, smoothing out his newspaper with lily-white workless hands, while I read the big words upside down: *Daily Telegraph.* "If you play ball with us, we'll play ball with you." (Honest to God, you'd have thought it was going to be one long tennis match.) "We want hard honest work and we want good athletics," he said as well. "And if you give us both these things you can be sure we'll do right by you and send you back into the world an honest man." Well, I could have died laughing, especially when straight after this I hear the barking sergeant-major's voice calling me and two others to attention and marching us off like we was Grenadier Guards. And when the governor kept saying how 'we' wanted you to do this, and 'we' wanted you to do that, I kept looking round for the other blokes, wondering how many of them there was. Of course, I knew there were thousands of them, but as far as I knew only one was in the room. And there *are* thousands of them, all over the poxeaten country, in shops, offices, railway stations, cars, houses, pubs—In-law blokes like you and them, all on the watch for Out-law blokes like me and us—and waiting to 'phone for the coppers as soon as we make a false move. And it'll always be there, I'll tell you that now, because I haven't finished making all my false moves yet, and I dare say I won't until I kick the bucket. If the In-laws are hoping to stop me making false moves they're wasting their time. They might as well stand me up against a wall and let fly with a dozen rifles. That's the only way they'll stop me, and a few million others. Because I've been doing a lot of thinking since coming here. They can spy on us all day to see if we're pulling our puddings and if we're working good or doing our 'athletics' but they can't make an X-ray of our guts to find out what we're telling ourselves. I've been asking myself all sorts of questions, and thinking about my life up to now. And I like doing all this. It's a treat. It passes the time away and don't make Borstal seem half so bad as the boys in our street used to say it was. And this long-distance running lark is the best of all, because it makes me think so good that I learn things even better than when I'm on my bed at night. And apart from that, what with thinking so much while I'm running I'm getting to be one of the best runners in the Borstal. I can go my five miles round better than anybody else I know.

So as soon as I tell myself I'm the first man ever to be dropped into the world, and as soon as I take that first flying leap out into the frosty grass of an early morning when even birds haven't the heart to whistle, I get to thinking, and that's what I like. I go my rounds in a dream, turning at lane or footpath corners without knowing I'm turning, leaping brooks without knowing they're there, and shouting good morning to the early cow-milker without seeing him. It's a treat, being a long-distance runner, out in the world by yourself with not a soul to make you bad-tempered or tell you what to do or that there's a shop to break and enter a bit back from the next street. Sometimes I think that I've never been so free as during that couple of hours when I'm trotting up the path out of the gates and turning by that bare-faced, big-bellied oak tree at the lane end. Everything's dead, but good, because it's dead before coming alive, not dead after being alive. That's how I look at it. Mind you, I often feel frozen stiff at first. I can't feel my hands or feet or flesh at all, like I'm a ghost who wouldn't know the earth was under him if he didn't see it now and again through the mist. But even though some people would call this frost-pain suffering if they wrote about it to their mams in a letter, I don't, because I know that in half an hour I'm going to be warm, that by the time I get to the main road and am turning on to the wheatfield footpath by the bus stop I'm going to feel as hot as a potbellied stove and as happy as a dog with a tin tail.

It's a good life, I'm saying to myself, if you don't give in to coppers and Borstal-bosses and the rest of them bastard-faced In-laws. Trot-trot-trot. Puff-puff-puff. Slap-slap-slap go my feet on the hard soil. Swish-swish-swish as my arms and side catch the bare branches of a bush. For I'm seventeen now, and when they let me out of this—if I don't make a break and see that things turn out otherwise—they'll try to get me in the army, and what's the difference between the army and this place I'm in now? They can't kid me, the bastards. I've seen the barracks near where I live, and if there weren't swaddies on guard outside with rifles you wouldn't know the difference between their high walls and the place I'm in now. Even though the swaddies come out at odd times a week for a pint of ale, so what? Don't I come out three mornings a week on my long-distance running, which is fifty times better than boozing. When they first said that I was to do my long-distance running without a guard pedalling beside me on a bike I couldn't believe it; but they called it a progressive and modern place, though they can't kid me because I know it's just like any other Borstal, going by the stories I've heard, except that they let me trot about like this. Borstal's Borstal no matter what they do; but anyway I moaned about it being a bit thick sending me out so early to run five miles on an empty stomach, until they talked me round to thinking it wasn't so bad —which I knew all the time—until they called me a good sport and patted me on the back when I said I'd do it and that I'd try to win them the Borstal Blue Ribbon Prize Cup For Long Distance Cross Country Running (All England). And now the governor talks to me when he comes on his rounds, almost as he'd talk to his prize race horse, if he had one.

"All right, Smith?" he asks.

"Yes, sir," I answer.

He flicks his grey moustache: "How's the running coming along?"

"I've set myself to trot round the grounds after dinner just to keep my hand in, sir," I tell him.

The pot-bellied pop-eyed bastard gets pleased at this: "Good show. I know you'll get us that cup," he says.

And I swear under my breath: "Like boggery, I will." No, I won't get them that cup, even though the stupid tash-twitching bastard has all his hopes in me. Because what does his barmy hope mean? I ask myself. Trot-trot-trot, slap-slap-slap, over the stream and into the wood where it's almost dark and frosty-dew twigs sting my legs. It don't mean a bloody thing to me, only to him, and it means as much to him as it would mean to me if I picked up the racing paper and put my bet on a hoss I didn't know, had never seen, and didn't care a sod if I ever did see. That's what it means to him. And I'll lose that race, because I'm not a race horse at all, and I'll let him know it when I'm about to get out—if I don't sling my hook even before the race. By Christ I will. I'm a human being and I've got thoughts and secrets and bloody life inside me that he doesn't know is there, and he'll never know what's there because he's stupid. I suppose you'll laugh at this, me saying the governor's a stupid bastard when I know hardly how to write and he can read and write and add-up like a professor. But what I say is true right enough. He's stupid, and I'm not, because I can see further into the likes of him than he can see into the likes of me. Admitted, we're both cunning, but I'm more cunning and I'll win in the end even if I die in gaol at eighty-two, because I'll have more fun and fire out of my life than he'll ever get out of his. He's read a thousand books I suppose, and for all I know he might even have written a few, but I know for a dead cert, as sure as I'm sitting here, that what I'm scribbling down is worth a million to what he could ever scribble down. I don't care what anybody says, but that's the truth and can't be denied. I know when he talks to me and I look into his army mug that I'm alive and he's dead. He's as dead as a doornail. If he ran ten yards he'd drop dead. If he got ten yards into what goes on in my guts he'd drop dead as well—with surprise. At the moment it's dead blokes like him as have the whip-hand over blokes like me, and I'm almost dead sure it'll always be like that, but even so, by Christ, I'd rather be like I am—always on the run and breaking into shops for a packet of fags and a jar of jam—than have the whip-hand over somebody else and be dead from the toe nails up. Maybe as soon as you get the whip-hand over somebody you do go dead. By God, to say that last sentence has needed a few hundred miles of long-distance running. I could no more have said that at first than I could have took a million-pound note from my back pocket. But it's true, you know, now I think of it again, and has always been true, and always will be true, and I'm surer of it every time I see the governor open that door and say Goodmorning lads.

As I run and see my smoky breath going out into the air as if I had ten cigars stuck in different parts of my body I think more on the little speech the governor made when I first came. Honesty. Be honest. I laughed so much one morning I went ten minutes down in my timing because I had to stop and get rid of the stitch in my side. The governor was so worried when I got back late that he sent me to the doctor's for an X-ray and heart check. Be honest. It's like saying: Be dead, like me, and then you'll have no more pain of leaving your nice slummy house for Borstal or prison. Be honest and settle down in a cosy six pounds a week job. Well, even with all this long-distance running I haven't yet been able to decide what he means by this, although I'm just about beginning to—and I don't like what it means. Because after all my thinking I found that it adds up to something that can't be true about me, being born and brought up as I was. Because another thing people like the governor will never understand is that I *am* honest, that I've never been anything else but honest, and that I'll always be honest. Sounds funny. But it's true because I know what honest means according to me and he only knows what it means according to him. I think my honesty is the only sort in the world, and he thinks his is the only sort in the world as well. That's why this dirty great walled-up and fenced-up manor house in the middle of nowhere has been used to coop-up blokes like me. And if I had the whip-hand I wouldn't even bother to build a place like this to put all the cops, governors, posh whores, penpushers, army officers, Members of Parliament in; no, I'd stick them up against a wall and let them have it, like they'd have done with blokes like us years ago, that is, if they'd ever known what it means to be honest, which they don't and never will so help me God Almighty.

I was nearly eighteen months in Borstal before I thought about getting out.

I can't tell you much about what it was like there because I haven't got the hang of describing buildings or saying how many crumby chairs and slatted windows make a room. Neither can I do much complaining, because to tell you the truth I didn't suffer in Borstal at all. I gave the same answer a pal of mine gave when someone asked him how much he hated it in the army. "I didn't hate it," he said. "They fed me, gave me a suit, and pocket-money, which was a bloody sight more than I ever got before, unless I worked myself to death for it, and most of the time they wouldn't let me work but sent me to the dole office twice a week." Well, that's more or less what I say. Borstal didn't hurt me in that respect, so since I've got no complaints I don't have to describe what they gave us to eat, what the dorms were like, or how they treated us. But in another way Borstal does something to me. No, it doesn't get my back up, because it's always been up, right from when I was born. What it does do is show me what they've been trying to frighten me with. They've got other things as well, like prison and, in the end, the rope. It's like me rushing up to thump a man and snatch the coat off his back when, suddenly, I pull up because he whips out a knife and lifts it to stick me like a pig if I come too close. That knife is Borstal, clink, the rope. But once you've seen the knife you learn a bit of unarmed combat. You have to, because you'll never get that sort of knife in your own hands, and this unarmed combat doesn't amount to much. Still, there it is, and you keep on rushing up to this man, knife or not, hoping to get one of your hands on his wrist and the other on his elbow both at the same time, and press back until he drops the knife.

You see, by sending me to Borstal they've shown me the knife, and from now on I know something I didn't know before: that it's war between me and them. I always knew this, naturally, because I was in Remand Homes as well and the boys there told me a lot about their brothers in Borstal, but it was only touch and go then, like kittens, like boxing-gloves, like dobbie. But now that they've shown me the knife, whether I ever pinch another thing in my life again or not, I know who my enemies are and what war is. They can drop all the atom bombs they like for all I care: I'll never call it war and wear a soldier's uniform, because I'm in a different sort of war, that they think is child's play. The war they think is war is suicide, and those that go and get killed in war should be put in clink for attempted suicide because that's the feeling in blokes' minds when they rush to join up or let themselves be called up. I know, because I've thought how good it would be sometimes to do myself in and the easiest way to do it, it occurred to me, was to hope for a big war so's I could join up and get killed. But I got past that when I knew I already was in a war of my own, that I was born into one, that I grew up hearing the sound of 'old soldiers' who'd been over the top at Dartmoor, half-killed at Lincoln, trapped in no-man's-land at Borstal, that sounded louder than any Jerry bombs. Government wars aren't my wars; they've got nowt to do with me, because my own war's all that I'll ever be bothered about. I remember when I was fourteen and I went out into the country with three of my cousins, all about the same age, who later went to different Borstals, and then to different regiments, from which they soon deserted, and then to different gaols where they still are as far as I know. But anyway, we were all kids then, and wanted to go out to the woods for a change, to get away from the roads of stinking hot tar one summer. We climbed over fences and went through fields, scrumping a few sour apples on our way, until we saw the wood about a mile off. Up Colliers' Pad we heard another lot of kids talking in high-school voices behind a hedge. We crept up on them and peeped through the brambles, and saw they were eating a picnic, a real posh spread out of baskets and flasks and towels. There must have been about seven of them, lads and girls sent out by their mams and dads for the afternoon. So we went on our bellies through the hedge like crocodiles and surrounded them, and then dashed into the middle, scattering the fire and batting their tabs and snatching up all there was to eat, then running off over Cherry Orchard fields into the wood, with a man chasing us who'd come up while we were ransacking their picnic. We got away all right, and had a good feed into the bargain, because we'd been clambed to death and couldn't wait long enough to get our chops ripping into them thin lettuce and ham sandwiches and creamy cakes.

Well, I'll always feel during every bit of my life like those daft kids should have felt before we broke them up. But they never dreamed that what happened was going to happen, just like the governor of this Borstal who spouts to us about honesty and all that wappy stuff don't know a bloody thing, while I know every minute of my life that a big boot is always likely to smash any nice picnic I might be barmy and dishonest enough to make for myself. I admit that there've been times when I've thought of telling the governor all this so as to put him on his guard, but when I've got as close as seeing him I've changed my mind, thinking to let him either find out for himself or go through the same mill as I've gone through. I'm not hard-hearted (in fact I've helped a few blokes in my time with the odd quid, lie, fag, or shelter from the rain when they've been on the run) but I'm boggered if I'm going to risk being put in the cells just for trying to give the governor a bit of advice he don't deserve. If my heart's soft I know the sort of people I'm going to save it for. And any advice I'd give the governor wouldn't do him the least bit of good; it'd only trip him up sooner than if he wasn't told at all, which I suppose is what I want to happen. But for the time being I'll let things go on as they are, which is something else I've learned in the last year or two. (It's a good job I can only think of these things as fast as I can write with this stub of pencil that's clutched in my paw, otherwise I'd have dropped the whole thing weeks ago.)

By the time I'm half-way through my morning course, when after a frost-bitten dawn I can see a phlegmy bit of sunlight hanging from the bare twigs of beech and sycamore, and when I've measured my half-way mark by the short-cut scrimmage down the steep bush-covered bank and into the sunken lane, when still there's not a soul in sight and not a sound except the neighing of a piebald foal in a cottage stable that I can't see, I get to thinking the deepest and daftest of all. The governor would have a fit if he could see me sliding down the bank because I could break my neck or ankle, but I can't not do it because it's the only risk I take and the only excitement I ever get, flying flat-out like one of them pterodactyls from the 'Lost World' I once heard on the wireless, crazy like a cut-balled cockerel, scratching myself to bits and almost letting myself go but not quite. It's the most wonderful minute because there's not one thought or word or picture of anything in my head while I'm going down. I'm empty, as empty as I was before I was born, and I don't let myself go, I suppose, because whatever it is that's farthest down inside me don't want me to die or hurt myself bad. And it's daft to think deep, you know, because it gets you nowhere, though deep is what I am when I've passed this half-way mark because the long-distance run of an early morning makes me think that every run like this is a life—a little life, I know—but a life as full of misery and happiness and things happening as you can ever get really around yourself—and I remember that after a lot of these runs I thought that it didn't need much know-how to tell how a life was going to end once it had got well started. But as usual I was wrong, caught first by the cops and then by my own bad brain, I could never trust myself to fly scot-free over these traps, was always tripped up sooner or later no matter how many I got over to the good without even knowing it. Looking back I suppose them big trees put their branches to their snouts and gave each other the wink, and there I was whizzing down the bank and not seeing a bloody thing.

II

I don't say to myself: "You shouldn't have done the job and then you'd have stayed away from Borstal"; no, what I ram into my runner-brain is that my luck had no right to scram just when I was on my way to making the coppers think I hadn't done the job after all. The time was autumn and the night foggy enough to set me and my mate Mike roaming the streets when we should have been rooted in front of the telly or stuck into a plush posh seat at the pictures, but I was restless after six weeks away from any sort of work, and well you might ask me why I'd been bone-idle for so long because normally I sweated my thin guts out on a milling-machine with the rest of them, but you see, my dad died from cancer of the throat, and mam collected a cool five hundred in insurance and benefits from the factory where he'd worked, "for your bereavement," they said, or words like that.

Now I believe, and my mam must have thought the same, that a wad of crisp blue-back fivers ain't a sight of good to a living soul unless they're flying out of your hand into some shopkeeper's till, and the shopkeeper is passing you tip-top things in exchange over the counter, so as soon as she got the money, mam took me and my five brothers and sisters out to town and got us dolled-up in new clothes. Then she ordered a twenty-one-inch telly, a new carpet because the old one was covered with blood from dad's dying and wouldn't wash out, and took a taxi home with bags of grub and a new fur coat. And do you know—you wain't believe me when I tell you—she'd still near three hundred left in her bulging handbag the next day, so how could any of us go to work after that? Poor old dad, he didn't get a look in, and he was the one who'd done the suffering and dying for such a lot of lolly.

Night after night we sat in front of the telly with a ham sandwich in one hand, a bar of chocolate in the other, and a bottle of lemonade between our boots, while mam was with some fancy-man upstairs on the new bed she'd ordered, and I'd never known a family as happy as ours was in that couple of months when we'd got all the money we needed. And when the dough ran out I didn't think about anything much, but just roamed the streets—looking for another job, I told mam—hoping I suppose to get my hands on another five hundred nicker so's the nice life we'd got used to could go on and on for ever. Because it's surprising how quick you can get used to a different life. To begin with, the adverts on the telly had shown us how much more there was in the world to buy than we'd ever dreamed of when we'd looked into shop windows but hadn't seen all there was to see because we didn't have the money to buy it with anyway. And the telly made all these things seem twenty times better than we'd ever thought they were. Even adverts at the cinema were cool and tame, because now we were seeing them in private at home. We used to cock our noses up at things in shops that didn't move, but suddenly we saw their real value because they jumped and glittered around the screen and had some pasty-faced tart going head over heels to get her nail-polished grabbers on to them or her lipstick lips over them, not like the crumby adverts you saw on posters or in newspapers as dead as doornails; these were flickering around loose, half-open packets and tins, making you think that all you had to do was finish opening them before they were yours, like seeing an unlocked safe through a shop window with the man gone away for a cup of tea without thinking to guard his lolly. The films they showed were good as well, in that way, because we couldn't get our eyes unglued from the cops chasing the robbers who had satchel-bags crammed with cash and looked like getting away to spend it—until the last moment. I always hoped they would end up free to blow the lot, and could never stop wanting to put my hand out, smash into the screen (it only looked a bit of rag-screen like at the pictures) and get the copper in a half-nelson so's he'd stop following the bloke with the money-bags. Even when he'd knocked off a couple of bank clerks I hoped he wouldn't get nabbed. In fact then I wished more than ever he wouldn't because it meant the hot-chair if he did, and I wouldn't wish that on anybody no matter what they'd done, because I'd read in a book where the hot-chair worn't a quick death at all, but that you just sat there scorching to death until you were dead. And it was when these cops were chasing the crooks that we played some good tricks with the telly, because when one of them opened his big gob to spout about getting their man I'd turn the sound down and see his mouth move like a goldfish or mackerel or a minnow mimicking what they were supposed to be acting—it was so funny the whole family nearly went into fits on the brand-new carpet that hadn't yet found its way to the bedroom. It was the best of all though when we did it to some Tory telling us about how good his government was going to be if we kept on voting for them—their slack chops rolling, opening and bumbling, hands lifting to twitch moustaches and touching their buttonholes to make sure the flower hadn't wilted, so that you could see they didn't mean a word they said, especially with not a murmur coming out because we'd cut off the sound. When the governor of the Borstal first talked to me I was reminded of those times so much that I nearly killed myself trying not to laugh. Yes, we played so many good stunts on the box of tricks that mam used to call us the Telly Boys, we got so clever at it.

My pal Mike got let off with probation because it was his first job—anyway the first they ever knew about—and because they said he would never have done it if it hadn't been for me talking him into it. They said I was a menace to honest lads like Mike—hands in his pockets so that they looked stone-empty, head bent forward as if looking for half-crowns to fill 'em with, a ripped jersey on and his hair falling into his eyes so that he could go up to women and ask them for a shilling because he was hungry—and that I was the brains behind the job, the guiding light when it came to making up anybody's mind, but I swear to God I worn't owt like that because really I ain't got no more brains than a gnat after hiding the money in the place I did. And I—being cranky like I am—got sent to Borstal because to tell you the honest truth I'd been to Remand Homes before—though that's another story and I suppose if ever I tell it it'll be just as boring as this one is. I was glad though that Mike got away with it, and I only hope he always will, not like silly bastard me.

So on this foggy night we tore ourselves away from the telly and slammed the front door behind us, setting off up our wide street like slow tugs on a river that'd broken their hooters, for we didn't know where the housefronts began what with the perishing cold mist all around. I was snatched to death without an overcoat: mam had forgotten to buy me one in the scrummage of shopping, and by the time I thought to remind her of it the dough was all gone. So we whistled 'The Teddy Boys Picnic' to keep us warm, and I told myself that I'd get a coat soon if it was the last thing I did. Mike said he thought the same about himself, adding that he'd also get some brand-new glasses with gold rims, to wear instead of the wire frames they'd given him at the school clinic years ago. He didn't twig it was foggy at first and cleaned his glasses every time I pulled him back from a lamp-post or car, but when he saw the lights on Alfreton Road looking like octopus eyes he put them in his pocket and didn't wear them again until we did the job. We hadn't got two ha-pennies between us, and though we weren't hungry we wished we'd got a bob or two when we passed the fish and chip shops because the delicious sniffs of salt and vinegar and frying fat made our mouths water. I don't mind telling you we walked the town from one end to the other and if our eyes worn't glued to the ground looking for lost wallets and watches they was swivelling around house windows and shop doors in case we saw something easy and worth nipping into.

Neither of us said as much as this to each other, but I know for a fact that that was what we was thinking. What I don't know—and as sure as I sit here I know I'll never know—is which of us was the first bastard to latch his peepers on to that baker's backyard. Oh yes, it's all right me telling myself it was me, but the truth is that I've never known whether it was Mike or not, because I do know that I didn't see the open window until he stabbed me in the ribs and pointed it out. "See it?" he said.

"Yes," I told him, "so let's get cracking."

"But what about the wall though?" he whispered, looking a bit closer.

"On your shoulders," I chipped in.

His eyes were already up there: "Will you be able to reach?" It was the only time he ever showed any life.

"Leave it to me," I said, ever-ready. "I can reach anywhere from your ham-hock shoulders."

Mike was a nipper compared to me, but underneath the scruffy draught-board jersey he wore were muscles as hard as iron, and you wouldn't think to see him walking down the street with glasses on and hands in pockets that he'd harm a fly, but I never liked to get on the wrong side of him in a fight because he's the sort that don't say a word for weeks on end—sits plugged in front of the telly, or reads a cowboy book, or just sleeps—when suddenly BIFF—half kills somebody for almost nothing at all, such as beating him in a race for the last Football Post on a Saturday night, pushing in before him at a bus stop, or bumping into him when he was day-dreaming about Dolly-on-the-Tub next door. I saw him set on a bloke once for no more than fixing him in a funny way with his eyes, and it turned out that the bloke was cockeyed but nobody knew it because he'd just that day come to live in our street. At other times none of these things would matter a bit, and I suppose the only reason why I was pals with him was because I didn't say much from one month's end to another either.

He put his hands up in the air like he was being covered with a Gatling-Gun, and moved to the wall like he was going to be mowed down, and I climbed up him like he was a stile or step-ladder, and there he stood, the palms of his upshot maulers flat and turned out so's I could step on 'em like they was the adjustable jack-spanner under a car, not a sound of a breath nor the shiver of a flinch coming from him. I lost no time in any case, took my coat from between my teeth, chucked it up to the glass-topped wall (where the glass worn't too sharp because the jags had been worn down by years of accidental stones) and was sitting astraddle before I knew where I was. Then down the other side, with my legs rammed up into my throat when I hit the ground, the crack coming about as hard as when you fall after a high parachute drop, that one of my mates told me was like jumping off a twelve-foot wall, which this must have been. Then I picked up my bits and pieces and opened the gate for Mike, who was still grinning and full of life because the hardest part of the job was already done. "I came, I broke, I entered," like that clever-dick Borstal song.

I didn't think about anything at all, as usual, because I never do when I'm busy, when I'm draining pipes, looting sacks, yaling locks, lifting latches, forcing my bony hands and lanky legs into making something move, hardly feeling my lungs going in-whiff and out-whaff, not realizing whether my mouth is clamped tight or gaping, whether I'm hungry, itching from scabies, or whether my flies are open and flashing dirty words like muck and spit into the late-night final fog. And when I don't know anything about all this then how can I honest-to-God say I think of anything at such times? When I'm wondering what's the best way to get a window open or how to force a door, how can I be thinking or have anything on my mind? That's what the four-eyed white-smocked bloke with the note-book couldn't understand when he asked me questions for days and days after I got to Borstal; and I couldn't explain it to him then like I'm writing it down now; and even if I'd been able to maybe he still wouldn't have caught on because I don't know whether I can understand it myself even at this moment, though I'm doing my best you can bet.

So before I knew where I was I was inside the baker's office watching Mike picking up that cash box after he'd struck a match to see where it was, wearing a tailor-made fifty-shilling grin on his square crew-cut nut as his paws closed over the box like he'd squash it to nothing. "Out," he suddenly said, shaking it so's it rattled. "Let's scram."

"Maybe there's some more," I said, pulling half a dozen drawers out of a rollertop desk.

"No," he said, like he'd already been twenty years in the game, "this is the lot," patting his tin box, "this is it."

I pulled out another few drawers, full of bills, books and letters. "How do you know, you loony sod?"

He barged past me like a bull at a gate. "Because I do."

Right or wrong, we'd both got to stick together and do the same thing. I looked at an ever-loving babe of a brand-new typewriter, but knew it was too traceable, so blew it a kiss, and went out after him. "Hang on," I said, pulling the door to, "we're in no hurry."

"Not much we aren't," he says over his shoulder.

"We've got months to splash the lolly," I whispered as we crossed the yard, "only don't let that gate creak too much or you'll have the narks tuning-in."

"You think I'm barmy?" he said, creaking the gate so that the whole street heard.

I don't know about Mike, but now I started to think, of how we'd get back safe through the streets with that money-box up my jumper. Because he'd clapped it into my hand as soon as we'd got to the main road, which might have meant that he'd started thinking as well, which only goes to show how you don't know what's in anybody else's mind unless you think about things yourself. But as far as my thinking went at that moment it wasn't up to much, only a bit of fright that wouldn't budge not even with a hot blow-lamp, about what we'd say if a copper asked us where we were off to with that hump in my guts.

"What is it?" he'd ask, and I'd say: "A growth." "What do you mean, a growth, my lad?" he'd say back, narky like. I'd cough and clutch myself like I was in the most tripe-twisting pain in the world, and screw my eyes up like I was on my way to the hospital, and Mike would take my arm like he was the best pal I'd got. "Cancer," I'd manage to say to Narker, which would make his slow punch-drunk brain suspect a thing or two. "A lad of your age?" So I'd groan again, and hope to make him feel a real bully of a bastard, which would be impossible, but anyway: "It's in the family. Dad died of it last month, and I'll die of it next month by the feel of it." "What, did he have it in the guts?" "No, in the throat. But it's got me in the stomach." Groan and cough. "Well, you shouldn't be out like this if you've got cancer, you should be in the hospital." I'd get ratty now: "That's where I'm trying to go if only you'd let me and stop asking so many questions. Aren't I, Mike?" Grunt from Mike as he unslung his cosh. Then just in time the copper would tell us to get on our way, kind and considerate all of a sudden, saying that the outpatient department of the hospital closes at twelve, so hadn't he better call us a taxi? He would if we liked, he says, and he'd pay for it as well. But we tell him not to bother, that he's a good bloke even if he is a copper, that we know a short cut anyway. Then just as we're turning a corner he gets it into his big batchy head that we're going the opposite way to the hospital, and calls us back. So we'd start to run . . . if you can call all that thinking.

Up in my room Mike rips open that money-box with a hammer and chisel, and before we know where we are we've got seventy-eight pounds fifteen and fourpence ha'penny *each* lying all over my bed like tea spread out on Christmas Day: cake and trifle, salad and sandwiches, jam tarts and bars of chocolate: all shared and shared alike between Mike and me because we believed in equal work and equal pay, just like the comrades my dad was in until he couldn't do a stroke anymore and had no breath left to argue with. I thought how good it was that blokes like that poor baker didn't stash all his cash in one of the big marble-fronted banks that take up every corner of the town, how lucky for us that he didn't trust them no matter how many millions of tons of concrete or how many iron bars and boxes they were made of, or how many coppers kept their blue pop-eyed peepers glued on to them, how smashing it was that he believed in money-boxes when so many shopkeepers thought it old-fashioned and tried to be modern by using a bank, which wouldn't give a couple of sincere, honest, hardworking, conscientious blokes like Mike and me a chance.

Now you'd think, and I'd think, and anybody with a bit of imagination would think, that we'd done as clean a job as could ever be done, that, with the baker's shop being at least a mile from where we lived, and with not a soul having seen us, and what with the fog and the fact that we weren't more than five minutes in the place, that the coppers should never have been able to trace us. But then, you'd be wrong, I'd be wrong, and everybody else would be wrong, no matter how much imagination was diced out between us.

Even so, Mike and I didn't splash the money about, because that would have made people think straightaway that we'd latched on to something that didn't belong to us. Which wouldn't do at all, because even in a street like ours there are people who love to do a good turn for the coppers, though I never know why they do. Some people are so mean-gutted that even if they've only got tuppence more than you and they think you're the sort that would take it if you have half the chance, they'd get you put inside if they saw you ripping lead out of a lavatory, even if it weren't their lavatory—just to keep their tuppence out of your reach. And so we didn't do anything to let on about how rich we were, nothing like going down town and coming back dressed in brand-new Teddy boy suits and carrying a set of skiffle-drums like another pal of ours who'd done a factory office about six months before. No, we took the odd bobs and pennies out and folded the notes into bundles and stuffed them up the drainpipe outside the door in the backyard. "Nobody'll ever think of looking for it there," I said to Mike. "We'll keep it doggo for a week or two, then take a few quid a week out till it's all gone. We might be thieving bastards, but we're not green."

Some days later a plain-clothes dick knocked at the door. And asked for me. I was still in bed, at eleven o'clock, and had to unroll myself from the comfortable black sheets when I heard mam calling me. "A man to see you," she said. "Hurry up, or he'll be gone."

I could hear her keeping him at the back door, nattering about how fine it had been but how it looked like rain since early this morning—and he didn't answer her except to snap out a snotty yes or no. I scrambled into my trousers and wondered why he'd come—knowing it was a copper because 'a man to see you' always meant just that in our house—and if I'd had any idea that one had gone to Mike's house as well at the same time I'd have twigged it to be because of that hundred and fifty quid's worth of paper stuffed up the drainpipe outside the back door about ten inches away from that plain-clothed copper's boot, where mam still talked to him thinking she was doing me a favour, and I wishing to God she'd ask him in, though on second thoughts realizing that that would seem more suspicious than keeping him outside, because they know we hate their guts and smell a rat if they think we're trying to be nice to them. Mam wasn't born yesterday, I thought, thumping my way down the creaking stairs.

I'd seen him before: Borstal Bernard in nicky-hat, Remand Home Ronald in rowing-boat boots. Probation Pete in a pit-prop mackintosh, three-months clink in collar and tie (all this out of a Borstal skiffle-ballad that my new mate made up, and I'd tell you it in full but it doesn't belong in this story), a 'tec who'd never had as much in his pockets as that drainpipe had up its jackses. He was like Hitler in the face, right down to the paint-brush tash, except that being six-foot tall made him seem worse. But I straightened my shoulders to look into his illiterate blue eyes—like I always do with any copper.

Then he started asking me questions, and my mother from behind said: "He's never left that television set for the last three months, so you've got nowt on him, mate. You might as well look for somebody else, because you're wasting the rates you get out of my rent and the income-tax that comes out of my pay-packet standing there like that"—which was a laugh because she'd never paid either to my knowledge, and never would, I hoped.

"Well, you know where Papplewick Street is, don't you?" the copper asked me, taking no notice of mam.

"Ain't it off Alfreton Road?" I asked him back, helpful and bright.

"You know there's a baker's half-way down on the left-hand side, don't you?"

"Ain't it next door to a pub, then?" I wanted to know.

He answered me sharp: "No, it bloody well ain't." Coppers always lose their tempers as quick as this, and more often than not they gain nothing by it. "Then I don't know it," I told him, saved by the bell.

He slid his big boot round and round on the doorstep. "Where were you last Friday night?" Back in the ring, but this was worse than a boxing match.

I didn't like him trying to accuse me of something he wasn't sure I'd done. "Was I at the baker's you mentioned? Or in the pub next door?"

"You'll get five years in Borstal if you don't give me a straight answer," he said, unbuttoning his mac even though it was cold where he was standing.

"I was glued to the telly, like mam says," I swore blind. But he went on and on with his looney questions: "Have you got a television?"

The things he asked wouldn't have taken in a kid of two, and what else could I say to the last one except: "Has the aerial fell down? Or would you like to come in and see it?"

He was liking me even less for saying that. "We know you weren't listening to the television set last Friday, and so do you, don't you?"

"P'raps not, but I was *looking* at it, because sometimes we turn the sound down for a bit of fun." I could hear mam laughing from the kitchen, and I hoped Mike's mam was doing the same if the cops had gone to him as well.

"We know you weren't in the house," he said, starting up again, cranking himself with the handle. They always say 'We' 'We', never 'I' 'I'—as if they feel braver and righter knowing there's a lot of them against only one.

"I've got witnesses," I said to him. "Mam for one. Her fancy-man, for two. Ain't that enough? I can get you a dozen more, or thirteen altogether, if it was a baker's that got robbed."

"I don't want no lies," he said, not catching on about the baker's dozen.

Where do they scrape cops up from anyway? "All I want is to get from you where you put that money."

Don't get mad, I kept saying to myself, don't get mad—hearing mam setting out cups and saucers and putting the pan on the stove for bacon. I stood back and waved him inside like I was a butler. "Come and search the house. If you've got a warrant."

"Listen, my lad," he said, like the dirty bullying jumped-up bastard he was, "I don't want too much of your lip, because if we get you down to the Guildhall you'll get a few bruises and black-eyes for your trouble." And I knew he wasn't kidding either, because I'd heard about all them sort of tricks. I hoped one day though that him and all his pals would be the ones to get the black-eyes and kicks; you never knew. It might come sooner than anybody thinks, like in Hungary. "Tell me where the money is, and I'll get you off with probation."

"What money?" I asked him, because I'd heard that one before as well.

"You know what money."

"Do I look as though I'd know owt about money?" I said, pushing my fist through a hole in my shirt.

"The money that was pinched, that you know all about," he said. "You can't trick me, so it's no use trying."

"Was it three-and-eightpence ha'penny?" I asked.

"You thieving young bastard. We'll teach you to steal money that doesn't belong to you."

I turned my head around: "Mam," I called out, "get my lawyer on the blower, will you?"

"Clever, aren't you?" he said in a very unfriendly way, "but we won't rest until we clear all this up."

"Look," I pleaded, as if about to sob my socks off because he'd got me wrong, "it's all very well us talking like this, it's like a game almost, but I wish you'd tell me what it's all about, because honest-to-God I've just got out of bed and here you are at the door talking about me having pinched a lot of money, money that I don't know anything about."

He swung around now as if he'd trapped me, though I couldn't see why he might think so. "Who said anything about money? I didn't. What made you bring money into this little talk we're having?"

"It's you," I answered, thinking he was going barmy, and about to start foaming at the chops, "you've got money on the brain, like all policemen. Baker's shops as well."

He screwed his face up. "I want an answer from you: where's that money?"

But I was getting fed-up with all this. "I'll do a deal."

Judging by his flash-bulb face he thought he was suddenly on to a good thing. "What sort of a deal?"

So I told him: "I'll give you all the money I've got, one and fourpence ha'penny, if you stop this third-degree and let me go in and get my breakfast.

Honest, I'm clambed to death. I ain't had a bite since yesterday. Can't you hear my guts rollin'?"

His jaw dropped, but on he went, pumping me for another half hour. A routine check-up, as they say on the pictures. But I knew I was winning on points.

Then he left, but came back in the afternoon to search the house. He didn't find a thing, not a French farthing. He asked me questions again and I didn't tell him anything except lies, lies, lies, because I can go on doing that forever without batting an eyelid. He'd got nothing on me and we both of us knew it, otherwise I'd have been down at the Guildhall in no time, but he kept on keeping on because I'd been in a Remand Home for a high-wall job before; and Mike was put through the same mill because all the local cops knew he was my best pal.

When it got dark me and Mike were in our parlour with a low light on and the telly off, Mike taking it easy in the rocking chair and me slouched out on the settee, both of us puffing a packet of Woods. With the door bolted and curtains drawn we talked about the dough we'd crammed up the drainpipe. Mike thought we should take it out and both of us do a bunk to Skegness or Cleethorpes for a good time in the arcades, living like lords in a boarding house near the pier, then at least we'd both have had a big beano before getting sent down.

"Listen, you daft bleeder," I said, "we aren't going to get caught at all, *and* we'll have a good time, later." We were so clever we didn't even go out to the pictures, though we wanted to.

In the morning old Hitler-face questioned me again, with one of his pals this time, and the next day they came, trying as hard as they could to get something out of me, but I didn't budge an inch. I know I'm showing off when I say this, but in me he'd met his match, and I'd never give in to questions no matter how long it was kept up. They searched the house a couple of times as well, which made me think they thought they really had something to go by, but I know now that they hadn't, and that it was all buckshee speculation. They turned the house upside down and inside out like an old sock, went from top to bottom and front to back but naturally didn't find a thing. The copper even poked his face up the front-room chimney (that hadn't been used or swept for years) and came down looking like Al Jolson so that he had to swill himself clean at the scullery sink. They kept tapping and pottering around the big aspidistra plant that grandma had left to mam, lifting it up from the table to look under the cloth, putting it aside so's they could move the table and get at the boards under the rug—but the big headed stupid ignorant bastards never once thought of emptying the soil out of the plant pot, where they'd have found the crumpled-up money-box that we'd buried the night we did the job. I suppose it's still there, now I think about it, and I suppose mam wonders now and again why the plant don't prosper like it used to—as if it could with a fistful of thick black tin lapped around its guts.

The last time he knocked at our door was one wet morning at five minutes to nine and I was sleep-logged in my crumby bed as usual. Mam had gone to work that day so I shouted for him to hold on a bit, and then went down to see who it was. There he stood, six-feet tall and sopping wet, and for the first time in my life I did a spiteful thing I'll never forgive myself for: I didn't ask him to come in out of the rain, because I wanted him to get double pneumonia and die. I suppose he could have pushed by me and come in if he'd wanted, but maybe he'd got used to asking questions on the doorstep and didn't want to be put off by changing his ground even though it was raining. Not that I don't like being spiteful because of any barmy principle I've got, but this bit of spite, as it turned out, did me no good at all. I should have treated him as a brother I hadn't seen for twenty years and dragged him in for a cup of tea and a fag, told him about the picture I hadn't seen the night before, asked him how his wife was after her operation and whether they'd shaved her moustache off to make it, and then sent him happy and satisfied out by the front door. But no, I thought, let's see what he's got to say for himself now.

He stood a little to the side of the door, either because it was less wet there, or because he wanted to see me from a different angle, perhaps having found it monotonous to watch a bloke's face always telling lies from the same side. "You've been identified," he said, twitching raindrops from his tash. "A woman saw you and your mate yesterday and she swears blind you are the same chaps she saw going into that bakery."

I was dead sure he was still bluffing, because Mike and I hadn't even seen each other the day before, but I looked worried. "She's a menace then to innocent people, whoever she is, because the only bakery I've been in lately is the one up our street to get some cut-bread on tick for mam."

He didn't bite on this. "So now I want to know where the money is"—as if I hadn't answered him at all.

"I think mam took it to work this morning to get herself some tea in the canteen." Rain was splashing down so hard I thought he'd get washed away if he didn't come inside. But I wasn't much bothered, and went on: "I remember I put it in the telly-vase last night—it was my only one-and-three and I was saving it for a packet of tips this morning—and I nearly had a jibbering black fit just now when I saw it had gone. I was reckoning on it for getting me through today because I don't think life's worth living without a fag, do you?"

I was getting into my stride and began to feel good, twigging that this would be my last pack of lies, and that if I kept it up for long enough this time I'd have the bastards beat: Mike and me would be off to the coast in a few weeks time having the fun of our lives, playing at penny football and latching on to a couple of tarts that would give us all they were good for. "And this weather's no good for picking-up fag-ends in the street," I said, "because they'd be sopping wet. Course, I know you could dry 'em out near the fire, but it don't taste the same you know, all said and done. Rainwater does summat to 'em that don't bear thinkin' about: it turns 'em back into hoss-tods without the taste though."

I began to wonder, at the back of my brainless eyes, why old copper-lugs didn't pull me up sharp and say he hadn't got time to listen to all this, but he wasn't looking at me anymore, and all my thoughts about Skegness went bursting to smithereens in my sludgy loaf. I could have dropped into the earth when I saw what he'd fixed his eyes on.

He was looking at *it,* an ever-loving fiver, and I could only jabber: "The one thing is to have some real fags because new hoss-tods is always better than stuff that's been rained on and dried, and I know how you feel about not being able to find money because one-and-three's one-and-three in anybody's pocket, and naturally if I see it knocking around I'll get you on the blower tomorrow straightaway and tell you where you can find it."

I thought I'd go down in a fit: three green-backs as well had been washed down by the water, and more were following, lying flat at first after their fall, then getting tilted at the corners by wind and rainspots as if they were alive and wanted to get back into the dry snug drainpipe out of the terrible weather, and you can't imagine how I wished they'd be able to. Old Hitler-face didn't know what to make of it but just kept staring down and down, and I thought I'd better keep on talking, though I knew it wasn't much good now.

"It's a fact, I know, that money's hard to come by and half-crowns don't get found on bus seats or in dustbins, and I didn't see any in bed last night because I'd 'ave known about it, wouldn't I? You can't sleep with things like that in the bed because they're too hard, and anyway at first they're. . . ." It took Hitler-boy a long time to catch on; they were beginning to spread over the yard a bit, reinforced by the third colour of a ten-bob note, before his hand clamped itself on to my shoulder.

III

The pop-eyed potbellied governor said to a pop-eyed potbellied Member of Parliament who sat next to his pop-eyed potbellied whore of a wife that I was his only hope for getting the Borstal Blue Ribbon Prize Cup For Long Distance Cross Country Running (All England), which I was, and it set me laughing to myself inside, and I didn't say a word to any potbellied pop-eyed bastard that might give them real hope, though I knew the governor anyway took my quietness to mean he'd got that cup already stuck on the bookshelf in his office among the few other mildewed trophies.

"He might take up running in a sort of professional way when he gets out," and it wasn't until he'd said this and I'd heard it with my own flap-tabs that I realized it might be possible to do such a thing, run for money, trot for wages on piece work at a bob a puff rising bit by bit to a guinea a gasp and retiring through old age at thirty-two because of lace-curtain lungs, a football heart, and legs like varicose beanstalks. But I'd have a wife and car and get my grinning long-distance clock in the papers and have a smashing secretary to answer piles of letters sent by tarts who'd mob me when they saw who I was as I pushed my way into Woolworth's for a packet of razor blades and a cup of tea. It was something to think about all right, and sure enough the governor knew he'd got me when he said, turning to me as if I would at any rate have to be consulted about it all: "How does this matter strike you, then, Smith, my lad?"

A line of potbellied pop-eyes gleamed at me and a row of goldfish mouths opened and wiggled gold teeth at me, so I gave them the answer they wanted because I'd hold my trump card until later. "It'd suit me fine, sir," I said.

"Good lad. Good show. Right spirit. Splendid."

"Well," the governor said, "get that cup for us today and I'll do all I can for you. I'll get you trained so that you whack every man in the Free World." And I had a picture in my brain of me running and beating everybody in the world, leaving them all behind until only I was trot-trotting across a big wide moor alone, doing a marvellous speed as I ripped between boulders and reed-clumps, when suddenly: CRACK! CRACK!—bullets that can go faster than any man running, coming from a copper's rifle planted in a tree, winged me and split my gizzard in spite of my perfect running, and down I fell.

The potbellies expected me to say something else. "Thank you, sir," I said.

Told to go, I trotted down the pavilion steps, out on to the field because the big cross-country was about to begin and the two entries from Gunthorpe had fixed themselves early at the starting line and were ready to move off like white kangaroos. The sports ground looked a treat: with big tea-tents all round and flags flying and seats for families—empty because no mam or dad had known what opening day meant—and boys still running heats for the hundred yards, and lords and ladies walking from stall to stall, and the Borstal Boys Brass Band in blue uniforms; and up on the stands the brown jackets of Hucknall as well as our own grey blazers, and then the Gunthorpe lot with shirt sleeves rolled. The blue sky was full of sunshine and it couldn't have been a better day, and all of the big show was like something out of Ivanhoe that we'd seen on the pictures a few days before.

"Come on, Smith," Roach the sports master called to me, "we don't want you to be late for the big race, eh? Although I dare say you'd catch them up if you were." The others cat-called and grunted at this, but I took no notice and placed myself between Gunthorpe and one of the Aylesham trusties, dropped on my knees and plucked a few grass blades to suck on the way round. So the big race it was, for them, watching from the grandstand under a fluttering Union Jack, a race for the governor, that he had been waiting for, and I hoped he and all the rest of his pop-eyed gang were busy placing big bets on me, hundred to one to win, all the money they had in their pockets, all the wages they were going to get for the next five years, and the more they placed the happier I'd be. Because here was a dead cert going to die on the big name they'd built for him, going to go down dying with laughter whether it choked him or not. My knees felt the cool soil pressing into them, and out of my eye's corner I saw Roach lift his hand. The Gunthorpe boy twitched before the signal was given; somebody cheered too soon; Medway bent forward; then the gun went, and I was away.

We went once around the field and then along a half-mile drive of elms, being cheered all the way, and I seemed to feel I was in the lead as we went out by the gate and into the lane, though I wasn't interested enough to find out. The five-mile course was marked by splashes of whitewash gleaming on gateposts and trunks and stiles and stones, and a boy with a waterbottle and bandage-box stood every half-mile waiting for those that dropped out or fainted. Over the first stile, without trying, I was still nearly in the lead but one; and if any of you want tips about running, never be in a hurry, and never let any of the other runners know you are in a hurry even if you are. You can always overtake on long-distance running without letting the others smell the hurry in you; and when you've used your craft like this to reach the two or three up front then you can do a big dash later that puts everybody else's hurry in the shade because you've not had to make haste up till then. I ran to a steady jog-trot rhythm, and soon it was so smooth that I forgot I was running, and I was hardly able to know that my legs were lifting and falling and my arms going in and out, and my lungs didn't seem to be working at all, and my heart stopped that wicked thumping I always get at the beginning of a run. Because you see I never race at all; I just run, and somehow I know that if I forget I'm racing and only jog-trot along until I don't know I'm running I always win the race. For when my eyes recognize that I'm getting near the end of the course—by seeing a stile or cottage corner—I put on a spurt, and such a fast big spurt it is because I feel that up till then I haven't been running and that I've used up no energy at all. And I've been able to do this because I've been thinking; and I wonder if I'm the only one in the running business with this system of forgetting that I'm running because I'm too busy thinking; and I wonder if any of the other lads are on to the same lark, though I know for a fact that they aren't. Off like the wind along the cobbled footpath and rutted lane, smoother than the flat grass track on the field and better for thinking because it's not too smooth, and I was in my element that afternoon knowing that nobody could beat me at running but intending to beat myself before the day was over. For when the governor talked to me of being honest when I first came in he didn't know what the word meant or he wouldn't have had me here in this race, trotting along in shimmy and shorts and sunshine. He'd have had me where I'd have had him if I'd been in his place: in a quarry breaking rocks until he broke his back. At least old Hitler-face the plain-clothes dick was honester than the governor, because he at any rate had had it in for me and I for him, and when my case was coming up in court a copper knocked at our front door at four o'clock in the morning and got my mother out of bed when she was paralytic tired, reminding her she had to be in court at dead on half past nine. It was the finest bit of spite I've ever heard of, but I would call it honest, the same as my mam's words were honest when she really told that copper what she thought of him and called him all the dirty names she'd ever heard of, which took her half an hour and woke the terrace up.

I trotted on along the edge of a field bordered by the sunken lane, smelling green grass and honeysuckle, and I felt as though I came from a long line of whippets trained to run on two legs, only I couldn't see a toy rabbit in front and there wasn't a collier's cosh behind to make me keep up the pace. I passed the Gunthorpe runner whose shimmy was already black with sweat and I could just see the corner of the fenced-up copse in front where the only man I had to pass to win the race was going all out to gain the half-way mark. Then he turned into a tongue of trees and bushes where I couldn't see him anymore, and I couldn't see anybody, and I knew what the loneliness of the long-distance runner running across country felt like, realizing that as far as I was concerned this feeling was the only honesty and realness there was in the world and I knowing it would be no different ever, no matter what I felt at odd times, and no matter what anybody else tried to tell me. The runner behind me must have been a long way off because it was so quiet, and there was even less noise and movement than there had been at five o'clock of a frosty winter morning. It was hard to understand, and all I knew was that you had to run, run, run, without knowing why you were running, but on you went through fields you didn't understand and into woods that made you afraid, over hills without knowing you'd been up and down, and shooting across streams that would have cut the heart out of you had you fallen into them. And the winning post was no end to it, even though crowds might be cheering you in, because on you had to go before you got your breath back, and the only time you stopped really was when you tripped over a tree trunk and broke your neck or fell into a disused well and stayed dead in the darkness forever. So I thought: they aren't going to get me on this racing lark, this running and trying to win, this jog-trotting for a bit of blue ribbon, because it's not the way to go on at all, though they swear blind that it is. You should think about nobody and go your own way, not on a course marked out for you by people holding mugs of water and bottles of iodine in case you fall and cut yourself so that they can pick you up—even if you want to stay where you are—and get you moving again.

On I went, out of the wood, passing the man leading without knowing I was going to do so. Flip-flap, flip-flap, jog-trot, jog-trot, crunchslap-crunchslap, across the middle of a broad field again, rhythmically running in my greyhound effortless fashion, knowing I had won the race though it wasn't half over, won it if I wanted it, could go on for ten or fifteen or twenty miles if I had to and drop dead at the finish of it, which would be the same, in the end, as living an honest life like the governor wanted me to. It amounted to: win the race and be honest, and on trot-trotting I went, having the time of my life, loving my progress because it did me good and set me thinking which by now I liked to do, but not caring at all when I remembered that I had to win this race as well as run it. One of the two, I had to win the race or run it, and I knew I could do both because my legs had carried me well in front—now coming to the short cut down the bramble bank and over the sunken road—and would carry me further because they seemed made of electric cable and easily alive to keep on slapping at those ruts and roots, but I'm not going to win because the only way I'd see I came in first would be if winning meant that I was going to escape the coppers after doing the biggest bank job of my life, but winning means the exact opposite, no matter how they try to kill or kid me, means running right into their white-gloved wall-barred hands and grinning mugs and staying there for the rest of my natural long life of stone-breaking anyway, but stone-breaking in the way I want to do it and not in the way they tell me.

Another honest thought that comes is that I could swing left at the next hedge of the field, and under its cover beat my slow retreat away from the sports ground winning post. I could do three or six or a dozen miles across the turf like this and cut a few main roads behind me so's they'd never know which one I'd taken; and maybe on the last one when it got dark I could thumb a lorry-lift and get a free ride north with somebody who might not give me away. But no, I said I wasn't daft didn't I? I won't pull out with only six months left, and besides there's nothing I want to dodge and run away from; I only want a bit of my own back on the In-laws and Potbellies by letting them sit up there on their big posh seats and watch me lose this race, though as sure as God made me I know that when I do lose I'll get the dirtiest crap and kitchen jobs in the months to go before my time is up. I won't be worth a threpp'ny-bit to anybody here, which will be all the thanks I get for being honest in the only way I know. For when the governor told me to be honest it was meant to be in his way not mine, and if I kept on being honest in the way he wanted and won my race for him he'd see I got the cushiest six months still left to run; but in my own way, well, it's not allowed, and if I find a way of doing it such as I've got now then I'll get what-for in every mean trick he can set his mind to. And if you look at it in my way, who can blame him? For this is war—and ain't I said so?—and when I hit him in the only place he knows he'll be sure to get his own back on me for not collaring that cup when his heart's been set for ages on seeing himself standing up at the end of the afternoon to clap me on the back as I take the cup from Lord Earwig or some such chinless wonder with a name like that. And so I'll hit him where it hurts a lot, and he'll do all he can to get his own back, tit for tat, though I'll enjoy it most because I'm hitting first, and because I planned it longer. I don't know why I think these thoughts are better than any I've ever had, but I do, and I don't care why. I suppose it took me a long time to get going on all this because I've had no time and peace in all my bandit life, and now my thoughts are coming pat and the only trouble is I often can't stop, even when my brain feels as if it's got cramp, frostbite and creeping paralysis all rolled into one and I have to give it a rest by slap-dashing down through the brambles of the sunken lane. And all this is another uppercut I'm getting in first at people like the governor, to show how—if I can—his races are never won even though some bloke always comes unknowingly in first, how in the end the governor is going to be doomed while blokes like me will take the pickings of his roasted bones and dance like maniacs around his Borstal's ruins. And so this story's like the race and once again I won't bring off a winner to suit the governor; no, I'm being honest like he told me to, without him knowing what he means, though I don't suppose he'll ever come in with a story of his own, even if he reads this one of mine and knows who I'm talking about.

I've just come up out of the sunken lane, kneed and elbowed, thumped and bramble-scratched, and the race is two-thirds over, and a voice is going like a wireless in my mind saying that when you've had enough of feeling good like the first man on earth of a frosty morning, and you've known how it is to be taken bad like the last man on earth on a summer's afternoon, then you get at last to being like the only man on earth and don't give a bogger about either good or bad, but just trot on with your slippers slapping the good dry soil that at least would never do you a bad turn. Now the words are like coming from a crystal-set that's broken down, and something's happening inside the shell-case of my guts that bothers me and I don't know why or what to blame it on, a grinding near my ticker as though a bag of rusty screws is loose inside me and I shake them up every time I trot forward. Now and again I break my rhythm to feel my left shoulderblade by swinging a right hand across my chest as if to rub the knife away that has somehow got stuck there. But I know it's nothing to bother about, that more likely it's caused by too much thinking that now and again I take for worry. For sometimes I'm the greatest worrier in the world I think (as you twigged I'll bet from me having got this story out) which is funny anyway because my mam don't know the meaning of the word so I don't take after her; though dad had a hard time of worry all his life up to when he filled his bedroom with hot blood and kicked the bucket that morning when nobody was in the house. I'll never forget it, straight I won't, because I was the one that found him and I often wished I hadn't. Back from a session on the fruit-machines at the fish-and-chip shop, jingling my three-lemon loot to a nail-dead house, as soon as I got in I knew something was wrong, stood leaning my head against the cold mirror above the mantelpiece trying not to open my eyes and see my stone-cold clock—because I knew I'd gone as white as a piece of chalk since coming in as if I'd been got at by a Dracula-vampire and even my penny-pocket winnings kept quiet on purpose.

Gunthorpe nearly caught me up. Birds were singing from the briar hedge, and a couple of thrushies flew like lightning into some thorny bushes. Corn had grown high in the next field and would be cut down soon with scythes and mowers; but I never wanted to notice much while running in case it put me off my stroke, so by the haystack I decided to leave it all behind and put on such a spurt, in spite of nails in my guts, that before long I'd left both Gunthorpe and the birds a good way off; I wasn't far now from going into that last mile and a half like a knife through margarine, but the quietness I suddenly trotted into between two pickets was like opening my eyes underwater and looking at the pebbles on a stream bottom, reminding me again of going back that morning to the house in which my old man had croaked, which is funny because I hadn't thought about it at all since it happened and even then I didn't brood much on it. I wonder why? I suppose that since I started to think on these long-distance runs I'm liable to have anything crop up and pester at my tripes and innards, and now that I see my bloody dad behind each grass-blade in my barmy runner-brain I'm not so sure I like to think and that it's such a good thing after all. I choke my phlegm and keep on running anyway and curse the Borstal-builders and their athletics—flappity-flap, slop-slop, crunchslap-crunchslap-crunchslap—who've maybe got their own back on me from the bright beginning by sliding magic-lantern slides into my head that never stood a chance before. Only if I take whatever comes like this in my runner's stride can I keep on keeping on like my old self and beat them back; and now I've thought on this far I know I'll win, in the crunchslap end. So anyway after a bit I went upstairs one step at a time not thinking anything about how I should find dad and what I'd do when I did. But now I'm making up for it by going over the rotten life mam led him ever since I can remember, knocking-on with different men even when he was alive and fit and she not caring whether he knew it or not, and most of the time he wasn't so blind as she thought and cursed and roared and threatened to punch her tab, and I had to stand up to stop him even though I knew she deserved it. What a life for all of us. Well, I'm not grumbling, because if I did I might just as well win this bleeding race, which I'm not going to do, though if I don't lose speed I'll win it before I know where I am, and then where would I be?

Now I can hear the sportsground noise and music as I head back for the flags and the lead-in drive, the fresh new feel of underfoot gravel going against the iron muscles of my legs. I'm nowhere near puffed despite that bag of nails that rattles as much as ever, and I can still give a big last leap like gale-force wind if I want to, but everything is under control and I know now that there ain't another long-distance cross-country running runner in England to touch my speed and style. Our doddering bastard of a governor, our half-dead gangrened gaffer is hollow like an empty petrol drum, and he wants me and my running life to give him glory, to put in him blood and throbbing veins he never had, wants his potbellied pals to be his witnesses as I gasp and stagger up to his winning post so's he can say: "My Borstal gets that cup, you see. I win my bet, because it pays to be honest and try to gain the prizes I offer to my lads, and they know it, have known it all along. They'll always be honest now, because I made them so." And his pals will think: "He trains his lads to live right, after all; he deserves a medal but we'll get him made a Sir"—and at this very moment as the birds come back to whistling I can tell myself I'll never care a sod what any of the chinless spineless In-laws think or say. They've seen me and they're cheering now and loudspeakers set around the field like elephant's ears are spreading out the big news that I'm well in the lead, and can't do anything else but stay there. But I'm still thinking of the Out-law death my dad died, telling the doctors to scat from the house when they wanted him to finish up in hospital (like a bleeding guinea-pig, he raved at them). He got up in bed to throw them out and even followed them down the stairs in his shirt though he was no more than skin and stick. They tried to tell him he'd want some drugs but he didn't fall for it, and only took the pain-killer that mam and I got from a herb-seller in the next street. It's not till now that I know what guts he had, and when I went into the room that morning he was lying on his stomach with the clothes thrown back, looking like a skinned rabbit, his grey head resting just on the edge of the bed, and on the floor must have been all the blood he'd had in his body, right from his toe-nails up, for nearly all of the lino and carpet was covered in it, thin and pink.

And down the drive I went, carrying a heart blocked up like Boulder Dam across my arteries, the nail-bag clamped down tighter and tighter as though in a woodwork vice, yet with my feet like birdwings and arms like talons ready to fly across the field except that I didn't want to give anybody that much of a show, or win the race by accident. I smell the hot dry day now as I run towards the end, passing a mountain-heap of grass emptied from cans hooked on to the fronts of lawnmowers pushed by my pals; I rip a piece of tree-bark with my fingers and stuff it in my mouth, chewing wood and dust and maybe maggots as I run until I'm nearly sick, yet swallowing what I can of it just the same because a little birdie whistled to me that I've got to go on living for at least a bloody sight longer yet but that for six months I'm not going to smell that grass or taste that dusty bark or trot this lovely path. I hate to have to say this but something bloody-well made me cry, and crying is a thing I haven't bloody-well done since I was a kid of two or three. Because I'm slowing down now for Gunthorpe to catch me up, and I'm doing it in a place just where the drive turns in to the sportsfield—where they can see what I'm doing, especially the governor and his gang from the grandstand, and I'm going so slow I'm almost marking time. Those on the nearest seats haven't caught on yet to what's happening and are still cheering like mad ready for when I make that mark, and I keep on wondering when the bleeding hell Gunthorpe behind me is going to nip by on to the field because I can't hold this up all day, and I think Oh Christ it's just my rotten luck that Gunthorpe's dropped out and that I'll be here for half an hour before the next bloke comes up, but even so, I say, I won't budge, I won't go for that last hundred yards if I have to sit down cross-legged on the grass and have the governor and his chinless wonders pick me up and carry me there, which is against their rules so you can bet they'd never do it because they're not clever enough to break the rules—like I would be in their place—even though they are their own. No, I'll show him what honesty means if it's the last thing I do, though I'm sure he'll never understand because if he and all them like him did it'd mean they'd be on my side which is impossible. By God I'll stick this out like my dad stuck out his pain and kicked them doctors down the stairs: if he had guts for that then I've got guts for this and here I stay waiting for Gunthorpe or Aylesham to bash that turf and go right slap-up against that bit of clothes-line stretched across the winning post. As for me, the only time I'll hit that clothes-line will be when I'm dead and a comfortable coffin's been got ready on the other side. Until then I'm a long-distance runner, crossing country all on my own no matter how bad it feels.

The Essex boys were shouting themselves blue in the face telling me to get a move on, waving their arms, standing up and making as if to run at that rope themselves because they were only a few yards to the side of it. You cranky lot, I thought, stuck at that winning post, and yet I knew they didn't mean what they were shouting, were really on my side and always would be, not able to keep their maulers to themselves, in and out of cop-shops and clink. And there they were now having the time of their lives letting themselves go in cheering me which made the governor think they were heart and soul on his side when he wouldn't have thought any such thing if he'd had a grain of sense. And I could hear the lords and ladies now from the grandstand, and could see them standing up to wave me in: "Run!" they were shouting in their posh voices. "Run!" But I was deaf, daft and blind, and stood where I was, still tasting the bark in my mouth and still blubbing like a baby, blubbing now out of gladness that I'd got them beat at last.

Because I heard a roar and saw the Gunthorpe gang throwing their coats up in the air and I felt the pat-pat of feet on the drive behind me getting closer and closer and suddenly a smell of sweat and a pair of lungs on their last gasp passed me by and went swinging on towards that rope, all shagged out and rocking from side to side, grunting like a Zulu that didn't know any better, like the ghost of me at ninety when I'm heading for that fat upholstered coffin. I could have cheered him myself: "Go on, go on, get cracking. Knot yourself up on that piece of tape." But he was already there, and so I went on, trot-trotting after him until I got to the rope, and collapsed, with a murderous sounding roar going up through my ears while I was still on the wrong side of it.

It's about time to stop; though don't think I'm not still running, because I am, one way or another. The governor at Borstal proved me right; he didn't respect my honesty at all; not that I expected him to, or tried to explain it to him, but if he's supposed to be educated then he should have more or less twigged it. He got his own back right enough, or thought he did, because he had me carting dustbins about every morning from the big full-working kitchen to the garden-bottoms where I had to empty them; and in the afternoon I spread out slops over spuds and carrots growing in the allotments. In the evenings I scrubbed floors, miles and miles of them. But it wasn't a bad life for six months, which was another thing he could never understand and would have made it grimmer if he could, and it was worth it when I look back on it, considering all the thinking I did, and the fact that the boys caught on to me losing the race on purpose and never had enough good words to say about me, or curses to throw out (to themselves) at the governor.

The work didn't break me; if anything it made me stronger in many ways, and the governor knew, when I left, that his spite had got him nowhere. For since leaving Borstal they tried to get me in the army, but I didn't pass the medical and I'll tell you why. No sooner was I out, after that final run and six-months hard, that I went down with pleurisy, which means as far as I'm concerned that I lost the governor's race all right, and won my own twice over, because I know for certain that if I hadn't raced my race I wouldn't have got this pleurisy, which keeps me out of khaki but doesn't stop me doing the sort of work my itchy fingers want to do.

I'm out now and the heat's switched on again, but the rats haven't got me for the last big thing I pulled. I counted six hundred and twenty-eight pounds and am still living off it because I did the job all on my own, and after it I had the peace to write all this, and it'll be money enough to keep me going until I finish my plans for doing an even bigger snatch, something up my sleeve I wouldn't tell to a living soul. I worked out my systems and hiding-places while pushing scrubbing-brushes around them Borstal floors, planned my outward life of innocence and honest work, yet at the same time grew perfect in the razor-edges of my craft for what I knew I had to do once free; and what I'll do again if netted by the poaching coppers.

In the meantime (as they say in one or two books I've read since, useless though because all of them ended on a winning post and didn't teach me a thing) I'm going to give this story to a pal of mine and tell him that if I do get captured again by the coppers he can try and get it put into a book or something, because I'd like to see the governor's face when he reads it, if he does, which I don't suppose he will; even if he did read it though I don't think he'd know what it was all about. And if I don't get caught the bloke I give this story to will never give me away; he's lived in our terrace for as long as I can remember, and he's my pal. That I do know.

JAMES BALDWIN (b. 1924)

Eldest of the nine children of a Harlem lay clergyman, James Baldwin was a preacher himself from ages fourteen to eighteen, at which point he left home, church, and Harlem to become an author. Like his mentor,

Richard Wright, he felt that he could not develop as a black writer in the repressive atmosphere of the United States. In 1948, therefore, he went to live and work in Paris, where he remained for the next ten years. His first book of essays, concerning racism in America and entitled Notes of a Native Son *(1956), was published during this time, as was his first novel,* Go Tell It On the Mountain *(1953), a semi-autobiographical account of a young boy's religious experiences in Harlem with flashbacks to the family's former life in the South.*

Since his return to the United States in 1958, Baldwin has published two more books of essays, Nobody Knows My Name *(1961) and* The Fire Next Time *(1964), as well as several novels and plays plus his collected short stories,* Going To Meet the Man *(1965). Although his recent works speak more in protest and rage, they explore like his earlier books the search for identity of black men to whom our society denies dignity and purpose.*

The conflict at the heart of the story "Sonny's Blues" results from Sonny's inability to live by the moral and social values of the white American society that his older brother has accepted.

Sonny's Blues

I READ ABOUT IT in the paper, in the subway, on my way to work. I read it, and I couldn't believe it, and I read it again. Then perhaps I just stared at it, at the newsprint spelling out his name, spelling out the story. I stared at it in the swinging lights of the subway car, and in the faces and bodies of the people, and in my own face, trapped in the darkness which roared outside.

It was not to be believed, and I kept telling myself that as I walked from the subway station to the high school. And at the same time I couldn't doubt it. I was scared, scared for Sonny. He became real to me again. A great block of ice got settled in my belly and kept melting there slowly all day long, while I taught my classes algebra. It was a special kind of ice. It kept melting, sending trickles of ice water all up and down my veins, but it never got less. Sometimes it hardened and seemed to expand until I felt my guts were going to come spilling out or that I was going to choke or scream. This would always be at a moment when I was remembering some specific thing Sonny had once said or done.

When he was about as old as the boys in my classes, his face had been bright and open, there was a lot of copper in it; and he'd had wonderfully direct brown eyes, and great gentleness and privacy. I wondered what he looked like now. He had been picked up, the evening before, in a raid on an apartment downtown, for peddling and using heroin.

I couldn't believe it: but what I mean by that is that I couldn't find any room for it anywhere inside me. I had kept it outside me for a long time. I hadn't wanted to know. I had had suspicions, but I didn't name them, I kept putting them away. I told myself that Sonny was wild, but he wasn't crazy. And he'd always been a good boy, he hadn't ever turned hard or evil or disrespectful, the way kids can, so quick, so quick, especially in Harlem. I didn't want to believe that I'd ever see my brother going down, coming to nothing, all that light in his face gone out, in the condition I'd already seen so many others. Yet it had happened and here I was, talking about algebra to a lot of boys who might, every one of them for all I knew, be popping off needles every time they went to the head. Maybe it did more for them than algebra could.

I was sure that the first time Sonny had ever had horse, he couldn't have been much older than these boys were now. These boys, now, were living as we'd been living then, they were growing up with a rush and their heads bumped abruptly against the low ceiling of their actual possibilities. They were filled with rage. All they really knew were two darknesses, the darkness of their lives, which was now closing in on them, and the darkness of the movies, which had blinded them to that other darkness, and in which they now, vindictively, dreamed, at once more together than they were at any other time, and more alone.

When the last bell rang, the last class ended, I let out my breath. It seemed I'd been holding it for all that time. My clothes were wet—I may have looked as though I'd been sitting in a steam bath, all dressed up, all afternoon. I sat alone in the classroom a long time. I listened to the boys outside, downstairs, shouting and cursing and laughing. Their laughter struck me for perhaps the first time. It was not the joyous laughter which—God knows why—one associates with children. It was mocking and insular, its intent was to denigrate. It was disenchanted, and in this, also, lay the authority of their curses. Perhaps I was listening to them because I was thinking about my brother and in them I heard my brother. And myself.

One boy was whistling a tune, at once very complicated and very simple, it seemed to be pouring out of him as though he were a bird, and it sounded very cool and moving through all that harsh, bright air, only just holding its own through all those other sounds.

I stood and walked over to the window and looked down into the courtyard. It was the beginning of the spring, and the sap was rising in the boys. A teacher passed through them every now and again, quickly, as though he or she couldn't wait to get out of that courtyard, to get those boys out of their sight and off their minds. I started collecting my stuff. I thought I'd better get home and talk to Isabel.

The courtyard was almost deserted by the time I got downstairs. I saw this boy standing in the shadow of a doorway, looking just like Sonny. I almost called his name. Then I saw that it wasn't Sonny, but somebody we used to know, a boy from around our block. He'd been Sonny's friend. He'd never been mine, having been too young for me, and, anyway, I'd never liked him. And now, even though he was a grown-up man, he still hung around that block, still spent hours on the street corner, was always high and raggy. I used to run into him from time to time, and he'd often work around to asking me for a quarter or fifty cents. He always had some real good excuse, too, and I always gave it to him, I don't know why.

But now, abruptly, I hated him. I couldn't stand the way he looked at me, partly like a dog, partly like a cunning child. I wanted to ask him what the hell he was doing in the school courtyard.

He sort of shuffled over to me, and he said, "I see you got the papers. So you already know about it."

"You mean about Sonny? Yes, I already know about it. How come they didn't get you?"

He grinned. It made him repulsive and it also brought to mind what he'd looked like as a kid. "I wasn't there. I stay away from them people."

"Good for you." I offered him a cigarette and I watched him through the smoke. "You come all the way down here just to tell me about Sonny?"

"That's right." He was sort of shaking his head and his eyes looked strange, as though they were about to cross. The bright sun deadened his damp dark brown skin and it made his eyes look yellow and showed up the dirt in his conked hair. He smelled funky. I moved a little away from him and I said, "Well, thanks. But I already know about it and I got to get home."

"I'll walk you a little ways," he said. We started walking. There were a couple of kids still loitering in the courtyard and one of them said good night to me and looked strangely at the boy beside me.

"What're you going to do?" he asked me. "I mean, about Sonny?"

"Look, I haven't seen Sonny for over a year, I'm not sure I'm going to do anything. Anyway, what the hell *can* I do?"

"That's right," he said quickly, "ain't nothing you can do. Can't much help old Sonny no more, I guess."

It was what I was thinking and so it seemed to me he had no right to say it.

"I'm surprised at Sonny, though," he went on—he had a funny way of talking, he looked straight ahead as though he were talking to himself—"I thought Sonny was a smart boy, I thought he was too smart to get hung."

"I guess he thought so, too," I said sharply, "and that's how he got hung. And how about you? You're pretty goddamn smart, I bet."

Then he looked directly at me, just for a minute. "I ain't smart," he said. "If I was smart, I'd have reached for a pistol a long time ago."

"Look. Don't tell *me* your sad story, if it was up to me, I'd give you one." Then I felt guilty—guilty probably, for never having supposed that the poor bastard *had* a story of his own, much less a sad one, and I asked, quickly, "What's going to happen to him now?"

He didn't answer this. He was off by himself someplace. "Funny thing," he said, and from his tone we might have been discussing the quickest way to get to Brooklyn, "when I saw the papers this morning, the first thing I asked myself was if I had anything to do with it. I felt sort of responsible."

I began to listen more carefully. The subway station was on the corner, just before us, and I stopped. He stopped, too. We were in front of a bar and he ducked slightly, peering in, but whoever he was looking for didn't seem to be there. The juke box was blasting away with something black and bouncy, and I half watched the barmaid as she danced her way from the juke box to her place behind the bar. And I watched her face as she laughingly responded to something someone said to her, still keeping time to the music. When she smiled one saw the little girl, one sensed the doomed, still-struggling woman beneath the battered face of the semi-whore.

"I never *give* Sonny nothing," the boy said finally, "but a long time ago I come to school high and Sonny asked me how it felt." He paused, I couldn't bear to watch him, I watched the barmaid, and I listened to the music which seemed to be causing the pavement to shake. "I told him it felt great." The music stopped, the barmaid paused and watched the juke box until the music began again. "It did."

All this was carrying me someplace I didn't want to go. I certainly didn't want to know how it felt. It filled everything, the people, the houses, the music, the dark, quicksilver barmaid, with menace; and this menace was their reality.

"What's going to happen to him now?" I asked again.

"They'll send him away someplace and they'll try to cure him." He shook his head. "Maybe he'll even think he's kicked the habit. Then they'll turn him loose"—He gestured, throwing his cigarette into the gutter. "That's all."

"What do you mean, that's *all?*"

But I knew what he meant.

"I *mean,* that's *all.*" He turned his head and looked at me, pulling down the corners of his mouth. "Don't you know what I mean?" he asked softly.

"How the hell *would* I know what you mean?" I almost whispered it, I don't know why.

"That's right," he said to the air, "how would *he* know what I mean?" He turned toward me again, patient and calm, and yet I somehow felt him shaking, shaking as though he were going to fall apart. I felt that ice in my guts again, the dread I'd felt all afternoon; and again I watched the barmaid, moving about the bar, washing glasses, and singing. "Listen. They'll let him out and then it'll just start over again. That's what I mean."

"You mean—they'll let him out. And then he'll just start working his way back in again. You mean he'll never kick the habit. Is that what you mean?"

"That's right," he said, cheerfully. "*You* see what I mean."

"Tell me," I said at last, "why does he want to die? He must want to die, he's killing himself, why does he want to die?"

He looked at me in surprise. He licked his lips. "He don't want to die. He wants to live. Don't nobody want to die, ever."

Then I wanted to ask him—too many things. He could not have answered, or if he had, I could not have borne the answers. I started walking. "Well, I guess it's none of my business."

"It's going to be rough on old Sonny," he said. We reached the subway station. "This is your station?" he asked. I nodded. I took one step down. "Damn!" he said, suddenly. I looked up at him. He grinned again. "Damn if I didn't leave all my money home. You ain't got a dollar on you, have you? Just for a couple of days, is all."

All at once something inside gave and threatened to come pouring out of me. I didn't hate him any more. I felt that in another moment I'd start crying like a child.

"Sure," I said. "Don't sweat." I looked in my wallet and didn't have a dollar, I only had a five. "Here," I said. "That hold you?"

He didn't look at it—he didn't want to look at it. A terrible, closed look came over his face, as though he were keeping the number on the bill a secret from him and me. "Thanks," he said, and now he was dying to see me go. "Don't worry about Sonny. Maybe I'll write him or something."

"Sure," I said. "You do that. So long."

"Be seeing you," he said. I went on down the steps.

And I didn't write Sonny or send him anything for a long time. When I finally did, it was just after my little girl died, he wrote me back a letter which made me feel like a bastard.

Here's what he said:

Dear brother,

You don't know how much I needed to hear from you. I wanted to write you many a time but I dug how much I must have hurt you and so I didn't write. But now I feel like a man who's been trying to climb up out of some deep, real deep and funky hole and just saw the sun up there, outside. I got to get outside.

I can't tell you much about how I got here. I mean I don't know how to tell you. I guess I was afraid of something or I was trying to escape from something and you know I have never been very strong in the head (smile). I'm glad Mama and Daddy are dead and can't see what's happened to their son and I swear if I'd known what I was doing I would never have hurt you so, you and a lot of other fine people who were nice to me and who believed in me.

I don't want you to think it had anything to do with me being a musician. It's more than that. Or maybe less than that. I can't get anything straight in my head down here and I try not to think about what's going to happen to me when I get outside again. Sometime I think I'm going to flip and *never* get outside and sometime I think I'll come straight back. I tell you one thing, though, I'd rather blow my brains out than go through this again. But that's what they all say, so they tell me. If I tell you when I'm coming to New York and if you could meet me, I sure would appreciate it. Give my love to Isabel and the kids and I was sure sorry to hear about little Gracie. I wish I could be like Mama and say the Lord's will be done, but I don't know it seems to me that trouble is the one thing that never does get stopped and I don't know what good it does to blame it on the Lord. But maybe it does some good if you believe it.

Your brother.
SONNY

Then I kept in constant touch with him and I sent him whatever I could and I went to meet him when he came back to New York. When I saw him, many things I thought I had forgotten came flooding back to me. This was because I had begun, finally, to wonder about Sonny, about the life that Sonny lived inside. This life, whatever it was, had made him older and thinner and it had deepened the distant stillness in which he had always moved. He looked very unlike my baby brother. Yet, when he smiled, when we shook hands, the baby brother I'd never known looked out from the depths of his private life, like an animal waiting to be coaxed into the light.

"How you been keeping?" he asked me.

"All right. And you?"

"Just fine." He was smiling all over his face. "It's good to see you again."

"It's good to see you."

The seven years' difference in our ages lay between us like a chasm: I wondered if these years would ever operate between us as a bridge. I was remembering, and it made it hard to catch my breath, that I had been there when he was born; and I had heard the first words he had ever spoken. When he started to walk, he walked from our mother straight to me. I caught him just before he fell when he took the first steps he ever took in this world.

"How's Isabel?"

"Just fine. She's dying to see you."

"And the boys?"

"They're fine, too. They're anxious to see their uncle."

"Oh, come on. You know they don't remember me."

"Are you kidding? Of course they remember you."

He grinned again. We got into a taxi. We had a lot to say to each other, far too much to know how to begin.

As the taxi began to move, I asked, "You still want to go to India?"

He laughed. "You still remember that. Hell, no. This place is Indian enough for me."

"It used to belong to them," I said.

And he laughed again. "They damn sure knew what they were doing when they got rid of it."

Years ago, when he was around fourteen, he'd been all hipped on the idea of going to India. He read books about people sitting on rocks, naked, in all kinds of weather, but mostly bad, naturally, and walking barefoot through hot coals and arriving at wisdom. I used to say that it sounded to me as though they were getting away from wisdom as fast as they could. I think he sort of looked down on me for that.

"Do you mind," he asked, "if we have the driver drive alongside the park? On the west side—I haven't seen the city in so long."

"Of course not," I said. I was afraid that I might sound as though I were humoring him, but I hoped he wouldn't take it that way.

So we drove along, between the green of the park and the stony, lifeless elegance of hotels and apartment buildings, toward the vivid, killing streets of our childhood. These streets hadn't changed, though housing projects jutted up out of them now like rocks in the middle of a boiling sea. Most of the houses in which we had grown up had vanished, as had the stores from which we had stolen, the basements in which we had first tried sex, the rooftops from which we had hurled tin cans and bricks. But houses exactly like the houses of our past yet dominated the landscape, boys exactly like the boys we once had been found themselves smothering in these houses, came down into the streets for light and air and found themselves encircled by disaster. Some escaped the trap, most didn't. Those who got out always left something of themselves behind, as some animals amputate a leg and leave it in the trap. It might be said, perhaps, that I had escaped, after all, I was a schoolteacher; or that Sonny had, he hadn't lived in Harlem for years. Yet, as the cab moved uptown through streets which seemed, with a rush, to darken with dark people, and as I covertly studied Sonny's face, it came to me that what we both were seeking through our separate cab windows was that part of ourselves which had been left behind. It's always at the hour of trouble and confrontation that the missing member aches.

We hit 110th Street and started rolling up Lenox Avenue. And I'd known this avenue all my life, but it seemed to me again, as it had seemed on the day I'd first heard about Sonny's trouble, filled with a hidden menace which was its very breath of life.

"We almost there," said Sonny.

"Almost." We were both too nervous to say anything more.

We live in a housing project. It hasn't been up long. A few days after it was up it seemed uninhabitably new, now, of course, it's already rundown. It looked like a parody of the good, clean, faceless life—God knows the people who live in it do their best to make it a parody. The beat-looking grass lying around isn't enough to make their lives green, the hedges will never hold out the streets, and they know it. The big windows fool no one, they aren't big enough to make space out of no space. They don't bother with the windows, they watch the TV screen instead. The playground is most popular with the children who don't play at jacks, or skip rope, or roller skate, or swing, and they can be found in it after dark. We moved in partly because it's not too far from where I teach, and partly for the kids; but it's really just like the houses in which Sonny and I grew up. The same things happen, they'll have the same things to remember. The moment Sonny and I started into the house I had the feeling that I was simply bringing him back into the danger he had almost died trying to escape.

Sonny has never been talkative. So I don't know why I was sure he'd be dying to talk to me when supper was over the first night. Everything went fine, the oldest boy remembered him, and the youngest boy liked him, and Sonny had remembered to bring something for each of them; and Isabel, who is really much nicer than I am, more open and giving, had gone to a lot of trouble about dinner and was genuinely glad to see him. And she'd always been able to tease Sonny in a way that I haven't. It was nice to see her face so vivid again and to hear her laugh and watch her make Sonny laugh. She wasn't, or, anyway, she didn't seem to be, at all uneasy or embarrassed. She chatted as though there were no subject which had to be avoided and she got Sonny past his first, faint stiffness. And thank God she was there, for I was filled with that icy dread again. Everything I did seemed awkward to me, and everything I said sounded freighted with hidden meaning. I was trying to remember everything I'd heard about dope addiction and I couldn't help watching Sonny for signs. I wasn't doing it out of malice. I was trying to find out something about my brother. I was dying to hear him tell me he was safe.

"Safe!" my father grunted, whenever Mama suggested trying to move to a neighborhood which might be safer for children. "Safe, hell! Ain't no place safe for kids, nor nobody."

He always went on like this, but he wasn't, ever, really as bad as he sounded, not even on weekends, when he got drunk. As a matter of fact, he was always on the lookout for "something a little better," but he died before he found it. He died suddenly, during a drunken weekend in the middle of the war, when Sonny was fifteen. He and Sonny hadn't ever got on too well. And this was partly because Sonny was the apple of his father's eye. It was because he loved Sonny so much and was frightened for him, that he was always fighting with him. It doesn't do any good to fight with Sonny. Sonny just moves back, inside himself, where he can't be reached. But the principal reason that they never hit it off is that they were so much alike. Daddy was big and rough and loud-talking, just the opposite of Sonny, but they both had—that same privacy.

Mama tried to tell me something about this, just after Daddy died. I was home on leave from the army.

This was the last time I ever saw my mother alive. Just the same, this picture gets all mixed up in my mind with pictures I had of her when she was younger. The way I always see her is the way she used to be on a Sunday afternoon, say, when the old folks were talking after the big Sunday dinner. I always see her wearing pale blue. She'd be sitting on the sofa. And my father would be sitting in the easy chair, not far from her. And the living room would be full of church folks and relatives. There they sit, in chairs all around the living room, and the night is creeping up outside, but nobody knows it yet.

You can see the darkness growing against the windowpanes and you hear the street noises every now and again, or maybe the jangling beat of a tambourine from one of the churches close by, but it's real quiet in the room. For a moment nobody's talking, but every face looks darkening, like the sky outside. And my mother rocks a little from the waist, and my father's eyes are closed. Everyone is looking at something a child can't see. For a minute they've forgotten the children. Maybe a kid is lying on the rug, half asleep. Maybe somebody's got a kid in his lap and is absent-mindedly stroking the kid's head. Maybe there's a kid, quiet and big-eyed, curled up in a big chair in the corner. The silence, the darkness coming, and the darkness in the faces frighten the child obscurely. He hopes that the hand which strokes his forehead will never stop—will never die. He hopes that there will never come a time when the old folks won't be sitting around the living room, talking about where they've come from, and what they've seen, and what's happened to them and their kinfolk.

But something deep and watchful in the child knows that this is bound to end, is already ending. In a moment someone will get up and turn on the light. Then the old folks will remember the children and they won't talk any more that day. And when light fills the room, the child is filled with darkness. He knows that every time this happens he's moved just a little closer to that darkness outside. The darkness outside is what the old folks have been talking about. It's what they've come from. It's what they endure. The child knows that they won't talk any more because if he knows too much about what's happened to *them,* he'll know too much too soon, about what's going to happen to *him.*

The last time I talked to my mother, I remember I was restless. I wanted to get out and see Isabel. We weren't married then and we had a lot to straighten out between us.

There Mama sat, in black, by the window. She was humming an old church song, *Lord, you brought me from a long ways off.* Sonny was out somewhere. Mama kept watching the streets.

"I don't know," she said, "if I'll ever see you again, after you go off from here. But I hope you'll remember the things I tried to teach you."

"Don't talk like that," I said, and smiled. "You'll be here a long time yet."

She smiled, too, but she said nothing. She was quiet for a long time. And I said, "Mama, don't you worry about nothing. I'll be writing all the time, and you be getting the checks. . . ."

"I want to talk to you about your brother," she said, suddenly. "If anything happens to me, he ain't going to have nobody to look out for him."

"Mama," I said, "ain't nothing going to happen to you *or* Sonny. Sonny's all right. He's a good boy and he's got good sense."

"It ain't a question of his being a good boy," Mama said, "nor of his having good sense. It ain't only the bad ones, nor yet the dumb ones that gets sucked under." She stopped, looking at me. "Your Daddy once had a brother," she said, and smiled in a way that made me feel she was in pain. "You didn't never know that, did you?"

"No," I said. "I never knew that," and I watched her face.

"Oh, yes," she said, "your Daddy had a brother." She looked out of the window again. "I know you never saw your Daddy cry. But *I* did—many a time, through all these years."

I asked her, "What happened to his brother? How come nobody's ever talked about him?"

This was the first time I ever saw my mother look old.

"His brother got killed," she said, "when he was just a little younger than you are now. I knew him. He was a fine boy. He was maybe a little full of the devil, but he didn't mean nobody no harm."

Then she stopped, and the room was silent, exactly as it had sometimes been on those Sunday afternoons. Mama kept looking out into the streets.

"He used to have a job in the mill," she said, "and, like all young folks, he just liked to perform on Saturday nights. Saturday nights, him and your father would drift around to different places, go to dances and things like that, or just sit around with people they knew, and your father's brother would sing, he had a fine voice, and play along with himself on his guitar. Well, this particular Saturday night, him and your father was coming home from some place, and they were both a little drunk and there was a moon that night, it was bright like day. Your father's brother was feeling kind of good, and he was whistling to himself, and he had his guitar slung over his shoulder. They was coming down a hill, and beneath them was a road that turned off from the highway. Well, your father's brother, being always kind of frisky, decided to run down this hill, and he did, with that guitar banging and clanging behind him, and he ran across the road, and he was making water behind a tree. And your father was sort of amused at him and he was still coming down the hill, kind of slow. Then he heard a car motor and that same minute his brother stepped from behind the tree, into the road, in the moonlight. And he started to cross the road. And your father started to run down the hill, he says he don't know why. This car was full of white men. They was all drunk, and when they seen your father's brother they let out a great whoop and holler and they aimed the car straight at him. They was having fun, they just wanted to scare him, the way they do sometimes, you know. But they was drunk. And I guess the boy, being drunk, too, and scared, kind of lost his head. By the time he jumped it was too late. Your father says he heard his brother scream when the car rolled over him, and he heard the wood of that guitar when it give, and he heard them strings go flying, and he heard them white men shouting, and the car kept on a-going and it ain't stopped till this day. And, time your father got down the hill, his brother weren't nothing but blood and pulp."

Tears were gleaming on my mother's face. There wasn't anything I could say.

"He never mentioned it," she said, "because I never let him mention it before you children. Your Daddy was like a crazy man that night and for many a night thereafter. He says he never in his life seen anything as dark as that road after the lights of that car had gone away. Weren't nothing, weren't nobody on that road, just your Daddy and his brother and that busted guitar. Oh, yes. Your Daddy never did really get right again. Till the day he died he weren't sure but that every white man he saw was the man that killed his brother."

She stopped and took out her handkerchief and dried her eyes and looked at me.

"I ain't telling you all this," she said, "to make you scared or bitter or to make you hate nobody. I'm telling you this because you got a brother. And the world ain't changed."

I guess I didn't want to believe this. I guess she saw this in my face. She turned away from me, toward the window again, searching those streets.

"But I praise my Redeemer," she said at last, "that he called your Daddy home before me. I ain't saying it to throw no flowers at myself, but, I declare, it keeps me from feeling too cast down to know I helped your father get safely through this world. Your father always acted like he was the roughest, strongest man on earth. And everybody took him to be like that. But if he hadn't had *me* there—to see his tears!"

She was crying again. Still, I couldn't move. I said, "Lord, Lord, Mama, I didn't know it was like that."

"Oh, honey," she said, "there's a lot that you don't know. But you are going to find it out." She stood up from the window and came over to me. "You got to hold on to your brother," she said, "and don't let him fall, no matter what it looks like is happening to him and no matter how evil you gets with him. You going to be evil with him many a time. But don't you forget what I told you, you hear?"

"I won't forget," I said. "Don't you worry, I won't forget. I won't let nothing happen to Sonny."

My mother smiled as though she were amused at something she saw in my face. Then, "You may not be able to stop nothing from happening. But you got to let him know you's *there*."

Two days later I was married, and then I was gone. And I had a lot of things on my mind and I pretty well forgot my promise to Mama until I got shipped home on a special furlough for her funeral.

And, after the funeral, with just Sonny and me alone in the empty kitchen, I tried to find out something about him.

"What do you want to do?" I asked him.

"I'm going to be a musician," he said.

For he had graduated, in the time I had been away, from dancing to the juke box to finding out who was playing what, and what they were doing with it, and he had bought himself a set of drums.

"You mean, you want to be a drummer?" I somehow had the feeling that being a drummer might be all right for other people but not for my brother Sonny.

"I don't think," he said, looking at me very gravely, "that I'll ever be a good drummer. But I think I can play a piano."

I frowned. I'd never played the role of the older brother quite so seriously before, had scarcely ever, in fact, *asked* Sonny a damn thing. I sensed myself in the presence of something I didn't really know how to handle, didn't understand. So I made my frown a little deeper as I asked: "What kind of musician do you want to be?"

He grinned. "How many kinds do you think there are?"

"Be *serious,*" I said.

He laughed, throwing his head back, and then looked at me. "I *am* serious."

"Well, then, for Christ's sake, stop kidding around and answer a serious question. I mean, do you want to be a concert pianist, you want to play classical music and all that, or—or, what?" Long before I finished he was laughing again. "For Christ's *sake,* Sonny!"

He sobered, but with difficulty. "I'm sorry. But you sound so—*scared!*" And he was off again.

"Well, you may think it's funny now, baby, but it's not going to be so funny when you have to make your living at it, let me tell you *that.*" I was furious because I knew he was laughing at me and I didn't know why.

"No," he said, very sober now, and afraid, perhaps, that he'd hurt me, "I don't want to be a classical pianist. That isn't what interests me. I mean"—he paused, looking hard at me, as though his eyes would help me to understand, and then gestured helplessly, as though perhaps his hand would help—"I mean, I'll have a lot of studying to do, and I'll have to study *everything,* but, I mean, I want to play *with*—jazz musicians." He stopped. "I want to play jazz," he said.

Well, the word had never before sounded as heavy, as real, as it sounded that afternoon in Sonny's mouth. I just looked at him and I was probably frowning a real frown by this time. I simply couldn't see why on earth he'd want to spend his time hanging around night clubs, clowning around on bandstands, while people pushed each other around a dance floor. It seemed —beneath him, somehow. I had never thought about it before, had never been forced to, but I suppose I had always put jazz musicians in a class with what Daddy called "good-time people."

"Are you *serious?*"

"Hell, *yes,* I'm serious."

He looked more helpless than ever, and annoyed, and deeply hurt.

I suggested, helpfully: "You mean—like Louis Armstrong?"

His face closed as though I'd struck him. "No. I'm not talking about none of that old-time, down home crap."

"Well, look, Sonny, I'm sorry, don't get mad. I just don't altogether get it, that's all. Name somebody—you know, a jazz musician you admire."

"Bird."

"Who?"

"Bird! Charlie Parker! Don't they teach you nothing in the goddamn army?"

I lit a cigarette. I was surprised and then a little amused to discover that I was trembling. "I've been out of touch," I said. "You'll have to be patient with me. Now. Who's this Parker character?"

"He's just one of the greatest jazz musicians alive," said Sonny, sullenly, his hands in his pockets, his back to me. "Maybe *the* greatest," he added bitterly, "that's probably why *you* never heard of him."

"All right," I said, "I'm ignorant. I'm sorry. I'll go out and buy all the cat's records right away, all right?"

"It don't," said Sonny, with dignity, "make any difference to me. I don't care what you listen to. Don't do me no favors."

I was beginning to realize that I'd never seen him so upset before. With another part of my mind I was thinking that this would probably turn out to be one of those things kids go through and that I shouldn't make it seem important by pushing it too hard. Still, I didn't think it would do any harm to ask: "Doesn't all this take a lot of time? Can you make a living at it?"

He turned back to me and half leaned, half sat, on the kitchen table. "Everything takes time," he said, "and—well, yes, sure, I can make a living at it. But what I don't seem to be able to make you understand is that it's the only thing I want to do."

"Well, Sonny," I said gently, "you know people can't always do exactly what they want to do—"

"*No,* I don't know that," said Sonny, surprising me. "I think people *ought* to do what they want to do, what else are they alive for?"

"You getting to be a big boy," I said desperately, "it's time you started thinking about your future."

"I'm thinking about my future," said Sonny, grimly. "I think about it all the time."

I gave up. I decided, if he didn't change his mind, that we could always talk about it later. "In the meantime," I said, "you got to finish school." We had already decided that he'd have to move in with Isabel and her folks. I knew this wasn't the ideal arrangement because Isabel's folks are inclined to be dicty and they hadn't especially wanted Isabel to marry me. But I didn't know what else to do. "And we have to get you fixed up at Isabel's."

There was a long silence. He moved from the kitchen table to the window. "That's a terrible idea. You know it yourself."

"Do you have a *better* idea?"

He just walked up and down the kitchen for a minute. He was as tall as I was. He had started to shave. I suddenly had the feeling that I didn't know him at all.

He stopped at the kitchen table and picked up my cigarettes. Looking at me with a kind of mocking, amused defiance, he put one between his lips. "You mind?"

"You smoking already?"

He lit the cigarette and nodded, watching me through the smoke. "I just wanted to see if I'd have the courage to smoke in front of you." He grinned and blew a great cloud of smoke to the ceiling. "It was easy." He looked at my face. "Come on, now. I bet you was smoking at my age, tell the truth."

I didn't say anything but the truth was on my face, and he laughed. But now there was something very strained in his laugh. "Sure. And I bet that ain't all you was doing."

He was frightening me a little. "Cut the crap," I said. "We already decided that you was going to go and live at Isabel's. Now what's got into you all of a sudden?"

"*You* decided it," he pointed out. "*I* didn't decide nothing." He stopped in front of me, leaning against the stove, arms loosely folded. "Look, brother. I don't want to stay in Harlem no more, I really don't." He was very earnest. He looked at me, then over toward the kitchen window. There was something in his eyes I'd never seen before, some thoughtfulness, some worry all his own. He rubbed the muscle of one arm. "It's time I was getting out of here."

"Where do you want to *go,* Sonny?"

"I want to join the army. Or the navy, I don't care. If I say I'm old enough, they'll believe me."

Then I got mad. It was because I was so scared. "You must be crazy. You goddamn fool, what the hell do you want to go and join the *army* for?"

"I just told you. To get out of Harlem."

"Sonny, you haven't even finished *school.* And if you really want to be a musician, how do you expect to study if you're in the *army?*"

He looked at me, trapped, and in anguish. "There's ways. I might be able to work out some kind of deal. Anyway, I'll have the G.I. Bill when I come out."

"*If* you come out." We stared at each other. "Sonny, please. Be reasonable. I know the setup is far from perfect. But we got to do the best we can."

"I ain't learning nothing in school," he said. "Even when I go." He turned away from me and opened the window and threw his cigarette out into the narrow alley. I watched his back. "At least, I ain't learning nothing you'd want me to learn." He slammed the window so hard I thought the glass would fly out, and turned back to me. "And I'm sick of the stink of these garbage cans!"

"Sonny," I said, "I know how you feel. But if you don't finish school now, you're going to be sorry later that you didn't." I grabbed him by the shoulders. "And you only got another year. It ain't so bad. And I'll come back and

I swear I'll help you do *whatever* you want to do. Just try to put up with it till I come back. Will you please do that? For me?"

He didn't answer and he wouldn't look at me.

"Sonny. You hear me?"

He pulled away. "I hear you. But you never hear anything *I* say."

I didn't know what to say to that. He looked out of the window and then back at me. "OK," he said, and sighed. "I'll try."

Then I said, trying to cheer him up a little, "They got a piano at Isabel's. You can practice on it."

And as a matter of fact, it did cheer him up for a minute. "That's right," he said to himself. "I forgot that." His face relaxed a little. But the worry, the thoughtfulness, played on it still, the way shadows play on a face which is staring into the fire.

But I thought I'd never hear the end of that piano. At first, Isabel would write me, saying how nice it was that Sonny was so serious about his music and how, as soon as he came in from school, or wherever he had been when he was supposed to be at school, he went straight to that piano and stayed there until suppertime. And, after supper, he went back to that piano and stayed there until everybody went to bed. He was at that piano all day Saturday and all day Sunday. Then he bought a record player and started playing records. He'd play one record over and over again, all day long sometimes, and he'd improvise along with it on the piano. Or he'd play one section of the record, one chord, one change, one progression, then he'd do it on the piano. Then back to the record. Then back to the piano.

Well, I really don't know how they stood it. Isabel finally confessed that it wasn't like living with a person at all, it was like living with sound. And the sound didn't make any sense to her, didn't make any sense to any of them—naturally. They began, in a way, to be afflicted by this presence that was living in their home. It was as though Sonny were some sort of god, or monster. He moved in an atmosphere which wasn't like theirs at all. They fed him and he ate, he washed himself, he walked in and out of their door; he certainly wasn't nasty or unpleasant or rude, Sonny isn't any of those things; but it was as though he were all wrapped up in some cloud, some fire, some vision all his own; and there wasn't any way to reach him.

At the same time, he wasn't really a man yet, he was still a child, and they had to watch out for him in all kinds of ways. They certainly couldn't throw him out. Neither did they dare to make a great scene about that piano because even they dimly sensed, as I sensed, from so many thousands of miles away, that Sonny was at that piano playing for his life.

But he hadn't been going to school. One day a letter came from the school board, and Isabel's mother got it—there had, apparently, been other letters but Sonny had torn them up. This day, when Sonny came in, Isabel's mother showed him the letter and asked where he'd been spending his time. And she finally got it out of him that he'd been down in Greenwich Village, with musicians and other characters, in a white girl's apartment. And this scared her and she started to scream at him, and what came up, once she began—though she denies it to this day—was what sacrifices they were making to give Sonny a decent home and how little he appreciated it.

Sonny didn't play the piano that day. By evening, Isabel's mother had calmed down but then there was the old man to deal with, and Isabel herself. Isabel says she did her best to be calm but she broke down and started crying. She says she just watched Sonny's face. She could tell, by watching him, what was happening with him. And what was happening was that they penetrated his cloud, they had reached him. Even if their fingers had been a thousand times more gentle than human fingers ever are, he could hardly help feeling that they had stripped him naked and were spitting on that nakedness. For he also had to see that his presence, that music, which was life or death to him, had been torture for them and that they had endured it, not at all for his sake, but only for mine. And Sonny couldn't take that. He can take it a little better today than he could then but he's still not very good at it and, frankly, I don't know anybody who is.

The silence of the next few days must have been louder than the sound of all the music ever played since time began. One morning, before she went to work, Isabel was in his room for something and she suddenly realized that all of his records were gone. And she knew for certain that he was gone. And he was. He went as far as the navy would carry him. He finally sent me a postcard from someplace in Greece, and that was the first I knew that Sonny was still alive. I didn't see him any more until we were both back in New York and the war had long been over.

He was a man by then, of course, but I wasn't willing to see it. He came by the house from time to time, but we fought almost every time we met. I didn't like the way he carried himself, loose and dreamlike all the time, and I didn't like his friends, and his music seemed to be merely an excuse for the life he led. It sounded just that weird and disordered.

Then we had a fight, a pretty awful fight, and I didn't see him for months. By and by I looked him up, where he was living, in a furnished room in the Village, and I tried to make it up. But there were lots of other people in the room, and Sonny just lay on his bed, and he wouldn't come downstairs with me, and he treated these other people as though they were his family and I weren't. So I got mad and then he got mad, and then I told him that he might just as well be dead as live the way he was living. Then he stood up and he told me not to worry about him any more in life, that he *was* dead as far as I was concerned. Then he pushed me to the door, and the other people looked on as though nothing were happening, and he slammed the door behind me. I stood in the hallway, staring at the door. I heard somebody laugh in the room and then the tears came to my eyes. I started down the steps, whistling to keep from crying, I kept whistling to myself, *You going to need me, baby, one of these cold, rainy days.*

I read about Sonny's trouble in the spring. Little Grace died in the fall. She was a beautiful little girl. But she only lived a little over two years. She died of polio and she suffered. She had a slight fever for a couple of days, but it didn't seem like anything and we just kept her in bed. And we would certainly have called the doctor, but the fever dropped, she seemed to be all right. So we thought it had just been a cold. Then, one day, she was up, playing, Isabel was in the kitchen fixing lunch for the two boys when they'd come in from school, and she heard Grace fall down in the living room. When you have a lot of children you don't always start running when one of them falls, unless they start screaming or something. And, this time, Grace was quiet. Yet, Isabel says that when she heard that *thump* and then that silence, something happened in her to make her afraid. And she ran to the living room and there was little Grace on the floor, all twisted up, and the reason she hadn't screamed was that she couldn't get her breath. And when she did scream, it was the worst sound, Isabel says, that she'd ever heard in all her life, and she still hears it sometimes in her dreams. Isabel will sometimes wake me up with a low, moaning, strangled sound, and I have to be quick to awaken her and hold her to me and where Isabel is weeping against me seems a mortal wound.

I think I may have written Sonny the very day that little Grace was buried. I was sitting in the living room in the dark, by myself, and I suddenly thought of Sonny. My trouble made his real.

One Saturday afternoon, when Sonny had been living with us, or, anyway, been in our house, for nearly two weeks, I found myself wandering aimlessly about the living room, drinking from a can of beer, and trying to work up the courage to search Sonny's room. He was out, he was usually out whenever I was home, and Isabel had taken the children to see their grandparents. Suddenly I was standing still in front of the living-room window, watching Seventh Avenue. The idea of searching Sonny's room made me still. I scarcely dared to admit to myself what I'd be searching for. I didn't know what I'd do if I found it. Or if I didn't.

On the sidewalk across from me, near the entrance to a barbecue joint, some people were holding an old-fashioned revival meeting. The barbecue cook, wearing a dirty white apron, his conked hair reddish and metallic in the pale sun, and a cigarette between his lips, stood in the doorway, watching them. Kids and older people paused in their errands and stood there, along with some older men and a couple of very tough-looking women who watched everything that happened on the avenue, as though they owned it, or were maybe owned by it. Well, they were watching this, too. The revival was being carried on by three sisters in black, and a brother. All they had were their voices and their Bibles and a tambourine. The brother was testifying and while he testified two of the sisters stood together, seeming to say, Amen, and the third sister walked around with the tambourine outstretched and a couple of people dropped coins into it. Then the brother's testimony ended, and the sister who had been taking up the collection dumped the coins into her palm and transferred them to the pocket of her long black robe. Then she raised both hands, striking the tambourine against the air, and then against one hand, and she started to sing. And the two other sisters and the brother joined in.

It was strange, suddenly, to watch, though I had been seeing these street meetings all my life. So, of course, had everybody else down there. Yet, they paused and watched and listened and I stood still at the window. " *'Tis the old ship of Zion,*" they sang, and the sister with the tambourine kept a steady, jangling beat, "*it has rescued many a thousand!*" Not a soul under the sound of their voices was hearing this song for the first time, not one of them had been rescued. Nor had they seen much in the way of rescue work being done around them. Neither did they especially believe in the holiness of the three sisters and the brother, they knew too much about them, knew where they lived, and how. The woman with the tambourine, whose voice dominated the air, whose face was bright with joy, was divided by very little from the woman who stood watching her, a cigarette between her heavy, chapped lips, her hair a cuckoo's nest, her face scarred and swollen from many beatings, and her black eyes glittering like coal. Perhaps they both knew this, which was why, when, as rarely, they addressed each other, they addressed each other as Sister. As the singing filled the air, the watching, listening faces underwent a change, the eyes focusing on something within; the music seemed to soothe a poison out of them; and time seemed, nearly, to fall away from the sullen, belligerent, battered faces, as though they were fleeing back to their first condition, while dreaming of their last. The barbecue cook half shook his head and smiled, and dropped his cigarette and disappeared into his joint. A man fumbled in his pockets for change and stood holding it in his hand impatiently, as though he had just remembered a pressing appointment further up the avenue. He looked furious. Then I saw Sonny, standing on the edge of the crowd. He was carrying a wide, flat notebook with a green cover, and it made him look, from where I was standing, almost like a schoolboy. The coppery sun brought out the copper in his skin, he was very faintly smiling, standing very still. Then the singing stopped, the tambourine turned into a collection plate again. The furious man dropped in his coins and vanished, so did a couple of the women, and Sonny dropped some change in the plate, looking directly at the woman with a little smile. He started across the avenue, toward the house. He has a slow, loping walk, something like the way Harlem hipsters walk, only he's imposed on this his own half-beat. I had never really noticed it before.

I stayed at the window, both relieved and apprehensive. As Sonny disappeared from my sight, they began singing again. And they were still singing when his key turned in the lock.

"Hey," he said.

"Hey, yourself. You want some beer?"

"No. Well, maybe." But he came up to the window and stood beside me, looking out. "What a warm voice," he said.

They were singing *If I could only hear my mother pray again!*

"Yes," I said, "and she can sure beat that tambourine."

"But what a terrible song," he said, and laughed. He dropped his notebook on the sofa and disappeared into the kitchen. "Where's Isabel and the kids?"

"I think they went to see their grandparents. You hungry?"

"No." He came back into the living room with his can of beer. "You want to come someplace with me tonight?"

I sensed, I don't know how, that I couldn't possibly say no. "Sure. Where?"

He sat down on the sofa and picked up his notebook and started leafing through it. "I'm going to sit in with some fellows in a joint in the Village."

"You mean, you're going to play, tonight?"

"That's right." He took a swallow of his beer and moved back to the window. He gave me a sidelong look. "If you can stand it."

"I'll try," I said.

He smiled to himself, and we both watched as the meeting across the way broke up. The three sisters and the brother, heads bowed, were singing *God be with you till we meet again.* The faces around them were very quiet. Then the song ended. The small crowd dispersed. We watched the three women and the lone man walk slowly up the avenue.

"When she was singing before," said Sonny, abruptly, "her voice reminded me for a minute of what heroin feels like sometimes—when it's in your veins. It makes you feel sort of warm and cool at the same time. And distant. And—and sure." He sipped his beer, very deliberately not looking at me. I watched his face. "It makes you feel—in control. Sometimes you've got to have that feeling."

"Do you?" I sat down slowly in the easy chair.

"Sometimes." He went to the sofa and picked up his notebook again. "Some people do."

"In order," I asked, "to play?" And my voice was very ugly, full of contempt and anger.

"Well"—he looked at me with great, troubled eyes, as though, in fact, he hoped his eyes would tell me things he could never otherwise say—"they *think* so. And *if* they think so—!"

"And what do *you* think?" I asked.

He sat on the sofa and put his can of beer on the floor. "I don't know," he said, and I couldn't be sure if he were answering my question or pursuing his thoughts. His face didn't tell me. "It's not so much to *play*. It's to *stand* it, to be able to make it at all. On any level." He frowned and smiled: "In order to keep from shaking to pieces."

"But these friends of yours," I said, "they seem to shake themselves to pieces pretty goddamn fast."

"Maybe." He played with the notebook. And something told me that I should curb my tongue, that Sonny was doing his best to talk, that I should listen. "But of course you only know the ones that've gone to pieces. Some don't—or at least they haven't *yet* and that's just about all *any* of us can say." He paused. "And then there are some who just live, really, in hell, and they know it and they see what's happening and they go right on. I don't know." He sighed, dropped the notebook, folded his arms. "Some guys, you can tell from the way they play, they on something *all* the time. And you can see that, well, it makes something real for them. But of course," he picked up his beer from the floor and sipped it and put the can down again, "they *want* to, too, you've got to see that. Even some of them that say they don't—*some,* not all."

"And what about you?" I asked. I couldn't help it. "What about you? Do *you* want to?"

He stood up and walked to the window and remained silent for a long time. Then he sighed. "Me," he said. Then: "While I was downstairs before, on my way here, listening to that woman sing, it struck me all of a sudden how much suffering she must have had to go through—to sing like that. It's *repulsive* to think you have to suffer that much."

I said: "But there's no way not to suffer—is there, Sonny?"

"I believe not," he said, and smiled, "but that's never stopped anyone from trying." He looked at me. "Has it?" I realized, with this mocking look, that there stood between us, forever, beyond the power of time or forgiveness, the fact that I had held silence—so long!—when he had needed human speech to help him. He turned back to the window. "No, there's no way not to suffer. But you try all kinds of ways to keep from drowning in it, to keep on top of it, and to make it seem—well, like *you.* Like you did something, all right, and now you're suffering for it. You know?" I said nothing. "Well you know," he said, impatiently, "why *do* people suffer? Maybe it's better to do something to give it a reason, *any* reason."

"But we just agreed," I said, "that there's no way not to suffer. Isn't it better, then, just to—take it?"

"But nobody just takes it," Sonny cried, "that's what I'm telling you! *Everybody* tries not to. You're just hung up on the *way* some people try—it's not *your* way!"

The hair on my face began to itch, my face felt wet. "That's not true," I said, "that's not true. I don't give a damn what other people do, I don't even care how they suffer. I just care how *you* suffer." And he looked at me. "Please believe me," I said, "I don't want to see you—die—trying not to suffer."

"I won't," he said, flatly, "die trying not to suffer. At least, not any faster than anybody else."

"But there's no need," I said, trying to laugh, "is there, in killing yourself?"

I wanted to say more, but I couldn't. I wanted to talk about will power and how life could be—well, beautiful. I wanted to say that it was all within; but was it? Or, rather, wasn't that exactly the trouble? And I wanted to promise that I would never fail him again. But it would all have sounded—empty words and lies.

So I made the promise to myself and prayed that I would keep it.

"It's terrible sometimes, inside," he said, "that's what's the trouble. You walk these streets, black and funky and cold, and there's not really a living ass to talk to, and there's nothing shaking, and there's no way of getting it out—that storm inside. You can't talk it and you can't make love with it, and when you finally try to get with it and play it, you realize *nobody's* listening. So *you've* got to listen. You got to find a way to listen."

And then he walked away from the window and sat on the sofa again, as though all the wind had suddenly been knocked out of him. "Sometimes you'll do *anything* to play, even cut your mother's throat." He laughed and looked at me. "Or your brother's." Then he sobered. "Or your own." Then: "Don't worry. I'm all right now and I think I'll *be* all right. But I can't forget—where I've been. I don't mean just the physical place I've been, I mean where I've *been.* And *what* I've been."

"What have you been, Sonny?" I asked.

He smiled—but sat sideways on the sofa, his elbow resting on the back, his fingers playing with his mouth and chin, not looking at me. "I've been something I didn't recognize, didn't know I could be. Didn't know anybody could be." He stopped, looking inward, looking helplessly young, looking old. "I'm not talking about it now because I feel *guilty* or anything like that—maybe it would be better if I did, I don't know. Anyway, I can't really talk about it. Not to you, not to anybody." And now he turned and faced me. "Sometimes, you know, and it was actually when I was most out of the world, I felt that I was in it, that I was *with* it, really, and I could play or I didn't really have to *play,* it just came out of me, it was there. And I don't know how I played, thinking about it now, but I know I did awful things, those times, sometimes, to people. Or it wasn't that I *did* anything to them—it was that they weren't real." He picked up the beer can; it was empty; he rolled it between his palms: "And other times—well, I needed a fix, I needed to find a place to lean, I needed to clear a space to *listen*—and I couldn't find it, and I—went crazy, I did terrible things to *me,* I was terrible *for* me." He began pressing the beer can between his hands, I watched the metal begin to give. It glittered, as he played with it, like a knife, and I was afraid he would cut himself, but I said nothing. "Oh well. I can never tell you. I was all by myself at the bottom of something, stinking and sweating and crying and shaking, and I smelled it, you know? *My* stink, and I thought I'd die if I couldn't get away from it and yet, all the same, I knew that everything I was doing was just locking me in with it. And I didn't know," he paused, still flattening the beer can, "I didn't know, I still *don't* know, something kept telling me that maybe it was good to smell your own stink, but I didn't think that *that* was what I'd been trying to do—and—who can stand it?" And he abruptly dropped the ruined beer can, looking at me with a small, still smile, and then rose, walking to the window as though it were the lodestone rock. I watched his face, he watched the avenue. "I couldn't tell you when Mama died—but the reason I wanted to leave Harlem so bad was to get away from drugs. And then, when I ran away, that's what I was running from—really. When I came back, nothing had changed. *I* hadn't changed, I was just—older." And he stopped, drumming with his fingers on the windowpane. The sun had vanished, soon darkness would fall. I watched his face. "It can come again," he said, almost as though speaking to himself. Then he turned to me. "It can come again," he repeated. "I just want you to know that."

"All right," I said at last. "So it can come again. All right."

He smiled, but the smile was sorrowful. "I had to try to tell you," he said.

"Yes," I said. "I understand that."

"You're my brother," he said, looking straight at me, and not smiling at all.

"Yes," I repeated, "yes. I understand that."

He turned back to the window, looking out. "All that hatred down there," he said, "all that hatred and misery and love. It's a wonder it doesn't blow the avenue apart."

We went to the only night club on a short, dark street, downtown. We squeezed through the narrow, chattering, jam-packed bar to the entrance of the big room, where the bandstand was. And we stood there for a moment, for the lights were very dim in this room and we couldn't see. Then, "Hello, boy," said a voice, and an enormous black man, much older than Sonny or myself, erupted out of all that atmospheric lighting and put an arm around Sonny's shoulder. "I been sitting right here," he said, "waiting for you."

He had a big voice, too, and heads in the darkness turned toward us.

Sonny grinned and pulled a little away, and said, "Creole, this is my brother. I told you about him."

Creole shook my hand. "I'm glad to meet you, son," he said, and it was clear that he was glad to meet me *there,* for Sonny's sake. And he smiled. "You got a real musician in *your* family," and he took his arm from Sonny's shoulder and slapped him, lightly, affectionately, with the back of his hand.

"Well. Now I've heard it all," said a voice behind us. This was another musician, and a friend of Sonny's, a coal-black, cheerful-looking man, built close to the ground. He immediately began confiding to me, at the top of his lungs, the most terrible things about Sonny, his teeth gleaming like a lighthouse and his laugh coming up out of him like the beginning of an earthquake. And it turned out that everyone at the bar knew Sonny, or almost everyone; some were musicians, working there, or nearby, or not working, some were simply hangers-on, and some were there to hear Sonny play. I was introduced to all of them and they were all very polite to me. Yet, it was clear that, for them, I was only Sonny's brother. Here, I was in Sonny's world. Or, rather: his kingdom. Here, it was not even a question that his veins bore royal blood.

They were going to play soon, and Creole installed me, by myself, at a table in a dark corner. Then I watched them, Creole, and the little black man, and Sonny, and the others, while they horsed around, standing just below the bandstand. The light from the bandstand spilled just a little short of them and, watching them laughing and gesturing and moving about, I had the feeling that they, nevertheless, were being most careful not to step into that circle of light too suddenly: that if they moved into the light too suddenly, without thinking, they would perish in flame. Then, while I watched, one of them, the small, black man, moved into the light and crossed the bandstand and started fooling around with his drums. Then—being funny and being, also, extremely ceremonious—Creole took Sonny by the arm and led him to the piano. A woman's voice called Sonny's name, and a few hands started clapping. And Sonny, also being funny and being ceremonious, and so touched, I think, that he could have cried, but neither hiding it nor showing it, riding it like a man, grinned, and put both hands to his heart and bowed from the waist.

Creole then went to the bass fiddle and a lean, very bright-skinned brown man jumped up on the bandstand and picked up his horn. So there they were, and the atmosphere on the bandstand and in the room began to change and tighten. Someone stepped up to the microphone and announced them. Then there were all kinds of murmurs. Some people at the bar shushed others. The waitress ran around, frantically getting in the last orders, guys and chicks got closer to each other, and the lights on the bandstand, on the quartet, turned to a kind of indigo. Then they all looked different there. Creole looked about him for the last time, as though he were making certain that all his chickens were in the coop, and then he—jumped and struck the fiddle. And there they were.

All I know about music is that not many people ever really hear it. And even then, on the rare occasions when something opens within, and the music enters, what we mainly hear, or hear corroborated, are personal, private, vanishing evocations. But the man who creates the music is hearing something else, is dealing with the roar rising from the void and imposing order on it as it hits the air. What is evoked in him, then, is of another order, more terrible because it has no words, and triumphant, too, for that same reason. And his triumph, when he triumphs, is ours. I just watched Sonny's face. His face was troubled, he was working hard, but he wasn't with it. And I had the feeling that, in a way, everyone on the bandstand was waiting for him, both waiting for him and pushing him along. But as I began to watch Creole, I realized that it was Creole who held them all back. He had them on a short rein. Up there, keeping the beat with his whole body, wailing on the fiddle, with his eyes half closed, he was listening to everything, but he was listening to Sonny. He was having a dialogue with Sonny. He wanted Sonny to leave the shore line and strike out for the deep water. He was Sonny's witness that deep water and drowning were not the same thing—he had been there, and he knew. And he wanted Sonny to know. He was waiting for Sonny to do the things on the keys which would let Creole know that Sonny was in the water.

And, while Creole listened, Sonny moved, deep within, exactly like someone in torment. I had never before thought of how awful the relationship must be between the musician and his instrument. He has to fill it, this instrument, with the breath of life, his own. He has to make it do what he wants it to do. And a piano is just a piano. It's made out of so much wood and wires and little hammers and big ones, and ivory. While there's only so much you can do with it, the only way to find this out is to try to try and make it do everything.

And Sonny hadn't been near a piano for over a year. And he wasn't on much better terms with his life, not the life that stretched before him now. He and the piano stammered, started one way, got scared, stopped; started another way, panicked, marked time, started again; then seemed to have found a direction, panicked again, got stuck. And the face I saw on Sonny I'd never seen before. Everything had been burned out of it, and, at the same time, things usually hidden were being burned in, by the fire and fury of the battle which was occurring in him up there.

Yet, watching Creole's face as they neared the end of the first set, I had the feeling that something had happened, something I hadn't heard. Then they finished, there was scattered applause, and then, without an instant's warning, Creole started into something else, it was almost sardonic, it was *Am I Blue.* And, as though he commanded, Sonny began to play. Something began to happen. And Creole let out the reins. The dry, low, black man said something awful on the drums, Creole answered, and the drums talked back. Then the horn insisted, sweet and high, slightly detached perhaps, and Creole listened, commenting now and then, dry, and driving, beautiful and calm and old. Then they all came together again, and Sonny was part of the family again. I could tell this from his face. He seemed to have found, right there beneath his fingers, a damn brand-new piano. It seemed that he couldn't get over it. Then, for a while, just being happy with Sonny, they seemed to be agreeing with him that brand-new pianos certainly were a gas.

Then Creole stepped forward to remind them that what they were playing was the blues. He hit something in all of them, he hit something in me, myself, and the music tightened and deepened, apprehension began to beat the air. Creole began to tell us what the blues were all about. They were not about anything very new. He and his boys up there were keeping it new, at the risk of ruin, destruction, madness, and death, in order to find new ways to make us listen. For, while the tale of how we suffer, and how we are delighted, and how we may triumph is never new, it always must be heard. There isn't any other tale to tell, it's the only light we've got in all this darkness.

And this tale, according to that face, that body, those strong hands on those strings, has another aspect in every country, and a new depth in every generation. Listen, Creole seemed to be saying, listen. Now these are Sonny's blues. He made the little black man on the drums know it, and the bright, brown man on the horn. Creole wasn't trying any longer to get Sonny in the water. He was wishing him Godspeed. Then he stepped back, very slowly, filling the air with the immense suggestion that Sonny speak for himself.

Then they all gathered around Sonny, and Sonny played. Every now and again one of them seemed to say, Amen. Sonny's fingers filled the air with life, his life. But that life contained so many others. And Sonny went all the way back, he really began with the spare, flat statement of the opening phrase of the song. Then he began to make it his. It was very beautiful because it wasn't hurried and it was no longer a lament. I seemed to hear with what burning he had made it his, with what burning we had yet to make it ours, how we could cease lamenting. Freedom lurked around us and I understood, at last, that he could help us to be free if we would listen, that he would never be free until we did. Yet, there was no battle in his face now. I heard what he had gone through, and would continue to go through until he came to rest in earth. He had made it his: that long line, of which we knew only Mama and Daddy. And he was giving it back, as everything must be given back, so that, passing through death, it can live forever. I saw my mother's face again, and felt, for the first time, how the stones of the road she had walked on must have bruised her feet. I saw the moonlit road where my father's brother died. And it brought something else back to me, and carried me past it. I saw my little girl again and felt Isabel's tears again, and I felt my own tears begin to rise. And I was yet aware that this was only a moment, that the world waited outside, as hungry as a tiger, and that trouble stretched above us, longer than the sky.

Then it was over. Creole and Sonny let out their breath, both soaking wet, and grinning. There was a lot of applause and some of it was real. In the dark, the girl came by and I asked her to take drinks to the bandstand. There was a long pause, while they talked up there in the indigo light and after a while I saw the girl put a Scotch and milk on top of the piano for Sonny. He didn't seem to notice it, but just before they started playing again, he sipped from it and looked toward me, and nodded. Then he put it back on top of the piano. For me, then, as they began to play again, it glowed and shook above my brother's head like the very cup of trembling.

PHILIP ROTH

(b. 1933)

Philip Roth has recorded with uncanny accuracy the dilemma of the emancipated, educated Eastern American Jew who has trouble defining his identity as a Jew and a human being. Born and raised in the Jewish section of Newark, New Jersey, which he graphically depicted in Portnoy's Complaint, *Roth has been a college student, teacher and writer-in-residence.*

The publication of Goodbye, Columbus *(1960), a collection of his short fiction, established Philip Roth as a vital new talent on the American literary scene. His novels, including* Letting Go *(1962) and* Portnoy's Complaint *(1969), have continued his exploration of the human condition.*

Sergeant Marx, in "Defender of the Faith," faces the question of the conflicting obligations that his Jewishness forces upon him in his position of responsibility to the larger society that the Army represents.

Defender of the Faith

IN MAY of 1945, only a few weeks after the fighting had ended in Europe, I was rotated back to the States, where I spent the remainder of the war with a training company at Camp Crowder, Missouri. Along with the rest of the Ninth Army, I had been racing across Germany so swiftly during the late winter and spring that when I boarded the plane, I couldn't believe its destination lay to the west. My mind might inform me otherwise, but there was an inertia of the spirit that told me we were flying to a new front, where we would disembark and continue our push eastward—eastward until we'd circled the globe, marching through villages along whose twisting, cobbled streets crowds of the enemy would watch us take possession of what, up to then, they'd considered their own. I had changed enough in two years not to mind the trembling of the old people, the crying of the very young, the uncertainty and fear in the eyes of the once arrogant. I had been fortunate enough to develop an infantryman's heart, which, like his feet, at first aches and swells but finally grows horny enough for him to travel the weirdest paths without feeling a thing.

Captain Paul Barrett was my C.O. in Camp Crowder. The day I reported for duty, he came out of his office to shake my hand. He was short, gruff, and fiery, and—indoors or out—he wore his polished helmet liner pulled down to his little eyes. In Europe, he had received a battlefield commission and a serious chest wound, and he'd been returned to the States only a few months before. He spoke easily to me, and at the evening formation he introduced me to the troops. "Gentlemen," he said, "Sergeant Thurston, as you know, is no longer with this company. Your new first sergeant is Sergeant Nathan Marx, here. He is a veteran of the European theatre, and consequently will expect to find a company of soldiers here, and not a company of *boys.*"

I sat up late in the orderly room that evening, trying half-heartedly to solve the riddle of duty rosters, personnel forms, and morning reports. The Charge of Quarters slept with his mouth open on a mattress on the floor. A trainee stood reading the next day's duty roster, which was posted on the bulletin board just inside the screen door. It was a warm evening, and I could hear radios playing dance music over in the barracks. The trainee, who had been staring at me whenever he thought I wouldn't notice, finally took a step in my direction.

"Hey, Sarge—we having a G.I. party tomorrow night?" he asked. A G.I. party is a barracks cleaning.

"You usually have them on Friday nights?" I asked him.

"Yes," he said, and then he added mysteriously, "That's the whole thing."

"Then you'll have a G.I. party."

He turned away, and I heard him mumbling. His shoulders were moving, and I wondered if he was crying.

"What's your name, soldier?" I asked.

He turned, not crying at all. Instead, his green-speckled eyes, long and narrow, flashed like fish in the sun. He walked over to me and sat on the edge of my desk. He reached out a hand. "Sheldon," he said.

"Stand on your feet, Sheldon."

Getting off the desk, he said, "Sheldon Grossbart." He smiled at the familiarity into which he'd led me.

"You against cleaning the barracks Friday night, Grossbart?" I said. "Maybe we shouldn't have G.I. parties. Maybe we should get a maid." My tone startled me. I felt I sounded like every top sergeant I had ever known.

"No, Sergeant." He grew serious, but with a seriousness that seemed to be only the stifling of a smile. "It's just—G.I. parties on Friday night, of all nights."

He slipped up onto the corner of the desk again—not quite sitting, but not quite standing, either. He looked at me with those speckled eyes flashing, and then made a gesture with his hand. It was very slight—no more than a movement back and forth of the wrist—and yet it managed to exclude from our affairs everything else in the orderly room, to make the two of us the center of the world. It seemed, in fact, to exclude everything even about the two of us except our hearts.

"Sergeant Thurston was one thing," he whispered, glancing at the sleeping C.Q., "but we thought that with you here things might be a little different."

"We?"

"The Jewish personnel."

"Why?" I asked, harshly. "What's on your mind?" Whether I was still angry at the "Sheldon" business, or now at something else, I hadn't time to tell, but clearly I was angry.

"We thought you—Marx, you know, like Karl Marx. The Marx Brothers. Those guys are all—M-a-r-x. Isn't that how *you* spell it, Sergeant?"

"M-a-r-x."

"Fishbein said—" He stopped. "What I mean to say, Sergeant—" His face and neck were red, and his mouth moved but no words came out. In a moment, he raised himself to attention, gazing down at me. It was as though he had suddenly decided he could expect no more sympathy from me than from Thurston, the reason being that I was of Thurston's faith, and not his. The young man had managed to confuse himself as to what my faith really was, but I felt no desire to straighten him out. Very simply, I didn't like him.

When I did nothing but return his gaze, he spoke, in an altered tone. "You see, Sergeant," he explained to me, "Friday nights, Jews are supposed to go to services."

"Did Sergeant Thurston tell you you couldn't go to them when there was a G.I. party?"

"No."

"Did he say you had to stay and scrub the floors?"

"No, Sergeant."

"Did the Captain say you had to stay and scrub the floors?"

"That isn't it, Sergeant. It's the other guys in the barracks." He leaned toward me. "They think we're goofing off. But we're not. That's when Jews go to services, Friday night. We have to."

"Then go."

"But the other guys make accusations. They have no right."

"That's not the Army's problem, Grossbart. It's a personal problem you'll have to work out yourself."

"But it's *unfair.*"

I got up to leave. "There's nothing I can do about it," I said.

Grossbart stiffened and stood in front of me. "But this is a matter of *religion,* sir."

"Sergeant," I said.

"I mean 'Sergeant,' " he said, almost snarling.

"Look, go see the chaplain. You want to see Captain Barrett, I'll arrange an appointment."

"No, no. I don't want to make trouble, Sergeant. That's the first thing they throw up to you. I just want my rights!"

"Damn it, Grossbart, stop whining. You have your rights. You can stay and scrub floors or you can go to shul*—"

The smile swam in again. Spittle gleamed at the corners of his mouth. "You mean church, Sergeant."

"I mean shul, Grossbart!"

I walked past him and went outside. Near me, I heard the scrunching of a

* *shul.* synagogue

guard's boots on gravel. Beyond the lighted windows of the barracks, young men in T shirts and fatigue pants were sitting on their bunks, polishing their rifles. Suddenly there was a light rustling behind me. I turned and saw Grossbart's dark frame fleeing back to the barracks, racing to tell his Jewish friends that they were right—that, like Karl and Harpo, I was one of them.

The next morning, while chatting with Captain Barrett, I recounted the incident of the previous evening. Somehow, in the telling, it must have seemed to the Captain that I was not so much explaining Grossbart's position as defending it. "Marx, I'd fight side by side with a nigger if the fella proved to me he was a man. I pride myself," he said, looking out the window, "that I've got an open mind. Consequently, Sergeant, nobody gets special treatment here, for the good *or* the bad. All a man's got to do is prove himself. A man fires well on the range, I give him a weekend pass. He scores high in P.T., he gets a weekend pass. He *earns* it." He turned from the window and pointed a finger at me. "You're a Jewish fella, am I right, Marx?"

"Yes, sir."

"And I admire you. I admire you because of the ribbons on your chest. I judge a man by what he shows me on the field of battle, Sergeant. It's what he's got *here,*" he said, and then, though I expected he would point to his heart, he jerked a thumb toward the buttons straining to hold his blouse across his belly. "Guts," he said.

"O.K., sir. I only wanted to pass on to you how the men felt."

"Mr. Marx, you're going to be old before your time if you worry about how the men feel. Leave that stuff to the chaplain—that's his business, not yours. Let's us train these fellas to shoot straight. If the Jewish personnel feels the other men are accusing them of goldbricking—well, I just don't know. Seems awfully funny that suddenly the Lord is calling so loud in Private Grossman's ear he's just got to run to church."

"Synagogue," I said.

"Synagogue is right, Sergeant. I'll write that down for handy reference. Thank you for stopping by."

That evening, a few minutes before the company gathered outside the orderly room for the chow formation, I called the C.Q., Corporal Robert LaHill, in to see me. LaHill was a dark, burly fellow whose hair curled out of his clothes wherever it could. He had a glaze in his eyes that made one think of caves and dinosaurs. "LaHill," I said, "when you take the formation, remind the men that they're free to attend church services *whenever* they are held, provided they report to the orderly room before they leave the area."

LaHill scratched his wrist, but gave no indication that he'd heard or understood.

"LaHill," I said, "*church.* You remember? Church, priest, Mass, confession."

He curled one lip into a kind of smile; I took it for a signal that for a second he had flickered back up into the human race.

"Jewish personnel who want to attend services this evening are to fall out in front of the orderly room at 1900," I said. Then, as an afterthought, I added, "By order of Captain Barrett."

A little while later, as the day's last light—softer than any I had seen that year—began to drop over Camp Crowder, I heard LaHill's thick, inflectionless voice outside my window: "Give me your ears, troopers. Toppie says for me to tell you that at 1900 hours all Jewish personnel is to fall out in front, here, if they want to attend the Jewish Mass."

At seven o'clock, I looked out the orderly-room window and saw three soldiers in starched khakis standing on the dusty quadrangle. They looked at their watches and fidgeted while they whispered back and forth. It was getting dimmer, and, alone on the otherwise deserted field, they looked tiny. When I opened the door, I heard the noises of the G.I. party coming from the surrounding barracks—bunks being pushed to the walls, faucets pounding water into buckets, brooms whisking at the wooden floors, cleaning the dirt away for Saturday's inspection. Big puffs of cloth moved round and round on the windowpanes. I walked outside, and the moment my foot hit the ground I thought I heard Grossbart call to the others, " 'Ten-*hut!*" Or maybe, when they all three jumped to attention, I imagined I heard the command.

Grossbart stepped forward. "Thank you, sir," he said.

" 'Sergeant,' Grossbart," I reminded him. "You call officers 'sir.' I'm not an officer. You've been in the Army three weeks—you know that."

He turned his palms out at his sides to indicate that, in truth, he and I lived beyond convention. "Thank you, anyway," he said.

"Yes," a tall boy behind him said. "Thanks a lot."

And the third boy whispered, "Thank you," but his mouth barely fluttered, so that he did not alter by more than a lip's movement his posture of attention.

"For what?" I asked.

Grossbart snorted happily. "For the announcement. The Corporal's announcement. It helped. It made it—"

"Fancier." The tall boy finished Grossbart's sentence.

Grossbart smiled. "He means formal, sir. Public," he said to me. "Now it won't seem as though we're just taking off—goldbricking because the work has begun."

"It was by order of Captain Barrett," I said.

"Aaah, but you pull a little weight," Grossbart said. "So we thank you." Then he turned to his companions. "Sergeant Marx, I want you to meet Larry Fishbein."

The tall boy stepped forward and extended his hand. I shook it. "You from New York?" he asked.

"Yes."

"Me, too." He had a cadaverous face that collapsed inward from his cheekbone to his jaw, and when he smiled—as he did at the news of our communal attachment—revealed a mouthful of bad teeth. He was blinking his eyes a good deal, as though he were fighting back tears. "What borough?" he asked.

I turned to Grossbart. "It's five after seven. What time are services?"

"Shul," he said, smiling, "is in ten minutes. I want you to meet Mickey Halpern. This is Nathan Marx, our sergeant."

The third boy hopped forward. "Private Michael Halpern." He saluted.

"Salute officers, Halpern," I said. The boy dropped his hand, and, on its way down, in his nervousness, checked to see if his shirt pockets were buttoned.

"Shall I march them over, sir?" Grossbart asked. "Or are you coming along?"

From behind Grossbart, Fishbein piped up. "Afterward, they're having refreshments. A ladies' auxiliary from St. Louis, the rabbi told us last week."

"The chaplain," Halpern whispered.

"You're welcome to come along," Grossbart said.

To avoid his plea, I looked away, and saw, in the windows of the barracks, a cloud of faces staring out at the four of us. "Hurry along, Grossbart," I said.

"O.K., then," he said. He turned to the others. "Double time, *march!*"

They started off, but ten feet away Grossbart spun around and, running backward, called to me, "Good *shabbus,** sir!" And then the three of them were swallowed into the alien Missouri dusk.

Even after they had disappeared over the parade ground, whose green was now a deep blue, I could hear Grossbart singing the doubletime cadence, and as it grew dimmer and dimmer, it suddenly touched a deep memory—as did the slant of the light—and I was remembering the shrill sounds of a Bronx playground where, years ago, beside the Grand Concourse, I played on long spring evenings such as this. It was a pleasant memory for a young man so far from peace and home, and it brought so many recollections with it that I began to grow exceedingly tender about myself. In fact, I indulged myself in a reverie so strong that I felt as though a hand were reaching down inside me. It had to reach so very far to touch me! It had to reach past those days in the forests of Belgium, and past the dying I'd refused to weep over; past the nights in German farmhouses whose books we'd burned to warm us; past endless stretches when I had shut off all softness I might feel for my fellows, and had managed even to deny myself the posture of a conqueror—the swagger that I, as a Jew, might well have worn as my boots whacked against the rubble of Wesel, Münster, and Braunschweig.

But now one night noise, one rumor of home and time past, and memory plunged down through all I had anesthetized, and came to what I suddenly remembered was myself. So it was not altogether curious that, in search of more of me, I found myself following Grossbart's tracks to Chapel No. 3, where the Jewish services were being held.

* *shabbus.* sabbath

I took a seat in the last row, which was empty. Two rows in front of me sat Grossbart, Fishbein, and Halpern, holding little white Dixie cups. Each row of seats was raised higher than the one in front of it, and I could see clearly what was going on. Fishbein was pouring the contents of his cup into Grossbart's, and Grossbart looked mirthful as the liquid made a purple arc between Fishbein's hand and his. In the glaring yellow light, I saw the chaplain standing on the platform at the front; he was chanting the first line of the responsive reading. Grossbart's prayer book remained closed on his lap; he was swishing the cup around. Only Halpern responded to the chant by praying. The fingers of his right hand were spread wide across the cover of his open book. His cap was pulled down low onto his brow, which made it round, like a *yarmulke.** From time to time, Grossbart wet his lips at the cup's edge; Fishbein, his long yellow face a dying light bulb, looked from here to there, craning forward to catch sight of the faces down the row, then of those in front of him, then behind. He saw me, and his eyelids beat a tattoo. His elbow slid into Grossbart's side, his neck inclined toward his friend, he whispered something, and then, when the congregation next responded to the chant, Grossbart's voice was among the others. Fishbein looked into his book now, too; his lips, however, didn't move.

Finally, it was time to drink the wine. The chaplain smiled down at them as Grossbart swigged his in one long gulp, Halpern sipped, meditating, and Fishbein faked devotion with an empty cup. "As I look down amongst the congregation"—the chaplain grinned at the word—"this night, I see many new faces, and I want to welcome you to Friday-night services here at Camp Crowder. I am Major Leo Ben Ezra, your chaplain." Though an American, the chaplain spoke deliberately—syllable by syllable, almost—as though to communicate, above all, with the lip readers in his audience. "I have only a few words to say before we adjourn to the refreshment room, where the kind ladies of the Temple Sinai, St. Louis, Missouri, have a nice setting for you."

Applause and whistling broke out. After another momentary grin, the chaplain raised his hands, palms out, his eyes flicking upward a moment, as if to remind the troops where they were and Who Else might be in attendance. In the sudden silence that followed, I thought I heard Grossbart cackle, "Let the goyim clean the floors!" Were those the words? I wasn't sure, but Fishbein, grinning, nudged Halpern. Halpern looked dumbly at him, then went back to his prayer book, which had been occupying him all through the rabbi's talk. One hand tugged at the black kinky hair that stuck out under his cap. His lips moved.

The rabbi continued. "It is about the food that I want to speak to you for a moment. I know, I know, I know," he intoned, wearily, "how in the mouths of most of you the *trafe*** food tastes like ashes. I know how you gag, some of

* *yarmulke.* skullcap
** *trafe.* opposite of *kosher;* unfit to eat

you, and how your parents suffer to think of their children eating foods unclean and offensive to the palate. What can I tell you? I can only say, close your eyes and swallow as best you can. Eat what you must to live, and throw away the rest. I wish I could help more. For those of you who find this impossible, may I ask that you try and try, but then come to see me in private. If your revulsion is so great, we will have to seek aid from those higher up."

A round of chatter rose and subsided. Then everyone sang "Ain Kelohainu;" after all those years, I discovered, I still knew the words. Then, suddenly, the service over, Grossbart was upon me. "Higher up? He means the General?"

"Hey, Shelly," Fishbein said, "he means God." He smacked his face and looked at Halpern. "How high can you go!"

"Sh-h-h!" Grossbart said. "What do you think, Sergeant?"

"I don't know," I said. "You better ask the chaplain."

"I'm going to. I'm making an appointment to see him in private. So is Mickey."

Halpern shook his head. "No, no, Sheldon—"

"You have rights, Mickey," Grossbart said. "They can't push us around."

"It's O.K.," said Halpern. "It bothers my mother, not me."

Grossbart looked at me. "Yesterday he threw up. From the hash. It was all ham and God knows what else."

"I have a cold—that was why," Halpern said. He pushed his *yarmulke* back into a cap.

"What about you, Fishbein?" I asked. "You kosher, too?"

He flushed. "A little. But I'll let it ride. I have a very strong stomach, and I don't eat a lot anyway." I continued to look at him, and he held up his wrist to reinforce what he'd just said; his watch strap was tightened to the last hole, and he pointed that out to me.

"But services are important to you?" I asked him.

He looked at Grossbart. "Sure, sir."

" 'Sergeant.' "

"Not so much at home," said Grossbart, stepping between us, "but away from home it gives one a sense of his Jewishness."

"We have to stick together," Fishbein said.

I started to walk toward the door; Halpern stepped back to make way for me.

"That's what happened in Germany," Grossbart was saying, loud enough for me to hear. "They didn't stick together. They let themselves get pushed around."

I turned. "Look, Grossbart. This is the Army, no summer camp."

He smiled. "So?"

Halpern tried to sneak off, but Grossbart held his arm.

"Grossbart, how old are you?" I asked.

"Nineteen."

"And you?" I said to Fishbein.

"The same. The same month, even."

"And what about him?" I pointed to Halpern, who had by now made it safely to the door.

"Eighteen," Grossbart whispered. "But like he can't tie his shoes or brush his teeth himself. I feel sorry for him."

"I feel sorry for all of us, Grossbart," I said, "but just act like a man. Just don't overdo it."

"Overdo what, sir?"

"The 'sir' business, for one thing. Don't overdo that," I said.

I left him standing there. I passed by Halpern, but he did not look at me. Then I was outside, but, behind, I heard Grossbart call, "Hey, Mickey, my *leben,** come on back. Refreshments!"

"*Leben!*" My grandmother's word for me!

One morning a week later, while I was working at my desk, Captain Barrett shouted for me to come into his office. When I entered, he had his helmet liner squashed down so far on his head that I couldn't even see his eyes. He was on the phone, and when he spoke to me, he cupped one hand over the mouthpiece. "Who the hell is Grossbart?"

"Third platoon, Captain," I said. "A trainee."

"What's all this stink about food? His mother called a goddam congressman about the food." He uncovered his mouthpiece and slid his helmet up until I could see his bottom eyelashes. "Yes, sir," he said into the phone. "Ycs, sir. I'm still here, sir. I'm asking Marx, here, right now—"

He covered the mouthpiece again and turned his head back toward me. "Lightfoot Harry's on the phone," he said, between his teeth. "This congressman calls General Lymans, who calls Colonel Sousa, who calls the Major, who calls me. They're just dying to stick this thing on me. Whatsa matter?" He shook the phone at me. "I don't feed the troops? What the hell is this?"

"Sir, Grossbart is strange—" Barrett greeted that with a mockingly indulgent smile. I altered my approach. "Captain, he's a very orthodox Jew, and so he's only allowed to eat certain foods."

"He throws up, the congressman said. Every time he eats something, his mother says, he throws up!"

"He's accustomed to observing the dietary laws, Captain."

"So why's his old lady have to call the White House?"

"Jewish parents, sir—they're apt to be more protective than you expect. I mean, Jews have a very close family life. A boy goes away from home, sometimes the mother is liable to get very upset. Probably the boy mentioned something in a letter, and his mother misinterpreted."

* *leben.* darling

"I'd like to punch him one right in the mouth," the Captain said. "There's a goddam war on, and he wants a silver platter!"

"I don't think the boy's to blame, sir. I'm sure we can straighten it out by just asking him. Jewish parents worry—"

"*All* parents worry, for Christ's sake. But they don't get on their high horse and start pulling strings—"

I interrupted, my voice higher, tighter than before. "The home life, Captain, is very important—but you're right, it may sometimes get out of hand. It's a very wonderful thing, Captain, but because it's so close, this kind of thing . . ."

He didn't listen any longer to my attempt to present both myself and Lightfoot Harry with an explanation for the letter. He turned back to the phone. "Sir?" he said. "Sir—Marx, here, tells me Jews have a tendency to be pushy. He says he thinks we can settle it right here in the company. . . . Yes, sir. . . . I *will* call back, sir, soon as I can." He hung up. "Where are the men, Sergeant?"

"On the range."

With a whack on the top of his helmet, he crushed it down over his eyes again, and charged out of his chair. "We're going for a ride," he said.

The Captain drove, and I sat beside him. It was a hot spring day, and under my newly starched fatigues I felt as though my armpits were melting down onto my sides and chest. The roads were dry, and by the time we reached the firing range, my teeth felt gritty with dust, though my mouth had been shut the whole trip. The Captain slammed the brakes on and told me to get the hell out and find Grossbart.

I found him on his belly, firing wildly at the five-hundred-feet target. Waiting their turns behind him were Halpern and Fishbein. Fishbein, wearing a pair of rimless G.I. glasses I hadn't seen on him before, had the appearance of an old peddler who would gladly have sold you his rifle and the cartridges that were slung all over him. I stood back by the ammo boxes, waiting for Grossbart to finish spraying the distant targets. Fishbein straggled back to stand near me.

"Hello, Sergeant Marx," he said.

"How are you?" I mumbled.

"Fine, thank you. Sheldon's really a good shot."

"I didn't notice."

"I'm not so good, but I think I'm getting the hang of it now. Sergeant, I don't mean to, you know, ask what I shouldn't—" The boy stopped. He was trying to speak intimately, but the noise of the shooting forced him to shout at me.

"What is it?" I asked. Down the range, I saw Captain Barrett standing up in the jeep, scanning the line for me and Grossbart.

"My parents keep asking and asking where we're going," Fishbein said. "Everybody says the Pacific. I don't care, but my parents—if I could relieve their minds, I think I could concentrate more on my shooting."

"I don't know where, Fishbein. Try to concentrate anyway."

"Sheldon says you might be able to find out."

"I don't know a thing, Fishbein. You just take it easy, and don't let Sheldon—"

"*I'm* taking it easy, Sergeant. It's at home—"

Grossbart had finished on the line, and was dusting his fatigues with one hand. I called to him. "Grossbart, the Captain wants to see you."

He came toward us. His eyes blazed and twinkled. "Hi!"

"Don't point that goddamn rifle!" I said.

"I wouldn't shoot you, Sarge." He gave me a smile as wide as a pumpkin, and turned the barrel aside.

"Damn you, Grossbart, this is no joke! Follow me."

I walked ahead of him, and had the awful suspicion that, behind me, Grossbart was *marching,* his rifle on his shoulder, as though he were a one-man detachment. At the jeep, he gave the Captain a rifle salute. "Private Sheldon Grossbart, sir."

"At ease, Grossman." The Captain sat down, slid over into the empty seat, and, crooking a finger, invited Grossbart closer.

"Bart, sir. Sheldon Gross*bart.* It's a common error." Grossbart nodded at me; I understood, he indicated. I looked away just as the mess truck pulled up to the range, disgorging a half-dozen K.P.'s with rolled-up sleeves. The mess sergeant screamed at them while they set up the chowline equipment.

"Grossbart, your mama wrote some congressman that we don't feed you right. Do you know that?" the Captain said.

"It was my father, sir. He wrote to Representative Franconi that my religion forbids me to eat certain foods."

"What religion is that, Grossbart?"

"Jewish."

" 'Jewish, *sir,*' " I said to Grossbart.

"Excuse me, sir. Jewish, sir."

"What have you been living on?" the Captain asked. "You've been in the Army a month already. You don't look to me like you're falling to pieces."

"I eat because I have to, sir. But Sergeant Marx will testify to the fact that I don't eat one mouthful more than I need in order to survive."

"Is that so, Marx?" Barrett asked.

"I've never seen Grossbart eat, sir," I said.

"But you heard the rabbi," Grossbart said. "He told us what to do, and I listened."

The captain looked at me. "Well, Marx?"

"I still don't know what he eats and doesn't eat, sir."

Grossbart raised his arms to plead with me, and it looked for a moment as though he were going to hand me his weapon to hold. "But, Sergeant—"

"Look, Grossbart, just answer the Captain's questions," I said sharply.

Barrett smiled at me, and I resented it. "All right, Grossbart," he said. "What is it you want? The little piece of paper? You want out?"

"No, sir. Only to be allowed to live as a Jew. And for the others, too."

"What others?"

"Fishbein, sir, and Halpern."

"They don't like the way we serve, either?"

"Halpern throws up, sir. I've seen it."

"I thought *you* throw up."

"Just once, sir. I didn't know the sausage was sausage."

"We'll give menus, Grossbart. We'll show training films about the food, so you can identify when we're trying to poison you."

Grossbart did not answer. The men had been organized into two long chow lines. At the tail end of one, I spotted Fishbein—or, rather, his glasses spotted me. They winked sunlight back at me. Halpern stood next to him, patting the inside of his collar with a khaki handkerchief. They moved with the line as it began to edge up toward the food. The mess sergeant was still screaming at the K.P.s. For a moment, I was actually terrified by the thought that somehow the mess sergeant was going to become involved in Grossbart's problem.

"Marx," the Captain said, "you're a Jewish fella—am I right?"

I played straight man. "Yes, sir."

"How long you been in the Army? Tell this boy."

"Three years and two months."

"A year in combat, Grossbart. Twelve goddamn months in combat all through Europe. I admire this man." The Captain snapped a wrist against my chest. "Do you hear him peeping about the food? Do you? I want an answer, Grossbart. Yes or no."

"No, sir."

"And why not? He's a Jewish fella."

"Some things are more important to some Jews than other things to other Jews."

Barrett blew up. "Look, Grossbart. Marx, here, is a good man—a goddam hero. When you were in high school, Sergeant Marx was killing Germans. Who does more for the Jews—you, by throwing up over a lousy piece of sausage, a piece of first-cut meat, or Marx, by killing those Nazi bastards? If I was a Jew, Grossbart, I'd kiss this man's feet. He's a goddamn hero, and *he* eats what we give him. Why, do you have to cause trouble is what I want to know! What is it you're buckin' for—a discharge?"

"No, sir."

"I'm talking to a wall! Sergeant, get him out of my way." Barrett swung himself back into the driver's seat. "I'm going to see the chaplain." The engine roared, the jeep spun around in a whirl of dust, and the Captain was headed back to camp.

For a moment, Grossbart and I stood side by side, watching the jeep. Then he looked at me and said, "I don't want to start trouble. That's the first thing they toss up to us."

When he spoke, I saw that his teeth were white and straight, and the sight of them suddenly made me understand that Grossbart actually did have parents—that once upon a time someone had taken little Sheldon to the dentist. He was their son. Despite all the talk about his parents, it was hard to believe in Grossbart as a child, an heir—as related by blood to anyone, mother, father, or, above all, to me. This realization led me to another.

"What does your father do, Grossbart?" I asked as we started to walk back toward the chow line.

"He's a tailor."

"An American?"

"Now, yes. A son in the Army," he said, jokingly.

"And your mother?" I asked.

He winked. "A *ballabusta.** She practically sleeps with a dust-cloth in her hand."

"She's also an immigrant?"

"All she talks is Yiddish, still."

"And your father, too?"

"A little English. 'Clean,' 'Press,' 'Take the pants in.' That's the extent of it. But they're good to me."

"Then, Grossbart—" I reached out and stopped him. He turned toward me, and when our eyes met, his seemed to jump back, to shiver in their sockets. "Grossbart—you were the one who wrote that letter, weren't you?"

It took only a second or two for his eyes to flash happy again. "Yes." He walked on, and I kept pace. "It's what my father *would* have written if he had known how. It was his name, though. *He* signed it. He even mailed it. I sent it home. For the New York postmark."

I was astonished, and he saw it. With complete seriousness, he thrust his right arm in front of me. "Blood is blood, Sergeant," he said, pinching the blue vein in his wrist.

"What the hell *are* you trying to do, Grossbart?" I asked. "I've seen you eat. Do you know that? I told the Captain I don't know what you eat, but I've seen you eat like a hound at chow."

"We work hard, Sergeant. We're in training. For a furnace to work, you've got to feed it coal."

"Why did you say in the letter that you threw up all the time?"

"I was really talking about Mickey there. I was talking *for* him. He would never write, Sergeant, though I pleaded with him. He'll waste away to nothing

* *ballabusta.* good housekeeper

if I don't help. Sergeant, I used my name—my father's name—but it's Mickey, and Fishbein, too, I'm watching out for."

"You're a regular Messiah, aren't you?"

We were at the chow line now.

"That's a good one, Sergeant," he said, smiling. "But who knows? Who can tell? Maybe you're the Messiah—a little bit. What Mickey says is the Messiah is a collective idea. He went to Yeshiva,* Mickey, for a while. He says *together* we're the Messiah. Me a little bit, you a little bit. You should hear that kid talk, Sergeant, when he gets going."

"Me a little bit, you a little bit," I said. "You'd like to believe that, wouldn't you, Grossbart? That would make everything so clean for you."

"It doesn't seem too bad a thing to believe, Sergeant. It only means we should all *give* a little, is all."

I walked off to eat my rations with the other noncoms.

Two days later, a letter addressed to Captain Barrett passed over my desk. It had come through the chain of command—from the office of Congressman Franconi, where it had been received, to General Lyman, to Colonel Sousa, to Major Lamont, now to Captain Barrett. I read it over twice. It was dated May 14th, the day Barrett had spoken with Grossbart on the rifle range.

DEAR CONGRESSMAN:

First let me thank you for your interest in behalf of my son, Private Sheldon Grossbart. Fortunately, I was able to speak with Sheldon on the phone the other night, and I think I've been able to solve our problem. He is, as I mentioned in my last letter, a very religious boy, and it was only with the greatest difficulty that I could persuade him that the religious thing to do—what God Himself would want Sheldon to do—would be to suffer the pangs of religious remorse for the good of his country and all mankind. It took some doing, Congressman, but finally he saw the light. In fact, what he said (and I wrote down the words on a scratch pad so as never to forget), what he said was "I guess you're right, Dad. So many millions of my fellow-Jews gave up their lives to the enemy, the least I can do is live for a while minus a bit of my heritage so as to help end this struggle and regain for all the children of God dignity and humanity." That, Congressman, would make any father proud.

By the way, Sheldon wanted me to know—and pass on to you—the name of a soldier who helped him reach this decision: SERGEANT NATHAN MARX. Sergeant Marx is a combat veteran who is Sheldon's first sergeant. This man has helped Sheldon over some of the first hurdles he's had to face in the Army, and is in part responsible for Sheldon's changing his mind about the dietary laws. I know Sheldon would appreciate any recognition Marx could receive.

Thank you and good luck. I look forward to seeing your name on the next election ballot.

Respectfully,
SAMUEL E. GROSSBART

* *Yeshiva.* Jewish parochial school

Attached to the Grossbart communiqué was another, addressed to General Marshall Lyman, the post commander, and signed by Representative Charles E. Franconi of the House of Representatives. The communiqué informed General Lyman that Sergeant Nathan Marx was a credit to the U.S. Army and the Jewish people.

What was Grossbart's motive in recanting? Did he feel he'd gone too far? Was the letter a strategic retreat—a crafty attempt to strengthen what he considered our alliance? Or had he actually changed his mind, via an imaginary dialogue between Grossbart *père* and Grossbart *fils?* I was puzzled, but only for a few days—that is, only until I realized that, whatever his reasons, he had actually decided to disappear from my life; he was going to allow himself to become just another trainee. I saw him at inspection, but he never winked; at chow formations, but he never flashed me a sign. On Sundays, with the other trainees, he would sit around watching the noncoms' softball team, for which I pitched, but not once did he speak an unnecessary word to me. Fishbein and Halpern retreated, too—at Grossbart's command, I was sure. Apparently he had seen that wisdom lay in turning back before he plunged over into the ugliness of privilege undeserved. Our separation allowed me to forgive him our past encounters, and, finally, to admire him for his good sense.

Meanwhile, free of Grossbart, I grew used to my job and my administrative tasks. I stepped on a scale one day, and discovered I had truly become a noncombatant; I had gained seven pounds. I found patience to get past the first three pages of a book. I thought about the future more and more, and wrote letters to girls I'd known before the war. I even got a few answers. I sent away to Columbia for a Law School catalogue. I continued to follow the war in the Pacific, but it was not my war. I thought I could see the end, and sometimes, at night, I dreamed that I was walking on the streets of Manhattan—Broadway, Third Avenue, 116th Street, where I had lived the three years I attended Columbia. I curled myself around these dreams and I began to be happy.

And then, one Saturday, when everybody was away and I was alone in the orderly room reading a month-old copy of the *Sporting News,* Grossbart reappeared.

"You a baseball fan, Sergeant?"

I looked up. "How are you?"

"Fine," Grossbart said. "They're making a soldier out of me."

"How are Fishbein and Halpern?"

"Coming along," he said. "We've got no training this afternoon. They're at the movies."

"How come you're not with them?"

"I wanted to come over and say hello."

He smiled—a shy regular-guy smile, as though he and I well knew that our friendship drew its sustenance from unexpected visits, remembered birthdays, and borrowed lawnmowers. At first it offended me, and then the feeling was swallowed by the general uneasiness I felt at the thought that everyone on the post was locked away in a dark movie theatre and I was here alone with Grossbart. I folded up my paper.

"Sergeant," he said, "I'd like to ask a favor. It is a favor, and I'm making no bones about it."

He stopped, allowing me to refuse him a hearing—which, of course, forced me into a courtesy I did not intend. "Go ahead."

"Well, actually it's two favors." I said nothing.

"The first one's about these rumors. Everybody says we're going to the Pacific."

"As I told your friend Fishbein, I don't know," I said. "You'll just have to wait to find out. Like everybody else."

"You think there's a chance of any of us going East?"

"Germany?" I said. "Maybe."

"I meant New York."

"I don't think so, Grossbart. Offhand."

"Thanks for the information, Sergeant," he said.

"It's not information, Grossbart. Just what I surmise."

"It certainly would be good to be near home. My parents—you know." He took a step toward the door and then turned back. "Oh, the other thing. May I ask the other?"

"What is it?"

"The other thing is—I've got relatives in St. Louis, and they say they'll give me a whole Passover dinner if I can get down there. God, Sergeant, that'd mean an awful lot to me."

I stood up. "No passes during basic, Grossbart."

"But we're off from now till Monday morning, Sergeant. I could leave the post and no one would even know."

"I'd know. You'd know."

"But that's all. Just the two of us. Last night, I called my aunt, and you should have heard her. 'Come—come,' she said. 'I got gefilte fish, *chrain**—the works!' Just a day, Sergeant. I'd take the blame if anything happened."

"The Captain isn't here to sign a pass."

"You could sign."

"Look, Grossbart—"

"Sergeant, for two months, practically, I've been eating *trafe* till I want to die."

"I thought you'd made up your mind to live with it. To be minus a little bit of heritage."

He pointed a finger at me. "You!" he said. "That wasn't for you to read."

"I read it. So what?"

"That letter was addressed to a congressman."

* *chrain.* horseradish

"Grossbart, don't feed me any baloney. You *wanted* me to read it."

"Why are you persecuting me, Sergeant?"

"Are you kidding!"

"I've run into this before," he said, "but never from my own!"

"Get out of here, Grossbart! Get the hell out of my sight!"

He did not move. "Ashamed, that's what you are," he said. "So you take it out on the rest of us. They say Hitler himself was half a Jew. Hearing you, I wouldn't doubt it."

"What are you trying to do with me, Grossbart?" I asked him. "What are you after? You want me to give you special privileges, to change the food, to find out about your orders, to give you weekend passes."

"You even talk like a goy!" Grossbart shook his fist. "Is this just a weekend pass I'm asking for? Is a Seder sacred, or not?"

Seder! It suddenly occurred to me that Passover had been celebrated weeks before. I said so.

"That's right," he replied. "Who says no? A month ago—and I was in the field eating hash! And now all I ask is a simple favor. A Jewish boy I thought would understand. My aunt's willing to go out of her way—to make a Seder a month later. . . ." He turned to go, mumbling.

"Come back here!" I called. He stopped and looked at me. "Grossbart, why can't you be like the rest? Why do you have to stick out like a sore thumb?"

"Because I'm a Jew, Sergeant. I *am* different. Better, maybe not. But different."

"This is a war, Grossbart. For the time being *be* the same."

"I refuse."

"What?"

"I refuse. I can't stop being me, that's all there is to it." Tears came to his eyes. "It's a hard thing to be a Jew. But now I understand what Mickey says—it's a harder thing to stay one." He raised a hand sadly toward me. "Look at *you.*"

"Stop crying!"

"Stop this, stop that, stop the other thing! *You* stop, Sergeant. Stop closing your heart to your own!" And, wiping his face with his sleeve, he ran out the door. "The least we can do for one another—the least . . ."

An hour later, looking out of the window, I saw Grossbart headed across the field. He wore a pair of starched khakis and carried a little leather ditty bag. I went out into the heat of the day. It was quiet; not a soul was in sight except, over by the mess hall, four K.P.s sitting around a pan, sloped forward from their waists, gabbing and peeling potatoes in the sun.

"Grossbart!" I called.

He looked toward me and continued walking.

"Grossbart, get over here!"

He turned and came across the field. Finally, he stood before me.

"Where are you going?" I asked.
"St. Louis. I don't care."
"You'll get caught without a pass."
"So I'll get caught without a pass."
"You'll go to the stockade."
"I'm *in* the stockade." He made an about-face and headed off.
I let him go only a step or two. "Come back here," I said, and he followed me into the office, where I typed out a pass and signed the Captain's name, and my own initials after it.
He took the pass and then, a moment later, reached out and grabbed my hand. "Sergeant, you don't know how much this means to me."
"O.K.," I said. "Don't get in any trouble."
"I wish I could show you how much this means to me."
"Don't do me any favors. Don't write any more congressmen for citations."
He smiled. "You're right, I won't. But let me do something."
"Bring me a piece of that gefilte fish. Just get out of here."
"I will!" he said. "With a slice of carrot and a little horseradish. I won't forget."
"All right. Just show your pass at the gate. And don't tell *anybody*."
"I won't. It's a month late, but a good Yom Tov to you."
"Good Yom Tov, Grossbart," I said.
"You're a good Jew, Sergeant. You like to think you have a hard heart, but underneath you're a fine, decent man. I mean that."
Those last three words touched me more than any words from Grossbart's mouth had the right to. "All right, Grossbart," I said. "Now call me 'sir,' and get the hell out of here."
He ran out the door and was gone. I felt very pleased with myself; it was a great relief to stop fighting Grossbart, and it had cost me nothing. Barrett would never find out, and if he did, I could manage to invent some excuse. For a while, I sat at my desk comfortable in my decision. Then the screen door flew back and Grossbart burst in again. "Sergeant!" he said. Behind him I saw Fishbein and Halpern, both in starched khakis, both carrying ditty bags like Grossbart's.
"Sergeant, I caught Mickey and Larry coming out of the movies. I almost missed them."
"Grossbart—did I say tell no one?" I said.
"But my aunt said I could bring friends. That I should, in fact."
"*I'm* the Sergeant, Grossbart—not your aunt!"
Grossbart looked at me in disbelief. He pulled Halpern up by his sleeve. "Mickey, tell the Sergeant what this would mean to you."
Halpern looked at me and, shrugging, said, "A lot."
Fishbein stepped forward without prompting. "This would mean a great deal to me and my parents, Sergeant Marx."

"No!" I shouted.

Grossbart was shaking his head. "Sergeant, I could see you denying me, but how you can deny Mickey, a Yeshiva boy—that's beyond me."

"I'm not denying Mickey anything," I said. "You just pushed a little too hard, Grossbart. *You* denied him."

"I'll give him my pass, then," Grossbart said. "I'll give him my aunt's address and a little note. At least let him go."

In a second, he had crammed the pass into Halpern's pants pocket. Halpern looked at me, and so did Fishbein. Grossbart was at the door, pushing it open. "Mickey, bring me a piece of gefilte fish, at least," he said, and then he was outside again.

The three of us looked at one another, and then I said, "Halpern, hand that pass over."

He took it from his pocket and gave it to me. Fishbein had now moved to the doorway, where he lingered. He stood there for a moment with his mouth slightly open, and then he pointed to himself. "And me?" he asked.

His utter ridiculousness exhausted me. I slumped down in my seat and felt pulses knocking at the back of my eyes. "Fishbein," I said, "you understand I'm not trying to deny you anything, don't you? If it was my Army, I'd serve gefilte fish in the mess hall. I'd sell *kugel** in the PX, honest to God."

Halpern smiled.

"You understand, don't you, Halpern?"

"Yes, Sergeant."

"And you, Fishbein? I don't want enemies. I'm just like you—I want to serve my time and go home. I miss the same things you miss."

"Then, Sergeant," Fishbein said, "why don't you come, too?"

"Where?"

"To St. Louis. To Shelly's aunt. We'll have a regular Seder. Play hide-the-matzo." He gave me a broad, black-toothed smile.

I saw Grossbart again, on the other side of the screen.

"Pst!" He waved a piece of paper. "Mickey, here's the address. Tell her I couldn't get away."

Halpern did not move. He looked at me, and I saw the shrug moving up his arms into his shoulders again. I took the cover off the typewriter and made out passes for him and Fishbein. "Go," I said. "The three of you."

I thought Halpern was going to kiss my hand.

That afternoon, in a bar in Joplin, I drank beer and listened with half an ear to the Cardinal game. I tried to look squarely at what I'd become involved in, and began to wonder if perhaps the struggle with Grossbart wasn't as much my fault as his. What was I that I had to *muster* generous feelings? Who

* *kugel.* pudding

was I to have been feeling so grudging, so tight-hearted? After all, I wasn't being asked to move the world. Had I a right, then, or a reason, to clamp down on Grossbart, when that meant clamping down on Halpern, too? And Fishbein—that ugly, agreeable soul? Out of the many recollections of my childhood that had tumbled over me these past few days, I heard my grandmother's voice: "What are you making a *tsimmes?* * " It was what she would ask my mother when, say, I had cut myself while doing something I shouldn't have done, and her daughter was busy bawling me out. I needed a hug and a kiss, and my mother would moralize. But my grandmother knew—mercy overrides justice. I should have known it, too. Who was Nathan Marx to be such a penny pincher with kindness? Surely, I thought, the Messiah himself—if He should ever come—won't niggle over nickels and dimes. God willing, he'll hug and kiss.

The next day, while I was playing softball over on the parade ground, I decided to ask Bob Wright, who was noncom in charge of Classification and Assignment, where he thought our trainees would be sent when their cycle ended, in two weeks. I asked casually, between innings, and he said, "They're pushing them all into the Pacific. Shulman cut the orders on your boys the other day."

The news shocked me, as though I were the father of Halpern, Fishbein, and Grossbart.

That night, I was just sliding into sleep when someone tapped on my door. "Who is it?" I asked.

"Sheldon."

He opened the door and came in. For a moment, I felt his presence without being able to see him. "How was it?" I asked.

He popped into sight in the near-darkness before me. "Great, Sergeant." Then he was sitting on the edge of the bed. I sat up.

"How about you?" he asked. "Have a nice weekend?"

"Yes."

"The others went to sleep." He took a deep, paternal breath. We sat silent for a while, and a homey feeling invaded my ugly little cubicle; the door was locked, the cat was out, the children were safely in bed.

"Sergeant, can I tell you something? Personal?"

I did not answer, and he seemed to know why. "Not about me. About Mickey. Sergeant, I never felt for anybody like I feel for him. Last night I heard Mickey in the bed next to me. He was crying so, it could have broken your heart. Real sobs."

"I'm sorry to hear that."

"I had to talk to him to stop him. He held my hand, Sergeant—he wouldn't let it go. He was almost hysterical. He kept saying if he only knew where we

* *tsimmes.* a dish made with carrots, involving complicated preparation; hence "to make a *tsimmes*" means to make a fuss

were going. Even if he knew it *was* the Pacific, that would be better than nothing. Just to know."

Long ago, someone had taught Grossbart the sad rule that only lies can get the truth. Not that I couldn't believe in the fact of Halpern's crying: his eyes *always* seemed red-rimmed. But, fact or not, it became a lie when Grossbart uttered it. He was entirely strategic. But then—it came with the force of indictment—so was I! There are strategies of aggression, but there are strategies of retreat as well. And so, recognizing that I myself had not been without craft and guile, I told him what I knew. "It is the Pacific."

He let out a small gasp, which was not a lie. "I'll tell him. I wish it was otherwise."

"So do I."

He jumped on my words. "You mean you think you could do something? A change, maybe?"

"No, I couldn't do a thing."

"Don't you know anybody over at C. and A.?"

"Grossbart, there's nothing I can do," I said. "If your orders are for the Pacific, then it's the Pacific."

"But Mickey—"

"Mickey, you, me—everybody, Grossbart. There's nothing to be done. Maybe the war'll end before you go. Pray for a miracle."

"But—"

"Good night, Grossbart." I settled back, and was relieved to feel the springs unbend as Grossbart rose to leave. I could see him clearly now; his jaw had dropped, and he looked like a dazed prize-fighter. I noticed for the first time a little paper bag in his hand.

"Grossbart," I smiled. "My gift?"

"Oh, yes, Sergeant. Here—from all of us." He handed me the bag. "It's egg roll."

"Egg roll?" I accepted the bag and felt a damp grease spot on the bottom. I opened it, sure that Grossbart was joking.

"We thought you'd probably like it. You know—Chinese egg roll. We thought you'd probably have a taste for—"

"Your aunt served egg roll?"

"She wasn't home."

"Grossbart, she invited you. You told me she invited you and your friends."

"I know," he said. "I just reread the letter. *Next* week."

I got out of bed and walked to the window. "Grossbart," I said. But I was not calling to him.

"What?"

"What are you, Grossbart? Honest to God, what are you?"

I think it was the first time I'd asked him a question for which he didn't have an immediate answer.

"How can you do this to people?" I went on.

"Sergeant, the day away did us all a world of good. Fishbein, you should see him, he *loves* Chinese food."

"But the Seder," I said.

"We took second best, Sergeant."

Rage came charging at me. I didn't sidestep. "Grossbart, you're a liar!" I said. "You're a schemer and a crook. You've got no respect for anything. Nothing at all. Not for me, for the truth—not even for poor Halpern! You use us all—"

"Sergeant, Sergeant, I feel for Mickey. Honest to God, I do. I *love* Mickey. I try—"

"You try! You feel!" I lurched toward him and grabbed his shirt front. I shook him furiously. "Grossbart, get out! Get out and stay the hell away from me. Because if I see you, I'll make your life miserable. *You understand that?*"

"Yes."

I let him free, and when he walked from the room, I wanted to spit on the floor where he had stood. I couldn't stop the fury. It engulfed me, owned me, till it seemed I could only rid myself of it with tears or an act of violence. I snatched from the bed the bag Grossbart had given me and, with all my strength, threw it out the window. And the next morning, as the men policed the area around the barracks, I heard a great cry go up from one of the trainees, who had been anticipating only his morning handful of cigarette butts and candy wrappers. "Egg roll!" he shouted. "Holy Christ, Chinese goddam egg roll!"

A week later, when I read the orders that had come down from C. and A., I couldn't believe my eyes. Every single trainee was to be shipped to Camp Stoneman, California, and from there to the Pacific—every trainee but one. Private Sheldon Grossbart. He was to be sent to Fort Monmouth, New Jersey. I read the mimeographed sheet several times. Dee, Farrell, Fishbein, Fuselli, Fylypowicz, Glinicki, Gromke, Gucwa, Halpern, Hardy, Helebrandt, right down to Anton Zygadlo—all were to be headed West before the month was out. All except Grossbart. He had pulled a string, and I wasn't it. I lifted the phone and called C. and A.

The voice on the other end said smartly, "Corporal Shulman, sir."

"Let me speak to Sergeant Wright."

"Who is this calling, sir?"

"Sergeant Marx."

And, to my surprise, the voice said, *"Oh!"* Then, "Just a minute, Sergeant."

Shulman's *"Oh!"* stayed with me while I waited for Wright to come to the phone. Why *"Oh!"?* Who was Shulman? And then, so simply, I knew I'd discovered the string that Grossbart had pulled. In fact, I could hear Grossbart the day he'd discovered Shulman in the PX, or in the bowling alley, or maybe even at services. "Glad to meet you. Where you from? Bronx? Me, too. Do you know So-and-So? And So-and-So? Me, too! You work at C. and A.? Really? Hey, how's chances of getting East? Could you do something? Change something? Swindle, cheat, lie? We gotta help each other, you know. If the Jews in Germany . . ."

Bob Wright answered the phone. "How are you, Nate? How's the pitching arm?"

"Good. Bob, I wonder if you could do me a favor." I heard clearly my own words, and they so reminded me of Grossbart that I dropped more easily than I could have imagined into what I had planned. "This may sound crazy, Bob, but I got a kid here on orders to Monmouth who wants them changed. He had a brother killed in Europe, and he's hot to go to the Pacific. Says he'd feel like a coward if he wound up Stateside. I don't know, Bob—can anything be done? Put somebody else in the Monmouth slot?"

"Who?" he asked cagily.

"Anybody. First guy in the alphabet. I don't care. The kid just asked if something could be done."

"What's his name?"

"Grossbart, Sheldon."

Wright didn't answer.

"Yeah," I said. "He's a Jewish kid, so he thought I could help him out. You know."

"I guess I can do something," he finally said. "The Major hasn't been around here for weeks. Temporary duty to the golf course. I'll try, Nate, that's all I can say."

"I'd appreciate it, Bob. See you Sunday." And I hung up, perspiring.

The following day, the corrected orders appeared: Fishbein, Fuselli, Fylypowicz, Glinicki, Gromke, Grossbart, Gucwa, Halpern, Hardy . . . Lucky Private Harley Alton was to go to Fort Monmouth, New Jersey, where, for some reason or other, they wanted an enlisted man with infantry training.

After chow that night, I stopped back at the orderly room to straighten out the guard-duty roster. Grossbart was waiting for me. He spoke first.

"You son of a bitch!"

I sat down at my desk, and while he glared at me, I began to make the necessary alterations in the duty roster.

"What do you have against me?" he cried. "Against my family? Would it kill you for me to be near my father, God knows how many months he has left to him?"

"Why so?"

"His heart," Grossbart said. "He hasn't had enough troubles in a lifetime, you've got to add to them. I curse the day I ever met you, Marx! Shulman told me what happened over there. There's no limit to your anti-Semitism, is there? The damage you've done here isn't enough. You have to make a special phone call! You really want me dead!"

I made the last few notations in the duty roster and got up to leave. "Good night, Grossbart."

"You owe me an explanation!" He stood in my path.

"Sheldon, you're the one who owes explanations."

He scowled. "To *you?*"

"To me, I think so—yes. Mostly to Fishbein and Halpern."

"That's right, twist things around. I owe nobody nothing, I've done all I could do for them. Now I think I've got the right to watch out for myself."

"For each other we have to learn to watch out, Sheldon. You told me yourself."

"You call this watching out for me—what you did?"

"No. For all of us."

I pushed him aside and started for the door. I heard his furious breathing behind me, and it sounded like a steam rushing from an engine of terrible strength.

"You'll be all right," I said from the door. And, I thought, so would Fishbein and Halpern be all right, even in the Pacific, if only Grossbart continued to see—in the obsequiousness of the one, the soft spirituality of the other—some profit for himself.

I stood outside the orderly room, and I heard Grossbart weeping behind me. Over in the barracks, in the lighted windows, I could see the boys in their T shirts sitting on their bunks talking about their orders, as they'd been doing for the past two days. With a kind of quiet nervousness, they polished shoes, shined belt buckles, squared away underwear, trying as best they could to accept their fate. Behind me, Grossbart swallowed hard, accepting his. And then, resisting with all my will an impulse to turn and seek pardon for my vindictiveness, I accepted my own.

3

The Search for Love

Venturing Outward

A universal element in the search for love is the ability that love has to exert an obsessive power, for good or ill, over the human spirit. The tiniest details of these times in our lives often remain with us for the rest of our life. Often the course of our search for love influences profoundly the course of our life as a whole.

EUDORA WELTY (b. 1909)

The South is the setting for Eudora Welty's work, as it has been for the numerous American writers who were born in that region. Still a resident of Jackson, Mississippi, where she was born and raised, she communicates a strong sense of place, while exploring on several levels the feelings of her characters as shaped by their setting and their situations.

Eudora Welty's first book, A Curtain of Green *(1941), a collection of short stories, was acclaimed for its extraordinary ability to portray character. Her novel* Delta Wedding *(1954) was well received, and another novel,* The Ponder Heart *(1954), won her the Howells Medal (1955), awarded by the American Academy of Arts to "the most distinguished work of American fiction" of the preceding five years.*

"Livvie" concerns a simple young bride in an isolated home deep in the Mississippi backwoods to which her aged husband has brought her.

Livvie

SOLOMON carried Livvie twenty-one miles away from her home when he married her. He carried her away up on the Old Natchez Trace into the deep country to live in his house. She was sixteen—an only girl, then. Once people said he thought nobody would ever come along there. He told her himself that it had been a long time, and a day she did not know about, since that road was a traveled road with *people* coming and going. He was good to her, but he kept her in the house. She had not thought that she could not get back. Where she came from, people said an old man did not want anybody in the world to ever find his wife, for fear they would steal her back from him. Solomon asked her before he took her. "Would she be happy?"—very dignified, for he was a colored man that owned his land and had it written down in the courthouse; and she said, "Yes, sir," since he was an old man and she was young and just listened and answered. He asked her, if she was choosing winter, would she pine for spring, and she said, "No indeed." Whatever she said, always, was because he was an old man . . . while nine years went by. All the time, he got old, and he got so old he gave out. At last he slept the whole day in bed, and she was young still.

It was a nice house, inside and outside both. In the first place, it had three rooms. The front room was papered in holly paper, with green palmettos from the swamp spaced at careful intervals over the walls. There was fresh newspaper cut with fancy borders on the mantel-shelf, on which were propped photographs of old or very young men printed in faint yellow—Solomon's people.

Solomon had a houseful of furniture. There was a double settee, a tall scrolled rocker and an organ in the front room, all around a three-legged table with a pink marble top, on which was set a lamp with three gold feet, besides a jelly glass with pretty hen feathers in it. Behind the front room, the other room had the bright iron bed with the polished knobs like a throne, in which Solomon slept all day. There were snow-white curtains of wiry lace at the window, and a lace bed-spread belonged on the bed. But what old Solomon slept so sound under was a big feather-stitched piece-quilt in the pattern "Trip Around the World," which had twenty-one different colors, four hundred and forty pieces, and a thousand yards of thread, and that was what Solomon's mother made in her life and old age. There was a table holding the Bible, and a trunk with a key. On the wall were two calendars, and a diploma from somewhere in Solomon's family, and under that Livvie's one possession was nailed, a picture of the little white baby of thc family she worked for, back in Natchez before she was married. Going through that room and on to the kitchen, there was a big wood stove and a big round table always with a wet top and with the knives and forks in one jelly glass and the spoons in another, and a cut-glass vinegar bottle between, and going out from those, many shallow dishes of pickled peaches, fig preserves, watermelon pickles and blackberry jam always sitting there. The churn sat in the sun, the doors of the safe were always both shut, and there were four baited mouse-traps in the kitchen, one in every corner.

The outside of Solomon's house looked nice. It was not painted, but across thc porch was an even balance. On each side there was one easy chair with high springs, looking out, and a fern basket hanging over it from the ceiling, and a dishpan of zinnia seedlings growing at its foot on the floor. By the door was a plow-wheel, just a pretty iron circle, nailed up on one wall and a square mirror on the other, a turquoise-blue comb stuck up in the frame, with the wash stand beneath it. On the door was a wooden knob with a pearl in the end, and Solomon's black hat hung on that, if he was in the house.

Out front was a clean dirt yard with every vestige of grass patiently uprooted and the ground scarred in deep whorls from the strike of Livvie's broom. Rose bushes with tiny blood-red roses blooming every month grew in threes on either side of the steps. On one side was a peach tree, on the other a pomegranate. Then coming around up the path from the deep cut of the Natchez Trace below was a line of bare crape-myrtle trees with every branch of them ending in a colored bottle, green or blue. There was no word that fell from Solomon's lips to say what they were for, but Livvie knew that there could be a spell put in trees, and she was familiar from the time she was born with the way bottle trees kept evil spirits from coming into the house—by luring them inside the colored bottles, where they cannot get out again. Solomon had made the bottle trees with his own hands over the nine years, in labor amounting to about a tree a year, and without a sign that he had any uneasiness in his heart, for he took as much pride in his precautions against spirits coming in the house as he took in the house, and sometimes in the sun the bottle trees looked prettier than the house did.

It was a nice house. It was in a place where the days would go by and surprise anyone that they were over. The lamplight and the firelight would shine out the door after dark, over the still and breathing country, lighting the roses and the bottle trees, and all was quiet there.

But there was nobody, nobody at all, not even a white person. And if there had been anybody, Solomon would not have let Livvie look at them, just as he would not let her look at a field hand, or a field hand look at her. There was no house near, except for the cabins of the tenants that were forbidden to her, and there was no house as far as she had been, stealing away down the still, deep Trace. She felt as if she waded a river when she went, for the dead leaves on the ground reached as high as her knees, and when she was all scratched and bleeding she said it was not like a road that went anywhere. One day, climbing up the high bank, she had found a graveyard without a church, with ribbon-grass growing about the foot of an angel (she had climbed up because she thought she saw angel wings), and in the sun, trees shining like burning flames through the great caterpillar nets which enclosed them. Scarey thistles stood looking like the prophets in the Bible in Solomon's house. Indian paint brushes grew over her head, and the mourning dove made the only sound in the world. Oh for a stirring of the leaves, and a breaking of the nets! But not by a ghost, prayed Livvie, jumping down the bank. After Solomon took to his bed, she never went out, except one more time.

Livvie knew she made a nice girl to wait on anybody. She fixed things to eat on a tray like a surprise. She could keep from singing when she ironed, and to sit by a bed and fan away the flies, she could be so still she could not hear herself breathe. She could clean up the house and never drop a thing, and wash the dishes without a sound, and she would step outside to churn, for churning sounded too sad to her, like sobbing, and if it made her home-sick and not Solomon, she did not think of that.

But Solomon scarcely opened his eyes to see her, and scarcely tasted his food. He was not sick or paralyzed or in any pain that he mentioned, but he was surely wearing out in the body, and no matter what nice hot thing Livvie would bring him to taste, he would only look at it now, as if he were past seeing how he could add anything more to himself. Before she could beg him, he would go fast asleep. She could not surprise him any more, if he would not taste, and she was afraid that he was never in the world going to taste another thing she brought him—and so how could he last?

But one morning it was breakfast time and she cooked his eggs and grits, carried them in on a tray, and called his name. He was sound asleep. He lay in a dignified way with his watch beside him, on his back in the middle of the bed. One hand drew the quilt up high, though it was the first day of spring. Through the white lace curtains a little puffy wind was blowing as if it came from round cheeks. All night the frogs had sung out in the swamp, like a commotion in the room, and he had not stirred, though she lay wide awake and saying "Shh, frogs!" for fear he would mind them.

He looked as if he would like to sleep a little longer, and so she put back the tray and waited a little. When she tiptoed and stayed so quiet, she surrounded herself with a little reverie, and sometimes it seemed to her when she was so stealthy that the quiet she kept was for a sleeping baby, and that she had a baby and was its mother. When she stood at Solomon's bed and looked down at him, she would be thinking, "He sleeps so well," and she would hate to wake him up. And in some other way, too, she was afraid to wake him up because even in his sleep he seemed to be such a strict man.

Of course, nailed to the wall over the bed—only she would forget who it was—there was a picture of him when he was young. Then he had a fan of hair over his forehead like a king's crown. Now his hair lay down on his head, the spring had gone out of it. Solomon had a lightish face, with eyebrows scattered but rugged, the way privet grows, strong eyes, with second sight, a strict mouth, and a little gold smile. This was the way he looked in his clothes, but in bed in the daytime he looked like a different and smaller man, even when he was wide awake, and holding the Bible. He looked like somebody kin to himself. And then sometimes when he lay in sleep and she stood fanning the flies away, and the light came in, his face was like new, so smooth and clear that it was like a glass of jelly held to the window, and she could almost look through his forehead and see what he thought.

She fanned him and at length he opened his eyes and spoke her name, but he would not taste the nice eggs she had kept warm under a pan.

Back in the kitchen she ate heartily, his breakfast and hers, and looked out the open door at what went on. The whole day, and the whole night before, she had felt the stir of spring close to her. It was as present in the house as a young man would be. The moon was in the last quarter and outside they were turning the sod and planting peas and beans. Up and down the red fields, over which smoke from the brush-burning hung showing like a little skirt of sky, a white horse and a white mule pulled the plow. At intervals hoarse shouts came through the air and roused her as if she dozed neglectfully in the shade, and they were telling her, "Jump up!" She could see how over each ribbon of field were moving men and girls, on foot and mounted on mules, with hats set on their heads and bright with tall hoes and forks as if they carried streamers on them and were going to some place on a journey—and how as if at a signal now and then they would all start at once shouting, hollering, cajoling, calling and answering back, running, being leaped on and breaking away, flinging to earth with a shout and lying motionless in the trance of twelve o'clock. The old women came out of the cabins and brought them the food they had ready for them, and then all worked together, spread evenly out. The little children came too, like a bouncing stream overflowing the fields, and set upon the men, the women, the dogs, the rushing birds, and the wave-like rows of earth, their little voices almost too high to be heard. In the middle distance like some white and gold towers were the haystacks, with black cows coming around to eat their edges. High above everything, the wheel of fields, house, and cabins, and the deep road surrounding like a moat to keep them in, was the turning sky, blue with long, far-flung white mare's-tail clouds, serene and still as high flames. And sound asleep while all this went around him that was his, Solomon was like a little still spot in the middle.

Even in the house the earth was sweet to breathe. Solomon had never let Livvie go any farther than the chicken house and the well. But what if she would walk now into the heart of the fields and take a hoe and work until she fell stretched out and drenched with her efforts, like other girls, and laid her cheek against the laid-open earth, and shamed the old man with her humbleness and delight? To shame him! A cruel wish could come in uninvited and so fast while she looked out the back door. She washed the dishes and scrubbed the table. She could hear the cries of the little lambs. Her mother, that she had not seen since her wedding day, had said one time, "I rather a man be anything, than a woman be mean."

So all morning she kept tasting the chicken broth on the stove, and when it was right she poured off a nice cup-ful. She carried it in to Solomon, and there he lay having a dream. Now what did he dream about? For she saw him sigh gently as if not to disturb some whole thing he held round in his mind, like a fresh egg. So even an old man dreamed about something pretty. Did he dream of her, while his eyes were shut and sunken, and his small hand with the wedding ring curled close in sleep around the quilt? He might be dreaming of what time it was, for even through his sleep he kept track of it like a clock, and knew how much of it went by, and waked up knowing where the hands were even before he consulted the silver watch that he never let go. He would sleep with the watch in his palm, and even holding it to his cheek like a child that loves a plaything. Or he might dream of journeys and travels on a steamboat to Natchez. Yet she thought he dreamed of her; but even while she scrutinized him, the rods of the foot of the bed seemed to rise up like a rail fence between them, and she could see that people never could be sure of anything as long as one of them was asleep and the other awake. To look at him dreaming of her when he might be going to die frightened her a little, as if he might carry her with him that way, and she wanted to run out of the room. She took hold of the bed and held on, and Solomon opened his eyes and called her name, but he did not want anything. He would not taste the good broth.

Just a little after that, as she was taking up the ashes in the front room for the last time in the year, she heard a sound. It was somebody coming. She pulled the curtains together and looked through the slit.

Coming up the path under the bottle trees was a white lady. At first she looked young, but then she looked old. Marvelous to see, a little car stood steaming like a kettle out in the field-track—it had come without a road.

Livvie stood listening to the long, repeated knockings at the door, and after a while she opened it just a little. The lady came in through the crack, though she was more than middle-sized and wore a big hat.

"My name is Miss Baby Marie," she said.

Livvie gazed respectfully at the lady and at the little suitcase she was holding close to her by the handle until the proper moment. The lady's eyes were running over the room, from palmetto to palmetto, but she was saying, "I live at home . . . out from Natchez . . . and get out and show these pretty cosmetic things to the white people and the colored people both . . . all around . . . years and years. . . . Both shades of powder and rouge. . . . It's the kind of work a girl can do and not go clear 'way from home . . ." And the harder she looked, the more she talked. Suddenly she turned up her nose and said, "It is not Christian or sanitary to put feathers in a vase," and then she took a gold key out of the front of her dress and began unlocking the locks on her suitcase. Her face drew the light, the way it was covered with intense white and red, with a little patty-cake of white between the wrinkles by her upper lip. Little red tassels of hair bobbed under the rusty wires of her picture-hat, as with an air of triumph and secrecy she now drew open her little suitcase and brought out bottle after bottle and jar after jar, which she put down on the table, the mantel-piece, the settee, and the organ.

"Did you ever see so many cosmetics in your life?" cried Miss Baby Marie.

"No'm," Livvie tried to say, but the cat had her tongue.

"Have you ever applied cosmetics?" asked Miss Baby Marie next.

"No'm," Livvie tried to say.

"Then look!" she said, and pulling out the last thing of all, "Try this!" she said. And in her hand was unclenched a golden lipstick which popped open like magic. A fragrance came out of it like incense, and Livvie cried out suddenly, "Chinaberry flowers!"

Her hand took the lipstick, and in an instant she was carried away in the air through the spring, and looking down with a half-drowsy smile from a purple cloud she saw from above a chinaberry tree, dark and smooth and neatly leaved, neat as a guinea hen in the dooryard, and there was her home that she had left. On one side of the tree was her mama holding up her heavy apron, and she could see it was loaded with ripe figs, and on the other side was her papa holding a fish-pole over the pond, and she could see it transparently, the little clear fishes swimming up to the brim.

"Oh, no, not chinaberry flowers—secret ingredients," said Miss Baby Marie. "My cosmetics have secret ingredients—not chinaberry flowers."

"It's purple," Livvie breathed, and Miss Baby Marie said, "Use it freely. Rub it on."

Livvie tiptoed out to the wash stand on the front porch and before the mirror put the paint on her mouth. In the wavery surface her face danced before her like a flame. Miss Baby Marie followed her out, took a look at what she had done, and said, "That's it."

Livvie tried to say "Thank you" without moving her parted lips where the paint lay so new.

By now Miss Baby Marie stood behind Livvie and looked in the mirror over her shoulder, twisting up the tassels of her hair. "The lipstick I can let you have for only two dollars," she said, close to her neck.

"Lady, but I don't have no money, never did have," said Livvie.

"Oh, but you don't pay the first time. I make another trip, that's the way I do. I come back again—later."

"Oh," said Livvie, pretending she understood everything so as to please the lady.

"But if you don't take it now, this may be the last time I'll call at your house," said Miss Baby Marie sharply. "It's far away from anywhere, I'll tell you that. You don't live close to anywhere."

"Yes'm. My husband, he keep the *money,*" said Livvie, trembling. "He is strict as he can be. He don't know *you* walk in here—Miss Baby Marie!"

"Where is he?"

"Right now, he in yonder sound asleep, an old man. I wouldn't ever ask him for anything."

Miss Baby Marie took back the lipstick and packed it up. She gathered up the jars for both black and white and got them all inside the suitcase, with the same little fuss of triumph with which she had brought them out. She started away.

"Goodbye," she said, making herself look grand from the back, but at the last minute she turned around in the door. Her old hat wobbled as she whispered, "Let me see your husband."

Livvie obediently went on tiptoe and opened the door to the other room. Miss Baby Marie came behind her and rose on her toes and looked in.

"My, what a little tiny old, old man!" she whispered, clasping her hands and shaking her head over them. "What a beautiful quilt! What a tiny old, old man!"

"He can sleep like that all day," whispered Livvie proudly.

They looked at him awhile so fast asleep, and then all at once they looked at each other. Somehow that was as if they had a secret, for he had never stirred. Livvie then politely, but all at once, closed the door.

"Well! I'd certainly like to leave you with a lipstick!" said Miss Baby Marie vivaciously. She smiled in the door.

"Lady, but I told you I don't have no money, and never did have."

"And never will?" In the air and all around, like a bright halo around the white lady's nodding head, it was a true spring day.

"Would you take eggs, lady?" asked Livvie softly.

"No, I have plenty of eggs—plenty," said Miss Baby Marie.

"I still don't have no money," said Livvie, and Miss Baby Marie took her suitcase and went on somewhere else.

Livvie stood watching her go, and all the time she felt her heart beating in her left side. She touched the place with her hand. It seemed as if her heart beat and her whole face flamed from the pulsing color of her lips. She went to sit by Solomon and when he opened his eyes he could not see a change in her. "He's fixin' to die," she said inside. That was the secret. That was when she went out of the house for a little breath of air.

She went down the path and down the Natchez Trace a way, and she did not know how far she had gone, but it was not far, when she saw a sight. It was a man, looking like a vision—she standing on one side of the Old Natchez Trace and he standing on the other.

As soon as this man caught sight of her, he began to look himself over. Starting at the bottom with his pointed toes, he began to look up, lifting his peg-top pants the higher to see fully his bright socks. His coat long and wide and leaf-green he opened like doors to see his high-up tawny pants and his pants he smoothed downward from the points of his collar, and he wore a luminous baby-pink satin shirt. At the end, he reached gently above his wide platter-shaped round hat, the color of a plum, and one finger touched at the feather, emerald green, blowing in the spring winds.

No matter how she looked, she could never look so fine as he did, and she was not sorry for that, she was pleased.

He took three jumps, one down and two up, and was by her side.

"My name is Cash," he said.

He had a guinea pig in his pocket. They began to walk along. She stared on and on at him, as if he were doing some daring spectacular thing, instead of just walking beside her. It was not simply the city way he was dressed that made her look at him and see hope in its insolence looking back. It was not only the way he moved along kicking the flowers as if he could break through everything in the way and destroy anything in the world, that made her eyes grow bright. It might be, if he had not appeared the way he did appear that day she would never have looked so closely at him, but the time people come makes a difference.

They walked through the still leaves of the Natchez Trace, the light and the shade falling through trees about them, the white irises shining like candles on the banks and the new ferns shining like green stars up in the oak branches. They came out at Solomon's house, bottle trees and all. Livvie stopped and hung her head.

Cash began whistling a little tune. She did not know what it was, but she had heard it before from a distance, and she had a revelation. Cash was a field hand. He was a transformed field hand. Cash belonged to Solomon. But he had stepped out of his overalls into this. There in front of Solomon's house he laughed. He had a round head, a round face, all of him was young, and he flung his head up, rolled it against the mare's-tail sky in his round hat, and he could laugh just to see Solomon's house sitting there. Livvie looked at it, and there was Solomon's black hat hanging on the peg on the front door, the blackest thing in the world.

"I been to Natchez," Cash said, wagging his head around against the sky. "*I* taken a trip, *I* ready for Easter!"

How was it possible to look so fine before the harvest? Cash must have stolen the money, stolen it from Solomon. He stood in the path and lifted his spread hand high and brought it down again and again in his laughter. He kicked up his heels. A little chill went through her. It was as if Cash was bringing that strong hand down to beat a drum or to rain blows upon a man, such an abandon and menace were in his laugh. Frowning, she went closer to him and his swinging arm drew her in at once and the fright was crushed from her body, as a little match-flame might be smothered out by what it lighted. She gathered the folds of his coat behind him and fastened her red lips to his mouth, and she was dazzled by herself then, the way he had been dazzled at himself to begin with.

In that instant she felt something that could not be told—that Solomon's death was at hand, that he was the same to her as if he were dead now. She cried out, and uttering little cries turned and ran for the house.

At once Cash was coming, following after, he was running behind her. He came close, and halfway up the path he laughed and passed her. He even picked up a stone and sailed it into the bottle trees. She put her hands over her head, and sounds clattered through the bottle trees like cries of outrage. Cash stamped and plunged zigzag up the front steps and in at the door.

When she got there, he had stuck his hands in his pockets and was turning slowly about in the front room. The little guinea pig peeped out. Around Cash, the pinned-up palmettos looked as if a lazy green monkey had walked up and down and around the walls leaving green prints of his hands and feet.

She got through the room and his hands were still in his pockets, and she fell upon the closed door to the other room and pushed it open. She ran to Solomon's bed, calling "Solomon! Solomon!" The little shape of the old man never moved at all, wrapped under the quilt as if it were winter still.

"Solomon!" She pulled the quilt away, but there was another one under that, and she fell on her knees beside him. He made no sound except a sigh, and then she could hear in the silence the light springy steps of Cash walking and walking in the front room, and the ticking of Solomon's silver watch, which came from the bed. Old Solomon was far away in his sleep, his face looked small, relentless, and devout, as if he were walking somewhere where she could imagine the snow falling.

Then there was a noise like a hoof pawing the floor, and the door gave a creak, and Cash appeared beside her. When she looked up, Cash's face was so black it was bright, and so bright and bare of pity that it looked sweet to her. She stood up and held up her head. Cash was so powerful that his presence gave her strength even when she did not need any.

Under their eyes Solomon slept. People's faces tell of things and places not known to the one who looks at them while they sleep, and while Solomon slept under the eyes of Livvie and Cash his face told them like a mythical story that all his life he had built, little scrap by little scrap, respect. A beetle could not have been more laborious or more ingenious in the task of its destiny. When Solomon was young, as he was in his picture overhead, it was the infinite thing with him, and he could see no end to the respect he would contrive and keep in a house. He had built a lonely house, the way he would make a cage, but it grew to be the same with him as a great monumental pyramid and sometimes in his absorption of getting it erected he was like the builder-slaves of Egypt who forgot or never knew the origin and meaning of the thing to which they gave all the strength of their bodies and used up all their days. Livvie and Cash could see that as a man might rest from a life-labor he lay in his bed, and they could hear how, wrapped in his quilt, he sighed to himself comfortably in sleep, while in his dreams he might have been an ant, a beetle, a bird, an Egyptian, assembling and carrying on his back and building with his hands, or he might have been an old man of India or a swaddled baby, about to smile and brush all away.

Then without warning old Solomon's eyes flew wide open under the hedge-like brows. He was wide awake.

And instantly Cash raised his quick arm. A radiant sweat stood on his temples. But he did not bring his arm down—it stayed in the air, as if something might have taken hold.

It was not Livvie—she did not move. As if something said "Wait," she stood waiting. Even while her eyes burned under motionless lids, her lips parted in a stiff grimace, and with her arms stiff at her sides she stood above the prone old man and the panting young one, erect and apart.

Movement when it came came in Solomon's face. It was an old and strict face, a frail face, but behind it, like a covered light, came an animation that could play hide and seek, that would dart and escape, had always escaped. The mystery flickered in him, and invited from his eyes. It was that very mystery that Cash with his quick arm would have to strike, and that Livvie could not weep for. But Cash only stood holding his arm in the air, when the gentlest flick of his great strength, almost a puff of his breath, would have been enough, if he had known how to give it, to send the old man over the obstruction that kept him away from death.

If it could not be that the tiny illumination in the fragile and ancient face caused a crisis, a mystery in the room that would not permit a blow to fall, at least it was certain that Cash, throbbing in his Easter clothes, felt a pang of shame that the vigor of a man would come to such an end that he could not be struck without warning. He took down his hand and stepped back behind Livvie, like a round-eyed schoolboy on whose unsuspecting head the dunce cap has been set.

"Young ones can't wait," said Solomon.

Livvie shuddered violently, and then in a gush of tears she stooped for a glass of water and handed it to him, but he did not see her.

"So here come the young man Livvie wait for. Was no prevention. No prevention. Now I lay eyes on young man and it come to be somebody I know all the time, and been knowing since he were born in a cotton patch, and watched grow up year to year, Cash McCord, growed to size, growed up to come in my house in the end—ragged and barefoot."

Solomon gave a cough of distaste. Then he shut his eyes vigorously, and his lips began to move like a chanter's.

"When Livvie married, her husband were already somebody. He had paid great cost for his land. He spread sycamore leaves over the ground from wagon to door, day he brought her home, so her foot would not have to touch ground. He carried her through his door. Then he growed old and could not lift her, and she were still young."

Livvie's sobs followed his words like a soft melody repeating each thing as he stated it. His lips moved for a little without sound, or she cried too fervently, and unheard he might have been telling his whole life, and then he said, "God forgive Solomon for sins great and small. God forgive Solomon for carrying away too young girl for wife and keeping her away from her people and from all the young people would clamor for her back."

Then he lifted up his right hand toward Livvie where she stood by the bed and offered her his silver watch. He dangled it before her eyes, and she hushed crying; her tears stopped. For a moment the watch could be heard ticking as it always did, precisely in his proud hand. She lifted it away. Then he took hold of the quilt; then he was dead.

Livvie left Solomon dead and went out of the room. Stealthily, nearly without noise, Cash went beside her. He was like a shadow, but his shiny shoes moved over the floor in spangles, and the green downy feather shone like a light in his hat. As they reached the front room, he seized her deftly as a long black cat and dragged her hanging by the waist round and round him, while he turned in a circle, his face bent down to hers. The first moment, she kept one arm and its hand stiff and still, the one that held Solomon's watch. Then the fingers softly let go, all of her was limp, and the watch fell somewhere on the floor. It ticked away in the still room, and all at once there began outside the full song of a bird.

They moved around and around the room and into the brightness of the open door, then he stopped and shook her once. She rested in silence in his trembling arms, unprotesting as a bird on a nest. Outside the redbirds were flying and crisscrossing, the sun was in all the bottles on the prisoned trees, and the young peach was shining in the middle of them with the bursting light of spring.

ROBERT BOLES (b. 1943)

Robert Boles spent most of his childhood abroad where his father was in the foreign service with the State Department. After serving in France as a United States Air Force medic, he returned to live with his family on Cape Cod, Massachusetts.

His fiction reflects much of his own experience. Boles' wealthy, cultured black heroes, isolated as they are from their Negro heritage, yet not really a part of the American way of life, seek their identities. In his first novel, The People One Knows *(1964), the main character, a soldier of interracial parentage, is shattered by his exposure to racial bigotry.* Curling *(1968) depicts the lonely attempt of its black protagonist to acquire a sense of worth as the adopted son of a white couple.*

The wealthy young man in "The Engagement Party," too, finds himself between two worlds—the false sophistication of his social class and the unpretentious simplicity of life in the kitchen, which he does not know how to achieve.

The Engagement Party

SHE WAS NOT a drinker, for she held her glass too carefully. My eyes fastened to a detail. Her fingernail polish. The red was put into check by its own too-even glaze, was held, suspended.

"Yes. Well, my husband's work is similar to yours," she continued.

"Is it really?" I asked, but not quite politely enough. Had it been the lines of her eyes which projected the effect of my lack of attention? Her makeup, though not overdone, was obvious. Immediately, a sense of having played this scene before.

I turned slightly away from her as a member of the combo walked by, and noticed Helen beckoning me.

"Excuse me, please," I said.

The woman smiled with closed jaws, shifted her weight and pivoted on a heel. Her last name was Nolan. I remembered that then. I had no intention of embarrassing her. One should be accustomed to that sort of thing at a party.

Smiling now, I worked my way towards Helen.

"By God! It's George! It's George himself!" The voice belonged to Helen's younger brother. I clapped him on the shoulder. "And you don't even have a drink!"

"I left it on the mantel!"

"Have you had enough already?"

"I've hardly begun," I said.

Helen appeared. Her arms were in front of her as if she were holding an imaginary purse with both hands. "There's someone you have to meet. My father's partner."

"I'm starved," I said.

She took my hand and led me across the room and into another. The people seemed plant-like, rooted in the carpet. Their motions seemed to have been caused by winds and crosswinds. Necks bent, backs; arms gestured in conversation. I had begun to perspire.

"I hope he doesn't get drunk," she confided without moving her lips or looking at me.

"Who?"

"My brother."

I bumped into the woman who wore the brocade dress, the one I had had the conversation with a moment before. Laughter and apologies, far in excess of what was called for. It was a brief bursting of her tension.

"Here he is," Helen announced.

"So, this is the young man who's going to carry you away." The man in his late forties or early fifties took my hand and shook it vigorously.

"Yes, sir," I said, assuming the bearing of a lower responding to an upper classman.

"It's about time I met you. Engineering, isn't it?"

"Yes, sir. Aeronautical."

"That's fine. You're a good-looking young man."

"Thank you, sir."

Helen moved away from me. I felt her absence as a hollow space beside me. Someone had asked her something and I had heard her say, "Certainly, Marie." That was all. I folded my arms, turned at the waist and followed her with my eyes. She escorted a woman to the foyer. The woman was a politician of some sort, I think. I believe I had seen her picture in the paper in regards to a "Culture March" on the Negro community.

"Wonderful girl, Helen."

"Yes, I agree," I said, and turned to face him again.

"Fine family."

"Yes, sir, I know," I said.

A group of men to my right were involved in a familiar and hearty political discussion. I tried to divide my attention.

"Your family's in . . . ?"

"California."

"Right. Ken told me. I had forgotten. Doctor, is he?"

"Not an M.D. He has a doctorate in education."

"I was in California for two years, you know."

"No, I didn't," I said. It was difficult for me to keep my eyes on him. His complexion was sallow, the color of coffee with heavy cream. I watched someone take a sip of a drink and felt thirsty again.

"I was in L.A.," he continued.

"We're from San Francisco."

"And what do you think of Boston?"

"It's fine. I like it," I said without much enthusiasm.

The music began. Bass throb, brushes on cymbals, then piano, vibes and saxophone in a long chorus. People separated. We stepped back. Some danced the High-Life, others the Bossa-Nova.

"I don't intend for us to stay here," I continued. "I've taken a job in Connecticut."

"I'm sure it's best. Best to get the bride away from her parents."

I nodded, then covered my mouth while belching.

I recognized the bellowing of Tommy's voice to my right. He was, perhaps, getting drunk. "Being colored doesn't have anything to do with color! It's a question of attitudes and history and all that crap!"

"It's a good life that's yours to lead," Helen's father's partner said. "When I was your age, I had to struggle. Not like you young people today."

"Yes," I said. "I realize how hard it must have been. I know how hard my father had to work."

The entire conversation was one often repeated. A needless formality. We were knowledgeably secure in the words we spoke. I felt a little disquiet.

"You youngsters have all of the opportunities, you know. And there are new ones opening every day. No worry about finding a job. If you're qualified, you'll get one."

Although it was not altogether true, I could do nothing but nod in solemn agreement and press my lips together in a gesture akin to a pout.

I thought I heard Helen call me, but I could not see her.

"What are your hobbies, son? I heard that you were a fine trackman in school."

"I swim, of course," I said, and struggled to say naturally, "and I'm a bit of a bug on sailing." It was the truth and it seemed to offend him. I had known that it would and that he would enjoy it.

A group of people parted in laughter. Helen entered between them. She came to my side. "Excuse me, Al. I'm going to take him away from you." Her voice sounded remarkably like her mother's.

"I understand." He extended his hand immediately and shook mine again quite vigorously.

Helen's hand was cool, as if it had been in cold water.

"You look fresh," I remarked.

"I just freshened up. I was wilting. It's so warm, and all of these people," she said. "Did you have a good conversation?"

"Yes. I suppose so. He's a very interesting man."

"What time is it?"

Instead of taking my hand away from her, I stood on my toes, stretched myself, and attempted to read the clock on the mantel in the other room. My drink had disappeared from in front of the mirror. "Quarter to eleven, I think."

There was a roar of laughter that was quickly muffled.

"Little brother is acting up again," she said.

"Leave Tommy alone," I said. "He's happy and well adjusted. Let him have some fun."

"You don't know what I go through with him!"

From across the room, a woman's voice calling Helen's name. The tone of it was comparable to the surface of a highly polished piece of wood. All of us, in a dense atmosphere of movements and poses, were beneath and supportive to it. "Helen!"

She looked.

Again, "Helen!"

I saw her at the other end of the room before Helen did. She sipped at a Manhattan and waved from her wrist as women, curiously, always wave.

Between smiles, I managed to repeat myself more forcefully than before. "I am starved, Helen. Famished!"

"You told me."

"I'm beginning to get a headache," I lied. "I didn't get a chance to eat this evening." But the evening was getting to me, the sensuous fugue, the cacophony of voices, the odors and light, the smoke. But something more than that. My disquietude.

"My poor dear," she mouthed, as she stroked my forehead with her fingertips. "I'm sure the caterer has some of those . . . things left. What were those things? Cabbage leaves stuffed with something and baked. Go into the kitchen."

"I think I will."

She had not really expected me to do so. "Dance with me first."

"No," I said. "You're cruel. I'm salivating and starved and you want me to burn more of my energy."

If she had pressed me, I would have danced. But she didn't.

"I'll see you in a few minutes."

We separated. She, it seemed, with misgivings. But I was relieved. I felt at once the dissolution of the effect of the hundred small embarrassments which had occurred between myself and others throughout the evening, the seconds of arbitrary inattentiveness which inflicted wounds, pinpricks, on each of us.

Perhaps I'm lying.

The kitchen door was on spring hinges. It closed itself after I had entered. I let my smile fall and imagined myself making an entrance onto a stage. I, as an actor with a small part in a play with Strindberg overtones.

I was at ease with the noise practically shut out. I hadn't noticed how sweaty I was. With a lot of room and air, it seemed to be present all at once. The white tiles of the floor and walls, glazed, flat and hard, made me doubly aware of my body and the bodies of the caterer and the girl. All of us were dark mobile beings set into this sterile chamber. The room was filled with the odors of smoke and powder and perfume in the other rooms.

"The groom-to-be is here!" the caterer said.

"You know it, dad," I said, slipping easily into the dialect to let him know that I was a member. "And I want me some f-o-o-d!"

"I hear you talkin', baby," the caterer said.

A metal chair painted white was against one of the walls. I sat in it and stretched out my legs. The caterer took a plate and began filling it. His white uniform was badly fitted. It was large. His arms were lean. The girl stood beside him and waited to help. She was very dark. Her bones were large, her hair coarse and beautiful.

"Get some salad for the man, Celestine," he said to her.

The name was right for her. It suggested fragility. Her bearing in some remarkable way suggested the same thing. She went to the refrigerator. I pretended that I had had slightly too much to drink. Her uniform played on my mind. The name Celestine did also. Her uniform was white. Starched. The material at the seams was doubled. Something easily noticeable for it was whiter there. The cloth played on her hips.

She looked at me briefly. I returned her glance with a smile and wondered, while I was doing so, what she thought of me. My complexion is agreeable with a black or charcoal gray suit. I am brown in the way a Mexican is brown. I had my jacket open, my vest unbuttoned part of the way.

Celestine put some salad into a wooden bowl. I raised my hand in a political gesture when enough had been placed there. She added a spoonful more and offered the words, "For your health."

"This is my daughter Celestine," the caterer said proudly.

"She's a very attractive girl."

Celestine turned away from me in modesty. It suddenly seemed right to speak of her with her father in this manner, the masculine dominant, the female subservient. I was particularly aware of the roles we had assumed and had heightened.

I noticed that the caterer continued to put food on my plate. "Enough!" I said. "Man, when I want food for next year, I'll let you know."

He accepted my criticism with gentle laughter, but I was vaguely aware that I had overstepped myself.

"And what do you want to drink with that, sir?" he asked.

"Either Scotch or bourbon on the rocks," I said, with the full, coarse, American aplomb.

"I'll have to go to the bar to get some." He put the plate on the table near me. The top of the table was porcelain.

Celestine went to a drawer, pulled it open and began to remove a table mat.

"I don't need that," I said with an unintended sharpness. I smiled idiotically afterwards.

Her father left the kitchen.

I pulled my chair to the table and began to eat.

"Sit down," I said to her after a moment. "You make me nervous standing there."

She obeyed me. My voice still had a residue of sharpness. It was her father who had gotten beneath my skin. All of us had accepted Southern attitudes in a minute.

I wanted to speak to her as I ate, but nothing seemed worth saying. It was difficult to cut through the cloth of pretension we had woven together. I ate in silence and she watched me in silence.

My thoughts turned to Helen, but it was clearly an alternative—something to compensate for my failure to communicate normally with the breathing girl seated next to me.

I ate too quickly and when I was almost done her father returned with a double light Scotch. I thanked him with a full mouth, then finished eating, and drank half of the drink slowly, with my eyes on the walls and ceiling.

I smiled to myself. I almost laughed.

In another moment I was in one of the large rooms again.

"So you're the fiancé!" a woman said, pointing her finger at my chest.

"I am," I said, and smiled.

"Well, dance with me, darling!" All of her *a*'s were broad, and her voice rasped pleasantly.

"Only the High-Life," I said. "I don't want to put my drink down."

We walked into the other room and began the lilting African dance which had gained so much favor. She danced well, if a bit stiffly, but it became her.

"You know, I just learned this," she said. "I think it's marvelous! And you must tell me about Helen. You two go so well together."

The combo ended the song. We had hardly begun. I hoped that I could separate myself from her without appearing to be rude. I excused myself but she gave no indication of having noticed. She continued as we walked to the side of the room, then she met someone I had met previously and introduced us. I slipped quietly away from her.

I wandered through groups of people as if I were looking for someone. I stopped briefly to chat with Helen's mother, and once again near a small group of men centered around a white civil rights worker who had just returned from the South. He emoted before his words as he told a story of an atrocity too vile to be printed in a newspaper.

It all seemed a circus I cared little about. Or a parade. I've never liked parades. I did something idiotic. I stamped my foot. When I did it, a little of the contents of my glass spilled out onto my thumb and fingers. There was no reason for it. Perhaps I wanted to hear the sound of my footstep beneath the carpet. And I didn't know any longer if I loved Helen. I'd marry her in any case, but I wondered if love was possible. It had disappeared in a second. It was like walking out in the middle of one of those romantic screen comedies. Of course, tomorrow I would feel differently. In all likelihood this pattern would stay with me for the next forty or fifty years.

After finishing my drink, I went to the bar and asked for a Scotch-and-quinine. I was slapped on the back.

"By Jove, it's Georgie!" Helen's brother said.

"Hello, Tommy."

"Great party, is it not?"

"It is that," I said.

He posed unwittingly against the bar. There was a serenity in the moment or him. "Who am I going to play tennis with on Saturdays when you're hooked up to Helen and in Connecticut?"

"Where is she, by the way?" I asked.

"Upstairs. Mrs. Williams spilled a drink on her dress . . . well, I kind of knocked her arm a little. You know how those things happen."

"I'll bet Helen has it in for you."

"What the hell! She's getting married in a couple of months," he said, then added, "You lucky son of a . . . So, what's going to happen to tennis and me on Saturdays?"

"You'll find a better player." I feinted a left to his jaw, bent my knees and jabbed at his stomach with my right. He jackknifed a bit. Then I mussed up his hair. "Judging by your reflexes, you haven't had as much to drink as I thought."

The bartender placed my drink on the counter. I didn't really want it, but picked it up and returned to the area in which couples danced. I watched without seeing and heard without listening. My preoccupation was with nothing. Maybe only the restlessness which had no outlet.

"Nice combo," someone said.

I tried, but not very hard, to remember his name. "Yes, they're very good."

In another moment I rested my glass and danced again. I found that this woman whose hand I had taken when I had stepped onto the floor was a fervent dancer. After our first words, all conversation stopped.

I danced with her several times. I got warm. My legs perspired. I saw Helen once and waved at her. She smiled obligingly and waved back. Tommy also danced a lot. We stopped when our foreheads and shirts were wet.

"To hell with being sedate!" he said. "I know we're supposed to, but it is a party."

Both of us went to the bar again, ordered and waited. Helen shook a finger of warning at him. I walked to her and kissed her. She recoiled from lack of privacy and said, "Not now, darling. Not here in front of all these people. Gracious!"

"Leave your brother alone," I said. "That's an order."

"Yes, dear."

I took my glass and began to mingle half-heartedly. The alcohol had worked its miniature wonder. I was dizzy. Still, I hadn't learned anything. I wanted to go swimming. That was all. The idea of it seized me at once. I could envision and feel it. I stood still in the center of the crowded room, closed my eyes and began a process of complete imagination. The voices, the laughter, the music intruded.

Upon opening my eyes, I walked without hesitation to the French doors that led to the patio and stepped out into the open. The air was much colder than I had expected it to be, and it took me a few seconds to get used to it. I sat in a deck lounge and closed my eyes. Who would be the first to disturb me?, I wondered. Helen might come looking for me. Tommy might want to tell me the latest dirty joke.

I felt myself sinking into the pulsating deepness of intoxication that precedes sleep, but pulled myself up and out of it at the sound of footsteps. I did not look behind me. I took a swallow of my drink. I followed the motion of the person behind me with my hearing. After a moment I realized that whoever it was had no interest in me. I closed my eyes again.

The footsteps moved from here to there, stopped, moved from here to there again. There was the sound of one glass touching another. When the sound moved to the side of me and a little in front of me, I opened my eyes. It was the caterer's daughter. I couldn't remember her name right away. Celestine. I should have guessed that it might have been either she or her father. She was putting empty glasses left by guests onto a tray.

I watched her, unnoticed. There was a certain dignity in her manner I find difficult to explain. It was feminine without the feminine embellishments of gesture. It was not decadent. Her uniform, her darkness, and that she worked contributed to it. But there was much more. I was at ease. I decided to finish my drink so that she would have to take my glass.

She heard me move, turned and seemed surprised by my presence. I smiled at her. She returned the smile and continued. She picked up glasses in front and then to the right of me. When she had almost finished, I held up my glass and turned it upside down to demonstrate its emptiness. She came and took it from me.

"Sit down for a while," I said.

She looked to the patio doors before deciding to accept.

I swung my legs over and put them on the ground to make room for her.

"I meant what I said to your father," I told her. My words were sincere. "It's a bit cold out here, don't you think?"

She did not answer.

I said nothing for the next few seconds. I reached for her bare arm. The contact, though brief, was electric. She did not move and was facing away from me. I wanted very much to see her face. I put my hand to her chin and forced her to look at me. I could not read her expression. I let go of her and waited for her to get up. She sat completely still.

"This is where my engagement was announced," I said. "Everyone was assembled here and a toast was made."

The night spun softly. I was not even able to hear her breathe. She sat rigidly, with her eyes fastened to some immobile bit of shadow. My need for her then urged me. I would give her something afterwards. Money. Fifty dollars perhaps. I had that much in my wallet.

The moment seemed to lick us with a broad tongue. I felt strangely like someone from the Southern past of masters and servants. I did love her for the moment. To make love with her once would be all that I needed. I would never have to see her again.

I stood and took her arm. "Let's go into the garden," I whispered.

I pulled her gently. I beckoned. My whispering voice trembled.

She broke away from me. "No," she said firmly. Her head was lowered. Her chin touched the top of her dress, her uniform, and although I could not see her eyes I detected a look of betrayal on her face.

Had I read the moment so inaccurately? She picked up the tray of unclean glasses and walked with quick, sure steps back to the house.

I waited for a decent length of time before returning. I wanted to smoke a cigarette, but had no matches. My disquietude was inert. The guests would begin to leave in an hour or so. Then the evening could be forgotten.

KATHERINE MANSFIELD (1888–1923)

Katherine Mansfield was born and raised in New Zealand but educated in England, where she returned at twenty-one to enter the literary world. She collaborated with John Middleton Murry, whom she later married, in several literary reviews and small magazines for which she wrote short stories and criticism. She gained popular success when her stories were collected and published, but poor health led to an untimely death at the age of thirty-five.

Mansfield's stories are delicate but sure probings, often centering around a moment of insight or understanding arising in a sharp, intense response to an event.

"The Dill Pickle" is a good example of her style. It presents a chance encounter which leads the main character to reappraise her earlier relationship with a lover.

A Dill Pickle

AND THEN, after six years, she saw him again. He was seated at one of those little bamboo tables decorated with a Japanese vase of paper daffodils. There was a tall plate of fruit in front of him, and very carefully, in a way she recognized immediately as his "special" way, he was peeling an orange.

He must have felt that shock of recognition in her for he looked up and met her eyes. Incredible! He didn't know her! She smiled; he frowned. She came towards him. He closed his eyes an instant, but opening them his face lit up as though he had struck a match in a dark room. He laid down the orange and pushed back his chair, and she took her little warm hand out of her muff and gave it to him.

"Vera!" he exclaimed. "How strange. Really, for a moment I didn't know you. Won't you sit down? You've had lunch? Won't you have some coffee?"

She hesitated, but of course she meant to.

"Yes, I'd like some coffee." And she sat down opposite him.

"You've changed. You've changed very much," he said, staring at her with that eager, lighted look. "You look so well. I've never seen you look so well before."

"Really?" She raised her veil and unbuttoned her high fur collar. "I don't feel very well. I can't bear this weather, you know."

"Ah, no. You hate the cold. . . ."

"Loathe it." She shuddered. "And the worst of it is that the older one grows . . ."

He interrupted her. "Excuse me," and tapped on the table for the waitress. "Please bring some coffee and cream." To her: "You are sure you won't eat anything? Some fruit, perhaps. The fruit here is very good."

"No, thanks. Nothing."

"Then that's settled." And smiling just a hint too broadly he took up the orange again. "You were saying—the older one grows—"

"The colder," she laughed. But she was thinking how well she remembered that trick of his—the trick of interrupting her—and of how it used to exasperate her six years ago. She used to feel then as though he, quite suddenly, in the middle of what she was saying, put his hand over her lips, turned from her, attended to something different, and then took his hand away, and with just the same slightly too broad smile, gave her his attention again. . . . Now we are ready. That is settled.

"The colder!" He echoed her words, laughing too. "Ah, ah. You still say the same things. And there is another thing about you that is not changed at all—your beautiful voice—your beautiful way of speaking." Now he was very grave; he leaned towards her, and she smelled the warm, stinging scent of the orange peel. "You have only to say one word and I would know your voice among all other voices. I don't know what it is—I've often wondered—that makes your voice such a—haunting memory. . . . Do you remember that first afternoon we spent together at Kew Gardens? You were so surprised because I did not know the names of any flowers. I am still just as ignorant for all your telling me. But whenever it is very fine and warm, and I see some bright colours—it's awfully strange—I hear your voice saying: 'Geranium, marigold and verbena.' And I feel those three words are all I recall of some forgotten, heavenly language. . . . You remember that afternoon?"

"Oh, yes, very well." She drew a long, soft breath, as though the paper daffodils between them were almost too sweet to bear. Yet, what had remained in her mind of that particular afternoon was an absurd scene over the tea table. A great many people taking tea in a Chinese pagoda, and he behaving like a maniac about the wasps—waving them away, flapping at them with his straw hat, serious and infuriated out of all proportion to the occasion. How delighted the sniggering tea drinkers had been. And how she had suffered.

But now, as he spoke, that memory faded. His was the truer. Yes, it had been a wonderful afternoon, full of geranium and marigold and verbena, and—warm sunshine. Her thoughts lingered over the last two words as though she sang them.

In the warmth, as it were, another memory unfolded. She saw herself sitting on a lawn. He lay beside her, and suddenly, after a long silence, he rolled over and put his head in her lap.

"I wish," he said, in a low, troubled voice, "I wish that I had taken poison and were about to die—here now!"

At that moment a little girl in a white dress, holding a long, dripping water lily, dodged from behind a bush, stared at them, and dodged back again. But he did not see. She leaned over him.

"Ah, why do you say that? I could not say that."

But he gave a kind of soft moan, and taking her hand he held it to his cheek.

"Because I know I am going to love you too much—far too much. And I shall suffer so terribly, Vera, because you never, never will love me."

He was certainly far better looking now than he had been then. He had lost all that dreamy vagueness and indecision. Now he had the air of a man who has found his place in life, and fills it with a confidence and an assurance which was, to say the least, impressive. He must have made money, too. His clothes were admirable, and at that moment he pulled a Russian cigarette case out of his pocket.

"Won't you smoke?"

"Yes, I will." She hovered over them. "They look very good."

"I think they are. I get them made for me by a little man in St. James's Street. I don't smoke very much. I'm not like you—but when I do, they must be delicious, very fresh cigarettes. Smoking isn't a habit with me; it's a luxury —like perfume. Are you still so fond of perfumes? Ah, when I was in Russia . . ."

She broke in: "You've really been to Russia?"

"Oh, yes. I was there for over a year. Have you forgotten how we used to talk of going there?"

"No, I've not forgotten."

He gave a strange half laugh and leaned back in his chair. "Isn't it curious. I have really carried out all those journeys that we planned. Yes, I have been to all those places that we talked of, and stayed in them long enough to—as you used to say, 'air oneself' in them. In fact, I have spent the last three years of my life travelling all the time. Spain, Corsica, Siberia, Russia, Egypt. The only country left is China, and I mean to go there, too, when the war is over."

As he spoke, so lightly, tapping the end of his cigarette against the ash-tray, she felt the strange beast that had slumbered so long within her bosom stir, stretch itself, yawn, prick up its ears, and suddenly bound to its feet, and fix its longing, hungry stare upon those far away places. But all she said was, smiling gently: "How I envy you."

He accepted that. "It has been," he said, "very wonderful—especially Russia. Russia was all that we had imagined, and far, far more. I even spent some days on a river boat on the Volga. Do you remember that boatman's song that you used to play?"

"Yes." It began to play in her mind as she spoke.

"Do you ever play it now?"

"No, I've no piano."

He was amazed at that. "But what has become of your beautiful piano?"

She made a little grimace. "Sold. Ages ago."

"But you were so fond of music," he wondered.

"I've no time for it now," said she.

He let it go at that. "That river life," he went on, "is something quite special. After a day or two you cannot realize that you have ever known another. And it is not necessary to know the language—the life of the boat creates a bond between you and the people that's more than sufficient. You eat with them, pass the day with them, and in the evening there is that endless singing."

She shivered, hearing the boatman's song break out again loud and tragic, and seeing the boat floating on the darkening river with melancholy trees on either side. . . . "Yes, I should like that," said she, stroking her muff.

"You'd like almost everything about Russian life," he said warmly. "It's so informal, so impulsive, so free without question. And then the peasants are so splendid. They are such human beings—yes, that is it. Even the man who drives your carriage has—has some real part in what is happening. I remember the evening a party of us, two friends of mine and the wife of one of them, went for a picnic by the Black Sea. We took supper and champagne and ate and drank on the grass. And while we were eating the coachman came up. 'Have a dill pickle,' he said. He wanted to share with us. That seemed to me so right, so—you know what I mean?"

And she seemed at that moment to be sitting on the grass beside the mysteriously Black Sea, black as velvet, and rippling against the banks in silent, velvet waves. She saw the carriage drawn up to one side of the road, and the little group on the grass, their faces and hands white in the moonlight. She saw the pale dress of the woman outspread and her folded parasol, lying on the grass like a huge pearl crochet hook. Apart from them, with his supper in a cloth on his knees, sat the coachman. "Have a dill pickle," said he, and although she was not certain what a dill pickle was, she saw the greenish glass jar with a red chili like a parrot's beak glimmering through. She sucked in her cheeks; the dill pickle was terribly sour. . . .

"Yes, I know perfectly what you mean," she said.

In the pause that followed they looked at each other. In the past when they had looked at each other like that they had felt such a boundless understanding between them that their souls had, as it were, put their arms round each other and dropped into the same sea, content to be drowned, like mournful lovers. But now, the surprising thing was that it was he who held back. He who said:

"What a marvellous listener you are. When you look at me with those wild eyes I feel that I could tell you things that I would never breathe to another human being."

Was there just a hint of mockery in his voice or was it her fancy? She could not be sure.

"Before I met you," he said, "I had never spoken of myself to anybody. How well I remember one night, the night that I brought you the little Christmas tree, telling you all about my childhood. And of how I was so miserable that I ran away and lived under a cart in our yard for two days without being discovered. And you listened, and your eyes shone, and I felt that you had even made the little Christmas tree listen too, as in a fairy story."

But of that evening she had remembered a little pot of caviare. It had cost seven and sixpence. He could not get over it. Think of it—a tiny jar like that costing seven and sixpence. While she ate it he watched her, delighted and shocked.

"No, really, that is eating money. You could not get seven shillings into a little pot that size. Only think of the profit they must make. . . ." And he had begun some immensely complicated calculations. . . . But now good-bye to the caviare. The Christmas tree was on the table, and the little boy lay under the cart with his head pillowed on the yard dog.

"The dog was called Bosun," she cried delightedly.

But he did not follow. "Which dog? Had you a dog? I don't remember a dog at all."

"No, no. I mean the yard dog when you were a little boy." He laughed and snapped the cigarette case to.

"Was he? Do you know I had forgotten that. It seems such ages ago. I cannot believe that it is only six years. After I had recognized you to-day—I had to take such a leap—I had to take a leap over my whole life to get back to that time. I was such a kid then." He drummed on the table. "I've often thought how I must have bored you. And now I understand so perfectly why you wrote to me as you did—although at the time that letter nearly finished my life. I found it again the other day, and I couldn't help laughing as I read it. It was so clever—such a true picture of me." He glanced up. "You're not going?"

She had buttoned her collar again and drawn down her veil.

"Yes, I am afraid I must," she said, and managed a smile. Now she knew that he had been mocking.

"Ah, no, please," he pleaded. "Don't go just for a moment," and he caught up one of her gloves from the table and clutched at it as if that would hold her. "I see so few people to talk to nowadays, that I have turned into a sort of barbarian," he said. "Have I said something to hurt you?"

"Not a bit," she lied. But as she watched him draw her glove through his fingers, gently, gently, her anger really did die down, and besides, at the moment he looked more like himself of six years ago. . . .

"What I really wanted then," he said softly, "was to be a sort of carpet—to make myself into a sort of carpet for you to walk on so that you need not be hurt by the sharp stones and the mud that you hated so. It was nothing more positive than that—nothing more selfish. Only I did desire, eventually, to turn into a magic carpet and carry you away to all those lands you longed to see."

As he spoke she lifted her head as though she drank something; the strange beast in her bosom began to purr. . . .

"I felt that you were more lonely than anybody else in the world," he went on, "and yet, perhaps, that you were the only person in the world who was really, truly alive. Born out of your time," he murmured, stroking the glove, "fated."

Ah, God! What had she done! How had she dared to throw away her happiness like this. This was the only man who had ever understood her. Was it too late? Could it be too late? *She* was that glove that he held in his fingers. . . .

"And then the fact that you had no friends and never had made friends with people. How I understood that, for neither had I. Is it just the same now?"

"Yes," she breathed. "Just the same. I am as alone as ever."

"So am I" he laughed gently, "just the same."

Suddenly with a quick gesture he handed her back the glove and scraped his chair on the floor. "But what seemed to me so mysterious then is perfectly plain to me now. And to you, too, of course. . . . It simply was that we were such egoists, so self-engrossed, so wrapped up in ourselves that we hadn't a corner in our hearts for anybody else. Do you know," he cried, naïve and hearty, and dreadfully like another side of that old self again, "I began studying a Mind System when I was in Russia, and I found that we were not peculiar at all. It's quite a well known form of . . ."

She had gone. He sat there, thunder-struck, astounded beyond words. . . . And then he asked the waitress for his bill.

"But the cream has not been touched," he said. "Please do not charge me for it."

SILVIO VILLAVICENCIO

Silvio Villavicencio operates a small used book store in Guadalajara, Jalisco, Mexico, and teaches Latin-American literature. He is little known to Americans but is considered by some to be one of the most articulate spokesmen for the "new wave" of contemporary Latin-American writers.

"The Mirror," originally written in Spanish, depicts the inner workings of a man's disjointed mind. The poem quoted at intervals in the story is by the Roman poet, Catullus (87—54 B.C.).

The Mirror

Translated by Octavio I. Romano—V.

I am a was and a will be and a is tired
—Quevedo

YESTERDAY, when Elena came looking for me, I tried to ignore her. I wanted her to leave quickly.

"I'll see you later—soon—when I can," I told her.

Fury rose to her mouth, then to her eyes. I heard her voice.

"Stupid!"

Then the silence came.

The corners of her eyes were painted, cat's eyes. Elena looked at the blue walls. I threw myself on the bed, looking up. Actually I saw nothing. I was thinking. There she was, immobile, empty, her eyes very distant and deep.

There is no point in bringing memories back. Perhaps I have invented everything, and nothing really happened. But it so happens that deeds trap me, and affect me. Each isolated thing, of course, signifies nothing. And all together, it is a great confusing mass. From another viewpoint, I would very much like to have done away with my memories. Such as I am, however, makes this futile, impossible. I can only escape myself by being different.

No, I am not here voluntarily. My destined role is empty and sinister. There is no escape. Every alternative is an absurdity. Am I really alive? Is it afternoon, or morning?

I do not remember when I met Elena. Two years ago? Three? Or is it that I have never known her? Anyway, two or three years ago I told her,

"Come with me?"

She did not say anything. Instead, she hugged me around the waist. The hotel was filthy, but I didn't notice that until the morning after. That was when I noticed Elena looking at her legs. She was doing this because Elena liked to look at herself. Seeing her close up, looking her over—was she pretty? Elena worked in a bar and she would bite my lips. At such times I felt like kicking her. But I would say nothing and fury would rush over me like a rabid bitch—like a needle in the tongue—like a cloud in the eye. I was afraid.

Blue veins on her wrists. Yesterday Elena looked at her arms, and then she looked at her hands again. Blue walls, almost black. I got up slowly, opened the window, and thought: *"The blind have no bodies, they have no shadows in the afternoon; but their night is ancient, more ancient than this beloved sun that floats in the sky."* Then I saw the books. I looked at them for a long time, saying nothing. I read slowly, only for myself:

"My tongue is still; throughout my limbs
a tenuous flame spreads; with sounds of you
my ears hum; cover my eyes
with double darkness."

Again, like being hit, the silence again.

I believed myself blind, so, when Elena decided to look at me it was too late. I was already blind.

"I am the man without eyes," I thought. But then I said to myself: "blue." And I saw *blue,* inside of my head.

It is in moments like this that the clarity of my deeds always invades and possesses me. Is this why I am such a man? Evidently. But to me this seems sad and obscene, or, almost anguished.

"I am blind," I said.

And I was blind for a long time until, outside, I heard a man making noise.

"It is Mr. Sánchez," said Elena.

Her anger had diminished, and all that remained was an immobile face, persistent and cold. The nose, the mouth, and the eyes horribly fixed.

"That's right," I answered.

Elena was a shadow. Vertigo. Elena was a stone on one's back, the loss of hope. *The blind are not aware of the night, because at midnight. . . .*

"What are you thinking?" she asked.

"Nothing," I replied.

More noises. Mr. Sánchez had to leave. I heard his footsteps going down the stairs and through the hall. I heard his coughing. Cough! Cough! Cough! I heard the noise of the closing door. Click! Then I imagined his heavy body walking along the street below, dragging its shadow along, until it disappears. It was then that Elena said,

"I want to vomit."

The lights in the street flickered and muffled noises could be heard in the distance. At such moments the air is charged with tension. The minutes become viscous and they drag. The silence grows and becomes menacing. Quickly then—like a gash—a scream. And that is exactly what happened yesterday.

"I want to vomit," she said again.

"It will cure you of what ails you," I answered.

But that was only an idea of hers, an idea that congested her face and made her veins swell. It was just an idea because, no, she never vomited anything. She was a tramp.

That is why, when she became pregnant, I said to her,

"That's the worst thing that can happen. It must be avoided. Some doctor can remove it, before it is born. . . ."

I could not convince her. Her mind was made up. Yesterday I tried to help her again.

"Never! Never!" she screamed.

The anger rose to her face again. And it was then that Elena tried to beat herself with something—or perhaps it was my fists that beat on her face. In any event, a small thread of blood broke out on her lips. Elena was a shadow, and that small thread of blood on her mouth was very becoming.

Thinking it over, actually I never wanted a son. I know that such small things are supposed to be important to me. But, what does it mean to have a son? Nothing. Absolutely nothing. That's quite clear. And furthermore, since I have no choice anyway, I must let things follow their own due course. I guess that's the way things should be. . . . No. No! I must not let my doubts get the better of me. Forget! Forget!

It may be absurd, but this explanation always calms me down. Then I feel nothing—neither sadness nor anguish. This sensation lasts only for a while, then I am myself again—my total existence again crowded with noises and fears. Memories rise from deep inside me.

Once, perhaps, I loved Elena. After all, I'm like other people. I go to the cafes and movies. I walk in the streets and look in store windows. In short, I am imprisoned. However, thinking it over, perhaps it was also desire that made me seek her out. Yes, that must have been it. But now all that has ended: I neither want her nor love her. She is a shadow, like everyone else.

Yesterday, after the noises, when she calmed down the shadow said,

"Mr. Sánchez is an imbecile. He is a pig. Today, when I was coming up, he tried to put his arms around me. And here I am, going to have your son. You hear? A son."

Sometimes Elena would look without seeing a thing, as if she was alone, as if she was dead. And yesterday she was alone—or dead—and she was trying to save herself, to save me. Vertigo. *Women who work in bars should not bite lips. . . .* Then I told her,

"But Elena, I like to greet him. Look. In the mornings I say to him, 'Good morning, Mr. Sánchez,' and I smile. I also greet him in the afternoons. It's been that way since I've known him. But more than that, once I had a beautiful dream: I kicked his eyes into a bloody pulp."

"Don't think of that. You are sneering. If I have a boy, I will give him your name," Elena said.

". . . and in the afternoons I also smile at him."

I looked at her face and sunk into her eyes. *I must not think. I must not think of anything! I must flee! A final escape. What are you thinking? What does anybody think?*

Elena was still talking.

"Did you know that I had gone to a doctor recently?"

I did not want to hear anything of that. Therefore, I was also deaf. That is why I said to her,

"Today I saw him again, Elena. . . ."

"And if it is a girl, I'll give her my name. Elena. We must think of our daughter!"

". . . and you must take into account that Mr. Sánchez is always faking. All faces are masks. I know that. I read it in some book."

"I don't want to know anything about that," she said. "I have come here to talk about something else."

Suppose that Elena would forget the whole affair. Would she still do the same things? Would she repeat the same acts and say the same words? I felt tired. I could neither see her nor close my eyes. Elena was an irritating ghost. She looked at her arms. She looked herself all over, in the mirror. She finally tired of looking at her own body, of looking at her own face so much. But then the result was worse. Elena said that we should live together, that it was not good to be alone. And she spoke again about our baby boy or girl.

"Someday you are going to go crazy. What are you thinking about? I want her to have your eyes. . . . My daughter!"

Her veins went up along her thin arms, to her neck. *Someday you will go crazy, you will go crazy, and you will be century upon century away from this world.* Elena raised her hands to her temples. To be with Elena would not have been any good. There she was, feeling hopeless, enduring her anguish, and seeking the tiniest bit of hope. I felt sad. Dizzy. I continued to think: *We are rotten, you and I, Elena. We are rotten. Do you know that? Rotten! No matter. Look. It is enough just to open these two eyes. We are like the creatures that live underground. Nothing is of much importance. I know that. And you and I are even less than that. Shit! That's what we are.* I was alone. Elena too. And in me she was looking for a hold on life.

What do all her words mean? Why are all the things that happen around a man so important. This is a stupid story, like a cheap pain, like a woman crying in a movie, like so many things that move in this world.

Life traps us and then drags us along. Aha! But, every now and then, I like to shatter this sinister order of tiny futilities. For example, the other day in the post office it occurred to me that the young lady at the window was an old whore. It occurred to me. So I told her. And she hit me on the nose with the little window. She screamed, and I left right away. That's all I know, except that even now I get a kick when I think of her stupid face behind that round glass.

No. It is not possible to destroy anything. We are always imprisoned. What if again you felt like destroying the order of things? What if you wanted to? Nothing. Always nothing.

We continued to talk, and Elena was saying,

"I'll buy the baby clothes right away. I don't want to be caught unprepared. . . ."

"Mr. Sánchez sometimes talks to himself. You ought to see him!"

". . . I'll buy some colored sheets. . . ."

". . . Nevertheless, the women around here say he is a degenerate, although personally I don't believe it. . . ."

". . . or, if you prefer, white sheets. . . ."

". . . because no one knows anything for certain. It's all gossip. Yes, in the afternoons he says obscene things to. . . ."

". . . and in addition to sheets, diapers and clothes. . . ."

It was futile. Inevitable. Our paths were already carved out. I knew it. Elena also wanted to remain deaf. And she was. Well, that was her business, so I continued to look up at the ceiling. Vertigo. I continued looking at nothing. I thought to myself: *Elena, you lie to me. You try to trap me. So he tried to hug you, eh? That's a lie! I rip your face, knock out your teeth, bloody your eyes, uri-*

nate in your mouth. You lie, you wretched whore. Everyone knows that that fat man is a queer. You don't know anything, Elena. He hugs little boys! Yes, little boys! But Elena was talking about something else.

"The doctor says I must take care of myself, for the baby's sake. I must be quiet. I need rest."

Dark and viscous butterflies are in the light of the street. Elena fixed her eyes on the window. *Look at your eyes. Look at yourself in the mirror and see those dark and viscous things in yourself, that red tongue. Then you will feel sick to your stomach Elena.* She was quiet, as if waiting. I expected nothing, so I relaxed. But it had to happen. It had to happen. It was inevitable.

When Elena looked again at the window I remembered the final words in the book: ". . . *with sounds of you my ears hum; cover my eyes with double darkness.*" She began to grit her teeth and bite out her words. Her eyes were like open windows through which emerged her loneliness. I swallowed saliva and began to sweat. I, too, was alone; alone to face everything. . . .

"I'll wear the loosest clothes. My womb grows each day."

That much I remember. Afterward, I felt a small pain in my back. A slight indisposition. What could have happened at that instant? What could have happened to me? In the puddles outside, the light was reflected. It was reflected. It was something muddled, debilitating, fascinating. . . . It was something circular, horribly fixed, immobile. Then a whirlwind and an echo: ". . . *with sounds of you my ears hum; cover my eyes with double darkness.*" A single instant was enough. Just an instant. Was that my one moment?

I was in a sweat. And there, beyond the glass, the muddled lights in the puddles. The moment froze. Foggy waves began to obscure everything. The noises grew louder. The fever increased and blood began to pound in my temples. Things began to rotate, first slowly, and then I saw Elena's face pass before mine. The fog returned. Then something inside of me broke. A person is a clock made to run by sinister hands. A single gear breaks, or a tiny screw, and then the whole thing explodes. I heard a dry thud, and a scream. I continued to sweat. Then the echo began to pound repeatedly in my head.

Sometimes impotence can tumble obstacles, leap over alleys, destroy things or the symbols of things. It is a road, a way out to nowhere. I felt anguished. And the anguish was in everything; in the walls, in Elena's contracted face, in her open white eyes, in the puddles, in the street. . . . Then I felt pity, pity for something without thinking of anything in particular. Pity for nothing. Then the anguish returned.

Rows of stacked books, a body lying stretched out on the floor with a still face, unmoving, free, or out of this world: Elena. I removed my shirt and wiped the sweat. But I continued to perspire. I looked down again. She looked dirty. I thought of the solitary streets. At that hour the voices cease, and noises recede little by little. Doors close, and everything is sinister and sweet under the pale light of the night.

I went downstairs slowly. No one could have heard the scream. No one. Or could they? It continued to echo in my head, over and over, amplifying, as if it would never stop.

Mr. Sánchez opened the outside door. I saw him drag his feet along mincingly. I smiled at him and said,

"Good evening, Mr. Sánchez."

He passed close to me, returning the greeting. *How ugly are the dead. You go to bed—goodnight—I am dead. Morning comes and you get up: I am a man. But you will never be able to wake up. You will never be able to move your body. And Mr. Sánchez is also dead. We are all dead, Elena.*

I opened and slammed the door closed. I walked along quietly, thinking almost of nothing, without hearing the scream. Up above, a small square of light interfered with the night. Then I took to the street below and disappeared into the shadows.

D. H. LAWRENCE (1885–1930)

David Herbert Lawrence was born in the English Midlands, the son of a rather coarse coal miner and a genteel former schoolteacher. He was a sickly child, strongly attached to his mother and repelled by the ugliness and brutality of his environment. He did not marry until after his mother's death, eloping with a professor's wife who left her three children behind. Lawrence's naturalistic, autobiographical novel Sons and Lovers *(1913) was an examination of the conflict within a young man between his love for a young woman and his attachment to his mother.*

Lawrence spent the rest of his short life, until he died at forty-five of tuberculosis, in conflict with literary censorship and in seeking to escape the decadence of civilization. His travels took him among primitive societies in Italy, Mexico, Ceylon, Australia, and New Mexico.

In probing of the relationships between people in love, Lawrence gave increasingly greater expression to his view that only through complete sexual realization could men and women rediscover themselves as whole human beings. The frankness with which he presented his material caused novels like The Rainbow *(1915),* Women in Love *(1920), and* Lady Chatterley's Lover *(1928) to be suppressed by the authorities and shunned by publishers.*

"The Horse Dealer's Daughter" shows D. H. Lawrence portraying the irrational and uncontrollable onset of physical love and its mystical power to overcome death.

The Horse Dealer's Daughter

"WELL, MABEL, and what are you going to do with yourself?" asked Joe, with foolish flippancy. He felt quite safe himself. Without listening for an answer, he turned aside, worked a grain of tobacco to the tip of his tongue, and spat it out. He did not care about anything, since he felt safe himself.

The three brothers and the sister sat round the desolate breakfast table, attempting some sort of desultory consultation. The morning's post had given the final tap to the family fortune, and all was over. The dreary dining-room itself, with its heavy mahogany furniture, looked as if it were waiting to be done away with.

But the consultation amounted to nothing. There was a strange air of ineffectuality about the three men, as they sprawled at table, smoking and reflecting vaguely on their own condition. The girl was alone, a rather short, sullen-looking young woman of twenty-seven. She did not share the same life as her brothers. She would have been good-looking, save for the impassive fixity of her face, "bulldog," as her brothers called it.

There was a confused tramping of horses' feet outside. The three men all sprawled round in their chairs to watch. Beyond the dark holly-bushes that separated the strip of lawn from the highroad, they could see a cavalcade of shire horses swinging out of their own yard, being taken for exercise. This was the last time. These were the last horses that would go through their hands. The young men watched with critical, callous look. They were all frightened at the collapse of their lives, and the sense of disaster in which they were involved left them no inner freedom.

Yet they were three fine, well-set fellows enough. Joe, the eldest, was a man of thirty-three, broad and handsome in a hot, flushed way. His face was red, he twisted his black moustache over a thick finger, his eyes were shallow and restless. He had a sensual way of uncovering his teeth when he laughed, and his bearing was stupid. Now he watched the horses with a glazed look of helplessness in his eyes, a certain stupor of downfall.

The great draught-horses swung past. They were tied head to tail, four of them, and they heaved along to where a lane branched off from the highroad, planting their great hoofs floutingly in the fine black mud, swinging their great rounded haunches sumptuously, and trotting a few sudden steps as they were led into the lane, round the corner. Every movement showed a massive, slumbrous strength, and a stupidity which held them in subjection. The groom at the head looked back, jerking the leading rope. And the cavalcade moved out of sight up the lane, the tail of the last horse, bobbed up tight and stiff, held out taut from the swinging great haunches as they rocked behind the hedges in a motion like sleep.

Joe watched with glazed hopeless eyes. The horses were almost like his own body to him. He felt he was done for now. Luckily he was engaged to a woman as old as himself, and therefore her father, who was steward of a neighbouring estate, would provide him with a job. He would marry and go into harness. His life was over, he would be a subject animal now.

He turned uneasily aside, the retreating steps of the horses echoing in his ears. Then, with foolish restlessness, he reached for the scraps of bacon-rind from the plates, and making a faint whistling sound, flung them to the terrier that lay against the fender. He watched the dog swallow them, and waited till the creature looked into his eyes. Then a faint grin came on his face, and in a high, foolish voice he said:

"You won't get much more bacon, shall you, you little bitch?"

The dog faintly and dismally wagged its tail, then lowered its haunches, circled round, and lay down again.

There was another helpless silence at the table. Joe sprawled uneasily in his seat, not willing to go till the family conclave was dissolved. Fred Henry, the second brother, was erect, clean-limbed, alert. He had watched the passing of the horses with more sangfroid. If he was an animal, like Joe, he was an animal which controls, not one which is controlled. He was master of any horse, and he carried himself with a well-tempered air of mastery. But he was not master of the situations of life. He pushed his coarse brown moustache upwards, off his lip, and glanced irritably at his sister, who sat impassive and inscrutable.

"You'll go and stop with Lucy for a bit, shan't you?" he asked. The girl did not answer.

"I don't see what else you can do," persisted Fred Henry.

"Go as a skivvy," Joe interpolated laconically.

The girl did not move a muscle.

"If I was her, I should go in for training for a nurse," said Malcolm, the youngest of them all. He was the baby of the family, a young man of twenty-two, with a fresh, jaunty *museau.*

But Mabel did not take any notice of him. They had talked at her and round her for so many years, that she hardly heard them at all.

The marble clock on the mantelpiece softly chimed the half-hour, the dog rose uneasily from the hearthrug and looked at the party at the breakfast table. But still they sat on in ineffectual conclave.

"Oh, all right," said Joe suddenly, apropos of nothing. "I'll get a move on."

He pushed back his chair, straddled his knees with a downward jerk, to get them free, in horsey fashion, and went to the fire. Still he did not go out of the room; he was curious to know what the others would do or say. He began to charge his pipe, looking down at the dog and saying, in a high, affected voice:

"Going wi' me? Going wi' me are ter? Tha'rt goin' further tha that counts on just now, dost hear?"

The dog faintly wagged its tail, the man stuck out his jaw and covered his pipe with his hands, and puffed intently, losing himself in the tobacco, looking down all the while at the dog with an absent brown eye. The dog looked up at him in mournful distrust. Joe stood with his knees stuck out, in real horsey fashion.

"Have you had a letter from Lucy?" Fred Henry asked of his sister.

"Last week," came the neutral reply.

"And what does she say?"

There was no answer.

"Does she *ask* you to go and stop there?" persisted Fred Henry.

"She says I can if I like."

"Well, then, you'd better. Tell her you'll come on Monday."

This was received in silence.

"That's what you'll do then, is it?" said Fred Henry, in some exasperation.

But she made no answer. There was a silence of futility and irritation in the room. Malcolm grinned fatuously.

"You'll have to make up your mind between now and next Wednesday," said Joe loudly, "or else find yourself lodgings on the kerbstone."

The face of the young woman darkened, but she sat on immutable.

"Here's Jack Fergusson!" exclaimed Malcolm, who was looking aimlessly out of the window.

"Where?" exclaimed Joe, loudly.

"Just gone past."

"Coming in?"

Malcolm craned his neck to see the gate.

"Yes," he said.

There was a silence. Mabel sat on like one condemned, at the head of the table. Then a whistle was heard from the kitchen. The dog got up and barked sharply. Joe opened the door and shouted:

"Come on."

After a moment a young man entered. He was muffled up in overcoat and a purple woollen scarf, and his tweed cap, which he did not remove, was pulled down on his head. He was of medium height, his face was rather long and pale, his eyes looked tired.

"Hello, Jack! Well, Jack!" exclaimed Malcolm and Joe. Fred Henry merely said, "Jack."

"What's doing?" asked the newcomer, evidently addressing Fred Henry.

"Same. We've got to be out by Wednesday. Got a cold?"

"I have—got it bad, too."

"Why don't you stop in?"

"*Me* stop in? When I can't stand on my legs, perhaps I shall have a chance." The young man spoke huskily. He had a slight Scotch accent.

"It's a knock-out, isn't it," said Joe, boisterously, "if a doctor goes round croaking with a cold. Looks bad for the patients, doesn't it?"

The young doctor looked at him slowly.

"Anything the matter with *you,* then?" he asked sarcastically.

"Not as I know of. Damn your eyes, I hope not. Why?"

"I thought you were very concerned about the patients, wondered if you might be one yourself."

"Damn it, no, I've never been patient to no flaming doctor, and hope I never shall be," returned Joe.

At this point Mabel rose from the table, and they all seemed to become aware of her existence. She began putting the dishes together. The young doctor looked at her, but did not address her. He had not greeted her. She went out of the room with the tray, her face impassive and unchanged.

"When are you off then, all of you?" asked the doctor.

"I'm catching the eleven-forty," replied Malcolm. "Are you goin' down wi' th' trap, Joe?"

"Yes, I've told you I'm going down wi' th' trap, haven't I?"

"We'd better be getting her in then. So long, Jack, if I don't see you before I go," said Malcolm, shaking hands.

He went out, followed by Joe, who seemed to have his tail between his legs.

"Well, this is the devil's own," exclaimed the doctor, when he was left alone with Fred Henry. "Going before Wednesday, are you?"

"That's the orders," replied the other.

"Where, to Northampton?"

"That's it."

"The devil!" exclaimed Fergusson, with quiet chagrin.

And there was silence between the two.

"All settled up, are you?" asked Fergusson.

"About."

There was another pause.

"Well, I shall miss yer, Freddy, boy," said the young doctor.

"And I shall miss thee, Jack," returned the other.

"Miss you like hell," mused the doctor.

Fred Henry turned aside. There was nothing to say. Mabel came in again, to finish clearing the table.

"What are *you* going to do, then, Miss Pervin?" asked Fergusson. "Going to your sister's, are you?"

Mabel looked at him with her steady, dangerous eyes, that always made him uncomfortable, unsettling his superficial ease.

"No," she said.

"Well, what in the name of fortune *are* you going to do? Say what you mean to do," cried Fred Henry, with futile intensity.

But she only averted her head, and continued her work. She folded the white table-cloth, and put on the chenille cloth.

"The sulkiest bitch that ever trod!" muttered her brother.

But she finished her task with perfectly impassive face, the young doctor watching her interestedly all the while. Then she went out.

Fred Henry stared after her, clenching his lips, his blue eyes fixing in sharp antagonism, as he made a grimace of sour exasperation.

"You could bray her into bits, and that's all you'd get out of her," he said in a small, narrowed tone.

The doctor smiled faintly.

"What's she *going* to do, then?" he asked.

"Strike me if *I* know!" returned the other.

There was a pause. Then the doctor stirred.

"I'll be seeing you to-night, shall I?" he said to his friend.

"Ay—where's it to be? Are we going over to Jessdale?"

"I don't know. I've got a cold on me. I'll come round to the Moon and Stars, anyway."

"Let Lizzie and May miss their night for once, eh?"

"That's it—if I feel as I do now."

"All's one—"

The two young men went through the passage and down to the back door together. The house was large, but it was servantless now, and desolate. At the back was a small bricked house-yard, and beyond that a big square, gravelled fine and red, and having stables on two sides. Sloping, dank, winter-dark fields stretched away on the open sides.

But the stables were empty. Joseph Pervin, the father of the family, had been a man of no education, who had become a fairly large horse dealer. The stables had been full of horses, there was a great turmoil and come-and-go of horses and of dealers and grooms. Then the kitchen was full of servants. But of late things had declined. The old man had married a second time, to retrieve his fortunes. Now he was dead and everything was gone to the dogs, there was nothing but debt and threatening.

For months, Mabel had been servantless in the big house, keeping the home together in penury for her ineffectual brothers. She had kept house for ten years. But previously it was with unstinted means. Then, however brutal and coarse everything was, the sense of money had kept her proud, confident. The men might be foul-mouthed, the women in the kitchen might have bad reputations, her brothers might have illegitimate children. But so long as there was money, the girl felt herself established, and brutally proud, reserved.

No company came to the house, save dealers and coarse men. Mabel had no associates of her own sex, after her sister went away. But she did not mind. She went regularly to church, she attended to her father. And she lived in the memory of her mother, who had died when she was fourteen, and whom she had loved. She had loved her father, too, in a different way, depending upon him, and feeling secure in him, until at the age of fifty-four he married again. And then she had set hard against him. Now he had died and left them all hopelessly in debt.

She had suffered badly during the period of poverty. Nothing, however, could shake the curious sullen, animal pride that dominated each member of the family. Now, for Mabel, the end had come. Still she would not cast about her. She would follow her own way just the same. She would always hold the keys of her own situation. Mindless and persistent, she endured from day to day. Why should she think? Why should she answer anybody? It was enough that this was the end, and there was no way out. She need not pass any more darkly along the main street of the small town, avoiding every eye. She need not demean herself any more, going into the shops and buying the cheapest food. This was at an end. She thought of nobody, not even of herself. Mindless and persistent, she seemed in a sort of ecstasy to be coming nearer to her fulfilment, her own glorification, approaching her dead mother, who was glorified.

In the afternoon she took a little bag, with shears and sponge and a small scrubbing brush, and went out. It was a grey, wintry day, with saddened, dark green fields and an atmosphere blackened by the smoke of foundries not far off. She went quickly, darkly along the causeway, heeding nobody, through the town to the churchyard.

There she always felt secure, as if no one could see her, although as a matter of fact she was exposed to the stare of every one who passed along under the churchyard wall. Nevertheless, once under the shadow of the great looming church, among the graves, she felt immune from the world, reserved within the thick churchyard wall as in another country.

Carefully she clipped the grass from the grave, and arranged the pinky white, small chrysanthemums in the tin cross. When this was done, she took an empty jar from a neighbouring grave, brought water, and carefully, most scrupulously sponged the marble headstone and the coping-stone.

It gave her sincere satisfaction to do this. She felt in immediate contact with the world of her mother. She took minute pains, went through the park in a state bordering on pure happiness, as if in performing this task she came into a subtle, intimate connection with her mother. For the life she followed here in the world was far less real than the world of death she inherited from her mother.

The doctor's house was just by the church. Fergusson, being a mere hired assistant, was slave to the country-side. As he hurried now to attend to the outpatients in the surgery, glancing across the graveyard with his quick eye, he saw the girl at her task at the grave. She seemed so intent and remote, it was like looking into another world. Some mystical element was touched in him. He slowed down as he walked, watching her as if spell-bound.

She lifted her eyes, feeling him looking. Their eyes met. And each looked away again at once, each feeling, in some way, found out by the other. He lifted his cap and passed on down the road. There remained distinct in his consciousness, like a vision, the memory of her face, lifted from the tombstone in the churchyard, and looking at him with slow, large, portentous eyes. It *was* portentous, her face. It seemed to mesmerize him. There was a heavy power in her eyes which laid hold of his whole being, as if he had drunk some powerful drug. He had been feeling weak and done before. Now the life came back into him, he felt delivered from his own fretted, daily self.

He finished his duties at the surgery as quickly as might be, hastily filling up the bottles of the waiting people with cheap drugs. Then, in perpetual haste, he set off again to visit several cases in another part of his round, before tea-time. At all times he preferred to walk if he could, but particularly when he was not well. He fancied the motion restored him.

The afternoon was falling. It was grey, deadened, and wintry, with a slow, moist, heavy coldness sinking in and deadening all the faculties. But why should he think or notice? He hastily climbed the hill and turned across the dark green fields, following the black cinder-track. In the distance, across a shallow dip in the country, the small town was clustered like smouldering ash, a tower, a spire, a heap of low, raw, extinct houses. And on the nearest fringe of the town, sloping into the dip, was Oldmeadow, the Pervins' house. He could see the stables and the outbuildings distinctly, as they lay towards him on the slope. Well, he would not go there many more times! Another resource would be lost to him, another place gone: the only company he cared for in the alien, ugly little town he was losing. Nothing but work, drudgery, constant hastening from dwelling to dwelling among the colliers and the iron-workers. It wore him out, but at the same time he had a craving for it. It was a stimulant to him to be in the homes of the working people, moving as it were through the innermost body of their life. His nerves were excited and gratified. He could come so near, into the very lives of the rough, inarticulate, powerfully emotional men and women. He grumbled, he said he hated the hellish hole. But as a matter of fact it excited him, the contact with the rough, strongly-feeling people was a stimulant applied direct to his nerves.

Below Oldmeadow, in the green, shallow, soddened hollow of fields, lay a square, deep pond. Roving across the landscape, the doctor's quick eye detected a figure in black passing through the gate of the field, down towards the pond. He looked again. It would be Mabel Pervin. His mind suddenly became alive and attentive.

Why was she going down there? He pulled up on the path on the slope above, and stood staring. He could just make sure of the small black figure moving in the hollow of the failing day. He seemed to see her in the midst of such obscurity, that he was like a clairvoyant, seeing rather with the mind's eye than with ordinary sight. Yet he could see her positively enough, whilst he kept his eye attentive. He felt, if he looked away from her, in the thick, ugly falling dusk, he would lose her altogether.

He followed her minutely as she moved, direct and intent, like something transmitted rather than stirring in voluntary activity, straight down the field towards the pond. There she stood on the bank for a moment. She never raised her head. Then she waded slowly into the water.

He stood motionless as the small black figure walked slowly and deliberately towards the centre of the pond, very slowly, gradually moving deeper into the motionless water, and still moving forward as the water got up to her breast. Then he could see her no more in the dusk of the dead afternoon.

"There!" he exclaimed. "Would you believe it?"

And he hastened straight down, running over the wet, soddened fields, pushing through the hedges, down into the depression of callous wintry obscurity. It took him several minutes to come to the pond. He stood on the bank, breathing heavily. He could see nothing. His eyes seemed to penetrate the dead water. Yes, perhaps that was the dark shadow of her black clothing beneath the surface of the water.

He slowly ventured into the pond. The bottom was deep, soft clay, he sank in, and the water clasped dead cold round his legs. As he stirred he could smell the cold, rotten clay that fouled up into the water. It was objectionable in his lungs. Still, repelled and yet not heeding, he moved deeper into the pond. The cold water rose over his thighs, over his loins, upon his abdomen. The lower part of his body was all sunk in the hideous cold element. And the bottom was so deeply soft and uncertain he was afraid of pitching with his mouth underneath. He could not swim, and was afraid.

He crouched a little, spreading his hands under the water and moving them round, trying to feel for her. The dead cold pond swayed upon his chest. He moved again, a little deeper, and again, with his hands underneath, he felt all around under the water. And he touched her clothing. But it evaded his fingers. He made a desperate effort to grasp it.

And so doing he lost his balance and went under, horribly, suffocating in the foul earthy water, struggling madly for a few moments. At last, after what seemed an eternity, he got his footing, rose again into the air and looked around. He gasped, and knew he was in the world. Then he looked at the water. She had risen near him. He grasped her clothing, and drawing her nearer, turned to take his way to land again.

He went very slowly, carefully, absorbed in the slow progress. He rose higher, climbing out of the pond. The water was now only about his legs; he was thankful, full of relief to be out of the clutches of the pond. He lifted her and staggered on to the bank, out of the horror of wet, grey clay.

He laid her down on the bank. She was quite unconscious and running with water. He made the water come from her mouth, he worked to restore her. He did not have to work very long before he could feel the breathing begin again in her; she was breathing naturally. He worked a little longer. He could feel her live beneath his hands; she was coming back. He wiped her face, wrapped her in his overcoat, looked round into the dim, dark grey world, then lifted her and staggered down the bank and across the fields.

It seemed an unthinkably long way, and his burden so heavy he felt he would never get to the house. But at last he was in the stable-yard, and then in the house-yard. He opened the door and went into the house. In the kitchen he laid her down on the hearthrug, and called. The house was empty. But the fire was burning in the grate.

Then again he kneeled to attend to her. She was breathing regularly, her eyes were wide open and as if conscious, but there seemed something missing in her look. She was conscious in herself, but unconscious of her surroundings.

He ran upstairs, took blankets from a bed, and put them before the fire to warm. Then he removed her saturated, earthy-smelling clothing, rubbed her dry with a towel, and wrapped her naked in the blankets. Then he went into the dining-room, to look for spirits. There was a little whisky. He drank a gulp himself, and put some into her mouth.

The effect was instantaneous. She looked full into his face, as if she had been seeing him for some time, and yet had only just become conscious of him.

"Dr. Fergusson?" she said.

"What?" he answered.

He was divesting himself of his coat, intending to find some dry clothing upstairs. He could not bear the smell of the dead, clayey water, and he was mortally afraid for his own health.

"What did I do?" she asked.

"Walked into the pond," he replied. He had begun to shudder like one sick, and could hardly attend to her. Her eyes remained full on him, he seemed to be going dark in his mind, looking back at her helplessly. The shuddering became quieter in him, his life came back in him, dark and unknowing, but strong again.

"Was I out of my mind?" she asked, while her eyes were fixed on him all the time.

"Maybe, for the moment," he replied. He felt quiet, because his strength had come back. The strange fretful strain had left him.

"Am I out of my mind now?" she asked.

"Are you?" he reflected a moment. "No," he answered truthfully, "I don't see that you are." He turned his face aside. He was afraid now, because he felt dazed, and felt dimly that her power was stronger than his, in this issue. And she continued to look at him fixedly all the time. "Can you tell me where I shall find some dry things to put on?" he asked.

"Did you dive into the pond for me?" she asked.

"No," he answered. "I walked in. But I went in overhead as well."

There was silence for a moment. He hesitated. He very much wanted to go upstairs to get into dry clothing. But there was another desire in him. And she seemed to hold him. His will seemed to have gone to sleep, and left him, standing there slack before her. But he felt warm inside himself. He did not shudder at all, though his clothes were sodden on him.

"Why did you?" she asked.

"Because I didn't want you to do such a foolish thing," he said.

"It wasn't foolish," she said, still gazing at him as she lay on the floor, with a sofa cushion under her head. "It was the right thing to do. *I* knew best, then."

"I'll go and shift these wet things," he said. But still he had not the power to move out of her presence, until she sent him. It was as if she had the life of his body in her hands, and he could not extricate himself. Or perhaps he did not want to.

Suddenly she sat up. Then she became aware of her own immediate condition. She felt the blankets about her, she knew her own limbs. For a moment it seemed as if her reason were going. She looked round, with wild eye, as if seeking something. He stood still with fear. She saw her clothing lying scattered.

"Who undressed me?" she asked, her eyes resting full and inevitable on his face.

"I did," he replied, "to bring you round."

For some moments she sat and gazed at him awfully, her lips parted.

"Do you love me, then?" she asked.

He only stood and stared at her, fascinated. His soul seemed to melt.

She shuffled forward on her knees, and put her arms round him, round his legs, as he stood there, pressing her breasts against his knees and thighs, clutching him with strange, convulsive certainty, pressing his thighs against her, drawing him to her face, her throat, as she looked up at him with flaring, humble eyes of transfiguration, triumphant in first possession.

"You love me," she murmured, in strange transport, yearning and triumphant and confident. "You love me. I know you love me, I know."

And she was passionately kissing his knees, through the wet clothing, passionately and indiscriminately kissing his knees, his legs, as if unaware of everything.

He looked down at the tangled wet hair, the wild, bare animal shoulders. He was amazed, bewildered, and afraid. He had never thought of loving her. He had never wanted to love her. When he rescued her and restored her, he was a doctor, and she was a patient. He had had no single personal thought of her. Nay, this introduction of the personal element was very distasteful to him, a violation of his professional honour. It was horrible to have her there embracing his knees. It was horrible. He revolted from it, violently. And yet—and yet—he had not the power to break away.

She looked at him again, with the same supplication of powerful love, and that same transcendent, frightening light of triumph. In view of the delicate flame which seemed to come from her face like a light, he was powerless. And yet he had never intended to love her. He had never intended. And something stubborn in him could not give way.

"You love me," she repeated, in a murmur of deep, rhapsodic assurance. "You love me."

Her hands were drawing him, drawing him down to her. He was afraid, even a little horrified. For he had, really, no intention of loving her. Yet her hands were drawing him towards her. He put out his hand quickly to steady himself, and grasped her bare shoulder. A flame seemed to burn the hand that grasped her soft shoulder. He had no intention of loving her: his whole will was against his yielding. It was horrible. And yet wonderful was the touch of her shoulders, beautiful the shining of her face. Was she perhaps mad? He had a horror of yielding to her. Yet something in him ached also.

He had been staring away at the door, away from her. But his hand remained on her shoulder. She had gone suddenly very still. He looked down at her. Her eyes were now wide with fear, with doubt, the light was dying from her face, a shadow of terrible greyness was returning. He could not bear the touch of her eyes' question upon him, and the look of death behind the question.

With an inward groan he gave way, and let his heart yield towards her. A sudden gentle smile came on his face. And her eyes, which never left his face, slowly, slowly filled with tears. He watched the strange water rise in her eyes, like some slow fountain coming up. And his heart seemed to burn and melt away in his breast.

He could not bear to look at her any more. He dropped on his knees and caught her head with his arms and pressed her face against his throat. She was very still. His heart, which seemed to have broken, was burning with a kind of agony in his breast. And he felt her slow, hot tears wetting his throat. But he could not move.

He felt the hot tears wet his neck and the hollows of his neck, and he remained motionless, suspended through one of man's eternities. Only now it had become indispensable to him to have her face pressed close to him; he could never let her go again. He could never let her head go away from the close clutch of his arm. He wanted to remain like that for ever, with his heart hurting him in a pain that was also life to him. Without knowing, he was looking down on her damp, soft brown hair.

Then, as it were suddenly, he smelt the horrid stagnant smell of that water. And at the same moment she drew away from him and looked at him. Her eyes were wistful and unfathomable. He was afraid of them, and he fell to kissing her, not knowing what he was doing. He wanted her eyes not to have that terrible, wistful, unfathomable look.

When she turned her face to him again, a faint delicate flush was glowing, and there was again dawning that terrible shining of joy in her eyes, which really terrified him, and yet which he now wanted to see, because he feared the look of doubt still more.

"You love me?" she said, rather faltering.

"Yes." The word cost him a painful effort. Not because it wasn't true. But because it was too newly true, the *saying* seemed to tear open again his newly-torn heart. And he hardly wanted it to be true, even now.

She lifted her face to him, and he bent forward and kissed her on the mouth, gently, with the one kiss that is an eternal pledge. And as he kissed her his heart strained again in his breast. He never intended to love her. But now it was over. He had crossed over the gulf to her, and all that he had left behind had shrivelled and become void.

After the kiss, her eyes again slowly filled with tears. She sat still, away from him, with her face drooped aside, and her hands folded in her lap. The tears fell very slowly. There was complete silence. He too sat there motionless and silent on the hearthrug. The strange pain of his heart that was broken seemed to consume him. That he should love her? That this was love! That he should be ripped open in this way! Him, a doctor! How they would all jeer if they knew! It was agony to him to think they might know.

In the curious naked pain of the thought he looked again to her. She was sitting there drooped into a muse. He saw a tear fall, and his heart flared hot. He saw for the first time that one of her shoulders was quite uncovered, one arm bare, he could see one of her small breasts; dimly, because it had become almost dark in the room.

"Why are you crying?" he asked, in an altered voice.

She looked up at him, and behind her tears the consciousness of her situation for the first time brought a dark look of shame to her eyes.

"I'm not crying, really," she said, watching him half frightened.

He reached his hand, and softly closed it on her bare arm.

"I love you! I love you!" he said in a soft, low vibrating voice, unlike himself.

She shrank, and dropped her head. The soft, penetrating grip of his hand on her arm distressed her. She looked up at him.

"I want to go," she said. "I want to go and get you some dry things."

"Why?" he said. "I'm all right."

"But I want to go," she said. "And I want you to change your things."

He released her arm, and she wrapped herself in the blanket, looking at him rather frightened. And still she did not rise.

"Kiss me," she said wistfully.

He kissed her, but briefly, half in anger.

Then, after a second, she rose nervously, all mixed up in the blanket. He watched her in her confusion, as she tried to extricate herself and wrap herself up so that she could walk. He watched her relentlessly, as she knew. And as she went, the blanket trailing, and as he saw a glimpse of her feet and her white leg, he tried to remember her as she was when he had wrapped her in the blanket. But then he didn't want to remember, because she had been nothing to him then, and his nature revolted from remembering her as she was when she was nothing to him.

A tumbling, muffled noise from within the dark house startled him. Then he heard her voice:—"There are clothes." He rose and went to the foot of the stairs, and gathered up the garments she had thrown down. Then he came back to the fire, to rub himself down and dress. He grinned at his own appearance when he had finished.

The fire was sinking, so he put on coal. The house was now quite dark, save for the light of a street-lamp that shone in faintly from beyond the holly trees. He lit the gas with matches he found on the mantelpiece. Then he emptied the pockets of his own clothes, and threw all his wet things in a heap into the scullery. After which he gathered up her sodden clothes, gently, and put them in a separate heap on the copper-top in the scullery.

It was six o'clock on the clock. His own watch had stopped. He ought to go back to the surgery. He waited, and still she did not come down. So he went to the foot of the stairs and called:

"I shall have to go."

Almost immediately he heard her coming down. She had on her best dress of black voile, and her hair was tidy, but still damp. She looked at him—and in spite of herself, smiled.

"I don't like you in those clothes," she said.

"Do I look a sight?" he answered.

They were shy of one another.

"I'll make you some tea," she said.

"No, I must go."

"Must you?" And she looked at him again with the wide, strained, doubtful eyes. And again, from the pain of his breast, he knew how he loved her. He went and bent to kiss her, gently, passionately, with his heart's painful kiss.

"And my hair smells so horrible," she murmured in distraction. "And I'm so awful, I'm so awful! Oh, no, I'm too awful." And she broke into bitter, heart-broken sobbing. "You can't want to love me, I'm horrible."

"Don't be silly, don't be silly," he said, trying to comfort her, kissing her, holding her in his arms. "I want you, I want to marry you, we're going to be married, quickly, quickly—tomorrow if I can."

But she only sobbed terribly, and cried:

"I feel awful. I feel awful. I feel I'm horrible to you."

"No, I want you, I want you," was all he answered, blindly, with that terrible intonation which frightened her almost more than her horror lest he should *not* want her.

BERNARD MALAMUD (b. 1914)

Bernard Malamud's upbringing and education in New York City have enabled him to capture accurately in his writing the feel and sound of big city Jewish life. In his short stories and in novels like The Assistant

(1957), The New Life *(1961),* The Fixer *(1966), and* Pictures of Fidelman *(1969), he celebrates man's affirmation of life in the face of afflictions that threaten to undermine his spirit. In fact, it is only through suffering that Malamud's heroes find peace.*

In "The Magic Barrel," he portrays the redemption of Leo Finkel, a young rabbinical student who discovers that to love God he must learn to love man.

The Magic Barrel

NOT LONG AGO there lived in uptown New York, in a small, almost meager room, though crowded with books, Leo Finkle, a rabbinical student in the Yeshivah University. Finkle, after six years of study, was to be ordained in June and had been advised by an acquaintance that he might find it easier to win himself a congregation if he were married. Since he had no present prospects of marriage, after two tormented days of turning it over in his mind, he called in Pinye Salzman, a marriage broker whose two-line advertisement he had read in the *Forward.**

The matchmaker appeared one night out of the dark fourth-floor hallway of the graystone rooming house where Finkle lived, grasping a black, strapped portfolio that had been worn thin with use. Salzman, who had been long in the business, was of slight but dignified build, wearing an old hat, and an overcoat too short and tight for him. He smelled frankly of fish, which he loved to eat, and although he was missing a few teeth, his presence was not displeasing, because of an amiable manner curiously contrasted with mournful eyes. His voice, his lips, his wisp of beard, his bony fingers were animated, but give him a moment of repose and his mild blue eyes revealed a depth of sadness, a characteristic that put Leo a little at ease although the situation, for him, was inherently tense.

He at once informed Salzman why he had asked him to come, explaining that his home was in Cleveland, and that but for his parents, who had married comparatively late in life, he was alone in the world. He had for six years devoted himself almost entirely to his studies, as a result of which, understandably, he had found himself without time for a social life and the company of young women. Therefore he thought it the better part of trial and error—of embarrassing fumbling—to call in an experienced person to advise him on these matters. He remarked in passing that the function of the marriage broker was ancient and honorable, highly approved in the Jewish community,

* *Forward.* a New York Jewish daily newspaper

because it made practical the necessary without hindering joy. Moreover, his own parents had been brought together by a matchmaker. They had made, if not a financially profitable marriage—since neither had possessed any worldly goods to speak of—at least a successful one in the sense of their everlasting devotion to each other. Salzman listened in embarrassed surprise, sensing a sort of apology. Later, however, he experienced a glow of pride in his work, an emotion that had left him years ago, and he heartily approved of Finkle.

The two went to their business. Leo had led Salzman to the only clear place in the room, a table near a window that overlooked the lamp-lit city. He seated himself at the matchmaker's side but facing him, attempting by an act of will to suppress the unpleasant tickle in his throat. Salzman eagerly unstrapped his portfolio and removed a loose rubber band from a thin packet of much-handled cards. As he flipped through them, a gesture and sound that physically hurt Leo, the student pretended not to see and gazed steadfastly out the window. Although it was still February, winter was on its last legs, signs of which he had for the first time in years begun to notice. He now observed the round white moon, moving high in the sky through a cloud menagerie, and watched with half-open mouth as it penetrated a huge hen, and dropped out of her like an egg laying itself. Salzman, though pretending through eyeglasses he had just slipped on, to be engaged in scanning the writing on the cards, stole occasional glances at the young man's distinguished face, noting with pleasure the long, severe scholar's nose, brown eyes heavy with learning, sensitive yet ascetic lips, and a certain, almost hollow quality of the dark cheeks. He gazed around at shelves upon shelves of books and let out a soft, contented sigh.

When Leo's eyes fell upon the cards, he counted six spread out in Salzman's hand.

"So few?" he asked in disappointment.

"You wouldn't believe me how much cards I got in my office," Salzman replied. "The drawers are already filled to the top, so I keep them now in a barrel, but is every girl good for a new rabbi?"

Leo blushed at this, regretting all he had revealed of himself in a curriculum vitae he had sent to Salzman. He had thought it best to acquaint him with his strict standards and specifications, but in having done so, felt he had told the marriage broker more than was absolutely necessary.

He hesitantly inquired, "Do you keep photographs of your clients on file?"

"First comes family, amount of dowry, also what kind promises," Salzman replied, unbuttoning his tight coat and settling himself in the chair. "After comes pictures, rabbi."

"Call me Mr. Finkle. I'm not yet a rabbi."

Salzman said he would, but instead called him doctor, which he changed to rabbi when Leo was not listening too attentively.

Salzman adjusted his horn-rimmed spectacles, gently cleared his throat and read in an eager voice the contents of the top card:

"Sophie P. Twenty-four years. Widow one year. No children. Educated high school and two years college. Father promises eight thousand dollars. Has wonderful wholesale business. Also real estate. On the mother's side comes teachers, also one actor. Well known on Second Avenue."

Leo gazed up in surprise. "Did you say a widow?"

"A widow don't mean spoiled, rabbi. She lived with her husband maybe four months. He was a sick boy she made a mistake to marry him."

"Marrying a widow has never entered my mind."

"This is because you have no experience. A widow, especially if she is young and healthy like this girl, is a wonderful person to marry. She will be thankful to you the rest of her life. Believe me, if I was looking now for a bride, I would marry a widow."

Leo reflected, then shook his head.

Salzman hunched his shoulders in an almost imperceptible gesture of disappointment. He placed the card down on the wooden table and began to read another:

"Lily H. High school teacher. Regular. Not a substitute. Has savings and new Dodge car. Lived in Paris one year. Father is successful dentist thirty-five years. Interested in professional man. Well Americanized family. Wonderful opportunity."

"I knew her personally," said Salzman. "I wish you could see this girl. She is a doll. Also very intelligent. All day you could talk to her about books and theyater and what not. She also knows current events."

"I don't believe you mentioned her age?"

"Her age?" Salzman said, raising his brows. "Her age is thirty-two years."

Leo said after a while, "I'm afraid that seems a little too old."

Salzman let out a laugh. "So how old are you, rabbi?"

"Twenty-seven."

"So what is the difference, tell me, between twenty-seven and thirty-two? My own wife is seven years older than me. So what did I suffer?—Nothing. If Rothschild's daughter wants to marry you, would you say on account her age, no?"

"Yes," Leo said dryly.

Salzman shook off the no in the yes. "Five years don't mean a thing. I give you my word that when you will live with her for one week you will forget her age. What does it mean five years—that she lived more and knows more than somebody who is younger? On this girl, God bless her, years are not wasted. Each one that it comes makes better the bargain."

"What subject does she teach in high school?"

"Languages. If you heard the way she speaks French, you will think it is music. I am in the business twenty-five years, and I recommend her with my whole heart. Believe me, I know what I'm talking, rabbi."

"What's on the next card?" Leo said abruptly.

Salzman reluctantly turned up the third card:

"Ruth K. Nineteen years. Honor student. Father offers thirteen thousand cash to the right bridegroom. He is a medical doctor. Stomach specialist with marvelous practice. Brother in law owns own garment business. Particular people."

Salzman looked as if he had read his trump card.

"Did you say nineteen?" Leo asked with interest.

"On the dot."

"Is she attractive?" He blushed. "Pretty?"

Salzman kissed his finger tips. "A little doll. On this I give you my word. Let me call the father tonight and you will see what means pretty."

But Leo was troubled. "You're sure she's that young?"

"This I am positive. The father will show you the birth certificate."

"Are you positive there isn't something wrong with her?" Leo insisted.

"Who says there is wrong?"

"I don't understand why an American girl her age should go to a marriage broker."

A smile spread over Salzman's face.

"So for the same reason you went, she comes."

Leo flushed. "I am pressed for time."

Salzman, realizing he had been tactless, quickly explained. "The father came, not her. He wants she should have the best, so he looks around himself. When we will locate the right boy he will introduce him and encourage. This makes a better marriage than if a young girl without experience takes for herself. I don't have to tell you this."

"But don't you think this young girl believes in love?" Leo spoke uneasily.

Salzman was about to guffaw but caught himself and said soberly, "Love comes with the right person, not before."

Leo parted dry lips but did not speak. Noticing that Salzman had snatched a glance at the next card, he cleverly asked, "How is her health?"

"Perfect," Salzman said, breathing with difficulty. "Of course, she is a little lame on her right foot from an auto accident that it happened to her when she was twelve years, but nobody notices on account she is so brilliant and also beautiful."

Leo got up heavily and went to the window. He felt curiously bitter and upbraided himself for having called in the marriage broker. Finally, he shook his head.

"Why not?" Salzman persisted, the pitch of his voice rising.

"Because I detest stomach specialists."

"So what do you care what is his business? After you marry her do you need him? Who says he must come every Friday night in your house?"

Ashamed of the way the talk was going, Leo dismissed Salzman, who went home with heavy, melancholy eyes.

Though he had felt only relief at the marriage broker's departure, Leo was in low spirits the next day. He explained it as arising from Salzman's failure to produce a suitable bride for him. He did not care for his type of clientele. But when Leo found himself hesitating whether to seek out another matchmaker, one more polished than Pinye, he wondered if it could be—his protestations to the contrary, and although he honored his father and mother—that he did not, in essence, care for the matchmaking institution? This thought he quickly put out of mind yet found himself still upset. All day he ran around in the woods—missed an important appointment, forgot to give out his laundry, walked out of a Broadway cafeteria without paying and had to run back with the ticket in his hand; had even not recognized his landlady in the street when she passed with a friend and courteously called out, "A good evening to you, Doctor Finkle." By nightfall, however, he had regained sufficient calm to sink his nose into a book and there found peace from his thoughts.

Almost at once there came a knock on the door. Before Leo could say enter, Salzman, commercial cupid, was standing in the room. His face was gray and meager, his expression hungry, and he looked as if he would expire on his feet. Yet the marriage broker managed, by some trick of the muscles, to display a broad smile.

"So good evening. I am invited?"

Leo nodded, disturbed to see him again, yet unwilling to ask the man to leave.

Beaming still, Salzman laid his portfolio on the table. "Rabbi, I got for you tonight good news."

"I've asked you not to call me rabbi. I'm still a student."

"Your worries are finished. I have for you a first-class bride."

"Leave me in peace concerning this subject." Leo pretended lack of interest.

"The world will dance at your wedding."

"Please, Mr. Salzman, no more."

"But first must come back my strength," Salzman said weakly. He fumbled with the portfolio straps and took out of the leather case an oily paper bag, from which he extracted a hard, seeded roll and a small, smoked white fish. With a quick motion of his hand he stripped the fish out of its skin and began ravenously to chew. "All day in a rush," he muttered.

Leo watched him eat.

"A sliced tomato you have maybe?" Salzman hesitantly inquired.

"No."

The marriage broker shut his eyes and ate. When he had finished he carefully cleaned up the crumbs and rolled up the remains of the fish, in the paper bag. His spectacled eyes roamed the room until he discovered, amid some piles of books, a one-burner gas stove. Lifting his hat he humbly asked, "A glass of tea you got, rabbi?"

Conscience-stricken, Leo rose and brewed the tea. He served it with a chunk of lemon and two cubes of lump sugar, delighting Salzman.

After he had drunk his tea, Salzman's strength and good spirits were restored.

"So tell me, rabbi," he said amiably, "you considered some more the three clients I mentioned yesterday?"

"There was no need to consider."

"Why not?"

"None of them suits me."

"What then suits you?"

Leo let it pass because he could give only a confused answer.

Without waiting for a reply, Salzman asked, "You remember this girl I talked to you—the high school teacher?"

"Age thirty-two?"

But, surprisingly, Salzman's face lit in a smile. "Age twenty-nine."

Leo shot him a look. "Reduced from thirty-two?"

"A mistake," Salzman avowed. "I talked today with the dentist. He took me to his safety deposit box and showed me the birth certificate. She was twenty-nine years last August. They made her a party in the mountains where she went for her vacation. When her father spoke to me the first time I forgot to write the age and I told you thirty-two, but now I remember this was a different client, a widow."

"The same one you told me about? I thought she was twenty-four?"

"A different. Am I responsible that the world is filled with widows?"

"No, but I'm not interested in them, nor for that matter, in school teachers."

Salzman pulled his clasped hand to his breast. Looking at the ceiling he devoutly exclaimed, "Yiddishe kinder, what can I say to somebody that he is not interested in high school teachers? So what then you are interested?"

Leo flushed but controlled himself.

"In what else will you be interested," Salzman went on, "if you not interested in this fine girl that she speaks four languages and has personally in the bank ten thousand dollars? Also her father guarantees further twelve thousand. Also she has a new car, wonderful clothes, talks on all subjects, and she will give you a first-class home and children. How near do we come in our life to paradise?"

"If she's so wonderful, why wasn't she married ten years ago?"

"Why?" said Salzman with a heavy laugh. "—Why? Because she is *partikiler.* This is why. She wants the *best.*"

Leo was silent, amused at how he had entangled himself. But Salzman had aroused his interest in Lily H., and he began seriously to consider calling on her. When the marriage broker observed how intently Leo's mind was at work on the facts he had supplied, he felt certain they would soon come to an agreement.

Late Saturday afternoon, conscious of Salzman, Leo Finkle walked with Lily Hirschorn along Riverside Drive. He walked briskly and erectly, wearing with distinction the black fedora he had that morning taken with trepidation out of the dusty hat box on his closet shelf, and the heavy black Saturday coat he had thoroughly whisked clean. Leo also owned a walking stick, a present from a distant relative, but quickly put temptation aside and did not use it. Lily, petite and not unpretty, had on something signifying the approach of spring. She was au courant, animatedly, with all sorts of subjects, and he weighed her words and found her surprisingly sound—score another for Salzman, whom he uneasily sensed to be somewhere around, hiding perhaps high in a tree along the street, flashing the lady signals with a pocket mirror; or perhaps a cloven-hoofed Pan, piping nuptial ditties as he danced his invisible way before them, strewing wild buds on the walk and purple grapes in their path, symbolizing fruit of a union, though there was of course still none.

Lily startled Leo by remarking, "I was thinking of Mr. Salzman, a curious figure, wouldn't you say?"

Not certain what to answer, he nodded.

She bravely went on, blushing, "I for one am grateful for his introducing us. Aren't you?"

He courteously replied, "I am."

"I mean," she said with a little laugh—and it was all in good taste, or at least gave the effect of being not in bad—"do you mind that we came together so?"

He was not displeased with her honesty, recognizing that she meant to set the relationship aright, and understanding that it took a certain amount of experience in life, and courage, to want to do it quite that way. One had to have some sort of past to make that kind of beginning.

He said that he did not mind. Salzman's function was traditional and honorable—valuable for what it might achieve, which, he pointed out, was frequently nothing.

Lily agreed with a sigh. They walked on for a while and she said after a long silence, again with a nervous laugh, "Would you mind if I asked you something a little bit personal? Frankly, I find the subject fascinating." Although Leo shrugged, she went on half embarrassedly, "How was it that you came to your calling? I mean was it a sudden passionate inspiration?"

Leo, after a time, slowly replied. "I was always interested in the Law."

"You saw revealed in it the presence of the Highest?"

He nodded and changed the subject. "I understand that you spent a little time in Paris, Miss Hirschorn?"

"Oh, did Mr. Salzman tell you, Rabbi Finkle?" Leo winced but she went on, "It was ages ago and almost forgotten. I remember I had to return for my sister's wedding."

And Lily would not be put off. "When," she asked in a trembly voice, "did you become enamored of God?"

He stared at her. Then it came to him that she was talking not about Leo Finkle, but of a total stranger, some mystical figure, perhaps even passionate prophet that Salzman had dreamed up for her—no relation to the living or dead. Leo trembled with rage and weakness. The trickster had obviously sold her a bill of goods, just as he had him, who'd expected to become acquainted with a young lady of twenty-nine, only to behold, the moment he laid eyes upon her strained and anxious face, a woman past thirty-five and aging rapidly. Only his self control had kept him this long in her presence.

"I am not," he said gravely, "a talented religious person," and in seeking words to go on, found himself possessed by shame and fear. "I think," he said in a strained manner, "that I came to God not because I loved Him, but because I did not."

This confession he spoke harshly because its unexpectedness shook him.

Lily wilted. Leo saw a profusion of loaves of bread go flying like ducks high over his head, not unlike the winged loaves by which he had counted himself to sleep last night. Mercifully, then, it snowed, which he would not put past Salzman's machinations.

He was infuriated with the marriage broker and swore he would throw him out of the room the minute he reappeared. But Salzman did not come that night, and when Leo's anger had subsided, an unaccountable despair grew in its place. At first he thought this was caused by his disappointment in Lily, but before long it became evident that he had involved himself with Salzman without a true knowledge of his own intent. He gradually realized—with an emptiness that seized him with six hands—that he had called in the broker to find him a bride because he was incapable of doing it himself. This terrifying insight he had derived as a result of his meeting and conversation with Lily Hirschorn. Her probing questions had somehow irritated him into revealing—to himself more than her—the true nature of his relationship to God, and from that it had come upon him, with shocking force, that apart from his parents, he had never loved anyone. Or perhaps it went the other way, that he did not love God so well as he might, because he had not loved man. It seemed to Leo that his whole life stood starkly revealed and he saw himself for the first time as he truly was—unloved and loveless. This bitter but somehow not fully unexpected revelation brought him to a point of panic, controlled only by extraorindary effort. He covered his face with his hands and cried.

The week that followed was the worst of his life. He did not eat and lost weight. His beard darkened and grew ragged. He stopped attending seminars and almost never opened a book. He seriously considered leaving the Yeshivah, although he was deeply troubled at the thought of the loss of all his years of study—saw them like pages torn from a book, strewn over the city—and at the devastating effect of his decision upon his parents. But he had lived without knowledge of himself, and never in the Five Books and all the Commentaries—mea culpa—had the truth been revealed to him. He did not know where to turn, and in all this desolating loneliness there was no *to whom,* although he often thought of Lily but not once could bring himself to go downstairs and make the call. He became touchy and irritable, especially with his landlady, who asked him all manner of personal questions; on the other hand, sensing his own disagreeableness, he waylaid her on the stairs and apologized abjectly, until mortified, she ran from him. Out of this, however, he drew the consolation that he was a Jew and that a Jew suffered. But gradually, as the long and terrible week drew to a close, he regained his composure and some idea of purpose in life: to go on as planned. Although he was imperfect, the ideal was not. As for his quest of a bride, the thought of continuing afflicted him with anxiety and heartburn, yet perhaps with this new knowledge of himself he would be more successful than in the past. Perhaps love would now come to him and a bride to that love. And for this sanctified seeking who needed a Salzman?

The marriage broker, a skeleton with haunted eyes, returned that very night. He looked, withal, the picture of frustrated expectancy—as if he had steadfastly waited the week at Miss Lily Hirschorn's side for a telephone call that never came.

Casually coughing, Salzman came immediately to the point: "So how did you like her?"

Leo's anger rose and he could not refrain from chiding the matchmaker: "Why did you lie to me, Salzman?"

Salzman's pale face went dead white, the world had snowed on him.

"Did you not state that she was twenty-nine?" Leo insisted.

"I give you my word—"

"She was thirty-five, if a day. *At least* thirty-five."

"Of this don't be too sure. Her father told me—"

"Never mind. The worst of it was that you lied to her."

"How did I lie to her, tell me?"

"You told her things about me that weren't true. You made me out to be more, consequently less than I am. She had in mind a totally different person, a sort of semi-mystical Wonder Rabbi."

"All I said, you was a religious man."

"I can imagine."

Salzman sighed. "This is my weakness that I have," he confessed. "My wife says to me I shouldn't be a salesman, but when I have two fine people that they would be wonderful to be married, I am so happy that I talk too much." He smiled wanly. "This is why Salzman is a poor man."

Leo's anger left him. "Well, Salzman, I'm afraid that's all."

The marriage broker fastened hungry eyes on him.

"You don't want any more a bride?"

"I do," said Leo, "but I have decided to seek her in a different way. I am no longer interested in an arranged marriage. To be frank, I now admit the necessity of premarital love. That is, I want to be in love with the one I marry."

"Love?" said Salzman, astounded. After a moment he remarked, "For us, our love is our life, not for the ladies. In the ghetto they—"

"I know, I know," said Leo. "I've thought of it often. Love, I have said to myself, should be a by-product of living and worship rather than its own end. Yet for myself I find it necessary to establish the level of my need and fulfill it."

Salzman shrugged but answered, "Listen, rabbi, if you want love, this I can find for you also. I have such beautiful clients that you will love them the minute your eyes will see them."

Leo smiled unhappily. "I'm afraid you don't understand."

But Salzman hastily unstrapped his portfolio and withdrew a manila packet from it.

"Pictures," he said, quickly laying the envelope on the table.

Leo called after him to take the pictures away, but as if on the wings of the wind, Salzman had disappeared.

March came. Leo had returned to his regular routine. Although he felt not quite himself yet—lacked energy—he was making plans for a more active social life. Of course it would cost something, but he was an expert in cutting corners; and when there were no corners left he would make circles rounder. All the while Salzman's pictures had lain on the table, gathering dust. Occasionally as Leo sat studying, or enjoying a cup of tea, his eyes fell on the manila envelope, but he never opened it.

The days went by and no social life to speak of developed with a member of the opposite sex—it was difficult, given the circumstances of his situation. One morning Leo toiled up the stairs to his room and stared out the window at the city. Although the day was bright his view of it was dark. For some time he watched the people in the street below hurrying along and then turned with a heavy heart to his little room. On the table was the packet. With a sudden relentless gesture he tore it open. For a half-hour he stood by the table in a state of excitement, examining the photographs of the ladies Salzman had included. Finally, with a deep sigh he put them down. There were six, of varying degrees of attractiveness, but look at them long enough and they all became Lily Hirschorn: all past their prime, all starved behind bright smiles, not a true personality in the lot. Life, despite their frantic yoohooings, had passed them by; they were pictures in a brief case that stank of fish. After a while, however, as Leo attempted to return the photographs into the envelope, he found in it another, a snapshot of the type taken by a machine for a quarter. He gazed at it a moment and let out a cry.

Her face deeply moved him. Why, he could at first not say. It gave him the impression of youth—spring flowers, yet age—a sense of having been used to the bone, wasted; this came from the eyes, which were hauntingly familiar, yet absolutely strange. He had a vivid impression that he had met her before, but try as he might he could not place her although he could almost recall her name, as if he had read it in her own handwriting. No, this couldn't be; he would have remembered her. It was not, he affirmed, that she had an extraordinary beauty—no, though her face was attractive enough; it was that *something* about her moved him. Feature for feature, even some of the ladies of the photographs could do better; but she leaped forth to his heart—had *lived,* or wanted to—more than just wanted, perhaps regretted how she had lived—had somehow deeply suffered: it could be seen in the depths of those reluctant eyes, and from the way the light enclosed and shone from her, and within her, opening realms of possibility: this was her own. Her he desired. His head ached and eyes narrowed with the intensity of his gazing, then as if an obscure fog had blown up in the mind, he experienced fear of her and was aware that he had received an impression, somehow, of evil. He shuddered, saying softly, it is thus with us all. Leo brewed some tea in a small pot and sat sipping it without sugar, to calm himself. But before he had finished drinking, again with excitement he examined the face and found it good: good for Leo Finkle. Only such a one could understand him and help him seek whatever he was seeking. She might, perhaps, love him. How she had happened to be among the discards in Salzman's barrel he could never guess, but he knew he must urgently go find her.

Leo rushed downstairs, grabbed up the Bronx telephone book, and searched for Salzman's home address. He was not listed, nor was his office. Neither was he in the Manhattan book. But Leo remembered having written down the address on a slip of paper after he had read Salzman's advertisement in the "personals" column of the *Forward.* He ran up to his room and tore through his papers, without luck. It was exasperating. Just when he needed the matchmaker he was nowhere to be found. Fortunately Leo remembered to look in his wallet. There on a card he found his name written and a Bronx address. No phone number was listed, the reason—Leo now recalled—he had originally communicated with Salzman by letter. He got on his coat, put a hat on over his skull cap and hurried to the subway station. All the way to the far end of the Bronx he sat on the edge of his seat. He was more than once tempted to take out the picture and see if the girl's face was as he remembered it, but he refrained, allowing the snapshot to remain in his inside coat pocket, content to have her so close. When the train pulled into the station he was waiting at the door and bolted out. He quickly located the street Salzman had advertised.

The building he sought was less than a block from the subway, but it was not an office building, nor even a loft, nor a store in which one could rent office space. It was a very old tenement house. Leo found Salzman's name in pencil on a soiled tag under the bell and climbed three dark flights to his apartment. When he knocked, the door was opened by a thin, asthmatic, gray-haired woman, in felt slippers.

"Yes?" she said, expecting nothing. She listened without listening. He could have sworn he had seen her, too, before but knew it was an illusion.

"Salzman—does he live here? Pinye Salzman," he said, "the matchmaker?"

She stared at him a long minute. "Of course."

He felt embarrassed. "Is he in?"

"No." Her mouth, though left open, offered nothing more.

"The matter is urgent. Can you tell me where his office is?"

"In the air." She pointed upward.

"You mean he has no office?" Leo asked.

"In his socks."

He peered into the apartment. It was sunless and dingy, one large room divided by a half-open curtain, beyond which he could see a sagging metal bed. The near side of a room was crowded with rickety chairs, old bureaus, a three-legged table, racks of cooking utensils, and all the apparatus of a kitchen. But there was no sign of Salzman or his magic barrel, probably also a figment of the imagination. An odor of frying fish made Leo weak to the knees.

"Where is he?" he insisted. "I've got to see your husband."

At length she answered, "So who knows where he is? Every time he thinks a new thought he runs to a different place. Go home, he will find you."

"Tell him Leo Finkle."

She gave no sign she had heard.

He walked downstairs, depressed.

But Salzman, breathless, stood waiting at his door.

Leo was astounded and overjoyed. "How did you get here before me?"

"I rushed."

"Come inside."

They entered. Leo fixed tea, and a sardine sandwich for Salzman. As they were drinking he reached behind him for the packet of pictures and handed them to the marriage broker.

Salzman put down his glass and said expectantly, "You found somebody you like?"

"Not among these."

The marriage broker turned away.

"Here is the one I want." Leo held forth the snapshot.

Salzman slipped on his glasses and took the picture into his trembling hand. He turned ghastly and let out a groan.

"What's the matter?" cried Leo.

"Excuse me. Was an accident this picture. She isn't for you."

Salzman frantically shoved the manila packet into his portfolio. He thrust the snapshot into his pocket and fled down the stairs.

Leo, after momentary paralysis, gave chase and cornered the marriage broker in the vestibule. The landlady made hysterical outcries but neither of them listened.

"Give me back the picture, Salzman."

"No." The pain in his eyes was terrible.

"Tell me who she is then."

"This I can't tell you. Excuse me."

He made to depart, but Leo, forgetting himself, seized the matchmaker by his tight coat and shook him frenziedly.

"Please," sighed Salzman. *"Please."*

Leo ashamedly let him go. "Tell me who she is," he begged. "It's very important for me to know."

"She is not for you. She is a wild one—wild, without shame. This is not a bride for a rabbi."

"What do you mean wild?"

"Like an animal. Like a dog. For her to be poor was a sin. This is why to me she is dead now."

"In God's name, what do you mean?"

"Her I can't introduce to you," Salzman cried.

"Why are you so excited?"

"Why, he asks," Salzman said, bursting into tears. "This is my baby, my Stella, she should burn in hell."

Leo hurried up to bed and hid under the covers. Under the covers he thought his life through. Although he soon fell asleep he could not sleep her out of his mind. He woke, beating his breast. Though he prayed to be rid of her, his prayers went unanswered. Through days of torment he endlessly struggled not to love her; fearing success, he escaped it. He then concluded to convert her to goodness, himself to God. The idea alternately nauseated and exalted him.

He perhaps did not know that he had come to a final decision until he encountered Salzman in a Broadway cafeteria. He was sitting alone at a rear table, sucking the bony remains of a fish. The marriage broker appeared haggard, and transparent to the point of vanishing.

Salzman looked up at first without recognizing him. Leo had grown a pointed beard and his eyes were weighted with wisdom.

"Salzman," he said, "love has at last come to my heart."

"Who can love from a picture?" mocked the marriage broker.

"It is not impossible."

"If you can love her, then you can love anybody. Let me show you some new clients that they just sent me their photographs. One is a little doll."

"Just her I want," Leo murmured.

"Don't be a fool, doctor. Don't bother with her."

"Put me in touch with her, Salzman," Leo said humbly. "Perhaps I can be of service."

Salzman had stopped eating and Leo understood with emotion that it was now arranged.

Leaving the cafeteria, he was, however, afflicted by a tormenting suspicion that Salzman had planned it all to happen this way.

* * *

Leo was informed by letter that she would meet him on a certain corner, and she was there one spring night, waiting under a street lamp. He appeared carrying a small bouquet of violets and rosebuds. Stella stood by the lamp post, smoking. She wore white with red shoes, which fitted his expectations, although in a troubled moment he had imagined the dress red, and only the shoes white. She waited uneasily and shyly. From afar he saw that her eyes—clearly her father's—were filled with desperate innocence. He pictured, in her, his own redemption. Violins and lit candles revolved in the sky. Leo ran forward with flowers outthrust.

Around the corner, Salzman, leaning against a wall, chanted prayers for the dead.

4

Marriage

The Shared Life

Good writers long ago abandoned the custom of ending a story, ". . . and they lived happily ever after"—as if growth, or discord, stopped at the happy conclusion of a youthful romance. Rather, life goes on and, far from growing simpler, usually becomes more complex. Marriage is difficult, demanding as it does that two adults share life together, yet preserve the essence of their separateness as persons.

JAMES THURBER (1894–1961)

James Thurber's versatility as a humorist is attested by the varied nature of his output. He contributed essays, short stories, and cartoons to The New Yorker *magazine, many of which have since been collected for book publication. He also wrote for children and for the stage.*

Thurber's theme, however, was constant: the battle between the sexes. Although his characters are often caricatures and his plots exaggerated, Thurber's understated irony and his obvious sympathy for the meek and the downtrodden (invariably husbands!) strike a responsive chord in all but the most staunch opponents of "light" writing.

"The Secret Life of Walter Mitty," one of his best known short stories, depicts one man's attempts to escape from harrowing reality into the never-never land of late-late show heroics.

The Secret Life of Walter Mitty

"WE'RE GOING THROUGH!" The Commander's voice was like thin ice breaking. He wore his full-dress uniform, with the heavily braided white cap pulled down rakishly over one cold gray eye. "We can't make it, sir. It's spoiling for a hurricane, if you ask me." "I'm not asking you, Lieutenant Berg," said the Commander. "Throw on the power lights! Rev her up to 8,500! We're going through!" The pounding of the cylinders increased; ta-pocketa-pocketa-pocketa-*pocketa-pocketa.* The Commander stared at the ice forming on the pilot window. He walked over and twisted a row of complicated dials. "Switch on No. 8 auxiliary!" he shouted. "Switch on No. 8 auxiliary!" repeated Lieutenant Berg. "Full strength in No. 3 turret!" shouted the Commander. "Full strength in No. 3 turret!" The crew, bending to their various tasks in the huge, hurtling eight-engined Navy hydroplane, looked at each other and grinned. "The Old Man'll get us through," they said to one another. "The Old Man ain't afraid of Hell!" . . .

"Not so fast! You're driving too fast!" said Mrs. Mitty. "What are you driving so fast for?"

"Hmm?" said Walter Mitty. He looked at his wife, in the seat beside him, with shocked astonishment. She seemed grossly unfamiliar, like a strange woman who had yelled at him in a crowd. "You were up to fifty-five," she said. "You know I don't like to go more than forty. You were up to fifty-five." Walter Mitty drove on toward Waterbury in silence, the roaring of the SN202 through the worst storm in twenty years of Navy flying fading in the remote, intimate airways of his mind. "You're tensed up again," said Mrs. Mitty. "It's one of your days. I wish you'd let Dr. Renshaw look you over."

Walter Mitty stopped the car in front of the building where his wife went to have her hair done. "Remember to get those overshoes while I'm having my hair done," she said. "I don't need overshoes," said Mitty. She put her mirror back into her bag. "We've been all through that," she said, getting out of the car. "You're not a young man any longer." He raced the engine a little. "Why don't you wear your gloves? Have you lost your gloves?" Walter Mitty reached in a pocket and brought out the gloves. He put them on, but after she had turned and gone into the building and he had driven on to a red light, he took them off again. "Pick it up, brother!" snapped a cop as the light changed, and Mitty hastily pulled on his gloves and lurched ahead. He drove around the streets aimlessly for a time, and then he drove past the hospital on his way to the parking lot.

. . . "It's the millionaire banker, Wellington McMillan," said the pretty nurse. "Yes?" said Walter Mitty, removing his gloves slowly. "Who has the case?" "Dr. Renshaw and Dr. Benbow, but there are two specialists here, Dr. Remington from New York and Dr. Pritchard-Mitford from London. He flew over." A door opened down a long, cool corridor and Dr. Renshaw came out. He looked distraught and haggard. "Hello, Mitty," he said. "We're having the devil's own time with McMillan, the millionaire banker and close personal friend of Roosevelt. Obstreosis of the ductal tract. Tertiary. Wish you'd take a look at him." "Glad to." said Mitty.

In the operating room there were whispered introductions: "Dr. Remington, Dr. Mitty. Dr. Pritchard-Mitford, Dr. Mitty." "I've read your book on streptothricosis," said Pritchard-Mitford, shaking hands. "A brilliant performance, sir." "Thank you," said Walter Mitty. "Didn't know you were in the States, Mitty," grumbled Remington. "Coals to Newcastle, bringing Mitford and me up here for a tertiary." "You are very kind," said Mitty. A huge, complicated machine, connected to the operating table, with many tubes and wires, began at this moment to go pocketa-pocketa-pocketa. "The new anaesthetizer is giving away!" shouted an interne. "There is no one in the East who knows how to fix it!" "Quiet, man!" said Mitty, in a low, cool voice. He sprang to the machine, which was now going pocketa-pocketa-queep-pocketa-queep. He began fingering delicately a row of glistening dials. "Give me a fountain pen!" he snapped. Someone handed him a fountain pen. He pulled a faulty piston out of the machine and inserted the pen in its place. "That will hold for ten minutes," he said. "Get on with the operation." A nurse hurried over and whispered to Renshaw, and Mitty saw the man turn pale. "Coreopsis has set in," said Renshaw nervously. "If you would take over, Mitty?" Mitty looked at him and at the craven figure of Benbow, who drank, and at the grave, uncertain faces of the two great specialists. "If you wish," he said. They slipped a white gown on him; he adjusted a mask and drew on thin gloves; nurses handed him shining . . .

"Back it up, Mac! Look out for that Buick!" Walter Mitty jammed on the brakes. "Wrong lane, Mac," said the parking-lot attendant, looking at Mitty closely. "Gee. Yeh," muttered Mitty. He began cautiously to back out of the lane marked "Exit Only." "Leave her sit there," said the attendant. "I'll put her away." Mitty got out of the car. "Hey, better leave the key." "Oh," said Mitty, handing the man the ignition key. The attendant vaulted into the car, backed it up with insolent skill, and put it where it belonged.

They're so damn cocky, thought Walter Mitty, walking along Main Street; they think they know everything. Once he had tried to take his chains off, outside New Milford, and he had got them wound around the axles. A man had had to come out in a wrecking car and unwind them, a young, grinning garage man. Since then Mrs. Mitty always made him drive to a garage to have the chains taken off. The next time, he thought, I'll wear my right arm in a sling; they won't grin at me then. I'll have my right arm in a sling and they'll see I couldn't possibly take the chains off myself. He kicked at the slush on the sidewalk. "Overshoes," he said to himself, and he began looking for a shoe store.

When he came out into the street again, with the overshoes in a box under his arm, Walter Mitty began to wonder what the other thing was his wife had told him to get. She had told him, twice before they set out from their house for Waterbury. In a way he hated these weekly trips to town—he was always getting something wrong. Kleenex, he thought, Squibb's, razor blades? No. Toothpaste, toothbrush, bicarbonate, carborundum, initiative and referendum? He gave it up. But she would remember it. "Where's the what's-its-name?" she would ask. "Don't tell me you forgot the what's-its-name." A newsboy went by shouting something about the Waterbury trial.

. . . "Perhaps this will refresh your memory." The District Attorney suddenly thrust a heavy automatic at the quiet figure on the witness stand. "Have you ever seen this before?" Walter Mitty took the gun and examined it expertly. "This is my Webley-Vickers 50.80," he said calmly. An excited buzz ran around the courtroom. The judge rapped for order. "You are a crack shot with any sort of firearms, I believe?" said the District Attorney, insinuatingly. "Objection!" shouted Mitty's attorney. "We have shown the defendant could not have fired the shot. We have shown that he wore his right arm in a sling on the night of the fourteenth of July." Walter Mitty raised his hand briefly and the bickering attorneys were stilled. "With any known make of gun," he said evenly, "I could have killed Gregory Fitzhurst at three hundred feet *with my left hand.*" Pandemonium broke loose in the courtroom. A woman's scream rose above the bedlam and suddenly a lovely, dark-haired girl was in Walter Mitty's arms. The District Attorney struck at her savagely. Without rising from his chair, Mitty let the man have it on the point of the chin. "You miserable cur!" . . .

"Puppy biscuit," said Walter Mitty. He stopped walking and the buildings of Waterbury rose up out of the misty courtroom and surrounded him again. A woman who was passing laughed. "He said 'Puppy biscuit,' " she said to her companion. "That man said 'Puppy biscuit' to himself." Walter Mitty hurried on. He went into an A. & P., not the first one he came to but a smaller one farther up the street. "I want some biscuit for small, young dogs," he said to the clerk. "Any special brand, sir?" The greatest pistol shot in the world thought a moment. "It says 'Puppies Bark for It' on the box," said Walter Mitty.

His wife would be through at the hairdresser's in fifteen minutes, Mitty saw in looking at his watch, unless they had trouble drying it; sometimes they had trouble drying it. She didn't like to get to the hotel first; she would want him to be there waiting for her as usual. He found a big leather chair in the lobby, facing a window, and he put the overshoes and the puppy biscuit on the floor beside it. He picked up an old copy of *Liberty* and sank down into the chair. "Can Germany Conquer the World through the Air?" Walter Mitty looked at the pictures of bombing planes and of ruined streets.

. . . "The cannonading has got the wind up in young Raleigh, sir," said the sergeant. Captain Mitty looked up at him through tousled hair. "Get him to bed," he said wearily, "with the others. I'll fly alone." "But you can't, sir," said the sergeant anxiously. "It takes two men to handle that bomber and the Archies are pounding hell out of the air. Von Richtman's circus is between here and Saulier." "Somebody's got to get that ammunition dump," said Mitty. "I'm going over. Spot of brandy?" He poured a drink for the sergeant and one for himself. War thundered and whined around the dugout and battered at the door. There was a rending of wood and splinters flew through the room. "A bit of a near thing," said Captain Mitty carelessly. "The box barrage is closing in," said the sergeant. "We only live once, sergeant," said Mitty, with his faint, fleeting smile. "Or do we?" He poured another brandy and tossed it off. "I never see a man could hold his brandy like you, sir," said the sergeant. "Begging your pardon, sir." Captain Mitty stood up and strapped on his huge Webley-Vickers automatic. "It's forty kilometers through hell, sir," said the sergeant. Mitty finished one last brandy. "After all," he said softly, "what isn't?" The pounding of the cannon increased; there was the ra-tat-tatting of machine guns, and from somewhere came the menacing pocketa-pocketa-pocketa of the new flame-throwers. Walter Mitty walked to the door of the dugout humming *"Après de Ma Blonde."* He turned and waved to the sergeant. "Cheerio!" he said. . . .

Something struck his shoulder. "I've been looking all over this hotel for you," said Mrs. Mitty. "Why do you have to hide in this old chair? How did you expect me to find you?" "Things close in," said Walter Mitty vaguely. "What?" Mrs. Mitty said. "Did you get the what's-its-name? The puppy biscuit? What's in that box?" "Overshoes," said Mitty. "Couldn't you have put them on in the store?" "I was thinking," said Walter Mitty. "Does it ever occur to you that I am sometimes thinking?" She looked at him. "I'm going to take your temperature when I get you home," she said.

They went out through the revolving doors that made a faintly derisive whistling sound when you pushed them. It was two blocks to the parking lot. At the drugstore on the corner she said, "Wait here for me. I forgot something. I won't be a minute." She was more than a minute. Walter Mitty lighted a cigarette. It began to rain, rain with sleet in it. He stood up against the wall of the drugstore, smoking. . . . He put his shoulders back and his heels together. "To hell with the handkerchief," said Walter Mitty scornfully. He took one last drag on his cigarette and snapped it away. Then, with that faint, fleeting smile playing about his lips, he faced the firing squad; erect and motionless, proud and disdainful, Walter Mitty the Undefeated, inscrutable to the last.

CYRUS COLTER (b. 1910)

At the age of sixty, Cyrus Colter celebrated the publication of his first book, The Beach Umbrella *(1970), a collection of short stories he had been writing in his spare time over the previous ten years. During that period he had built a career as senior member of the Illinois Commerce Commission and as an active participant in other governmental committees, plus various cultural and public service organizations. His book won the Iowa School of Letters Award for the best book-length collection of short fiction by a writer who had not yet published a volume of fiction.*

Although Colter's stories center around the tragedies and ironies of everyday life in the black community of Chicago, the elements of humanity he depicts are universal. He catches critical moments in his characters' lives when they reveal their inner selves in frustrated efforts to overcome the desperation of their existence.

"The Beach Umbrella" presents just such a moment, when the possession of a beach umbrella comes to represent escape from the drabness of Elijah's day-to-day existence.

The Beach Umbrella

THE THIRTY-FIRST STREET beach lay dazzling under a sky so blue that Lake Michigan ran to the horizon like a sheet of sapphire silk, studded with little barbed white sequins for sails; and the heavy surface of the water lapped gently at the boulder "sea wall" which had been cut into, graded, and sanded to make the beach. Saturday afternoons were always frenzied: three black lifeguards, giants in sunglasses, preened in their towers and chaperoned the bathers—adults, teen-agers, and children—who were going through every physical gyration of which the human body is capable. Some dove, swam, some hollered, rode inner tubes, or merely stood waist-deep and pummeled the water; others—on the beach—sprinted, did handsprings and somersaults, sucked Eskimo pies, or just buried their children in the sand. Then there were the lollers—extended in their languor under a garish variety of beach umbrellas.

Elijah lolled too—on his stomach in the white sand, his chin cupped in his palm; but under no umbrella. He had none. By habit, though, he stared in awe at those who did, and sometimes meddled in their conversation: "It's gonna be gettin' hot pretty soon—if it ain't careful," he said to a Bantu-looking fellow and his girl sitting nearby with an older woman. The temperature was then in the nineties. The fellow managed a negligent smile. "Yeah," he said, and persisted in listening to the women. Buoyant still, Elijah watched them. But soon his gaze wavered, and then moved on to other lollers of interest. Finally he got up, stretched, brushed sand from his swimming trunks, and scanned the beach for a new spot. He started walking.

He was not tall. And he appeared to walk on his toes—his nut-colored legs were bowed and skinny and made him hobble like a jerky little spider. Next he plopped down near two men and two girls—they were hilarious about something—sitting beneath a big purple and white umbrella. The girls, chocolate brown and shapely, emitted squeals of laughter at the wisecracks of the men. Elijah was enchanted. All summer long the rambunctious gaiety of the beach had fastened on him a curious charm, a hex, that brought him gawking and twiddling to the lake each Saturday. The rest of the week, save Sunday, he worked. But Myrtle, his wife, detested the sport and stayed away. Randall, the boy, had been only twice and then without little Susan, who during the summer was her mother's own midget reflection. But Elijah came regularly, especially whenever Myrtle was being evil, which he felt now was almost always. She was getting worse, too—if that was possible. The woman was money-crazy.

"You gotta sharp-lookin' umbrella there!" he cut in on the two laughing couples. They studied him—the abruptly silent way. Then the big-shouldered fellow smiled and lifted his eyes to their spangled roof. "Yeah? . . . Thanks," he said. Elijah carried on: "I see a lot of 'em out here this summer—much more'n last year." The fellow meditated on this, but was noncommittal. The others went on gabbing, mostly with their hands. Elijah, squinting in the hot sun, watched them. He didn't see how they could be married; they cut the fool too much, acted like they'd itched to get together for weeks and just now made it. He pondered going back in the water, but he'd already had an hour of that. His eyes traveled the sweltering beach. Funny about his folks; they were every shape and color a God-made human could be. Here was a real sample of variety—pink white to jetty black. Could you any longer call that a race of people? It was a complicated complication—for some real educated guy to figure out. Then another thought slowly bore in on him: the beach umbrellas blooming across the sand attracted people—slews of friends, buddies; and gals, too. Wherever the loudest racket tore the air, a big red, or green, or yellowish umbrella—bordered with white fringe maybe—flowered in the middle of it all and gave shade to the happy good-timers.

Take, for instance, that tropical-looking pea-green umbrella over there, with the Bikinied brown chicks under it, and the portable radio jumping. A real beach party! He got up, stole over, and eased down in the sand at the fringe of the jubilation—two big thermos jugs sat in the shade and everybody had a paper cup in hand as the explosions of buffoonery carried out to the water. Chief provoker of mirth was a bulging-eyed old gal in a white bathing suit who, encumbered by big flabby overripe thighs, cavorted and pranced in the sand. When, perspiring from the heat, she finally fagged out she flopped down almost on top of him. So far he had gone unnoticed. But now, as he craned in at closer range, she brought him up: "Whatta you want, Pops?" She grinned, but with a touch of hostility.

Pops! Where'd she get that stuff? He was only forty-one, not a day older than that boozy bag. But he smiled. "Nothin'," he said brightly, "but you sure got one goin' here." He turned and viewed the noise-makers.

"An' you wanta get in on it!" she wrangled.

"Oh, I was just lookin'—"

"—You was just lookin'. Yeah, you was just lookin' at them young chicks there!" She roared a laugh and pointed at the sexy-looking girls under the umbrella.

Elijah grinned weakly.

"Beat it!" she catcalled, and turned back to the party.

He sat like a rock—the hell with her. But soon he relented, and wandered down to the water's edge—remote now from all inhospitality—to sit in the sand and hug his raised knees. Far out, the sailboats were pinned to the horizon and, despite all the close-in fuss, the wide miles of lake lay impassive under a blazing calm; far south and east down the long curving lake shore, miles in the distance, the smoky haze of the Whiting plant of the Youngstown Sheet and Tube Company hung ominously in an otherwise bright sky. And so it was that he turned back and viewed the beach again—and suddenly caught his craving. Weren't they something—the umbrellas! The flashy colors of them! And the swank! No wonder folks ganged round them. Yes . . . yes, he too must have one. The thought came slow and final, and seared him. For there stood Myrtle in his mind. She nagged him now night and day, and it was always money that got her started; there was never enough—for Susan's shoes, Randy's overcoat, for new kitchen linoleum, Venetian blinds, for a better car than the old Chevy. "I just don't understand you!" she had said only night before last. "Have you got any plans at all for your family? You got a family, you know. If you could only bear to pull yourself away from that deaf old tightwad out at that warehouse, and go get yourself a real job . . . But no! Not you!"

She was talking about old man Schroeder, who owned the warehouse where he worked. Yes, the pay could be better, but it still wasn't as bad as she made out. Myrtle could be such a fool sometimes. He had been with the old man nine years now; had started out as a freight handler, but worked up to doing inventories and a little paper work. True, the business had been going down recently, for the old man's sight and hearing were failing and his key people had left him. Now he depended on him, Elijah—who of late wore a necktie on the job, and made his inventory rounds with a ball-point pen and clipboard. The old man was friendlier, too—almost "hat in hand" to him. He liked everything about the job now—except the pay. And that was only because of Myrtle. She just wanted so much; even talked of moving out of their rented apartment and buying out in the Chatham area. But one thing had to be said for her: she never griped about anything for herself; only for the family, the kids. Every payday he endorsed his check and handed it over to her, and got back in return only gasoline and cigarette money. And this could get pretty tiresome. About six weeks ago he'd gotten a ten-dollar-a-month raise out of the old man, but that had only made her madder than ever. He'd thought about looking for another job all right; but where would he go to get another white-collar job? There weren't many of them for him. She wouldn't care if he went back to the steel mills, back to pouring that white-hot ore out at Youngstown Sheet and Tube. It would be okay with her—so long as his paycheck was fat. But that kind of work was no good, undignified; coming home on the bus you were always so tired you went to sleep in your seat, with your lunch pail in your lap.

Just then two wet boys, chasing each other across the sand, raced by him into the water. The cold spray on his skin made him jump, jolting him out of his thoughts. He turned and slowly scanned the beach again. The umbrellas were brighter, gayer, bolder than ever—each a hiving center of playful people. He stood up finally, took a long last look, and then started back to the spot where he had parked the Chevy.

The following Monday evening was hot and humid as Elijah sat at home in their plain living room and pretended to read the newspaper; the windows were up, but not the slightest breeze came through the screens to stir Myrtle's fluffy curtains. At the moment she and nine-year-old Susan were in the kitchen finishing the dinner dishes. For twenty minutes now he had sat waiting for the furtive chance to speak to Randall. Randall, at twelve, was a serious, industrious boy, and did deliveries and odd jobs for the neighborhood grocer. Soon he came through—intent, absorbed—on his way back to the grocery for another hour's work.

"Gotta go back, eh, Randy?" Elijah said.

"Yes, sir." He was tall for his age, and wore glasses. He paused with his hand on the doorknob.

Elijah hesitated. Better wait, he thought—wait till he comes back. But Myrtle might be around then. Better ask him now. But Randall had opened the door. "See you later, Dad," he said—and left.

Elijah, shaken, again raised the newspaper and tried to read. He should have called him back, he knew, but he had lost his nerve—because he couldn't tell how Randy would take it. Fifteen dollars was nothing though, really—Randy probably had fifty or sixty stashed away somewhere in his room. Then he thought of Myrtle, and waves of fright went over him—to be even thinking about a beach umbrella was bad enough; and to buy one, especially now, would be to her some kind of crime; but to borrow even a part of the money for it from Randy . . . well, Myrtle would go out of her mind. He had never lied to his family before. This would be the first time. And he had thought about it all day long. During the morning, at the warehouse, he had gotten out the two big mail-order catalogues to look at the beach umbrellas; but the ones shown were all so small and dinky-looking he was contemptuous. So at noon he drove the Chevy out to a sporting-goods store on West Sixty-third Street. There he found a gorgeous assortment of yard and beach umbrellas. And there he found his prize. A beauty, a big beauty, with wide red and white stripes, and a white fringe. But oh the price! Twenty-three dollars! And he with nine.

"What's the matter with you?" Myrtle had walked in the room. She was thin, and medium brown-skinned with a saddle of freckles across her nose, and looked harried in her sleeveless housedress with her hair unkempt.

Startled, he lowered the newspaper. "Nothing," he said.

"How can you read looking over the paper?"

"Was I?"

Not bothering to answer, she sank in a chair. "Susie," she called back into the kitchen, "bring my cigarettes in here, will you, baby?"

Soon Susan, chubby and solemn, with the mist of perspiration on her forehead, came in with the cigarettes. "Only three left, Mama," she said, peering into the pack.

"Okay," Myrtle sighed, taking the cigarettes. Susan started out "Now, scour the sink good, honey—and then go take your bath. You'll feel cooler."

Before looking at him again, Myrtle lit a cigarette. "School starts in three weeks," she said, with a forlorn shake of her head. "Do you realize that?"

"Yeah? . . . Jesus, times flies." He could not look at her.

"Susie needs dresses, and a couple of pairs of good shoes—and she'll need a coat before it gets cold."

"Yeah, I know." He patted the arm of the chair.

"Randy—bless his heart—has already made enough to get most of his things. That boy's something; he's all business—I've never seen anything like it." She took a drag on her cigarette. "And old man Schroeder giving you a ten-dollar raise! What was you thinkin' about? What'd you say to him?"

He did not answer at first. Finally he said, "Ten dollars is ten dollars, Myrtle. You know business is slow."

"I'll say it is! And there won't be any business before long—and then where'll you be? I tell you over and over again, you better start looking for something now! I been preachin' it to you for a year."

He said nothing.

"Ford and International Harvester are hiring every man they can lay their hands on! And the mills out in Gary and Whiting are going full blast—you see the red sky every night. The men make good money."

"They earn every nickel of it, too," he said in gloom.

"But they get it! Bring it home! It spends! Does that mean anything to you? Do you know what some of them make? Well, ask Hawthorne—or ask Sonny Milton. Sonny's wife says his checks some weeks run as high as a hundred twenty, hundred thirty dollars. One week! Take-home pay!"

"Yeah? . . . And Sonny told me he wished he had a job like mine."

Myrtle threw back her head with a bitter gasp. "Oh-h-h, God! Did you tell him what you made? Did you tell him that?"

Suddenly Susan came back into the muggy living room. She went straight to her mother and stood as if expecting an award. Myrtle absently patted her on the side of the head. "Now, go and run your bath water, honey," she said.

Elijah smiled at Susan. "Susie," he said, "d'you know your tummy is stickin' way out—you didn't eat too much, did you?" He laughed.

Susan turned and observed him; then looked at her mother. "No," she finally said.

"Go on now, baby," Myrtle said. Susan left the room.

Myrtle resumed. "Well, there's no use going through all this again. It's plain as the nose on your face. You got a family—a good family, I think. The only question is, do you wanta get off your hind end and do somethin' for it. It's just that simple."

Elijah looked at her. "You can talk real crazy sometimes, Myrtle."

"I think it's that old man!" she cried, her freckles contorted. "He's got you answering the phone, and taking inventory—wearing a necktie and all that. You wearing a necktie and your son mopping in a grocery store, so he can buy his own clothes." She snatched up her cigarettes, and walked out of the room.

His eyes did not follow her, but remained off in space. Finally he got up and went into the kitchen. Over the stove the plaster was thinly cracked, and in spots the linoleum had worn through the pattern; but everything was immaculate. He opened the refrigerator, poured a glass of cold water, and sat down at the kitchen table. He felt strange and weak, and sat for a long time sipping the water.

Then after a while he heard Randall's key in the front door, sending tremors of dread through him. When Randall came into the kitchen, he seemed to him as tall as himself; his glasses were steamy from the humidity outside, and his hands were dirty.

"Hi, Dad," he said gravely without looking at him, and opened the refrigerator door.

Elijah chuckled. "Your mother'll get after you about going in there without washing your hands.

But Randall took out the water pitcher and closed the door.

Elijah watched him. Now was the time to ask him. His heart was hammering. Go on—now! But instead he heard his husky voice saying, "What'd they have you doing over at the grocery tonight?"

Randall was drinking the glass of water. When he finished, he said, "Refilling shelves."

"Pretty hot job tonight, eh?"

"It wasn't so bad." Randall was matter-of-fact as he set the empty glass over the sink, and paused before leaving.

"Well . . . you're doing fine, son. Fine. Your mother sure is proud of you . . ." Purpose had lodged in his throat.

The praise embarrassed Randall. "Okay, Dad," he said, and edged from the kitchen.

Elijah slumped back in his chair, near prostration. He tried to clear his mind of every particle of thought, but the images became only more jumbled, oppressive to the point of panic.

Then before long Myrtle came into the kitchen—ignoring him. But she seemed not so hostile now as coldly impassive, exhibiting a bravado he had not seen before. He got up and went back into the living room and turned on the television. As the TV-screen lawmen galloped before him, he sat oblivious, admitting the failure of his will. If only he could have gotten Randall to himself long enough—but everything had been so sudden, abrupt; he couldn't just ask him out of the clear blue. Besides, around him Randall always seemed so busy, too busy to talk. He couldn't understand that; he had never mistreated the boy, never whipped him in his life; had shaken him a time or two, but that was long ago, when he was little.

He sat and watched the finish of the half-hour TV show. Myrtle was in the bedroom now. He slouched in his chair, lacking the resolve to get up and turn off the television.

Suddenly he was on his feet.

Leaving the television on, he went back to Randall's room in the rear. The door was open and Randall was asleep, lying on his back on the bed, perspiring, still dressed except for his shoes and glasses. He stood over the bed and looked at him. He was a good boy; his own son. But how strange—he thought for the first time—there was no resemblance between them. None whatsoever. Randy had a few of his mother's freckles on his thin brown face, but he could see none of himself in the boy. Then his musings were scattered by the return of his fear. He dreaded waking him. And he might be cross. If he didn't hurry, though, Myrtle or Susie might come strolling out any minute. His bones seemed rubbery from the strain. Finally he bent down and touched Randall's shoulder. The boy did not move a muscle, except to open his eyes. Elijah smiled at him. And he slowly sat up.

"Sorry, Randy—to wake you up like this."

"What's the matter?" Randall rubbed his eyes.

Elijah bent down again, but did not whisper. "Say, can you let me have fifteen bucks—till I get my check? . . . I need to get some things—and I'm a little short this time." He could hardly bring the words up.

Randall gave him a slow, queer look.

"I'll get my check a week from Friday," Elijah said, ". . . and I'll give it back to you then—sure."

Now instinctively Randall glanced toward the door, and Elijah knew Myrtle had crossed his thoughts. "You don't have to mention anything to your mother," he said with casual suddenness.

Randall got up slowly off the bed, and in his socks walked to the little table where he did his homework. He pulled the drawer out, fished far in the back a moment, and brought out a white business envelope secured by a rubber band. Holding the envelope close to his stomach, he took out first a ten-dollar bill, and then a five, and, sighing, handed them over.

"Thanks, old man," Elijah quivered, folding the money. "You'll get this back the day I get my check. . . . That's for sure."

"Okay," Randall finally said.

Elijah started out. Then he could see Myrtle on payday—her hand extended for his check. He hesitated, and looked at Randall, as if to speak. But he slipped the money in his trousers pocket and hurried from the room.

The following Saturday at the beach did not begin bright and sunny. By noon it was hot, but the sky was overcast and angry, the air heavy. There was no certainty whatever of a crowd, raucous or otherwise, and this was Elijah's chief concern as, shortly before twelve o'clock, he drove up in the Chevy and parked in the bumpy, graveled stretch of high ground that looked down eastward over the lake and was used for a parking lot. He climbed out of the car, glancing at the lake and clouds, and prayed in his heart it would not rain—the water was murky and restless, and only a handful of bathers had showed. But it was early yet. He stood beside the car and watched a bulbous, brown-skinned woman, in bathing suit and enormous straw hat, lugging a lunch basket down toward the beach, followed by her brood of children. And a fellow in swimming trunks, apparently the father, took a towel and sandals from his new Buick and called petulantly to his family to "just wait a minute, please." In another car, two women sat waiting, as yet fully clothed and undecided about going swimming. While down at the water's edge there was the usual cluster of dripping boys who, brash and boisterous, swarmed to the beach every day in fair weather or foul.

Elijah took off his shirt, peeled his trousers from over his swimming trunks, and started collecting the paraphernalia from the back seat of the car: a frayed pink rug filched from the house, a towel, sunglasses, cigarettes, a thermos jug filled with cold lemonade he had made himself, and a dozen paper cups. All this he stacked on the front fender. Then he went around to the rear and opened the trunk. Ah, there it lay—encased in a long, slim package trussed with heavy twine, and barely fitting athwart the spare tire. He felt prickles of excitement as he took the knife from the tool bag, cut the twine, and pulled the wrapping paper away. Red and white stripes sprang at him. It was even more gorgeous than when it had first seduced him in the store. The white fringe gave it style; the wide red fillets were cardinal and stark, and the white stripes glared. Now he opened it over his head for the full thrill of its colors, and looked around to see if anyone else agreed. Finally after a while he gathered up all his equipment and headed down for the beach, his short, nubby legs seeming more bowed than ever under the weight of their cargo.

When he reached the sand, a choice of location became a pressing matter. That was why he had come early. From past observation it was clear that the center of gaiety shifted from day to day; last Saturday it might have been nearer the water, this Saturday, well back; or up, or down, the beach a ways. He must pick the site with care, for he could not move about the way he did when he had no umbrella; it was too noticeable. He finally took a spot as near the center of the beach as he could estimate, and dropped his gear in the sand. He knelt down and spread the pink rug, then moved the thermos jug over onto it, and folded the towel and placed it with the paper cups, sunglasses, and cigarettes down beside the jug. Now he went to find a heavy stone or brick to drive down the spike for the hollow umbrella stem to fit over. So it was not until the umbrella was finally up that he again had time for anxiety about the weather. His whole morning's effort had been an act of faith, for, as yet, there was no sun, although now and then a few azure breaks appeared in the thinning cloud mass. But before very long this brighter texture of the sky began to grow and spread by slow degrees, and his hopes quickened. Finally he sat down under the umbrella, lit a cigarette, and waited.

It was not long before two small boys came by—on their way to the water. He grinned, and called to them, "Hey, fellas, been in yet?"—their bathing suits were dry.

They stopped, and observed him. Then one of them smiled, and shook his head.

Elijah laughed. "Well, whatta you waitin' for? Go on in there and get them suits wet!" Both boys gave him silent smiles. And they lingered. He thought this a good omen—it had been different the Saturday before.

Once or twice the sun burst through the weakening clouds. He forgot the boys now in watching the skies, and soon they moved on. His anxiety was not detectable from his lazy posture under the umbrella, with his dwarfish, gnarled legs extended and his bare heels on the little rug. But then soon the clouds began to fade in earnest, seeming not to move away laterally, but slowly to recede into a lucent haze, until at last the sun came through hot and bright. He squinted at the sky and felt delivered. They would come, the folks would come!—were coming now; the beach would soon be swarming. Two other umbrellas were up already, and the diving board thronged with wet, acrobatic boys. The lifeguards were in their towers now, and still another launched his yellow rowboat. And up on the Outer Drive, the cars, one by one, were turning into the parking lot. The sun was bringing them out all right; soon he'd be in the middle of a field day. He felt a low-key, welling excitement, for the water was blue and far out the sails were starched and white.

Soon he saw the two little boys coming back. They were soaked. Their mother—a thin, brown girl in a yellow bathing suit—was with them now, and the boys were pointing to his umbrella. She seemed dignified for her youth, as she gave him a shy glance and then smiled at the boys.

"Ah, ha!" he cried to the boys. "You've been in now all right!" And then laughing to her, "I was kiddin' them a while ago about their dry bathing suits."

She smiled at the boys again. "They like for me to be with them when they go in," she said.

"I got some lemonade here," he said abruptly, slapping the thermos jug. "Why don't you have some?" His voice was anxious.

She hesitated.

He jumped up. "Come on, sit down." He smiled at her and stepped aside.

Still she hesitated. But her eager boys pressed close behind her. Finally she smiled and sat down under the umbrella.

"You fellas can sit down under there too—in the shade," he said to the boys, and pointed under the umbrella. The boys flopped down quickly in the shady sand. He started at once serving them cold lemonade in the paper cups.

"Whew! I thought it was goin' to rain there for a while," he said, making conversation after passing out the lemonade. He had squatted on the sand and lit another cigarette. "Then there wouldn't a been much goin' on. But it turned out fine after all—there'll be a mob here before long."

She sipped the lemonade, but said little. He felt she had sat down only because of the boys, for she merely smiled and gave short answers to his questions. He learned the boys' names, Melvin and James; their ages, seven and nine; and that they were still frightened by the water. But he wanted to ask her name, and inquire about her husband. But he could not capture the courage.

Now the sun was hot and the sand was hot. And an orange and white umbrella was going up right beside them—two fellows and a girl. When the fellow who had been kneeling to drive the umbrella spike in the sand stood up, he was string-bean tall, and black, with his glistening hair freshly processed. The girl was a lighter brown, and wore a lilac bathing suit, and although her legs were thin, she was pleasant enough to look at. The second fellow was medium, really, in height, but short beside his tall, black friend. He was yellow-skinned, and fast getting bald, although still in his early thirties. Both men sported little shoestring moustaches.

Elijah—watched them in silence as long as he could. "You picked the right spot all right!" he laughed at last, putting on his sunglasses.

"How come, man?" The tall, black fellow grinned, showing his mouthful of gold teeth.

"You see everybody here!" happily rejoined Elijah. "They all come here!"

"Man, I been coming here for years," the fellow reproved, and sat down in his khaki swimming trunks to take off his shoes. Then he stood up. "But right now, in the water I goes." He looked down at the girl. "How 'bout you, Lois, baby?"

"No, Caesar," she smiled, "not yet; I'm gonna sit here awhile and relax.

"Okay, then—you just sit right there and relax. And Little Joe"—he turned and grinned to his shorter friend—"you sit there an' relax right along with her. You all can talk with this gentleman here"—he nodded at Elijah—"an' his nice wife." Then, pleased with himself, he trotted off toward the water.

The young mother looked at Elijah, as if he should have hastened to correct him. But somehow he had not wanted to. Yet too, Caesar's remark seemed to amuse her, for she soon smiled. Elijah felt the pain of relief—he did not want her to go; he glanced at her with a furtive laugh, and then they both laughed. The boys had finished their lemonade now, and were digging in the sand. Lois and Little Joe were busy talking.

Elijah was not quite sure what he should say to the mother. He did not understand her, was afraid of boring her, was desperate to keep her interested. As she sat looking out over the lake, he watched her. She was not pretty; and she was too thin. But he thought she had poise; he liked the way she treated her boys—tender, but casual; how different from Myrtle's frantic herding.

Soon she turned to the boys. "Want to go back in the water?" she laughed.

The boys looked at each other, and then at her. "Okay," James said finally, in resignation.

"Here, have some more lemonade," Elijah cut in.

The boys, rescued for the moment, quickly extended their cups. He poured them more lemonade, as she looked on smiling.

Now he turned to Lois and Little Joe sitting under their orange and white umbrella. "How 'bout some good ole cold lemonade?" he asked with a mushy smile. "I got plenty of cups." He felt he must get something going.

Lois smiled back. "No thanks," she said, fluttering her long eyelashes, "not right now."

He looked anxiously at Little Joe.

"I'll take a cup!" said Little Joe, and turned and laughed to Lois: "Hand me that bag there, will you?" He pointed to her beach bag in the sand. She passed it to him, and he reached in and pulled out a pint of gin. "We'll have some *real* lemonade," he vowed with a daredevilish grin.

Lois squealed with pretended embarrassment. "Oh, Joe!"

Elijah's eyes were big now; he was thinking of the police. But he handed Little Joe a cup and poured the lemonade, to which Joe added gin. Then Joe, grinning, thrust the bottle at Elijah. "How 'bout yourself, chief?" he said.

Elijah, shaking his head, leaned forward and whispered, "You ain't suppose to drink on the beach y'know."

"This ain't a drink, man—it's a taste!" said Little Joe, laughing and waving the bottle around toward the young mother. "How 'bout a little taste for your wife here?" he said to Elijah.

The mother laughed and threw up both hands. "No, not for me!"

Little Joe gave her a rakish grin. "What'sa matter? You 'fraid of that guy?" He jerked his thumb toward Elijah. "You 'fraid of gettin' a whippin', eh?"

"No, not exactly," she laughed.

Elijah was so elated with her his relief burst up in hysterical laughter. His laugh became strident and hoarse and he could not stop. The boys gaped at him, and then at their mother. When finally he recovered, Little Joe asked him, "Whut's so funny 'bout that?" Then Little Joe grinned at the mother. "You beat him up sometimes, eh?"

This started Elijah's hysterics all over again. The mother looked concerned now, and embarrassed; her laugh was nervous and shadowed. Little Joe glanced at Lois, laughed, and shrugged his shoulders. When Elijah finally got control of himself again he looked spent and demoralized.

Lois now tried to divert attention by starting a conversation with the boys. But the mother showed signs of restlessness and seemed ready to go. At this moment Caesar returned. Glistening beads of water ran off his long, black body; and his hair was unprocessed now. He surveyed the group and then flashed a wide, gold-toothed grin. "One big, happy family, like I said." Then he spied the paper cup in Little Joe's hand. "Whut you got there, man?"

Little Joe looked down into his cup with a playful smirk. "Lemonade, lover boy, lemonade."

"Don't hand me that jive, Joey. You ain't never had any straight lemonade in your life."

This again brought uproarious laughter from Elijah. "I got the straight lemonade here!" He beat the thermos jug with his hand. "Come on—have some!" He reached for a paper cup.

"Why, sure," said poised Caesar. He held out the cup and received the lemonade. "Now, gimme that gin," he said to Little Joe. Joe handed over the gin, and Caesar poured three fingers into the lemonade and sat down in the sand with his legs crossed under him. Soon he turned to the two boys, as their mother watched him with amusement. "Say, ain't you boys goin' in any more? Why don't you tell your daddy there to take you in?" He nodded toward Elijah.

Little Melvin frowned at him. "My daddy's workin'," he said.

Caesar's eyebrows shot up. "Oooh, la, la!" he crooned. "Hey, now!" And he turned and looked at the mother and then at Elijah, and gave a clownish little snigger.

Lois tittered before feigning exasperation at him. "There you go again," she said, "talkin' when you shoulda been listening."

Elijah laughed along with the rest. But he felt deflated. Then he glanced at the mother, who was laughing too. He could detect in her no sign of dismay. Why then had she gone along with the gag in the first place, he thought—if now she didn't hate to see it punctured?

"Hold the phone!" softly exclaimed Little Joe. "Whut is this?" He was staring over his shoulder. Three women, young, brown, and worldly looking, wandered toward them, carrying an assortment of beach paraphernalia and looking for a likely spot. They wore scant bathing suits, and were followed, but slowly, by an older woman with big, unsightly thighs. Elijah recognized her at once. She was the old gal who the Saturday before had chased him away from her beach party. She wore the same white bathing suit, and one of her girls carried the pea-green umbrella.

Caesar forgot his whereabouts ogling the girls. The older woman, observing this, paused to survey the situation. "How 'bout along in here?" she finally said to one of the girls. The girl carrying the thermos jug set it in the sand so close to Caesar it nearly touched him. He was rapturous. The girl with the umbrella had no chance to put it up, for Caesar and Little Joe instantly encumbered her with help. Another girl turned on a portable radio, and grinning, feverish Little Joe started snapping his fingers to the music's beat.

Within a half hour, a boisterous party was in progress. The little radio, perched on a hump of sand, blared out hot jazz, as the older woman—whose name turned out to be Hattie—passed around some cold, rum-spiked punch; and before long she went into her dancing-prancing act—to the riotous delight of all, especially Elijah. Hattie did not remember him from the Saturday past, and he was glad, for everything was so different today! As different as milk and ink. He knew no one realized it, but this was his party really—the wildest, craziest, funniest, and best he had ever seen or heard of. Nobody had been near the water—except Caesar, and the mother and boys much earlier. It appeared Lois was Caesar's girl friend, and she was hence more capable of reserve in face of the come-on antics of Opal, Billie, and Quanita—Hattie's girls. But Little Joe, to Caesar's tortured envy, was both free and aggressive. Even the young mother, who now volunteered her name to be Mrs. Green, got frolicsome, and twice jabbed Little Joe in the ribs.

Finally Caesar proposed they all go in the water. This met with instant, tipsy acclaim; and Little Joe, his yellow face contorted from laughing, jumped up, grabbed Billie's hand and made off with her across the sand. But Hattie would not budge. Full of rum, and stubborn, she sat sprawled with her flaccid thighs spread in an obscene V, and her eyes half shut. Now she yelled at her departing girls: "You all watch out, now! Don'tcha go in too far. . . . Just wade! None o' you can swim a lick!"

Elijah now was beyond happiness. He felt a floating, manic glee. He sprang up and jerked Mrs. Green splashing into the water, followed by her somewhat less ecstatic boys. Caesar had to paddle about with Lois and leave Little Joe unassisted to caper with Billie, Opal, and Quanita. Billie was the prettiest of the three, and despite Hattie's contrary statement, she could swim; and Little Joe, after taking her out in deeper water, waved back to Caesar in triumph. The sun was brazen now, and the beach and lake thronged with a variegated humanity. Elijah, a strong but awkward, country-style swimmer, gave Mrs. Green a lesson in floating on her back, and though she too could swim, he often felt obligated to place both his arms under her young body and buoy her up.

And sometimes he would purposely let her sink to her chin, whereupon she would feign a happy fright and utter faint simian screeches. Opal and Quanita sat in the shallows and kicked up their heels at Caesar, who, fully occupied with Lois, was a grinning, water-threshing study in frustration.

Thus the party went—on and on—till nearly four o'clock. Elijah had not known the world afforded such joy; his homely face was a wet festoon of beams and smiles. He went from girl to girl, insisting she learn to float on his outstretched arms. Once begrudging Caesar admonished him, "Man, you gonna drown one o' them pretty chicks." And Little Joe bestowed his highest accolade by calling him "lover boy," as Elijah nearly strangled from laughter.

At last they looked up to see old Hattie as she reeled down to the water's edge, coming to fetch her girls. Both Caesar and Little Joe ran out of the water to meet her, seized her by the wrists, and, despite her struggles and curses, dragged her in. "Turn me loose! You big galoots!" she yelled and gasped as the water hit her. She was in knee-deep before she wriggled and fought herself free, with such force she sat down in the wet sand with a thud. She roared a laugh now, and spread her arms for help, as her girls came sprinting and splashing out of the water and tugged her to her feet. Her eyes narrowed to vengeful, grinning slits as she turned on Caesar and Little Joe: "I know whut you two're up to!" She flashed a glance around toward her girls. "I been watchin' both o' you studs! Yeah, yeah, but your eyes may shine, an' your teeth may grit . . ." She went limp in a sneering, raucous laugh. Everybody laughed now—except Lois and Mrs. Green.

They had all come out of the water now, and soon the whole group returned to their three beach umbrellas. Hattie's girls immediately prepared to break camp. They took down their pea-green umbrella, folded some wet towels, and donned their beach sandals, as Hattie still bantered Caesar and Little Joe.

"Well, you sure had yourself a ball today," she said to Little Joe, who was sitting in the sand.

"Coming back next Saturday?" asked grinning Little Joe.

"I jus' might at that," surmised Hattie. "We wuz here last Saturday."

"Good! Good!" Elijah broke in. "Let's all come back—next Saturday!" He searched every face.

"I'll be here," chimed Little Joe, grinning to Caesar. Captive Caesar glanced at Lois, and said nothing.

Lois and Mrs. Green were silent. Hattie, insulted, looked at them and started swelling up. "Never mind," she said pointedly to Elijah, "you jus' come on anyhow. You'll run into a slew o' folks lookin' for a good time. You don't need no certain people." But a little later, she and her girls all said friendly goodbyes and walked off across the sand.

The party now took a sudden downturn. All Elijah's efforts at resuscitation seemed unavailing. The westering sun was dipping toward the distant buildings of the city, and many of the bathers were leaving. Caesar and Little Joe had become bored; and Mrs. Green's boys, whining to go, kept a reproachful eye on their mother.

"Here, you boys, take some more lemonade," Elijah said quickly, reaching for the thermos jug. "Only got a little left—better get while gettin's good!" He laughed. The boys shook their heads.

On Lois he tried cajolery. Smiling and pointing to her wet, but trim bathing suit, he asked, "What color would you say that is?"

"Lilac," said Lois, now standing.

"It sure is pretty! Prettiest on the beach!" he whispered.

Lois gave him a weak smile. Then she reached down for her beach bag, and looked at Caesar.

Caesar stood up. "Let's cut," he turned and said to Little Joe, and began taking down their orange and white umbrella.

Elijah was desolate. "Whatta you goin' for? It's getting cooler! Now's the time to enjoy the beach!"

"I've got to go home," Lois said.

Mrs. Green got up now; her boys had started off already. "Just a minute, Melvin," she called, frowning. Then, smiling, she turned and thanked Elijah.

He whirled around to them all. "Are we comin' back next Saturday? Come on—let's all come back! Wasn't it great! It was great! Don't you think? Whatta you say?" He looked now at Lois and Mrs. Green.

"We'll see," Lois said, smiling. "Maybe."

"Can you come?" He turned to Mrs. Green.

"I'm not sure," she said. "I'll try."

"Fine! Oh, that's fine!" He turned on Caesar and Little Joe. "I'll be lookin' for you guys, hear?"

"Okay, chief," grinned Little Joe. "An' put somethin' in that lemonade, will ya?"

Everybody laughed . . . and soon they were gone.

Elijah slowly crawled back under his umbrella, although the sun's heat was almost spent. He looked about him. There was only one umbrella on the spot now, his own, where before there had been three. Cigarette butts and paper cups lay strewn where Hattie's girls had sat, and the sandy imprint of Caesar's enormous street shoes marked his site. Mrs. Green had dropped a bobby pin. He too was caught up now by a sudden urge to go. It was hard to bear much longer—the lonesomeness. And most of the people were leaving anyway. He stirred and fidgeted in the sand, and finally started an inventory of his belongings. . . . Then his thoughts flew home, and he reconsidered. Funny—he hadn't thought of home all afternoon. Where had the time gone anyhow? . . . It seemed he'd just pulled up in the Chevy and unloaded his gear; now it was time to go home again. Then the image of solemn Randy suddenly formed in his mind, sending waves of guilt through him. He forgot where he was as the duties of his existence leapt on his back—where would he ever get Randy's fifteen dollars? He felt squarely confronted by a great blank void. It was an awful thing he had done—all for a day at the beach . . . with some sporting girls. He thought of his family and felt tiny—and him itching to come back next Saturday! Maybe Myrtle was right about him after all. Lord, if she knew what he had done . . .

He sat there for a long time. Most of the people were gone now. The lake was quiet save for a few boys still in the water. And the sun, red like blood, had settled on the dark silhouettes of the housetops across the city. He sat beneath the umbrella just as he had at one o'clock . . . and the thought smote him. He was jolted. Then dubious. But there it was—quivering, vital, swelling inside his skull like an unwanted fetus. So this was it! He mutinied inside. So he must sell it . . . his umbrella. Sell it for anything—only as long as it was enough to pay back Randy. For fifteen dollars even, if necessary. He was dogged; he couldn't do it; that wasn't the answer anyway. But the thought clawed and clung to him, rebuking and coaxing him by turns, until it finally became conviction. He must do it; it was the right thing to do; the only thing to do. Maybe then the awful weight would lift, the dull commotion in his stomach cease. He got up and started collecting his belongings; placed the thermos jug, sunglasses, towel, cigarettes, and little rug together in a neat pile, to be carried to the Chevy later. Then he turned to face his umbrella. Its red and white stripes stood defiant against the wide, churned-up sand. He stood for a moment mooning at it. Then he carefully let it down, and carrying it in his right hand, went off across the sand.

The sun now had gone down behind the vast city in a shower of crimson-golden glints, and on the beach only a few stragglers remained. For his first prospects he approached two teen-age boys, but suddenly realizing they had no money he turned away and went over to an old woman, squat and black, in street clothes—a spectator—who stood gazing eastward out across the lake. She held in her hand a little black book, with red-edged pages, which looked like the New Testament. He smiled at her. "Wanna buy a nice new beach umbrella?" He held out the collapsed umbrella toward her.

She gave him a beatific smile, but shook her head. "No, son," she said, "that ain't what I want." And she turned to gaze out on the lake again.

For a moment he still held the umbrella out, with a question mark on his face. "Okay, then," he finally said, and went on.

Next he hurried down to the water's edge, where he saw a man and two women preparing to leave. "Wanna buy a nice new beach umbrella?" His voice sounded high-pitched, as he opened the umbrella over his head. "It's brand-new. I'll sell it for fifteen dollars—it cost a lot more'n that."

The man was hostile, and glared. Finally he said, "Whatta you take me for —a fool?"

Elijah looked bewildered, and made no answer. He observed the man for a moment. Finally he let the umbrella down. As he moved away, he heard the man say to the women, "It's hot—he stole it somewhere."

Close by another man sat alone in the sand. Elijah started toward him. The man wore trousers, but was stripped to the waist, and bent over intent on some task in his lap. When Elijah reached him he looked up from half a hatful of cigarette butts he was breaking open for the tobacco he collected in a little paper bag. He grinned at Elijah, who meant now to pass on.

"No, I ain't interested either, buddy," the man insisted as Elijah passed him. "Not me. I jus' got outa jail las' week—an' ain't goin' back for no umbrella." He laughed, as Elijah kept on.

Now he saw three women, still in their bathing suits, sitting together near the diving board. They were the only people he had not yet tried—except the one lifeguard left. As he approached them, he saw that all three wore glasses and were sedate. Some schoolteachers maybe, he thought, or office workers. They were talking—until they saw him coming; then they stopped. One of them was plump, but a smooth dark brown, and sat with a towel around her shoulders. Elijah addressed them through her: "Wanna buy a nice beach umbrella?" And again he opened the umbrella over his head.

"Gee! It's beautiful," the plump woman said to the others. "But where'd you get it?" she suddenly asked Elijah, polite mistrust entering her voice.

"I bought it—just this week."

The three women looked at each other. "Why do you want to sell it so soon then?" a second woman said.

Elijah grinned. "I need the money."

"Well!" The plump woman was exasperated. "No, we don't want it." And they turned from him. He stood for a while, watching them; finally he let the umbrella down and moved on.

Only the lifeguard was left. He was a huge youngster, not over twenty, and brawny and black as he bent over cleaning out his beached rowboat. Elijah approached him so suddenly he looked up startled.

"Would you be interested in this umbrella?" Elijah said, and proffered the umbrella. "It's brand-new—I just bought it Tuesday. I'll sell it cheap." There was urgency in his voice.

The lifeguard gave him a queer stare; and then peered off toward the Outer Drive, as if looking for help. "You're lucky as hell," he finally said. "The cops just now cruised by—up on the Drive. I'd have turned you in so quick it'd make your head swim. Now you get the hell outa here." He was menacing.

Elijah was angry. "Whatta you mean? I bought this umbrella—it's mine."

The lifeguard took a step toward him. "I said you better get the hell outa here! An' I mean it! You thievin' bastard, you!"

Elijah, frightened now, gave ground. He turned and walked away a few steps; and then slowed up, as if an adequate answer had hit him. He stood for a moment. But finally he walked on, the umbrella drooping in his hand.

He walked up the gravelly slope now toward the Chevy, forgetting his little pile of belongings left in the sand. When he reached the car, and opened the trunk, he remembered; and went back down and gathered them up. He returned, threw them in the trunk and, without dressing, went around and climbed under the steering wheel. He was scared, shaken; and before starting the motor sat looking out on the lake. It was seven o'clock; the sky was waning pale, the beach forsaken, leaving a sense of perfect stillness and approaching night; the only sound was a gentle lapping of the water against the sand—one moderate hallo-o-o-o would have carried across to Michigan. He looked down at the beach. Where were they all now—the funny, proud, laughing people? Eating their dinners, he supposed, in a variety of homes. And all the beautiful umbrellas—where were they? Without their colors the beach was so deserted. Ah, the beach . . . after pouring hot ore all week out at Youngstown Sheet and Tube, he would probably be too fagged out for the beach. But maybe he wouldn't—who knew? It was great while it lasted . . . great. And his umbrella . . . he didn't know what he'd do with that . . . he might never need it again. He'd keep it, though—and see. Ha! . . . hadn't he sweat to get it! . . . and they thought he had stolen it . . . stolen it . . . ah . . . and maybe they were right. He sat for a few moments longer. Finally he started the motor, and took the old Chevy out onto the Drive in the pink-hued twilight. But down on the beach the sun was still shining.

IRWIN SHAW (b. 1913)

A native of Brooklyn, Irwin Shaw has been successful as a playwright, screenwriter, novelist, and short story writer. His first success was a one-act anti-war play, "Bury the Dead," which was staged by the Group Theater in the thirties. He has published six collections of short stories and several novels including The Young Lions *(1948), one of the finest war novels to come out of World War II, and* Rich Man, Poor Man *(1971), a panorama of post–World War II America.*

Shaw's greatest strengths as a writer are usually said to be the technical skill with which he can swiftly sketch in a character or a setting, judiciously using a few simple details, plus his accurate ear for dialogue, especially that which can be overheard on the sidewalks of New York.

"The Girls in Their Summer Dresses," records a verbal conflict between a husband and wife that gives a penetrating glimpse of their underlying relationship.

The Girls in Their Summer Dresses

FIFTH AVENUE was shining in the sun when they left the Brevoort. The sun was warm, even though it was February, and everything looked like Sunday morning—the buses and the well-dressed people walking slowly in couples and the quiet buildings with the windows closed.

Michael held Frances' arm tightly as they walked toward Washington Square in the sunlight. They walked lightly, almost smiling, because they had slept late and had a good breakfast and it was Sunday. Michael unbuttoned his coat and let it flap around him in the mild wind.

"Look out," Frances said as they crossed Eighth Street. "You'll break your neck." Michael laughed and Frances laughed with him.

"She's not so pretty," Frances said. "Anyway, not pretty enough to take a chance of breaking your neck."

Michael laughed again. "How did you know I was looking at her?"

Frances cocked her head to one side and smiled at her husband under the brim of her hat. "Mike, darling," she said.

"O.K.," he said. "Excuse me."

Frances patted his arm lightly and pulled him along a little faster toward Washington Square. "Let's not see anybody all day," she said. "Let's just hang around with each other. You and me. We're always up to our neck in people, drinking their Scotch or drinking our Scotch; we only see each other in bed. I want to go out with my husband all day long. I want him to talk only to me and listen only to me."

"What's to stop us?" Michael asked.

"The Stevensons. They want us to drop by around one o'clock and they'll drive us into the country."

"The cunning Stevensons," Mike said. "Transparent. They can whistle. They can go driving in the country by themselves."

"Is it a date?"

"It's a date."

Frances leaned over and kissed him on the tip of the ear.

"Darling," Michael said, "this is Fifth Avenue."

"Let me arrange a program," Frances said. "A planned Sunday in New York for a young couple with money to throw away."

"Go easy."

"First let's go to the Metropolitan Museum of Art," Frances suggested, because Michael had said during the week he wanted to go. "I haven't been there in three years and there're at least ten pictures I want to see again. Then we can take the bus down to Radio City and watch them skate. And later we'll go down to Cavanagh's and get a steak as big as a blacksmith's apron, with a bottle of wine, and after that there's a French picture at the Filmarte that everybody says—say, are you listening to me?"

"Sure," he said. He took his eyes off the hatless girl with the dark hair, cut dancer-style like a helmet, who was walking past him.

"That's the program for the day," Frances said flatly. "Or maybe you'd just rather walk up and down Fifth Avenue."

"No," Michael said. "Not at all."

"You always look at other women," Frances said. "Everywhere. Every damned place we go."

"No, darling," Michael said, "I look at everything. God gave me eyes and I look at women and men in subway excavations and moving pictures and the little flowers of the field. I casually inspect the universe."

"You ought to see the look in your eye," Frances said, "as you casually inspect the universe on Fifth Avenue."

"I'm a happily married man." Michael pressed her elbow tenderly. "Example for the whole twentieth century—Mr. and Mrs. Mike Loomis. Hey, let's have a drink," he said, stopping.

"We just had breakfast."

"Now listen, darling," Mike said, choosing his words with care, "it's a nice day and we both felt good and there's no reason why we have to break it up. Let's have a nice Sunday."

"All right. I don't know why I started this. Let's drop it. Let's have a good time."

They joined hands consciously and walked without talking among the baby carriages and the old Italian men in their Sunday clothes and the young women with Scotties in Washington Square Park.

"At least once a year everyone should go to the Metropolitan Museum of Art," Frances said after a while, her tone a good imitation of the tone she had used at breakfast and at the beginning of their walk. "And it's nice on Sunday. There're a lot of people looking at the pictures and you get the feeling maybe Art isn't on the decline in New York City, after all—"

"I want to tell you something," Michael said very seriously. "I have not touched another woman. Not once. In all the five years."

"All right," Frances said.

"You believe that, don't you?"

"All right."

They walked between the crowded benches, under the scrubby city-park trees.

"I try not to notice it," Frances said, "but I feel rotten inside, in my stomach, when we pass a woman and you look at her and I see that look in your eye and that's the way you looked at me the first time. In Alice Maxwell's house. Standing there in the living room, next to the radio, with a green hat on and all those people."

"I remember the hat," Michael said.

"The same look," Frances said. "And it makes me feel bad. It makes me feel terrible."

"Sh-h-h, please, darling, sh-h-h."

"I think I would like a drink now," Frances said.

They walked over to a bar on Eighth Street, not saying anything. Michael automatically helping her over curbstones and guiding her past automobiles. They sat near a window in the bar and the sun streamed in and there was a small, cheerful fire in the fireplace. A little Japanese waiter came over and put down some pretzels and smiled happily at them.

"What do you order after breakfast?" Michael asked.

"Brandy, I suppose," Frances said.

"Courvoisier," Michael told the waiter, "Two Courvoisiers."

The waiter came with the glasses and they sat drinking the brandy in the sunlight. Michael finished half his and drank a little water.

"I look at women," he said. "Correct. I don't say it's wrong or right. I look at them. If I pass them on the street and I don't look at them, I'm fooling you, I'm fooling myself."

"You look at them as though you want them," Frances said, playing with her brandy glass. "Every one of them."

"In a way," Michael said, speaking softly and not to his wife, "in a way that's true. I don't do anything about it, but it's true."

"I know it. That's why I feel bad."

"Another brandy," Michael called. "Waiter, two more brandies."

He sighed and closed his eyes and rubbed them gently with his fingertips. "I love the way women look. One of the things I like best about New York is the battalions of women. When I first came to New York from Ohio that was the first thing I noticed, the million wonderful women, all over the city. I walked around with my heart in my throat."

"A kid," Frances said. "That's a kid's feeling."

"Guess again," Michael said. "Guess again. I'm older now. I'm a man getting near middle age, putting on a little fat, and I still love to walk along Fifth Avenue at three o'clock on the east side of the street between Fiftieth and the

Fifty-seventh Streets. They're all out then, shopping, in their furs and their crazy hats, everything all concentrated from all over the world into seven blocks—the best furs, the best clothes, the handsomest women, out to spend money and feeling good about it."

The Japanese waiter put the two drinks down, smiling with great happiness. "Everything is all right?" he asked.

"Everything is wonderful," Michael said.

"If it's just a couple of fur coats," Frances said, "and forty-five dollar hats —"

"It's not the fur coats. Or the hats. That's just the scenery for that particular kind of women. Understand," he said, "you don't have to listen to this."

"I want to listen."

"I like the girls in the offices. Neat, with their eyeglasses, smart, chipper, knowing what everything is about. I like the girls on Forty-fourth Street at lunchtime, the actresses, all dressed up on nothing a week. I like the salesgirls in the stores, paying attention to you first because you're a man, leaving lady customers waiting. I got all this stuff accumulated in me because I've been thinking about it for ten years and now you've asked for it and here it is."

"Go ahead," Frances said.

"When I think of New York City, I think of all the girls on parade in the city. I don't know whether it's something special with me or whether every man in the city walks around with the same feeling inside him, but I feel as though I'm at a picnic in this city. I like to sit near the women in the theatres, the famous beauties who've taken six hours to get ready and look it. And the young girls at the football games, with the red cheeks, and when the warm weather comes, the girls in their summer dresses." He finished his drink. "That's the story."

Frances finished her drink and swallowed two or three times extra. "You say you love me?"

"I love you."

"I'm pretty, too," Frances said. "As pretty as any of them."

"You're beautiful," Michael said.

"I'm good for you," Frances said, pleading. "I've made a good wife, a good housekeeper, a good friend. I'd do any damn thing for you."

"I know," Michael said. He put his hand out and grasped hers.

"You'd like to be free to—" Frances said.

"Sh-h-h."

"Tell the truth." She took her hand away from under his.

Michael flicked the edge of his glass with his finger. "O.K.," he said gently. "Sometimes I feel I would like to be free."

"Well," Frances said, "any time you say."

"Don't be foolish." Michael swung his chair around to her side of the table and patted her thigh.

She began to cry silently into her handkerchief, bent over just enough so that nobody else in the bar would notice. "Someday," she said, crying, "you're going to make a move."

Michael didn't say anything. He sat watching the bartender slowly peel a lemon.

"Aren't you?" Frances asked harshly. "Come on, tell me. Talk. Aren't you?"

"Maybe," Michael said. He moved his chair back again. "How the hell do I know?"

"You know," Frances persisted. "Don't you know?"

"Yes," Michael said after a while, "I know."

Frances stopped crying then. Two or three snuffles into the handkerchief and she put it away and her face didn't tell anything to anybody. "At least do me one favor," she said.

"Sure."

"Stop talking about how pretty this woman is or that one. Nice eyes, nice breasts, a pretty figure, good voice." She mimicked his voice. "Keep it to yourself. I'm not interested."

Michael waved to the waiter. "I'll keep it to myself," he said.

Frances flicked the corners of her eyes. "Another brandy," she told the waiter.

"Two," Michael said.

"Yes, Ma'am, yes, sir," said the waiter, backing away.

Frances regarded Michael coolly across the table. "Do you want me to call the Stevensons?" she asked. "It'll be nice in the country."

"Sure," Michael said. "Call them."

She got up from the table and walked across the room toward the telephone. Michael watched her walk, thinking what a pretty girl, what nice legs.

KATHERINE ANNE PORTER (b. 1894)

Although Katherine Anne Porter grew up in Texas and New Orleans, she spent much of her adult life in Paris and Mexico, the setting of many of her stories. Her first published works were novellas: "Hacienda" (1934), "Noon Wine" (1937), "Pale Horse, Pale Rider" (1937, considered by most critics as her best work), and "No Safe Harbor" (1939). Her Collected Short Stories *won the National Book Award and the Pulitzer Prize in 1965. A full-length novel,* Ship of Fools *(1963), though a best seller, disappointed some critics and admirers.*

Porter's reputation was first established through the superb craftsmanship she employed in portraying inner turmoil in her characters in order to reveal their essential natures.

On the surface, "Rope" might appear to be merely a recounting of a trivial argument between a husband and wife. Through Porter's skill as a writer, however, deeper dynamics of the underlying relationship are exposed.

Rope

ON THE third day after they moved to the country he came walking back from the village carrying a basket of groceries and a twenty-four-yard coil of rope. She came out to meet him, wiping her hands on her green smock. Her hair was tumbled, her nose was scarlet with sunburn; he told her that already she looked like a born country woman. His gray flannel shirt stuck to him, his heavy shoes were dusty. She assured him he looked like a rural character in a play.

Had he brought the coffee? She had been waiting all day long for coffee. They had forgot it when they ordered at the store the first day.

Gosh, no, he hadn't. Lord, now he'd have to go back. Yes, he would if it killed him. He thought, though, he had everything else. She reminded him it was only because he didn't drink coffee himself. If he did he would remember it quick enough. Suppose they ran out of cigarettes? Then she saw the rope. What was that for? Well, he thought it might do to hang clothes on, or something. Naturally she asked him if he thought they were going to run a laundry? They already had a fifty-foot line hanging right before his eyes? Why, hadn't he noticed it, really? It was a blot on the landscape to her.

He thought there were a lot of things a rope might come in handy for. She wanted to know what, for instance. He thought a few seconds, but nothing occurred. They could wait and see, couldn't they? You need all sorts of strange odds and ends around a place in the country. She said, yes, that was so; but she thought just at that time when every penny counted, it seemed funny to buy more rope. That was all. She hadn't meant anything else. She hadn't just seen, not at first, why he felt it was necessary.

Well, thunder, he had bought it because he wanted to, and that was all there was to it. She thought that was reason enough, and couldn't understand why he hadn't said so, at first. Undoubtedly it would be useful, twenty-four yards of rope, there were hundreds of things, she couldn't think of any at the moment, but it would come in. Of course. As he had said, things always did in the country.

But she was a little disappointed about the coffee, and oh, look, look, look at the eggs! Oh, my, they're all running! What had he put on top of them? Hadn't he known eggs mustn't be squeezed? Squeezed, who had squeezed them, he wanted to know. What a silly thing to say. He had simply brought them along in the basket with the other things. If they got broke it was the grocer's fault. He should know better than to put heavy things on top of eggs.

She believed it was the rope. That was the heaviest thing in the pack, she saw him plainly when he came in from the road, the rope was a big package on top of everything. He desired the whole wide world to witness that this was not a fact. He had carried the rope in one hand and the basket in the other, and what was the use of her having eyes, if that was the best they could do for her?

Well, anyhow, she could see one thing plain: no eggs for breakfast. They'd have to scramble them now, for supper. It was too damned bad. She had planned to have steak for supper. No ice, meat wouldn't keep. He wanted to know why she couldn't finish breaking the eggs in a bowl and set them in a cool place.

Cool place! if he could find one for her, she'd be glad to set them there. Well, then, it seemed to him they might very well cook the meat at the same time they cooked the eggs and then warm up the meat for tomorrow. The idea simply choked her. Warmed-over meat, when they might as well have had it fresh. Second best and scraps and makeshifts, even to the meat! He rubbed her shoulder a little. It doesn't really matter so much, does it, darling? Sometimes when they were playful, he would rub her shoulder and she would arch and purr. This time she hissed and almost clawed. He was getting ready to say that they could surely manage somehow when she turned on him and said, if he told her they could manage somehow she would certainly slap his face.

He swallowed the words red hot, his face burned. He picked up the rope and started to put it on the top shelf. She would not have it on the top shelf, the jars and tins belonged there; positively she would not have the top shelf cluttered up with a lot of rope. She had borne all the clutter she meant to bear in the flat in town, there was space here at least and she meant to keep things in order.

Well, in that case, he wanted to know what the hammer and nails were doing up there? And why had she put them there when she knew very well he needed that hammer and those nails upstairs to fix the window sashes? She simply slowed down everything and made double work on the place with her insane habit of changing things around and hiding them.

She was sure she begged his pardon, and if she had had any reason to believe he was going to fix the sashes this summer she would have left the hammer and nails right where he put them; in the middle of the bedroom floor where they could step on them in the dark. And now if he didn't clear the whole mess out of there she would throw them down the well.

Oh, all right, all right—could he put them in the closet? Naturally not, there were brooms and mops and dustpans in the closet, and why couldn't he find a place for his rope outside her kitchen? Had he stopped to consider there were seven God-forsaken rooms in the house, and only one kitchen?

He wanted to know what of it? And did she realize she was making a complete fool of herself? And what did she take him for, a three-year-old idiot? The whole trouble with her was she needed something weaker than she was to heckle and tyrannize over. He wished to God now they had a couple of children she could take it out on. Maybe he'd get some rest.

Her face changed at this, she reminded him he had forgot the coffee and had bought a worthless piece of rope. And when she thought of all the things they actually needed to make the place even decently fit to live in, well, she could cry, that was all. She looked so forlorn, so lost and despairing he couldn't believe it was only a piece of rope that was causing all the racket. What *was* the matter, for God's sake?

Oh, would he please hush and go away, and *stay* away, if he could, for five minutes? By all means, yes, he would. He'd stay away indefinitely if she wished. Lord, yes, there was nothing he'd like better than to clear out and never come back. She couldn't for the life of her see what was holding him, then. It was a swell time. Here she was, stuck, miles from a railroad, with a half-empty house on her hands, and not a penny in her pocket, and everything on earth to do; it seemed the God-sent moment for him to get out from under. She was surprised he hadn't stayed in town as it was until she had come out and done the work and got things straightened out. It was his usual trick.

It appeared to him that this was going a little far. Just a touch out of bounds, if she didn't mind his saying so. Why the hell had he stayed in town the summer before? To do a half-dozen extra jobs to get the money he had sent her. That was it. She knew perfectly well they couldn't have done it otherwise. She had agreed with him at the time. And that was the only time so help him he had ever left her to do anything by herself.

Oh, he could tell that to his great-grandmother. She had her notion of what had kept him in town. Considerably more than a notion, if he wanted to know. So, she was going to bring all that up again, was she? Well, she could just think what she pleased. He was tired of explaining. It may have looked funny but he had simply got hooked in, and what could he do? It was impossible to believe that she was going to take it seriously. Yes, yes, she knew how it was with a man: if he was left by himself a minute, some woman was certain to kidnap him. And naturally he couldn't hurt her feelings by refusing!

Well, what was she raving about? Did she forget she had told him those two weeks alone in the country were the happiest she had known for four years? And how long had they been married when she said that? All right, shut up! If she thought that hadn't stuck in his craw.

She hadn't meant she was happy because she was away from him. She meant she was happy getting the devilish house nice and ready for him. That was what she had meant, and now look! Bringing up something she had said a year ago simply to justify himself for forgetting her coffee and breaking the eggs and buying a wretched piece of rope they couldn't afford. She really thought it was time to drop the subject, and now she wanted only two things in the world. She wanted him to get that rope from underfoot, and go back to the village and get her coffee, and if he could remember it, he might bring a metal mitt for the skillets, and two more curtain rods, and if there were any rubber gloves in the village, her hands were simply raw, and a bottle of milk of magnesia from the drugstore.

He looked out at the dark blue afternoon sweltering on the slopes, and mopped his forehead and sighed heavily and said, if only she could wait a minute for *anything,* he was going back. He had said so, hadn't he, the very instant they found he had overlooked it?

Oh, yes, well . . . run along. She was going to wash windows. The country was so beautiful! She doubted they'd have a moment to enjoy it. He meant to go, but he could not until he had said that if she wasn't such a hopeless melancholiac she might see that this was only for a few days. Couldn't she remember anything pleasant about the other summers? Hadn't they ever had any fun? She hadn't time to talk about it, and now would he please not leave that rope lying around for her to trip on? He picked it up, somehow it had toppled off the table, and walked out with it under his arm.

Was he going this minute? He certainly was. She thought so. Sometimes it seemed to her he had second sight about the precisely perfect moment to leave her ditched. She had meant to put the mattresses out to sun, if they put them out this minute they would get at least three hours, he must have heard her say that morning she meant to put them out. So of course he would walk off and leave her to it. She supposed he thought the exercise would do her good.

Well, he was merely going to get her coffee. A four-mile walk for two pounds of coffee was ridiculous, but he was perfectly willing to do it. The habit was making a wreck of her, but if she wanted to wreck herself there was nothing he could do about it. If he thought it was coffee that was making a wreck of her, she congratulated him: he must have a damned easy conscience.

Conscience or no conscience, he didn't see why the mattresses couldn't very well wait until tomorrow. And anyhow, for God's sake, were they living *in* the house, or were they going to let the house ride them to death? She paled at this, her face grew livid about the mouth, she looked quite dangerous, and reminded him that housekeeping was no more her work than it was his: she had other work to do as well, and when did he think she was going to find time to do it at this rate?

Was she going to start on that again? She knew as well as he did that his work brought in the regular money, hers was only occasional, if they depended on what *she* made—and she might as well get straight on this question once for all!

That was positively not the point. The question was, when both of them were working on their own time, was there going to be a division of the housework, or wasn't there? She merely wanted to know, she had to make her plans. Why, he thought that was all arranged. It was understood that he was to help. Hadn't he always, in summers?

Hadn't he, though? Oh, just hadn't he? And when, and where, and doing what? Lord, what an uproarious joke!

It was such a very uproarious joke that her face turned slightly purple, and she screamed with laughter. She laughed so hard she had to sit down, and finally a rush of tears spurted from her eyes and poured down into the lifted corners of her mouth. He dashed towards her and dragged her up to her feet and tried to pour water on her head. The dipper hung by a string on a nail and he broke it loose. Then he tried to pump water with one hand while she struggled in the other. So he gave it up and shook her instead.

She wrenched away, crying out for him to take his rope and go to hell, she had simply given him up: and ran. He heard her high-heeled bedroom slippers clattering and stumbling on the stairs.

He went out around the house and into the lane; he suddenly realized he had a blister on his heel and his shirt felt as if it were on fire. Things broke so suddenly you didn't know where you were. She could work herself into a fury about simply nothing. She was terrible, damn it: not an ounce of reason. You might as well talk to a sieve as that woman when she got going. Damned if he'd spend his life humoring her! Well, what to do now? He would take back the rope and exchange it for something else. Things accumulated, things were mountainous, you couldn't move them or sort them out or get rid of them. They just lay and rotted around. He'd take it back. Hell, why should he? He wanted it. What was it anyhow? A piece of rope. Imagine anybody caring more about a piece of rope than about a man's feelings. What earthly right had she to say a word about it? He remembered all the useless, meaningless things she bought for herself: Why? because I wanted it, that's why! He stopped and selected a large stone by the road. He would put the rope behind it. He would put it in the tool-box when he got back. He'd heard enough about it to last him a life-time.

When he came back she was leaning against the post box beside the road waiting. It was pretty late, the smell of broiled steak floated nose high in the cooling air. Her face was young and smooth and fresh-looking. Her unmanageable funny black hair was all on end. She waved to him from a distance, and he speeded up. She called out that supper was ready and waiting, was he starved?

You bet he was starved. Here was the coffee. He waved it at her. She looked at his other hand. What was that he had there?

Well, it was the rope again. He stopped short. He had meant to exchange it but forgot. She wanted to know why he should exchange it, if it was something he really wanted. Wasn't the air sweet now, and wasn't it fine to be here?

She walked beside him with one hand hooked into his leather belt. She pulled and jostled him a little as he walked, and leaned against him. He put his arm clear around her and patted her stomach. They exchanged wary smiles. Coffee, coffee for the Ootsum-Wootsums! He felt as if he were bringing her a beautiful present.

He was a love, she firmly believed, and if she had had her coffee in the morning, she wouldn't have behaved so funny. . . . There was a whippoorwill still coming back, imagine, clear out of season, sitting in the crab-apple tree calling all by himself. Maybe his girl stood him up. Maybe she did. She hoped to hear him once more, she loved whippoorwills. . . . He knew how she was, didn't he?

Sure, he knew how she was.

CLAUDE McKAY (1890–1948)

Claude McKay was born in Jamaica, British West Indies, and was brought up by a schoolmaster brother who introduced him to the writings of the outstanding social thinkers of the time. It was McKay's discovery of British and American poetry, however, that influenced him most and started him writing.

Dissatisfied with the restricted opportunities in the islands, he came to the United States in 1912 but found Tuskegee Institute and Kansas State University equally restrictive. While supporting himself at a variety of menial jobs in and around Harlem, he continued to write and publish his poetry. In the 1920's, McKay lived and wrote in London, Russia, and the south of France, as well as in New York. He turned more and more to prose fiction.

In novels like Home to Harlem *(1928) and* Banjo *(1929), and in his short stories (collected in 1932 in* Gingertown*), Claude McKay was one of the first Negro writers to depict black life realistically, debunking the exotic portrayals of Harlem and Jamaica which were rampant in the writing of his day. He was especially concerned with the soul-destroying effect of the materialistic values of white men's civilization upon the inherent joy and freedom of the fundamentally rural black culture.*

"Truant," from Gingertown, *follows the frustrations of a Jamaican who has drifted into a respectable marriage, a home in Harlem, and a steady job—against all of which his free soul rebels.*

Truant

THE WARBLING of a mother's melody had just ended, and the audience was in a sentimental state and ready for the scene that the curtain, slowly drawn, disclosed. A mother in calico print jigged on her knee a little baby, crooning the while some Gaelic folk-words. A colleen sat on a red-covered box, mending a chemise; sitting at her feet, a younger sister with a picture book. Three boys in shirt sleeves and patched pantaloons playing with a red-and-green train on a lacquer-black railroad. A happy family. An antique sitting room, torn wallpaper, two comic chairs, and the Holy Virgin on the mantelpiece. A happy family. Father, fat and round like a chianti bottle, skips into the picture and up leaps boys and girls and mother with baby. The Merry Mulligans!

The orchestra starts at the pointing baton. Squeaky-burlesque family singing. Dancing. Stunting. A performing wonder, that little baby. Charming family of seven. American-famous. The Merry Mulligans, beloved of all lovers of clean vaudeville.

With them the show finished. Barclay Oram and his wife Rhoda descended from Nigger Heaven, walked up to 50th Street, and caught the local subway train for Harlem. He took the slower train, hoping there would be seats and the passengers not jammed together as always.

Perhaps others had hoped for the same thing. The cars were packed. Rhoda broke up a piece of chewing gum and chewed. She had a large mouth, and she chewed the gum as if she were eating food, opening her mouth so wide that people could see the roof. When they were first married, Barclay had detested her way of chewing gum and told her so. But she replied that it was absurd to let a little thing like chewing gum irritate him.

"Oh, you brown baby!" she had cried, taking his face in her hands and kissing him with the perfumed flavor of her favorite chewing gum on her breath. . . .

"The show was pretty nice, eh?" said Rhoda.

"I am fed up with them; a cabaret in Harlem is better," replied Barclay.

"I don't think so. Anything downtown for a change is preferable to the cheap old colored shows. I'm dead sick of them."

She chewed the gum vigorously, dropping a few pointless phrases that were half-swallowed up in the roar of the train though the enormous gut of the city and the strange staccato talk of voices half-lifted above and half-caught in the roar. Barclay gazed moodily at the many straphangers who were jammed together. None seemed standing on his feet. All seemed like fat bags and lean boxes piled up indiscriminately in a warehouse. Penned up like cattle, the standing closely pressing the seated passengers, kneading them with their knees and blotting out their sight, so that those who had been fortunate to find seats were as uncomfortable as those who had not.

"I thought we'd have a little air in this local box," he said.

"It'll be better at 72nd Street," she said. "Some of them will get out."

"And others will push in. New York City is swarming with people like a beehive."

"Getting thicker and thicker every day," she agreed.

At 135th Street they left the train. Rhoda, as usual, put her hand through her husband's arm as they walked home. The saloons, restaurants, candy stores of the Avenue were crowded. The Chop Suey Palace was doing a good after-theater business.

"Might have some chop suey," suggested Barclay.

"Not tonight," she said. "Betsy's with the Howlands, and they might want to go to bed."

"Ah yes!" He had forgotten about Betsy, their four-year-old child. Always he forgot about her. Never could he quite realize that he was the father of a family. A railroad waiter, although he was thirty-six, he always felt himself just a boy—a servant boy. His betters whom he served treated him always as a boy—often as a nice dog. And when he grew irritated and snapped, they turned on him as upon a bad dog. It was better for him, then, that, although he was a husband and father, he should feel like an irresponsible boy. Even when sometimes he grew sad, sullen, and disquieted, these were the moods of a boy. Rhoda bossed him a little and never took his moods seriously. . . .

They went straight home. Barclay lighted up the three-room apartment. Rhoda went across the hall to the Howlands' for Betsy. She brought the child in, sleeping on her breast, and bent down that Barclay might kiss her. Then she put her to bed in her little cot beside the dresser.

They had a little supper, cold chicken and beer. . . . They went to bed in the front room that they had made their bedroom. Another room was let to a railroad porter, and the dining room served for eating and sitting room.

Rhoda undressed, rubbed her face and her limbs with cold cream, slipped on a long white gown with pink ribbon around the neck, and lay down against the wall. Barclay laid himself down beside her in his underclothes. During the first six months of their union he had slept regularly in pyjamas. Then he ignored them and began sleeping in his underclothes, returning to the habit of his village boyhood. Rhoda protested at first. Afterwards she accepted it quietly. . . .

Sleep, sweet sleep. . . .

The next morning Rhoda shook Barclay at five o'clock. "O God!" He stretched himself, turned over, and rested his head on her breast.

"Time to get up," she said.

"Yes," he sighed. "God! I feel tired." He stretched his arms, touched, fondled her face, and fell into a slight doze.

Ten minutes more. Rhoda gave him a dig in the back with her knee and cried, "You just must get up, Barclay."

"All right." He turned out of bed. Six o'clock in the Pennsylvania Station for duty, that was life itself. A dutiful black boy among proud and sure white men, so that he could himself be a man in Harlem with purchasing power for wife, child, flat, movie, food, liquor. . . .

He went to the bathroom and washed. Dressed, he entered the dining room, opened a cabinet, and poured out a glass of whisky. That peppered him up and opened his eyes wide. It was not necessary for Rhoda to make coffee. He would breakfast with the other waiters in the dining car. Mechanically he kissed her good-by. She heard him close the door, and she moved over into the middle of the bed, comfortably alone, for an early-morning nap.

It was a disastrous trip for Barclay. On the dining car he was the first waiter and in charge of the pantry. As pantryman he received five dollars a month more than the other waiters. It was his job to get the stores (with the steward and chef) from the commissary. He was responsible for the stuff kept in the pantry. There were some waiters and cooks addicted to petty stealing. Butter, cream, cheese, sugar, fruit. They stole for their women in New York. They stole for their women-on-the-side in the stopover cities. Always Barclay had to mount guard quietly. Between him and the raw-voiced, black-bull chef there was an understanding to watch out for the nimble-fingered among the crew. For if they were short in the checking up of the stores, the steward held them responsible. And the commissary held the steward responsible.

This trip Barclay had one of his moody-boy spells. He would not watch the pantry. Let the boys swipe the stuff. He had no pleasure waiting on the passengers. It was often a pleasure, something of an anticipated adventure, each day to meet new passengers, remark the temperature of their looks, and sometimes make casual conversation with a transient acquaintance. But today it was all wrong from the moment he observed them, impatient, crowding the corridor, and the rushing of the dining room as soon as the doors were opened. They filled him with loathing, made him sick of service. SERVICE. A beautiful word fallen upon bad days. No place for true human service in these automatic-serving days.

Mechanically Barclay picked up the dimes and quarters that were left for service. For Rhoda and Betsy. It pleasured him when Rhoda wore pretty clothes. And Betsy loved him more each time he remembered to bring home colored bonbons. What was he going to do with the child? He wondered if he would be able to give her a good education like her mother's. And what would she do? Perhaps marry a railroad waiter like her mother and raise up children to carry on the great tradition of black servitude.

Philadelphia, Harrisburg, Altoona, Pittsburgh. No dice, no coon-can, this trip. His workmates coaxed. Nothing could lift him out of himself. He was a moody boy this trip. The afternoon of the fourth day from New York brought the dining car to Washington. Washington reminded Barclay of a grave. He had sharp, hammering memories of his university days there. For there he had fallen in love. . . .

He went up to 7th Street, loitering through the Negro district, stopping curiously before a house, leaning against a stoop, sniffing here and there like a stray hound. He went into a barrel-house and drank a glass of whisky. The place was sour-smelling, full of black men, dim and smoky, close, but friendly warm.

The hour of his train's departure, approached. Barclay continued drinking. He felt pleased with himself in doing something irregular. Oh, he had been regular for such a long time! A good waiter, an honest pantryman. Never once had he sneaked a packet of sugar nor a pound of butter for his flat. Rhoda would have flung it in the street. He had never given to the colored girls who worked in the yards and visited the dining cars with their teasing smiles. Oh, it was hard to be responsible, hard to be regular.

What would the steward say about his being left in Washington? Maybe he would be drunk himself, for he was a regular souser. Barclay recalled the day when he got helplessly stewed on the Washington run, and the waiters managed the dining car, handed out checks, made change among themselves, and gave the best service they ever did as a crew. At Philadelphia an inspector hopped on the train and took charge of the service. The dining car was crowded. The steward half-roused himself out of his stupor and came lurching through the jam of passengers in the corridor into the diner, to dispute the stewardship with the inspector.

"I'm in charge of this diner," he said in a nerve-biting, imey-wimey voice. "Give a man a chance; treat me like a gen'leman."

Tears trickled down his cheeks. He staggered and swayed in the corridor, blocking the entrance and exit of the guests. Like a challenged mastiff, the inspector eyed him, at the same time glancing quickly from the waiters to the amazed guests. Then he gripped the steward by the scruff of the collar and, with the help of the Pullman conductor, locked him up in a drawing room until the train reached New York.

The crew did not like the steward and hoped they would be rid of him at last. But he was back with them the next trip. The inspector was known as a hard guy, quick to report a waiter if a flask of gin were discovered in his locker. But it was different with the steward. Both men were peers, the inspector being a promoted steward.

"Well, I'm off duty, anyhow," murmured Barclay. He smiled and ordered another drink. The train must have passed Baltimore by then, on its way to New York. What waiter was waiting on the first two tables? "I should worry." He had the warm, luxurious feelings of a truant. He drank himself drunk.

"Something for a change. I've been regular too long. Too awfully regular," he mused.

He rocked heavily out of the barrel-house to a little fried-chicken restaurant. He ate. His stomach appeased, his thoughts turned to a speakeasy. May as well finish the thing in style—be grandly irregular, he thought. He found a speakeasy. Bold-eyed chocolate girls, brown girls, yellow girls. Blues. Pianola blues, gramophone blues. Easy-queasy, daddy-mammy, honey-baby, brown-gal, black-boy, hot-dog blues. . . .

The next day he reported himself at the restaurant-car department in Washington, and was sent home to New York. There at the commissary the superintendent looked him over and said: "Well, you're a case. You wanted a little time off, eh? Well, take ten days."

That was his punishment—ten idle days. He left the commissary walking on air. For three years he had worked on the railroad without taking a holiday. Why? He did not himself know. He had often yearned for a few entirely free days. But he had never had the courage to take them, not for fear of forfeiting the nominal wages, but the tips—his real wages. Nor had he wanted to lose his former dining car. He had liked his work-pals there. A good crew teaming splendidly along together, respectful to and respected by the steward, who was a decent-minded man. Moreover, there was the flat with Rhoda and Betsy. Every day was precious, every tip necessary. . . . Ten days gratuitously thrust upon him with malicious intent. No wages-and-food, no tips. Let him cool his heels and tighten his belt. Yet he was happy, happy like a truant suspended from school.

Freedom! Ten days. What would he do with them? There would be parties. Rhoda loved parties. She had friends in New York who knew her when she was a schoolteacher. Whist. Dancing. Movies.

He nosed around the tenderloin district. When he first came to New York he had lived in 40th Street.

He met a pal he had once worked with as elevator boy in a department store. They drank two glasses of beer each and walked up to San Juan Hill.

When Barclay got home, Rhoda, in an orange evening dress, was just leaving for a party. They embraced.

"I phoned up the commissary yesterday and they said you were left in Washington. Bad boy!" She laughed. "Guess I'll fix you something to eat."

"Don't bother. I'm not hungry," said Barclay.

"All right. I'm going on to Mame Dixon's for whist and a little dancing afterwards. You might dress up and come on down and have a little fun."

"Not tonight, honey. We'll have plenty of time to go around together. They gave me ten days."

"Ten days!" she cried. "The rent is due on Friday and the insurance on—on—Ten days! But why did you get left, Barclay?"

"I don't know. Felt rotten the whole trip—tired, blue. Been too punctual all along. Just had to break the habit. Feel a little irresponsible."

"But you might get in bad with the company. How could you, when there's Betsy and me to think of and our social position?"

She broke up a stick of chewing gum and vigorously chewed. "Well, anyway, come on along to Mame's if you feel like it." She rolled the gum with her tongue. "But if you don't, you can bring Betsy over from the Howlands'."

Chewing, chewing, she went out.

"Kill-joy," murmured Barclay. Riding on the subway from San Juan Hill to Harlem, he had been guessing chucklingly at what she would say. Perhaps: "All right, honey-stick, why slave every day? Let's play around together for ten days."

Chewing, chewing. Always chewing. Yet that mouth was the enchanting thing about her. . . . Her mouth. It made me marry her. Her skin was brown and beautiful. Like cat's fur, soft to the fingers. But it was not her fruit-ripe skin. It was her mouth that made me.

Ordinary her face would have been, if it were not for the full, large mouth that was mounted on the ample plane of her features like an exquisite piece of bas-relief.

He went across the hall to the Howlands' and brought back Betsy.

"Candy, daddy, candy!" The happy brown thing clapped her hands and pulled at his pantaloons. He set her on his knee and gave her a little paper packet. He danced her up and down: "Betsy, wupsy, mupsy, pretsy, eatsy plentsy candy."

She wriggled off his knee with the packet and dropped the candies one by one into a small glass jar, gurgling over the colors and popping one into her mouth at intervals. . . . She returned again to Barclay's knee, squeezing a brown rubber doll. For a little while she made a rocking horse of him. Then she scratched her head and yawned. Barclay undressed her and put her in the crib.

"Betsy and me and our social position." That social position! Alone he brooded, moody, unreasonable. Resentment gripped his heart. He hated his love of Rhoda's mouth. He hated the flat and his pitiable "social position." He hated fatherhood. He resented the sleeping child.

"Betsy and me and——" Should he go on forever like that? Round the circle of the Eastern field? New York, Boston, Buffalo, Pittsburgh, Harrisburg, Washington, Baltimore, Philadelphia, again New York.

Forever? Getting off nowhere?

Forever fated to the lifelong tasks of the unimaginative? Why was he, a West Indian peasant boy, held prisoner within the huge granite-gray walls of New York? Dreaming of tawny tasseled fields of sugar cane, and silver-gray John-tuhits among clusters of green and glossy-blue berries of pimento. The husbands and fathers of his village were not mechanically driven servant boys. They were hardy, independent tillers of the soil or struggling artisans.

What enchantment had lured him away from the green intimate life that clustered round his village—the simple African-transplanted life of the West Indian hills? Why had he hankered for the hard-slabbed streets, the vertical towers, the gray complex life of this steel-tempered city? Stone and steel! Steel and stone! Mounting in heaven-pursuing magnificence. Feet piled upon feet, miles circling miles, of steel and stone. A tree seemed absurd and a garden queer in this iron-gray majesty of man's imagination. He was a slave to it. A part of him was in love with this piling grandeur. And that was why he was a slave to it.

From the bedroom came a slight stirring and a sleepy murmur of child-language. Barclay was lost in the past. Step by step he retraced his life. . . . His fever-like hunger for book knowledge, for strange lands and great cities. His grand adolescent dream.

The evening of his departure from the village came back star-blue and clear. He had trudged many miles to the railroad with his bright-patterned carpet bag on his shoulder. For three years in the capital of his island he had worked in a rum warehouse. Happy. On the road to his beautiful dream. Later he had crossed over to Santiago in Cuba. And at twenty-five he had reached New York, found his strange land—a great city of great books.

Two years of elevator-running and switchboard-operating had glanced by like a magic arrow against the gaunt gray walls of the city. Time was a radiant servant working for his dream.

His dream, of course, was the Negro university. Now he remembered how he turned green cold like a cucumber when he was told that he could not enter the university course. Two years preparatory work was needed. Undaunted, he had returned to New York and crammed for a year. And the next fall he swept through the entrance examinations.

For Barclay then the highroad to wisdom led necessarily by way of a university. It had never occurred to him that he might have also attained his goal in his own free, informal way.

He had been enchanted by the words: University, Seat of Learning. He had seen young men of the insular island villages returned from the native colleges. They all brought back with them a new style of clothes, a different accent, a new gait, the exciting, intoxicating smell of the city—so much more intriguing than the ever-fresh accustomed smell of the bright-green hill-valley village. Style and accent and exotic smell—all those attractive fruits of college training, fundamental forms of the cultural life. Home study could not give him the stamp. . . . His disillusion had not embittered him. . . .

My college days were happy, he reflected. A symmetrical group of buildings, gray walls supporting in winter stout, dark-brown leafless creepers. An all-Negro body of students—men and women—of many complexions, all intensely active. The booklore was there, housed in a kind of Gothic building with a projecting façade resting on Grecian pillars. The names of Aristotle, Solon, Virgil, Shakespeare, Dante, and Longfellow were cut in the façade. The building was one of the many symbols, scattered over America and the world, summing up the dream of a great romantic king of steel.

Barclay found no romance in textbooks, of course. But he found plenty of it in the company of the jolly girls and chummy chaps of his widened acquaintance. And the barbaric steps of the turkey-trot and the bunny-hug (exciting dances of that period) he had found more enchanting than the library. He was amorously touched by the warm, intimate little dances he attended—the spontaneous outburst of group-singing when the dancers were particularly drunk on a rich, tintinnabulating melody.

Then one day he was abruptly pulled up in his fantastic steps. No more money in the box. He had to wheel round about and begin the heavy steps of working his way through college.

The next fall he met Rhoda. It was at one of those molasses-thick Aframerican affairs that had rendered university life so attractive to him, at the home of a very generous fawn-brown widow who enjoyed giving a few students a nice time at her flat. The widow entertained her guests in a free kind of way. She did not belong to the various divisions that go to the making of nice Negro society, for she was merely the widow of a Pullman porter, who had saved up his tips and paid up on a good insurance policy. She had been too fine for the non-discriminating parlor-social sets, and too secular for the prayer-meeting black ladies. So she had cleverly gone in for the non-snobbish young intellectuals—poor students who could not afford to put on airs.

Barclay recalled the warm roomful of young Negro men and girls. Copper and chocolate and fine anthracite, with here and there a dash of cream, all warmly dancing. One night he was attracted to Rhoda. He danced with her all the time and she was warm to him, loving to him. She was the first American girl with whom he began a steady intimacy. All the ardors of him were stirred to her, and simply, impetuously he had rushed into deep love, like a bee that darts too far into the heart of a flower and, unable to withdraw, dies at the bottom of the juice.

Rhoda, who had been earning her own living as a teacher, helped him, and the problem of money was lifted from his mind. Oh, he was very happy then! Books and parties and Rhoda. . . .

In the middle of his junior year she told him she was with child. They discussed whether she should have the child or operate it away. If she had it without being married, she would lose her job. He remembered a school-teaching girl of his village who had tried to conceal her pregnancy and died under an operation in the city. The other girls, the free peasant girls, always bore their children when they were gotten with child. Perhaps it was better that way.

Rhoda was pleased that Barclay wanted the thing to develop in the natural way. She desired a child. She was at that vague age when some women feel that marriage is more than the grim pursuit of a career. So they went to New York together and got married.

But Barclay did not fully realize the responsibility, perhaps could not, of marriage. Never fully understood its significance.

Barclay remembered now that he was as keen as Rhoda for the marriage. Carried away by the curiosity to take up a new role, there had been something almost of eagerness in his desire to quit the university. And it had seemed a beautiful gesture. Rhoda had helped him when he was in great need, and he felt splendid now to come to her support when she was incapacitated for work. He would have hated to see her drop down to menial tasks. As a Jack-of-all-trades he had met many refined colored girls having a rough time, jammed at the bottom of the common scramble to survive.

He had been happy that Rhoda was not pushed to leave Betsy in one of those dime dumps where poor colored children were guarded while their mothers worked, happy that from his job on the railroad he was earning enough for the family to live simply and comfortably.

About that job he had never taken serious thought. Where was it leading him? What was it making of his character? He had taken it as if he were acting in a play rather than working at a job. It met the necessary bill of being in love. For he was really in love with Rhoda. The autumn-leaf mellowness of her body. Her ripe-ripe accent and richness of laughter. And her mouth: the full form of it, its strength and beauty, its almost unbearable sweetness, magnetic, drawing, sensuous, exquisite, a dark pagan piece of pleasure. . . . How fascinated and enslaved he had been to what was now stale with chewing gum and banal remarks on "social position."

Barclay's attitude to the railroad was about the same toward the modern world in general. He had entered light-heartedly into the whirl and crash and crush, the grand babel of building, the suction and spouting, groaning and whining and breaking of steel—all the riotous, contagious movement around him.

He had entered into the rough camaraderie of the railroad with all the hot energy of youth. It was a rugged, new experience that kindled his vagabonding mind and body. There was rude poetry in the roar and rush and rattle of trains, the sharp whistle of engines and racing landscapes, the charm of a desolate mining town and glimpses of faces lost as soon as seen. He had even tried to capture some of those fleeting piled-up images. Some he had read to his workmates, which they appreciated, but teased him for writing:

We are out in the field, the vast wide-open field,
Thundering through from city to city
Where factories grow like jungle trees
Yielding new harvests for the world.
Through Johnstown glowing like a world aflame,
And Pittsburgh, Negro-black, brooding in iron smoke,
Philly's Fifteenth street of wenches, speakeasies, and cops.
Out in the field, new fields of life
Where machines spin flowers like tropic trees
And coal and steel are blazing suns—
And darkly we wonder, night-wrapped in the light.

The steel-framed poetry of cities did not crowd out but rather intensified in him the singing memories of his village life. He loved both, the one complementing the other. Against the intricate stone-and-steel flights of humanity's mass spirit, misty in space and time, hovered the green charm of his village. Yellow-eyed and white-lidded Spanish needles coloring the grassy hillsides, barefooted black girls, straight like young sweet-woods, tramping to market with baskets of mangoes or star-apples poised unsupported on their heads. The native cockish liquor juice of the sugar cane, fermented in bamboo joints for all-night carousal at wakes and tea meetings. Heavy drays loaded with new-made sugar, yams, and plantains, rumbling along the chalky country road away down and over the hills under the starshine and the hot-free love songs of the draymen.

He remembered all, regretting nothing, since his life was a continual fluxion from one state to another. His deepest regret was always momentary, arising from remaining in a rut after he had exhausted the experience.

Rhoda now seemed only another impasse into which he had drifted. Just a hole to pull out of again and away from the road, that arena of steel rushing him round and round in the same familiar circle. He had to evade it and be irresponsible again.

But there was the child and the Moral Law. The cold white law. Rhoda seemed more than he to be subject to it with her constant preoccupation about social position.

Spiritually he was subject to another law. Other gods of strange barbaric glory claimed his allegiance, and not the grim frock-coated gentleman of the Moral Law of the land. The Invisible Law that upheld those magnificent machines and steel-spired temples and new cathedrals erected to the steel-flung traffic plan of man. Oh, he could understand and love the poetry of them, but not their law that held humanity gripped in fear.

His thought fell to a whisper within him. He could never feel himself more than a stranger within these walls. His body went through the mechanical process, but untamed, for his spirit was wandering far. . . .

Rhoda at the party and the child asleep. He could hear her breathing and wondered if it were breath of his breath. For he had often felt to himself a breath of his own related to none. Suppose he should start now on the trail again with that strange burning thought. Related to none.

There was the Liberty Bonds in his trunk. Rhoda would need them. He remembered how he had signed for them. All the waiters herded together in one of the commissary rooms and lectured by one of the special war men.

"Buy a bond, boys. All you boys will buy a bond because you all believe in the Allied cause. We are in the war to make the world safe for Democracy. You boys on the railroad are enjoying the blessings of Democracy like all real Americans. Your service is inestimable. Keep on doing your part and do your best by buying a bond because you believe in the Allied cause and you want America to win the war and the banner of Democracy float over the world. Come on, take your bond."

For the Moral Law. Buy a bond.

Well it was all right; he had subscribed. One way of saving money, although the bonds were woth so much less now. There was the bankbook with a couple hundred dollars. Leave that, too. Insurance policies. Forget them.

He thought he heard the child stir. He dared not look. He clicked the door and stepped out. Where? Destination did not matter. Maybe his true life lay in eternal inquietude.

ERNEST HEMINGWAY (1899–1961)

With his first novel, The Sun Also Rises *(1926), Ernest Hemingway became the acknowledged spokesman for the post–World War I "lost generation," a generation which began to question traditional American values. In his short stories, and in later novels such as* A Farewell to Arms *(1929),* For Whom the Bell Tolls *(1940), and* The Old Man and the Sea *(1952), Hemingway dealt with man's need to affirm his courage in order to live with dignity. Much of his writing reflected his own experiences as an ambulance driver during the first World War, as a foreign correspondent during the Spanish Civil War, and as a devotee of big game hunting, deep sea fishing, and bull fighting. His detached, realistic style, with its short sentences and understated emotions, has found many imitators in modern fiction.*

"The Short Happy Life of Francis Macomber" is a typical Hemingway short story in that it confronts its main character with the need to demonstrate his courage in the face of death in order to prove himself as a man.

The Short Happy Life of Francis Macomber

IT WAS NOW lunch time and they were all sitting under the double green fly of the dining tent pretending that nothing had happened.

"Will you have lime juice or lemon squash?" Macomber asked.

"I'll have a gimlet," Robert Wilson told him.

"I'll have a gimlet too. I need something," Macomber's wife said.

"I suppose it's the thing to do," Macomber agreed. "Tell him to make three gimlets."

The mess boy had started them already, lifting the bottles out of the canvas cooling bags that sweated wet in the wind that blew through the trees that shaded the tents.

"What had I ought to give them?" Macomber asked.

"A quid would be plenty," Wilson told him. "You don't want to spoil them."

"Will the headman distribute it?"

"Absolutely."

Francis Macomber had, half an hour before, been carried to his tent from the edge of the camp in triumph on the arms and shoulders of the cook, the personal boys, the skinner and the porters. The gun-bearers had taken no part in the demonstration. When the native boys put him down at the door of his tent, he had shaken all their hands, received their congratulations, and then gone into the tent and sat on the bed until his wife came in. She did not speak to him when she came in and he left the tent at once to wash his face and hands in the portable wash basin outside and go over to the dining tent to sit in a comfortable canvas chair in the breeze and the shade.

"You've got your lion," Robert Wilson said to him, "and a damned fine one too."

Mrs. Macomber looked at Wilson quickly. She was an extremely handsome and well-kept woman of the beauty and social position which had, five years before, commanded five thousand dollars as the price of endorsing, with photographs, a beauty product which she had never used. She had been married to Francis Macomber for eleven years.

"He is a good lion, isn't he?" Macomber said. His wife looked at him now. She looked at both these men as though she had never seen them before.

One, Wilson, the white hunter, she knew she had never truly seen before. He was about middle height with sandy hair, a stubby mustache, a very red face and extremely cold blue eyes with faint white wrinkles at the corners that grooved merrily when he smiled. He smiled at her now and she looked away from his face at the way his shoulders sloped in the loose tunic he wore with the four big cartridges held in loops where the left breast pocket should have been, at his big brown hands, his old slacks, his very dirty boots and back to his red face again. She noticed where the baked red of his face stopped in a white line that marked the circle left by his Stetson hat that hung now from one of the pegs of the tent pole.

"Well, here's to the lion," Robert Wilson said. He smiled at her again and, not smiling, she looked curiously at her husband.

Francis Macomber was very tall, very well built if you did not mind that length of bone, dark, his hair cropped like an oarsman, rather thin-lipped, and was considered handsome. He was dressed in the same sort of safari clothes that Wilson wore except that his were new, he was thirty-five years old, kept himself very fit, was good at court games, had a number of big-game fishing records, and had just shown himself, very publicly, to be a coward.

"Here's to the lion," he said. "I can't ever thank you for what you did."

Margaret, his wife, looked away from him and back to Wilson.

"Let's not talk about the lion," she said.

Wilson looked over at her without smiling and now she smiled at him.

"It's been a very strange day," she said. "Hadn't you ought to put your hat on even under the canvas at noon? You told me that, you know."

"Might put it on," said Wilson.

"You know you have a very red face, Mr. Wilson," she told him and smiled again.

"Drink," said Wilson.

"I don't think so," she said. "Francis drinks a great deal, but his face is never red."

"It's red today," Macomber tried a joke.

"No," said Margaret. "It's mine that's red today. But Mr. Wilson is always red."

"Must be racial," said Wilson. "I say, you wouldn't like to drop my beauty as a topic, would you?"

"I've just started on it."

"Let's chuck it," said Wilson.

"Conversation is going to be so difficult," Margaret said.

"Don't be silly, Margot," her husband said.

"No difficulty," Wilson said. "Got a damn fine lion."

Margot looked at them both and they both saw that she was going to cry. Wilson had seen it coming for a long time and he dreaded it. Macomber was past dreading it.

"I wish it hadn't happened. Oh, I wish it hadn't happened," she said and started for her tent. She made no noise of crying but they could see that her shoulders were shaking under the rose-colored, sun-proofed shirt she wore.

"Women upset," said Wilson to the tall man. "Amounts to nothing. Strain on the nerves and one thing'n another."

"No," said Macomber. "I suppose that I rate that for the rest of my life now."

"Nonsense. Let's have a spot of the giant killer," said Wilson. "Forget the whole thing. Nothing to it anyway."

"We might try," said Macomber. "I won't forget what you did for me though."

"Nothing," said Wilson. "All nonsense."

So they sat there in the shade where the camp was pitched under some wide-topped acacia trees with a boulder-strewn cliff behind them, and a stretch of grass that ran to the bank of a boulder-filled stream in front with forest beyond it, and drank their just-cool lime drinks and avoided one another's eyes while the boys set the table for lunch. Wilson could tell that the boys all knew about it now and when he saw Macomber's personal boy looking curiously at his master while he was putting dishes on the table he snapped at him in Swahili. The boy turned away with his face blank.

"What were you telling him?" Macomber asked.

"Nothing. Told him to look alive or I'd see he got about fifteen of the best."

"What's that? Lashes?"

"It's quite illegal," Wilson said. "You're supposed to fine them."

"Do you still have them whipped?"

"Oh, yes. They could raise a row if they chose to complain. But they don't. They prefer it to the fines."

"How strange!" said Macomber.

"Not strange, really," Wilson said. "Which would you rather do? Take a good birching or lose your pay?"

Then he felt embarrassed at asking it and before Macomber could answer he went on, "We all take a beating every day, you know, one way or another."

This was no better. "Good God," he thought. "I am a diplomat, aren't I?"

"Yes, we take a beating," said Macomber, still not looking at him. "I'm awfully sorry about that lion business. It doesn't have to go any further, does it? I mean no one will hear about it, will they?"

"You mean will I tell it at the Mathaiga Club?" Wilson looked at him now coldly. He had not expected this. So he's a bloody four-letter man as well as a bloody coward, he thought. I rather liked him too until today. But how is one to know about an American?

"No," said Wilson. "I'm a professional hunter. We never talk about our clients. You can be quite easy on that. It's supposed to be bad form to ask us not to talk though."

He had decided now that to break would be much easier. He would eat, then, by himself and could read a book with his meals. They would eat by themselves. He would see them through the safari on a very formal basis—what was it the French called it? Distinguished consideration—and it would be a damn sight easier than having to go through this emotional trash. He'd insult him and make a good clean break. Then he could read a book with his meals and he'd still be drinking their whisky. That was the phrase for it when a safari went bad. You ran into another white hunter and you asked, "How is everything going?" and he answered, "Oh, I'm still drinking their whisky," and you knew everything had gone to pot.

"I'm sorry," Macomber said and looked at him with his American face that would stay adolescent until it became middle-aged, and Wilson noted his crew-cropped hair, fine eyes only faintly shifty, good nose, thin lips and handsome jaw. "I'm sorry I didn't realize that. There are lots of things I don't know."

So what could he do, Wilson thought. He was all ready to break it off quickly and neatly and here the beggar was apologizing after he had just insulted him. He made one more attempt. "Don't worry about me talking," he said. "I have a living to make. You know in Africa no woman ever misses her lion and no white man ever bolts."

"I bolted like a rabbit," Macomber said.

Now what in hell were you going to do about a man who talked like that, Wilson wondered.

Wilson looked at Macomber with his flat, blue, machine-gunner's eyes and the other smiled back at him. He had a pleasant smile if you did not notice how his eyes showed when he was hurt."

"Maybe I can fix it up on buffalo," he said. "We're after them next, aren't we?"

"In the morning if you like," Wilson told him. Perhaps he had been wrong. This was certainly the way to take it. You most certainly could not tell a damned thing about an American. He was all for Macomber again. If you could forget the morning. But, of course, you couldn't. The morning had been about as bad as they come.

"Here comes the Memsahib," he said. She was walking over from her tent looking refreshed and cheerful and quite lovely. She had a very perfect oval face, so perfect that you expected her to be stupid. But she wasn't stupid, Wilson thought, no, not stupid.

"How is the beautiful red-faced Mr. Wilson? Are you feeling better, Francis, my pearl?"

"Oh, much," said Macomber.

"I've dropped the whole thing," she said, sitting down at the table. "What importance is there to whether Francis is any good at killing lions? That's not his trade. That's Mr. Wilson's trade. Mr. Wilson is really very impressive killing anything. You do kill anything, don't you?"

"Oh, anything," said Wilson. "Simply anything." They are, he thought, the hardest in the world; the hardest, the cruelest, the most predatory and the most attractive and their men have softened or gone to pieces nervously as they have hardened. Or is it that they pick men they can handle? They can't know that much at the age they marry, he thought. He was grateful that he had gone through his education on American women before now because this was a very attractive one.

"We're going after buff in the morning," he told her.

"I'm coming," she said.

"No, you're not."

"Oh, yes, I am. Mayn't I, Francis?"

"Why not stay in camp?"

"Not for anything," she said. "I wouldn't miss something like today for anything."

When she left, Wilson was thinking, when she went off to cry, she seemed a hell of a fine woman. She seemed to understand, to realize, to be hurt for him and for herself and to know how things really stood. She is away for twenty minutes and now she is back, simply enamelled in that American female cruelty. They are the damnedest women. Really the damnedest.

"We'll put on another show for you tomorrow," Francis Macomber said.

"You're not coming," Wilson said.

"You're very mistaken," she told him. "And I want *so* to see you perform again. You were lovely this morning. That is if blowing things' heads off is lovely."

"Here's the lunch," said Wilson. "You're very merry, aren't you?"

"Why not? I didn't come out here to be dull."

"Well, it hasn't been dull," Wilson said. He could see the boulders in the river and the high bank beyond with the trees and he remembered the morning.

"Oh, no," she said. "It's been charming. And tomorrow. You don't know how I look forward to tomorrow."

"That's eland he's offering you," Wilson said.

"They're the big cowy things that jump like hares, aren't they?"

"I suppose that describes them," Wilson said.

"It's very good meat," Macomber said.

"Did you shoot it, Francis?" she asked.

"Yes."

"They're not dangerous, are they?"

"Only if they fall on you," Wilson told her.

"I'm so glad."

"Why not let up on the bitchery just a little, Margot," Macomber said, cutting the eland steak and putting some mashed potato, gravy and carrot on the down-turned fork that tined through the piece of meat.

"I suppose I could," she said, "since you put it so prettily."

"Tonight we'll have champagne for the lion," Wilson said. "It's a bit too hot at noon."

"Oh, the lion," Margot said. "I'd forgotten the lion!"

So, Robert Wilson thought to himself, she *is* giving him a ride, isn't she? Or do you suppose that's her idea of putting up a good show? How should a woman act when she discovers her husband is a bloody coward? She's damn cruel but they're all cruel. They govern, of course, and to govern one has to be cruel sometimes. Still, I've seen enough of their damn terrorism.

"Have some more eland," he said to her politely.

That afternoon, late, Wilson and Macomber went out in the motor car with the native driver and the two gun-bearers. Mrs. Macomber stayed in the camp. It was too hot to go out, she said, and she was going with them in the early morning. As they drove off Wilson saw her standing under the big tree, looking pretty rather than beautiful in her faintly rosy khaki, her dark hair drawn back off her forehead and gathered in a knot low on her neck, her face as fresh, he thought, as though she were in England. She waved to them as the car went off through the swale of high grass and curved around through the trees into the small hills of orchard bush.

In the orchard bush they found a herd of impala, and leaving the car they stalked one old ram with long, wide-spread horns and Macomber killed it with a very creditable shot that knocked the buck down at a good two hundred yards and sent the herd off bounding wildly and leaping over one another's backs in long, leg-drawn-up leaps as unbelievable and as floating as those one makes sometimes in dreams.

"That was a good shot," Wilson said. "They're a small target."

"Is it a worth-while head?" Macomber asked.

"It's excellent," Wilson told him. "You shoot like that and you'll have no trouble."

"Do you think we'll find buffalo tomorrow?"

"There's a good chance of it. They feed out early in the morning and with luck we may catch them in the open."

"I'd like to clear away that lion business," Macomber said. "It's not very pleasant to have your wife see you do something like that."

I should think it would be even more unpleasant to do it, Wilson thought, wife or no wife, or to talk about it having done it. But he said, "I wouldn't think about that any more. Any one could be upset by his first lion. That's all over."

But that night after dinner and a whisky and soda by the fire before going to bed, as Francis Macomber lay on his cot with the mosquito bar over him and listened to the night noises it was not all over. It was neither all over nor was it beginning. It was there exactly as it happened with some parts of it indelibly emphasized and he was miserably ashamed at it. But more than shame he felt cold, hollow fear in him. The fear was still there like a cold slimy hollow in all the emptiness where once his confidence had been and it made him feel sick. It was still there with him now.

It had started the night before when he had wakened and heard the lion roaring somewhere up along the river. It was a deep sound and at the end there were sort of coughing grunts that made him seem just outside the tent, and when Francis Macomber woke in the night to hear it he was afraid. He could hear his wife breathing quietly, asleep. There was no one to tell he was afraid, nor to be afraid with him, and, lying alone, he did not know the Somali proverb that says a brave man is always frightened three times by a lion; when he first sees his track, when he first hears him roar and when he first confronts him. Then while they were eating breakfast by lantern light out in the dining tent, before the sun was up, the lion roared again and Francis thought he was just at the edge of camp.

"Sounds like an old-timer," Robert Wilson said, looking up from his kippers and coffee. "Listen to him cough."

"Is he very close?"

"A mile or so up the stream."

"Will we see him?"
"We'll have a look."
"Does his roaring carry that far? It sounds as though he were right in camp."
"Carries a hell of a long way," said Robert Wilson. "It's strange the way it carries. Hope he's a shootable cat. The boys said there was a very big one about here."
"If I get a shot, where should I hit him," Macomber asked, "to stop him?"
"In the shoulders," Wilson said. "In the neck if you can make it. Shoot for bone. Break him down."
"I hope I can place it properly," Macomber said.
"You shoot very well," Wilson told him. "Take your time. Make sure of him. The first one in is the one that counts."
"What range will it be?"
"Can't tell. Lion has something to say about that. Won't shoot unless it's close enough so you can make sure."
"At under a hundred yards?" Macomber asked.
Wilson looked at him quickly.
"Hundred's about right. Might have to take him a bit under. Shouldn't chance a shot at much over that. A hundred's a decent range. You can hit him wherever you want at that. Here comes the Memsahib."
"Good morning," she said. "Are we going after that lion?"
"As soon as you deal with your breakfast," Wilson said. "How are you feeling?"
"Marvellous," she said. "I'm very excited."
"I'll just go and see that everything is ready," Wilson went off. As he left the lion roared again.
"Noisy beggar," Wilson said. "We'll put a stop to that."
"What's the matter, Francis?" his wife asked him.
"Nothing," Macomber said.
"Yes, there is," she said. "What are you upset about?"
"Nothing," he said.
"Tell me," she looked at him. "Don't you feel well?"
"It's that damned roaring," he said. "It's been going on all night, you know."
"Why didn't you wake me," she said. "I'd love to have heard it."
"I've got to kill the damned thing," Macomber said, miserably.
"Well, that's what you're out here for, isn't it?"
"Yes. But I'm nervous. Hearing the thing roar gets on my nerves."
"Well then, as Wilson said, kill him and stop his roaring."
"Yes, darling," said Francis Macomber. "It sounds easy, doesn't it?"
"You're not afraid, are you?"
"Of course not. But I'm nervous from hearing him roar all night."

"You'll kill him marvellously," she said. "I know you will. I'm awfully anxious to see it."

"Finish your breakfast and we'll be starting."

"It's not light yet," she said. "This is a ridiculous hour."

Just then the lion roared in a deep-chested moaning, suddenly guttural, ascending vibration that seemed to shake the air and ended in a sigh and a heavy, deep-chested grunt.

"He sounds almost here," Macomber's wife said.

"My God," said Macomber. "I hate that damned noise."

"It's very impressive."

"Impressive. It's frightful."

Robert Wilson came up then carrying his short, ugly, shockingly big-bored .505 Gibbs and grinning.

"Come on," he said. "Your gun-bearer has your Springfield and the big gun. Everything's in the car. Have you solids?"

"Yes."

"I'm ready," Mrs. Macomber said.

"Must make him stop that racket," Wilson said. "You get in front. The Memsahib can sit back here with me."

They climbed into the motor car and, in the gray first daylight, moved off up the river through the trees. Macomber opened the breech of his rifle and saw he had metal-cased bullets, shut the bolt and put the rifle on safety. He saw his hand was trembling. He felt in his pocket for more cartridges and moved his fingers over the cartridges in the loops of his tunic front. He turned back to where Wilson sat in the rear seat of the doorless, box-bodied motor car beside his wife, them both grinning with excitement, and Wilson leaned forward and whispered,

"See the birds dropping. Means the old boy has left his kill."

On the far bank of the stream Macomber could see, above the trees, vultures circling and plummeting down.

"Chances are he'll come to drink along here," Wilson whispered. "Before he goes to lay up. Keep an eye out."

They were driving slowly along the high bank of the stream which here cut deeply to its boulder-filled bed, and they wound in and out through big trees as they drove. Macomber was watching the opposite bank when he felt Wilson take hold of his arm. The car stopped.

"There he is," he heard the whisper. "Ahead and to the right. Get out and take him. He's a marvellous lion."

Macomber saw the lion now. He was standing almost broadside, his great head up and turned toward them. The early morning breeze that blew toward them was just stirring his dark mane, and the lion looked huge, silhouetted on the rise of bank in the gray morning light, his shoulders heavy, his barrel of a body bulking smoothly.

"How far is he?" asked Macomber, raising his rifle.

"About seventy-five. Get out and take him."

"Why not shoot from where I am?"

"You don't shoot them from cars," he heard Wilson saying in his ear. "Get out. He's not going to stay there all day."

Macomber stepped out of the curved opening at the side of the front seat, onto the step and down onto the ground. The lion still stood looking majestically and coolly toward this object that his eyes only showed in silhouette, bulking like some super-rhino. There was no man smell carried toward him and he watched the object, moving his great head a little from side to side. Then watching the object, not afraid, but hesitating before going down the bank to drink with such a thing opposite him, he saw a man figure detach itself from it and he turned his heavy head and swung away toward the cover of the trees as he heard a cracking crash and felt the slam of a .30-06 220-grain solid bullet that bit his flank and ripped in sudden hot scalding nausea through his stomach. He trotted, heavy, big-footed, swinging wounded full-bellied, through the trees toward the tall grass and cover, and the crash came again to go past him ripping the air apart. Then it crashed again and he felt the blow as it hit his lower ribs and ripped on through, blood sudden hot and frothy in his mouth, and he galloped toward the high grass where he could crouch and not be seen and make them bring the crashing thing close enough so he could make a rush and get the man that held it.

Macomber had not thought how the lion felt as he got out of the car. He only knew his hands were shaking and as he walked away from the car it was almost impossible for him to make his legs move. They were stiff in the thighs, but he could feel the muscles fluttering. He raised the rifle, sighted on the junction of the lion's head and shoulders and pulled the trigger. Nothing happened though he pulled until he thought his finger would break. Then he knew he had the safety on and as he lowered the rifle to move the safety over he moved another frozen pace forward, and the lion seeing his silhouette now clear of the silhouette of the car, turned and started off at a trot, and, as Macomber fired, he heard a whunk that meant that the bullet was home; but the lion kept on going. Macomber shot again and every one saw the bullet throw a spout of dirt beyond the trotting lion. He shot again, remembering to lower his aim, and they all heard the bullet hit, and the lion went into a gallop and was in the tall grass before he had the bolt pushed forward.

Macomber stood there feeling sick at his stomach, his hands that held the Springfield still cocked, shaking, and his wife and Robert Wilson were standing by him. Beside him too were the two gun-bearers chattering in Wakamba.

"I hit him," Macomber said. "I hit him twice."

"You gut-shot him and you hit him somewhere forward," Wilson said without enthusiasm. The gun-bearers looked very grave. They were silent now.

"You may have killed him," Wilson went on. "We'll have to wait a while before we go in to find out."

"What do you mean?"

"Let him get sick before we follow him up."

"Oh," said Macomber.

"He's a hell of a fine lion," Wilson said cheerfully. "He's gotten into a bad place though."

"Why is it bad?"

"Can't see him until you're on him."

"Oh," said Macomber.

"Come on," said Wilson. "The Memsahib can stay here in the car. We'll go to have a look at the blood spoor."

"Stay here, Margot," Macomber said to his wife. His mouth was very dry and it was hard for him to talk.

"Why?" she asked.

"Wilson says to."

"We're going to have a look," Wilson said. "You stay here. You can see even better from here."

"All right."

Wilson spoke in Swahili to the driver. He nodded and said,

"Yes, Bwana."

Then they went down the steep bank and across the stream, climbing over and around the boulders and up the other bank, pulling up by some projecting roots, and along it until they found where the lion had been trotting when Macomber first shot. There was dark blood on the short grass that the gun-bearers pointed out with grass stems, and that ran away behind the river bank trees.

"What do we do?" asked Macomber.

"Not much choice," said Wilson. "We can't bring the car over. Bank's too steep. We'll let him stiffen up a bit and then you and I'll go in and have a look for him."

"Can't we set the grass on fire?" Macomber asked.

"Too green."

"Can't we send beaters?"

Wilson looked at him appraisingly. "Of course we can," he said. "But it's just a touch murderous. You see we know the lion's wounded. You can drive an unwounded lion—he'll move on ahead of a noise—but a wounded lion's going to charge. You can't see him until you're right on him. He'll make himself perfectly flat in cover you wouldn't think would hide a hare. You can't very well send boys in there to that sort of a show. Somebody bound to get mauled."

"What about the gun-bearers?"

"Oh, they'll go with us. It's their *shauri.** You see, they signed on for it. They don't look too happy though, do they?"

"I don't want to go in there," said Macomber. It was out before he knew he'd said it.

* *shauri.* agreement

"Neither do I," said Wilson very cheerily. "Really no choice though." Then, as an afterthought, he glanced at Macomber and saw suddenly how he was trembling and the pitiful look on his face.

"You don't have to go in, of course," he said. "That's what I'm hired for, you know. That's why I'm so expensive."

"You mean you'd go in by yourself? Why not leave him there?"

Robert Wilson, whose entire occupation had been with the lion and the problem he presented, and who had not been thinking about Macomber except to note that he was rather windy, suddenly felt as though he had opened the wrong door in a hotel and seen something shameful.

"What do you mean?"

"Why not just leave him?"

"You mean pretend to ourselves he hasn't been hit?"

"No. Just drop it."

"It isn't done."

"Why not?"

"For one thing, he's certain to be suffering. For another, some one else might run onto him."

"I see."

"But you don't have to have anything to do with it."

"I'd like to," Macomber said. "I'm just scared, you know."

"I'll go ahead when we go in," Wilson said, "with Kongoni tracking. You keep behind me and a little to one side. Chances are we'll hear him growl. If we see him we'll both shoot. Don't worry about anything. I'll keep you backed up. As a matter of fact, you know, perhaps you'd better not go. It might be much better. Why don't you go over and join the Memsahib while I just get it over with?"

"No, I want to go."

"All right," said Wilson. "But don't go in if you don't want to. This is my *shauri* now, you know."

"I want to go," said Macomber.

They sat under a tree and smoked.

"Want to go back and speak to the Memsahib while we're waiting?" Wilson asked.

"No."

"I'll just step back and tell her to be patient."

"Good," said Macomber. He sat there, sweating under his arms, his mouth dry, his stomach hollow feeling, wanting to find courage to tell Wilson to go on and finish off the lion without him. He could not know that Wilson was furious because he had not noticed the state he was in earlier and sent him back to his wife. While he sat there Wilson came up. "I have your big gun," he said. "Take it. We've given him time, I think. Come on."

Macomber took the big gun and Wilson said:

"Keep behind me and about five yards to the right and do exactly as I tell you." Then he spoke in Swahili to the two gun-bearers who looked the picture of gloom.

"Let's go," he said.

"Could I have a drink of water?" Macomber asked. Wilson spoke to the older gun-bearer, who wore a canteen on his belt, and the man unbuckled it, unscrewed the top and handed it to Macomber, who took it noticing how heavy it seemed and how hairy and shoddy the felt covering was in his hand. He raised it to drink and looked ahead at the high grass with the flat-topped trees behind it. A breeze was blowing toward them and the grass rippled gently in the wind. He looked at the gun-bearer and he could see the gun-bearer was suffering too with fear.

Thirty-five yards into the grass the big lion lay flattened out along the ground. His ears were back and his only movement was a slight twitching up and down of his long, black-tufted tail. He had turned at bay as soon as he had reached this cover and he was sick with the wound through his full belly, and weakening with the wound through his lungs that brought a thin foamy red to his mouth each time he breathed. His flanks were wet and hot and flies were on the little openings the solid bullets had made in his tawny hide, and his big yellow eyes, narrowed with hate, looked straight ahead, only blinking when the pain came as he breathed, and his claws dug in the soft baked earth. All of him, pain, sickness, hatred and all of his remaining strength, was tightening into an absolute concentration for a rush. He could hear the men talking and he waited, gathering all of himself into this preparation for a charge as soon as the men would come into the grass. As he heard their voices his tail stiffened to twitch up and down, and, as they came into the edge of the grass, he made a coughing grunt and charged.

Kongoni, the old gun-bearer, in the lead watching the blood spoor, Wilson watching the grass for any movement, his big gun ready, the second gun-bearer looking ahead and listening, Macomber close to Wilson, his rifle cocked, they had just moved into the grass when Macomber heard the blood-choked coughing grunt, and saw the swishing rush in the grass. The next thing he knew he was running; running wildly, in panic in the open, running toward the stream.

He heard the *ca-ra-wong!* of Wilson's big rifle, and again in a second crashing *carawong!* and turning saw the lion, horrible-looking now, with half his head seeming to be gone, crawling toward Wilson in the edge of the tall grass while the red-faced man worked the bolt on the short ugly rifle and aimed carefully as another blasting *carawong!* came from the muzzle, and the crawling, heavy, yellow bulk of the lion stiffened and the huge, mutilated head slid forward and Macomber, standing by himself in the clearing where he had run, holding a loaded rifle, while two black men and a white man looked back at him in contempt, knew the lion was dead. He came toward Wilson, his tallness all seeming a naked reproach, and Wilson looked at him and said:

"Want to take pictures?"

"No," he said.

That was all any one had said until they reached the motor car. Then Wilson had said:

"Hell of a fine lion. Boys will skin him out. We might as well stay here in the shade."

Macomber's wife had not looked at him nor he at her and he had sat by her in the back seat with Wilson sitting in the front seat. Once he had reached over and taken his wife's hand without looking at her and she had removed her hand from his. Looking across the stream to where the gun-bearers were skinning out the lion he could see that she had been able to see the whole thing. While they sat there his wife had reached forward and put her hand on Wilson's shoulder. He turned and she had leaned forward over the low seat and kissed him on the mouth.

"Oh, I say," said Wilson, going redder than his natural baked color.

"Mr. Robert Wilson," she said. "The beautiful red-faced Mr. Robert Wilson."

Then she sat down beside Macomber again and looked away across the stream to where the lion lay, with uplifted, white-muscled, tendon-marked naked forearms, and white bloating belly, as the black men fleshed away the skin. Finally the gun-bearers brought the skin over, wet and heavy, and climbed in behind with it, rolling it up before they got in, and the motor car started. No one had said anything more until they were back in camp.

That was the story of the lion. Macomber did not know how the lion had felt before he started his rush, nor during it when the unbelievable smash of the .505 with a muzzle velocity of two tons had hit him in the mouth, nor what kept him coming after that, when the second ripping crash had smashed his hind quarters and he had come crawling on toward the crashing, blasting thing that had destroyed him. Wilson knew something about it and only expressed it by saying, "Damned fine lion," but Macomber did not know how Wilson felt about things either. He did not know how his wife felt except that she was through with him.

His wife had been through with him before but it never lasted. He was very wealthy, and would be much wealthier, and he knew she would not leave him ever now. That was one of the few things that he really knew. He knew about that, about motor cycles—that was earliest—about motor cars, about duck-shooting, about fishing, trout, salmon and big-sea, about sex in books, many books, too many books, about all court games, about dogs, not much about horses, about hanging on to his money, about most of the other things his world dealt in, and about his wife not leaving him. His wife had been a great beauty and she was still a great beauty in Africa, but she was not a great enough beauty any more at home to be able to leave him and better herself and she knew it and he knew it. She had missed the chance to leave him and he knew it. If he had been better with women she would probably have started to worry about him getting another new, beautiful wife; but she knew too much about him to worry about him either. Also, he had always had a great tolerance which seemed the nicest thing about him if it were not the most sinister.

All in all they were known as a comparatively happily married couple, one of those whose disruption is often rumored but never occurs, and as the society columnist put it, they were adding more than a spice of *adventure* to their much envied and ever-enduring *Romance* by a *Safari* in what was known as *Darkest Africa* until the Martin Johnsons lighted it on so many silver screens where they were pursuing *Old Simba* the lion, the buffalo, *Tembo* the elephant and as well collecting specimens for the Museum of Natural History. This same columnist had reported them *on the verge* at least three times in the past and they had been. But they always made it up. They had a sound basis of union. Margot was too beautiful for Macomber to divorce her and Macomber had too much money for Margot ever to leave him.

It was now about three o'clock in the morning and Francis Macomber, who had been asleep a little while after he had stopped thinking about the lion, wakened and then slept again, woke suddenly, frightened in a dream of the bloody-headed lion standing over him, and listening while his heart pounded, he realized that his wife was not in the other cot in the tent. He lay awake with that knowledge for two hours.

At the end of that time his wife came into the tent, lifted her mosquito bar and crawled cozily into bed.

"Where have you been?" Macomber asked in the darkness.

"Hello," she said. "Are you awake?"

"Where have you been?"

"I just went out to get a breath of air."

"You did, like hell."

"What do you want me to say, darling?"

"Where have you been?"

"Out to get a breath of air."

"That's a new name for it. You *are* a bitch."

"Well, you're a coward."

"All right," he said. "What of it?"

"Nothing as far as I'm concerned. But please let's not talk, darling, because I'm very sleepy."

"You think that I'll take anything."

"I know you will, sweet."

"Well, I won't."

"Please, darling, let's not talk. I'm so very sleepy."

"There wasn't going to be any of that. You promised there wouldn't be."

"Well, there is now," she said sweetly.

"You said if we made this trip that there would be none of that. You promised."

"Yes, darling. That's the way I meant it to be. But the trip was spoiled yesterday. We don't have to talk about it do we?"

"You don't wait long when you have an advantage, do you?"

"Please let's not talk. I'm so sleepy, darling."

"I'm going to talk."

"Don't mind me then, because I'm going to sleep." And she did.

At breakfast they were all three at the table before daylight and Francis Macomber found that, of all the many men that he had hated, he hated Robert Wilson the most.

"Sleep well?" Wilson asked in his throaty voice, filling a pipe.

"Did you?"

"Topping," the white hunter told him.

You bastard, thought Macomber, you insolent bastard.

So she woke him when she came in, Wilson thought, looking at them both with his flat, cold eyes. Well, why doesn't he keep his wife where she belongs? What does he think I am, a bloody plaster saint? Let him keep her where she belongs. It's his own fault.

"Do you think we'll find buffalo?" Margot asked, pushing away a dish of apricots.

"Chance of it," Wilson said and smiled at her. "Why don't you stay in camp?"

"Not for anything," she told him.

"Why not order her to stay in camp?" Wilson said to Macomber.

"You order her," said Macomber coldly.

"Let's not have any ordering, nor," turning to Macomber, "any silliness, Francis," Margot said quite pleasantly.

"Are you ready to start?" Macomber asked.

"Any time," Wilson told him. "Do you want the Memsahib to go?"

"Does it make any difference whether I do or not?"

The hell with it, thought Robert Wilson. The utter complete hell with it. So this is what it's going to be like. Well, this is what it's going to be like, then.

"Makes no difference," he said.

"You're sure you wouldn't like to stay in camp with her yourself and let me go out and hunt the buffalo?" Macomber asked.

"Can't do that," said Wilson. "Wouldn't talk rot if I were you."

"I'm not talking rot. I'm disgusted."

"Bad word, disgusted."

"Francis, will you please try to speak sensibly!" his wife said.

"I speak too damned sensibly," Macomber said. "Did you ever eat such filthy food?"

"Something wrong with the food?" asked Wilson quietly.

"No more than with everything else."

"I'd pull yourself together, laddybuck," Wilson said very quietly. "There's a boy waits at table that understands a little English."

"The hell with him."

Wilson stood up and puffing on his pipe strolled away, speaking a few words in Swahili to one of the gun-bearers who was standing waiting for him. Macomber and his wife sat on at the table. He was staring at his coffee cup.

"If you make a scene I'll leave you, darling," Margot said quietly.

"No, you won't."

"You can try it and see."

"You won't leave me."

"No," she said. "I won't leave you and you'll behave yourself."

"Behave myself? That's a way to talk. Behave myself."

"Yes. Behave yourself."

"Why don't *you* try behaving?"

"I've tried it so long. So very long."

"I hate that red-faced swine," Macomber said. "I loathe the sight of him."

"He's really *very* nice."

"Oh, *shut up,*" Macomber almost shouted. Just then the car came up and stopped in front of the dining tent and the driver and the two gun-bearers got out. Wilson walked over and looked at the husband and wife sitting there at the table.

"Going shooting?" he asked.

"Yes," said Macomber, standing up. "Yes."

"Better bring a woolly. It will be cool in the car," Wilson said.

"I'll get my leather jacket," Margot said.

"The boy has it," Wilson told her. He climbed into the front with the driver and Francis Macomber and his wife sat, not speaking, in the back seat.

Hope the silly beggar doesn't take a notion to blow the back of my head off, Wilson thought to himself. Women *are* a nuisance on safari.

The car was grinding down to cross the river at a pebbly ford in the gray daylight and then climbed, angling up the steep bank, where Wilson had ordered a way shovelled out the day before so they could reach the parklike wooded rolling country on the far side.

It was a good morning, Wilson thought. There was a heavy dew and as the wheels went through the grass and low bushes he could smell the odor of the crushed fronds. It was an odor like verbena and he liked this early morning smell of the dew, the crushed bracken and the look of the tree trunks showing black through the early morning mist, as the car made its way through the untracked, parklike country. He had put the two in the back seat out of his mind now and was thinking about buffalo. The buffalo that he was after stayed in the daytime in a thick swamp where it was impossible to get a shot, but in the night they fed out into an open stretch of country and if he could come between them and their swamp with the car, Macomber would have a good chance at them in the open. He did not want to hunt buff with Macomber in thick cover. He did not want to hunt buff or anything else with Macomber at all, but he was a professional hunter and he had hunted with some rare ones in his time. If they got buff today there would only be rhino to come and the poor man would have gone through his dangerous game and things might pick up. He'd have nothing more to do with the woman and Macomber would get over that too. He must have gone through plenty of that before by the look of things. Poor beggar. He must have a way of getting over it. Well, it was the poor sod's own bloody fault.

He, Robert Wilson, carried a double size cot on safari to accommodate any windfalls he might receive. He had hunted for a certain clientele, the international, fast, sporting set, where the women did not feel they were getting their money's worth unless they had shared that cot with the white hunter. He despised them when he was away from them although he liked some of them well enough at the time, but he made his living by them; and their standards were his standards as long as they were hiring him.

They were his standards in all except the shooting. He had his own standards about the killing and they could live up to them or get some one else to hunt them. He knew, too, that they all respected him for this. This Macomber was an odd one though. Damned if he wasn't. Now the wife. Well, the wife. Yes, the wife. Hm, the wife. Well he'd dropped all that. He looked around at them. Macomber sat grim and furious. Margot smiled at him. She looked younger today, more innocent and fresher and not so professionally beautiful. What's in her heart God knows, Wilson thought. She hadn't talked much last night. At that it was a pleasure to see her.

The motor car climbed up a slight rise and went on through the trees and then out into a grassy prairie-like opening and kept in the shelter of the trees along the edge, the driver going slowly and Wilson looking carefully out across the prairie and all along its far side. He stopped the car and studied the opening with his field glasses. Then he motioned to the driver to go on and the car moved slowly along, the driver avoiding wart-hog holes and driving around the mud castles ants had built. Then, looking across the opening, Wilson suddenly turned and said,

"By God, there they are!"

And looking where he pointed, while the car jumped forward and Wilson spoke in rapid Swahili to the driver, Macomber saw three huge, black animals looking almost cylindrical in their long heaviness, like big black tank cars, moving at a gallop across the far edge of the open prairie. They moved at a stiff-necked, stiff-bodied gallop and he could see the upswept wide black horns on their heads as they galloped heads out; the heads not moving.

"They're three old bulls," Wilson said. "We'll cut them off before they get to the swamp."

The car was going a wild forty-five miles an hour across the open and as Macomber watched, the buffalo got bigger and bigger until he could see the gray, hairless, scabby look of one huge bull and how his neck was a part of his shoulders and the shiny black of his horns as he galloped a little behind the others that were strung out in that steady plunging gait; and then, the car swaying as though it had just jumped a road, they drew up close and he could see the plunging hugeness of the bull, and the dust in his sparsely haired hide, the wide boss of horn and his outstretched, wide-nostrilled muzzle, and he was raising his rifle when Wilson shouted, "Not from the car, you fool!" and he had no fear, only hatred of Wilson, while the brakes clamped on and the car skidded, plowing sideways to an almost stop and Wilson was out on one side and he on the other, stumbling as his feet hit the still speeding-by of the earth, and then he was shooting at the bull as he moved away, hearing the bullets whunk into him, emptying his rifle at him as he moved steadily away, finally remembering to get his shots forward into the shoulder, and as he fumbled to reload, he saw the bull was down. Down on his knees, his big head tossing, and seeing the other two still galloping he shot at the leader and hit him. He shot again and missed and he heard the *carawonging* roar as Wilson shot and saw the leading bull slide forward onto his nose.

"Get that other," Wilson said. "Now you're shooting!"

But the other bull was moving steadily at the same gallop and he missed, throwing a spout of dirt, and Wilson missed and the dust rose in a cloud and Wilson shouted, "Come on. He's too far!" and grabbed his arm and they were in the car again, Macomber and Wilson hanging on the sides and rocketing swayingly over the uneven ground, drawing up on the steady, plunging, heavy-necked, straight-moving gallop of the bull.

They were behind him and Macomber was filling his rifle, dropping shells onto the ground, jamming it, clearing the jam, then they were almost up with the bull when Wilson yelled "Stop," and the car skidded so that it almost swung over and Macomber fell forward onto his feet, slammed his bolt forward and fired as far forward as he could aim into the galloping, rounded black back, aimed and shot again, then again, then again, and the bullets, all of them hitting, had no effect on the buffalo that he could see. Then Wilson shot, the roar deafening him, and he could see the bull stagger. Macomber shot again, aiming carefully, and down he came, onto his knees.

"All right," Wilson said. "Nice work. That's the three."

Macomber felt a drunken elation.

"How many times did you shoot?" he asked.

"Just three," Wilson said. "You killed the first bull. The biggest one. I helped you finish the other two. Afraid they might have got into cover. You had them killed. I was just mopping up a little. You shot damn well."

"Let's go to the car," said Macomber. "I want a drink."

"Got to finish off that buff first," Wilson told him. The buffalo was on his knees and he jerked his head furiously and bellowed in pig-eyed, roaring rage as they came toward him.

"Watch he doesn't get up," Wilson said. Then, "Get a little broadside and take him in the neck just behind the ear."

Macomber aimed carefully at the center of the huge, jerking, rage-driven neck and shot. At the shot the head dropped forward.

"That does it," said Wilson. "Got the spine. They're a hell of a looking thing, aren't they?"

"Let's get the drink," said Macomber. In his life he had never felt so good.

In the car Macomber's wife sat very white faced. "You were marvellous, darling," she said to Macomber. "What a ride."

"Was it rough?" Wilson asked.

"It was frightful. I've never been more frightened in my life."

"Let's all have a drink," Macomber said.

"By all means," said Wilson. "Give it to the Memsahib." She drank the neat whisky from the flask and shuddered a little when she swallowed. She handed the flask to Macomber who handed it to Wilson.

"It was frightfully exciting," she said. "It's given me a dreadful headache. I didn't know you were allowed to shoot them from cars though."

"No one shot from cars," said Wilson coldly.

"I mean chase them from cars."

"Wouldn't ordinarily," Wilson said. "Seemed sporting enough to me though while we were doing it. Taking more chance driving that way across the plain full of holes and one thing and another than hunting on foot. Buffalo could have charged us each time we shot if he liked. Gave him every chance. Wouldn't mention it to any one though. It's illegal if that's what you mean."

"It seemed very unfair to me," Margot said, "chasing those big helpless things in a motor car."

"Did it?" said Wilson.

"What would happen if they heard about it in Nairobi?"

"I'd lose my licence for one thing. Other unpleasantnesses," Wilson said, taking a drink from the flask. "I'd be out of business."

"Really?"

"Yes, really."

"Well," said Macomber, and he smiled for the first time all day. "Now she has something on you."

"You have such a pretty way of putting things, Francis," Margot Macomber said. Wilson looked at them both. If a four-letter man marries a five-letter woman, he was thinking, what number of letters would their children be? What he said was, "We lost a gun-bearer. Did you notice it?"

"My God, no," Macomber said.

"Here he comes," Wilson said. "He's all right. He must have fallen off when we left the first bull."

Approaching them was the middle-aged gun-bearer, limping along in his knitted cap, khaki tunic, shorts and rubber sandals, gloomy-faced and disgusted looking. As he came up he called out to Wilson in Swahili and they all saw the change in the white hunter's face.

"What does he say?" asked Margot.

"He says the first bull got up and went into the bush," Wilson said with no expression in his voice.

"Oh," said Macomber blankly.

"Then it's going to be just like the lion," said Margot, full of anticipation.

"It's not going to be a damned bit like the lion," Wilson told her. "Did you want another drink, Macomber?"

"Thanks, yes," Macomber said. He expected the feeling he had had about the lion to come back but it did not. For the first time in his life he really felt wholly without fear. Instead of fear he had a feeling of definite elation.

"We'll go and have a look at the second bull," Wilson said. "I'll tell the driver to put the car in the shade."

"What are you going to do?" asked Margaret Macomber.

"Take a look at the buff," Wilson said.

"I'll come."

"Come along."

The three of them walked over to where the second buffalo bulked blackly in the open, head forward on the grass, the massive horns swung wide.

"He's a very good head," Wilson said. "That's close to a fifty-inch spread."

Macomber was looking at him with delight.

"He's hateful looking," said Margot. "Can't we go into the shade?"

"Of course," Wilson said. "Look," he said to Macomber, and pointed. "See that patch of bush?"

"Yes."

"That's where the first bull went in. The gun-bearer said when he fell off the bull was down. He was watching us helling along and the other two buff galloping. When he looked up there was the bull up and looking at him. Gun-bearer ran like hell and the bull went off slowly into that bush."

"Can we go in after him now?" asked Macomber eagerly.

Wilson looked at him appraisingly. Damned if this isn't a strange one, he thought. Yesterday he's scared sick and today he's a ruddy fire eater.

"No, we'll give him a while."

"Let's please go into the shade," Margot said. Her face was white and she looked ill.

They made their way to the car where it stood under a single, wide-spreading tree and all climbed in.

"Chances are he's dead in there," Wilson remarked. "After a little we'll have a look."

Macomber felt a wild unreasonable happiness that he had never known before.

"By God, that was a chase," he said. "I've never felt any such feeling. Wasn't it marvellous, Margot?"

"I hated it."

"Why?"

"I hated it," she said bitterly. "I loathed it."

"You know I don't think I'd ever be afraid of anything again," Macomber said to Wilson. "Something happened in me after we first saw the buff and started after him. Like a dam bursting. It was pure excitement."

"Cleans out your liver," said Wilson. "Damn funny things happen to people."

Macomber's face was shining. "You know something did happen to me," he said. "I feel absolutely different."

His wife said nothing and eyed him strangely. She was sitting far back in the seat and Macomber was sitting forward talking to Wilson who turned sideways talking over the back of the front seat.

"You know, I'd like to try another lion," Macomber said. "I'm really not afraid of them now. After all, what can they do to you?"

"That's it," said Wilson. "Worst one can do is kill you. How does it go? Shakespeare. Damned good. See if I can remember. Oh, damned good. Used to quote it to myself at one time. Let's see. 'By my troth, I care not; a man can die but once; we owe God a death and let it go which way it will he that dies this year is quit for the next.' Damned fine, eh?"

He was very embarrassed, having brought out this thing he had lived by, but he had seen men come of age before and it always moved him. It was not a matter of their twenty-first birthday.

It had taken a strange chance of hunting, a sudden precipitation into action without opportunity for worrying beforehand, to bring this about with Macomber, but regardless of how it had happened it had most certainly happened. Look at the beggar now, Wilson thought. It's that some of them stay little boys so long, Wilson thought. Sometimes all their lives. Their figures stay boyish when they're fifty. The great American boy-men. Damned strange people. But he liked this Macomber now. Damned strange fellow. Probably meant the end of cuckoldry too. Well, that would be a damned good thing. Damned good thing. Beggar had probably been afraid all his life. Don't know what started it. But over now. Hadn't had time to be afraid with the buff. That and being angry too. Motor car too. Motor cars made it familiar. Be a damn fire eater now. He'd seen it in the war work the same way. More of a change than any loss of virginity. Fear gone like an operation. Something else grew in its place. Main thing a man had. Made him into a man. Women knew it too. No bloody fear.

From the far corner of the seat Margaret Macomber looked at the two of them. There was no change in Wilson. She saw Wilson as she had seen him the day before when she had first realized what his great talent was. But she saw the change in Francis Macomber now.

"Do you have that feeling of happiness about what's going to happen?" Macomber asked, still exploring his new wealth.

"You are not supposed to mention it," Wilson said, looking in the other's face. "Much more fashionable to say you're scared. Mind you, you'll be scared too, plenty of times."

"But you *have* a feeling of happiness about action to come?"

"Yes," said Wilson. "There's that. Doesn't do to talk too much about all this. Talk the whole thing away. No pleasure in anything if you mouth it up too much."

"You're both talking rot," said Margot. "Just because you've chased some helpless animals in a motor car you talk like heroes."

"Sorry," said Wilson. "I have been gassing too much." She's worried about it already, he thought.

"If you don't know what we're talking about why not keep out of it?" Macomber asked his wife.

"You've gotten awfully brave, awfully suddenly," his wife said contemptuously, but her contempt was not secure. She was very afraid of something.

Macomber laughed, a very natural hearty laugh. "You know I *have,*" he said. "I really have."

"Isn't it sort of late?" Margot said bitterly. Because she had done the best she could for many years back and the way they were together now was no one person's fault.

"Not for me," said Macomber.

Margot said nothing but sat back in the corner of the seat.

"Do you think we've given him time enough?" Macomber asked Wilson cheerfully.

"We might have a look," Wilson said. "Have you any solids left?"

"The gun-bearer has some."

Wilson called in Swahili and the older gun-bearer, who was skinning out one of the heads, straightened up, pulled a box of solids out of his pocket and brought them over to Macomber, who filled his magazine and put the remaining shells in his pocket.

"You might as well shoot the Springfield," Wilson said. "You're used to it. We'll leave the Mannlicher in the car with the Memsahib. Your gun-bearer can carry your heavy gun. I've this damned cannon. Now let me tell you about them." He had saved this until the last because he did not want to worry Macomber. "When a buff comes he comes with his head high and thrust straight out. The boss of the horns covers any sort of a brain shot. The only shot is straight into the nose. The only other shot is into his chest or, if you're to one side, into the neck or the shoulders. After they've been hit once they take a hell of a lot of killing. Don't try anything fancy. Take the easiest shot there is. They've finished skinning out that head now. Should we get started?"

He called to the gun-bearers, who came up wiping their hands, and the older one got into the back.

"I'll only take Kongoni," Wilson said. "The other can watch to keep the birds away."

As the car moved slowly across the open space toward the island of brushy trees that ran in a tongue of foliage along a dry water course that cut the open swale, Macomber felt his heart pounding and his mouth was dry again, but it was excitement, not fear.

"Here's where he went in," Wilson said. Then to the gun-bearer in Swahili, "Take the blood spoor."

The car was parallel to the patch of bush. Macomber, Wilson and the gun-bearer got down. Macomber, looking back, saw his wife, with the rifle by her side, looking at him. He waved to her and she did not wave back.

The brush was very thick ahead and the ground was dry. The middle-aged gun-bearer was sweating heavily and Wilson had his hat down over his eyes and his red neck showed just ahead of Macomber. Suddenly the gun-bearer said something in Swahili to Wilson and ran forward.

"He's dead in there," Wilson said. "Good work," and he turned to grip Macomber's hand and as they shook hands, grinning at each other, the gun-bearer shouted wildly and they saw him coming out of the bush sideways, fast as a crab, and the bull coming, nose out, mouth tight closed, blood dripping, massive head straight out, coming in a charge, his little pig eyes bloodshot as he looked at them. Wilson, who was ahead was kneeling shooting, and Macomber, as he fired, unhearing his shot in the roaring of Wilson's gun, saw fragments like slate burst from the huge boss of the horns, and the head jerked, he shot again at the wide nostrils and saw the horns jolt again and fragments fly, and he did not see Wilson now and, aiming carefully, shot again with the buffalo's huge bulk almost on him and his rifle almost level with the on-coming head, nose out, and he could see the little wicked eyes and the head started to lower and he felt a sudden white-hot, blinding flash explode inside his head and that was all he ever felt.

Wilson had ducked to one side to get in a shoulder shot. Macomber had stood solid and shot for the nose, shooting a touch high each time and hitting the heavy horns, splintering and chipping them like hitting a slate roof, and Mrs. Macomber, in the car, had shot at the buffalo with the 6.5 Mannlicher as it seemed about to gore Macomber and had hit her husband about two inches up and a little to one side of the base of his skull.

Francis Macomber lay now, face down, not two yards from where the buffalo lay on his side and his wife knelt over him with Wilson beside her.

"I wouldn't turn him over," Wilson said.

The woman was crying hysterically.

"I'd get back in the car," Wilson said. "Where's the rifle?"

She shook her head, her face contorted. The gun-bearer picked up the rifle.

"Leave it as it is," said Wilson. Then, "Go get Abdulla so that he may witness the manner of the accident."

He knelt down, took a handkerchief from his pocket, and spread it over Francis Macomber's crew-cropped head where it lay. The blood sank into the dry, loose earth.

Wilson stood up and saw the buffalo on his side, his legs out, his thinly-haired belly crawling with ticks. "Hell of a good bull," his brain registered automatically. "A good fifty inches, or better. Better." He called to the driver and told him to spread a blanket over the body and stay by it. Then he walked over to the motor car where the woman sat crying in the corner.

"That was a pretty thing to do," he said in a toneless voice. "He *would* have left you too."

"Stop it," she said.

"Of course it's an accident," he said. "I know that."

"Stop it," she said.

"Don't worry," he said. "There will be a certain amount of unpleasantness but I will have some photographs taken that will be very useful at the inquest. There's the testimony of the gun-bearers and the driver too. You're perfectly all right."

"Stop it," she said.

"There's a hell of a lot to be done," he said. "And I'll have to send a truck off to the lake to wireless for a plane to take the three of us into Nairobi. Why didn't you poison him? That's what they do in England."

"Stop it. Stop it. Stop it," the woman cried.

Wilson looked at her with his flat blue eyes.

"I'm through now," he said. "I was a little angry. I'd begun to like your husband."

"Oh, please stop it," she said. "Please, please stop it."

"That's better," Wilson said. "Please is much better. Now I'll stop."

F. SCOTT FITZGERALD (1896–1940)

F. Scott Fitzgerald's best writing is intensely autobiographical, sometimes perhaps painfully so. Chronicler of "the jazz age" of the twenties and thirties, he reflects sharply and poignantly the high life and the disillusionments of those years. Because he often spent money faster than he earned it, many of Fitzgerald's works (especially two of his novels, The Great Gatsby *and* Tender Is the Night*) examine the effect on people of the possession—or lack—of money. His own financial problems caused him to dash off sometimes inferior stories. Eventually he ended as a screen writer in Hollywood.*

"Babylon Revisited" examines a once affluent, heavy drinking American who returns to Paris in the aftermath of the 1929 stock market crash. Sobered by the realization of the mess he has made of his life, he attempts to piece together a new existence out of the fragments of his past.

Babylon Revisited

"AND WHERE'S Mr. Campbell?" Charlie asked.

"Gone to Switzerland. Mr. Campbell's a pretty sick man, Mr. Wales."

"I'm sorry to hear that. And George Hardt?" Charlie inquired.

"Back in America, gone to work."

"And where is the snow bird?"

"He was in here last week. Anyway, his friend, Mr. Schaeffer, is in Paris."

Two familiar names from the long list of a year and a half ago. Charlie scribbled an address in his notebook and tore out the page.

"If you see Mr. Schaeffer, give him this," he said. "It's my brother-in-law's address. I haven't settled on a hotel yet."

He was not really disappointed to find Paris was so empty. But the stillness in the bar was strange, almost portentous.

It was not an American bar any more—he felt polite in it, and not as if he owned it. It had gone back into France. He had felt the stillness from the moment he got out of the taxi and saw the doorman, usually in a frenzy of activity at this hour, gossiping with a *chasseur** by the servants' entrance.

Passing through the corridor, he heard only a single, bored voice in the once-clamorous women's room. When he turned into the bar he traveled the twenty feet of green carpet with his eyes fixed straight ahead by old habit; and then, with his foot firmly on the rail, he turned and surveyed the room, encountering only a single pair of eyes that fluttered up from a newspaper in the corner. Charlie asked for the head barman, Paul, who in the latter days of the bull market had come to work in his own custom-built car—disembarking, however, with due nicety at the nearest corner. But Paul was at his country house to-day and Alix was giving him his information.

"No, no more. I'm going slow these days."

Alix congratulated him: "Hope you stick to it, Mr. Wales. You were going pretty strong a couple of years ago."

"I'll stick to it all right," Charlie assured him. "I've stuck to it for over a year and a half now."

"How do you find conditions in America?"

"I haven't been to America for months. I'm in business in Prague, representing a couple of concerns there. They don't know about me down there." He smiled faintly. "Remember the night of George Hardt's bachelor dinner here? . . . By the way, what's become of Claude Fessenden?"

Alix lowered his voice confidentially: "He's in Paris, but he doesn't come here any more. Paul doesn't allow it. He ran up a bill of thirty thousand francs, charging all his drinks and his lunches, and usually his dinner, for

* *chasseur.* bellboy

more than a year. And when Paul finally told him he had to pay, he gave him a bad check."

Alix pressed his lips together and shook his head.

"I don't understand it, such a dandy fellow. Now he's all bloated up—" He made a plump apple of his hands.

A thin world, resting on a common weakness, shredded away now like tissue paper. Turning, Charlie saw a group of effeminate young men installing themselves in a corner.

"Nothing affects them," he thought. "Stocks rise and fall, people loaf or work, but they go on forever." The place oppressed him. He called for the dice and shook with Alix for the drink.

"Here for long, Mr. Wales?"

"I'm here for four or five days to see my little girl."

"Oh-h! You have a little girl?"

Outside, the fire-red, gas-blue, ghost-green signs shone smokily through the tranquil rain. It was late afternoon and the streets were in movement; the *bistros** gleamed. At the corner of the Boulevard des Capucines he took a taxi. The Place de la Concorde moved by in pink majesty; they crossed the logical Seine, and Charlie felt the sudden provincial quality of the left bank.

"I spoiled this city for myself," he thought. "I didn't realize it, but the days came along one after another, and then two years were gone, and everything was gone, and I was gone."

He was thirty-five, a handsome man, with the Irish mobility of his face sobered by a deep wrinkle between his eyes. As he rang his brother-in-law's bell in the Rue Palatine, the wrinkle deepened till it pulled down his brows; he felt a cramping sensation in his belly. From behind the maid who opened the door darted a lovely little girl of nine who shrieked "Daddy!" and flew up, struggling like a fish, into his arms. She pulled his head around by one ear and set her cheek against his.

"My old pie," he said.

"Oh, daddy, daddy, daddy, daddy, dads, dads, dads!"

She drew him into the salon, where the family waited, a boy and girl his daughter's age, his sister-in-law and her husband. He greeted Marion with his voice pitched carefully to avoid either feigned enthusiasm or dislike, but her response was more frankly tepid, and she minimized her expression of unshakable distrust by directing her regard toward his child. The two men clasped hands in a friendly way and Lincoln Peters rested his for a moment on Charlie's shoulder.

The room was warm and comfortably American. The three children moved intimately about, playing through the yellow oblongs that led to other rooms; the cheer of six o'clock spoke in the eager smacks of the fire and the sounds of French activity in the kitchen. But Charlie did not relax; his heart sat up rig-

* *bistros.* restaurants

idly in his body and he drew confidence from his daughter, who from time to time came close to him, holding in her arms the doll he had brought.

"Really extremely well," he declared in answer to Lincoln's question. "There's a lot of business there that isn't moving at all, but we're doing even better than ever. In fact, damn well. I'm bringing my sister over from America next month to keep house for me. In fact, my income is bigger than it was when I had money. You see, the Czechs—"

His boasting was for a specific purpose; but after a moment, seeing a faint restiveness in Lincoln's eye, he changed the subject:

"Those are fine children of yours, well brought up, good manners."

"We think Honoria's a great little girl too."

Marion Peters came back into the little salon. She was a tall woman with worried eyes, who had once possessed a fresh American loveliness. Charlie had never been sensitive to it and was always surprised when people spoke of how pretty she had been. From the first there had been an instinctive antipathy between them.

"Well, how do you find Honoria?" she asked.

"Wonderful. I was astonished how much she's grown in ten months. All the children are looking well."

"We haven't had a doctor for a year. How do you like being back in Paris?"

"It seems very funny to see so few Americans around."

"I'm delighted," Marion said vehemently. "Now at least you can go into a store without their assuming you're a millionaire. We've suffered like everybody, but on the whole it's a good deal pleasanter."

"But it was nice while it lasted," Charlie said. "We were a sort of royalty, almost infallible, with a sort of magic around us. In the bar this afternoon"—he stumbled, seeing his mistake—"there wasn't a man I knew."

She looked at him keenly. "I should think you'd have had enough of bars."

"I only stayed a minute. I take one drink every afternoon, and no more."

"Don't you want a cocktail before dinner?" Lincoln asked.

"I take only one drink every afternoon, and I've had that."

"I hope you keep to it," said Marion.

Her dislike was evident in the coldness with which she spoke, but Charlie only smiled; he had larger plans. Her very aggressiveness gave him an advantage, and he knew enough to wait. He wanted them to initiate the discussion of what they knew had brought him to Paris.

Honoria was to spend the following afternoon with him. At dinner he couldn't decide whether she was most like him or her mother. Fortunate if she didn't combine the traits of both that had brought them to disaster. A great wave of protectiveness went over him. He thought he knew what to do for her. He believed in character; he wanted to jump back a whole generation and trust in character again as the eternally valuable element. Everything wore out now. Parents expected genius, or at least brilliance, and both the forcing of children and the fear of forcing them, the fear of warping natural abilities, were poor substitutes for that long, careful watchfulness, that checking and balancing and reckoning of accounts, the end of which was that there should be no slipping below a certain level of duty and integrity.

That was what the elders had been unable to teach plausibly since the break between the generations ten or twelve years ago.

He left soon after dinner, but not to go home. He was curious to see Paris by night with clearer and more judicious eyes. He bought a *strapontin** for the Casino and watched Josephine Baker go through her chocolate arabesques.

After an hour he left and strolled toward Montmartre, up the Rue Pigalle into the Place Blanche. The rain had stopped and there were a few people in evening clothes disembarking from taxis in front of cabarets, and *cocottes*** prowling singly or in pairs, and many Negroes. He passed a lighted door from which issued music, and stopped with the sense of familiarity; it was Bricktop's, where he had parted with so many hours and so much money. A few doors farther on he found another ancient rendezvous and incautiously put his head inside. Immediately an eager orchestra burst into sound, a pair of professional dancers leaped to their feet and a maître d'hôtel swooped toward him, crying, "Crowd just arriving, sir!" But he withdrew quickly.

"You have to be damn drunk," he thought.

Zelli's was closed, the bleak and sinister cheap hotels surrounding it were dark; up in the Rue Blanche there was more light and a local, coloquial French crowd. The Poet's Cave had disappeared, but the two great mouths of the Café of Heaven and the Café of Hell still yawned—even devoured, as he watched, the meager contents of a tourist bus—a German, a Japanese, and an American couple who glanced at him with frightened eyes.

So much for the effort and ingenuity of Montmartre. All the catering to vice and waste was on an utterly childish scale, and he suddenly realized the meaning of the word "dissipate"—to dissipate into thin air; to make nothing out of something. In the little hours of the night every move from place to place was an enormous human jump, an increase of paying for the privilege of slower and slower motion.

He remembered thousand-franc notes given to an orchestra for playing a single number, hundred-franc notes tossed to a doorman for calling a cab.

But it hadn't been given for nothing.

It had been given, even the most wildly squandered sum, as an offering to destiny that he might not remember the things most worth remembering, the things that now he would always remember—his child taken from his control, his wife escaped to a grave in Vermont.

In the glare of a *brasserie**** a woman spoke to him. He bought her some eggs and coffee, and then, eluding her encouraging stare, gave her a twenty-franc note and took a taxi to his hotel.

* *strapontin.* seat
** *cocottes.* tarts
*** *brasserie.* tavern

II

He woke upon a fine fall day—football weather. The depression of yesterday was gone and he liked the people on the streets. At noon he sat opposite Honoria at the Grand Vatel, the only restaurant he could think of not reminiscent of champagne dinners and long luncheons that began at two and ended in a blurred and vague twilight.

"Now, how about vegetables? Oughtn't you to have some vegetables?"

"Well, yes."

"Here's *épinards** and *chou-fleur*** and carrots and *haricots.*" ***

"I'd like *choux-fleurs.*"

"Wouldn't you like to have two vegetables?"

"I usually only have one at lunch."

The waiter was pretending to be inordinately fond of children. *"Qu'elle est mignonne la petite? Elle parle exactment comme une française."* †

"How about dessert? Shall we wait and see?"

The waiter disappeared. Honoria looked at him expectantly.

"What are we going to do?"

"First we're going to that toy store in the Rue St. Honoré and buy you anything you like. And then we're going to the vaudeville at the Empire."

She hesitated. "I like it about the vaudeville, but not the toy store."

"Why not?"

"Well, you brought me this doll." She had it with her. "And I've got lots of things. And we're not rich any more, are we?"

"We never were. But to-day you are to have anything you want."

"All right," she agreed resignedly.

He had always been fond of her, but when there had been her mother and a French nurse he had been inclined to be strict; now he extended himself, reached out for a new tolerance; he must be both parents to her and not shut any of her out of communication.

"I want to get to know you," he said gravely. "First let me introduce myself. My name is Charles J. Wales, of Prague."

"Oh, daddy!" her voice cracked with laughter.

"And who are you, please?" he persisted, and she accepted a rôle immediately: "Honoria Wales, Rue Palatine, Paris."

"Married or single?"

"No, not married. Single."

He indicated the doll. "But I see you have a child, madame."

Unwilling to disinherit it, she took it to her heart and thought quickly: "Yes, I've been married, but I'm not married now. My husband is dead."

* *épinards.* spinach
** *chou-fleur.* cauliflower
*** *haricots.* beans
† *Qu'elle est mignonne la petite? Elle parle exactment comme une française.* Isn't she a sweet little girl? She speaks exactly like a Frenchwoman.

He went on quickly, "And the child's name?"

"Simone. That's after my best friend at school."

"I'm very pleased that you're doing so well at school."

"I'm third this month," she boasted. "Elsie"—that was her cousin—"is only about eighteenth, and Richard is about at the bottom."

"You like Richard and Elsie, don't you?"

"Oh, yes. I like Richard quite well and I like her all right."

Cautiously and casually he asked: "And Aunt Marion and Uncle Lincoln—which do you like best?"

"Oh, Uncle Lincoln, I guess."

He was increasingly aware of her presence. As they came in, a murmur of "What an adorable child" followed them, and now the people at the next table bent all their silences upon her, staring as if she were something no more conscious than a flower.

"Why don't I live with you?" she asked suddenly. "Because mamma's dead?"

"You must stay here and learn more French. It would have been hard for daddy to take care of you so well."

"I don't really need much taking care of any more. I do everything for myself."

Going out of the restaurant, a man and a woman unexpectedly hailed him!

"Well, the old Wales!"

"Hello there, Lorraine . . . Dunc."

Sudden ghosts out of the past: Duncan Schaeffer, a friend from college. Lorraine Quarrles, a lovely, pale blond of thirty; one of a crowd who had helped them make months into days in the lavish times of two years ago.

"My husband couldn't come this year," she said, in answer to his question. "We're poor as hell. So he gave me two hundred a month and told me I could do my worst on that . . . This your little girl?"

"What about sitting down?" Duncan asked.

"Can't do it." He was glad for an excuse. As always, he felt Lorraine's passionate, provocative attraction, but his own rhythm was different now.

"Well, how about dinner?" she asked.

"I'm not free. Give me your address and let me call you."

"Charlie, I believe you're sober," she said judicially. "I honestly believe he's sober, Dunc. Pinch him and see if he's sober."

Charlie indicated Honoria with his head. They both laughed.

"What's your address?" said Duncan skeptically.

He hesitated, unwilling to give the name of his hotel.

"I'm not settled yet. I'd better call you. We're going to see the vaudeville at the Empire."

"There! That's what I want to do," Lorraine said. "I want to see some clowns and acrobats and jugglers. That's just what we'll do, Dunc."

"We've got to do an errand first," said Charlie. "Perhaps we'll see you there."

"All right, you snob. . . . Good-by, beautiful little girl."

"Good-by." Honoria bobbed politely.

Somehow, an unpleasant encounter, Charlie thought. They liked him because he was functioning, because he was serious; they wanted to see him, because he was stronger than they were now, because they wanted to draw a certain sustenance from his strength.

At the Empire, Honoria proudly refused to sit upon her father's folded coat. She was already an individual with a code of her own, and Charlie was more and more absorbed by the desire of putting a little of himself into her before she crystallized utterly. It was hopeless to try to know her in so short a time.

Between the acts they came upon Duncan and Lorraine in the lobby where the band was playing.

"Have a drink?"

"All right, but not up at the bar. We'll take a table."

"The perfect father."

Listening abstractedly to Lorraine, Charlie watched Honoria's eyes leave them all, and he followed them wistfully about the room, wondering what they saw. He met them and she smiled.

"I liked that lemonade," she said.

What had she said? What had he expected? Going home in a taxi afterward, he pulled her over until her head rested against his chest.

"Darling, do you ever think about your mother?"

"Yes, sometimes," she answered vaguely.

"I don't want you to forget her. Have you got a picture of her?"

"Yes, I think so. Anyhow, Aunt Marion has. Why don't you want me to forget her?"

"She loved you very much."

"I loved her too."

They were silent for a moment.

"Daddy, I want to come and live with you," she said suddenly.

His heart leaped; he had wanted it to come like this.

"Aren't you perfectly happy?"

"Yes, but I love you better than anybody. And you love me better than anybody, don't you, now that mummy's dead?"

"Of course I do. But you won't always like me best, honey. You'll grow up and meet somebody your own age and go marry him and forget you ever had a daddy."

"Yes, that's true," she agreed tranquilly.

He didn't go in. He was coming back at nine o'clock and he wanted to keep himself fresh and new for the thing he must say then.

"When you're safe inside, just show yourself in that window."

"All right. Good-by, dads, dads, dads, dads."

He waited in the dark street until she appeared, all warm and glowing, in the window above and kissed her fingers out into the night.

III

They were waiting. Marion sat behind empty coffee cups in a dignified black dinner dress that just faintly suggested mourning. Lincoln was walking up and down with the animation of one who had already been talking. They were as anxious as he was to get into the question. He opened it almost immediately:

"I suppose you know what I want to see you about—why I really came to Paris."

Marion fiddled with the glass grapes on her necklace and frowned.

"I'm awfully anxious to have a home," he continued. "And I'm awfully anxious to have Honoria in it. I appreciate your taking in Honoria for her mother's sake, but things have changed now"—he hesitated and then continued strongly—"changed radically with me, and I want to ask you to reconsider the matter. It would be silly for me to deny that about two years ago I was acting badly—"

Marion looked up at him with hard eyes.

"—but all that's over. As I told you, I haven't had more than a drink a day for over a year, and I take that drink deliberately, so that the idea of alcohol won't get too big in my imagination. You see the idea?"

"No," said Marion succinctly.

"It's a sort of stunt I set myself. It keeps the matter in proportion."

"I get you," said Lincoln. "You don't want to admit it's got any attraction for you."

"Something like that. Sometimes I forget and don't take it. But I try to take it. Anyhow, I couldn't afford to drink in my position. The people I represent are more than satisfied with what I've done, and I'm bringing my sister over from Burlington to keep house for me, and I want awfully to have Honoria too. You know that even when her mother and I weren't getting along well I never let anything that happened touch Honoria. I know she's fond of me and I know I'm able to take care of her and—well, there you are. How do you feel about it?"

He knew that now he would have to take a beating. It would last an hour or two hours, and it would be difficult, but if he modulated his inevitable resentment to the chastened attitude of the reformed sinner, he might win his point in the end. "Keep your temper," he told himself. "You don't want to be justified. You want Honoria."

Lincoln spoke first: "We've been talking it over ever since we got your letter last month. We're happy to have Honoria here. She's a dear little thing, and we're glad to be able to help her, but of course that isn't the question—"

Marion interrupted suddenly. "How long are you going to stay sober, Charlie?" she asked.

"Permanently, I hope."

"How can anybody count on that?"

"You know I never did drink heavily until I gave up business and came over here with nothing to do. Then Helen and I began to run around with—"

"Please leave Helen out of it. I can't bear to hear you talk about her like that."

He stared at her grimly; he had never been certain how fond of each other the sisters were in life.

"My drinking only lasted about a year and a half—from the time we came over until I—collapsed."

"It was time enough."

"It was time enough," he agreed.

"My duty is entirely to Helen," she said. "I try to think what she would have wanted me to do. Frankly, from the night you did that terrible thing you haven't really existed for me. I can't help that. She was my sister."

"Yes."

"When she was dying she asked me to look out for Honoria. If you hadn't been in a sanitarium then, it might have helped matters."

He had no answer.

"I'll never in my life be able to forget the morning when Helen knocked at my door, soaked to the skin and shivering, and said you'd locked her out."

Charlie gripped the sides of the chair. This was more difficult than he expected; he wanted to launch out into a long expostulation and explanation, but he only said: "The night I locked her out—" and she interrupted, "I don't feel up to going over that again."

After a moment's silence Lincoln said: "We're getting off the subject. You want Marion to set aside her legal guardianship and give you Honoria. I think the main point for her is whether she has confidence in you or not."

"I don't blame Marion," Charlie said slowly, "but I think she can have entire confidence in me. I had a good record up to three years ago. Of course, it's within human possibilities I might go wrong any time. But if we wait much longer I'll lose Honoria's childhood and my chance for a home. I'll simply lose her, don't you see?"

"Yes, I see," said Lincoln.

"Why didn't you think of all this before?" Marion asked.

"I suppose I did, from time to time, but Helen and I were getting along badly. When I consented to the guardianship, I was flat on my back in a sanitarium and the market had cleaned me out of every sou. I knew I'd acted badly, and I thought if it would bring any peace to Helen, I'd agree to anything. But now it's different. I'm well, I'm functioning, I'm behaving damn well, so far as—"

"Please don't swear at me," Marion said.

He looked at her, startled. With each remark the force of her dislike became more and more apparent. She had built up all her fear of life into one wall and faced it toward him. This trivial reproof was possibly the result of some trouble with the cook several hours before. Charlie became increasingly alarmed at leaving Honoria in this atmosphere of hostility against himself; sooner or later it would come out, in a word here, a shake of the head there, and some of that distrust would be irrevocably implanted in Honoria. But he pulled his temper down out of his face and shut it up inside him; he had won a point, for Lincoln realized the absurdity of Marion's remark and asked her lightly since when she had objected to the word "damn."

"Another thing," Charlie said: "I'm able to give her certain advantages now. I'm going to take a French governess to Prague with me. I've got a lease on a new apartment—"

He stopped, realizing that he was blundering. They couldn't be expected to accept with equanimity the fact that his income was again twice as large as their own.

"I suppose you can give her more luxuries than we can," said Marion. "When you were throwing away money we were living along watching every ten francs. . . . I suppose you'll start doing it again."

"Oh, no," he said. "I've learned. I worked hard for ten years, you know—until I got lucky in the market, like so many people. Terribly lucky. It didn't seem any use working any more, so I quit. It won't happen again."

There was a long silence. All of them felt their nerves straining, and for the first time in a year Charlie wanted a drink. He was sure now that Lincoln Peters wanted him to have his child.

Marion shuddered suddenly; part of her saw that Charlie's feet were planted on the earth now, and her own maternal feeling recognized the naturalness of his desire; but she had lived for a long time with a prejudice—a prejudice founded on a curious disbelief in her sister's happiness, and which, in the shock of one terrible night, had turned to hatred for him. It had all happened at a point in her life where the discouragement of ill-health and adverse circumstances made it necessary for her to believe in tangible villainy and a tangible villain.

"I can't help what I think!" she cried out suddenly. "How much you were responsible for Helen's death, I don't know. It's something you'll have to square with your own conscience."

An electric current of agony surged through him; for a moment he was almost on his feet, an unuttered sound echoing in his throat. He hung on to himself for a moment, another moment.

"Hold on there," said Lincoln uncomfortably. "I never thought you were responsible for that."

"Helen died of heart trouble," Charlie said dully.

"Yes, heart trouble." Marion spoke as if the phrase had another meaning for her.

Then, in the flatness that followed her outburst, she saw him plainly and she knew he had somehow arrived at control over the situation. Glancing at her husband, she found no help from him, and as abruptly as if it were a matter of no importance, she threw up the sponge.

"Do what you like!" she cried, springing up from her chair. "She's your child. I'm not the person to stand in your way. I think if it were my child I'd rather see her—" She managed to check herself. "You two decide it. I can't stand this. I'm sick. I'm going to bed."

She hurried from the room; after a moment Lincoln said:

"This has been a hard day for her. You know how strongly she feels—" His voice was almost apologetic: "When a woman gets an idea in her head."

"Of course."

"It's going to be all right. I think she sees now that you—can provide for the child, and so we can't very well stand in your way or Honoria's way."

"Thank you, Lincoln."

"I'd better go along and see how she is."

"I'm going."

He was still trembling when he reached the street, but a walk down the Rue Bonaparte to the *quais** set him up, and as he crossed the Seine, dotted with many cold moons, he felt exultant. But back in his room he couldn't sleep. The image of Helen haunted him. Helen whom he had loved so until they had senselessly begun to abuse each other's love and tear it into shreds. On that terrible February night that Marion remembered so vividly, a slow quarrel that had gone on for hours. There was a scene at the Florida, and then he attempted to take her home, and then Helen kissed Ted Wilder at a table, and what she had hysterically said. Charlie's departure and, on his arrival home, his turning the key in the lock in wild anger. How could he know she would arrive an hour later alone, that there would be a snowstorm in which she wandered about in slippers for an hour, too confused to find a taxi? Then the aftermath, her escaping pneumonia by a miracle, and all the attendant horror. They were "reconciled," but that was the beginning of the end, and Marion, who had seen with her own eyes and who imagined it to be one of many scenes from her sister's martyrdom, never forgot.

Going over it again brought Helen nearer, and in the white, soft light that steals upon half sleep near morning he found himself talking to her again. She said that he was perfectly right about Honoria and that she wanted Honoria to be with him. She said she was glad he was being good and doing better. She said a lot of other things—very friendly things—but she was in a swing in a white dress, and swinging faster and faster all the time, so that at the end he could not hear clearly all that she said.

* *quais.* docks

IV

He woke up feeling happy. The door of the world was open again. He made plans, vistas, futures for Honoria and himself, but suddenly he grew sad, remembering all the plans he and Helen had made. She had not planned to die. The present was the thing—work to do and someone to love. But not to love too much, for Charlie had read in D. H. Lawrence about the injury that a father can do to a daughter or a mother to a son by attaching them too closely. Afterward, out in the world, the child would seek in the marriage partner the same blind, unselfish tenderness and, failing in all human probability to find it, develop a grudge against love and life.

It was another bright, crisp day. He called Lincoln Peters at the bank where he worked and asked if he could count on taking Honoria when he left for Prague. Lincoln agreed that there was no reason for delay. One thing—the legal guardianship. Marion wanted to retain that a while longer. She was upset by the whole matter, and it would oil things if she felt that the situation was still in her control for another year. Charlie agreed, wanting only the tangible, visible child.

Then the question of a governess. Charlie sat in a gloomy agency and talked to a buxom Breton peasant whom he knew he couldn't endure. There were others whom he could see to-morrow.

He lunched with Lincoln Peters at the Griffon, trying to keep down his exultation.

"There's nothing quite like your own child," Lincoln said. "But you understand how Marion feels too."

"She's forgotten how hard I worked for seven years there," Charlie said. "She just remembers one night."

"There's another thing." Lincoln hesitated. "While you and Helen were tearing around Europe throwing money away, we were just getting along. I didn't touch any of the prosperity because I never got ahead enough to carry anything but my insurance. I think Marion felt there was some kind of injustice in it—you not even working and getting richer and richer."

"It went just as quick as it came," said Charlie.

"A lot did. And a lot of it stayed in the hands of *chasseurs* and saxophone players and maîtres d'hôtel—well, the big party's over now. I just said that to explain Marion's feeling about those crazy years. If you drop in about six o'clock to-night before Marion's too tired, we'll settle the details on the spot."

Back at his hotel, Charlie took from his pocket a *pneumatique** that Lincoln had given him at luncheon. It had been redirected by Paul from the hotel bar.

DEAR CHARLIE: You were so strange when we saw you the other day that I wondered if I did something to offend you. If so, I'm not conscious of it. In fact, I have thought

* *pneumatique.* express letter

about you too much for the last year, and it's always been in the back of my mind that I might see you if I came over here. We did have such good times that crazy spring, like the night you and I stole the butcher's tricycle, and the time we tried to call on the president and you had the old derby and the wire cane. Everybody seems so old lately, but I don't feel old a bit. Couldn't we get together sometime to-day for old time's sake? I've got a vile hang-over for the moment, but will be feeling better this afternoon and will look for you about five at the bar.

Always devotedly,
LORRAINE.

His first feeling was one of awe that he had actually, in his mature years, stolen a tricycle and pedaled Lorraine all over the Étoile between the small hours and dawn. In retrospect it was a nightmare. Locking out Helen didn't fit in with any other act of his life, but the tricycle incident did—it was one of many. How many weeks or months of dissipation to arrive at that condition of utter irresponsibility?

He tried to picture how Lorraine had appeared to him then—very attractive; so much so that Helen had been jealous. Yesterday, in the restaurant, she had seemed trite, blurred, worn away. He emphatically did not want to see her, and he was glad no one knew at what hotel he was staying. It was a relief to think of Honoria, to think of Sundays spent with her and of saying good morning to her and of knowing she was there in his house at night, breathing quietly in the darkness.

At five he took a taxi and bought presents for all the Peterses—a piquant cloth doll, a box of Roman soldiers, flowers for Marion, big linen handkerchiefs for Lincoln.

He saw, when he arrived in the apartment, that Marion had accepted the inevitable. She greeted him now as though he were a recalcitrant member of the family, rather than a menacing outsider. Honoria had been told she was going, and Charlie was glad to see that her tact was sufficient to conceal her excessive happiness. Only on his lap did she whisper her delight and the question "When?" before she slipped away.

He and Marion were alone for a minute in the room, and on an impulse he spoke out boldly:

"Family quarrels are bitter things. They don't go according to my rules. They're not like aches or wounds; they're more like splits in the skin that won't heal because there's not enough material. I wish you and I could be on better terms."

"Some things are hard to forget," she answered. "It's a question of confidence. If you behave yourself in the future I won't have any criticism." There was no answer to this, and presently she asked, "When do you propose to take her?"

"As soon as I can get a governess. I hoped the day after to-morrow."

"That's impossible. I've got to get her things in shape. Not before Saturday."

He yielded. Coming back into the room, Lincoln offered him a drink.

"I'll take my daily whisky," he said.

It was warm here, it was a home, people together by a fire. The children felt very safe and important; the mother and father were serious, watchful. They had things to do for the children more important than his visit here. A spoonful of medicine was, after all, more important than the strained relations between Marion and himself. They were not dull people, but they were very much in the grip of life and circumstances, and their gestures as they turned in a cramped space lacked largeness and grace. He wondered if he couldn't do something to get Lincoln out of that rut at the bank.

There was a long peal at the doorbell; the maid crossed the room and went down the corridor. The door opened upon another long ring, and then voices, and the three in the salon looked up expectantly; Richard moved to bring the corridor within his range of vision, and Marion rose. Then the maid came along the corridor, closely followed by the voices, which developed under the light into Duncan Schaeffer and Lorraine Quarrles.

They were gay, they were hilarious, they were roaring with laughter. For a moment Charlie was astounded; then he realized they had got the address he had left at the bar.

"Ah-h-h!" Duncan wagged his finger roguishly at Charlie. "Ah-h-h!"

They both slid down into another cascade of laughter. Anxious and at a loss, Charlie shook hands with them quickly and presented them to Lincoln and Marion. Marion nodded, scarcely speaking. She had drawn back a step toward the fire; her little girl stood beside her, and Marion put an arm about her shoulder.

With growing annoyance at the intrusion, Charlie waited for them to explain themselves. After some concentration Duncan said:

"We came to take you to dinner. Lorraine and I insist that all this shi-shi, cagy business got to stop."

Charlie came closer to them, as if to force them backward down the corridor.

"Sorry, but I can't. Tell me where you'll be and we'll call you in half an hour."

This made no impression. Lorraine sat down suddenly on the side of a chair, and focusing her eyes on Richard, cried, "Oh, what a nice little boy! Come here, little boy." Richard glanced at his mother, but did not move. With a perceptible shrug of her shoulders, Lorraine turned back to Charlie:

"Come on out to dinner. Be yourself, Charlie. Come on."

"How about a little drink?" said Duncan to the room at large.

Lincoln Peters had been somewhat uneasily occupying himself by swinging Honoria from side to side with her feet off the ground.

"I'm sorry, but there isn't a thing in the house," he said. "We just this minute emptied the only bottle."

"All the more reason for coming to dinner," Lorraine assured Charlie.

"I can't," said Charlie almost sharply. "You two go have dinner and I'll phone you."

"Oh, you will, will you?" Her voice became suddenly unpleasant. "All right, we'll go along. But I remember, when you used to hammer on my door, I used to be enough of a good sport to give you a drink. Come on, Dunc."

Still in slow motion, with blurred, angry faces, with uncertain feet, they retired along the corridor.

"Good night," Charlie said.

"Good night!" responded Lorraine emphatically.

When he went back into the salon Marion had not moved, only now her son was standing in the circle of her other arm. Lincoln was still swinging Honoria back and forth like a pendulum from side to side.

"What an outrage!" Charlie broke out. "What an absolute outrage!"

Neither of them answered. Charlie dropped down into an armchair, picked up his drink, set it down again and said:

"People I haven't seen for two years having the colossal nerve—"

He broke off. Marion had made the sound "Oh!" in one swift, furious breath, turned her body from him with a jerk and left the room.

Lincoln set down Honoria carefully.

"You children go in and start your soup," he said, and when they obeyed, he said to Charlie:

"Marion's not well and she can't stand shocks. That kind of people make her really physically sick."

"I didn't tell them to come here. They wormed this address out of Paul at the bar. They deliberately—"

"Well, it's too bad. It doesn't help matters. Excuse me a minute."

Left alone, Charlie sat tense in his chair. In the next room he could hear the children eating, talking in monosyllables, already oblivious of the scene among their elders. He heard a murmur of conversation from a farther room and then the ticking bell of a phone picked up, and in a panic he moved to the other side of the room and out of earshot.

In a minute Lincoln came back. "Look here, Charlie. I think we'd better call off dinner for to-night. Marion's in bad shape."

"Is she angry with me?"

"Sort of," he said, almost roughly. "She's not strong and—"

"You mean she's changed her mind about Honoria?"

"She's pretty bitter right now. I don't know. You phone me at the bank tomorrow."

"I wish you'd explain to her I never dreamed these people would come here. I'm just as sore as you are."

"I couldn't explain anything to her now."

Charlie got up. He took his coat and hat and started down the corridor. Then he opened the door of the dining room and said in a strange voice, "Good night, children."

Honoria rose and ran around the table to hug him.

"Good night, sweetheart," he said vaguely, and then trying to make his voice more tender, trying to conciliate something, "Good night, dear children."

V

Charlie went directly to the bar with the furious idea of finding Lorraine and Duncan, but they were not there, and he realized that in any case there was nothing he could do. He had not touched his drink at the Petcrses', and now he ordered a whisky-and-soda. Paul came over to say hello.

"It's a great change," he said sadly. "We do about half the business we did. So many fellows I hear about back in the States lost everything, maybe not in the first crash, but then in the second, and now when everything keeps going down. Your friend George Hardt lost every cent, I hear. Are you back in the States?"

"No, I'm in business in Prague."

"I heard that you lost a lot in the crash."

"I did," and he added grimly, "but I lost everything I wanted in the boom."

"Selling short."

"Something like that."

Again the memory of those days swept over him like a nightmare—the people they had met traveling; then people who couldn't add a row of figures or speak a coherent sentence. The little man Helen had consented to dance with at the ship's party, who had insulted her ten feet from the table; the human mosaic of pearls who sat behind them at the Russian ballet and, when the curtain rose on a scene, remarked to her companion: "Luffly; just luffly. Zomebody ought to baint a bicture of it." Men who locked their wives out in the snow, because the snow of twenty-nine wasn't real snow. If you didn't want it to be snow, you just paid some money.

He went to the phone and called the Peters apartment; Lincoln himself answered.

"I called up because, as you can imagine, this thing is on my mind. Has Marion said anything definite?"

"Marion's sick," Lincoln answered shortly. "I know this thing isn't altogether your fault, but I can't have her go to pieces about this. I'm afraid we'll have to let it slide for six months; I can't take the chance of working her up to this state again."

"I see."

"I'm sorry, Charlie."

He went back to his table. His whisky glass was empty, but he shook his head when Alix looked at it questioningly. There wasn't much he could do now except send Honoria some things; he would send her a lot of things tomorrow. He thought rather angrily that that was just money—he had given so many people money.

"No, no more," he said to another waiter. "What do I owe you?"

He would come back some day; they couldn't make him pay forever. But he wanted his child, and nothing was much good now, beside that fact. He wasn't young any more, with a lot of nice thoughts and dreams to have by himself. He was absolutely sure Helen wouldn't have wanted him to be so alone.

5

Later Life

New Joys, New Sorrows

Man is mortal. Yet he spends much of his life attempting to evade that basic fact of his existence. Rare is the man who faces his declining years with dignity and self-respect—accepting his ultimate fate, yet working to preserve vitality and energy in the face of physical and psychological deterioration. But for the man who continues to grow, to seek further meanings in the journey between birth and death, the rewards may go beyond all expectation.

JONATHAN KARIARA (b. 1935)

In response to our invitation to discuss his life and work directly with his readers, Jonathan Kariara has written as follows:

"I was born in Kenya in 1935 and graduated with an Honours Degree in English at Makerere University College in 1960. In the same year I joined the East African Literature Bureau as an assistant book production officer. In 1966 I left the Bureau to work as senior editor with the Eastern Africa Branch of the Oxford University Press. I am the Editor of ZUKA, the Branch's journal of creative writing.

"I strongly believe that it is the duty of the black writer to communicate directly with his reader, by going straight to the subject and by drawing as little attention to himself as possible. I dislike any simplification, of people and events: I can't abide 'innocence.'

" 'Her Warrior' is very much based on my grandmother (strictly she wasn't my *grandmother in the European sense, as she was not my father's mother but his step-brother's), a fiery, independent woman who, in spite of all the talk about the submissiveness of the African woman, was having no nonsense from anybody. She was feared and respected in the village, too! But of course I have used episodes from real life or imagined to create the mood I wanted—for instance the real woman lived quite near us."*

Her Warrior

SHE WAS a tall woman with high cheekbones, now more emphasized than ever by the loss of her molar teeth. Her lips were finer than most of her tribe's and wore a shut, rather sour expression. Her eyes seemed to be always fixed on the distance, as though she didn't "see" or mind the immediate, but dwelt in the eternal. She was not like other children's grandmothers we knew, who would spoil their grandchildren and had their huts "just outside the hedge" of their sons' homesteads. Grandmother lived three hills away, which was inexplicable.

All the other grandmothers had some relationship with their aging husbands. Some had strange dreams of how their dead ones had visited them in their dreams, and would repeat their last night's experience in great detail, time and time again, thus relieving the monotony of their existence. There was Grandma Wacu who was always rescuing her husband from toppling into the fire as he dozed and would scold him with a mighty wrath in spite of her neighbours' constant protestations that her husband was stone deaf. There were the "Lizards," so called for their daylong basking in the sun. Their life now consisted of following the course of the sun; outside their respective huts in the morning, under the Mukoigo tree at noon, at the back of their huts at sunset, taking in the last rays of the sun. There was Gacucu (Little Grandmother) who after forty years of married life was still having fights with her husband, and indiscriminately would tell her troubles in great detail to us children, to our great joy but so much to the embarrassment of her married daughters.

Grandmother was different. She never mentioned her husband. If ever she heard any of us refer to him she would instantly snort and push away any small object near her with an impatient sweep of her long arm. If any of us dared ask her why she never mentioned him she would instantly lose her temper and like a broody hen ruffling her feathers would rise to gather her few possessions, for a return journey to her hut three hills away. She had been insulted.

On this occasion, though, she had been asked to come, to see him. He was dying. "Tell her she must come," my father had told the man he sent to her. When she arrived she was greatly changed. She who before had walked with such a firm step for her age, who had such a haughty face, was now in a state of nervous excitement. My mother hurried to meet her at the gate as she arrived. "You must see . . ." "See what?" snapped Grandmother, pushing her aside and confronting my father. "And so I must come, Karanja. So I'm wanted now?" she almost jeered. He, fearing she might say something which would sorrow both for the rest of their lives, left the house immediately and left Mother to face the old woman. "Who wants me here?" she demanded, stamping here and there with a stick like a blind man "looking" for his way. "Who wants me here?" she repeated. We had always enjoyed her tantrums before, we knew they always ended in her either shortening her visit to us, or in a wonderful mood when simply and vividly she would tell us strange stories of her adventures as a girl, before she married. But now it was different, although she was raving, her mind was not on what she was saying, rather she was like a receiver of bad news who puts off the announcement with gibberish. She kept on looking furtively in the direction of his hut, and Mother, guessing what was worrying her, had to break the news she feared. "He is not there. We persuaded him to go to the mission hospital, Mother," she said. For a few seconds the other woman was like somebody choking. She gasped and swayed and would have fallen unconscious had Mother not done what was very unexpected of her. She who always feared the older woman rushed to where she was standing and gripped her by the shoulders, turning Grandmother to face her. Steadily she gazed into Grandmother's face, as though searching for a clue that would thaw the cold resentment the old woman had built up towards her husband. And her eyes also seemed to accuse the older woman, as if saying, "You too were responsible, even to sending him to the mission hospital." The other woman might have understood her for she did not rave now but was leaning on Mother, helplessly. Mother took her into the house.

This is the story as we came to learn later. They married "outside the tribe". That means, she saw her man and decided in her heart to marry him. He saw her heart's decision, and quietly but finally accepted it. Thus they disregarded all the tribal forms of courting and marriage and let it be known they were going to marry. She simply told her parents she was marrying him, so wounding their pride in the implication that they did not count, tribal customs did not count. A girl must not decide for herself finally whom she is going to marry. But she was marrying Wanyoike, the great warrior, so their pride was partly mollified. He on the other hand could have chosen any bride he wanted to marry. He was a war leader, a great but short-lived war leader.

They were not married for long when the Masai declared war on the Kikuyu. They had cunningly chosen their moment, for the Kikuyus had just been through a period of famine and were rather weakened. Anger that the Masai should so cunningly involve them, when it was usual for them to be the cunning party, gave them greater courage than they normally possessed when fighting the dreaded Maitha.

The war was fought and the Kikuyu were being driven from hill to hill. Wanyoike, one of the Kikuyu leaders, was blind with anger. For days he had fought, never uttering a word, but as the conviction grew that they would lose the battle his anger grew into such a frenzied hatred of the Masai that he would do anything to see them retreat. Next day he did the unexpected, the unprecedented. He gripped the long arm of a Kikuyu warrior who had fallen dead beside him and chopped it off at the shoulder blade. His living hand gripped the dead one and, waving it aloft, he charged into a group of Masai warriors, striking right and left with the dead man's arm. At first they did not understand what was happening, until one after the other they felt the clammy touch of the dead arm. Then they saw. And fear spread among them, a primeval fear of warm blood coming in contact with the disintegrating dead. One after the other they let out a cry, the inhuman cry of a trapped wild animal. It spread like fire with a wind behind it; it echoed in every warrior, Kikuyu or Masai, so that the Kikuyu paused, paralysed with fear, and the Masai, afraid of "evil-let-loose", took to flight. Seeing them flee the Kikuyu fell to, and made history that day for grandmothers to repeat to their grandchildren of the day the Masai were wholly defeated. But it was curious that not one of them mentioned Wanyoike who caused the victory. To them as to the defeated Masai it was greatly shocking, therefore taboo, that the living blood in a man should so dare to come into such close contact with the dead.

Wanyoike came back from a war a lonely man. Once the victory was won they were all afraid of him. Deadly afraid. Many of them said later that they all wanted to be religiously cleansed after that battle, although they should have been singing victorious. They hurried on to their respective huts, who should have come back one body, united in and drunk with victory. Wanyoike crept back to his young wife, afraid of himself. So she took to protecting him, fiercely. "The battle she fought!" the old women in the village would say. "You did not dare ask her how the child she was carrying kicked. It was Wanyoike's so what interest could you have in it? We never knew the little things she liked during her time of waiting. She was proud and foolish and had a way of making you look just like a shrivelled leaf floating on the wind, with a wave of her hand. You did not dare show up at her house. 'What do you want?' she would demand, sweeping out like a mad thing, even though you might have been carrying anointing oil to her. When the child arrived she had 'no woman with her'." Then they would add with a shudder: "Some people think he helped her with the birth of the child."

When the child was a few days old Wanyoike killed a fat ram and invited his relations to come and meet the "new guest" arrived. There was no beer at the feast, for his wife would not agree to the feasting and said she would rather go through what she had recently been through than debase herself by asking any of those women to help her with beer making. So the feast Wanyoike provided never came to life, for not even birds can sing on dry throats. The party was rather flagging when she came out. "You should have seen her fury, that their relations should come to bless the child! And she would not eat the meat, would not touch her special portion, but went about like a sheep suffering from lock-jaw. We had all sympathized with her in the past but now we were not sorry to see that her husband was very angry with her, and we knew what his anger meant. It was then that their fights started. She would bow to no man, but would lift her long strong arms and with fury would strike. He would get hold of her and shake her until there was no wind in her. And they are the ones who had walked together in the cool of the evening, as no other woman dare with her husband. Their fights were still and terrible, like quicksands, each keen to destroy the other. Then one day he decided they could not live together and soon after built her a hut where she now lives. He never called her back but something went out of him with her departure. He quickly grew old and started cooking for himself, ay, one of our warriors ended cooking for himself!"

Mother must have succeeded in persuading Grandmother to see her dying husband. "What are we waiting for, then?" we heard her demand of Mother impatiently. Soon they were outside, ready to go to the hospital. But she was not destined to see her husband any more. As they came out at the door my father came in at the gate. Something in his face must have broken the news to the women. Grandmother looked steadily in his face and something, as it were, snapped in the very core of her being. She did not break down in weeping as many women would have done. She simply turned to pick the little bag she always carried which had fallen when she saw my father. "It is well," she said, "that I did not see him in those ridiculous things they give them to wear at the hospital. I would never have forgiven him if I had seen him in those—

those . . ." She could not continue but walked to the gate. And as she fumbled to open it she was no longer a proud old lady. She was a tottering old woman who would from now on sit outside her hut, looking at the horizon. "She is watching her girlhood dance in the horizon," her neighbours would say if they saw her sitting thus. But most of the time she saw nothing, nothing.

NICK C. VACA (B. 1943)

In reply to our invitation to discuss his life and work with his readers, Nick C. Vaca has reponded: "I was born in Deming, New Mexico on November 19, 1943. Within three months of my birth my family moved to California where I have spent the remainder of my years. Graduation from high school in Stockton, California was followed by attendance at the University of California at Berkeley where I received my M.A. in sociology. I am presently working on my thesis in completion for the doctorate in sociology. I am also a Fellow at College V at the University of California at Santa Cruz.

"My intent in 'The Visit' was to fuse an experience born within the Chicano cultural matrix with two universal leitmotifs. First, the theme of intent and actuality. This theme was expressed by Ralph's desire to help his father, but only in the most dramatic way possible, while it was in the most prosaic manner that aid was needed and should have been offered. In spite of the generous mental offers that Ralph makes about sacrificing his arm for his father's life, he leaves in the end with his head still in the dreamy world of chivalrous acts while his father is left to suffer the pains of his illness.

"Second, I wished to focus on the fraility that old age visits on all. In particular, however, I wished to show the frailness of the male, who, at times, by virtue of living out the role of man set by society, is often destined to be deprived of the family—that social cushion that so often softens the decline into old age of the female. It was with the use of the Spanish sentence with its different symbolic system, by which the story became the unique product of the Chicano experience in the United States. It was with these symbolic codes that I hope to touch all those who have shared the same cultural background and have had a similar experiential history."

The Visit

THE GRAY SKIES of winter had covered the San Joaquin Valley for three months. A hazy sunlight had managed to filter through the dark surface of the clouds only twice in the three months, forcing the rest of the days to march on in a dreary procession that made one look much like any other. It was the time of year when darkness came early in the day, the clouds and fog obliging dull lights to be ignited in the streets and houses, and children dressed in thick woolens to be called in early from play.

Today was December 14. On the floor of the San Joaquin Valley the evening fog was beginning its nightly ritual, slowly seeping from the exhausted farming fields on to the roads, gradually moistening the shadows of night. Jogging along a desolate dirt road in the outskirts of Tracy two head lights cut a dull, white path. To anyone not acquainted with the farming area in this part of Tracy the road would have proven difficult to travel, but Ralph Sanchez knew the area well, and the road very well. He had been born, played, worked and only left this area three years ago. Except for his brother Miguel, who still lived in Tracy, Ralph probably knew the area better than anyone else.

Half humming, half singing a Mexican corrido to himself, Ralph squinted to see through the fog trying to find and mentally place old familiar markers that would tell him exactly where he was, and what to expect. To the left he spotted the old eucalyptus tree that had served as the target for his first air rifle; further ahead on the left was the gutted, rusting car in which he and Miguel had played when they were young. In those days the upholstery was worn and cotton bulged out everywhere; the doors were on the verge of falling off; the tires were flat and the body was dented on all sides, but it nevertheless resembled very much the car it once must have been. Now all that remained was the frame and scaling rust. Beyond the car Ralph crossed a small, wooden bridge that spanned one of the irrigation canals that provided the water for the farms in this part of Tracy. As he drove over the murky waters of the canal, he knew that he was close to his destination. Passing a rotting redwood fence, the headlights stopped abruptly, illuminating a trailer in a circular clearing. It was Don Pedro's, who was Ralph's father. In spite of the heavy fog, the words "Hunts," "Heinz 76," and "Del Monte," could clearly be made out on the side of the trailer. These were the names of well known canneries whose boxes were used to pack fruits, make tables, chairs, and even trailer houses. The roof on the trailer was a rusted sheet of corrugated steel. The whole structure stood on four large, wooden spoke wheels which Don Pedro declared to anyone who had not known him in his earlier years, that at one time they had actually served to move the trailer from place to place. Now the wheels had sunk deep into the earth, the spokes partially hidden by the wild grass and weeds that immobility had allowed to grow. Two years ago both back wheels gave way to the erosion of the years and crumbled, making the trailer sit like some animal on its haunches. The door to the trailer was a house door that had replaced the original door made from the same "Hunts," "Heinz 76," and "Del Monte" boxes. Somehow, so Don Pedro tells it, the original door was lost near El Paso in the winter of '37 and some concerned and kind neighbor in the labor camp where Don Pedro and his family were staying donated a spare house door for the trailer. Its leather hinges were now nearly rotted away and it looked as if a swift stroke could pull the door off what now seemed its natural place.

This was the second visit within the last two months for Ralph. It marked a display of the love that he had for his father, because Ralph did *indeed* love his father. Such was his love that it knew no boundaries, no limits. He would have sacrificed anything for his father—his right arm, his car, his last bit of money. These were not idle thoughts that came into Ralph's head. No, not likely. They took up a great deal of Ralph's time. Because out of Don Pedro's twelve children only Ralph came to visit the old man. The reasons for Don Pedro's isolation are too complicated, too old to drag out into the sun to examine, but as it was only Ralph who came to see Don Pedro, it was natural that he should concern himself so much with his father's welfare. The thought of sacrificing his arm pleased Ralph very much. Probably because he had read or been told that someone had actually done such a thing, and the grandeur of such an act struck his fancy. The honor of being placed in a position where he could actually give up his right arm for his father filled him with such pride that he often lamented the lack of opportunity to commit such an act. His best and favorite arm, as he always noted to himself, was not too much to give up for the sake of his father's welfare. He would have dearly loved to be able to walk up to his father's persecutor and calmly but courageously announce that his father be set free and that his right, his favorite arm, could be taken in exchange. If he could only do such a thing, then he could show his father that the love of his only faithful son was not of a weak or fragile nature.

The mist from the fog had built up on the windshield of Ralph's car and though the wipers were working normally Ralph nevertheless had to strain to see if there was any sign that would tell him that his father was at home. Unable to detect any movements within the trailer, Ralph turned off the headlights and stepped out into the moist night air. At the door of the trailer Ralph knocked quietly and cautiously. There was no answer. He knocked again, heavily, the force of the knocks threatening to demolish the leather hinges. A silence followed, then muffled sounds and a,

"¿Quien es?" *

Quickly Ralph blurted, *"Soy yo su hijo, Rafael!"* **

Impatiently Ralph waited in the cold night air, while his father impatiently tried to unlock the door.

* *¿Quien es?* Who is it?
** *Soy yo su hijo, Rafael!* It's me, your son, Ralph!

Throwing the door wide open, Don Pedro embraced Ralph then scruffed him by neck as he pulled him inside. It was dark, cold and damp in the "Hunts," "Heinz 76," "Del Monte" trailer, with only a small kerosene lamp to light the windowless enclosure. On the far side of the trailer where the slant created by the two collapsed wheels began stood a small black stove with a small pile of wood at its side. A dresser drawer separated the stove and a small table and a stool where Don Pedro ate his meals. Tacked along the walls of the trailer were faded news clippings and magazine articles and pictures concerning Mexico's Revolution of 1910. Inside a vertically placed "Hunts" tomato box was a small stack of paper back books all done in Spanish and thoroughly dog-eared with broken bindings. Above Don Pedro's bed were some pictures of his less faithful children. There were girls dressed in first communion dresses and many school pictures, mostly of his sons displaying missing teeth and slicked hair. To this man who lived in this trailer Ralph had brought a new book dealing with the Revolution of 1910. It would have been difficult to get Don Pedro a book about anything else. He was consumed by the Revolution. His conversations never extended beyond ten minutes before the name of a general, a battle, a treaty or a name of an important town in the Revolution would casually be stringed into the conversation. Ralph's contribution to Don Pedro's library was also in Spanish and a bit dated. He had found the book in a small used book store in San Jose underneath a stack of old Life and Look magazines. He knew that it would be appreciated by his father, and be read carefully and repeatedly.

Within his circle of old friends, Don Pedro was considered something of a scholar on the Revolution. He was often called upon to settle arguments concerning fine points of the Revolution—what battle was fought where, what town fell when, what general led what troops. Along with his knowledge of the historical facts of the Revolution, Don Pedro was also knowledgeable of some of the most rudimentary political philosophies that were popular during the Revolution. Upon close questioning, Don Pedro could make a clear exposition of communism in relation to the writings of Marx, Lenin, and Trotsky. Trotsky particularly delighted Don Pedro because he was killed in Mexico.

"Come here, *hijo!*" * shouted Don Pedro.

"What are you doing in these parts? You come so rarely to see me. You're like a stranger. Don't you know the road to my house any more? Did you forget?"

Every time Ralph came to visit the old man, Don Pedro always reprimanded him for not coming to see him more often. Ralph would respond by grinning sheepishly while he muttered excuses of being too busy and that he came more often than did his other children who didn't come at all.

"*Viejito,*** don't start that. Everytime I come to see you it's the same thing. Not today, eh? Look what I got," said Ralph, pulling out a recently opened

* *hijo.* son
** *Viejito.* old man (used affectionately when referring to parents)

bottle of whiskey. Ralph had been drinking heavily and his speech and actions showed the initial effects of the whiskey. He was very affectionate. He kept embracing his father, while Don Pedro kept trying to pull away from him, explaining that he had to get his pants on over his longjohns. Ralph just kept hugging him. Don Pedro saw that his attempt at getting his pants on was futile. He good naturedly got back into bed.

From underneath the bed two empty Mason fruit jars were produced, filled with whiskey and quickly emptied. Don Pedro, relegated to the bed by Ralph's affectionate attacks settled himself in for a conversation. At his side on the bed sat Ralph.

"Well what do you have to say for yourself, son?" opened Don Pedro.

"Say for myself, what do you mean? I've been working, you know, in the cannery in San Jose. Working long hours. This is my first day off in two months and what do I do with it? I come to see you. That's what I have to say for myself, *viejito.* And what do I get for it? Nothing but *pedos** from you for not coming to see you sooner, when it's impossible for me to come sooner. *Pedos, pedos, pedos. Puros pedos,*" said Ralph.

"But that's alright, *viejito,*" continued Ralph, "I know how you feel about having people visit you. Besides, I'm not important. What *is* important is how you feel. How are your legs now? Have they gotten any better since the last time I saw you?"

Don Pedro had been suffering from rheumatism for about ten years now and each year the pain got worse until last year it drove him to Mexico in search for a cure. Had someone explained to him that rheumatism was incurable it would probably have done no good. He still would have gone to Mexico as he did, spent $200.00 for an hour's diagnosis, a hypodermic needle and fifteen bottles of a creamy liquid that he was instructed to inject into his kneecap when the pain hit him. Ever since he returned from Mexico he faithfully injected the liquid into his kneecap at least once a month, but by his own admission the injections did very little to relieve the pain.

"I can hardly walk now. This fog makes things even worse. If I walk for a while the pain increases to the point where I almost can't bear it. I've been getting the injections but they don't seem to do any good," said Don Pedro.

"Just what is the matter, *viejito?* I know you keep telling me that your legs hurt. But I don't know what that means except that your legs hurt and that doesn't tell me much. I mean do you really know what the trouble with your legs is? Have you been examined by a doctor?" inquired Ralph.

"No, I don't really know what it is that causes the pain. Someone told me that it was rheumatism, but they weren't certain, and neither am I. I haven't gone to a doctor because right now I don't have enough money for it. Anyway, even if I did have the money I've no way of getting to a doctor. All my

* *pedos.* complaints (slang)

friends are as old as I, if not older, and they can't drive and even if they could drive they wouldn't be of much help to me because they can't speak English. English is all the doctors around here speak. Right now I'm at the mercy of the weather and my pain."

Ralph leaned over and grasped his father's hands tightly in a show of appreciation for both his situation and the pain that he suffered.

The tinkling of glass again and two gulps. Ralph wiped his mouth with the back of his hand, stood up, straightened his shoulders, and began to pace the small area of the trailer. His lips were drawn tight and his forehead was furrowed in display of his concern over his father's position. The warped, dusty floor creaked under his weight. At the far end of the trailer, where the stove stood, Ralph stopped, turned quickly and a smile appeared on his face. He quickly walked over to his father, sat down on the edge of the bed and asked, "*Oye, padre,** how come you got two names, eh? I bet you didn't even think I knew. But I do. Old Don Diego told me about two months ago when I last came to visit you. *Viejito chingado*** knows more than he should, eh? You know, I thought about it ever since he told me about it: I couldn't think of any reason why you would have two names. You're not a bandit, are you *viejito?*" added Ralph with a deep laugh.

The question startled Don Pedro. Though it was generally known that he had two names, it was also tacitly known that no one should ever question him about the reasons for it.

Don Pedro moved his legs beneath the blanket, sat upright, adjusted the blankets but did not answer Ralph. A long silence followed with an occasional embarrassed cough interrupting the quietness of the trailer. Shifting his legs once more, Don Pedro spoke in a quiet voice.

"I've never told the reasons for both my names to anyone before. Mostly for personal reasons of pride and honor. For the past forty years I've kept these reasons celled inside of me. But I guess I'll die soon and what I say here tonight to you and the cockroaches won't affect me when my body lies cold and buried in the earth. You know I've always talked about the Revolution of 1910 and how grand it was. I guess it was something I had to do. You know, to make both me and Mexico look good to you. In many ways that Revolution was both Mexico's and my great adventure in life. And like all adventures, the Revolution not only had to be exciting but also noble. If I squint through the eyes of my memory the Revolution *was* grand and noble. But if I open them wide, as I must now do, its beauty and nobility are marred by flaws that cannot be denied.

"I was sixteen years old when I first heard of the Revolution. This is a measure of my ignorance then because the Revolution had been going on for six months before I heard about it. I had no reason to be aware of such things.

* *Oye, padre.* Listen, Father
** *Viejito chingado.* The old son of a bitch (affectionately)

I and your Uncle Manuel were farm boys in the country. Our only concern was tending the sheep that were placed in our care. When I returned to my village I found that it had been raided five times within three months and each time by different armies. In those days a farm was not a safe place to be. It could be plundered by anyone who took such a thought in mind. After the sixth raid on our village, I saw the advantage was clearly on the side of the men with guns. For that reason and probably for that reason alone, I joined the army. I joined Carranza's forces. I did this in spite of the fact that I admired Villa and Zapata tremendously. In those days one heard great things about both men, but especially about Villa. There was a rumor that Villa had a whole train just for his men. Fifty cars, so the rumor went, of nothing but food, ammunition, clothing and women. His army lacked nothing and could lose to no one. Yet I chose Carranza, mostly because of your grandfather Don Francisco who admired the brilliance of this man just as most men admired the courage and military capabilities of Zapata and Villa. A pensive man, Don Francisco would call Carranza, a man who planned the future of modern Mexico. I don't regret joining Carranza. In Carranza's forces there were many men like your grandfather. In my squad alone we had three schoolteachers, two writers, two poets and four artists."

Don Pedro paused, took another drink from his Mason fruit jar, wiped his mouth with the edge of the blanket, looked straight into the dancing light of the kerosene lamp and continued.

"In the beginning things were good. I had my rifle, ammunition, a horse, food and no fear. Then it was I, I'm very sorry to say, who frightened the people in the villages, menacing them with my prancing black horse and waving my pistol in the air. For such acts I hope I am forgiven. Eight months after I joined the forces we fought three heavy battles. The rifles became rusty, the horse worn, ammunition scarce and both fear and hunger returned. I was young, remember, sixteen years is not very old. What I said about the goodness of the ideals of the Revolution still holds, *hijo.* Don't get me wrong about that. That I don't deny because look at Mexico now. No, the Revolution, the real Revolution is not what I disliked or found less noble than I have painted in your mind over the years. In every Revolution, however, there are wars that are fought within the minds of men that have little or nothing to do with the fighting outside. These are wars that are fought at all times but that intensify and become momentous during times of conflict. Then the mind, the heart and the soul struggle to keep as one. The teachers, writers, poets and artists would sit around the camp fire with the thin, yellow-red tongue of the flames licking at their feet and discuss the ideals of the Revolution and its significance not only for Mexico, but for all of mankind. But what did I know of such things, I was young and ignorant. It made more sense to me to eat and sleep rather than to sit and talk. To me the only significant things were food, warmth and the knowledge that we were winning our campaign or that the Revolution was going to be over. It was after one year in Carranza's army and fighting in the Revolution for the glory of Mexico that the *true* Revolution was beginning to be overshadowed by the war in my head. It was difficult to keep the ideals of the Revolution in mind when all I saw were people dying, the land drying up, crops failing and my village decaying. Was this the sacrifice that was to be made for the sake of the Revolution? The ideals of the Revolution were good, but they seemed nicer once the dying was over. When my cousin, Manuel, who was only fourteen, died in my arms the ideals became nothing but words in the wind. They couldn't bring Manuel back, you couldn't eat ideals and they didn't protect you much from the cold, the hot sun or the bullets of your enemy.

"I tried to hold myself together. Still desperately trying to hold on to the ideals of the Revolution, I would talk with the circle of thinkers asking them to explain in detail the reasons for the Revolution—land reform, democracy, communism, despotism. I tried to learn how to think like they did so that my faith in the Revolution would be as strong as theirs. But even as I tried I knew I was losing the war. The final battle that turned the tide in my mind was fought and lost when I found out that there were great differences between all of the generals that I so admired. Carranza, Villa, Obregon, and Zapata, all of them seemed to be pulling in all different directions. One night while the writers, poets, teachers and artists were defining some important aspects of the Revolution, Don Diego and I got on our horses and rode two days into El Paso. I didn't want anyone to track me down so I changed my name to Sanchez. You know that there are many Sanchez'. With such a name it would have been difficult to trace me."

The dank trailer was filled with silence once more. Only the tinkling of the whiskey bottle touching the lip of Ralph's fruit jar and the gurgling sound of the liquid falling into the jar could be heard. Again and again. Ralph was motionless, his eyes brimming with tears.

"Ay, que viejito." * he finally managed to say.

Don Pedro sat in his bed entranced and exhausted. He had relieved himself of a large burden. He had admitted not only deserting his country, but more importantly the ideals of the Revolution. His romance with life lasted a mere year and ended in an ignoble act.

Again Ralph got up from bed, walked to the end of the trailer, turned and said, "What did you say was wrong with you, father? You still can't walk?"

Don Pedro was still entranced, his eyes fixed on the kerosene lamp. He did not answer for some time, then lifting his eyes he managed a soft reply.

"No, I still can't walk very well, son."

"You say you haven't seen a doctor?" continued Ralph.

"No, I haven't been able to see a doctor, because there's no way for me to get to town and because no one can talk to the doctor for me. You know that the doctors around here don't speak Spanish," said Don Pedro.

* *Ay, que viejito.* Oh, what an old man

Ralph became more interested and moved.

"How bad is the pain you say?"

"Bad, *hijo,* very bad. I can't even take a trip into town until the summer comes because of the pain that such a trip would cause. Don Chapo, *pobre** Don Chapo, has to bring me my groceries every day," answered Don Pedro.

"And you say the injections don't work?" asked Ralph.

"No, they don't," said Don Pedro.

The pain was indeed bad. It probably could not have been worse, and Don Pedro was not exaggerating when he spoke of not being able to leave his bed at times without suffering the consequences of not being able to walk for days after. There were often nights when the pain in his legs was the sole reason for his inability to sleep. Years ago when he was traveling the migrant route his health was among the best. He never suffered from any illness and was never hospitalized for any type of treatment. It was only in the last ten years when his friends began dying, and his family deserted him, that illness and fragile health came to him. First there was the kidney trouble, then the trouble with his back followed by innumerable smaller ailments that kept Don Pedro in constant pain. But when he had these ailments he still had friends to care for him, to come and visit him in the hospital and look after his trailer while he was away. Now it was rheumatism, something that could not be cured and which pained him more than did his other ailments. Worst of all there was no one to advise him on what to do, or, once advised, to help him. Yes, the pain was terrible and the hope that perhaps Ralph could help him sparked him to press Ralph for definite action.

"Well," spoke Ralph, "what about if I took you to the doctor. Would you go?"

Don Pedro answered quickly, "Yes, of course I would. I just need someone to take me. To help me while I talk with the doctor. They don't understand Spanish, you know. Of course I would go."

"Okay, then I'll take you," said Ralph. Having resolved the issue, Ralph hugged Don Pedro again.

Pushing Ralph away gently, Don Pedro asked, "When?"

"When what?" answered Ralph.

"When are you going to take me to see the doctor," said Don Pedro.

"Well, do you have a doctor first of all," hedged Ralph. "I mean we just can't go into any doctor's office just like that. You have to warn him or something like that."

Don Pedro had kept the name of the doctor that had operated on his kidney. From underneath the mattress, Don Pedro pulled out a multi-folded paper with the name Doctor Jones on it and his address in Tracy. He handed it to Ralph. Ralph opened it, ripping it slightly with unsteady hands. He looked at it for what seemed an unreasonably long time, then nodding his

* *pobre.* poor

head he refolded it and stuck it in his shirt pocket. He poured the last drink in the bottle and when that was finished he stood up and began to pace the floor. It was time for Ralph to leave.

"Well, *viejito,* I have to go. I've got a long way to travel tonight. The fog's bad. Can't hardly see more than ten feet in front of you. It's as bad as it was two years ago about Thanksgiving time, when they had that accident with twenty-two cars," said Ralph in a timid voice.

Don Pedro was startled. He did not expect Ralph to leave so soon after having promised to take him to the doctor. Don Pedro wanted to set a date for the visit to the doctor.

"*Ya,** so quickly. You just got here and you're leaving?" said Don Pedro.

"It's a long way, *viejito.* I got to get going," said Ralph meekly.

Don Pedro attempted to finalize the matter of the doctor before Ralph left by saying, "Well, if you must go then that's the way it must be. But before you go tell me when we're going to see the doctor."

"The doctor? Oh yes, the doctor. Well, let's see, next week I have the night shift which means that I'll have to sleep during the day. So that's out. Let's see, next week I have the night shift, and then . . ." Ralph's mind blurred as it tried to think beyond the week of his night shift duty.

"Don't worry, *viejito,* I'll take care of it. Pretty soon I'll take you to see the doctor," said Ralph with a note of finality.

"But when?" pressed Don Pedro.

"Well, you know that next week I have the night shift so I can't go then . . . I'll figure it out and then let you know."

Don Pedro knew that he had lost. He knew that the promise would never be fulfilled. Tomorrow when the whiskey had worn off, Ralph would recall nothing of tonight's conversation. Ralph gave Don Pedro one last hug and told him, "You know you're the only *viejito* I've got so take care of yourself."

With that Ralph opened the door to the trailer and stepped out into the fog. As he drove past the decaying car he lingered a while shaking his head in sympathetic regret that what obviously once was a fine car should have met with such a sad end. Moving on to the highway well beyond the trailer in the clearing, Ralph wondered if he would ever have the chance to sacrifice his right arm, his favorite arm, for his father.

PAULE MARSHALL (b. 1929)

Although Paule Marshall is a Brooklyn-born Brooklyn College graduate, her parents' West Indian heritage has played a large part in her writing. Her first novel, Brown Girl, Brownstones *(1959), portrays a ten year old*

* *Ya.* Already

girl growing up in Brooklyn in a Barbadian family and community, and the conflicts arising from their attempt to reconcile their old and new ways of life. Her latest novel, The Chosen Place, The Timeless People *(1969), traces the impact on a remote West Indian island community of the sudden intrusion of the age of technology in the form of an American research and development team.*

Marshall's collection Soul Clap Hands and Sing *(1961) contains four novellas, in four different settings, on a single theme: the approach of death for an aging man who is unready to face the greater unknown. In "Brazil," one of these four stories, Caliban's search for his identity proves as fruitless as it is harrowing.*

Brazil

THREE TRUMPETS, two saxophones, a single trombone; a piano, drums and a bass fiddle. Together in the dimness of the night club they shaped an edifice of sound glittering with notes and swaying to the buffeting of the drums the way a tall building sways imperceptibly to the wind when, suddenly, one of the trumpets sent the edifice toppling with a high, whinnying chord that seemed to reach beyond sound into silence. It was a signal and the other instruments quickly followed, the drums exploding into the erotic beat of a samba, the bass becoming a loud pulse beneath the shrieking horns—and in the midst of the hysteria, a voice announced, first in Portuguese and then in English, "Ladies and gentlemen, the Casa Samba presents *O Grande Caliban e a Pequena Miranda*—The Great Caliban and the Tiny Miranda!"

The music ended in a taut, expectant silence and in the darkness a spotlight poured a solid cone of light onto the stage with such force smoke seemed to rise from its wide edge and drift out across the audience. Miranda stood within the cone of light, alone but for the shadowy forms of the musicians behind her, as rigid and stiff-faced as a statue. She was a startlingly tall, long-limbed woman with white skin that appeared luminous in the spotlight and blond hair piled like whipped cream above a face that was just beginning to slacken with age and was all the more handsome and arresting because of this. Her brief costume of sequins and tulle gave off what seemed an iridescent dust each time she breathed, and a smile was affixed like a stamp to her mouth, disguising an expression that was, at once, calculating and grasping—but innocently so, like a child who has no sense of ownership and claims everything to be his. Blue eye shadow sprinkled with gold dust and a pair of dramatic, blue-tinged eyelashes hid her sullen, bored stare.

She filled the night club with a powerful animal presence, with a decisive, passionless air that was somehow Germanic. And she was part German, one of those Brazilians from Rio Grande do Sul who are mixed German, Portuguese, native Indian and sometimes African. With her the German had triumphed. She was a Brunhild without her helmet and girdle of mail, without her spear.

There was a rap on the drums and Miranda clutched one of her buttocks as if she had been struck there; another rap, louder this time, and she clutched the other, feigning shock and outrage.

"Hey, lemme in, stupid!" a rough male voice called in Portuguese behind her, and she whirled like a door that had been kicked open as a dark, diminutive figure burst around her thigh, wearing a scarlet shirt with billowing sleeves and a huge *C* embroidered on the breast like the device of a royal house, a pair of oversized fighter's trunks of the same scarlet which fell past his knees and a prize fighter's high laced shoes.

He was an old man. His hair beneath the matted wig he wore had been gray for years now and his eyes under crumpled lids were almost opaque with rheum and innocent with age. Yet, as he turned to Miranda with a motion of kicking the door shut, his movements were deft and fluid—his body was still young, it seemed—and as he turned to the audience his face, despite the wrinkles which like fine incisions had drawn his features into an indistinct knot, was still mobile, eloquent, subtle, each muscle beneath the black skin under his absolute control.

Applause greeted him and he assumed the stance of a prize fighter, his body dropping to a wary, menacing crouch, his head ducking and weaving and his tiny fists cocked as he did a dazzling swift dance on his toes. . . . Suddenly he unleashed a flurry of savage jabs, first in the direction of Miranda, who quailed, then at the audience. He pommeled the air and when the knockout blow finally came, it was an uppercut so brilliantly timed, so visually lethal, that those in the audience who had never seen him before jerked their heads out of the way of that fist. "Joe Louis, the champion," he cried, and held up a triumphant right hand.

He always opened his act this way and the caricature had made him famous and become his trademark. But he had burlesqued at other times in his long career, and just as effectively, a rustic gazing up at Rio's high buildings of tinted glass and steel for the first time (this was his favorite since fifty years ago he had himself come to Rio from a small jewel-mining town in Minas Gerais), an American who had just missed his plane (and it had never mattered that his skin was black or that he spoke Portuguese, the illusion had held), a matron from the Brazilian upper class whose costume had begun unraveling during the carnival ball at Copacabana palace . . . and others.

He had been Everyman, so much so that it had become difficult over his thirty-five years in show business to separate out of the welter of faces he could assume his face, to tell where O Grande Caliban ended and he, Heitor

Baptista Guimares, began. He had begun to think about this dimly ever since the night he had decided to retire—and to be vaguely disturbed.

Their act was mostly slapstick, with Caliban using the cowed Miranda as a butt for his bullying and abuse. And it was this incongruous and contradictory relationship—Caliban's strength, his bossiness despite his age and shriveled body and Miranda's weakness, which belied her imposing height and massive limbs—that was the heart of their act. It shaped everything they did. When they sang, as they were doing now, his voice was an ominous bass rumble beneath her timid soprano. They broke into a dance routine and Miranda took little mincing steps while Caliban spurred his body in a series of impressive leaps and spins, and forced his legs wide in a split.

It looked effortless, but he felt his outraged muscles rebel as he repeated the split, his joints stiffen angrily. He smiled to disguise both his pain and the disgust he felt for his aging body. He was suddenly overwhelmed by rage and, as usual when his anger became unbearable and he felt helpless, he blamed Miranda. She caught his angry scowl and paused for an instant that was no longer than the natural pause between her dance steps, bewildered, thinking that she had done something wrong and then understanding (she knew him far better now that they openly hated each other), and her own anger streaked across her eyes even as her smile remained intact.

Halfway through their act Miranda left the stage and, alone with the spotlight narrowed to just his face, Caliban spun off a ream of old off-color jokes and imitations. Everything he did was flawlessly timed and full of the subtlety and slyness he had perfected over the years, but he was no longer funny. The audience laughed, but for reasons other than his jokes: the Brazilians out of affection and loyalty, and the tourists, mostly Americans from a Moore-McCormack ship in the harbor, out of a sense of their own well-being and in relief—relief because in the beginning when Caliban's dark face had appeared around Miranda's white thigh they had tensed, momentarily outraged and alarmed until, with smiles that kept slipping out of place, they had reminded each other that this was Brazil after all, where white was never wholly white, no matter how pure it looked. They had begun laughing then in loud, self-conscious gusts, turning to each other for cues and reassurance, whispering, "I don't know why I'm laughing. I don't understand a word of Spanish. Or is this the place where they speak Portuguese?"

Miranda returned for a brief, noisy finale and at the very end she reversed the roles by scooping Caliban up with one hand and marching triumphantly off stage with him kicking, his small arms flailing, high above her head.

"*Senhor* and *Senhoras, O Grande Caliban e a Pequena Miranda!*"

Usually, they took two curtain calls, the first with Miranda still holding the protesting Caliban aloft and the other with Caliban on the ground and in command again, chasing the frightened Miranda across the stage. But, tonight, as soon as they were behind the wing, he ordered her to set him down and when she did, he turned and walked toward his dressing room without a word, his legs stiff with irritability and his set shoulders warning her off.

"Hey, are you crazy, where are you going? The curtain call . . ."

"You take it," he said, without turning. "You think it's your show, so you take it."

She stared after him, helpless and enraged, her eyes a vaporous gray which somehow suggested that her mind was the same gray swirl, and her hair shining like floss in the dimness and dust backstage. Then she bounded after him, an animal about to attack. "Now what did I do wrong?" she shouted against the dwindling sound of the applause.

He turned abruptly and she stopped. "Everything," he said quietly. "You did everything wrong. You were lousy."

"So were you."

"Yes, but only because of you."

"Bastard, whenever something's worrying you or you feel sick, you take it out on me. I swear you're like a woman changing life. Nobody told you to try doing the split out there tonight, straining yourself. You're too old. You should retire. You're finished."

"Shut up."

"Why don't you take out your worries on the little mamita you have home, your holiest of virgins . . . ?" He walked rapidly away and she cried after him, gesturing furiously, her voice at a scathing pitch, "Yes, go home to mamita, your child bride. And has the holiest of virgins given birth to your little Jesus yet?"

"Pig," he said, and opened the door to his dressing room.

"Children of old men come out crooked." She began to cry, the false eyelashes staining her cheeks blue.

"Barren bitch."

"Runt! Despoiler of little girls."

He slammed the door on her, jarring the mirror on his dressing table so that his reflection wavered out of shape within its somber, mottled depth. He remained near the door, waiting for the mirror to settle and his own anger to subside, aware, as always, of a critical silence in the room. It was a pleasant silence, welcoming him when his performance was good, but mocking and cold—as it was now—when he failed. And he was aware of something else in the room, a subtle disturbance he had sensed there ever since the night, two months ago, when he had decided to retire. He had thought, at first, that the disturbance was due to something out of place within the familiar disorder or to some new object which had been placed there without his knowing it. But after searching and finding nothing, he had come to believe that what he felt was really a disturbance within himself, some worry he could not define which had become dislodged and escaped along with his breath and taken a vague, elusive form outside of him. Each night it awaited him in the cubicle of a dressing room and watched him while he took off his make-up and dressed, mute yet somehow plaintive, like the memory of someone he had known at another time, but whose face he could no longer remember.

Taking off the scarlet shirt, he tossed it among the other costumes littering the room and, sitting at the dressing table, began taking off the make-up, pausing each time the bulb over the mirror flickered out as the music, playing now for the patrons' dancing, jarred the walls. As his face emerged it was clear that it had once been appealing—the way a child's face is—with an abrupt little nose flattened at the tip, a wry mouth and softly molded contours which held dark shadows within their hollows—a face done in miniature over which the black skin had been drawn tight and eyes which held like a banked fire the intensity of the Latin.

He avoided looking at his face now that he was old. Without the make-up it reminded him of a piece of old fruit so shriveled and spotted with decay that there was no certainty as to what it had been originally. Above all, once he removed the make-up, his face was without expression, bland, as though only on stage made up as Caliban in the scarlet shirt and baggy trunks was he at all certain of who he was. Caliban might have become his reality.

So that now, while his hands did the work of his eyes, he gazed absently at his body, imposing on his slack shoulders and on the sunken chest which barely stirred with his breathing the dimmed memory of his body at the height of his fame (he could not remember what it had looked like before becoming Caliban). He had held himself like a military man then, very erect, his small shoulders squared, all of him stretching it seemed toward the height which had been denied him—and this martial stance, so incongruous somehow, had won him the almost hysterical admiration of the crowds. Yet in the midst of this admiration, he had always felt vaguely like a small animal who had been fitted out in an absurd costume and trained to amuse, some Lilliputian in a kingdom of giants who had to play the jester in order to survive. The world had been scaled without him in mind—and his rage and contempt for it and for those who belonged was always just behind his smile, in the vain, superior lift of his head, in his every gesture.

He pulled on a robe of the same red satin, with a large *C* embroidered on the breast, hiding himself. He flung aside the towel he was using and the light flickered and then flickered again as the door opened and the porter, Henriques, who also served as Caliban's valet, entered with the cup of *café Sinho* he always brought him after the last show.

Caliban watched the reflection take shape behind his in the mirror: the bloated form dressed in a discarded evening jacket with a cummerbund spanning his vast middle, the face a white globule until the beaked nose which absorbed it appeared, and then the fringe of black hair which Henriques kept waved and pomaded. Caliban felt comforted and younger suddenly, so that as Henriques placed the coffee beside him he motioned him to a chair and, turning, said, his voice loud and casual but strained:

"Henriques, we are in business, old man. Or better out of business. The signs are finished. I saw them today. And they are good. Very bold. They used my red and it hits the eye like one of Caliban's uppercuts"—his fist cut through the air and, although Henriques laughed and nodded, no smile stirred within his old eyes.

"And, thank God, they got the *C* in Caliban right. I was worried about that because they got it all wrong on the posters they made for my tour last year. But it pleased me the way they did the *C* this time. Very large and sweeping. Up at the top it says, 'O Grande Caliban retiring,' in big print to catch the eye, with the *C* coming at you like a fist, then below that 'Brazil's greatest and most beloved comedian leaving the stage after thirty-five years,' and at the bottom, 'See him perform for the last time this month at the Casa Samba.' That's all. And enough, I think. It is more dramatic that way . . ."

"And when will they be put on display, Senhor Caliban?" Henriques asked with elaborate courtesy.

"The day after tomorrow. The posters will go up all over the city, but the big signs only downtown and in Copacabana. There'll be announcements in all the papers of course—a full-page ad which will run for a week, and on radio and television."

"I have a confession, senhor," Henriques said, his voice edging in beside Caliban's, which had grown louder, filling the room. "I personally did not believe it. You know, senhor, how you sometimes talk about retiring but . . . well, you know. But now with the signs and the announcements . . ."

"The talk has ended, Henriques. Two more weeks. The signs are ready, old man!" He shouted as though informing someone beyond the room and held up two fingers the color and shape of dried figs. "Two weeks from tonight Caliban does his last boxing match. That night will mark my anniversary. Thirty-five years ago that same night I won the amateur contest at the Teatro Municipal. Do you remember the old Teatro Municipal? There's a clinic there now for the children of the poor. The night I won, the producer, Julio Baretos, right away booked me in his regular show and christened me O Grande Caliban. After that . . ." His gesture summed up the success which had followed that night.

"And what is your real name, Senhor Caliban?" Henriques said.

Caliban paused, surprised for the moment, and then quickly said, "Guimares. Heitor Guimares. Heitor Baptista Guimares." He gave an embarrassed laugh. "I haven't used it for so long I had to stop and think."

"Perhaps you will begin using it now that you are retiring."

"Of course," he said, and sat back, his smile and gesture dying, his eyes becoming troubled again under their crumpled lids. He quickly drank the *café Sinho* and, as his glance met Henriques' over the cup, he gave a shapeless smile. "Of course," he repeated loudly, even as his gaze wandered over the costumes hung like the bright skins of imaginary animals on the walls, over the trunks containing his juggling and magician equipment. His eyes lingered on each object, possessing it. He tied the scarlet robe more securely around him.

"You are wise to retire," Henriques said quietly. "After all, you are not that old yet and you have a new life ahead what with a young wife and a child soon."

"Of course," Caliban murmured, and for a moment could not remember what his wife looked like.

"How many your age have that? Look at me. I haven't been able to have a woman for years now. And children? All my children have forgotten me. And you have money, Senhor Caliban, while we who are old and without must keep dragging around a dead carcass, breathing death over everybody, working till our end . . ." Henriques stirred heavily in the chair, looking, with the costumes draped behind him and the cummerbund girding his middle, like some old, sated regent.

"Yes," he said, and followed Caliban's stare into space. "You are retiring at the right time, senhor, and with dignity. Putting up the signs all over the city shows style. You are saying good-by to Rio in the proper way, which is only right, since it was here that you became famous. Rio made you, after all."

"Of course."

"Now once a year during carnival you will perform before the President at Copacabana Palace Hotel and all of Rio will weep remembering your greatness . . ."

Caliban restrained him with a gesture and in the silence his dark skin seemed to grow ashen as if inside some abstract terror had cramped his heart. "What to do, Henriques," he said, and shrugged. "I am an old man. Did you see me tonight? The last show especially? I could hardly move. I forgot lines so that the jokes didn't make sense. I was all right in the beginning, but once I gave the knockout punch I was through. That punch took all my strength. I feel it here," he touched his right shoulder, his chest. "Oh, I know I could go on working at the Casa Samba for a while longer, I am an institution here, but I don't love it any more. I don't feel the crowd. And then that pig Miranda has gotten so lousy."

"Did you have her name put on the signs?"

"To hell with her. No," he shouted, swept suddenly by the same anger he had felt on stage. He jumped up and began dressing under Henriques' somnolent eye, wonder at the intensity of his anger, knowing remotely that it reached beyond Miranda to something greater.

"But haven't you told her?"

"I told her. I even told her about the signs. But like you she didn't believe me. She just laughed. The pig," he cried suddenly, and the light flickered. "Did you hear her cursing me just now, and cursing my wife and my unborn child. She has become crazy this past year. All because I married." Suddenly, facing the door, he shouted, "It's my business that I married, pig, not yours. And if I chose to marry a child of twenty-five, it is my business still."

He waited, quivering, as though expecting Miranda to burst into the room. Then, turning again to Henriques, he said, "You would not believe it, Henriques, but I still give her everything she wants even though I married. Last month she saw one of those fancy circular beds in a magazine from Hollywood and I had one custom made for her. A while back, she took out all the light fixtures and put in chandeliers, even in the kitchen, so that her place looks like the grand ballroom of the Copacabana Palace Hotel. I bought the chandeliers for her, of course, as I have bought nearly everything she has—while she has been saving her money all these years. And even though I married I still go and spend part of the evening with her before we come to the club . . . So she complains I will have nothing to do with her any more. But after all, Henriques, I am an old man and I have a young wife. Besides it was always a little grotesque with her . . ."

"They say it's never good to keep a woman around once you're finished with her."

"I should have kicked her out, yes—and long ago. She was never any good for me or for the act. From the very beginning she tried to take over both of us. And I only included her in the act for effect. She wasn't supposed to do anything more than stand there like a mannequin. But she kept insisting—she would wake me at night begging me to let her do more. And so . . ." He motioned hopelessly and sat down.

"I should have never taken up with her." Then he said softly, "But she was a weakness with me in the beginning." He gave Henriques an oblique, almost apologetic glance. "And what I said just now was not true. She was good for me in the beginning—and we were good together. We were the same, you see. Me, as I am—" and with a gesture he offered Henriques his shrunken body—"and she, so tall, and she was skinny then. They were laughing at her the first time I saw her in a show at the Miramar almost fifteen years ago now. She couldn't dance. She couldn't sing. She hadn't bleached her hair yet and she looked lousy . . . I understood what it was for her being so tall—" His voice dropped, becoming entangled with the memory. "And she was good for the act in the beginning. She had imagination and the comic touch. She was the one who thought up the prize-fighter routine, which is still the most famous. But then something went wrong with her, Henriques, and she began doing everything wrong. I've been carrying her for years now. Perhaps I would have had another five, ten years left, if not for her. She has become a bane. She has used me till I'm dry, the pig!"

"But what of her now?"

Caliban, dressed in an expensive mohair suit with a white handkerchief embroidered with a red *C* in the breast pocket, patent-leather shoes with built-up heels and diamond cuff links glinting in turn with the many rings he wore, turned sharply toward the door as if to rush from the room and the question. "What of her? That's not my worry. The day those signs go up is the day I finish with her, the parasite. Let her spend some of the money she sits on. She has talked for years about doing her own act. Now she'll have a chance to do it."

"But does she have the talent for that?"

"No, and she knows it. Do you think she would have stayed with me all this time if she had, Henriques? Not Miranda."

"Well, she will find someone to keep her. She is like Rio. There will always be somebody to admire her." Henriques heaved up from the chair, and, as his unwieldy bulk filled the small room, the dusk whirred up like frightened birds and settled further away. He began picking up Caliban's clothes.

"Yes," Caliban said thoughtfully, "she will find somebody to use, the bitch. For a while anyway." He hurried to the door, eager to escape the room which had suddenly become crowded with the image of Miranda and hot from his anger. As he opened it, he sensed the vague, illusory form of his fear rush past him like a draft and lead him through the clutter backstage, out the back door and across the denuded yard to the entrance, where the neon lights pulsed the name CASA SAMBA into the night and a large sign at the door announced the nightly appearance of O Grande Caliban.

The club was closing; the last of the crowd clustered under the awning while the doorman called up the taxis. Beyond the radius of neon lights the night itself was a vast awning under which the city slept, exhausted from its nightly revelry, its few remaining lights like dull reflections of the stars. Its mountains, like so many dark breasts thrusting into the sky, gave height and prominence and solidity to the night.

The Casa Samba had been built on the sloping street leading to the *Pão de Açúcar* and as Caliban walked toward his car he was aware, as if for the first time, of the mountain's high, solid cone, black against the lesser blackness of the sky, benevolent, rising protectively over the sleeping city. He could make out the cable line of the aerial railway looped in a slender thread between *Pão de Açúcar* and its satellite, Mount Urca. What had been for years just another detail in the familiar frieze that was Rio was suddenly separate and distinct, restored . . . He paused beside his car, hoping (but unaware of the hope) that a part of himself which he had long since ceased to see might emerge into consciousness as the mountain had emerged, thinking (and he was aware of this) that there might be a wind the day after tomorrow when the signs announcing his retirement went up, a wind strong enough to tear them down before they could be read and whip them out to sea. He was half smiling, his worn eyelids closing with pleasure at the thought, when a taxi with a group of Americans from the night club stopped and one of them called to him in English, "Say, do you speak English?"

He turned, annoyed. The man's voice, the harsh, unmelodic, almost guttural English he spoke, his pale face floating in the darkness seemed to snatch his pleasure, to declare that there would be no wind the day after tomorrow and the signs would remain. As the taxi's headlights singled him out, he felt as if he had been caught on stage without the armor of his scarlet shirt and loose trunks—suddenly defenseless, shorter than his five feet, insignificant. He quickly assumed his martial pose.

"I speak some little English," he said stiffly.

"Well, then maybe you can explain to our driver here—" and the driver protested in Portuguese to Caliban that he had understood them and could speak English—"that we want to go someplace else, not back to the hotel, but to another night club. Are there any that stay open all night? Do you understand what I'm saying? Some place where we can dance."

Without answering, Caliban turned and told the driver where to take them. Then he said in English, "He will take you to a place."

"Thanks. Say, aren't you the comedian from the club? What's your name again?"

He wanted to fling the full title—O Grande Caliban—in the man's face and walk away, but he could not even say Caliban. For some reason he felt suddenly divested of that title and its distinction, no longer entitled to use it.

The man was whispering to the others in the car. "What was his name again? You know, the old guy telling the jokes. With the blonde."

"The name is Heitor Guimares," Caliban said suddenly.

"No, I mean your stage name."

"Hey, wait, I remember," someone in the car called. "It was from Shakespeare. Caliban . . ."

"Heitor Baptista Guimares," he cried, his voice loud and severe, addressed not only to them but to the mountain and the night. Turning, he walked to his car.

He did not drive away but remained perched like a small, ruffled bird on the cushions he used to raise the driver's seat, his rings winking angrily in the dimness as he watched the taillights of the taxi define the slope as it sped down, trying to order his breathing, which had suddenly become a conscious and complex act. The taillights vanished and with them the momentary annoyance he had felt with the tourists. He was alone then, with only the vague form of his anxiety (and he had never felt such loneliness) and the unfamiliar name echoing in his mind.

"Heitor Guimares," he said slowly. "Heitor Guimares." But although he repeated it until his tongue was heavy, it had no reality. It was the name of a stranger who had lived at another time.

By the time Caliban reached the modern house of glass walls and stone he had built in a suburb near Corcovado, the mountain of Christ, a thin, opalescent dawn had nudged aside the darkness, and, as he walked hesitantly across the patio, through the living room, down the hall to the bedrooms, the sound of his raised heels on the tiles was like the failing pulse of the dying night.

He paused at the opened door of the master bedroom. He could not hear his wife's breathing but he could see it in the small, steady flame of the candle before the Madonna in the niche near the bed. In the faint light he made out her stomach, like a low hill on the wide plain of the bed, and the dark outline of her face framed by the pillows. He did not have to see that face to know its mildness and repose. The first time he had met her on the tour last year which had taken him through the small town in Minas Gerais where he had been born (she was the granddaughter of a distant cousin of his and it had been easy to arrange the marriage), he had almost, instinctively, crossed himself. She had looked like a Madonna painted black. He had wanted to confess to her as to a priest, seeing her that first time. He would have confessed now if he could have named his fear—whispering to her while she slept. And she would have, blindly in her sleep, curved her body to receive him, nesting him within the warm hollow of her back as if he were the child she bore. He hesitated though, feeling, oddly, that he was no longer entitled to her comfort, just as he was no longer entitled to use the name Caliban.

He closed the door and went to the small room at the end of the hall which he used as a den and stretched out on the cot there without undressing. As always when he was troubled, he slept quickly and his dream was that he was caught in a mine shaft without a lantern to light his way.

As quickly, light rushed at him from one end of the shaft and he awoke to the afternoon sun which had invaded the room. Like a reveler the sunlight did a sprightly dance on the framed photographs on the walls (they were all of Caliban, one with the President of Brazil during the carnival of 1946 and another with Carmen Miranda the year before she died), on the mementoes and awards on top of the desk; it leaped across the floor and landed in the arms of his wife as she opened the door.

She did not enter the room but stood, like a petitioner, in the doorway, holding a cup of coffee as though it was an offering. She had already been to Mass, yet a thin haze from her long sleep filmed her eyes; her body, Caliban knew, would still be warm and pliant from the bed. He felt neither pleasure nor passion at the thought, though—and as if she understood this and blamed herself, she bowed her head.

"Caliban . . ." she said finally, and hesitated. Then: "You have slept in all your clothes and in your rings."

"It's nothing," he said, and sat up, waving her off as she started forward to help him. "I was tired last night, that's all."

His body felt strange: sore as though he had been beaten while he slept, constricted by the clothes which seemed to have shrunk overnight. The taste of the name he had spoken aloud in the car was still in his mouth. "Let me have the coffee," he said.

The coffee was the color and texture of his sleep and he drank it quickly, wishing that it was a potion which would bring on that sleep again. "Is there a wind today?"

"Only at the top of the road, near the church." And she quickly added, "But I wore a coat."

His thought had been of the signs, not of her, and, ashamed suddenly, he said in the paternal, indulgent tone he used with her, "Tell me, Clara, how would you like to live somewhere else for a while? Somewhere in Minas again perhaps . . ."

She could not disguise her reluctance. "Back to Minas? But what of your work?"

"You let me worry about that, little Clara."

"And this house?"

"Sell it and build a bigger one there."

"Yes, of course. But then Rio is nice too. I mean there is carnival here and . . ."

"We will come down for carnival each year."

"Of course. Then there is the child. It would be nice if it were born in Rio. Perhaps after the child we could return to Minas . . ."

"No, I don't want a child of mine to be born in Rio and be called a *Carioca.*"

"Yes, Caliban."

"Say Heitor," he said sharply, startling her.

"Heitor?" She frowned.

"Don't you know my real name?"

"Of course."

"Well, then, you can begin using it."

She would have asked why (he could see the question stir within the haze), but she was not bold enough.

For the first time her timidity annoyed him and he leaped up, his movement so abrupt that she drew back. "Tell me," he said, appealing to her suddenly, "did your mother ever speak about me? Or your grandmother? Did they ever talk about me as a young man? About Heitor?"

"Of course."

"What did they say I was like?"

She was silent for so long he repeated the question, his voice high and urgent. "What did they say?"

"I know they used to talk about how big a success you were . . ." she said hesitantly.

"As a young man, I said. Before I came to Rio. I was different then . . ."

"I know they used to talk, but I can't remember all that they said. I only know that when you were famous they always looked for your name in the papers."

He sat down on the edge of the cot, showing his disgust with her by a limp wave and feeling unreasonably that she had failed him. It was as if he had married her hoping that she would bring, like a dowry, the stories and memories of him as a young man, as Heitor, only to discover that he had been cheated.

"Heitor Guimares . . . Senhora Guimares," she was murmuring, touching herself and smiling abstractly.

"What are you laughing about? You don't like the name?"

"No, it's just that until I get used to it I will keep looking for someone else when I say it because I'm so used to you being Caliban."

It was not clear whether he hurled the cup at her or at the floor, but it missed her and, as it broke on the tiles, the sunlight scuttled from the room and the spilled coffee spread in a dark stain between them. "And who will you be looking for?" His shout was strident with the same abstract rage of the night before. "Who? Tell me. Some boy your age perhaps? Some tall, handsome boy, eh, some *Carioca* who will dance with you in the streets during carnival and jounce you on my bed behind my back? Is he the one you will be looking for?"

She said nothing. She had uttered a muted cry when the cup broke, but now, as he leaped up again, she calmly placed her hands over her swollen stomach, protecting it from the violence of his movement and, as he shouted, her fat child's fingers spread wider, deflecting the sound.

"Tell me!" he charged her. "Who is this person you will be looking for when you call my name?"

She remained as silent and resigned as the Virgin in their bedroom, her head bent in submission, her hands guarding the stomach.

Her silence was a defense he could not shake and as he stood there, menacing her with his shouts, he felt his anger rebound from the thick, invisible wall of silence which shielded her and flail him. He was the victim of his own rage, and bruised, beaten, he rushed from the room, from her, his heels clattering like small hoofs on the tile.

"Caliban!" He heard her cry over the sound of the motor as he started the car, and then a snatch of words as he drove off: "You have not changed your clothes."

He realized this when he was some distance from the house and had calmed a little. And the feel of the stale, sodden clothes recalled the time when he had first come to Rio and had had to wear secondhand clothes that were invariably too large for him and shiny from long wear and smelling always of the former owners. That had been the time, of course, when he had been only Heitor Guimares and people calling him by that name had not looked for anyone else, nor had he felt strange saying it. He tried to restore those years in his mind, but the memories were without form or coherence. They filtered down at random, blown like dust through his mind, and as he reached out to snatch them—desperate suddenly to recapture that time and that self—they eluded his fingers.

One memory paused though: he saw a street, the Rua Gloria, and the restaurant where he had worked until he had won the contest at the Teatro Municipal. The pattern of the tile floor over which he had swung the mop three times a day, the tables—slabs of cheap white marble upon which he had placed the food—were suddenly clear. He had left a part of himself there. Suddenly he brought his foot down on the accelerator, standing up and gripping the steering wheel to give himself leverage, and the big car bounded forward, bearing him to the city and the Rua Gloria.

As the car swept down the mountain roads, the sea appeared, vast and benign, mirroring the sky's paleness and breaking the sun's image into fragments, then the bays—sure, graceful curves, forming an arabesque design with the hills between—and finally the city itself—white, opulent, languorous under the sun's caress, taking its afternoon rest now in preparation for the night.

The Rua Gloria was in the old section of Rio and Caliban found it easily, recognizing the house on the corner with its Moorish-style balcony and checker-pane windows. The house was a ruin but somehow it promised that he would find the restaurant at the other end of the street. Parking the car, he started down, eager suddenly. Instinctively, as if the years had not passed, his legs made the slight adjustment to the sloping street and his feet sought out the old holes in the pavement; halfway down he passed the boys' school and his head turned automatically, expecting the boys in the yard to wave and shout, "*Ohlá,* Senhor Heitor, when are you going to stop growing?"

There were boys in the yard now, playing soccer in the eddying dust, and they looked no different from those he had known. But they did not wave, and, although they shouted and rushed out the gate when he passed, it was only because he was a stranger. They pointed to his mohair suit, his shoes with the raised heels, his rings dancing in the sunlight, whispering among themselves. And then one of them cried, "O Grande Caliban," and, with that abruptness which Caliban had perfected, dropped to a fighter's crouch. The others took up his cry and the name O Grande Caliban rose in a piercing chorale.

They trailed him, trumpeting the name, a scuffing retinue in their school uniforms. Caliban stiffened each time they tossed his name into the air like a football, but he welcomed them. They were a solid wall between him and the apprehensiveness which trailed him. Because of them he was certain that he would find the restaurant intact, like the setting of a play which had not been dismantled.

And it was there, but unrecognizable save for the glazed tiles in the entrance way which were all broken now and the stone doorsill in which the old groove had been worn deeper. Where the awning had been, a huge sign said BEBE COCA-COLA and below that, on the modern glass front, was the new name of the restaurant: O RESTAURANTE GRANDE CALIBAN.

The boys crowded behind him, pressing him inside, and he saw that the tile floor whose every imperfection he could have traced in the dark had been covered in bright linoleum; chrome chairs and tables had replaced the marble tables and wire-back chairs, while booths covered in simulated leather lined one wall. The air smelled of stale coffee and as Caliban, jarred by the sight of faded newspaper photographs of himself crowding the walls and a garish oil painting of him in the scarlet shirt hanging over the bar, placed his hand on a table to steady himself, a fly there stirred its wings but did not move.

The only occupant was a man—the waiter or owner perhaps—half-asleep at the bar, his stout haunches overlapping the stool. He stirred into wakefulness now with the same blind, stubborn movement as the fly. He was a *sarará* with an abundance of sandy hair curling out of the sweat-shirt he wore, fair skin pitted from smallpox and small, agate-colored eyes set within morose features. He turned, querulous with sleep, and missing Caliban, who was, after all, no taller than most of the boys, he shouted, "Get out of here, you little bandits, before you let in the flies."

"We come with Caliban," they hurled at him, "O Grande Caliban."

The man started suspiciously and peered, his head lowered as though he was about to charge, through the fog of sleep. As he spotted Caliban his agate-colored eyes glittered like one of Caliban's rings, and an awed smile groped its way around his mouth. "Senhor Caliban . . . ?" he whispered, and slipped from the stool into a bow so fluid and perfect it looked rehearsed.

"Senhor Caliban, it is a great honor . . ." With a proud wave he presented Caliban with the large portrait over the bar, the photographs, the chrome chairs and the linoleum. "Please . . ." He motioned him to a booth, then to a table.

Caliban would have turned and left if the boys had not been behind him, barring his way. He wanted to escape, for the restaurant had profaned his past with chrome and simulated leather, and the portrait, the faded photographs, his name on the window had effaced the Heitor Guimares who had wielded the mop over the tiles.

"Who put up those pictures?" he asked sharply.

The man's smile faltered and he said, puzzled, "I found them here when I bought the place, Senhor Caliban, all except the portrait. I did that. I am something of a painter—an artist like yourself, Senhor Caliban. I did it in your honor . . ." He gave the supple bow again.

"Who owned the place before you?"

"A man named DaCruz. He had many debts so I got it cheap . . ."

"Did he put them up?"

"No, I think it was his great-uncle, old Nacimento, the one, Senhor Caliban, who must have owned the restaurant when you worked here. Perhaps you've forgotten him?"

"Yes, I had forgotten," Caliban said, and paused, trying to summon Nacimento's face from the blurred assortment of faces in his mind. "Is he still alive?"

"He was the last time I heard, Senhor Caliban, but he is very sick because of course he is so old. And he has nothing now, I hear, and lives in the *favelas.*"

"Which one?"

"The one above Copacabana . . . Senhor Caliban, a *café Sinho* perhaps?"

But Caliban had already turned and with an abrupt wave scattered the boys out of his way.

"A *café Sinho,* at least!" The man shouted from the doorway over the heads of the boys, but Caliban, his small back slanted forward, was already rushing up the street, his patent-leather shoes flashing in the sunlight.

Later, as Caliban climbed the first slope leading to the *favela,* his shoes became covered with red dust and clay. He could see just above him the beginning of the slums—a vast, squalid rookery for the poor of Rio clinging to the hill above Copacabana, a nest of shacks built with the refuse of the city: the discarded crates and boxes, bits of galvanized iron and tin, old worm-eaten boards and shingles—and all of this piled in confused, listing tiers along the hillside, the wood bleached gray by the sun. The *favela* was another city above Rio which boldly tapped its electricity from below—so that at night the hills were strewn with lights—and repulsed the government's efforts to remove it. It was an affront—for that squalor rising above Rio implied that Rio herself was only a pretense; it was a threat—for it seemed that at any moment the *favela* would collapse and hurtle down, burying the city below.

Caliban had long ago ceased to see the *favelas.* He would glance up at the hills occasionally to watch them shift miraculously as the shadows moving across then shifted, but his eye passed quickly over the ugliness there: it was too much a reminder of what he had known. Now the *favela* claimed his eye. It seemed to rush down at him, bringing with it a sure and violent death—and he remembered the stories of strangers who had ventured into the *favelas* and had either disappeared or been found garroted the next day at the foot of the hill.

In pursuing the old man, it was as if, suddenly, he was pursuing his own death. And because he was exhausted, the thought of that death was almost pleasurable. He imagined the thronged cathedral, the crowds standing a thousand deep outside, the city hung in crape; he heard the priest intoning his name—and at the thought that perhaps no one would recognize the name Heitor Guimares, he stumbled and nearly fell.

The children of the *favela* appeared, slipping quietly down amid the scrub which lined the path, some of them balancing gallon tins of water on their heads or smaller children on their hips. They seemed born of the dust which covered them, like small, tough plants sprung from the worn soil, and their flat, incurious eyes seemed to mirror the defeated lives they had yet to live.

They watched him climb without comment, recognizing that he was a stranger from the city below who brought with him the trappings of that world: the flashing rings and stylish clothes. Their empty stares seemed to push him up the hill toward some final discovery.

Caliban could not look at them, and said, his eyes averted, "*Ohlá,* can any of you tell me where to find Nacimento, the old man?"

Their answer was a stolid silence and he called down the line, addressing each one in turn: "Do you know him? Which is his house? Do you know who

I'm talking about?" Finally he cried, his voice strained thin by the dust and his exertion, "Do you know him; he is an old friend!"

"His house is the one there," a boy said finally, pointing. "The one beside the tree without a head."

Caliban saw the tree, a dead palm without its headdress of fronds, starting out of the ground like a derisive finger, and then the house beside it, a makeshift of old boards and tin and dried fronds. It looked untenanted: Nacimento might have died and left the house as a monument. Caliban turned to the children, the fear dropping like a weight inside him.

"He's there," the boy said. "He doesn't like the sun."

And suddenly Caliban remembered Nacimento sending him to roll down the restaurant awning against the sun each afternoon. The warped door he pushed open now seemed to declare the age of the man inside and, as he entered the room, shutting out the glare behind him, it was as if the night was in hiding there, waiting for the sun to set before it rushed out and, charging down the hill, lay siege to the city.

"Nacimento . . ." he called softly. He could not see the old man but he heard his breathing—a thin *râle* like the fluting of an instrument Nacimento played to ease his loneliness. Presently Caliban made out a table because of a white cup there, then a cot whose legs had been painted white and finally the dark form of the old man.

He was seated before the boarded-up window, facing it as though it was open, and he was watching the sun arching down the sky or the children waiting around the dead palm for Caliban to emerge.

"Nacimento," Caliban said, and knew that the old man was blind. "Senhor Nacimento."

"Is there someone?" the old man asked uncertainly, as though he could no longer distinguish between those voices which probably filled his fantasies sitting there alone and those that were real. He did not turn from the window.

"Yes, it is Heitor Guimares."

"Who is the person?" the old man said formally, turning now.

"Heitor."

"Heitor?"

"Yes, from the restaurant years ago. You remember. He . . . I used to be the waiter . . ."

"Heitor . . ." the old man said slowly, as though searching for the face to which the name belonged.

Hopeful, Caliban drew closer. He could see Nacimento's eyes now, two yellow smears in the dimness which reflected nothing and the face wincing, it seemed, in unrelieved pain.

"Yes, Heitor," Caliban said coaxingly. "You used to call me Little Heitor from Minas. You remember . . ."

"I know no Heitor," the old man said sorrowfully, and then, starting apprehensively, he cried, "Is the door closed? The sun ruins everything."

Caliban's voice rose, tremulous and insistent. "But of course you remember. After all, every day you used to tell me the same thing—to close the door, to roll down the awning against the sun. It was I—Heitor Guimares—who would sometimes tell a few jokes at night to keep the customers drinking. But then, you must remember because it was you, after all, who made me enter the amateur contest at the Teatro Municipal. You even went with me that night and gave me a shirt to wear with ruffles down the front like a movie star. The Teatro Municipal!" he shouted as the old man shook his head confusedly. "We wept on each other's shoulder when they told me I had won and put me in the regular show with the name of Caliban . . ."

"O Grande Caliban," the old man said severely.

"Yes, but I was Heitor Guimares when I worked for you, not Caliban."

"O Grande Caliban. He was the best they ever had at the Teatro Municipal. I told him he would win and he was the best . . ."

"But I was Heitor then!"

"I know no Heitor," Nacimento cried piteously, and turned to the boarded-up window, reaching up as though he would open it and call for help. "I know no Heitor. . . ."

Caliban believed him. It was no use. The old man, he understood, going suddenly limp, had retained only a few things: his fear of the sun, the name O Grande Caliban, a moment of success in a crowded theater in which he had shared. That was all. The rest had been stripped away in preparation for his death which, in a way, had already begun. Caliban smelled its stench in the room suddenly and wanted to flee as he had fled the restaurant earlier. Groping toward the door, he jarred against the table and the cup there fell and brokc. The old man whimpered at the sound and Caliban remembered his wife's muted outcry that morning over the other cup he had broken. The day seemed to be closing in on him, squeezing his life from him, and his panic was like a stitch in his side as he rushed out, forgetting to close the door behind him.

The night might have escaped through the open door and followed him down the hill, for as he sat in his car, crumpled with exhaustion, knowing that his search had been futile and he could do nothing now but go to Miranda as he did each evening at this time, he saw the first of the dusk surge across the hill in a dark, purposeful wave, drowning out the *favela,* and then charge down the slopes, deepening into night as it came.

The city, in quick defense, turned on her lights, and as Caliban drove out of the tunnel onto the road which followed the wide arc of Copacabana Bay he saw the lights go on in the apartment buildings and hotels piled like white angular cliffs against the black hills. Seen from a distance those lighted windows resembled very large, fine diamonds, an iridescent amber now in the last of the sunlight, which would turn to a fiery yellow once the darkness settled. Rio—still warm from the sun, murmurous with the cadence of the sea, bejeweled with lights—was readying herself for the nightly carousal, waiting for the wind to summon her lovers.

Caliban had been one of her lovers, but as he drove through her midst, he felt her indifference to his confusion, to his sense of a loss which remained nameless; moreover, he suspected that she had even been indifferent to his success. "After all Rio has made you," Henriques had said, but he had not added that she would quickly choose another jester to her court once he was gone. Caliban hated the city suddenly—and as that hate became unbearable he shifted its weight onto Miranda. He accused her. Hadn't Henriques said that she and Rio were the same? He brought his foot down on the accelerator and the car leaped forward like a startled horse, leaving black streaks on the road.

Oddly enough, Miranda's apartment, in a new building at the end of Copacabana, reflected in the city. The great squares of black and white tile in the foyer suggested not only the stark white buildings reared against the dark hills and the sidewalks of Copacabana—a painstaking mosaic of small black and white stones, but the faces of the *Cariocas* themselves—endless combinations of black and white. The green rug in the living room could have been a swatch cut from one of the hills, while the other furnishings there—elaborate period pieces of an ivory finish, marble tables cluttered with figurines, sofas of pale silk and down, white drapes and gilt-edged mirrors—repeated the opulence, self-indulgence, the lavish whiteness of the city. And the chandeliers with their fiery crystal spears, which rustled like frosted leaves as Caliban slammed the door, caught the brilliance of Rio at night.

For the first time Caliban was aware of how the room expressed the city, and of himself, reflected in one of the mirrors, in relation to it. He was like a house pet, a tiny dog, who lent the room an amusing touch but had no real place there. The pale walls and ivory furniture, the abundance of white throughout stripped him of importance, denied him all significance. He felt like whimpering as the old man, Nacimento, had whimpered when the cup broke—and he must have unknowingly, for Miranda suddenly called from the adjoining bedroom, "What in the hell are you muttering to yourself about out there?"

He turned and through the half-opened door saw her enthroned amid a tumble of pink satin cushions on the circular bed he had bought her, while her maid massaged her feet in a basin of scented water—the girl's black hands wavering out of shape under the water. Miranda had already dressed her hair for the night club—the stiff froth of blond curls piled high above her white brow—and applied her make-up (she had spent the afternoon at it, Caliban knew), but her body beneath the sheer pink dressing gown was still bare, the tops of the breasts a darker pink than the gown. Knowing how slack those breasts had become, Caliban felt repelled, weary and then angry again; he understood suddenly that her refusal ever to leave him and marry, to have children and use those ample breasts, was, simply, her desire to remain the child herself—willful, dependent, indulged—and that she had used him to this end, just as she would use someone else now that she had exhausted him.

As always when he was truly angry, he became calm, and in that calm he could always feel his nerves, the muscles of his abrupt little arms and legs, his heart, quietly marshaling their force for the inevitable outburst. He came and stood in the doorway, very still, the only exterior signs of his anger a tightness around his mouth, a slight tension to his wide nose and a chill light within his even gaze.

Without looking up from polishing her nails, Miranda said querulously, "You come in late slamming my doors and then you stand outside talking to yourself. Where have you been all day anyway? People have been calling here looking for you after they called your house and that stupid child you married said she didn't know where you had gone."

She glanced up, still sullen and truculent from their quarrel the night before—and stiffened. Her maid felt her foot go taut and turned, puzzled.

"Go home, Luiz," he said quietly.

Miranda screamed, the sound jarring the bottle of nail polish from her hand and it spilled, staining the pink covers red. "No, Luiz . . ." She reached toward the girl. "Wait, Luiz . . ."

"Go home, Luiz," he repeated.

The girl stood up then as though jerked to her feet and, holding the basin of water, looked from him to Miranda for a single distraught moment and then broke for the door, the water sloshing on the rug. As she passed him, Caliban said gently, "Good night, Luiz," and closed the door behind her.

"Luiz!"

Caliban came and sat across the bed from her and deliberately placed his trouser leg with the red dust and clay from the *favela* against the pink coverlet.

Miranda stared at the leg, her gray eyes dull with hysteria and disbelief, at the nail polish streaked like fresh blood on the bedclothes and her hands, at the trail of water the maid had left on the rug and then across to the closed door. Her skin blanched with terror and her scream convulsed the air again, higher this time, so that the chandelier over her bed swayed anxiously. And still screaming, cursing incoherently, she frantically began drawing up the sheet around her.

"Tell me," Caliban said evenly, "do you know a Heitor Guimares?"

She did not hear him at first and he waited until her scream broke off and then repeated in the same quiet tone, "I asked you if you know somebody named Heitor Guimares?"

"Who?" The word was uttered at the same high pitch as her scream.

"Heitor Guimares."

"Heitor who . . . ? Guimares. No. Who is that? I don't know anybody by that name. Guimares . . . ?" Wary, suspicious, she said after a pause, "Why do you ask?" and then emboldened by his silence, shouted, "What is this? Why do you come asking me about someone I don't know? Who's this Heitor

Guimares anyway? Why do you come in here looking as if you slept in the sewers and muttering to yourself, scaring me, scaring my maid, slamming my doors and ruining my bed with your dirt? Oh, God, what's wrong now? It's going to be hell tonight. You'll do everything wrong in the show and blame me. You're old!" she screamed, and started up in the bed. "And losing your mind. You should retire. Go back to Minas, peasant . . . And that little bitch, she's fired. I won't pay her a cent for ruining the rug. Everything ruined . . ." she said tragically, and paused, looking tearfully down at the spilled nail polish on her hands, quiet for the moment, and then her head snapped up. "Who is this Heitor Guimares now? I lie here alone all day, all night, alone, always alone, and then you come in here accusing me of someone I don't know. Bastard! Suppose I did know someone by that name. It would be my business. You don't own me. I'm not your scared little mamita. Heitor Guimares! Who is he? Somebody has been feeding you lies."

"I am Heitor Guimares."

She stared at him, the rest of what she had to say lying dead on her lips and the wildness still in her eyes. Then her bewilderment collapsed into a laugh that was as shrill, in relief, as her scream had been. The sheet she was holding around her dropped and her arm shot out, stiff with scorn. "You? No, senhor, you are Caliban. O Grande Caliban!" And leaping from the bed, her great breasts swinging, she dropped to his familiar fighter's crouch, her fists cocked menacingly and her smile confirming what the others—his wife that morning, the boys on the Rua Gloria chanting behind him, the man in the restaurant that had been made into a shrine, and, finally, the old man, Nacimento—had all insisted was true, and what he, and certainly Miranda, had really known all along: simply, that Caliban had become his only reality and anything else he might have been was lost. The image Miranda had created for him was all he had now and once that was taken—as it would be tomorrow when the signs announcing his retirement went up—he would be left without a self.

Miranda did not see him pick up the small boudoir chair, for her head was lowered over her fists and she was doing the little shuffling fighter's dance he had made famous. But as the chair cut the air above her, her head snapped up, her hand started up and she watched its flight with the mocking smile her shock and stupefaction had fixed on her face. She tried to move but could not. It was too late anyway; the chair smashed into the low-hanging chandelier and brought it down in a roar of shattered crystal onto the bed—and in the light from the small lamps along the walls the bed seemed to explode in a thick, mushrooming cloud of pink dust.

Caliban's destruction of the apartment was swift and complete. It was as if the illusion of strength he had created on stage for so long had been finally given to him. While Miranda stood transfixed, a dazed horror spreading like a patina over her face (and she was never to lose that expression), he hauled down drapes and curtains, overturned furniture, scattered drawers and their frivolous contents across the floor, broke the figurines against the white walls, smashed the mirrors and his reflection there—and then, with a jagged piece of glass, slashed open the silk sofas and chairs so that the down drifted up over the wreckage like small kites. Finally, wielding a heavy curtain rod as if it were a lance, he climbed onto a marble table and swung repeatedly at the large chandelier in the living room, sending the glass pendants winging over the room. With each blow he felt the confusion and despair congested within him fall away, leaving an emptiness which, he knew, would remain with him until he died. He wanted to sleep suddenly, beside his wife, in the room with the Madonna.

A glass spear struck Miranda, who had staggered, weeping and impotent, to the door, and she shrieked. Her outcry was the sound of the trumpet the night before, a high, whinnying note that reached beyond all sound into a kind of silence. The scream broke her paralysis and she rushed at him with a powerful animal grace, the gown flaring open around her bare body, and reaching up caught the rod.

He let it go, but from his high place he leaned down and struck her with his small fist on her head, and the hair cascaded down like a curtain over her stunned face.

He was at the elevator, the automatic door sliding open in front of him, when he heard her frightened, tearful voice calling him down the hall. "Caliban! Caliban! Where are you going? The show! Are you crazy—what about the show tonight? Oh, Mary, full of grace, look what the bastard's done. The place! He's killed me inside. Oh, God, where is he going? Crazy bastard, come back here. What did I do? Was it me, Caliban? Caliban, *meu negrinho,* was it me . . . ?"

RICHARD RIVE (b. 1931)

Richard Rive has become an important figure in African literature, not only for his own excellent short stories in the collection African Songs *(1963) and his novel* Emergency *(1964), but also for his anthologies of the works of African writers:* Quartet *(1963) and* Modern African Prose *(1964). Born and educated in Cape Town, South Africa, where he for a time taught high school English and Latin, he received a Farfield Foundation Fellowship in 1962 which enabled him to travel widely throughout Africa and Europe—lecturing, teaching, broadcasting, and studying contemporary African literature.*

In "Resurrection," Rive depicts the mixed community in South Africa where fairer children force their darker-skinned mother and sister to stay in the kitchen and to use the back door.

Resurrection

THE PEOPLE SANG. And one by one the voices joined in and the volume rose. Tremulously at first, thin and tenuous, and then swelling till it filled the tiny dining room, pulsated into the two bedrooms, stacked high with hats and overcoats, and spent itself in the kitchen where fussy housewives, dressed in black, were making wreaths.

"Jesu lover of my soul,
Let me to Thy bo-som fly . . ."

A blubbery woman in the corner nearest the cheap, highly polished chest of drawers wept hysterically. Above her head hung a cheap reproduction of a Karroo scene. A dazzling white-gabled farmhouse baking in the hot African sun, in the distance kopjes shimmering against a hazy blue sky. Her bosom heaved and her lips quivered as she refused to be placated. Her tears proved infectious and handkerchiefs were convulsively sought.

"Hide me, O my Saviour, hide,
Till the storm of life is past;
Safe into the haven guide . . ."

sang a small boy in a freshly laundered Eton collar who shared a stiff Ancient and Modern Hymnbook with his mother. His voice was wiry and weak and completely dominated by the strong soprano next to him. All the people joined in and sang. Except Mavis. Only Mavis sat silent, glossy-eyed, staring down at her rough though delicately shaped brown hands. Her eyes hot and red, but tearless, with a slightly contemptuous sneer around the closed, cruel mouth. Only Mavis sat silent. Staring at her hands and noticing that the left thumbnail was scarred and broken. She refused to raise her eyes, refused to look at the coffin, at the hymnbook open and neglected on her lap. Her mouth was tightly shut, as if determined not to open, not to say a word. Tensely she sat and stared at her broken fingernail. The room did not exist. The fat woman blubbered unnoticed. The people sang but Mavis heard nothing.

"Other refuge have I none,
Hangs my helpless soul on Thee . . ."

they began the second verse. The fat woman had sufficiently recovered to attempt to add a tremulous contralto. The boy in the Eton collar laboriously followed the line with his finger. Mavis vaguely recognized Rosie as she fussily hurried in with a tray of fresh flowers, passed a brief word with an overdressed woman nearest the door, and busily hurried out again. Mavis sensed things happening but saw without seeing and felt without feeling. Nothing registered, but she could feel the Old Woman's presence, could feel the room becoming her dead mother, becoming full of Ma, crowded with Ma, swirling with Ma. Ma of the gnarled hands and frightened eyes. Those eyes that had asked questioningly, "Mavis, why do they treat me so? Please Mavis, why do they treat me so?"

And Mavis had known the answer and had felt the anger well up inside her, till her mouth felt hot and raw. And she had spat out at the Old Woman, "Because you're colored! You're colored, Ma, but you gave birth to white children. It's your fault, Ma, all your fault. . . . You gave birth to white children. White children, Ma. White Children!"

Mavis felt dimly aware that the room was overcrowded, overbearingly overcrowded. Hot, stuffy, crammed, overflowing. And, of course, Ma. Squeezed in. Occupying a tiny place in the center. Right in the center. Pride of place in a coffin of pinewood that bore the economical legend:

Maria Loupser
1889–1961
R.I.P.

Rest in peace. With people crowding around and sharing seats and filling the doorway. And Ma had been that Maria Loupser who must now rest in peace. Maria Loupser. Maria Wilhelmina Loupser. Mavis looked up quickly to see if the plaque was really there, then automatically shifted her gaze to her broken nail. No one noticed her self-absorption, and the singing continued uninterruptedly.

"Other refuge have I none,
Hangs my helpless soul on Thee . . ."

Flowers. Hot, oppressive smell of flowers. Flowers, death, and the people singing. A florid red-faced man in the doorway singing so that his veins stood out purple against the temples. People bustling in and out. Fussily. Coming to have a look at Ma. A last look at Ma. To put a flower in the coffin for Ma. Then opening hymnbooks and singing a dirge for Ma. Poor deceived Ma of the tragic eyes and twisted hands who had given birth to white children, and Mavis. Now they raised their voices and sang for Ma.

"Leave, ah, leave me not alone,
Still support and comfort me! . . ."

And it had been only a month earlier when Mavis had looked into those bewildered eyes.

"Mavis, why do they treat me so?"

And Mavis had become angry so that her saliva had turned hot in her mouth.

"Please Mavis, why do they treat me so?"

And then she had driven the words into the Old Woman with a skewer.

"Because you are old and black, and your children want you out of the way."

And yet what Mavis had wanted to add was, "They want me out of the way too, Ma, because you made me black like you. I am also your child, Ma. I belong to you. They want me also to stay in the kitchen and use the back door. We must not be seen, Ma, their friends must not see us. We embarrass them, Ma, so they hate us. They hate us because we're black. You and I, Ma."

But she had not said so, and had only stared cruelly into the eyes of the Old Woman. Eyes that did not understand. Eyes already dying. And she had continued to torture the Old Woman.

"You're no longer useful, Ma. You're a nuisance, a bloody nuisance, a bloody black nuisance. You might come out of your kitchen and shock the white scum they bring here. You're a bloody nuisance, Ma!"

But still the Old Woman could not understand, and looked helplessly at Mavis.

"But I don't want to go in the dining room. It's true, Mavis, I don't want to go in the dining room."

And as she spoke tears flooded her eyes and she whimpered like a child who had lost a toy.

"It's my dining room, Mavis, it's true. It's my dining room."

And Mavis had felt such a dark and hideous pleasure overwhelming her that she had screamed hysterically at the Old Woman.

"You're black and your bloody children's white. Jim and Rosie and Sonny are white, white, white! And you made me. You made me black!"

Then Mavis had broken down exhausted at her self-revealing and had cried like a baby.

"Ma, why did you make me black?"

And then only had a vague understanding strayed into those milky eyes, and Ma had taken her youngest into her arms and rocked and soothed her. And crooned to her in a cracked, broken voice the songs she had sung years before she had come to Cape Town.

"Slaap my kindjie slaap sag,
Onder engele vannag. . . ."

And the voice of the Old Woman had become stronger and more perceptive as her dull eyes saw her childhood, and the stream running through Wolfgat, and the broken-down church, and the moon rising in the direction of Solitaire.

And Ma had understood and rocked Mavis in her arms like years before. And now Ma was back in the dining room as shadows crept across the wall.

"Abide with me! Fast falls the eventide. . . ."

Shadows creeping across the room. Shadows gray and deep. As deep as Ma's ignorance.

"The darkness deepens: Lord, with me abide. . . ."

Shadows filtering through the drawn blind. Rosie tight-lipped and officious. Sonny. Jim, who had left his white wife at home. Pointedly ignoring Mavis, speaking in hushed tones to the florid man in the doorway. Mavis a small inconspicuous brown figure in the corner. The only other brown face in the crowded dining room besides Ma. Even the Old Woman was paler in death. Ma's friends in the kitchen. A huddled, frightened group around the stove.

"Mavis, why do they tell my friends not to visit me?"

And Mavis had shrugged her shoulders indifferently.

"Please, Mavis, why do they tell my friends not to visit me?"

And Mavis had turned on her.

"Do you want Soufie with her black skin to sit in the dining room? Or Ou-Kaar with his kroeskop? Or Eva or Leuntjie? Do you? Do you want Sonny's wife to see them? Or the white dirt Rosie picks up? Do you want to shame your children? Humiliate them? Expose their black blood?"

And the Old Woman had blubbered. "I only want my friends to visit. They can sit in the kitchen."

And Mavis had sighed helplessly at the simplicity of the doddering Old Woman and had felt like saying, "And what of my friends, my colored friends? Must they also sit in the kitchen?"

And tears had shot into those milky eyes and the mother had looked even older.

"Mavis, I want my friends to visit me, even if they sit in the kitchen. Please, Mavis, they're all I got."

And now Ma's friends sat in the kitchen, a cowering timid group around the fire, speaking the raw guttural Afrikaans of the Caledon District. They spoke of Ma and their childhood together. Ou-Kaar and Leuntjie and Eva and Ma. Of the Caledon District, cut off from bustling Cape Town. Where the Moravian mission church was crumbling, and the sweet water ran past Wolfgat, and past Karwyderskraal, and lost itself near Grootkop. And the moon rose rich and yellow from the hills behind Solitaire. And now they sat frightened and huddled around the stove, speaking of Ma. Tant Soufie in a new kopdoek, and Ou-Kaar conspicuous in borrowed yellow shoes, sizes too small. And Leuntjie and Eva.

And in the dining room sat Dadda's relations, singing. Dadda's friends who had ignored Ma while she had lived. Dadda's white friends and relations, and a gloss-eyed Mavis, a Mavis who scratched meaninglessly at her broken thumbnail. And now the singing rose in volume as still more people filed in.

"When other helpers fail, and comforts flee,
Help of the helpless, O abide with me! . . ."

they sang to the dead woman.

Mavis could have helped Ma, could have given the understanding she needed, could have protected Ma, could have tried to stop the petty tyranny. But she had never tried to reason with them. Rosie, Sonny, and Jim. She had never pleaded with them, explained to them that the Old Woman was dying. Her own soul ate her up. Gnawed her inside. She was afraid of their reactions lest they should notice her. Preferred to play a shadow, seen but never heard. A vague entity, part of the furniture. If only they could somehow be aware of her emotions. The feelings bottled up inside her, the bubbling volcano below. She was afraid they might openly say, "Why don't you both clear out and leave us in peace, you bloody black bastards!" She could then have cleared out, should then have cleared out, sought a room in Woodstock or Salt River and have forgotten her frustration. But there was Ma. There was the Old Woman. Mavis had never spoken to them, but had vented her spleen on her helpless mother.

"You sent them to a white school. You were proud of your white brats and hated me, didn't you?"

And the mother had stared with oxlike dumbness.

"You encouraged them to bring their friends to the house, to your house, and told me to stay in the kitchen. And you had a black skin yourself. You hated me, Ma, hated me! And now they've pushed you also in the kitchen. There's no one to blame but you. You're the cause of all this."

And she had tormented the Old Woman, who did not retaliate. Who could not retaliate. Who could not understand. Now she sat tortured with memories as they sang hymns for Ma.

The room assumed a sepulchral appearance. Shadows deepened, gray, then darker. Tears, flowers, handkerchiefs, and dominating everything, the simple, bewildered eyes of Ma. Bewildered even in death. So that Mavis had covered them with two pennies, that others might not see.

"I need Thy presence every passing hour. . . ."

sang Dadda's eldest brother, who sat with eyes tightly shut near the head of the coffin. He had bitterly resented Dadda's marriage to a colored woman. Living in sin! A Loupser married to a Hottentot! He had boasted of his refusal to greet Ma socially while she lived, and he attended the funeral only because his brother's wife had died. This was the second time he had been in the dining room. The first time was Dadda's funeral. And now this. A colored girl—his niece, he believed—sitting completely out of place and saying nothing . . . annoying, most annoying.

"What but Thy Grace can foil the tempter's power . . ."

sang the boy in the Eton collar, whose mother had not quite recovered from the shock that Mr. Loupser had had a colored wife. All sang except Mavis, torturing herself with memories.

"I am going to die, Mavis," those milky eyes had told her a week before, "I think I am going to die."

"Ask your white brats to bury you. You slaved for them."

"They are my children but they do not treat me right."

"Do you know why? Shall I tell you why?" And she had driven home every word with an ugly ferocity. "Because they're ashamed of you. Afraid of you, afraid the world might know of their colored mother!"

"But I did my best for them!"

"You did more than your best, you encouraged them, but you were ashamed of me, weren't you? So now we share a room at the back where we can't be seen. And you are going to die, and your white children will thank God that you're out of the way."

"They are your brothers and sisters, Mavis."

"What's that you're saying?" Mavis gasped, amazed at the hypocrisy. "What's that? I hate them and I hate you! I hate you!"

And the Old Woman had whimpered, "But you are my children, you are all my children. Please, Mavis, don't let me die so?"

"You will die in the back room and be buried from the kitchen!"

"It's a sin, Mavis, it's a sin!"

But they had not buried her from the kitchen. They had removed the table from the dining room and borrowed chairs from the neighbors. And now, while they waited for the priest from Dadda's church, they sang hymns.

> *"Heaven's morning breaks, and earth's vain shadows*
> *flee: . . ."*

sang the boy in the Eton collar.

> *"In life and death, O Lord, abide with me! . . ."*

the florid man sang loudly, to end the verse. There was an expectant bustle at the door, and then the priest from Dadda's church, St. John the Divine, appeared. All now crowded into the dining room, those who were making wreaths, and Tant Soufie holding Ou-Kaar's trembling hand.

"Please, Mavis, ask Father Josephs at the mission to bury me."

"Ask your brats to fetch him themselves. See them ask a black man to bury you!"

"Please, Mavis, see that Father Josephs buries me!"

"It's not my business, you fool! You did nothing for me!"

"I am your mother, my girl," the Old Woman had sobbed, "I raised you."

"Yes, you raised me, and you taught me my place! You took me to the mission with you, because we were too black to go to St. John's. Let them see Father Josephs for a change. Let them enter our mission and see our God."

And Ma had not understood but whimpered, "Please, Mavis, let Father Josephs bury me."

So now the priest from Dadda's church stood at the head of her coffin, sharp and thin, clutching his cassock with his left hand, while his right held an open prayer book.

"I said I will take heed to my ways: that I offend not in my tongue. I will keep my mouth as it were with a bridle: while the ungodly is in my sight."

Mavis felt the cruel irony of the words.

"I held my tongue and spake nothing. I kept silent, yea even from good words but it was pain and grief to me. . . ."

The fat lady stroked her son's head and sniffed loudly.

"My heart was hot within me, and while I was thus musing the fire kindled, and at the last I spake with my tongue . . ."

Mavis now stared entranced at her broken fingernail. The words seared, and filling, dominated the room.

It was true. Rosie had consulted her about going to the mission and asking for Father Josephs, but she had turned on her heel without a word and walked out into the streets, and walked and walked. Through the cobbled streets of older Cape Town, up beyond the mosque in the Malay quarter on the slopes of Signal Hill. Thinking of the dead woman in the room.

A mother married to a white man and dying in a back room. Walking the streets, the Old Woman with her, followed by the Old Woman's eyes. Eating out her soul. Let them go to the mission and see our God. Meet Father Josephs. But they had gone for Dadda's priest, who now prayed at the coffin of a broken colored woman. And the back room was empty.

"I heard a voice from heaven, Saying unto me, Write, From henceforth blessed are the dead which die in the Lord; even so saith the Spirit; for they rest from their labors. . . ."

"Lord, take Thy servant, Maria Wilhelmina Loupser, into Thy eternal care. Grant her Thy eternal peace and understanding. Thou are our refuge and our rock. Look kindly upon her children who even in this time of trial and suffering look up to Thee for solace. Send Thy eternal blessing upon them, for they have heeded Thy commandment which is 'Honour thy father and thy mother, that thy days may be long. . . .' "

Mavis felt hot, strangely, unbearably hot. Her saliva turned to white heat in her mouth and her head rolled drunkenly. The room was filled with her mother's presence, her mother's eyes, body, soul. Flowing into her, filling every pore, becoming one with her, becoming a living condemnation.

"Misbelievers!" she screeched hoarsely. "Liars! You killed me! You murdered me! Hypocrites! Don't you know your God!"

THOMAS WILLIAMS (b. 1926)

In response to our invitation to discuss his life and work with his readers, Thomas Williams has replied as follows:

"Born 1926 in Duluth, Minnesota. Lived in Minnesota, New York City, went to New Hampshire when I was 14, and have used this state as a base, more or less, ever since. U. S. Army, 1944–46. I've attended the Universities of Chicago, New Hampshire, Iowa and Paris. An M.A. from New Hampshire in 1958, and I've been teaching here ever since, now a professor of English, teaching writing and a contemporary genre course, sometimes short stories, sometimes novels. Married (20 years, no less), two children. My wife and I built this cabin I write from now, out of stone and logs from our own land, with hand tools, and we are still building it 16 years later, so it grows much bigger and dramatic than the prosaic house we live in in the winter. We are isolated here; the road in looks more like a cliff of granite than a road.

"My books are Ceremony of Love *(1955),* Town Burning *(1959),* The Night of Trees *(1961),* Whipple's Castle *(1969), all novels, and a collection of short stories,* A High New House *(1963). In progress is a novel,* The Hair of Harold Roux. *Short stories have been in* Esquire, The New Yorker, Saturday Evening Post; *poetry in the little magazines; articles, columns and essays in* Esquire. *I've also done a few reviews but I don't like them and don't do them any more except in odd circumstances.*

"I don't know what to say about 'Goose Pond.' I've certainly thought about it enough. It was my first published short story, and though I like others as well or better, it does seem the most durable in terms of publication. It has been included in several collections and anthologies. And I've even taught it—so I should know something about it, anyway.

"I wrote it in Iowa, among the alien corn, missing my cabin and my New Hampshire mountains. I think that might account for some of the intensity of the nature details. Nostalgia can be a powerful thing. And of course death is always with us. We cause it and we suffer it and see our friends suffer it. I cause it because I'm a hunter, though a very ambivalent one, and I love what I kill, if that is possible to understand. Is the story one in which hunting is used to illustrate life and death, or is death used to say something about the depth-perceiving, hunting animals that we are, whether we like it or not? I think maybe both. The idea for the story (not its 'theme,' or 'meaning,' or anything like that) came to me in the form of the man, just having suffered helplessly while his wife died, cleaning the beautiful body of the deer. This seemed to me so paradoxically right, wrong, horrifying and perfectly logical that I had to write the story to find out why."

Goose Pond

ROBERT HURLEY's wife died in September, and by the middle of October he had more or less settled everything. His son and daughter were both married and lived far away from New York; his son in Los Angeles, his daughter in Toledo. They came East for the funeral and each wanted him to come and visit. "I'm not about to retire. I won't be an old man in a guest room," he told them, knowing the great difference between the man he looked at fifty-eight and the man he felt himself to be. It had taken Mary six months to die, and during the last few of those months he began quietly to assume many of her symptoms. The doctors noticed it and understood, but his children, accustomed to a father who had always been to them a common-sense, rather unimaginative figure, were shocked by his loss of weight, by a listlessness as unlike him, as unsettling to them as if the earth's rotation had begun to slow down.

But he would do no visiting, even though his business did not need him. "I know what visiting is," he wrote to his son. "I don't do it very well. Please don't call so much. You know how to write letters." "Daddy," his daughter said, long distance. "The children are crazy to have their grandfather come and see them."

And he thought, there is one place I would like to go, and there are no children I know there: "I'm going to New Hampshire, to Leah."

"All by yourself? What for?" She began to get excited, almost hysterical. He could see her biting her lower lip—a habit of her mother's. Afterwards she would be calling Charles in Los Angeles.

"I was born there. Your mother and I lived there before you were born. Do I need any other reason? It's October. Anyway, I'll be back in a couple of weeks."

"But, Daddy, we felt that you shouldn't be alone. . . ."

"I haven't been alone for thirty years," he said. "I want to try it again. Now go back to whatever you were doing. I can hear a baby crying in your house. Go take care of it. I'm going to stay with the Pedersens. Do you remember the old people in the big house on the mountain? If they still take boarders, that's where I'll be." *If they're still alive,* he thought. He wanted to walk in the woods again, but he had other reasons. The sight of his grandchildren, the hundred times a day when their small disasters caused screaming, tears; he couldn't stand it. They were always about to hurt themselves, they nearly fell so many times. They had so many deadly years to make. Automobiles, knives, leukemia, fire. . . . On the afternoon of the funeral he had watched his granddaughter, Ann, and suddenly he saw her having his wife's senseless pain, saw her crying not because of a bumped knee, but at more serious wounds. And the Pedersens? They were so old, they had somehow escaped, and as he remembered them they lived dried-up and careful, in a kind of limbo. He would go to the Pedersens, on Cascom Mountain.

Nana fussed with the Edison lamp, turning the white flame up in the mantle, moving the broad base across the crack made by the table leaf; then with the side of her hand she wiped the shiny surface of the table where it had been. The light shone past the tinted shade, up the glass chimney and sharpened her old face, made her glasses glint for a second until she moved away, tall and always busy, her small eyes always alert. She rarely sat down, and even then seemed poised, ready for busy duty. The old man settled himself cautiously, as he did now, one piece at a time. Nana had his zither out of its case, the light just right, made sure he had his hearing aid, his pick, an ash tray near. In spite of his age, he smoked cigarettes.

Back in the shadows, between a lacy, drooping vine and the narrow window, Nana's older sister, blue dress and high black shoes, composed and fragile face, sat in a rocker and never spoke. Nana herself was seventy-nine. For forty years she had bossed the seven-mile trek down to Leah in the late fall, back up the mountain again to this high old house in the spring. It was Nana who dealt with the world, who shut the windows when it rained, herded great-grandchildren when the family came in the summer, locked the house for the winter. In a few weeks they would be going down to their small apartment in Leah, to take their chances on another winter.

The old man tuned his zither, humming in a dry, crackly falsetto and turning his wrench as he picked the short strings. Tuned against the windy old voice, the crisp notes of the zither were startling, clear and metallic. There seemed to be no connection between the voice and the sounds of the strings, as if the old man heard other notes, the sounds of memory to check his instrument against.

"German *concert* zither," Nana said proudly, still hovering over the lamp. She rearranged his cigarettes, the coffee cup. She spoke from behind him, "He don't hear so good," nodding vigorously. "But he got the hearing aid." She pointed into his ear, where the pink button shone like a flower against brown freckles. "He don't wear it all the time, like he should." She moved quickly away on some sudden errand, and the old man looked up and winked at Hurley.

"Sometimes it makes too much noise," he said, smiling benevolently at his wife. She began to move the table. "It's all right. It's all right!" he said. In his fifty years in America he had mastered the sounds of English, but the rhythms of his speech were Scandinavian. "I'm going to play first a Norwegian song."

Nana poised herself upon a chair, folded her hands firmly, set herself for a moment and then began energetically to smooth her apron down her long thighs. The old lady against the wall stopped rocking. It always startled Hurley when, out of her silent effacement, she responded.

The old man bent over his zither, his shiny face as ruddy as a baby's. His mottled, angular fingers worked over the strings; he swayed back and forth to keep time and snorted, gave little gasps and grunts he evidently did not hear himself, in time with the music. Beneath, occasionally overcoming the sibilant, involuntary breaths, the music was poignantly clear, ordered, cascading, vivid as little knives in the shadowy room. At the end they all applauded, and the old man bowed, very pleased.

That night Hurley climbed the staircase that angled around the central chimney, an oil lamp to light his way, and entered his cold room in moonlight almost as bright as the lamp, but colder, whiter against the lamp's yellow. Two little windows looked down across the old man's garden—"Mostly for the deer," the old man had said of it—then over the one still-mown pasture left to the farm, down the long hills silvery in moonlight to Lake Cascom in the valley, white among black surrounding spruce. Behind, on the other side of the house, he could feel the dark presence of Cascom Mountain.

He wondered if it would be a night for sleep. He was tired enough. In the last few days he had taken many of the familiar trails, especially following those that he remembered led through hardwood. Although the leaves had turned and mostly fallen, here or there one tree flamed late among the bare ones, catching light and casting it in all directions as if it were an orange or soft red sun. He stopped often in the woods, surprised by each molten maple branch, even the smallest bright veins of each leaf golden and precious against a gnarled black trunk or the green twilight of a spruce grove. He walked carefully, resting often, sampling the few cold, sweet apples from the abandoned mountain trees, eating Nana's sandwiches a little at a time. He wanted the day to last as long as possible. At night he thought of his wife.

The high, sloping bed was wide and lonesome as a field of snow. During his wife's illness he could not sleep in their own bed, but slept every night on a studio couch where he could reach the sides, holding himself down, remember exactly where he was and why she was not beside him. If he woke in the night and for a second forgot, he had to learn over again from the beginning that Mary was going to die. It was always the first time over again, when they had left the doctor (the poor doctor, according to Mary) at the cancer hospital and walked together to Grant's Tomb. Mary finally said, "You know? They should pay a man a thousand dollars a minute for having to say those words."

Then the inevitable sequence of hours came through his mind, one after the other, until the afternoon when she was not so brave any more and shook her head back and forth as if to throw off the plastic tube that went into her nose and down, jiggling the clamps and the bottle on its hanger. Tears rolled from the outside corners of her drowned eyes and she cried pettishly, "Help me, help me."

She had taken pain better than most, was better at taking it by far than her husband or her children. When she had the compound fracture of her wrist she had been the calm one, the strong one. And he thought, *My God, how much pain she must have if she is caused to do this—if it is Mary who is caused to do this. . . .*

As they cut nerves, cutting off pain in little bits and pieces, it was as if they cut off her life, too, by shreds—the pain, the possibility of it forever gone; the life forever gone. But new pain took the place of the old. She lived for six months and died almost weightless, ageless, the little lines and wrinkles of her familiar body smoothed as if by a filling pulp. Her arms turned to thin tubes, her forehead waxed as taut, as translucent as a yellow apple. Her eyes, before the final cutting, watched him, blameful as a beaten child's. She whined for help: "What is happening to me?" And being a man only, he could stand, and stand, and stand, helpless at the foot of her crank-operated bed, the simple handle drawing his eyes, mocking, it seemed to him, telling him to crank, to grasp the handle in his strong hands and crank, sweat at it, crank faster and harder, crank until she is well again.

He turned and his hand touched the firm, virginal pillow next to his. The linen smelled country new, of washdays and clotheslines.

At midnight he heard what he first supposed to be a hundred dogs barking in the distance, and as the barking changed on the wind he suddenly knew, in exactly the same way he had known in his childhood that it was the Canada geese flying over, low here because of the height of the land, streaming over in the darkness. *Lorlorn, lorlorn, lorlorn,* the geese called to each other as they passed. He ran to the window—remembering an old excitement, feet numb on the cold boards—but the geese did not cross the moon. He remembered them well enough that way: the long wavering files of geese, necks thrust out straight, dark wings arching tirelessly on their long journey over the guns, through all the deadly traps set for them—the weather, the ice, the hunting animals and the traitor decoys. Each one its own warm life deep in the cold sky, and they called to each other, kept close and on course together, facing with disciplined bravery that impossible journey.

He came awake in the indeterminate time when night was breaking and the small windows were luminous squares upon the wall. He lay on his back and watched the light grow, the corners arrange themselves and the moldings darken, wondering at a curved shape above the closet door. As the morning increased (he heard pans banging down in the kitchen, Nana's sharp morning voice) he finally saw that the curved shape was a bow hung on pegs. This room evidently had been a young boy's during the summer: a huge fungus platter hung between the windows and in the back of the closet he had found a fly rod enmeshed in kinky leader. Nana had missed a trout hook crusted with dried worm, stuck high on a curtain.

Before he went downstairs he remembered the bow, took it down and, wondering at the easy memories of his youth, strung it. He instinctively placed the lower end against the inside of his right foot, his left hand slid easily up the wood with the string lightly guided by his finger tips. The string vibrated tautly, and he remembered, too, how a bow seemed lighter after being strung, the tense pressure communicating energy to the arm. He estimated the pull at sixty pounds—quite a powerful bow.

"Oh, you found the bow'n arrow!" Nana said when he came into the kitchen with it. "You going to shoot? Say, how did you cock it?"

He placed the bow against his foot, pulled with his right hand and pushed with the heel of his left hand, his fingers working the string out of the notch.

"Nobody could fix it. The children going crazy they couldn't shoot, nobody could cock it," Nana said admiringly.

"Do you have any arrows?"

The old man had decided to listen. "In the umbrella stand is some arrows," he said, and Nana rushed out after them. After breakfast she insisted they all go out and watch him shoot, and he was surprised at his own excitement when he fitted the nock of one of the warped target arrows to the string. He drew and loosed the arrow across the thirty yards between the driveway and the barn. *Whap* as the arrow hit the silvery, unpainted wood of the barn and stuck, quivering. A cloud of swallows streamed out of a sashless window, and shreds of dusty hay fell from between the boards. The old people were impressed.

As he drew his second arrow the bow split apart above the grip. Arrow, string, half the bow fell loosely over his arms.

"Ooooh!" the old people sighed. "The wood was too old," the old man said. "It all dries up and it got no give to it."

"I'll get you another one," Hurley said. They shushed him up, said it wasn't any good, that nobody could cock it anyway. But later when he drove his Drive-Ur-Self Chevrolet down into Leah for groceries and the mail, he stopped in at Follansbees' hardware store.

Old Follansbee remembered him from the times he and Mary had come up to ski, possibly not from the earlier time when Follansbee was a young man working in his father's store and Hurley was a boy.

"Do for you?" Old Follansbee's bald head (once covered with black, bushy hair, parted in the middle) gleamed softly, approximately the same color and texture as his maple roll-top desk.

"I'd like to buy a bow—and some arrows," Hurley added in order to specify what kind of bow he meant. In Leah he had always been constrained to come immediately to the point. The old man led him to the sporting-goods corner where rifles and shotguns, fish poles and outboard motors, knives, rubber boots, decoys, pistols lay in cases on counters, hung on racks. He remembered this part of the store and the objects he had fallen in love with as a boy. No girl had meant as much to him at fifteen as had the beautifully angular lines of a Winchester model 62, .22 pump. He even remembered the model number, but from this distance he wondered how a number could have meant so much.

He tried out a few of the pretty, too-modern bows until he found one that seemed to have the same pull as the one he had broken.

"That one's glass," Old Follansbee said. "My boy says it don't want to break."

"Glass? It's made of glass?"

"Correct. Strange, ain't it? What they can do these days? You'll want some arrows, did you say?"

He bought two arrows. When he'd pulled the one out of the barn it came apart in his hands, split all the way up the shaft. He decided to replace it with two, even though he knew the New Hampshire way was to resent such prodigality. He bought a leather arm guard and finger tabs; then he saw the hunting arrows. The slim, three-bladed heads suggested Indians and his youth. The target arrows, beside them, seemed to have no character, no honest function. He bought two hunting arrows and, under old Follansbee's suspicious conventional eye, a bow-hunting license, feeling like a child who had spent his Sunday-school money on a toy.

At the Post Office he found a joint communiqué from his worried children. "We have decided that it would be best . . ." the words went. He sent two identical telegrams: *Having wonderful time. Tend your business. Love, Dad.* They all believed in the therapy of youth—in this case, grandchildren. He couldn't think of a way to tell them that he loved them all too much.

Nana and the old man walked with him as far as the ledges at the top of the wild orchard, careful in their white tennis shoes. Nana stood splayfooted on the granite, queen of the hill, and surveyed the valley, the advancing forest with a disapproving eye.

"I see Holloways is letting their north pasture go back," she said, shaking her head. She had seen whole hills go back to darkness, many fine houses fall into their cellar holes. She turned toward Hurley accusingly, he being from the outside and thus responsible for such things. "You got to pay money to have them take the hay!"

"Tell me it's cheaper to buy it off the truck," the old man said. "But I told them it don't grow on trucks." He stood beside his tall wife, in his baggy pants and old mackinaw. His new tennis shoes were startlingly white. "I call this 'the hill of agony,' " he said, winking at Hurley.

"You see where the deer come down to eat our garden?" Nana said, pointing to the deer trails through the apple trees. "We tell the game warden to shoot. Nothing. They hang bangers in the trees. All night, 'Bang! Bang!' Nobody can sleep."

"Neither could the deer. They stayed up all night and et my lettuce," the old man said. He laughed and whacked his thigh.

"You shoot me a nice young deer," Nana said. "I make mincemeat, roasts, nice sausage for your breakfast.

He had tried to tell them that he didn't want to shoot anything with the bow, just carry it. Could he tell them that it gave a peculiar strength to his arm, that it seemed to be a kind of dynamo? When he was a boy in these same woods he and his friends had not been spectators, but actors. Their bows, fish poles, skis, rifles had set them apart from the mere hikers, the summer people.

"I won't be back tonight unless the weather changes," he said. The sun was warm on the dry leaves, but the air was crisply cool in the shadows. He said good-by to the old people, took off his pack and waited on the ledges to see them safely back to the house below, then unrolled his sleeping bag and rolled it tighter. The night before he had noticed on his geodetic map a small, five-acre pond high in the cleft between Cascom and Gilman mountains. It was called Goose Pond, and he seemed to remember having been there once, long ago, perhaps trout fishing. He remembered being very tired, yet not wanting to leave; he remembered the cat tails and alders and a long beaver dam, the pond deep in a little basin. He was sure he could follow the brook that issued from the pond—if he could pick the right one from all the little brooks that came down between Gilman and Cascom.

His pack tightened so that it rode high on his back, he carried his bow and the two hunting arrows in one hand. He soon relearned that arrows pass easily through the brush only if they go points first.

Stopping often to rest he climbed past the maples into ground juniper and pine, hearing often the soft explosions of partridge, sometimes seeing them as they burst up and whistled through the trees. He passed giant beeches crossing their noisy leaves, then walked silently through softwood until he came to a granite knob surrounded by stunted, wind-grieved hemlock. To the northwest he could see the Presidential Range, but Leah, the lake and the Pedersens' farm were all out of sight. He ate a hard-boiled egg and one of the bittersweet wild apples he had collected on the way. The wind was delightfully cool against his face, but he knew his sweat would soon chill. At two o'clock the sun was fairly low in the hard blue sky—whole valleys were in shadow below.

He took out his map. He had crossed three little brooks, and the one he could hear a short way ahead must be Goose Pond's overflow. By the sound it was a fair-sized brook. When he climbed down through the hemlock and saw it he was sure. White water angled right and left, dropping over boulders into narrow sluices and deep, clear pools. He knelt down and lowered his head into the icy water. His forehead turned numb, as if it were made of rubber. A water beetle darted to the bottom. A baby trout flashed green and pink beside a stone. It was as if he were looking through a giant lens into an alien world, where life was cold and cruel, and even the light had a quality of darkness about it. Odd little sticks on the bottom were the camouflaged larvae of insects, waiting furtively to hatch or to be eaten. Fish hid in the shadows under stones, their avid little mouths ready to snap. He shuddered and raised his head—a momentary flash of panic, as if some carnivorous animal with a gaping mouth might come darting up to tear his face.

Following the brook, jumping from stone to stone, sometimes having to leave it for the woods in order to get around tangles of blowdown or waterfalls, he came suddenly into the deep silence of the spruce, where the channel was deep. In the moist, cathedral silence of the tall pillars of spruce he realized how deafening the white water had been. The wind stirred the tops of the trees and made the slim trunks move slowly, but could not penetrate the dim, yet luminous greenness of the place.

And he saw the deer. He saw the face of the deer beside a narrow tree, and for a moment there was nothing but the face: a smoky-brown eye deep as a tunnel, it seemed, long delicate lashes, a black whisker or two along the white-shaded muzzle. The black nose quivered at each breath, the nostrils rounded. Then he began to follow the light brown line, motionless and so nearly invisible along the back, down along the edge of the white breast. One large ear turned slowly toward him. It was a doe, watching him carefully, perfect in the moment of fine innocence and wonder—a quality he suddenly remembered—the expressionless readiness of the deer. But other instincts had been working on him. He hadn't moved, had breathed slowly, put his weight equally on both legs. The light sharpened as if it had been twilight and the sun had suddenly flashed. Every detail—the convolutions of the bark on the trees, tiny twigs, the fine sheen of light on each hair of the doe, each curved, precious eyelash—became vivid and distinct. Depth grew, color brightened; his hunter's eyes became painfully efficient, as if each needle-like detail pierced him. The world became polarized on the axis of their eyes. He was alone with the doe in a green world that seemed to cry for rich red, and he did not have time to think: it was enough that he sensed the doe's quick decision to leave him. An onyx hoof snapped, her white flag rose and the doe floated in a slow arc, broadside to him, clear of the trees for an endless second. He watched down the long arrow, three blades moved ahead of the doe and at the precise moment all tension stopped; his arms, fingers, eyes and the bow were all one instrument. The arrow sliced through the deer.

Her white flag dropped. Gracefully, in long, splendid leaps, hoofs stabbing the hollow-sounding carpet of needles, the doe flickered beyond the trees. One moment of crashing brush, then silence. A thick excitement rose like fluid into his face, his arms seemed to grow to twice their normal size, become twice as strong. And still his body was governed by the old, learned patterns. He walked silently forward and retrieved his bloody arrow, snapped the feathers alive again. The trail was a vivid line of jewels, brighter than the checkerberries against their shiny green leaves, unmistakable. He rolled the bright blood between his fingers as he slowly moved forward. He must let the doe stop and lie down, let her shock-born strength dissipate in calm bleeding. Watching each step, figuring out whole series of steps, of brush bendings in advance, he picked the silent route around snags and under the blowdown.

In an hour he had gone a hundred yards, still tight and careful, up out of the spruce and onto a small rise covered with birch and poplar saplings. The leaves were loud underfoot and, as he carefully placed one foot, the doe rose in front of him and crashed downhill, obviously weak, staggering against the whippy birch. A fine mist of blood sprayed at each explosion of breath from the holes in her ribs. He ran after her, leaping over brush, running along fallen limbs, sliding under low branches that flicked his cheeks like claws. His bow caught on a branch and jerked him upright. After one impatient pull he left it. He drew his knife. The brown shape ahead had disappeared, and he dove through the brush after it, witch hobble grabbing at his legs.

The doe lay against a stump, one leg twitching. He knelt down and put one hard arm around her neck and, not caring for the dangerous hoofs, the spark of life, raised the firm, warm neck against his chest and, sighing, stabbed carefully into the sticking place. Blood was hot on the knife and on his hand.

He rolled over into the leaves, long breaths bending him, making his back arch. His shirt vibrated over his heart, his body turned heavy and pressed with unbelievable weight into the earth. He let his arms melt into the ground, and a cool, lucid sadness came over his flesh.

He made himself get up. In order to stand he had to fight gravity, to use all his strength—a quick fear for his heart. His joints ached and had begun to stiffen. He must keep moving. Shadows were long and he had much to do before dark. He followed the blood trail back and found his bow and one arrow. He limped going back down the hill; at a certain angle his knees tended to jackknife, as if gears were slipping.

He stood over the clean body of the doe, the white belly snowy against brown leaves. One hind leg he hooked behind a sapling, and he held the other with his knee as he made the first long incision through the hair and skin, careful not to break the peritoneum. He ran the incision from the breast to the tail, then worked the skin back with his fingers before making the second cut through the warm membrane, the sticky blue case for the stomach and entrails. He cut, and the steamy innards rolled unbroken and still working out onto the ground. A few neat berries of turd rattled on the leaves. He cut the anus and organs of reproduction clear of the flesh, then found the kidneys and liver and reached arm-deep into the humid chest cavity, the hot smell of blood close in his nostrils, and removed the yellow lungs in handfuls. Then he pulled out the dark red heart. Kidneys, liver and heart he wrapped carefully in his sandwich wrappings, then rose and painfully stretched. Goose Pond lay just below; he could see a flicker of water through the skein of branches, and there he would make camp.

With his belt looped around the neck and front hoofs, he slid the doe down toward the pond. It was dusk by the time he found a dry platform of soft needles beneath a hemlock, next to the water. The doe had become stiff enough so that he could hang it in a young birch, head wedged in a fork. He spread his sleeping bag, tried it for roots and stones, and found none. The last high touch of sun on the hill above him had gone; he had even prepared ground for a fire when he realized that he had no energy left, no appetite to eat the liver of the doe.

Darkness had settled in along the ground, but the sky was still bright; one line of cirrus clouds straight overhead still caught orange sunlight. Across the silver water the alder swamp was jet black, and the steep hill rose behind, craggy with spruce. A beaver's nose broke water and even, slow circles spread across the pond. The dark woods filled with cold, and one of his legs began to jerk uncontrollably. He took off his boots and slid into his sleeping bag.

The doe was monstrous, angular against the sky, her neck stretched awkwardly, head canted to one side. The black hole in her belly gaped empty. He drew his sleeping bag up around his face.

If he were twenty again he would be happy. To have shot a deer with a bow—he'd be a hero, a woodsman, famous in Leah. How it would have impressed Mary! She would have said little about it—she went to great lengths never to flatter him; her compliments had been more tangible, seldom in words. He must think of something else. The world was too empty. The cold woods, the darkening water were empty. He was too cold, too tired to manipulate his thoughts. And the progression of hours began again. Mary's eyes watched him, deep in sick hollows. How could her flesh turn so brown? Why could he do nothing to stop the pain? She watched him, in torment, her frail body riven, cut beyond endurance. The disease had killed her bravery with pain and left her gruesomely alive, without dignity, whimpering like a spoiled brat, asking for help she should have known did not exist. And he stood by and watched, doing nothing. Nothing. He was not a man to do nothing. *Mary, did I do nothing to help you?*

He heard, far away, the lonely cry of the Canada geese. He was alone, hidden in the blind night, high on the stony mass of Cascom Mountain.

And then they came in, circling, calling to each other above the doubtful ground. Perhaps they had seen the reflected circle of fading sky, or remembered; generations remembering that geese had rested safely in the high pond and found food there. The scouts came whistling on their great wings, searching and listening. They sent their messages back to the flock waiting above, then planed down, braking, smeared the water with wind and came to rest in a flash of spray. The flock circled down after, careless now it was safe, honking gaily, giving the feeding call prematurely, echoing the messages of the leaders and landing masters. "Come in, come down and rest," they seemed to call, until everyone had landed safely. Then the voices grew softer, less excited, and only an occasional word drifted across the water.

Robert Hurley lay in the warm hollow of his sleeping bag, where the hours had stopped. He thought for a moment of the doe's death, and of his knife. The geese spoke softly to each other on the water—a small splash, a flutter of wings and the resting, contented voices in the deep basin of the pond. As sleep washed over him he seemed to be among them; their sentinels guarded him.

When they had rested well they would rise and continue the dangerous journey down the world.

LEO TOLSTOI (1828–1910)

Count Leo Nikolaievich Tolstoi's early life was typical of the youth of all younger sons of the Russian aristocracy: French tutors, the university, boredom with country life, dissipation in Moscow, some Army service. At nineteen, however, the young landowner had begun to keep a journal which led, five years later, to the publication of the first of many stories—the start of his prosperous career as a writer.

Tolstoi's first novel, War and Peace, *considered by many as the greatest novel ever written, was published in 1869; his other great novel,* Anna Karenina, *in 1877. Despite the vast sweep of historic events that form the backdrop for these works, Tolstoi manages to make his characters come vividly to life, and he probes them deeply to expose their inner lives.*

As he approached the age of fifty, Tolstoi began to turn away from the material values he had always lived by and to evolve a new kind of Christianity emphasizing love, compassion for all living things, and the rejection of property and violence. He changed his way of life, renouncing his worldly goods, dressing and working like a peasant. His religious conversion could not but affect his writing, which he believed must now serve his new-found creed.

"The Death of Ivan Ilych" (1884) is one of these later works. It reflects Tolstoi's rejection of worldly values in the knowledge that death makes us all equal.

The Death of Ivan Ilych

Translated by Louise and Aylmer Maude

1

DURING AN INTERVAL in the Melvinski trial in the large building of the Law Courts, the members and public prosecutor met in Ivan Egorovich Shebek's private room, where the conversation turned on the celebrated Krasovski case. Fëdor Vasilievich warmly maintained that it was not subject to their jurisdiction, Ivan Egorovich maintained the contrary, while Peter Ivanovich, not having entered into the discussion at the start, took no part in it but looked through the *Gazette* which had just been handed in.

"Gentlemen," he said, "Ivan Ilych has died!"

"You don't say so!"

"Here, read it yourself," replied Peter Ivanovich, handing Fëdor Vasilievich the paper still damp from the press. Surrounded by a black border were the words: "Praskovya Fëdorovna Golovina, with profound sorrow, informs relatives and friends of the demise of her beloved husband Ivan Ilych Golovin, Member of the Court of Justice, which occurred on February the 4th of this year 1882. The funeral will take place on Friday at one o'clock in the afternoon."

Ivan Ilych had been a colleague of the gentlemen present and was liked by them all. He had been ill for some weeks with an illness said to be incurable. His post had been kept open for him, but there had been conjectures that in case of his death Alexeev might receive his appointment, and that either Vinnikov or Shtabel would succeed Alexeev. So on receiving the news of Ivan Ilych's death the first thought of each of the gentlemen in that private room was of the changes and promotions it might occasion among themselves or their acquaintances.

"I shall be sure to get Shtabel's place or Vinnikov's," thought Fëdor Vasilievich. "I was promised that long ago, and the promotion means an extra eight hundred rubles a year for me besides the allowance."

"Now I must apply for my brother-in-law's transfer from Kaluga," thought Peter Ivanovich. "My wife will be very glad, and then she won't be able to say that I never do anything for her relations."

"I thought he would never leave his bed again," said Peter Ivanovich aloud. "It's very sad."

"But what really was the matter with him?"

"The doctors couldn't say—at least they could, but each of them said something different. When last I saw him I thought he was getting better."

"And I haven't been to see him since the holidays. I always meant to go."

"Had he any property?"

"I think his wife had a little—but something quite trifling."

"We shall have to go to see her, but they live so terribly far away."

"Far away from you, you mean. Everything's far away from your place."

"You see, he never can forgive my living on the other side of the river," said Peter Ivanovich, smiling at Shebek. Then, still talking of the distances between different parts of the city, they returned to the Court.

Besides considerations as to the possible transfers and promotions likely to result from Ivan Ilych's death, the mere fact of the death of a near acquaintance aroused, as usual, in all who heard of it the complacent feeling that, "it is he who is dead and not I."

Each one thought or felt, "Well, he's dead but I'm alive!" But the more intimate of Ivan Ilych's acquaintances, his so-called friends, could not help thinking also that they would now have to fulfil the very tiresome demands of propriety by attending the funeral service and paying a visit of condolence to the widow.

Fëdor Vasilievich and Peter Ivanovich had been his nearest acquaintances. Peter Ivanovich had studied law with Ivan Ilych and had considered himself to be under obligations to him.

Having told his wife at dinner-time of Ivan Ilych's death and of his conjecture that it might be possible to get her brother transferred to their circuit, Peter Ivanovich sacrificed his usual nap, put on his evening clothes, and drove to Ivan Ilych's house.

At the entrance stood a carriage and two cabs. Leaning against the wall in the hall downstairs near the cloak-stand was a coffin-lid covered with cloth of gold, ornamented with gold cord and tassels, that had been polished up with metal powder. Two ladies in black were taking off their fur cloaks. Peter Ivanovich recognized one of them as Ivan Ilych's sister, but the other was a stranger to him. His colleague Schwartz was just coming downstairs, but on seeing Peter Ivanovich enter he stopped and winked at him, as if to say: "Ivan Ilych has made a mess of things—not like you and me."

Schwartz's face with his Piccadilly whiskers and his slim figure in evening dress, had as usual an air of elegant solemnity which contrasted with the playfulness of his character and had a special piquancy here, or so it seemed to Peter Ivanovich.

Peter Ivanovich allowed the ladies to precede him and slowly followed them upstairs. Schwartz did not come down but remained where he was, and Peter Ivanovich understood that he wanted to arrange where they should play bridge that evening. The ladies went upstairs to the widow's room, and Schwartz with seriously compressed lips but a playful look in his eyes, indicated by a twist of his eyebrows the room to the right where the body lay.

Peter Ivanovich, like everyone else on such occasions, entered feeling uncertain what he would have to do. All he knew was that at such times it is always safe to cross oneself. But he was not quite sure whether one should make obeisances while doing so. He therefore adopted a middle course. On entering the room he began crossing himself and made a slight movement resembling a bow. At the same time, as far as the motion of his head and arm allowed, he surveyed the room. Two young men—apparently nephews, one of whom was a high-school pupil—were leaving the room, crossing themselves as they did so. An old woman was standing motionless, and a lady with strangely arched eyebrows was saying something to her in a whisper. A vigorous, resolute Church Reader, in a frock-coat, was reading something in a loud voice with an expression that precluded any contradiction. The butler's assistant, Gerasim, stepping lightly in front of Peter Ivanovich, was strewing something on the floor. Noticing this, Peter Ivanovich was immediately aware of a faint odour of a decomposing body.

The last time he had called on Ivan Ilych, Peter Ivanovich had seen Gerasim in the study. Ivan Ilych had been particularly fond of him and he was performing the duty of a sick nurse.

Peter Ivanovich continued to make the sign of the cross slightly inclining his head in an intermediate direction between the coffin, the Reader, and the icons on the table in a corner of the room. Afterwards, when it seemed to him that this movement of his arm in crossing himself had gone on too long, he stopped and began to look at the corpse.

The dead man lay, as dead men always lie, in a specially heavy way, his rigid limbs sunk in the soft cushions of the coffin, with the head forever bowed on the pillow. His yellow waxen brow with bald patches over his sunken temples was thrust up in the way peculiar to the dead, the protruding nose seeming to press on the upper lip. He was much changed and had grown even thinner since Peter Ivanovich had last seen him, but, as is always the case with the dead, his face was handsomer and above all more dignified than when he was alive. The expression on the face said that what was necessary had been accomplished, and accomplished rightly. Besides this there was in that expression a reproach and a warning to the living. This warning seemed to Peter Ivanovich out of place, or at least not applicable to him. He felt a certain discomfort and so he hurriedly crossed himself once more and turned and went out of the door—too hurriedly and too regardless of propriety, as he himself was aware.

Schwartz was waiting for him in the adjoining room with legs spread wide apart and both hands toying with his top-hat behind his back. The mere sight of that playful, well-groomed, and elegant figure refreshed Peter Ivanovich. He felt that Schwartz was above all these happenings and would not surrender to any depressing influences. His very look said that this incident of a church service for Ivan Ilych could not be a sufficient reason for infringing the order of the session—in other words, that it would certainly not prevent his unwrapping a new pack of cards and shuffling them that evening while a footman placed four fresh candles on the table: in fact, that there was no reason for supposing that this incident would hinder their spending the evening agreeably. Indeed he said this in a whisper as Peter Ivanovich passed him, proposing that they should meet for a game at Fëdor Vasilievich's. But apparently Peter Ivanovich was not destined to play bridge that evening. Praskovya Fëdorovna (a short, fat woman who despite all efforts to the contrary had continued to broaden steadily from her shoulders downward and who had the same extraordinarily arched eyebrows as the lady who had been standing by the coffin), dressed all in black, her head covered with lace, came out of her own room with some other ladies, conducted them to the room where the dead body lay, and said: "The service will begin immediately. Please go in."

Schwartz, making an indefinite bow, stood still, evidently neither accepting nor declining this invitation, Praskovya Fëdorovna, recognizing Peter Ivanovich, sighed, went close up to him, took his hand, and said: "I know you were a true friend to Ivan Ilych . . ." and looked at him awaiting some suitable response. And Peter Ivanovich knew that, just as it had been the right thing to cross himself in that room, so what he had to do here was to press her hand, sigh, and say, "Believe me. . . ." So he did all this and as he did it felt that the desired result had been achieved: that both he and she were touched.

"Come with me. I want to speak to you before it begins," said the widow. "Give me your arm."

Peter Ivanovich gave her his arm and they went to the inner rooms, passing Schwartz, who winked at Peter Ivanovich compassionately.

"That does for our bridge! Don't object if we find another player. Perhaps you can cut in when you do escape," said his playful look.

Peter Ivanovich sighed still more deeply and despondently, and Praskovya Fëdorovna pressed his arm gratefully. When they reached the drawing-room, upholstered in pink cretonne and lighted by a dim lamp, they sat down at the table—she on a sofa and Peter Ivanovich on a low pouffe, the springs of which yielded spasmodically under his weight. Praskovya Fëdorovna had been on the point of warning him to take another seat, but felt that such a warning was out of keeping with her present condition and so changed her mind. As he sat down on the pouffe Peter Ivanovich recalled how Ivan Ilych had arranged this room and had consulted him regarding this pink cretonne with green leaves. The whole room was full of furniture and knick-knacks, and on her way to the sofa the lace of the widow's black shawl caught on the carved edge of the table. Peter Ivanovich rose to detach it, and the springs of the pouffe, relieved of his weight, rose also and gave him a push. The widow began detaching her shawl herself, and Peter Ivanovich again sat down, suppressing the rebellious springs of the pouffe under him. But the widow had not quite freed herself and Peter Ivanovich got up again, and again the pouffe rebelled and even creaked. When this was all over she took out a clean cambric handkerchief and began to weep. The episode with the shawl and the struggle with the pouffe had cooled Peter Ivanovich's emotions and he sat there with a sullen look on his face. This awkward situation was interrupted by Sokolov, Ivan Ilych's butler, who came to report that the plot in the cemetery that Praskovya Fëdorovna had chosen would cost two hundred rubles. She stopped weeping and, looking at Peter Ivanovich with the air of a victim, remarked in French that it was very hard for her. Peter Ivanovich made a silent gesture signifying his full conviction that it must indeed be so.

"Please smoke," she said in a magnanimous yet crushed voice, and turned to discuss with Sokolov the price of the plot for the grave.

Peter Ivanovich while lighting his cigarette heard her inquiring very circumstantially into the prices of different plots in the cemetery and finally decide which she would take. When that was done she gave instructions about engaging the choir. Sokolov then left the room.

"I look after everything myself," she told Peter Ivanovich, shifting the albums that lay on the table; and noticing that the table was endangered by his cigarette-ash, she immediately passed him an ash-tray, saying as she did so: "I consider it an affectation to say that my grief prevents my attending to practical affairs. On the contrary, if anything can—I won't say console me, but—distract me, it is seeing to everything concerning him." She again took out her handkerchief as if preparing to cry, but suddenly, as if mastering her feeling, she shook herself and began to speak calmly. "But there is something I want to talk to you about."

Peter Ivanovich bowed, keeping control of the springs of the pouffe, which immediately began quivering under him.

"He suffered terribly the last few days."

"Did he?" said Peter Ivanovich.

"Oh, terribly! He screamed unceasingly, not for minutes but for hours. For the last three days he screamed incessantly. It was unendurable. I cannot understand how I bore it; you could hear him three rooms off. Oh, what I have suffered!"

"Is it possible that he was conscious all that time?" asked Peter Ivanovich.

"Yes," she whispered. "To the last moment. He took leave of us a quarter of an hour before he died, and asked us to take Volodya away."

The thought of the sufferings of this man he had known so intimately, first as a merry little boy, then as a school-mate, and later as a grown-up colleague, suddenly struck Peter Ivanovich with horror, despite an unpleasant consciousness of his own and this woman's dissimulation. He again saw that brow, and that nose pressing down on the lip, and felt afraid for himself.

"Three days of frightful suffering and then death! Why, that might suddenly, at any time, happen to me," he thought, and for a moment felt terrified. But—he did not himself know how—the customary reflection at once occurred to him that this had happened to Ivan Ilych and not to him, and that it should not and could not happen to him, and to think that it could would be yielding to depression which he ought not to do, as Schwartz's expression plainly showed. After which reflection Peter Ivanovich felt reassured, and began to ask with interest about the details of Ivan Ilych's death, as though death was an accident natural to Ivan Ilych but certainly not to himself.

After many details of the really dreadful physical sufferings Ivan Ilych had endured (which details he learnt only from the effect those sufferings had produced on Praskovya Fëdorovna's nerves) the widow apparently found it necessary to get to business.

"Oh, Peter Ivanovich, how hard it is! How terribly, terribly hard!" and she again began to weep.

Peter Ivanovich sighed and waited for her to finish blowing her nose. When she had done so he said, "Believe me . . ." and she again began talking and brought out what was evidently her chief concern with him—namely to question him as to how she could obtain a grant of money from the government on the occasion of her husband's death. She made it appear that she was asking Peter Ivanovich's advice about her pension, but he soon saw that she already knew about that to the minutest detail, more even than he did himself. She knew how much could be got out of the government in consequence of her husband's death, but wanted to find out whether she could not possibly extract something more. Peter Ivanovich tried to think of some means of doing so, but after reflecting for a while and, out of propriety, condemning the government for its niggardliness, he said he thought that nothing more could be got. Then she sighed and evidently began to devise means of getting rid of her visitor. Noticing this, he put out his cigarette, rose, pressed her hand, and went out into the anteroom.

In the dining-room where the clock stood that Ivan Ilych had liked so much and had bought at an antique shop, Peter Ivanovich met a priest and a few acquaintances who had come to attend the service, and he recognized Ivan Ilych's daughter, a handsome young woman. She was in black and her slim figure appeared slimmer than ever. She had a gloomy, determined, almost angry expression, and bowed to Peter Ivanovich as though he were in some way to blame. Behind her, with the same offended look, stood a wealthy young man, an examining magistrate, whom Peter Ivanovich also knew and who was her fiancé, as he had heard. He bowed mournfully to them and was about to pass into the death-chamber, when from under the stairs appeared the figure of Ivan Ilych's schoolboy son, who was extremely like his father. He seemed a little Ivan Ilych, such as Peter Ivanovich remembered when they studied law together. His tear-stained eyes had in them the look that is seen in the eyes of boys of thirteen or fourteen who are not pure-minded. When he saw Peter Ivanovich he scowled morosely and shamefacedly. Peter Ivanovich nodded to him and entered the death-chamber. The service began: candles, groans, incense, tears, and sobs. Peter Ivanovich stood looking gloomily down at his feet. He did not look once at the dead man, did not yield to any depressing influence, and was one of the first to leave the room. There was no one in the anteroom, but Gerasim darted out of the dead man's room, rummaged with his strong hands among the fur coats to find Peter Ivanovich's and helped him on with it.

"Well, friend Gerasim," said Peter Ivanovich, so as to say something. "It's a sad affair, isn't it?"

"It's God's will. We shall all come to it some day," said Gerasim, displaying his teeth—the even, white teeth of a healthy peasant—and, like a man in the thick of urgent work, he briskly opened the front door, called the coachman, helped Peter Ivanovich into the sledge, and sprang back to the porch as if in readiness for what he had to do next.

Peter Ivanovich found the fresh air particularly pleasant after the smell of incense, the dead body, and carbolic acid.

"Where to, sir?" asked the coachman.

"It's not too late even now. . . . I'll call round on Fëdor Vasilievich."

He accordingly drove there and found them just finishing the first rubber, so that it was quite convenient for him to cut in.

2

Ivan Ilych's life had been most simple and most ordinary and therefore most terrible.

He had been a member of the Court of Justice, and died at the age of forty-five. His father had been an official who after serving in various ministries and departments in Petersburg had made the sort of career which brings men to positions from which by reason of their long service they cannot be dismissed, though they are obviously unfit to hold any responsible position, and for whom therefore posts are especially created, which though fictitious carry salaries of from six to ten thousand rubles that are not fictitious, and in receipt of which they live on to a great age.

Such was the Privy Councillor and superfluous member of various superfluous insitutions, Ilya Epimovich Golovin.

He had three sons, of whom Ivan Ilych was the second. The eldest son was following in his father's footsteps only in another department, and was already approaching that stage in the service at which a similar sinecure would be reached. The third son was a failure. He had ruined his prospects in a number of positions and was now serving in the railway department. His father and brothers, and still more their wives, not merely disliked meeting him, but avoided remembering his existence unless compelled to do so. His sister had married Baron Greff, a Petersburg official of her father's type. Ivan Ilych was *le phénix de la famille** as people said. He was neither as cold and formal as his elder brother nor as wild as the younger, but was a happy mean between them—an intelligent, polished, lively and agreeable man. He had studied with his younger brother at the School of Law, but the latter had failed to complete the course and was expelled when he was in the fifth class. Ivan Ilych finished the course well. Even when he was at the School of Law he was just what he remained for the rest of his life: a capable, cheerful, good-natured, and sociable man, though strict in the fulfilment of what he considered to be his duty: and he considered his duty to be what was so considered by those in authority. Neither as a boy nor as a man was he a toady, but from early youth was by nature attracted to people of high station as a fly is drawn to the light, assimilating their ways and views of life and establishing friendly relations with

* *le phénix de la famille.* the perfect member of the family; as unique as the phoenix, the bird which rises from ashes to be reborn

them. All the enthusiasms of childhood and youth passed without leaving much trace on him; he succumbed to sensuality, to vanity, and latterly among the highest classes to liberalism, but always within limits which his instinct unfailingly indicated to him as correct.

At school he had done things which had formerly seemed to him very horrid and made him feel disgusted with himself when he did them; but when later on he saw that such actions were done by people of good position and that they did not regard them as wrong, he was able not exactly to regard them as right, but to forget about them entirely or not be at all troubled at remembering them.

Having graduated from the School of Law and qualified for the tenth rank of the civil service, and having received money from his father for his equipment, Ivan Ilych ordered himself clothes at Scharmer's, the fashionable tailor, hung a medallion inscribed *respice finem** on his watchchain, took leave of his professor and the prince who was patron of the school, had a farewell dinner with his comrades at Donon's first-class restaurant, and with his new and fashionable portmanteau, linen, clothes, shaving and other toilet appliances, and a travelling rug, all purchased at the best shops, he set off for one of the provinces where, through his father's influence, he had been attached to the Governor as an official for special service.

In the province Ivan Ilych soon arranged as easy and agreeable a position for himself as he had had at the School of Law. He performed his official tasks, made his career, and at the same time amused himself pleasantly and decorously. Occasionally he paid official visits to country districts, where he behaved with dignity both to his superiors and inferiors, and performed the duties entrusted to him, which related chiefly to the sectarians, with an exactness and incorruptible honesty of which he could not but feel proud.

In official matters, despite his youth and taste for frivolous gaiety, he was exceedingly reserved, punctilious, and even severe; but in society he was often amusing and witty, and always good-natured, correct in his manner, and *bon enfant,*** as the governor and his wife—with whom he was like one of the family—used to say of him.

In the province he had an affair with a lady who made advances to the elegant young lawyer, and there was also a milliner; and there were carousals with aides-de-camp who visited the district, and after-supper visits to a certain outlying street of doubtful reputation; and there was too some obsequiousness to his chief and even to his chief's wife, but all this was done with such a tone of good breeding that no hard names could be applied to it. It all came under the heading of the French saying: *"Il faut que jeunesse se passe."* *** It was all done with clean hands, in clean linen, with French phrases, and above all among people of the best society and consequently with the approval of people of rank.

* *respice finem.* prepare for the end
** *bon enfant.* a good child
*** *Il faut que jeunesse se passe.* Youth will pass

So Ivan Ilych served for five years and then came a change in his official life. The new and reformed judicial institutions were introduced, and new men were needed. Ivan Ilych became such a new man. He was offered the post of examining magistrate, and he accepted it though the post was in another province and obliged him to give up the connexions he had formed and to make new ones. His friends met to give him a send-off; they had a group-photograph taken and presented him with a silver cigarette-case, and he set off to his new post.

As examining magistrate Ivan Ilych was just as *comme il faut** and decorous a man, inspiring general respect and capable of separating his official duties from his private life, as he had been when acting as an official on special service. His duties now as examining magistrate were far more interesting and attractive than before. In his former position it had been pleasant to wear an undress uniform made by Scharmer, and to pass through the crowd of petitioners and officials who were timorously awaiting an audience with the governor, and who envied him as with free and easy gait he went straight into his chief's private room to have a cup of tea and a cigarette with him. But not many people had then been directly dependent on him—only police officials and the sectarians when he went on special missions—and he liked to treat them politely, almost as comrades, as if he were letting them feel that he who had the power to crush them was treating them in this simple, friendly way. There were then but few such people. But now, as an examining magistrate, Ivan Ilych felt that everyone without exception, even the most important and self-satisfied, was in his power, and that he need only write a few words on a sheet of paper with a certain heading, and this or that important, self-satisfied person would be brought before him in the role of an accused person or a witness, and if he did not choose to allow him to sit down, would have to stand before him and answer his questions. Ivan Ilych never abused his power; he tried on the contrary to soften its expression, but the consciousness of it and of the possibility of softening its effect, supplied the chief interest and attraction of his office. In his work itself, especially in his examinations, he very soon acquired a method of eliminating all considerations irrelevant to the legal aspect of the case, and reducing even the most complicated case to a form in which it would be presented on paper only in its externals, completely excluding his personal opinion of the matter, while above all observing every prescribed formality. The work was new and Ivan Ilych was one of the first men to apply the new Code of 1864.

On taking up the post of examining magistrate in a new town, he made new acquaintances and connexions, placed himself on a new footing, and assumed a somewhat different tone. He took up an attitude of rather dignified aloofness towards the provincial authorities, but picked out the best circle of legal

* *comme il faut.* proper

gentlemen and wealthy gentry living in the town and assumed a tone of slight dissatisfaction with the government, of moderate liberalism, and of enlightened citizenship. At the same time, without at all altering the elegance of his toilet, he ceased shaving his chin and allowed his beard to grow as it pleased.

Ivan Ilych settled down very pleasantly in this new town. The society there, which inclined towards opposition to the Governor, was friendly, his salary was larger, and he began to play *vint,** which he found added not a little to the pleasure of life, for he had a capacity for cards, played good-humouredly, and calculated rapidly and astutely, so that he usually won.

After living there for two years he met his future wife, Praskovya Fëdorovna Mikhel, who was the most attractive, clever, and brilliant girl of the set in which he moved, and among other amusements and relaxations from his labours as examining magistrate, Ivan Ilych established light and playful relations with her.

While he had been an official on special service he had been accustomed to dance, but now as an examining magistrate it was exceptional for him to do so. If he danced now, he did it as if to show that though he served under the reformed order of things, and had reached the fifth official rank, yet when it came to dancing he could do it better than most people. So at the end of an evening he sometimes danced with Praskovya Fëdorovna, and it was chiefly during these dances that he captivated her. She fell in love with him. Ivan Ilych had at first no definite intention of marrying, but when the girl fell in love with him he said to himself: "Really, why shouldn't I marry?"

Praskovya Fëdorovna came of a good family, was not bad looking, and had some little property. Ivan Ilych might have aspired to a more brilliant match, but even this was good. He had his salary, and she, he hoped, would have an equal income. She was well connected, and was a sweet, pretty, and thoroughly correct young woman. To say that Ivan Ilych married because he fell in love with Praskovya Fëdorovna and found that she sympathized with his views of life would be as incorrect as to say that he married because his social circle approved of the match. He was swayed by both these considerations: the marriage gave him personal satisfaction, and at the same time it was considered the right thing by the most highly placed of his associates.

So Ivan Ilych got married.

The preparations for marriage and the beginning of married life, with its conjugal caresses, the new furniture, new crockery, and new linen, were very pleasant until his wife became pregnant—so that Ivan Ilych had begun to think that marriage would not impair the easy, agreeable, gay and always decorous character of his life, approved of by society and regarded by himself as natural, but would even improve it. But from the first months of his wife's pregnancy, something new, unpleasant, depressing, and unseemly, and from which there was no way of escape, unexpectedly showed itself.

* *vint.* a form of bridge

His wife, without any reason—*de gaieté de coeur** as Ivan Ilych expressed it to himself—began to disturb the pleasure and propriety of their life. She began to be jealous without any cause, expected him to devote his whole attention to her, found fault with everything, and made coarse and ill-mannered scenes.

At first Ivan Ilych hoped to escape from the unpleasantness of this state of affairs by the same easy and decorous relation to life that had served him heretofore: he tried to ignore his wife's disagreeable moods, continued to live in his usual easy and pleasant way, invited friends to his house for a game of cards, and also tried going out to his club or spending his evenings with friends. But one day his wife began upbraiding him so vigorously, using such coarse words, and continued to abuse him every time he did not fulfil her demands, so resolutely and with such evident determination not to give way till he submitted—that is, till he stayed at home and was bored just as shc was—that he became alarmed. He now realized that matrimony—at any rate with Praskovya Fëdorovna—was not always conducive to the pleasures and amenities of life, but on the contrary often infringed both comfort and propriety, and that he must therefore entrench himself against such infringement. And Ivan Ilych began to seek for means of doing so. His official duties were the one thing that imposed upon Praskovya Fëdorovna, and by means of his official work and the duties attached to it he began struggling with his wife to secure his own independence.

With the birth of their child, the attempts to feed it and the various failures in doing so, and with the real and imaginary illnesses of mother and child, in which Ivan Ilych's sympathy was demanded but about which he understood nothing, the need of securing for himself an existence outside his family life became still more imperative.

As his wife grew more irritable and exacting and Ivan Ilych transferred the centre of gravity of his life more and more to his official work, so did he grow to like his work better and became more ambitious than before.

Very soon, within a year of his wedding, Ivan Ilych had realized that marriage, though it may add some comforts to life, is in fact, a very intricate and difficult affair towards which in order to perform one's duty, that is, to lead a decorous life approved of by society, one must adopt a definite attitude just as towards one's official duties.

And Ivan Ilych evolved such an attitude towards married life. He only required of it those conveniences—dinner at home, housewife, and bed—which it could give him, and above all that propriety of external forms required by public opinion. For the rest he looked for light-hearted pleasure and propriety, and was very thankful when he found them, but if he met with antagonism and querulousness he at once retired into his separate fenced-off world of official duties, where he found satisfaction.

* *de gaieté de coeur.* frivolously

Ivan Ilych was esteemed a good official, and after three years was made Assistant Public Prosecutor. His new duties, their importance, the possibility of indicting and imprisoning anyone he chose, the publicity his speeches received, and the success he had in all these things, made his work still more attractive.

More children came. His wife became more and more querulous and ill-tempered, but the attitude Ivan Ilych had adopted towards his home life rendered him almost impervious to her grumbling.

After seven years' service in that town he was transferred to another province as Public Prosecutor. They moved, but were short of money and his wife did not like the place they moved to. Though the salary was higher the cost of living was greater, besides which two of their children died and family life became still more unpleasant for him.

Praskovya Fëdorovna blamed her husband for every inconvenience they encountered in their new home. Most of the conversations between husband and wife, especially as to the children's education, led to topics which recalled former disputes, and those disputes were apt to flare up again at any moment. There remained only those rare periods of amorousness which still came to them at times but did not last long. These were islets at which they anchored for a while and then again set out upon that ocean of veiled hostility which showed itself in their aloofness for one another. This aloofness might have grieved Ivan Ilych had he considered that it ought not to exist, but he now regarded the position as normal, and even made it the goal at which he aimed in family life. His aim was to free himself more and more from those unpleasantnesses and to give them a semblance of harmlessness and propriety. He attained this by spending less and less time with his family, and when obliged to be at home he tried to safeguard his position by the presence of outsiders. The chief thing however was that he had his official duties. The whole interest of his life now centred in the official world and that interest absorbed him. The consciousness of his power, being able to ruin anybody he wished to ruin, the importance, even the external dignity of his entry into court, or meetings with his subordinates, his success with superiors and inferiors, and above all his masterly handling of cases, of which he was conscious—all this gave him pleasure and filled his life, together with chats with his colleagues, dinners, and bridge. So that on the whole Ivan Ilych's life continued to flow as he considered it should do—pleasantly and properly.

So things continued for another seven years. His eldest daughter was already sixteen, another child had died, and only one son was left, a schoolboy and a subject of dissension. Ivan Ilych wanted to put him in the School of Law, but to spite him Praskovya Fëdorovna entered him at the High School. The daughter had been educated at home and had turned out well: the boy did not learn badly either.

3

So Ivan Ilych lived for seventeen years after his marriage. He was already a Public Prosecutor of long standing, and had declined several proposed transfers while awaiting a more desirable post, when an unanticipated and unpleasant occurrence quite upset the peaceful course of his life. He was expecting to be offered the post of presiding judge in a University town, but Happe somehow came to the front and obtained the appointment instead. Ivan Ilych became irritable, reproached Happe, and quarrelled both with him and with his immediate superiors—who became colder to him and again passed him over when other appointments were made.

This was in 1880, the hardest year of Ivan Ilych's life. It was then that it became evident on the one hand that his salary was insufficient for them to live on, and on the other that he had been forgotten, and not only this, but that what was for him the greatest and most cruel injustice appeared to others a quite ordinary occurrence. Even his father did not consider it his duty to help him. Ivan Ilych felt himself abandoned by everyone, and that they regarded his position with a salary of 3,500 rubles as quite normal and even fortunate. He alone knew that with the consciousness of the injustices done him, with his wife's incessant nagging, and with the debts he had contracted by living beyond his means, his position was far from normal.

In order to save money that summer he obtained leave of absence and went with his wife to live in the country at her brother's place.

In the country, without his work, he experienced *ennui** for the first time in his life, and not only *ennui* but intolerable depression, and he decided that it was impossible to go on living like that, and that it was necessary to take energetic measures.

Having passed a sleepless night pacing up and down the veranda, he decided to go to Petersburg and bestir himself, in order to punish those who had failed to appreciate him and to get transferred to another ministry.

Next day, despite many protests from his wife and her brother, he started for Petersburg with the sole object of obtaining a post with a salary of five thousand rubles a year. He was no longer bent on any particular department or tendency, or kind of activity. All he now wanted was an appointment to another post with a salary of five thousand rubles, either in the administration, in the banks, with the railways, in one of the Empress Marya's Institutions, or even in the customs—but it had to carry with it a salary of five thousand rubles and be in a ministry other than that in which they had failed to appreciate him.

And this quest of Ivan Ilych's was crowned with remarkable and unexpected success. At Kursk an acquaintance of his, F. I. Ilyin, got into the first-class carriage, sat down beside Ivan Ilych, and told him of a telegram just re-

* *ennui.* restless boredom

ceived by the Governor of Kursk announcing that a change was about to take place in the ministry: Peter Ivanovich was to be superseded by Ivan Semënovich.

The proposed change, apart from its significance for Russia, had a special significance for Ivan Ilych, because by bringing forward a new man, Peter Petrovich, and consequently his friend Zachar Ivanovich, it was highly favourable for Ivan Ilych, since Zachar Ivanovich was a friend and colleague of his.

In Moscow this news was confirmed, and on reaching Petersburg Ivan Ilych found Zachar Ivanovich and received a definite promise of an appointment in his former department of Justice.

A week later he telegraphed to his wife: "Zachar in Miller's place. I shall receive appointment on presentation of report."

Thanks to this change of personnel, Ivan Ilych had unexpectedly obtained an appointment in his former ministry which placed him two stages above his former colleagues besides giving him five thousand rubles salary and three thousand five hundred rubles for expenses connected with his removal. All his ill humour towards his former enemies and the whole department vanished, and Ivan Ilych was completely happy.

He returned to the country more cheerful and contented than he had been for a long time. Praskovya Fëdorovna also cheered up and a truce was arranged between them. Ivan Ilych told of how he had been fêted by everybody in Petersburg, how all those who had been his enemies were put to shame and now fawned on him, how envious they were of his appointment, and how much everybody in Petersburg had liked him.

Praskovya Fëdorovna listened to all this and appeared to believe it. She did not contradict anything, but only made plans for their life in the town to which they were going. Ivan Ilych saw with delight that these plans were his plans, that he and his wife agreed, and that, after a stumble, his life was regaining its due and natural character of pleasant lightheartedness and decorum.

Ivan Ilych had come back for a short time only, for he had to take up his new duties on the 10th of September. Moreover, he needed time to settle into the new place, to move all his belongings from the province, and to buy and order many additional things: in a word, to make such arrangements as he had resolved on, which were almost exactly what Praskovya Fëdorovna too had decided on.

Now that everything had happened so fortunately, and that he and his wife were at one in their aims and moreover saw so little of one another, they got on together better than they had done since the first years of marriage. Ivan Ilych had thought of taking his family away with him at once, but the insistence of his wife's brother and her sister-in-law, who had suddenly become particularly amiable and friendly to him and his family, induced him to depart alone.

So he departed, and the cheerful state of mind induced by his success and by the harmony between his wife and himself, the one intensifying the other, did not leave him. He found a delightful house, just the thing both he and his wife had dreamt of. Spacious, lofty reception rooms in the old style, a convenient and dignified study, rooms for his wife and daughter, a study for his son —it might have been specially built for them. Ivan Ilych himself superintended the arrangements, chose the wallpapers, supplemented the furniture (preferably with antiques which he considered particularly *comme il faut*), and supervised the upholstering. Everything progressed and progressed and approached the ideal he had set himself: even when things were only half completed they exceeded his expectations. He saw what a refined and elegant character, free from vulgarity, it would all have when it was ready. On falling asleep he pictured to himself how the reception-room would look. Looking at the yet unfinished drawing-room he could see the fireplace, the screen, the what-not, the little chairs dotted here and there, the dishes and plates on the walls, and the bronzes, as they would be when everything was in place. He was pleased by the thought of how his wife and daughter, who shared his taste in this matter, would be impressed by it. They were certainly not expecting as much. He had been particularly successful in finding, and buying cheaply, antiques which gave a particularly aristocratic character to the whole place. But in his letters he intentionally understated everything in order to be able to surprise them. All this so absorbed him that his new duties—though he liked his official work—interested him less than he had expected. Sometimes he even had moments of absent-mindedness during the Court Sessions, and would consider whether he should have straight or curved cornices for his curtains. He was so interested in it all that he often did things himself, rearranging the furniture, or rehanging the curtains. Once when mounting a step-ladder to show the upholsterer, who did not understand, how he wanted the hangings draped, he made a false step and slipped, but being a strong and agile man he clung on and only knocked his side against the knob of the window frame. The bruised place was painful but the pain soon passed, and he felt particularly bright and well just then. He wrote: "I feel fifteen years younger." He thought he would have everything ready by September, but it dragged on till mid-October. But the result was charming not only in his eyes but to everyone who saw it.

In reality it was just what is usually seen in the houses of people of moderate means who want to appear rich, and therefore succeed only in resembling others like themselves: there were damasks, dark wood, plants, rugs, and dull and polished bronzes—all the things people of a certain class have in order to resemble other people of that class. His house was so like the others that it would never have been noticed, but to him it all seemed to be quite exceptional. He was very happy when he met his family at the station and brought them to the newly furnished house all lit up, where a footman in a white tie opened the door into the hall decorated with plants, and when they went on into the drawingroom and the study uttering exclamations of delight. He conducted them everywhere, drank in their praises eagerly, and beamed with pleasure. At tea that evening, when Praskovya Fëdorovna among other things asked him about his fall, he laughed and showed them how he had gone flying and had frightened the upholsterer.

"It's a good thing I'm a bit of an athlete. Another man might have been killed, but I merely knocked myself, just here; it hurts when it's touched, but it's passing off already—it's only a bruise."

So they began living in their new home—in which, as always happens, when they got thoroughly settled in they found they were just one room short—and with the increased income, which as always was just a little (some five hundred rubles) too little, but it was all very nice.

Things went particularly well at first, before everything was finally arranged and while something had still to be done: this thing bought, that thing ordered, another thing moved, and something else adjusted. Though there were some disputes between husband and wife, they were both so well satisfied and had so much to do that it all passed off without any serious quarrels. When nothing was left to arrange it became rather dull and something seemed to be lacking, but they were then making acquaintances, forming habits, and life was growing fuller.

Ivan Ilych spent his mornings at the law court and came home to dinner, and at first he was generally in a good humour, though he occasionally became irritable just on account of his house. (Every spot on the tablecloth or the upholstery, and every broken window-blind string, irritated him. He had devoted so much trouble to arranging it all that every disturbance of it distressed him.) But on the whole his life ran its course as he believed life should do: easily, pleasantly, and decorously.

He got up at nine, drank his coffee, read the paper, and then put on his undress uniform and went to the law courts. There the harness in which he worked had already been stretched to fit him and he donned it without a hitch: petitioners inquiries at the chancery, the chancery itself, and the sittings public and administrative. In all this the thing was to exclude everything fresh and vital, which always disturbs the regular course of official business, and to admit only official relations with people, and then only on official grounds. A man would come, for instance, wanting some information. Ivan Ilych, as one in whose sphere the matter did not lie, would have nothing to do with him: but if the man had some business with him in his official capacity, something that could be expressed on officially stamped paper, he would do everything, positively everything he could within the limits of such relations, and in doing so would maintain the semblance of friendly human relations, that is, would observe the courtesies of life. As soon as the official relations ended, so did everything else. Ivan Ilych possessed this capacity to separate his real life from the official side of affairs and not mix the two, in the highest degree, and by long practice and natural aptitude had brought it to such a pitch that sometimes, in the manner of a virtuoso, he would even allow himself to let the human and official relations mingle. He let himself do this just because he felt that he could at any time he chose resume the strictly official attitude again and drop the human relation. And he did it all easily, pleasantly, correctly, and even artistically. In the intervals between the sessions he smoked, drank tea, chatted a little about politics, a little about general topics, a little about cards, but most of all about official appointments. Tired, but with the feelings of a virtuoso—one of the first violins who has played his part in an orchestra with precision—he would return home to find that his wife and daughter had been out paying calls, or had a visitor, and that his son had been to school, had done his homework with his tutor, and was duly learning what is taught at High Schools. Everything was as it should be. After dinner, if they had no visitors, Ivan Ilych sometimes read a book that was being much discussed at the time, and in the evening settled down to work, that is, read official papers, compared the depositions of witnesses, and noted paragraphs of the Code applying to them. This was neither dull nor amusing. It was dull when he might have been playing bridge, but if no bridge was available it was at any rate better than doing nothing or sitting with his wife. Ivan Ilych's chief pleasure was giving little dinners to which he invited men and women of good social position, and just as his drawing-rooms resembled all other drawing-rooms so did his enjoyable little parties resemble all other such parties.

Once they even gave a dance. Ivan Ilych enjoyed it and everything went off well, except that it led to a violent quarrel with his wife about the cakes and sweets. Praskovya Fëdorovna had made her own plans, but Ivan Ilych insisted on getting everything from an expensive confectioner and ordered too many cakes, and the quarrel occurred because some of those cakes were left over and the confectioner's bill came to forty-five rubles. It was a great and disagreeable quarrel. Praskovya Fëdorovna called him "a fool and an imbecile," and he clutched at his head and made angry allusions to divorce.

But the dance itself had been enjoyable. The best people were there, and Ivan Ilych had danced with Princess Trufonova, a sister of the distinguished founder of the Society "Bear my Burden."

The pleasures connected with his work were pleasures of ambition; his social pleasures were those of vanity; but Ivan Ilych's greatest pleasure was playing bridge. He acknowledged that whatever disagreeable incident happened in his life, the pleasure that beamed like a ray of light above everything else was to sit down to bridge with good players, not noisy partners, and of course to four-handed bridge (with five players it was annoying to have to stand out, though one pretended not to mind), to play a clever and serious game (when the cards allowed it) and then to have supper and drink a glass of wine. After a game of bridge, especially if he had won a little (to win a large sum was unpleasant), Ivan Ilych went to bed in specially good humour.

So they lived. They formed a circle of acquaintances among the best people and were visited by people of importance and by young folk. In their views as to their acquaintances, husband, wife and daughter were entirely agreed, and tacitly and unanimously kept at arm's length and shook off the shabby friends and relations who, with much show of affection, gushed into the drawing-room with its Japanese plates on the walls. Soon these shabby friends ceased to obtrude themselves and only the best people remained in the Golovins' set.

Young men made up to Lisa, the Petrishchev, an examining magistrate and Dmitri Ivanovich Petrishchev's son and sole heir, began to be so attentive to her that Ivan Ilych had already spoken to Praskovya Fëdorovna about it, and considered whether they should not arrange a party for them, or get up some private theatricals.

So they lived, and all went well, without change, and life flowed pleasantly.

4

They were all in good health. It could not be called ill health if Ivan Ilych sometimes said he had a queer taste in his mouth and felt some discomfort in his left side.

But this discomfort increased and, though not exactly painful, grew into a sense of pressure in his side accompanied by ill humour. And his irritability became worse and worse and began to mar the agreeable, easy, and correct life that had established itself in the Golovin family. Quarrels between husband and wife became more and more frequent, and soon the ease and amenity disappeared and even the decorum was barely maintained. Scenes again became frequent, and very few of those islets remained on which husband and wife could meet without an explosion. Praskovya Fëdorovna now had good reason to say that her husband's temper was trying. With characteristic exaggeration she said he had always had a dreadful temper, and that it had needed all her good nature to put up with it for twenty years. It was true that now the quarrels were started by him. His bursts of temper always came just before dinner, often just as he began to eat his soup. Sometimes he noticed that a plate or dish was chipped, or the food was not right, or his son put his elbow on the table, or his daughter's hair was not done as he liked it, and for all this he blamed Praskovya Fëdorovna. At first she retorted and said disagreeable things to him, but once or twice he fell into such a rage at the beginning of dinner that she realized it was due to some physical derangement brought on by taking food, and so she restrained herself and did not answer, but only hurried to get the dinner over. She regarded this self-restraint as highly praiseworthy. Having come to the conclusion that her husband had a dreadful temper and made her life miserable, she began to feel sorry for herself, and the more she pitied herself the more she hated her husband. She began to wish he would die; yet she did not want him to die because then his salary would cease. And this irritated her against him still more. She considered herself dreadfully unhappy just because not even his death could save her, and though she concealed her exasperation, that hidden exasperation of hers increased his irritation also.

After one scene in which Ivan Ilych had been particularly unfair and after which he had said in explanation that he certainly was irritable but that it was due to his not being well, she said that if he was ill it should be attended to, and insisted on his going to see a celebrated doctor.

He went. Everything took place as he had expected and as it always does. There was the usual waiting and the important air assumed by the doctor, with which he was so familiar (resembling that which he himself assumed in court), and the sounding and listening, and the questions which called for answers that were foregone conclusions and were evidently unnecessary, and the look of importance which implied that "if only you put yourself in our hands we will arrange everything—we know indubitably how it has to be done, always in the same way for everybody alike." It was all just as it was in the law courts. The doctor put on just the same air towards him as he himself put on towards an accused person.

The doctor said that so-and-so indicated that there was so-and-so inside the patient, but if the investigation of so-and-so did not confirm this, then he must assume that and that. If he assumed that and that, then . . . and so on. To Ivan Ilych only one question was important: was his case serious or not? But the doctor ignored that inappropriate question. From his point of view it was not the one under consideration, the real question was to decide between a floating kidney, chronic catarrh, or appendicitis. It was not a question of Ivan Ilych's life or death, but one between a floating kidney and appendicitis. And that question the doctor solved brilliantly, as it seemed to Ivan Ilych, in favour of the appendix, with the reservation that should an examination of the urine give fresh indications the matter would be reconsidered. All this was just what Ivan Ilych had himself brilliantly accomplished a thousand times in dealing with men on trial. The doctor summed up just as brilliantly, looking over his spectacles triumphantly and even gaily at the accused. From the doctor's summing up Ivan Ilych concluded that things were bad, but that for the doctor, and perhaps for everybody else, it was a matter of indifference, though for him it was bad. And this conclusion struck him painfully, arousing in him a great feeling of pity for himself and of bitterness towards the doctor's indifference to a matter of such importance.

He said nothing of this, but rose, placed the doctor's fee on the table, and remarked with a sigh: "We sick people probably often put inappropriate questions. But tell me, in general, is this complaint dangerous, or not? . . ."

The doctor looked at him sternly over his spectacles with one eye, as if to say: "Prisoner, if you will not keep to the questions put to you, I shall be obliged to have you removed from the court."

"I have already told you what I consider necessary and proper. The analysis may show something more." And the doctor bowed.

Ivan Ilych went out slowly, seated himself disconsolately in his sledge, and drove home. All the way home he was going over what the doctor had said, trying to translate those complicated, obscure, scientific phrases into plain language and find in them an answer to the question: "Is my condition bad? Is it very bad? Or is there as yet nothing much wrong?" And it seemed to him that the meaning of what the doctor had said was that it was very bad. Everything in the streets seemed depressing. The cabmen, the houses, the passers-by, and the shops, were dismal. His ache, this dull gnawing ache that never ceased for a moment, seemed to have acquired a new and more serious significance from the doctor's dubious remarks. Ivan Ilych now watched it with a new and oppressive feeling.

He reached home and began to tell his wife about it. She listened, but in the middle of his account his daughter came in with her hat on, ready to go out with her mother. She sat down reluctantly to listen to this tedious story, but could not stand it long, and her mother too did not hear him to the end.

"Well, I am very glad," she said. "Mind now to take your medicine regularly. Give me the prescription and I'll send Gerasim to the chemist's." And she went to get ready to go out.

While she was in the room Ivan Ilych had hardly taken time to breathe, but he sighed deeply when she left it.

"Well," he thought, "perhaps it isn't so bad after all."

He began taking his medicine and following the doctor's directions, which had been altered after the examination of the urine. But then it happened that there was a contradiction between the indications drawn from the examination of the urine and the symptoms that showed themselves. It turned out that what was happening differed from what the doctor had told him, and that he had either forgotten, or blundered, or hidden something from him. He could not, however, be blamed for that, and Ivan Ilych still obeyed his orders implicitly and at first derived some comfort from doing so.

From the time of his visit to the doctor, Ivan Ilych's chief occupation was the exact fulfilment of the doctor's instructions regarding hygiene and the taking of medicine, and the observation of his pain and his excretions. His chief interests came to be people's ailments and people's health. When sickness, deaths, or recoveries were mentioned in his presence, especially when the illness resembled his own, he listened with agitation which he tried to hide, asked questions, and applied what he heard to his own case.

The pain did not grow less, but Ivan Ilych made efforts to force himself to think that he was better. And he could do this so long as nothing agitated him. But as soon as he had any unpleasantness with his wife, any lack of success in his official work, or held bad cards at bridge, he was at once acutely sensible of his disease. He had formerly borne such mischances, hoping soon to adjust what was wrong, to master it and attain success, or make a grand slam. But now every mischance upset him and plunged him into despair. He would say to himself: "There now, just as I was beginning to get better and the medicine had begun to take effect, comes this accursed misfortune, or unpleasantness. . . ." And he was furious with the mishap, or with the people who were causing the unpleasantness and killing him, for he felt that this fury was killing him but could not restrain it. One would have thought that it should have been clear to him that this exasperation with circumstances and people aggravated his illness, and that he ought therefore to ignore unpleasant occurrences. But he drew the very opposite conclusion: he said that he needed peace, and he watched for everything that might disturb it and became irritable at the slightest infringement of it. His condition was rendered worse by the fact that he read medical books and consulted doctors. The progress of his disease was so gradual that he could deceive himself when comparing one day with another—the difference was so slight. But when he consulted the doctors it seemed to him that he was getting worse, and even very rapidly. Yet despite this he was continually consulting them.

That month he went to see another celebrity, who told him almost the same as the first had done but put his questions rather differently, and the interview with this celebrity only increased Ivan Ilych's doubts and fears. A friend of a friend of his, a very good doctor, diagnosed his illness again quite differently from the others, and though he predicted recovery, his questions and suppositions bewildered Ivan Ilych still more and increased his doubts. A homeopathist diagnosed the disease in yet another way, and prescribed medicine which Ivan Ilych took secretly for a week. But after a week, not feeling any improvement and having lost confidence both in the former doctor's treatment and in this one's, he became still more despondent. One day a lady acquaintance mentioned a cure effected by a wonder-working icon. Ivan Ilych caught himself listening attentively and beginning to believe that it had occurred. This incident alarmed him. "Has my mind really weakened to such an extent?" he asked himself. "Nonsense! It's all rubbish. I mustn't give way to nervous fears but having chosen a doctor must keep strictly to his treatment. That is what I will do. Now it's all settled. I won't think about it, but will follow the treatment seriously till summer, and then we shall see. From now there must be no more of this wavering!" This was easy to say but impossible to carry out. The pain in his side oppressed him and seemed to grow worse and more incessant, while the taste in his mouth grew stranger and stranger. It seemed to him that his breath had a disgusting smell, and he was conscious of a loss of appetite and strength. There was no deceiving himself: something terrible, new, and more important than anything before in his life, was taking place within him of which he alone was aware. Those about him did not understand or would not understand it, but thought everything in the world was going on as usual. That tormented Ivan Ilych more than anything. He saw that his household, especially his wife and daughter who were in a perfect whirl of visiting, did not understand anything of it and were annoyed that he was so depressed and so exacting, as if he were to blame for it. Though they tried to disguise it he saw that he was an obstacle in their path, and that his wife had adopted a definite line in regard to his illness and kept to it regardless of anything he said or did. Her attitude was this: "You know," she would say to her friends, "Ivan Ilych can't do as other people do, and keep to the treatment prescribed for him. One day he'll take his drops and keep strictly to his diet and go to bed in good time, but the next day unless I watch him he'll suddenly forget his medicine, eat sturgeon—which is forbidden—and sit up playing cards till one o'clock in the morning."

"Oh, come, when was that?" Ivan Ilych would ask in vexation. "Only once at Peter Ivanovich's."

"And yesterday with Shebek."

"Well, even if I hadn't stayed up, this pain would have kept me awake."

"Be that as it may you'll never get well like that, but will always make us wretched."

Praskovya Fëdorovna's attitude to Ivan Ilych's illness, as she expressed it both to others and to him, was that it was his own fault and was another of the annoyances he caused her. Ivan Ilych felt that this opinion escaped her involuntarily—but that did not make it easier for him.

At the law courts too, Ivan Ilych noticed, or thought he noticed, a strange attitude towards himself. It sometimes seemed to him that people were watching him inquisitively as a man whose place might soon be vacant. Then again, his friends would suddenly begin to chaff him in a friendly way about his low spirits, as if the awful, horrible, and unheard-of thing that was going on within him, incessantly gnawing at him and irresistibly drawing him away, was a very agreeable subject for jests. Schwartz in particular irritated him by his jocularity, vivacity, and *savoir-faire,** which reminded him of what he himself had been ten years ago.

Friends came to make up a set and they sat down to cards. They dealt, bending the new cards to soften them, and he sorted the diamonds in his hand and found he had seven. His partner said "No trumps" and supported him with two diamonds. What more could be wished for? It ought to be jolly and lively. They would make a grand slam. But suddenly Ivan Ilych was conscious of that gnawing pain, that taste in his mouth, and it seemed ridiculous that in such circumstances he should be pleased to make a grand slam.

He looked at his partner Mikhail Mihaylovich, who rapped the table with his strong hand and instead of snatching up the tricks pushed the cards courteously and indulgently towards Ivan Ilych that he might have the pleasure of gathering them up without the trouble of stretching out his hand for them. "Does he think I am too weak to stretch out my arm?" thought Ivan Ilych, and forgetting what he was doing he over-trumped his partner, missing the grand slam by three tricks. And what was most awful of all was that he saw how upset Mikhail Mihaylovich was about it but did not himself care. And it was dreadful to realize why he did not care.

They all saw that he was suffering, and said: "We can stop if you are tired.

* *savoir-faire.* confident air of always doing the right thing

Take a rest." Lie down? No, he was not at all tired, and he finished the rubber. All were gloomy and silent. Ivan Ilych felt that he had diffused this gloom over them and could not dispel it. They had supper and went away, and Ivan Ilych was left alone with the consciousness that his life was poisoned and was poisoning the lives of others, and that this poison did not weaken but penetrated more and more deeply into his whole being.

With this consciousness, and with physical pain besides that terror, he must go to bed, often to lie awake the greater part of the night. Next morning he had to get up again, dress, go to the law courts, speak, and write; or if he did not go out, spend at home those twenty-four hours a day each of which was a torture. And he had to live thus all alone on the brink of an abyss, with no one who understood or pitied him.

5

So one month passed and then another. Just before the New Year his brother-in-law came to town and stayed at their house. Ivan Ilych was at the law courts and Praskovya Fëdorovna had gone shopping. When Ivan Ilych came home and entered his study he found his brother-in-law there—a healthy, florid man—unpacking his portmanteau himself. He raised his head on hearing Ivan Ilych's footsteps and looked up at him for a moment without a word. That stare told Ivan Ilych everything. His brother-in-law opened his mouth to utter an exclamation of surprise but checked himself, and that action confirmed it all.

"I have changed, eh?"

"Yes, there is a change."

And after that, try as he would to get his brother-in-law to return to the subject of his looks, the latter would say nothing about it. Praskovya Fëdorovna came home and her brother went out to her. Ivan Ilych locked the door and began to examine himself in the glass, first full face, then in profile. He took up a portrait of himself taken with his wife, and compared it with what he saw in the glass. The change in him was immense. Then he bared his arms to the elbow, looked at them, drew the sleeves down again, sat down on an ottoman, and grew blacker than night.

"No, no, this won't do!" he said to himself, and jumped up, went to the table, took up some law papers and began to read them, but could not continue. He unlocked the door and went into the reception-room. The door leading to the drawing-room was shut. He approached it on tiptoe and listened.

"No, you are exaggerating!" Praskovya Fedorovna was saying.

"Exaggerating! Don't you see it? Why, he's a dead man! Look at his eyes—there's no light in them. But what is it that is wrong with him?"

"No one knows. Nikolaevich [that was another doctor] said something, but I don't know what. And Leshchetitsky [this was the celebrated specialist] said quite the contrary . . ."

Ivan Ilych walked away, went to his own room, lay down, and began musing: "The kidney, a floating kidney." He recalled all the doctors had told him of how it detached itself and swayed about. And by an effort of imagination he tried to catch that kidney and arrest it and support it. So little was needed for this, it seemed to him. "No, I'll go to see Peter Ivanovich again." [That was the friend whose friend was a doctor.] He rang, ordered the carriage, and got ready to go.

"Where are you going, Jean?" asked his wife, with a specially sad and exceptionally kind look.

This exceptionally kind look irritated him. He looked morosely at her.

"I must go to see Peter Ivanovich."

He went to see Peter Ivanovich, and together they went to see his friend, the doctor. He was in, and Ivan Ilych had a long talk with him.

Reviewing the anatomical and physiological details of what in the doctor's opinion was going on inside him, he understood it all.

There was something, a small thing, in the vermiform appendix. It might all come right. Only stimulate the energy of one organ and check the activity of another, then absorption would take place and everything would come right. He got home rather late for dinner, ate his dinner, conversed cheerfully, but could not for a long time bring himself to go back to work in his room. At last, however, he went to his study and did what was necessary, but the consciousness that he had put something aside—an important, intimate matter which he would revert to when his work was done—never left him. When he had finished his work he remembered that this intimate matter was the thought of his vermiform appendix. But he did not give himself up to it, and went to the drawing-room for tea. There were callers there, including the examining magistrate who was a desirable match for his daughter, and they were conversing, playing the piano, and singing. Ivan Ilych, as Praskovya Fëdorovna remarked, spent that evening more cheerfully than usual, but he never for a moment forgot that he had postponed the important matter of the appendix. At eleven o'clock he said good-night and went to his bedroom. Since his illness he had slept alone in a small room next to his study. He undressed and took up a novel by Zola, but instead of reading it fell into thought, and in his imagination that desired improvement in the vermiform appendix occurred. There was the absorption and evacuation and the re-establishment of normal activity. "Yes, that's it!" he said to himself. "One need only assist nature, that's all." He remembered his medicine, rose, took it, and lay down on his back watching for the beneficent action of the medicine and for it to lessen the pain. "I need only take it regularly and avoid all injurious influences. I am already feeling better, much better." He began touching his side: it was not painful to the touch. "There, I really don't feel it. It's much better already."

He put out the light and turned on his side. . . . "The appendix is getting better, absorption is occurring." Suddenly he felt the old, familiar, dull, gnawing pain, stubborn and serious. There was the same familiar loathsome taste in his mouth. His heart sank and he felt dazed. "My God! My God!" he muttered. "Again, again! and it will never cease." And suddenly the matter presented itself in a quite different aspect. "Vermiform appendix! Kidney!" he said to himself. "It's not a question of appendix or kidney, but of life and . . . death. Yes, life was there and now it is going, going and I cannot stop it. Yes. Why deceive myself? Isn't it obvious to everyone but me that I'm dying, and that it's only a question of weeks, days . . . it may happen this moment. There was light and now there is darkness. I was here and now I'm going there! Where?" A chill came over him, his breathing ceased, and he felt only the throbbing of his heart.

"When I am not, what will there be? There will be nothing. Then where shall I be when I am no more? Can this be dying? No, I don't want to!" He jumped up and tried to light the candle, felt for it with trembling hands, dropped candle and candlestick on the floor, and fell back on his pillow.

"What's the use? It makes no difference," he said to himself, staring with wide-open eyes into the darkness. "Death. Yes, death. And none of them know or wish to know it, and they have no pity for me. Now they are playing." (He heard through the door the distant sound of a song and its accompaniment.) "It's all the same to them, but they will die too! Fools! I first, and they later, but it will be the same for them. And now they are merry . . . the beasts!"

Anger choked him and he was agonizingly, unbearably, miserable. "It is impossible that all men have been doomed to suffer this awful horror!" He raised himself.

"Something must be wrong. I must calm myself—must think it all over from the beginning." And he again began thinking. "Yes, the beginning of my illness: I knocked my side, but I was quite well that day and the next. It hurt a little, then rather more. I saw the doctor, then followed despondency and anguish, more doctors, and I drew nearer to the abyss. My strength grew less and I kept coming nearer and nearer, and now I have wasted away and there is no light in my eyes. I think of the appendix—but this is death! I think of mending the appendix, and all the while here is death! Can it really be death?" Again terror seized him and he gasped for breath. He leant down and began feeling for the matches, pressing with his elbow on the stand beside the bed. It was in the way and hurt him, he grew furious with it, pressed on it still harder, and upset it. Breathless and in despair he fell on his back, expecting death to come immediately.

Meanwhile the visitors were leaving. Praskovya Fëdorovna was seeing them off. She heard something fall and came in.

"What has happened?"

"Nothing. I knocked it over accidentally."

She went out and returned with a candle. He lay there panting heavily, like a man who has run a thousand yards, and stared upwards at her with a fixed look.

"What is it, Jean?"

"No . . . o . . . thing. I upset it." ("Why speak of it? She won't understand," he thought.)

And in truth she did not understand. She picked up the stand, lit his candle, and hurried away to see another visitor off. When she came back he still lay on his back, looking upwards.

"What is it? Do you feel worse?"

"Yes."

She shook her head and sat down.

"Do you know, Jean, I think we must ask Leshchetitsky to come and see you here."

This meant calling in the famous specialist, regardless of expense. He smiled malignantly and said "No." She remained a little longer and then went up to him and kissed his forehead.

While she was kissing him he hated her from the bottom of his soul and with difficulty refrained from pushing her away.

"Good-night. Please God you'll sleep."

"Yes."

6

Ivan Ilych saw that he was dying, and he was in continual despair.

In the depth of his heart he knew he was dying, but not only was he not accustomed to the thought, he simply did not and could not grasp it.

The syllogism he had learnt from Kiezewetter's Logic: "Caius is a man, men are mortal, therefore Caius is mortal," had always seemed to him correct as applied to Caius, but certainly not as applied to himself. That Caius—man in the abstract—was mortal, was perfectly correct, but he was not Caius, not an abstract man, but a creature quite, quite separate from all others. He had been little Vanya, with a mamma and a papa, with Mitya and Volodya, with the toys, a coachman and a nurse, afterwards with Katenka and with all the joys, griefs, and delights of childhood, boyhood, and youth. What did Caius know of the smell of that striped leather ball Vanya had been so fond of? Had Caius kissed his mother's hand like that, and did the silk of her dress rustle so for Caius? Had he rioted like that at school when the pastry was bad? Had Caius been in love like that? Could Caius preside at a session as he did? "Caius really was mortal, and it was right for him to die, but for me, little Vanya, Ivan Ilych, with all my thoughts and emotions, it's altogether a different matter. It cannot be that I ought to die. That would be too terrible."

Such was his feeling.

"If I had to die like Caius, I should have known it was so. An inner voice would have told me so, but there was nothing of the sort in me and I and all my friends felt that our case was quite different from that of Caius. And now here it is!" he said to himself. "It can't be. It's impossible! But here it is. How is this? How is one to understand it?"

He could not understand it, and tried to drive this false, incorrect, morbid thought away and to replace it by other proper and healthy thoughts. But that thought, and not the thought only but the reality itself, seemed to come and confront him.

And to replace that thought he called up a succession of others, hoping to find in them some support. He tried to get back into the former current of thoughts that had once screened the thought of death from him. But strange to say, all that had formerly shut off, hidden, and destroyed, his consciousness of death, no longer had that effect. Ivan Ilych now spent most of his time in attempting to re-establish that old current. He would say to himself: "I will take up my duties again—after all I used to live by them." And banishing all doubts he would go to the law courts, enter into conversation with his colleagues, and sit carelessly as was his wont, scanning the crowd with a thoughtful look and leaning both his emaciated arms on the arms of his oak chair; bending over as usual to a colleague and drawing his papers nearer he would interchange whispers with him, and then suddenly raising his eyes and sitting erect would pronounce certain words and open the proceedings. But suddenly in the midst of those proceedings the pain in his side, regardless of the stage the proceedings had reached, would begin its own gnawing work. Ivan Ilych would turn his attention to it and try to drive the thought of it away, but without success. *It* would come and stand before him and look at him, and he would be petrified and the light would die out of his eyes, and he would again begin asking himself whether *It* alone was true. And his colleagues and subordinates would see with surprise and distress that he, the brilliant and subtle judge, was becoming confused and making mistakes. He would shake himself, try to pull himself together, manage somehow to bring the sitting to a close, and return home with the sorrowful consciousness that his judicial labours could not as formerly hide from him what he wanted them to hide, and could not deliver him from *It.* And what was worst of all was that *It* drew his attention to itself not in order to make him take some action but only that he should look at *It,* look it straight in the face: look at it and without doing anything, suffer inexpressibly.

And to save himself from this condition Ivan Ilych looked for consolations —new screens—and new screens were found and for a while seemed to save him, but then they immediately fell to pieces or rather became transparent, as if *It* penetrated them and nothing could veil *It.*

In these latter days he would go into the drawing-room he had arranged—

that drawing-room where he had fallen and for the sake of which (how bitterly ridiculous it seemed) he had sacrificed his life—for he knew that his illness originated with that knock. He would enter and see that something had scratched the polished table. He would look for the cause of this and find that it was the bronze ornamentation of an album, that had got bent. He would take up the expensive album which he had lovingly arranged, and feel vexed with his daughter and her friends for their untidiness—for the album was torn here and there and some of the photographs turned upside down. He would put it carefully in order and bend the ornamentation back into position. Then it would occur to him to place all those things in another corner of the room, near the plants. He would call the footman, but his daughter or wife would come to help him. They would not agree, and his wife would contradict him, and he would dispute and grow angry. But that was all right, for then he did not think about *It*. *It* was invisible.

But then, when he was moving something himself, his wife would say: "Let the servants do it. You will hurt yourself again." And suddenly *It* would flash through the screen and he would see it. It was just a flash, and he hoped it would disappear, but he would involuntarily pay attention to his side. "It sits there as before, gnawing just the same!" And he could no longer forget *It,* but could distinctly see it looking at him from behind the flowers. "What is it all for?"

"It really is so! I lost my life over that curtain as I might have done when storming a fort. Is that possible? How terrible and how stupid. It can't be true! It can't, but it is."

He would go to his study, lie down, and again be alone with *It:* face to face with *It*. And nothing could be done with *It* except to look at it and shudder.

7

How it happened it is impossible to say because it came about step by step, unnoticed, but in the third month of Ivan Ilych's illness, his wife, his daughter, his son, his acquaintances, the doctors, the servants, and above all he himself, were aware that the whole interest he had for other people was whether he would soon vacate his place, and at last release the living from the discomfort caused by his presence and be himself released from his sufferings.

He slept less and less. He was given opium and hypodermic injections of morphine, but this did not relieve him. The dull depression he experienced in a somnolent condition at first gave him a little relief, but only as something new, afterwards it became as distressing as the pain itself or even more so.

Special foods were prepared for him by the doctors' orders, but all those foods became increasingly distasteful and disgusting to him.

For his excretions also special arrangements had to be made, and this was a torment to him every time—a torment from the uncleanliness, the unseemliness, and the smell, and from knowing that another person had to take part in it.

But just through this most unpleasant matter, Ivan Ilych obtained comfort. Gerasim, the butler's young assistant, always came in to carry the things out. Gerasim was a clean, fresh peasant lad, grown stout on town food and always cheerful and bright. At first the sight of him, in his clean Russian peasant costume, engaged in that disgusting task embarrassed Ivan Ilych.

Once when he got up from the commode too weak to draw up his trousers, he dropped into a soft armchair and looked with horror at his bare, enfeebled thighs with the muscles so sharply marked on them.

Gerasim with a firm light tread, his heavy boots emitting a pleasant smell of tar and fresh winter air, came in wearing a clean Hessian apron, the sleeves of his print shirt tucked up over his strong bare young arms; and refraining from looking at his sick master out of consideration for his feelings, and restraining the joy of life that beamed from his face, he went up to the commode.

"Gerasim!" said Ivan Ilych in a weak voice.

Gerasim started, evidently afraid he might have committed some blunder, and with a rapid movement turned his fresh, kind, simple young face which just showed the first downy signs of a beard.

"Yes, sir?"

"That must be very unpleasant for you. You must forgive me. I am helpless."

"Oh, why, sir," and Gerasim's eyes beamed and he showed his glistening white teeth, "what's a little trouble? It's a case of illness with you, sir."

And his deft strong hands did their accustomed task, and he went out of the room stepping lightly. Five minutes later he as lightly returned.

Ivan Ilych was still sitting in the same position in the armchair.

"Gerasim," he said when the latter had replaced the freshly-washed utensil. "Please come here and help me." Gerasim went up to him. "Lift me up. It is hard for me to get up, and I have sent Dmitri away."

Gerasim went up to him, grasped his master with his strong arms deftly but gently, in the same way that he stepped—lifted him, supported him with one hand, and with the other drew up his trousers and would have set him down again, but Ivan Ilych asked to be led to the sofa. Gerasim, without an effort and without apparent pressure, led him, almost lifting him, to the sofa and placed him on it.

"Thank you. How easily and well you do it all!"

Gerasim smiled again and turned to leave the room. But Ivan Ilych felt his presence such a comfort that he did not want to let him go.

"One thing more, please move up that chair. No, the other one—under my feet. It is easier for me when my feet are raised."

Gerasim brought the chair, set it down gently in place, and raised Ivan

Ilych's legs on to it. It seemed to Ivan Ilych that he felt better while Gerasim was holding up his legs.

"It's better when my legs are higher," he said. "Place that cushion under them."

Gerasim did so. He again lifted the legs and placed them, and again Ivan Ilych felt better while Gerasim held his legs. When he set them down Ivan Ilych fancied he felt worse.

"Gerasim," he said. "Are you busy now?"

"Not at all, sir," said Gerasim, who had learnt from the townfolk how to speak to gentlefolk.

"What have you still to do?"

"What have I to do? I've done everything except chopping the logs for to-morrow."

"Then hold my legs up a bit higher, can you?"

"Of course I can. Why not?" And Gerasim raised his master's legs higher and Ivan Ilych thought that in that position he did not feel any pain at all.

"And how about the logs?"

"Don't trouble about that, sir. There's plenty of time."

Ivan Ilych told Gerasim to sit down and hold his legs, and began to talk to him. And strange to say it seemed to him that he felt better while Gerasim held his legs up.

After that Ivan Ilych would sometimes call Gerasim and get him to hold his legs on his shoulders, and he liked talking to him. Gerasim did it all easily, willingly, simply, and with a good nature that touched Ivan Ilych. Health, strength, and vitality in other people were offensive to him, but Gerasim's strength and vitality did not mortify but soothed him.

What tormented Ivan Ilych most was the deception, the lie, which for some reason they all accepted, that he was not dying but was simply ill, and that he only need keep quiet and undergo a treatment and then something very good would result. He however knew that do what they would nothing would come of it, only still more agonizing suffering and death. This deception tortured him—their not wishing to admit what they all knew and what he knew, but wanting to lie to him concerning his terrible condition, and wishing and forcing him to participate in that lie. Those lies—lies enacted over him on the eve of his death and destined to degrade this awful, solemn act to the level of their visitings, their curtains, their sturgeon for dinner—were a terrible agony for Ivan Ilych. And strangely enough, many times when they were going through their antics over him he had been within a hairbreadth of calling out to them: "Stop lying! You know and I know that I am dying. Then at least stop lying about it!" But he had never had the spirit to do it. The awful, terrible act of his dying was, he could see, reduced by those about him to the level of a casual, unpleasant, and almost indecorous incident (as if someone entered a drawing-room diffusing an unpleasant odour) and this was done by that very decorum which he had served all his life long. He saw that no one felt for him, because no one even wished to grasp his position. Only Gerasim recognized it and pitied him. And so Ivan Ilych felt at ease only with him. He felt comforted when Gerasim supported his legs (sometimes all night long) and refused to go to bed, saying: "Don't you worry, Ivan Ilych. I'll get sleep enough later on," or when he suddenly became familiar and exclaimed: "If you weren't sick it would be another matter, but as it is, why should I grudge a little trouble?" Gerasim alone did not lie; everything showed that he alone understood the facts of the case and did not consider it necessary to disguise them, but simply felt sorry for his emaciated and enfeebled master. Once when Ivan Ilych was sending him away he even said straight out: "We shall all of us die, so why should I grudge a little trouble?"—expressing the fact that he did not think his work burdensome, because he was doing it for a dying man and hoped someone would do the same for him when his time came.

Apart from this lying, or because of it, what most tormented Ivan Ilych was that no one pitied him as he wished to be pitied. At certain moments after prolonged suffering he wished most of all (though he would have been ashamed to confess it) for someone to pity him as a sick child is pitied. He longed to be petted and comforted. He knew he was an important functionary, that he had a beard turning grey, and that therefore what he longed for was impossible, but still he longed for it. And in Gerasim's attitude towards him there was something akin to what he wished for, and so that attitude comforted him. Ivan Ilych wanted to weep, wanted to be petted and cried over, and then his colleague Shebek would come, and instead of weeping and being petted, Ivan Ilych would assume a serious, severe, and profound air, and by force of habit would express his opinion on a decision of the Court of Cassation and would stubbornly insist on that view. This falsity around him and within him did more than anything else to poison his last days.

8

It was morning. He knew it was morning because Gerasim had gone, and Peter the footman had come and put out the candles, drawn back one of the curtains, and begun quietly to tidy up. Whether it was morning or evening, Friday or Sunday, made no difference, it was all just the same: the gnawing, unmitigated, agonizing pain, never ceasing for an instant, the consciousness of life inexorably waning but not yet extinguished, the approach of that ever dreaded and hateful Death which was the one reality, and always the same falsity. What were days, weeks, hours, in such a case?

"Will you have some tea, sir?"

"He wants things to be regular, and wishes the gentlefolk to drink tea in the morning," thought Ivan Ilych, and only said "No."

"Wouldn't you like to move onto the sofa, sir?"

"He wants to tidy up the room, and I'm in the way. I am uncleanliness and disorder," he thought, and said only:

"No, leave me alone."

The man went on bustling about. Ivan Ilych stretched out his hand. Peter came up, ready to help.

"What is it, sir?"

"My watch."

Peter took the watch which was close at hand and gave it to his master.

"Half-past eight. Are they up?"

"No, sir, except Vladimir Ivanich" (the son) "who has gone to school. Praskovya Fëdorovna ordered me to wake her if you asked for her. Shall I do so?"

"No, there's no need to." "Perhaps I'd better have some tea," he thought, and added aloud: "Yes, bring me some tea."

Peter went to the door, but Ivan Ilych dreaded being left alone. "How can I keep him here? Oh yes, my medicine." "Peter, give me my medicine." "Why not? Perhaps it may still do me some good." He took a spoonful and swallowed it. "No, it won't help. It's all tomfoolery, all deception," he decided as soon as he became aware of the familiar, sickly, hopeless taste. "No, I can't believe in it any longer. But the pain, why this pain? If it would only cease just for a moment!" And he moaned. Peter turned towards him. "It's all right. Go and fetch me some tea."

Peter went out. Left alone Ivan Ilych groaned not so much with pain, terrible though that was, as from mental anguish. Always and for ever the same, always these endless days and nights. If only it would come quicker! If only *what* would come quicker? Death, darkness? . . . No, no! Anything rather than death!

When Peter returned with the tea on a tray, Ivan Ilych stared at him for a time in perplexity, not realizing who and what he was. Peter was disconcerted by that look and his embarrassment brought Ivan Ilych to himself.

"Oh, tea! All right, put it down. Only help me to wash and put on a clean shirt."

And Ivan Ilych began to wash. With pauses for rest, he washed his hands and then his face, cleaned his teeth, brushed his hair, and looked in the glass. He was terrified by what he saw, especially by the limp way in which his hair clung to his pallid forehead.

While his shirt was being changed he knew that he would be still more frightened at the sight of his body, so he avoided looking at it. Finally he was ready. He drew on a dressing-gown, wrapped himself in a plaid, and sat down in the armchair to take his tea. For a moment he felt refreshed, but as soon as he began to drink the tea he was again aware of the same taste, and the pain also returned. He finished it with an effort, and then lay down stretching out his legs, and dismissed Peter.

Always the same. Now a spark of hope flashes up, then a sea of despair rages, and always pain; always pain, always despair, and always the same. When alone he had a dreadful and distressing desire to call someone, but he knew beforehand that with others present it would be still worse. "Another dose of morphine—to lose consciousness. I will tell him, the doctor, that he must think of something else. It's impossible, impossible, to go on like this."

An hour and another pass like that. But now there is a ring at the door bell. Perhaps it's the doctor? It is. He comes in fresh, hearty, plump, and cheerful, with that look on his face that seems to say: "There now, you're in a panic about something, but we'll arrange it all for you directly!" The doctor knows this expression is out of place here, but he has put it on once for all and can't take it off—like a man who has put on a frock-coat in the morning to pay a round of calls.

The doctor rubs his hands vigorously and reassuringly.

"Brr! How cold it is! There's such a sharp frost; just let me warm myself!" he says, as if it were only a matter of waiting till he was warm, and then he would put everything right.

"Well now, how are you?"

Ivan Ilych feels that the doctor would like to say: "Well, how are your affairs?" but that even he feels that this would not do, and says instead: "What sort of a night have you had?"

Ivan Ilych looks at him as much as to say: "Are you really never ashamed of lying?" But the doctor does not wish to understand this question, and Ivan Ilych says: "Just as terrible as ever. The pain never leaves me and never subsides. If only something . . ."

"Yes, you sick people are always like that. . . . There, now I think I am warm enough. Even Praskovya Fëdorovna, who is so particular, could find no fault with my temperature. Well, now I can say good-morning," and the doctor presses his patient's hand.

Then, dropping his former playfulness, he begins with a most serious face to examine the patient, feeling his pulse and taking his temperature, and then begins the sounding and auscultation.

Ivan Ilych knows quite well and definitely that all this is nonsense and pure deception, but when the doctor, getting down on his knee, leans over him, putting the ear first higher then lower, and performs various gymnastic movements over him with a significant expression on his face, Ivan Ilych submits to it all as he used to submit to the speeches of the lawyers, though he knew very well that they were all lying and why they were lying.

The doctor, kneeling on the sofa, is still sounding him when Praskovya Fëdorovna's silk dress rustles at the door and she is heard scolding Peter for not having let her know of the doctor's arrival.

She comes in, kisses her husband, and at once proceeds to prove that she has been up a long time already, and only owing to a misunderstanding failed to be there when the doctor arrived.

Ivan Ilych looks at her, scans her all over, sets against her the whiteness and plumpness and cleanness of her hands and neck, the gloss of her hair, and the sparkle of her vivacious eyes. He hates her with his whole soul. And the thrill of hatred he feels for her makes him suffer from her touch.

Her attitude towards him and his disease is still the same. Just as the doctor had adopted a certain relation to his patient which he could not abandon, so had she formed one towards him—that he was not doing something he ought to do and was himself to blame, and that she reproached him lovingly for this—and she could not now change that attitude.

"You see he doesn't listen to me and doesn't take his medicine at the proper time. And above all he lies in a position that is no doubt bad for him—with his legs up."

She described how he made Gerasim hold his legs up.

The doctor smiled with a contemptuous affability that said: "What's to be done? These sick people do have foolish fancies of that kind, but we must forgive them."

When the examination was over the doctor looked at his watch, and then Praskovya Fëdorovna announced to Ivan Ilych that it was of course as he pleased, but she had sent today for a celebrated specialist who would examine him and have a consultation with Michael Danilovich (their regular doctor).

"Please don't raise any objections. I am doing this for my own sake," she said ironically, letting it be felt that she was doing it all for his sake and only said this to leave him no right to refuse. He remained silent, knitting his brows. He felt that he was so surrounded and involved in a mesh of falsity that it was hard to unravel anything.

Everything she did for him was entirely for her own sake, and she told him she was doing for herself what she actually was doing for herself, as if that was so incredible that he must understand the opposite.

At half-past eleven the celebrated specialist arrived. Again the sounding began and the significant conversations in his presence and in another room, about the kidneys and the appendix, and the questions and answers, with such an air of importance that again, instead of the real question of life and death which now alone confronted him, the question arose of the kidney and appendix which were not behaving as they ought to and would now be attacked by Michael Danilovich and the specialist and forced to mend their ways.

The celebrated specialist took leave of him with a serious though not hopeless look, and in reply to the timid question Ivan Ilych, with eyes glistening with fear and hope, put to him as to whether there was a chance of recovery, said that he could not vouch for it but there was a possibility. The look of hope with which Ivan Ilych watched the doctor out was so pathetic that Praskovya Fëdorovna, seeing it, even wept as she left the room to hand the doctor his fee.

The gleam of hope kindled by the doctor's encouragement did not last long. The same room, the same pictures, curtains, wall-paper, medicine bottles, were all there, and the same aching suffering body, and Ivan Ilych began to moan. They gave him a subcutaneous injection and he sank into oblivion.

It was twilight when he came to. They brought him his dinner and he swallowed some beef tea with difficulty, and then everything was the same again and night was coming on.

After dinner, at seven o'clock, Praskovya Fëdorovna came into the room in evening drcss, her full bosom pushed up by her corset, and with traces of powder on her face. She had reminded him in the morning that they were going to the theatre. Sarah Bernhardt was visiting the town and they had a box, which he had insisted on their taking. Now he had forgotten about it and her toilet offended him, but he concealed his vexation when he remembered that he had himself insisted on their securing a box and going because it would be an instructive and aesthetic pleasure for the children.

Praskovya Fëdorovna came in, self-satisfied but yet with a rather guilty air. She sat down and asked how he was, but, as he saw, only for the sake of asking and not in order to learn about it, knowing that there was nothing to learn—and then went on to what she really wanted to say: that she would not on any account have gone but that the box had been taken and Helen and their daughter were going, as well as Petrishchev (the examining magistrate, their daughter's fiancé) and that it was out of the question to let them go alone; but that she would have much preferred to sit with him for a while; and he must be sure to follow the doctor's orders while she was away.

"Oh, and Fëdor Petrovich" (the fiancé) "would like to come in. May he? And Lisa?"

"All right."

Their daughter came in in full evening dress, her fresh young flesh exposed (making a show of that very flesh which in his own case caused so much suffering), strong, healthy, evidently in love, and impatient with illness, suffering, and death, because they interfered with her happiness.

Fëdor Petrovich came in too, in evening dress, his hair curled *à la Capoul,* a tight stiff collar round his long sinewy neck, an enormous white shirt-front and narrow black trousers tightly stretched over his strong thighs. He had one white glove tightly drawn on, and was holding his opera hat in his hand.

Following him the schoolboy crept in unnoticed, in a new uniform, poor little fellow, and wearing gloves. Terribly dark shadows showed under his eyes, the meaning of which Ivan Ilych knew well.

His son had always seemed pathetic to him, and now it was dreadful to see the boy's frightened look of pity. It seemed to Ivan Ilych that Vasya was the only one besides Gerasim who understood and pitied him.

They all sat down and again asked how he was. A silence followed. Lisa asked her mother about the opera-glasses, and there was an altercation between mother and daughter as to who had taken them and where they had been put. This occasioned some unpleasantness.

Fëdor Petrovich inquired of Ivan Ilych whether he had ever seen Sarah

Bernhardt. Ivan Ilych did not at first catch the question, but then replied: "No, have you seen her before?"

"Yes, in *Adrienne Lecouvreur.*"

Praskovya Fëdorovna mentioned some rôles in which Sarah Bernhardt was particularly good. Her daughter disagreed. Conversation sprang up as to the elegance and realism of her acting—the sort of conversation that is always repeated and is always the same.

In the midst of the conversation Fëdor Petrovich glanced at Ivan Ilych and became silent. Ivan Ilych was staring with glittering eyes straight before him, evidently indignant with them. This had to be rectified, but it was impossible to do so. The silence had to be broken, but for a time no one dared to break it and they all became afraid that the conventional deception would suddenly become obvious and the truth become plain to all. Lisa was the first to pluck up courage and break that silence, but by trying to hide what everybody was feeling, she betrayed it.

"Well, if we are going it's time to start," she said, looking at her watch, a present from her father, and with a faint and significant smile at Fëdor Petrovich relating to something known only to them. She got up with a rustle of her dress.

They all rose, said good-night, and went away.

When they had gone it seemed to Ivan Ilych that he felt better; the falsity had gone with them. But the pain remained—that same pain and that same fear that made everything monotonously alike, nothing harder and nothing easier. Everything was worse.

Again minute followed minute and hour followed hour. Everything remained the same and there was no cessation. And the inevitable end of it all became more and more terrible.

"Yes, send Gerasim here," he replied to a question Peter asked.

9

His wife returned late at night. She came in on tiptoe, but he heard her, opened his eyes, and made haste to close them again. She wished to send Gerasim away and to sit with him herself, but he opened his eyes and said: "No, go away."

"Are you in great pain?"

"Always the same."

"Take some opium."

He agreed and took some. She went away.

Till about three in the morning he was in a state of stupefied misery. It seemed to him that he and his pain were being thrust into a narrow, deep black sack, but though they were pushed further and further in they could not be pushed to the bottom. And this, terrible enough in itself, was accompanied by suffering. He struggled but yet co-operated. And suddenly he broke through, fell, and regained consciousness. Gerasim was sitting at the foot of the bed dozing quietly, while he himself lay with his emaciated stockinged legs resting on Gerasim's shoulders; the same shaded candle was there and the same unceasing pain.

"Go away, Gerasim," he whispered.

"It's all right, sir. I'll stay a while."

"No. Go away."

He removed his legs from Gerasim's shoulders, turned sideways onto his arm, and felt sorry for himself. He only waited till Gerasim had gone into the next room and then restrained himself no longer but wept like a child. He wept on account of his helplessness, his terrible loneliness, the cruelty of man, the cruelty of God, and the absence of God.

"Why hast Thou done all this? Why hast Thou brought me here? Why, why dost Thou torment me so terribly?"

He did not expect an answer and yet wept because there was no answer and could be none. The pain again grew more acute, but he did not stir and did not call. He said to himself: "Go on! Strike me! But what is it for? What have I done to Thee? What is it for?"

Then he grew quiet and not only ceased weeping but even held his breath and became all attention. It was as though he were listening not to an audible voice but to the voice of his soul, to the current of thoughts arising within him.

"What is it you want?" was the first clear conception capable of expression in words, that he heard.

"What do you want? What do you want?" he repeated to himself.

"What do I want? To live and not to suffer," he answered.

And again he listened with such concentrated attention that even his pain did not distract him.

"To live? How?" asked his inner voice.

"Why, to live as I used to—well and pleasantly."

"As you lived before, well and pleasantly?" the voice repeated.

And in imagination he began to recall the best moments of his pleasant life. But strange to say none of those best moments of his pleasant life now seemed at all what they had then seemed—none of them except the first recollections of childhood. There, in childhood, there had been something really pleasant with which it would be possible to live if it could return. But the child who had experienced that happiness existed no longer, it was like a reminiscence of somebody else.

As soon as the period began which had produced the present Ivan Ilych, all that had then seemed joys now melted before his sight and turned into something trivial and often nasty.

And the further he departed from childhood and the nearer he came to the present the more worthless and doubtful were the joys. This began with the School of Law. A little that was really good was still found there—there was light-heartedness, friendship, and hope. But in the upper classes there had already been fewer of such good moments. Then during the first years of his official career, when he was in the service of the Governor, some pleasant moments again occurred: there were the memories of love for a woman. Then all became confused and there was still less of what was good; later on again there was still less that was good, and the further he went the less there was. His marriage, a mere accident, then the disenchantment that followed it, his wife's bad breath and the sensuality and hypocrisy: then that deadly official life and those preoccupations about money, a year of it, and two, and ten, and twenty, and always the same thing. And the longer it lasted the more deadly it became. "It is as if I had been going downhill while I imagined I was going up. And that is really what it was. I was going up in public opinion, but to the same extent life was ebbing away from me. And now it is all done and there is only death."

"Then what does it mean? Why? It can't be that life is so senseless and horrible. But if it really has been so horrible and senseless, why must I die and die in agony? There is something wrong!"

"Maybe I did not live as I ought to have done," it suddenly occurred to him. "But how could that be, when I did everything properly?" he replied, and immediately dismissed from his mind this, the sole solution of all the riddles of life and death, as something quite impossible.

"Then what do you want now? To live? Live how? Live as you lived in the law courts when the usher proclaimed 'The judge is coming!' The judge is coming, the judge!" he repeated to himself. "Here he is, the judge. But I am not guilty!" he exclaimed angrily. "What is it for?" And he ceased crying, but turning his face to the wall continued to ponder on the same question: Why, and for what purpose, is there all this horror? But however much he pondered he found no answer. And whenever the thought occurred to him, as if often did, that it all resulted from his not having lived as he ought to have done, he at once recalled the correctness of his whole life and dismissed so strange an idea.

10

Another fortnight passed. Ivan Ilych now no longer left his sofa. He would not lie in bed but lay on the sofa, facing the wall nearly all the time. He suffered ever the same unceasing agonies and in his loneliness pondered always on the same insoluble question: "What is this? Can it be that it is Death?" And the inner voice answered: "Yes, it is Death."

"Why these sufferings?" And the voice answered, "For no reason—they just are so." Beyond and besides this there was nothing.

From the very beginning of his illness, ever since he had first been to see the doctor, Ivan Ilych's life had been divided between two contrary and alternating moods: now it was despair and the expectation of this uncomprehended and terrible death, and now hope and an intently interested observation of the functioning of his organs. Now before his eyes there was only a kidney or an intestine that temporarily evaded its duty, and now only that incomprehensible and dreadful death from which it was impossible to escape.

These two states of mind had alternated from the very beginning of his illness, but the further it progressed the more doubtful and fantastic became the conception of the kidney, and the more real the sense of impending death.

He had but to call to mind what he had been three months before and what he was now, to call to mind with what regularity he had been going downhill, for every possibility of hope to be shattered.

Latterly during that loneliness in which he found himself as he lay facing the back of the sofa, a loneliness in the midst of a populous town and surrounded by numerous acquaintances and relations but that yet could not have been more complete anywhere—either at the bottom of the sea or under the earth—during that terrible loneliness Ivan Ilych had lived only in memories of the past. Pictures of his past rose before him one after another. They always began with what was nearest in time and then went back to what was the most remote—to his childhood—and rested there. If he thought of the stewed prunes that had been offered him that day, his mind went back to the raw shrivelled French plums of his childhood, their peculiar flavour and the flow of saliva when he sucked their stones, and along with the memory of that taste came a whole series of memories of those days: his nurse, his brother, and their toys. "No, I mustn't think of that. . . . It is too painful," Ivan Ilych said to himself, and brought himself back to the present—to the button on the back of the sofa and the creases in its morocco. "Morocco is expensive, but it does not wear well: there had been a quarrel about it. It was a different kind of quarrel and a different kind of morocco that time when we tore father's portfolio and were punished, and Mamma brought us some tarts. . . ." And again his thoughts dwelt on his childhood, and again it was painful and he tried to banish them and fix his mind on something else.

Then again together with that chain of memories another series passed through his mind—of how his illness had progressed and grown worse. There also the further back he looked the more life there had been. There had been more of what was good in life and more of life itself. The two merged together. "Just as the pain went on getting worse and worse, so my life grew worse and worse," he thought. "There is one bright spot there at the back, at the beginning of life, and afterwards all becomes blacker and blacker and proceeds more and more rapidly—in inverse ratio to the square of the distance from death," thought Ivan Ilych. And the example of a stone falling downwards with increasing velocity entered his mind. Life, a series of increasing sufferings, flies further and further towards its end—the most terrible suffering. "I am flying. . . ." He shuddered, shifted himself, and tried to resist, but was already aware that resistance was impossible, and again with eyes weary of gazing but unable to cease seeing what was before them, he stared at the back of the sofa and waited—awaiting that dreadful fall and shock and destruction.

"Resistance is impossible!" he said to himself. "If I could only understand what it is all for! But that too is impossible. An explanation would be possible if it could be said that I have not lived as I ought to. But it is impossible to say that," and he remembered all the legality, correctitude, and propriety of his life. "That at any rate can certainly not be admitted," he thought, and his lips smiled ironically as if someone could see that smile and be taken in by it. "There is no explanation! Agony, death . . . What for?"

11

Another two weeks went by in this way and during that fortnight an event occurred that Ivan Ilych and his wife had desired. Petrishchev formally proposed. It happened in the evening. The next day Praskovya Fëdorovna came into her husband's room considering how best to inform him of it, but that very night there had been a fresh change for the worse in his condition. She found him still lying on the sofa but in a different position. He lay on his back, groaning and staring fixedly in front of him.

She began to remind him of his medicines, but he turned his eyes toward her with such a look that she did not finish what she was saying; so great an animosity, to her in particular, did that look express.

"For Christ's sake let me die in peace!" he said.

She would have gone away, but just then their daughter came in and went up to say good morning. He looked at her as he had done at his wife, and in reply to her inquiry about his health said dryly that he would soon free them all of himself. They were both silent and after sitting with him for a while went away.

"Is it our fault?" Lisa said to her mother. "It's as if we were to blame! I am sorry for papa, but why should we be tortured?"

The doctor came at his usual time. Ivan Ilych answered "Yes" and "No," never taking his angry eyes from him, and at last said: "You know you can do nothing for me, so leave me alone."

"We can ease your sufferings."

"You can't even do that. Let me be."

The doctor went into the drawing-room and told Praskovya Fëdorovna that the case was very serious and that the only resource left was opium to allay her husband's sufferings, which must be terrible.

It was true, as the doctor said, that Ivan Ilych's physical sufferings were terrible, but worse than the physical sufferings were his mental sufferings, which were his chief torture.

His mental sufferings were due to the fact that that night, as he looked at Gerasim's sleepy, good-natured face with its prominent cheek-bones, the question suddenly occurred to him: "What if my whole life has really been wrong?"

It occurred to him that what had appeared perfectly impossible before, namely that he had not spent his life as he should have done, might after all be true. It occurred to him that his scarcely perceptible attempts to struggle against what was considered good by the most highly placed people, those scarcely noticeable impulses which he had immediately suppressed, might have been the real thing, and all the rest false. And his professional duties and the whole arrangement of his life and of his family, and all his social and official interests, might all have been false. He tried to defend all those things to himself and suddenly felt the weakness of what he was defending. There was nothing to defend.

"But if that is so," he said to himself, "and I am leaving this life with the consciousness that I have lost all that was given me and it is impossible to rectify it—what then?"

He lay on his back and began to pass his life in review in quite a new way. In the morning when he saw first his footman, then his wife, then his daughter, and then the doctor, their every word and movement confirmed to him the awful truth that had been revealed to him during the night. In them he saw himself—all that for which he had lived—and saw clearly that it was not real at all, but a terrible and huge deception which had hidden both life and death. This consciousness intensified his physical suffering tenfold. He groaned and tossed about, and pulled at his clothing which choked and stifled him. And he hated them on that account.

He was given a large dose of opium and became unconscious, but at noon his sufferings began again. He drove everybody away and tossed from side to side.

His wife came to him and said:

"Jean, my dear, do this for me. It can't do any harm and often helps. Healthy people often do it."

He opened his eyes wide.

"What? Take communion? Why? It's unnecessary! However . . ."

She began to cry.

"Yes, do, my dear. I'll send for our priest. He is such a nice man."

"All right. Very well," he muttered.

When the priest came and heard his confession, Ivan Ilych was softened and seemed to feel a relief from his doubts and consequently from his sufferings, and for a moment there came a ray of hope. He again began to think of the vermiform appendix and the possibility of correcting it. He received the sacrament with tears in his eyes.

When they laid him down again afterwards he felt a moment's ease, and the hope that he might live awoke in him again. He began to think of the operation that had been suggested to him. "To live! I want to live!" he said to himself.

His wife came to congratulate him after his communion, and when uttering the usual conventional words she added:

"You feel better, don't you?"

Without looking at her he said "Yes."

Her dress, her figure, the expression of her face, the tone of her voice, all revealed the same thing. "This is wrong, it is not as it should be. All you have lived for and still live for is falsehood and deception, hiding life and death from you." And as soon as he admitted that thought, his hatred and his agonizing physical suffering again sprang up, and with that suffering a consciousness of the unavoidable, approaching end. And to this was added a new sensation of grinding shooting pain and a feeling of suffocation.

The expression of his face when he uttered that "yes" was dreadful. Having uttered it, he looked her straight in the eyes, turned on his face with a rapidity extraordinary in his weak state and shouted:

"Go away! Go away and leave me alone!"

12

From that moment the screaming began that continued for three days, and was so terrible that one could not hear it through two closed doors without horror. At the moment he answered his wife he realized that he was lost, that there was no return, that the end had come, the very end, and his doubts were still unsolved and remained doubts.

"Oh! Oh! Oh!" he cried in various intonations. He had begun by screaming "I won't!" and continued screaming on the letter *O*.

For three whole days, during which time did not exist for him, he struggled in that black sack into which he was being thrust by an invisible, resistless force. He struggled as a man condemned to death struggles in the hands of the executioner, knowing that he cannot save himself. And every moment he felt that despite all his efforts he was drawing nearer and nearer to what terrified him. He felt that his agony was due to his being thrust into that black hole and still more to his not being able to get right into it. He was hindered from getting into it by his conviction that his life had been a good one. That very justification of his life held him fast and prevented his moving forward, and it caused him most torment of all.

Suddenly some force struck him in the chest and side, making it still harder to breathe, and he fell through the hole and there at the bottom was a light. What had happened to him was like the sensation one sometimes experiences in a railway carriage when one thinks one is going backwards while one is really going forwards and suddenly becomes aware of the real direction.

"Yes, it was all not the right thing," he said to himself, "but that's no matter. It can be done. But what *is* the right thing?" he asked himself, and suddenly grew quiet.

This occurred at the end of the third day, two hours before his death. Just then his schoolboy son had crept softly in and gone up to the bedside. The dying man was still screaming and waving his arms. His hand fell on the boy's head, and the boy caught it, pressed it to his lips, and began to cry.

At that very moment Ivan Ilych fell through and caught sight of the light, and it was revealed to him that though his life had not been what it should have been, this could still be rectified. He asked himself, "What *is* the right thing?" and grew still, listening. Then he felt that someone was kissing his hand. He opened his eyes, looked at his son, and felt sorry for him. His wife came up to him and he glanced at her. She was gazing at him open-mouthed, with undried tears on her nose and cheek and a despairing look on her face. He felt sorry for her too.

"Yes, I am making them wretched," he thought. "They are sorry, but it will be better for them when I die." He wished to say this but had not the strength to utter it. "Besides, why speak? I must act," he thought. With a look at his wife he indicated his son and said: "Take him away . . . sorry for him . . . sorry for you too. . . ." He tried to add, "forgive me," but said "forgo" and waved his hand, knowing that He whose understanding mattered would understand.

And suddenly it grew clear to him that what had been oppressing him and would not leave him was dropping away at once from two sides, from ten sides, and from all sides. He was sorry for them, he must act so as not to hurt them and free himself from these sufferings. "How good and how simple!" he thought. "And the pain?" he asked himself. "What has become of it? Where are you, pain?"

He turned his attention to it.

"Yes, here it is. Well, what of it? Let the pain be."

"And death . . . where is it?"

He sought his former accustomed fear of death and did not find it. "Where is it? What death?" There was no fear because there was no death.

In place of death there was light.

"So that's what it is!" he suddenly exclaimed aloud. "What joy!"

To him all this happened in a single instant, and the meaning of that instant did not change. For those present his agony continued for another two hours. Something rattled in his throat, his emaciated body twitched, then the gasping and rattle became less and less frequent.

"It is finished!" said someone near him.

He heard these words and repeated them in his soul.

"Death is finished," he said to himself. "It is no more!"

He drew in a breath, stopped in the midst of a sigh, stretched out, and died.

ISAAC LOEB PERETZ (1852–1917)

Although I. L. Peretz was born in Poland and raised in the orthodox Jewish tradition, he had a broad understanding of the variegated experiences and problems of all East European Jews and a rather sophisticated knowledge of the world, stemming from his wide reading, his work as an archivist, and his contacts with many phases of Polish Jewish life in his career as a lawyer.

He is generally regarded as the supreme literary artist of his people and as a leader in the elevation of Yiddish, the everyday language of European Jews, into a medium of literary expression. Peretz' short stories and poems are a fascinating mixture of the commonplace and the supernatural. In describing the world of suffering, sin, and injustice which he felt the Jews must resist in order to gain their freedom, he employed themes and characters from the Bible, from folklore, and from the beliefs of the mystical Hassidic sect.

"Bontsha the Silent," especially, reflects Peretz' sympathy for the downtrodden. Bontsha, most miserable of God's creatures, whose death on earth has gone almost unnoticed, surprisingly finds himself exalted in heaven.

Bontsha the Silent

HERE ON EARTH the death of Bontsha the Silent made no impression at all. Ask anyone: Who was Bontsha, how did he live, and how did he die? Did his strength slowly fade, did his heart slowly give out—or did the very marrow of his bones melt under the weight of his burdens? Who knows? Perhaps he just died from not eating—starvation, it's called.

If a horse, dragging a cart through the streets, should fall, people would run from blocks around to stare, newspapers would write about this fascinating event, a monument would be put up to mark the very spot where the horse had fallen. Had the horse belonged to a race as numerous as that of human beings, he wouldn't have been paid this honor. How many horses are there, after all? But human beings—there must be a thousand million of them!

Bontsha was a human being; he lived unknown, in silence, and in silence he died. He passed through our world like a shadow. When Bontsha was born no one took a drink of wine; there was no sound of glasses clinking. When he was confirmed he made no speech of celebration. He existed like a grain of sand at the rim of a vast ocean, amid millions of other grains of sand exactly similar, and when the wind at last lifted him up and carried him across to the other shore of that ocean, no one noticed, no one at all.

During his lifetime his feet left no mark upon the dust of the streets; after his death the wind blew away the board that marked his grave. The wife of the gravedigger came upon that bit of wood, lying far off from the grave, and she picked it up and used it to make a fire under the potatoes she was cooking; it was just right. Three days after Bontsha's death no one knew where he lay, neither the gravedigger nor anyone else. If Bontsha had had a headstone, someone, even after a hundred years, might have come across it, might still have been able to read the carved words, and his name, Bontsha the Silent, might not have vanished from this earth.

His likeness remained in no one's memory, in no one's heart. A shadow! Nothing! Finished!

In loneliness he lived, and in loneliness he died. Had it not been for the infernal human racket someone or other might have heard the sound of Bontsha's bones cracking under the weight of his burdens; someone might have glanced around and seen that Bontsha was also a human being, that he had two frightened eyes and a silent trembling mouth; someone might have noticed how, even when he bore no actual load upon his back, he still walked with his head bowed down to earth, as though while living he was already searching for his grave.

When Bontsha was brought to the hospital ten people were waiting for him to die and leave them his narrow little cot; when he was brought from the hospital to the morgue twenty were waiting to occupy his pall; when he was taken out of the morgue forty were waiting to lie where he would lie forever. Who knows how many are now waiting to snatch from him that bit of earth?

In silence he was born, in silence he lived, in silence he died—and in an even vaster silence he was put into the ground.

Ah, but in the other world it was not so! No! In Paradise the death of Bontsha was an overwhelming event. The great trumpet of the Messiah announced through the seven heavens: Bontsha the Silent is dead! The most exalted angels, with the most imposing wings, hurried, flew, to tell one another, "Do you know who has died? Bontsha! Bontsha the Silent!"

And the new, the young little angels with brilliant eyes, with golden wings and silver shoes, ran to greet Bontsha, laughing in their joy. The sound of their wings, the sound of their silver shoes, as they ran to meet him, and the bubbling of their laughter, filled all Paradise with jubilation, and God Himself knew that Bontsha the Silent was at last here.

In the great gateway to heaven Abraham, our father, stretched out his arms in welcome and benediction. "Peace be with you!" And on his old face a deep sweet smile appeared.

What, exactly, was going on up there in Paradise?

There, in Paradise, two angels came bearing a golden throne for Bontsha to sit upon, and for his head a golden crown with glittering jewels.

"But why the throne, the crown, already?" two important saints asked. "He hasn't even been tried before the heavenly court of justice to which each new arrival must submit." Their voices were touched with envy. "What's going on here, anyway?"

And the angels answered the two important saints that, yes, Bontsha's trial hadn't started yet, but it would only be a formality, even the prosecutor wouldn't dare open his mouth. Why, the whole thing wouldn't take five minutes!

"What's the matter with you?" the angels asked. "Don't you know whom you're dealing with? You're dealing with Bontsha, Bontsha the Silent!"

When the young, the singing angels encircled Bontsha in love, when Abraham, our father, embraced him again and again, as a very old friend, when Bontsha heard that a throne waited for him, and for his head a crown, and that when he would stand trial in the court of heaven no one would say a word against him—when he heard all this, Bontsha, exactly as in the other world, was silent. He was silent with fear. His heart shook, in his veins ran ice, and he knew this must all be a dream or simply a mistake.

He was used to both, to dreams and mistakes. How often, in that other world, had he not dreamed that he was wildly shoveling up money from the street, that whole fortunes lay there on the street beneath his hands—and then he would wake and find himself a beggar again, more miserable than before the dream.

How often in that other world had someone smiled at him, said a pleasant word—and then, passing and turning back for another look, had seen his mistake and spat at Bontsha.

Wouldn't that be just my luck, he thought now, and he was afraid to lift his eyes, lest the dream end, lest he awake and find himself again on earth, lying somewhere in a pit of snakes and loathesome vipers, and he was afraid to make the smallest sound, to move so much as an eyelash; he trembled and he could not hear the paeans of the angels; he could not see them as they danced in stately celebration about him; he could not answer the loving greeting of Abraham, our father, "Peace be with you!" And when at last he was led into the great court of justice in Paradise he couldn't even say "Good morning." He was paralyzed with fear.

And when his shrinking eyes beheld the floor of the courtroom of justice, his fear, if possible, increased. The floor was of purest alabaster, embedded with glittering diamonds. On such a floor stand my feet, thought Bontsha. My feet! He was beside himself with fear. Who knows, he thought, for what very rich man, or great learned rabbi, or even saint, this whole thing's meant? The rich man will arrive, and then it will all be over. He lowered his eyes; he closed them.

In his fear he did not hear when his name was called out in the pure angelic voice: "Bontsha the Silent!" Through the ringing in his ears he could make out no words, only the sound of that voice like the sound of music, of a violin.

Yet did he, perhaps, after all, catch the sound of his own name, "Bontsha the Silent?" And then the voice added, "To him that name is as becoming as a frock coat to a rich man."

What's that? What's he saying? Bontsha wondered, and then he heard an impatient voice interrupting the speech of his defending angel. "Rich man! Frock coat! No metaphors, please! And no sarcasm!"

"He never," began the defending angel again, "complained, not against God, not against man; his eye never grew red with hatred, he never raised a protest against heaven."

Bontsha couldn't understand a word, and the harsh voice of the prosecuting angel broke in once more. "Never mind the rhetoric, please!"

"His sufferings were unspeakable. Here, look upon a man who was more tormented than Job!"

Who? Bontsha wondered. Who is this man?

"Facts! Facts! Never mind the flowery business and stick to the facts, please!" the judge called out.

"When he was eight days old he was circumcised—"

"Such realistic details are unnecessary—"

"The knife slipped, and he did not even try to staunch the flow of blood—"

"—are distasteful. Simply give us the important facts."

"Even then, an infant, he was silent, he did not cry out his pain," Bontsha's defender continued. "He kept his silence, even when his mother died, and he was handed over, a boy of thirteen, to a snake, a viper—a stepmother!"

Hm, Bontsha thought, could they mean me?

"She begrudged him every bite of food, even the moldy rotten bread and the gristle of meat that she threw at him, while she herself drank coffee with cream."

"Irrelevant and immaterial," said the judge.

"For all that, she didn't begrudge him her pointed nails in his flesh—flesh that showed black and blue through the rags he wore. In winter, in the bitterest cold, she made him chop wood in the yard, barefoot! More than once were his feet frozen, and his hands, that were too young, too tender, to lift the heavy logs and chop them. But he was always silent, he never complained, not even to his father—"

"Complain! To that drunkard!" The voice of the prosecuting angel rose derisively, and Bontsha's body grew cold with the memory of fear.

"He never complained," the defender continued, "and he was always lonely. He never had a friend, never was sent to school, never was given a new suit of clothes, never knew one moment of freedom."

"Objection! Objection!" the prosecutor cried out angrily. "He's only trying to appeal to the emotions with these flights of rhetoric!"

"He was silent even when his father, raving drunk, dragged him out of the house by the hair and flung him into the winter night, into the snowy, frozen night. He picked himself up quietly from the snow and wandered into the distance where his eyes led him.

"During his wanderings he was always silent; during his agony of hunger he begged only with his eyes. And at last, on a damp spring night, he drifted to a great city, drifted there like a leaf before the wind, and on his very first night, scarcely seen, scarcely heard, he was thrown into jail. He remained silent, he never protested, he never asked, Why, what for? The doors of the jail were opened again, and, free, he looked for the most lowly filthy work, and still he remained silent.

"More terrible even than the work itself was the search for work. Tormented and ground down by pain, by the cramp of pain in an empty stomach, he never protested, he always kept silent.

"Soiled by the filth of a strange city, spat upon by unknown mouths, driven from the streets, into the roadways, where, a human beast of burden, he pursued his work, a porter, carrying the heaviest loads upon his back, scurrying between carriages, carts, and horses, staring death in the eyes every moment, he still kept silent.

"He never reckoned up how many pounds he must haul to earn a penny; how many times, with each step, he stumbled and fell for that penny. He never reckoned up how many times he almost vomited out his very soul, begging for his earnings. He never reckoned up his bad luck, the other's good luck. No, never. He remained silent. He never even demanded his own earnings; like a beggar, he waited at the door for what was rightfully his, and only in the depths of his eyes was there an unspoken longing. 'Come back later!' they'd order him; and, like a shadow, he would vanish, and then, like a shadow, would return and stand waiting, his eyes begging, imploring, for what was his. He remained silent even when they cheated him, keeping back, with one excuse or another, most of his earnings, or giving him bad money. Yes, he never protested, he always remained silent.

"Once," the defending angel went on, "Bontsha crossed the roadway to the fountain for drink, and in that moment his whole life was miraculously changed. What miracle happened to change his whole life? A splendid coach, with tires of rubber, plunged past, dragged by runaway horses; the coachman, fallen, lay in the street, his head split open. From the mouths of the frightened horses spilled foam, and in their wild eyes sparks struck like fire in a dark night, and inside the carriage sat a man, half alive, half dead, and Bontsha caught at the reins and held the horses. The man who sat inside and whose life was saved, a Jew, a philanthropist, never forgot what Bontsha had done for him. He handed him the whip of the dead driver, and Bontsha, then and there, became a coachman—no longer a common porter! And what's more, his great benefactor married him off, and what's still more, this great philanthropist himself provided a child for Bontsha to look after.

"And still Bontsha never said a word, never protested."

They mean me, I really do believe they mean me, Bontsha encouraged himself, but still he didn't have the gall to open his eyes, to look up at his judge.

"He never protested. He remained silent even when that great philanthropist shortly thereafter went into bankruptcy without even having paid Bontsha one cent of his wages.

"He was silent even when his wife ran off and left him with her helpless infant. He was silent when, fifteen years later, that same helpless infant had grown up and become strong enough to throw Bontsha out of the house."

They mean me, Bontsha rejoiced, they really mean me.

"He even remained silent," continued the defending angel, "when that same benefactor and philanthropist went out of bankruptcy, as suddenly as he'd gone into it, and still didn't pay Bontsha one cent of what he owed him. No, more than that. This person, as befits a fine gentleman who has gone through bankruptcy, again went driving the great coach with the tires of rubber, and now, now he had a new coachman, and Bontsha, again a porter in the roadway, was run over by coachman, carriage, horses. And still, in his agony, Bontsha did not cry out; he remained silent. He did not even tell the police who had done this to him. Even in the hospital, where everyone is allowed to scream, he remained silent. He lay in utter loneliness on his cot, abandoned by the doctor, by the nurse; he had not the few pennies to pay them—and he made no murmur. He was silent in that awful moment just before he was about to die, and he was silent in that very moment when he did die. And never one murmur of protest against man, never one murmur of protest against God!"

Now Bontsha begins to tremble again. He senses that after his defender has finished, his prosecutor will rise to state the case against him. Who knows of what he will be accused? Bontsha, in that other world on earth, forgot each present moment as it slipped behind him to become the past. Now the defending angel has brought everything back to his mind again—but who knows what forgotten sins the prosecutor will bring to mind?

The prosecutor rises. "Gentlemen!" he begins in a harsh and bitter voice, and then he stops. "Gentlemen—" he begins again, and now his voice is less harsh, and again he stops. And finally, in a very soft voice, the same prosecutor says, "Gentlemen, he was always silent—and now I too will be silent."

The great court of justice grows very still, and at last from the judge's chair a new voice rises, loving, tender. "Bontsha my child, Bontsha"—the voice swells like a great harp—"my heart's child . . ."

Within Bontsha his very soul begins to weep. He would like to open his eyes, to raise them, but they are darkened with tears. It is so sweet to cry. Never until now has it been sweet to cry.

"My child, my Bontsha . . ."

Not since his mother died has he heard such words, and spoken in such a voice.

"My child," the judge begins again, "you have always suffered, and you have always kept silent. There isn't one secret place in your body without its bleeding wound; there isn't one secret place in your soul without its wound and blood. And you never protested. You always were silent.

"There, in that other world, no one understood you. You never understood yourself. You never understood that you need not have been silent, that you could have cried out and that your outcries would have brought down the world itself and ended it. You never understood your sleeping strength. There in that other world, that world of lies, your silence was never rewarded, but here in Paradise is the world of truth, here in Paradise you will be rewarded. You, the judge can neither condemn nor pass sentence upon. For you there is not only one little portion of Paradise, one little share. No, for you there is everything! Whatever you want! Everything is yours!"

Now for the first time Bontsha lifts his eyes. He is blinded by light. The splendor of light lies everywhere, upon the walls, upon the vast ceiling, the angels blaze with light, the judge. He drops his weary eyes.

"Really?" he asks, doubtful, and a little embarrassed.

"Really!" the judge answers. "Really! I tell you, everything is yours. Everything in Paradise is yours. Choose! Take! Whatever you want! You will only take what is yours!"

"Really?" Bontsha asks again, and now his voice is stronger, more assured.

And the judge and all the heavenly host answer, "Really! Really! Really!"

"Well then"—and Bontsha smiles for the first time—"well then, what I would like, Your Excellency, is to have, every morning for breakfast, a hot roll with fresh butter."

A silence falls upon the great hall, and it is more terrible than Bontsha's has ever been, and slowly the judge and the angels bend their heads in shame at this unending meekness they have created on earth.

Then the silence is shattered. The prosecutor laughs aloud, a bitter laugh.

ALTERNATE TABLE OF CONTENTS ARRANGED BY FORM

THE FOLLOWING REARRANGEMENT of the contents of this book suggests appropriate stories for the study of fictional *forms* discussed in the following pages. Although in this way we seem to treat each element of fiction as if it were separate and distinct, the success of a good story depends upon how all these elements are interwoven. It is useful to look at each in isolation, but in the final analysis they all work together.

SOME NOTES ON FORM IN FICTION

THROUGH THE SHORT stories and novellas (short novels) in this book, you may achieve the satisfactions that come from sharing an author's experiences, and a corresponding growth in awareness about universal truths he depicts. You may also gain a fuller understanding of your own experiences and those of others.

At some point, readers who become intrigued with fiction grow interested not only in what an author says but in how he says it—what it is that makes a story so moving, how the author arranges his material to create a stunning effect. These are questions of *form*, or structure. These "Notes on Form" are here to guide you if you should want to understand more about an author's structural devices after you have read his story. Attention to formal elements will deepen your enjoyment and understanding of all good fiction. The "Notes" touch on seven key aspects of form in fiction:

- Plot
- Character
- Setting
- Thematic Devices
- Point of View
- Symbolism
- Style

As illustrations under each element of form, we shall make reference to one or more stories from this book. The preceding Alternate Table of Contents Arranged by Form can assist you further.

What Is Form in Fiction?

Whenever it was that man first learned to communicate, he seems to have demonstrated the very human need to hear and to tell stories. The form in which stories have been—and are being—told has varied widely, often depending on the method of presentation. Primitive man thought storytelling close to magic. Later, as stories became part of religious rituals to be performed on special occasions accompanied by music and dance, more formal elements (particularly rhythm and drama) were added. With the growth of the ceremonial tradition, which required that stories be repeated in exactly the same form, from generation to generation, memory aids such as rhyme and meter appeared. The first literary forms imposed on storytelling were, in fact, those of poetry and drama. Prose storytelling had to wait for the development of written language.

Even then, into the eighteenth century, prose narrative remained largely the simple recounting of a popular tale, or the retelling of fables and parables intended to teach moral lessons. Occasionally these tales reached lofty heights in *The Arabian Nights,* the *Decameron,* and *Don Quixote,* but by and large most serious thoughts were still reserved for poetry. In Shakespeare's plays, for example, kings and noblemen usually speak blank verse; coarse commoners and clowns use prose.

In the eighteenth and nineteenth centuries, the growth of industry and trade created a new, educated middle class seeking common tales in plain language. It was for this audience that prose fiction, first in the novel and later in the short story, developed its own unique form and gained acceptance as a literary art form.

But what is the difference between a story someone "tells" and a literary work of fiction? The key word, again, is *form.* All art seeks to find meaning in the apparently formless reality of everyday life. In every work of art, the artist takes this raw material and gives it a form, in order to make some structural comment on the world as he sees it. His aim is that the form he imposes upon reality will help his audience better to understand themselves and their world.

A straightforward narration of actual events is therefore not necessarily a work of art. Neither is much "escape fiction," whose only interest for us involves the outcome of the action (for example, a detective story).

The serious work of fiction does not present us with life as it actually is. It rearranges behavior. It takes a character, places him in a situation, and stirs things up—often internally as well as externally. The change this brings about in the character, in his view of the world, or in our view of him and his world, frequently suggests conclusions about the general condition of humankind.

In a work of fiction, then, something happens to someone, at some time, in some place, and something significant changes as a result. The space restrictions of the short story and the novella often limit the author to a single major character involved in one sequence of events revealing an insight into one aspect of life.

What Is "Plot"?

The conscious arrangement of incidents for a significant purpose is usually referred to as the plot of a story: what *happens* in it. If nothing happens, if there is no action, there is no story.

What causes things to happen in fiction is usually some disturbance of the normal pattern of a person's existence which places him in opposition to people or forces that interfere with the former progression of his life. This opposition, without which there probably can be no plot, is called *conflict.* The main character may be forced to choose between courses of action or sets of values in an attempt to recapture his once-peaceful existence.

At a key moment in the story, the conflict reaches its climax, its point of no return, where the opposing forces must meet, where a choice of action must be made and the future course of someone's life determined. This is the moment when Hemingway's Francis Macomber faces the charging bull buffalo; when Faulkner's young boy, gun in hand, confronts the bear at twenty yards, when Roth's Sergeant Marx reads the order sending everyone except Grossbart to the Pacific.

For a plot to be effective, everything that has happened up to the moment of climax must have made that moment inevitable, and the outcome of that moment must be logical in terms of everything that has preceded it.

The complexity of life is reflected in the many types of conflicts we meet in literature. The main character may have to struggle against opposing forces within himself as well as those in the outside world. Often, a character's internal conflicts and the external conflicts inflicted by the outside world are intertwined. Francis Macomber not only faces the charging beast but also his own value as an individual. In Baldwin's story, Sonny's difficulty in resolving his inner problems cannot be separated from his conflict with the values of the racist society which asks him to conform. Similarly, the boy's conflict with the forces of nature in "The Bear," or Bobby's conflict with his parents' values in "Cutting Edge," or George's conflict with the way of life his coming marriage will force upon him in "The Engagement Party," reflect internal crises which must also be resolved externally.

A conflict may be largely physical like Big Boy's escape in Richard Wright's story. It may be emotional like the argument between husband and wife in "Rope." The dilemma faced by the main character may involve a moral choice like the one facing Sergeant Marx in "Defender of the Faith." Conflict may be simple and clear like Smith's hatred of authority in "The Loneliness of the Long-Distance Runner" or it may be multiple and complex as when Charlie copes with his own nature, echoes of the past, and the opposition of his sister-in-law in "Babylon Revisited." The main character may not even be aware of the true nature of his conflict, as is the case with the young boy in "My Oedipus Complex." But whatever shape it takes, the conflict of a story is the center of its plot, and it determines how the formal elements of the story will be arranged.

If we take note of the incidents an author chooses to depict, the positioning, length, and development of each incident, we can get very close to the heart of his skill as a plot craftsman. Hemingway's "The Short Happy Life of Francis Macomber" provides an excellent example of skillful plot development. Like many short stories, this one starts *in media res,* in the middle of things, rather than at the very beginning of the first incident of the story. Three people carefully avoid a touchy subject, "pretending that nothing had happened." We learn only gradually of Macomber's cowardice. By the time we understand it fully, we will incidentally have been introduced to the three main characters—significantly, largely through their reactions to the incident with the lion. When we do see Macomber's panicky retreat from the charging lion, the relationship among the three has been established and the conflict has emerged: Macomber confronting his need to assert his masculinity against his inner fears, against the contempt of his wife, and against the virile rivalry of Robert Wilson.

Only after the lengthy recounting of the lion hunt and a brief, sarcastic summary of the Macombers' eleven years of marriage, which is fully halfway through the story, do we know enough of what has gone before so that the plot can move forward. The buffalo hunt can now be depicted, in as vivid and exacting detail as the lion hunt was. Simultaneously, we become aware of changing relationships among the three characters. Tension mounts as the wounded buffalo, like the lion of the previous day, must be uncovered and disposed of. The parallel pattern of both hunts builds the suspense. Because the wounded lion proved to be the first test of Macomber's manliness, once we hear of a second wounded animal, we anticipate a second moment of truth. When the bull charges at Macomber, we reach the point of no return, but with a twist—it is Margot who must act, not Francis. Francis Macomber's conflicts have all been successfully resolved—for the last thirty minutes of his life he has experienced true happiness. Although Margot resolves a particular problem, she must still live with much that has remained unresolved. Given the relationship between the Macombers that the author established in the first half of the story, the ending is inevitable.

What an author *omits* can also be significant. Eleven years of marriage are summarized in a couple of paragraphs, as are the details of Margot's affair with Wilson.

Through his skillful manipulation of plot elements, Hemingway succeeds in communicating some of his insights into human behavior. If we examine most successful works of fiction, we will find similar examples of the author's manipulation of scene and incident to produce his intended effect.

In a successfully developed plot, all the elements are interrelated, each incident following logically from the preceding ones to bring about some significant change in the characters or the situation that existed at the beginning of the story. The best test of a good plot is its plausibility. Could it really have happened? Is it consistent with our experience of human behavior?

What Is "Character"?

A story does not merely happen. It happens *to someone*: someone in action, reacting to a situation. It is especially significant in fiction to understand the choices available to a character in a critical spot and how and why he chooses one particular course of action or decision over others. In this way, character and plot are interrelated. The author structures his plot so that it reveals truths about his main character. Yet what happens to that character must be consistent with the kind of person he has been shown to be.

A character must conform to the reader's experience and expectation of human behavior. We can accept Barclay Oram's desertion of his family in McKay's "Truant" after we have witnessed his carefree course through life: into the city, in and out of the university, into marriage. A character should behave as people usually do. A stroll down any crowded city street will yield more than one Mike Loomis ogling the girls as he does in Shaw's story.

What a character does and why must always be motivated by understandable reasons. Given the wife he has, Walter Mitty can find release only in his exotic "secret life".

If a character is to be recognizably human yet interesting enough to hold our attention, the author must avoid extremes. No reader can identify with a character who is *too* unusual. Similarly, a character so ordinary as to lack any individuality will turn the reader off. Even the most common of common characters must possess some individual characteristic to bring him to life as a person rather than a type. Colter's Elijah in "The Beach Umbrella" is more than just a hen-pecked husband. His ambivalent feelings toward life and his yearning for broader experience reveal him as more than a mere stereotype.

Short fiction usually contains one central character only: the one who is involved in the conflict, the one whose fate is the significant element in the story. The meaning of most stories, as we saw in ". . . Francis McComber," lies in the change that occurs in the main character as a result of action in the story. For example, something snaps "in the very core of her being" when Grandmother is told of her husband's death in Kariara's "Her Warrior." Seeing this transformation, we learn much about her relationship with her man.

In other cases, the very failure of a character to change can be as significant as any transformation. The unchanging consistency of Peretz' Bontsha in Heaven is necessary to an understanding of his character.

Minor characters, on the other hand, are rarely presented in all their dimensions. A sentence or two out of Mrs. Mitty's mouth tell us all we need to know about her.

We learn about a main character in a variety of ways. Early in Vaca's "The Visit," the author describes Don Pedro's crippling ailments and his obsession with the Mexican Revolution. More often, however, character is implied and suggested through what is said, thought, or done. Mrs. Zeller's first words in Purdy's "Cutting Edge" characterize her clearly. The inner thoughts of the narrator in Villavicencio's "Mirror" show us the form of his madness. In "The Engagement Party" George's change of speech pattern into Southern dialect reveals a change of his attitude as he steps into the kitchen. The record of everything that Tolstoi's Ivan Ilych did in his lifetime sums up the person he is at his death.

In some stories, the main character may tell us what he is really like without even being aware of what he is revealing. Much of the enjoyment of "My Oedipus Complex" stems from the young boy's naïveté as to the significance of what he describes. The contrast between the supposedly great love that the son in "The Visit" expresses for his father and his callous disregard of Don Pedro's need to be taken to a doctor reveals his nature.

In Baldwin's "Sonny's Blues" we see how an author reveals character using several of these techniques. Sonny's character doesn't really change during the course of the narrative. What changes is his brother's (and the reader's) perception and understanding of that character. As a result, there is a change in the narrator's attitude toward Sonny.

Early in the story, James Baldwin swiftly sketches the father and mother of the main characters. The father had alienated Sonny. The mother's description of a callous murder by a car of joy-riding whites adds another layer of pent-up rage to the texture of the story.

At the very outset, the contrast between brothers is sharp. The narrator reacts internally to his disreputable brother's arrest on a drug charge, contrasting it with his own respectable job teaching a high school algebra class. In a conversation with Sonny's friend, he shies away from involvement ("What the hell can I do?"). But we catch a glimpse of Sonny through his friend's eyes: "He don't want to die. He wants to live."

Sonny's repentant and confused return to his brother, their strained conversation during the slow ride through Harlem, evoke memories that clarify the background of their relationship and lack of communication. Especially revealing is the brother's inability to relate to Sonny's commitment to jazz ("It's the only thing I want to do.") that leads to Sonny's plaintive cry, "I hear you. But you never hear anything *I* say."

The earlier split between the brothers is related only indirectly, when the narrator explains the incident as his wife wrote him about it. Sonny's cutting school and spending his time with musicians clashed with the respectable values of his brother's wife's family. Sonny couldn't take that and cut himself loose.

Ultimately, Baldwin fuses plot, mood, and a multiple point of view to generate a change of character in the narrator. The sudden death of the narrator's baby daughter brings about a new understanding of suffering and he writes to him ("My trouble made his real."). As they watch a street corner revival meeting together, the barriers suddenly disappear. Sonny reveals the storm inside him that he has tried to cope with through drugs and through music. His brother cannot tell Sonny directly of his own self-realization of the silence between them—it would sound empty. But he promises to himself never to fail Sonny again.

In the final scene, set in Sonny's world of music, the narrator finally experiences not only what Sonny has lived through but also the "long line" of suffering his people have gone through, and the promise of redemption in the very lamentation of Sonny's blues.

What Is "Setting"?

The fact is that a story must, obviously, take place *somewhere* at some definite time. This, together with the atmosphere or mood created, is usually referred to as a story's setting. Setting furthers the reader's understanding of the characters, the plot, and the thematic elements.

Just as an author cannot hope to put down on paper a total description of an action or a character encompassing every detail, neither can he always portray the total scene in which an action takes place. A single detail or a combination of significant details often provides all the reader needs to know to visualize the whole. The look and feel of the wilderness in Faulkner's "The Bear" is communicated early by the simple phrase "unaxed woods." The atmosphere of a Sunday morning on Fifth Avenue in "The Girls in Their Summer Dresses" needs no more detail than "the buses and the well-dressed people walking slowly in couples and the quiet buildings with the windows closed."

At other times, however, an accumulation of detail is necessary to produce the full effect of the setting on the story. Elijah's isolation from the gaiety on the beach is accentuated by a detailed depiction of the frenzied scenes under the beach umbrellas.

An author's choice of setting and his choice of how much of that setting to depict is determined by the part the setting is to play in the story. In some fiction the setting is relatively unimportant. In "Rope," for example, we know only that the couple live in the country in seven rooms and a kitchen. No more detail is necessary.

The setting of "Defender of the Faith" is given more specifically: Camp Crowder, Missouri. But, having stated this, the author simply assumes our knowledge of the general atmosphere of an army camp. Any camp will do.

In a story like Fitzgerald's "Babylon Revisited," however, time and place are at the core of the story's meaning, as the title points up. The early scenes abound with details about the look, the sound, and the mood of Paris in the early 30's—and of Charlie's inner thoughts about the contrast to the Paris of a year and a half before.

Beyond its primary function, to tell us where and when the story takes place, setting serves other purposes. It can help illuminate character, as in Sillitoe's "The Loneliness of the Long-Distance Runner." We understand Smith's inner conflict and final act of defiance better when we see the drab surroundings of his home, the oppressive atmosphere of the Borstal, and the long-distance run early in the morning.

Setting can also play an important part in the plot, as in Wright's "Big Boy Leaves Home." The racial atmosphere of the South brings about all that happens. The key places—the forbidden swimming hole and the kiln in which Big Boy spends the night—affect very directly what happens in the story.

Even the theme of a work of fiction can be underscored through setting. The bleak disappointment of the boy's first look at the bazaar in "Araby," in contrast to his expectations of its romance, mark his initiation into the disillusionment that comes with growing up. The untouched, primal wilderness of "The Bear," the cheerless streets of the small Louisiana town in "The Sky Is Gray," the peace of the woods in "Goose Pond"—all contribute to their stories as much as do the characters or incidents.

When setting changes within a story, the resulting contrast is usually significant. In Marshall's "Brazil," Caliban leaves the nightclub, his natural setting for many years, to seek his true self in scenes of his youth. But he finds he no longer has an identity there, and the story moves forward accordingly. In Boles' "The Engagement Party" and Rive's "Resurrection," a kitchen door sharply separates two aspects of the main characters' lives.

Eudora Welty uses every detail of the setting in "Livvie" to point up Livvie's imprisonment and the change that Cash brings. The contents of the three rooms of the house to which old Solomon takes his young bride are catalogued down to the jelly glasses and the bed knobs, creating an effect of Livvie's suffocation through Solomon's accumulation of possessions.

Every detail is revealing. Livvie's only treasure, pitiful evidence of the emptiness of her life, is the picture of a white baby belonging to a family she once worked for. Dominating the bedroom is the piecework quilt that was the prime accomplishment of Solomon's mother's life: is this what Livvie's married life will add up to? Before the house lies a barren dirt yard, every trace of grass uprooted. Trees hung with colored bottles to ward off evil spirits, the product of nine years' labor by Solomon, surround the house. In her fruitless attempts to escape these sterile surroundings, Livvie stumbles in knee-high dead leaves and hidden gravestones.

In the face of details such as these, we are not surprised that Livvie feels life calling her from distant fields as nature comes alive in the spring. Her one successful foray down the road ends in the coming of Cash, dressed in life-giving green, and the death of Solomon. At the end of the story, flowers and ferns shine and sun touches the bottles on the prisoned trees. Welty has not used her descriptive power merely as an end in itself but to heighten the significance of the other elements of her story.

What Are "Thematic Devices"?

When an author places his characters in a context of human experiences, his purpose is usually to make some point, to reveal some meaning, to provide some insight about life. The statement about life which comes out of the experience of the people in the story is called the *theme,* and the varied ways in which the author exposes his theme can be referred to as *thematic* devices.

Not every story has a serious "message" by any means. An author may wish merely to produce an emotional response or to communicate the quality of an experience without suggesting a deep meaning. He may be content to say, "This is what I see."

Most serious fiction, however, attempts to go beyond the immediate experience to point up some universal understanding of man and his world. It should provide growing awareness, deepening discovery, or new insights into human behavior. If it offers nothing new, it should, at least, cause the reader to reassess or extend his old interpretations of the universe.

Every element of a story—plot, character, setting, point of view, style—contributes to the expression of the theme, for the theme is a major reason for the existence of most stories. If we examine Lawrence's "The Horse Dealer's Daughter," we can see an author using all these elements to support his theme.

As a first reading of this story clearly shows, Lawrence is concerned with the power of love, passionate, unthinking love, as a life-giving force which, nevertheless, cannot be attained until one has first touched death. The first half of the story is a realistic depiction of an atmosphere of death. The family business has died. Mabel's spirit has been dead for years while she performed family chores like an automaton. The day is dark, her future obscure. Little wonder that, after visiting her mother's grave, she walks silently into the dark waters of a rank, foul-smelling pond.

Dr. Fergusson also seems to lack life as he pursues his harried schedule. He can only yearn for the vitality he glimpses in his young, working-class patients. It is therefore logical that in the depths of the murky pond, as both touch bottom coming close to dying, they should establish a mystical bond that frees them to live.

Here Lawrence shifts from the dark, sullen, animal-like realism of the early scenes to a tender passion, reflected in the flames of the fireplace, that goes beyond reality, as first she, and then, against all will and reason, he, discover love. At the end, although they have returned to sights and smells of the real world, life has prevailed: their love has survived.

We need not agree with Lawrence's theme. His view of life, like that of any author, comes out of his own experience. But if he has succeeded in involving us in his story, we have gained in our ability to recognize other ways of looking at life and love.

The theme of a story is not its topic, not a mere statement of its general subject (love, war, death, etc.). When attempting to identify a story's theme, it is useful to examine the outcome of the conflict in the story: the change in the main character and what he has learned from his experience. A story's title may also suggest a clue. Titles like "Defender of the Faith," "Cutting Edge," "Resurrection," and "Truant" provide such clues. When trying to restate an author's theme, you might attempt a general statement of a sentence or two, in line with all details in the story and not contradicted by any of them, which can be applied to your own experience of people and situations. Don't lapse into a moral, a proverb, a saying, or a cliché ("Love conquers all." "Honesty is the best policy."). Do say something significant. If an author has gone to all the trouble to construct a plot, people it with characters, and has carried you more or less willingly through it, it is unlikely that there is little one can say about the story.

What Is "Point of View"?

Christopher Isherwood very appropriately has the narrator of one of his books, a writer, describe his function in the first sentence of the story by stating: "I am a camera." Just as a motion-picture camera is an eye through which we view the action of a film, the author of a work of fiction controls what we see and how we view it. The location of the author's eye in the framework of the narrative, the determination of who sees or tells the story, is referred to as the story's "point of view."

There are advantages and limitations involved in any choice of point of view. Having one of the characters tell the story makes it more immediate for the reader. But telling the story through the detached eye of the author lends more range and freedom. The final choice of which point of view to employ must be determined by which best serves the needs of the plot, characterization, and theme.

If the story is told in the "first person" by one of the characters, using an "I" or "we," the author is restricted to depicting only those observations and occurrences within the range of the narrator's own experience. Be careful not to identify the "I" of this kind of story with the author—it is a character speaking. In fact, the author cannot directly intrude his own comments or any knowledge of events or characters that would not be known by the narrator. In addition, only a style and intelligence appropriate to the narrator can be used in the writing of the story. These restrictions, however, can serve the author well since every line he writes helps to characterize the narrator—often unwittingly—as in Baldwin's "Sonny's Blues." The boy in O'Connor's "My Oedipus Complex" is unaware of the cases and the implications of what he describes through the eyes of a child, yet the reader's major enjoyment and insight into childhood stem from precisely this distorted view.

The main character need not always be the narrator, as we have seen in "Sonny's Blues." If he is a secondary character who is affected by what happens to the main character, he can lend added insights through his reactions to the main character's actions.

A minor character not directly involved in the main conflict of the story may function as narrator, sometimes even as commentator and clarifier. We see and hear the grandmother's story in "Her Warrior" through the eyes of her grandchild, who tells us of the past and permits us to see its consequence in the present.

When an author uses a first-person point of view to give the reader a sense of immediacy, he will have a narrator relate the story as if it were happening at that moment. When immediacy is not required, he will have the narrator recall a story that happened in his past. As can be seen in Joyce's "Araby," this retrospecive point of view permits the narrator to comment with the insights of maturity on what happened years before.

A good example of the use of first-person point of view to add this extra dimension of understanding is Gaines' "The Sky Is Gray." Told by eight-year-old James as it is happening in the present tense, in the appropriate dialect, the story allows us to view through James' discerning yet naive eyes the love, the stubborn pride, and the dogged will to survive, of his Mama. It is James' comments on and reactions to what his Mama says (and leaves unsaid) that convince us that he is being well prepared for the manhood he must assume so prematurely.

Because of the first-person narration, we experience the cold, the hunger, the playfully flirtatious wrangling with the little girl on the bus, and the grudging acceptance of the old white lady's kindness as pointedly as James does. We participate directly in his precocious growth into manhood.

On the other hand, when an author tells his story *as author,* in the third person, what he loses in immediacy he gains in scope. He now stands over his material knowing all. He can interject his own interpretations, thoughts, and comments. He can show us as much or as little as suits his purpose. And we readers, joined with him in his lofty point of view, are as omniscient as he, knowing more than any character in the story. Tolstoi writes in this grand manner in "The Death of Ivan Ilych," making us privy to the conversations and thoughts of all the characters and aware of the imminence of death before any of them.

Some stories use the third person to heighten realism by having the author remain detached from the characters and action. In a story like Porter's "Rope," for example, the author does not interpret the action and intrudes no comments of her own. The reader, too, is detached, seeing and hearing only external happenings and drawing his own conclusions as to their significance.

Some have said there is a way for an author to have the best of both points of view: by writing in the third person but following the action through the eyes of one of the characters. This kind of story contains the immediacy of the first person while allowing the author to view the main character externally and interpret his actions and thoughts. In Malamud's "The Magic Barrel," for example, we travel through the story perched on

Leo Finkel's shoulder, seeing only as much as he does. But the implications we draw are expanded by the presence of Bernard Malamud at our side as well.

In first-person stories, the point of view generally remains fixed. Third-person stories, however, may shift back and forth from detached storytelling into the mind and eyes of one or more of the characters. Much of the effect of Mansfield's "The Dill Pickle," for example, stems from the different picture each character presents of past moments they shared.

When an author chooses his point of view wisely and carries it out realistically and consistently, it heightens the reader's perception and understanding of all the elements in a story.

What Is "Symbolism"?

A creative author attempts to say as much as possible as briefly as possible, encouraging the reader to draw upon his own insights and experiences. A common device in fiction to bring about this creative reading experience is symbolism.

A symbol is an object, person, situation, action, even name or color, that has a literal meaning in the story but suggests or represents other, more abstract meanings as well. Many obvious symbols are immediately recognizable: a bird represents freedom; a sword, warfare; the color white, purity; a child, innocence. Although conventional symbols such as these are often used in literature, in many cases the author also invests a particular element of the story with a unique symbolic meaning in order to amplify the theme, the characterization, or the atmosphere.

Several examples of symbolism occur in stories in this book. For Colter's Elijah, the beach umbrella represents more than protection from the sun. It is a symbol of freedom from the everyday rut of life, of a yearning to escape into the youthful gaiety of the beach crowd. In a similar sense, life for Vera, in Mansfield's "A Dill Pickle" is like her experience with a pickle in Russia: an eager anticipation of a new experience that, like the pickle, has proved sour when tasted. And Peretz represents Bontsha's lifetime of deprivation in his choice of a hot roll with butter every morning as his final reward.

Characters can be used symbolically to represent abstract qualities in a story. Cash McCord in "Livvie," arriving in the spring dressed in green, the color of growing things, dominates the stifling aura of death surrounding Livvie. Miranda in Marshall's "Brazil" becomes identified in Caliban's mind with the city of Rio: he has loved both, but, as he sees himself reflected against the lights of Rio in the mirrors of her apartment, he realizes how grotesque the relationships have been. Both Miranda and Rio will quickly choose another once he is gone. In destroying Miranda's apartment he attempts to purge that part of himself which both Miranda and Rio represent.

Symbolic use of animals is seen strongly in Faulkner's "The Bear" where the beast takes on all the mystical strength and spiritual beauty of nature that man can never destroy. In Williams' "Goose Pond," Robert Hurley's reaffirmation of life is represented symbolically by the annual return of the Canada Geese to the pond to rest before they continue "the dangerous journey down the world."

Actions occurring in a story often carry abstract meanings apart from their literal significance in the plot. In Sillitoe's "The Loneliness of the Long-Distance Runner," Smith has been on the run all his life—from his environment, from the values society has attempted to impose upon him, and from the police. Ironically, his second-place finish in the long-distance run is his first successful symbolic run.

In other cases action in a story brings to mind religious or mythological parallels that add significance to what has occurred. Fergusson's rescue of Mabel from the dark pond in Lawrence's "The Horse Dealer's Daughter," his struggle to drag her out at the risk of his own life, and the resultant awakening of love between them harks back to the earliest religious rituals of purification and resurrection through water.

Even places and names may be intended symbolically by some authors. In Vaca's "The Visit," Don Pedro's trailer represents the helpless stagnation of his life—its wheels sunk into the earth, immobile. The train on which Barclay Oram works in McKay's "Truant" is in constant motion, but it only brings Barclay back to where he started. What more appropriate name for the misshapen protagonist of Marshall's "Brazil" than "O Grande Caliban"—the great monster—and how heartrending his inability to rid himself of this identity! The ordinariness of a name like Smith in "The Loneliness of the Long-Distance Runner" is equally significant, as is the anonymity of main characters in "Sonny's Blues," "The Mirror," and "Rope." Anonymity here might be intended to emphasize the universality of their lives or to emphasize their unfulfilled natures.

In a story like Purdy's "Cutting Edge," the author seemingly intends several elements of the story to be taken symbolically. The title itself has a double meaning: the literal cutting edge of a razor and the figurative use of the expression to mean sharp, biting use of language. Bobby's beard, his symbol of independence and maturity, estranges him from his mother and brings him closer, for a moment, to his father. It makes him a stranger to his own parents, in which guise he learns the true nature of their relationship. He walks naked among them, almost as if they did not exist, while the beard threatens to shake the already tenuous truce between his father and mother. When Bobby uses the cutting edge of his razor, shedding some of his blood as well as his beard, it is too late to be of much use. But, as Bobby says, "I can't think of any more I can do for you." Their relationship is beyond redemption through sacrifice.

Any discussion of literary symbolism warrants a strong caution. The temptation to read symbolic meaning into every detail of everything one reads can become strong. All symbolic interpretation must be supported by the context of the story. Not every character taking a swim is engaging in a purification ritual. If a detail is to be taken symbolically, the story must furnish additional clues to support that interpretation. Most important, the symbolic meaning must add something significant to the literal meaning of characters or events. Even a story containing symbolic elements will eventually stand or fall on its qualities as a story, not as a puzzle.

What Is Style?

When you come down to fundamentals, all an author has at his disposal to begin with are words. In order to convey action, character, setting, and theme to his reader, an author manipulates words to create desired effects. We are perhaps most aware of an author's style when it is *not* appropriate, when it disturbs us. Becoming aware of why what is right, is right—is something else again.

An author's first concern is that his words suit the subject of his story and the characters who mouth them. In a first-person narrative, especially, the use of language must be appropriate to the supposed narrator. In Gaines' "The Sky Is Gray," James not only sees the events around him as an eight-year-old Louisiana black child would, but he also tells us about them in a dialect and vocabulary that makes us feel we are hearing them from his own lips. Joyce, in "Araby," on the other hand, does not pretend to write as if the narrator were an innocent lad. The language is too well-wrought, the insights too mature. But that is precisely the significance of that story's point of view: it is told in retrospect by the intellectual adult that the boy has become. The narrator in Villavicencio's "The Mirror," who quotes Catullus while fighting off spells of vertigo, speaks a richly poetic yet violently disjointed language that parallels the disturbance of his mind.

Creative use of dialect and idiom heighten the reality of language in Wright's "Big Boy Leaves Home," Vaca's "The Visit," Malamud's "The Magic Barrel," and Boles, "The Engagement Party," to name a few.

In some stories the author chooses to let the characters' conversation carry most of the burden of the story. The state of the Loomis marriage in Shaw's "The Girls in Their

Summer Dresses" is revealed largely through their argument. "The Short Happy Life of Francis Macomber," creates one atmosphere of tension through terse patches of conversation and yet another, later, when the character reveals his inner thoughts through another common device, the internal monologue. Almost every story in this book employs internal monologues at some point.

An author's use of language in narrative and descriptive passages also adds to the overall effect of the story. The rather colorless, literal storytelling in Purdy's "Cutting Edge" and Porter's "Rope" reflects the cold and detached mood of each. In sharp contrast is the profusion of description and the lyrical use of language in Williams' "Goose Pond," Lawrence's "The Horse Dealer's Daughter," and Faulkner's "The Bear."

A problem every author faces is the inherent limitations of language for making the reader actually experience what is being described. One literary technique for thrusting the reader directly into a scene is the reproduction of the sense impressions that accompanied the experience. Sharp, accurate rendering of the descriptive details of a scene help us to visualize it in our mind's eye. The squalid trailer in Vaca's "The Visit," the healing calm of the forest in "Goose Pond," Miranda's lush apartment in "Brazil," the house and stables in "The Horse Dealer's Daughter" come to life through the authors' use of visual detail.

Other senses can also be brought into play. Walter Mitty's dream world seems filled with mechanical devices going "pocketa pocketa pocketa." The snatches of conversation at "The Engagement Party" merge into a cacophony of meaningless sound that matches George's feelings of futility. Sounds emerging from Sonny's piano provide a glimpse of the truth about him. An odor of frying fish seems to follow Salzman around in "The Magic Barrel."

Another effective technique for making a literary experience more immediate is the use of comparison. By holding up the detail of description or feeling he wishes to communicate next to a related detail that may have evoked a similar sensory or emotional response in his reader, an author can add a new associational dimension to the reader's perception of the scene, as in the first paragraph of "The Beach Umbrella," when we are told that ". . . Lake Michigan ran to the horizon like a sheet of sapphire silk, studded with little barbed white sequins for sails." Or as when Wilson suddenly notices Francis Macomber's fear as they stalk the wounded lion; here Hemingway vividly communicates, through a comparison, Wilson's reaction: ". . . [he] suddenly felt as though he had opened the wrong door in a hotel and seen something shameful."

You will perhaps have noticed that both comparisons above used the notion of *like.* This is the most direct form of comparison and is called a *simile.* Although a relatively brief comparison, the simile is not a simple thing. Its language and frame of reference must be appropriate to the mood and setting of the story. Elijah's yearning to escape the drabness of his life *would* make him imagine sequined silks at the beach where he seeks romance. Wilson's lonely life *would* produce comparisons with seedy hotels. A rural black *would* describe the scream emanating from the dentist's office as "Hollering like a pig under a gate."

A more subtle form of comparison, in which not all of the elements compared are directly stated and the reader must supply the missing links, is a *metaphor.* "Goose Pond" affords an example when, after the doe has been wounded, the author states: "The trail was a vivid line of jewels. . . ." From the context, we quickly supply the unstated drops of blood. And economy of expression is achieved by eliminating the unnecessary half of the comparison.

A particularly effective metaphoric device is *personification:* endowing animals or inanimate objects with human qualities. In "The Loneliness of the Long-Distance Runner," for example, Sillitoe describes a "bare-faced, big-bellied oak tree." To see it as he does, we must imagine a bare-faced, big-bellied person superimposed over that of the oak tree he is describing. Richard Wright, in "Big Boy Leaves Home," metaphorically communicates the joy of Big Boy's escape at the story's end by having the very dust dance: "The truck sped over the asphalt miles, sped northward, jolting him, shaking out of his bosom the crumbs of corn bread, making them dance with the splinters and the sawdust in the golden blades of sunshine."

Simile and metaphor are used to maximum effect in a story like "The Mirror" where the mad narrator's distortions of reality and his suppressed violence are graphically depicted in grotesque simile on simile: ". . . fury would rush over me like a rabid bitch—like a needle in the tongue—like a cloud in the eye." His metaphors are distorted images: "The minutes become viscous and they drag." Vivid allusions of blindness, deafness, and shadows recur frequently in crazed thoughts evoked by remembered lines from a poem by Catullus. And when metaphor fails, when he finds he cannot blot out the words and the presence of his pregnant mistress metaphorically, the narrator must destroy her physically.

It is important that the tone of a story be established early. The reader must know whether it is to be taken seriously or satirically, tragically or comically. Tone can be revealed through all formal elements of a story, but most particularly through use of language and incident to show the author's feeling toward his characters and their situations. The tender, folk-tale quality of "Bontsha the Silent," written as if the author were telling it to us personally, establishes his gentle compassion for Bontsha and makes the patriarchs of Heaven seem as human as next-door neighbors. In contrast, the absurd fantasies of Walter Mitty's dream world and the equally exaggerated nagging wife of his real world preclude our viewing his problems with anything stronger than mild sympathy and quiet amusement. Both Poston's "The Revolt of the Evil Fairies" and Crayton's "The Day the World Almost Came to an End" depict experiences that, though frightening or frustrating to the children involved at the time, are now converted into a different tone established by narrators who recall these incidents with the tolerant humor of later years. Our minds are at ease from the start.

There is one important element of style and tone to be dealt with: *irony.* Occurring whenever there is a discrepancy between what we might normally expect and what actually happens, irony mirrors the contradictions of human experience. The happy life of Francis Macomber lasts but thirty minutes. For the momentary pleasure the beach umbrella has given Elijah, he condemns himself to life in the steel mills. "Resurrection" offers the supreme irony of the black daughter of a black mother and a white father who has rejected and condemned her mother during her lifetime for the sin of blackness. Having remained silent at her mother's funeral, thereby denying her mother's dying request that she be buried by her black church, she is entered by her mother's spirit who cries out against the hypocrisy of the white priest and the mourners who eulogize her without having known her.

Irony is also useful in producing humorous or sarcastic effects. Thurber, for example, juxtaposes fantasy and reality in two sentences that net a comic result: "The greatest pistol shot in the world thought a moment. 'It says, "Puppies Bark for It" on the box,' said Walter Mitty."

Dramatic irony is an effective device for increasing insight into a character's behavior when the reader knows more about a situation than the character does—thus, everything the character says or does can be evaluated in reference to the reader's superior knowledge. A well-written story will provide this kind of insight on rereading when the reader can reevaluate lines and actions in light of his foreknowledge of the outcome. In "My Oedipus Complex," O'Connor's entire effect depends upon our mature realization of the true state of affairs in the household contrasted to the very limited understanding provided by the boy telling the story.

The extreme form of irony is paradox, where two apparent opposites seem to be true at the same time. Sergeant Marx becomes a true "defender of the faith" when he stops being the defender that Grossbart expects. Smith really wins his long-distance run by finishing second. The boy is victor over the bear when he does *not* shoot him.

No author's style should be considered an end in itself. Stories that are self-consciously "well written" are rarely popular. Style, like all formal elements of fiction, is best judged primarily on its contribution to our understanding and appreciation of the total story.

TEN WAYS INTO A STORY

The following ten general questions, applied to virtually any work of fiction, should help a reader to analyze and judge its effectiveness:

1. What is the author's purpose in this story?
2. How significant is that purpose, in your opinion?
3. How effective is the plot in conveying the author's ideas, beliefs, and feelings over to the reader? How is this handled?
4. What methods of characterization does the author use? How does his method of characterization assist him in making a comment on the human condition?
5. What does the choice of time and setting accomplish for the story?
6. Has the story given you any new insights into human behavior, or has it confirmed or expanded earlier insights? If so, which ones?
7. How does the point of view from which the story is told affect what the author is saying?
8. How does the style—the author's choice and arrangement of language and situation—affect your understanding and appreciation of the story?
9. Would a rereading clarify or add to your understanding?
10. Did you like the story? Why or why not?